BAEN BOOKS
by CORDWAINER SMITH

We the Underpeople
When the People Fell

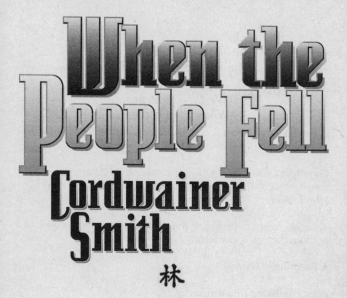

When the People Fell

Cordwainer Smith

林

白

樂

Compiled by
Hank Davis

BAEN

WHEN THE PEOPLE FELL

This is a work of fiction. All the characters and events portrayed in this book are fictional, and any resemblance to real people or incidents is purely coincidental.

A Baen Books Original

Baen Publishing Enterprises
P.O. Box 1403
Riverdale, NY 10471
www.baen.com

ISBN: 978-1-4516-3829-5

Cover art by Tom Kidd

First Baen paperback printing, September 2012

Distributed by Simon & Schuster
1230 Avenue of the Americas
New York, NY 10020

Library of Congress Cataloging-in-Publication Data:
2007016200

Printed in the United States of America

10 9 8 7 6 5 4 3 2 1

When the People Fell

∽ CONTENTS ∽

INTRODUCTION
by Frederik Pohl

Once, a good many years ago, I had a story in a magazine called *Fantasy Book*. Actually, it was only about half a story (it was a collaboration with Isaac Asimov called "Little Man on the Subway"), and for that matter *Fantasy Book* was only about half a magazine. It didn't last very long or reach a very big audience. It might not even have reached me if I hadn't been a contributor—half a contributor. But, by gosh, it had some good stories. And the best of them all was a piece called "Scanners Live in Vain" by an author called Cordwainer Smith.

"Cordwainer Smith," forsooth! The instant question that burned in my mind was who lay behind that disguise. Henry Kuttner had played hide-and-seek games with pennames in those days. So had Robert A. Heinlein, and "Scanners Live in Vain" seemed inventive enough, and *good* enough, to do credit to either of them. But it wasn't in the style, or any of the styles, that I had associated with them. Besides, they denied it. Theodore Sturgeon? A. E. van Vogt? No, neither of them. Then who?

It really did not seem probable that this was someone wholly new. Apart from the coyness of the by-line, there was too great a wealth of color and innovation and conceptually stimulating thought in "Scanners" for me to believe for one second that it was the creation of any but a top master in science fiction. It was not only good. It was expert. Even excellent writers are not usually that excellent the first time around.

Not long afterward I signed a contract to edit a science-fiction anthology for Doubleday's paperback subsidiary, to be entitled *Beyond the End of Time*. That pleased me a lot, not least because it meant I had a chance to display "Scanners Live in Vain" to an audience a hundred times larger than *Fantasy Book* had commanded. And there was a valuable fringe benefit. Somebody would have to sign the publishing agreement for the story. And then I would have him!

Only I didn't. The permission came back signed by Forrest J. Ackerman, as Cordwainer Smith's literary agent. For a brief, crazed period I suspected Forry of having written the story himself, but he assured me he hadn't. And there it rested. For the better part of a decade. Until the time came when I was doing some editorial work for *Galaxy* and my phone rang. The man on the other end said, "Mr. Pohl? I'm Paul Linebarger."

I said, "Yes?" in a tone that he easily translated to mean, *And who the hell is Paul Linebarger*? He quickly added: "I write under the name of Cordwainer Smith."

So who is Paul Linebarger, then?

Well, let me tell you a story. I was once traveling

around Eastern Europe on behalf of the U.S. State Department, talking about science fiction to audiences of Poles and Macedonians and Soviet Georgians. Among others. American science fiction is kindly received in almost all parts of the world, that one included. I was received with cordial hospitality. By the Eastern Europeans, anyway; and often, but not always, by the American diplomats charged with keeping me busy and out of trouble. The least welcome I was ever made to feel was at an embassy dinner, at a post where the American ambassador was a stuffed shirt of the old school, had never read any science fiction, never intended to ready any, and was visibly displeased with the malign turn of fate that compelled him to make dinner-table conversation with a person who made his living by writing the stuff. He didn't thaw until we got to the brandy, and Cordwainer Smith's name came up. I mentioned his real name. The ambassador almost dropped his snifter. "*Doctor* Paul Linebarger? The professor from Johns Hopkins?" the very one, I agreed. "But he was my *teacher*!" said the ambassador. And for what was left of the evening he could not have been more charming.

Professor Linebarger did not teach foreign affairs only to the ambassador; he taught any number of others. He didn't only teach events. He played a part in shaping them. Bilingual in Chinese (he grew up there) and fluent in half a dozen other languages, he was on call to the State Department to lecture, explain, discuss, or negotiate. Even in English. He once gave me his explanation of that. "It's because," he said, "I can speak a . . . lot . . . more . . . slowly . . . and . . . distinctly . . . than . . . most . . . people."

And so he could. And I'm sure that was helpful with many persons who owned rusty or incomplete English. But I don't for one second believe that was the reason. What the State Department treasured was what we all treasure: not the habit of speech, but the mind that shaped it, wise, quick, and comprehending.

Traveler, teacher, writer, diplomat, scholar, Paul Linebarger led a fascinating life. It was as colorful as his novels.

If you have not happened to read a lot of science fiction, the next question that might come to your mind is: "So who is Cordwainer Smith, then?" So let me tell you something about what he wrote, and why to so many of us he was, and is, something special.

Start with this. All of science fiction is special. Not every person likes any of it. Hardly any one likes all of it. It comes in a wide variety of shapes and flavors. Some are bland and familiar, like vanilla. Some are strange and at first glance hardly assimilable, like a Tinguely sculpture happening. That is one of the things that attracts me to science fiction: its mind stretching employment of incongruities. When this trait is pushed as far as it can go, it is a precarious tightrope-dance, daring balanced against disaster; the imagination of the writer and the tolerance of the reader stand stretched right up to the point of catastrophic collapse. One tiny millimeter more, and it would all fall apart. What was mind-bending and fresh would become simply absurd. A. E. van Vogt walked that narrow path marvelously, so did Jack Vance; Samuel R. Delany and Vernor Vinge do it now; but no one, ever, has done it with more daredevil success than Cordwainer Smith. The outrageousness of his concepts, characters, and even words

Congohelium and stroon. Cat-people and laminated-mouse-brain roots. Mile-high abandoned freeways, and dead people who move and act and think and feel. Smith made wonderlands. And he made us believe they could be real.

Part of it was his finely tuned ear for the sound and sense of words. He had a prose style that changed and grew over the few years of his short career, and proved over and over that the right word was the unexpected word. The Smith word-selection is so privately his own, that it can be detected even in the titles of his stories— though perhaps not as straightforwardly as one might imagine. Once James Blish looked up delightedly from the latest issue of *Galaxy* and said, "What I remember best about Cordwainer Smith is those marvelously individual titles." Which titles in particular? I asked, and Jim said, "Why all of them. 'The Dead Lady of Clown town,' 'The Ballad of Lost C'Mell, and Think Blue, Count Two,'" for three. That was funny, and I told him so, because not one of those had been Smith's original title. I had put them on the stories when I published them. But Jim wasn't wrong, because I hadn't made any of them up. They had simply come out of Smith's own text.

Paul Linebarger was not at all a recluse. In fact the opposite. He was gregarious and conversational, traveled immensely, spent a great deal of his time in classes and meetings. But he did not want to meet many science-fiction people. It was not that he did not like them. It was almost a superstition. Once before he had begun a career as a writer. He had published two novels—*Carola* and *Ria*, neither of them science fiction; what they remind me of most are Robert Briffault's novels of European politics, *Europa* and *Europa in Limbo*. He had had every intention of continuing, but he couldn't. The novels had been published under the pseudonym of Felix C. Forrest. They had attracted enough attention to make a number of people wonder who "Felix C. Forrest" was, and a few of them had found out. Unfortunately. What was unfortunate was that when Paul found himself in face-to-face contact with "Forrest"'s audience, he could no longer write for them. Would the same thing happen with science fiction under the same circumstances? He didn't know. But he did not want to risk it.

So Paul Linebarger kept his pseudonym private. He stayed away from gatherings where science-fiction readers and writers were present. When the World Science Fiction Convention was in Washington in 1963, not more than a mile or two from his home, I urged him to drop in and test the water. I would not tell a soul who he was. If he chose, he could turn around and leave. If not . . . well, then not.

Paul weighed the thought and then, reluctantly, decided against the risk. But, he said, there were a couple of individuals whom he would like to meet if they wouldn't mind coming to his house. And so it happened. And of course it was a marvelous afternoon. It had to be. Paul was a fine host, and Genevieve—once his student, then his wife—a splendid hostess. Under the scarlet and gold birth scroll calligraphed by Paul's godfather, Sun Yat-sen, drinking "pukka pegs" (ginger ale and brandy highball, which, Paul said, were what had kept the British army alive in India), in that discovering company the vibrations were optimal.

And it did not trouble his writing at all, then or thereafter. He kept on writing, if anything better than ever. He enjoyed his guests—particularly, he said, Judith Merril and Algis Budrys—enough so that he felt easier about meeting others in the field. Little by little he did. Some in person, some only by mail, most by phone, and I think that the time was not far off when Paul Linebarger would have made an appearance at a science-fiction convention. Maybe a lot of them. But time ran out. He died of a stroke in 1966, at the bitterly unfair age of fifty-three.

Every important work of fiction is written partly in code. What we read in a sentence is not always what the author had in mind when he wrote it, and there are times—oh, *many* times—when the author's meaning may be unclear even to him. This is not always a flaw. It is sometimes a necessity. When a human mind, boxed inside its skull, perceiving the universe only through deceitful senses and communicating with it only in imprecise words, reaches for complex meanings and patterns of understanding, explicit statement is hard to achieve. The higher the reach, the harder the task. Cordwainer Smith's reach sometimes went clear out of sight.

Paul taught me how to decrypt some of his messages, but only the easy ones. Somewhere in the files of the manuscript collection at Syracuse University there is, or ought to be, an annotated copy of some of his manuscripts with decoding instructions. The particular stories were a parable of Middle-Eastern politics. He had taken the trouble to note in the margins for me which story characters from the remote future represented what current Egyptian and Lebanese political figures.

That is a game many writers play. It is sometimes fun, but I don't happen to consider it a whole *lot* of fun. What I wish I could decode in the work of Cordwainer Smith is far more complicated. His concerns went beyond current life and contemporary politics, and maybe beyond human experience entirely. Religion. Metaphysics. Ultimate meaning. The search for truth. When you set out to catch ultimate truth in a net of words, you need a lot of patience and a lot of skill. The quarry is elusive. Worse than that. You need a lot of faith, too, and a lot of stubbornness, because what you are seeking may not exist at all. Does religion refer to anything "real?" *Is* there such a thing in the universe as "meaning?"

The Cordwainer Smith stories are science fiction, all right. But they are, at least the best of them are, science fiction of the special sort that C. S. Lewis called "eschatological fiction." They aren't about the future of human beings like us. They are about what comes *after* human beings like us. They don't answer questions. They ask them and command us to ask them too.

Cordwainer Smith's whole science-fiction writing career essentially took place in less than a decade. But how many writers in a full lifetime can match it?

—Frederik Pohl

Section I: Instrumentality Stories

No, No, Not Rogov!

That golden shape on the golden steps shook and fluttered like a bird gone mad—like a bird imbued with an intellect and a soul, and, nevertheless, driven mad by ecstasies and terrors beyond human understanding— ecstasies drawn momentarily down into reality by the consummation of superlative art. A thousand worlds watched.

Had the ancient calendar continued this would have been A.D. 13,582. After defeat, after disappointment, after ruin and reconstruction, mankind had leapt among the stars.

Out of meeting inhuman art, out of confronting non-human dances, mankind had made a superb esthetic effort and had leapt upon the stage of all the worlds.

The golden steps reeled before the eyes. Some eyes had retinas. Some had crystalline cones. Yet all eyes were fixed upon the golden shape which interpreted The Glory and Affirmation of Man *in the Inter-World Dance Festival of what might have been A.D. 13,582.*

Once again mankind was winning the contest. Music

11

*and dance were hypnotic beyond the limits of systems,
compelling, shocking to human and inhuman eyes. The
dance was a triumph of shock—the shock of dynamic
beauty.*

*The golden shape on the golden steps executed
shimmering intricacies of meaning. The body was gold and
still human. The body was a woman, but more than a
woman. On the golden steps, in the golden light, she
trembled and fluttered like a bird gone mad.*

∞ | ∞

The Ministry of State Security had been positively
shocked when they found that a Nazi agent, more heroic
than prudent, had almost reached N. Rogov.

Rogov was worth more to the Soviet armed forces than
any two air armies, more than three motorized divisions.
His brain was a weapon, a weapon for the Soviet power.

Since the brain was a weapon, Rogov was a prisoner.
He didn't mind. Rogov was a pure Russian type, broad-
faced, sandy-haired, blue-eyed, with whimsey in his smile
and amusement in the wrinkles of the tops of his cheeks.

"Of course I'm a prisoner," Rogov used to say. "I
am a prisoner of State service to the Soviet peoples.
But the workers and peasants are good to me. I am an
academician of the All Union Academy of Sciences, a
major general in the Red Air Force, a professor in the
University of Kharkov, a deputy works manager of the
Red Flag Combat Aircraft Production Trust. From each
of these I draw a salary."

Sometimes he would narrow his eyes at his Russian scientific colleagues and ask them in dead earnest, "Would I serve capitalists?"

The affrighted colleagues would try to stammer their way out of the embarrassment, protesting their common loyalty to Stalin or Beria, or Zhukov, or Molotov, or Bulganin, as the case may have been.

Rogov would look very Russian: calm, mocking, amused. He would let them stammer.

Then he'd laugh. Solemnity transformed into hilarity, he would explode into bubbling, effervescent, good-humored laughter. "Of course I could not serve the capitalists. My little Anastasia would not let me."

The colleagues would smile uncomfortably and would wish that Rogov did not talk so wildly, or so comically, or so freely.

Even Rogov might wind up dead. Rogov didn't think so. They did. Rogov was afraid of nothing.

Most of his colleagues were afraid of each other, of the Soviet system, of the world, of life, and of death.

Perhaps Rogov had once been ordinary and mortal like other people, and full of fears.

But he had become the lover, the colleague, the husband of Anastasia Fyodorovna Cherpas.

Comrade Cherpas had been his rival, his antagonist, his competitor, in the struggle for scientific eminence in the daring Slav frontiers of Russian science. Russian science could never overtake the inhuman perfection of German method, the rigid intellectual and moral discipline of German teamwork, but the Russians could and did get ahead of the Germans by giving vent to their bold, fantastic imaginations. Rogov had pioneered the first rocket launchers of 1939. Cherpas had finished the job by making the best of the rockets radio-directed.

Rogov in 1942 had developed a whole new system of photo-mapping. Comrade Cherpas had applied it to color film. Rogov, sandy-haired, blue-eyed, and smiling, had recorded his criticisms of Comrade Cherpas's naïveté and unsoundness at the top-secret meetings of Russian scientists during the black winter nights of 1943. Comrade Cherpas, her butter-yellow hair flowing down like living water to her shoulders, her unpainted face gleaming with fanaticism, intelligence, and dedication, would snarl her own defiance at him, deriding his Communist theory, pinching at his pride, hitting his intellectual hypotheses where they were weakest.

By 1944 a Rogov-Cherpas quarrel had become something worth traveling to see.

In 1945 they were married.

Their courtship was secret, their wedding a surprise, their partnership a miracle in the upper ranks of Russian science.

The emigré press had reported that the great scientist, Peter Kapitza, once remarked, "Rogov and Cherpas, there is a team. They're Communists, good Communists; but they're better than that! They're *Russian*, Russian enough to beat the world. Look at them. That's the future, our Russian future!" Perhaps the quotation was an exaggeration, but it did show the enormous respect in which both Rogov and Cherpas were held by their colleagues in Soviet science.

Shortly after their marriage strange things happened to them.

Rogov remained happy. Cherpas was radiant.

Nevertheless, the two of them began to have haunted expressions, as though they had seen things which words could not express, as though they had stumbled upon secrets too important to be whispered even to the most secure agents of the Soviet State Police.

In 1947 Rogov had an interview with Stalin. As he left Stalin's office in the Kremlin, the great leader himself came to the door, his forehead wrinkled in thought, nodding, "Da, *da, da.*"

Even his own personal staff did not know why Stalin was saying "Yes, yes, yes," but they did see the orders that went forth marked ONLY BY SAFE HAND, and TO BE READ AND RETURNED, NOT RETAINED, and furthermore stamped FOR AUTHORIZED EYES ONLY AND UNDER NO CIRCUMSTANCES TO BE COPIED.

Into the true and secret Soviet budget that year by the direct personal order of a noncommittal Stalin, an item was added for "Project Telescope." Stalin tolerated no inquiry, brooked no comment.

A village which had had a name became nameless.

A forest which had been opened to the workers and peasants became military territory.

Into the central post office in Kharkov there went a new box number for the *village of Ya. Ch.*

Rogov and Cherpas, comrades and lovers, scientists both and Russians both, disappeared from the everyday lives of their colleagues. Their faces were no longer seen at scientific meetings. Only rarely did they emerge.

On the few times they were seen, usually going to and from Moscow at the time the All Union budget was made up each year, they seemed smiling and happy. But they did not make jokes.

What the outside world did not know was that Stalin in giving them their own project, granting them a paradise restricted to themselves, had seen to it that a snake went with them in the paradise. The snake this time was not one, but two personalities—Gausgofer and Gauck.

∽ II ∾

Stalin died.

Beria died too—less willingly.

The world went on.

Everything went into the forgotten village of Ya. Ch. and nothing came out.

It was rumored that Bulganin himself visited Rogov and Cherpas. It was even whispered that Bulganin said as he went to the Kharkov airport to fly back to Moscow, "It's big, big, big. There'll be no cold war if they do it. There won't be any war of any kind. We'll finish capitalism before the capitalists can ever begin to fight. If they do it. If they do it." Bulganin was reported to have shaken his head slowly in perplexity and to have said nothing more but to have put his initials on the unmodified budget of Project Telescope when a trusted messenger next brought him an envelope from Rogov.

Anastasia Cherpas became a mother. Their first boy looked like his father. He was followed by a little girl. Then another little boy. The children didn't stop

Cherpas's work. They had a large dacha and trained nursemaids took over the household.

Every night the four of them dined together.

Rogov, Russian, humorous, courageous, amused.

Cherpas, older, more mature, more beautiful than ever but just as biting, just as cheerful, just as sharp as she had ever been.

But then the other two, the two who sat with them across the years of all their days, the two colleagues who had been visited upon them by the all-powerful word of Stalin himself.

Gausgofer was a female: bloodless, narrow-faced, with a voice like a horse's whinny. She was a scientist and a policewoman, and competent at both jobs. In 1917 she had reported her own mother's whereabouts to the Bolshevik Terror Committee. In 1924 she had commanded her father's execution. He had been a Russian German of the old Baltic nobility and he had tried to adjust his mind to the new system, but he had failed. In 1930 she had let her lover trust her a little too much. He had been a Roumanian Communist, very high in the Party, but he had whispered into her ear in the privacy of their bedroom, whispered with the tears pouring down his face; she had listened affectionately and quietly and had delivered his words to the police the next morning.

With that she had come to Stalin's attention.

Stalin had been tough. He had addressed her brutally. "Comrade, you have some brains. I can see you know what Communism is all about. You understand loyalty. You're going to get ahead and serve the Party and the working class, but is that all you want?" He had spat the question at her.

She had been so astonished that she gaped.

The old man had changed his expression, favoring her with leering benevolence. He had put his forefinger on her chest. "Study science, Comrade. Study science. Communism plus science equals victory. You're too clever to stay in police work."

Gausgofer took a reluctant pride in the fiendish program of her German namesake, the wicked old geographer who made geography itself a terrible weapon in the Nazi anti-Soviet struggle.

Gausgofer would have liked nothing better than to intrude on the marriage of Cherpas and Rogov.

Gausgofer fell in love with Rogov the moment she saw him.

Gausgofer fell in hate—and hate can be as spontaneous and miraculous as love—with Cherpas the moment she saw *her*.

But Stalin had guessed that too.

With the bloodless, fanatic Gausgofer he had sent a man named B. Gauck.

Gauck was solid, impassive, blank-faced. In body he was about the same height as Rogov. Where Rogov was muscular, Gauck was flabby. Where Rogov's skin was fair and shot through with the pink and health of exercise, Gauck's skin was like stale lard, greasy, gray-green, sickly even on the best of days.

Gauck's eyes were black and small. His glance was as cold and sharp as death. Gauck had no friends, no enemies, no beliefs, no enthusiasm. Even Gausgofer was afraid of him.

Gauck never drank, never went out, never received

mail, never sent mail, never spoke a spontaneous word. He was never rude, never kind, never friendly, never really withdrawn: he couldn't withdraw any more than the constant withdrawal of all his life.

Rogov had turned to his wife in the secrecy of their bedroom soon after Gausgofer and Gauck came and had said, "Anastasia, is that man sane?"

Cherpas intertwined the fingers of her beautiful, expressive hands. She who had been the wit of a thousand scientific meetings was now at a loss for words. She looked up at her husband with a troubled expression. "I don't know, Comrade . . . I just don't know . . ."

Rogov smiled his amused Slavic smile. "At the least then I don't think Gausgofer knows either."

Cherpas snorted with laughter and picked up her hairbrush. "That she doesn't. She really doesn't know, does she? I'll wager she doesn't even know to whom he reports."

That conversation had receded into the past. Gauck, Gausgofer, the bloodless eyes and the black eyes—they remained.

Every dinner the four sat down together.

Every morning the four met in the laboratory.

Rogov's great courage, high sanity, and keen humor kept the work going.

Cherpas's flashing genius fueled him whenever the routine overloaded his magnificent intellect.

Gausgofer spied and watched and smiled her bloodless smiles; sometimes, curiously enough, Gausgofer made genuinely constructive suggestions. She never understood the whole frame of reference of their work, but she knew enough of the mechanical and engineering details to be very useful on occasion.

Gauck came in, sat down quietly, said nothing, did nothing. He did not even smoke. He never fidgeted. He never went to sleep. He just watched.

The laboratory grew and with it there grew the immense configuration of the espionage machine.

∾ III ∾

In theory what Rogov had proposed and Cherpas seconded was imaginable. It consisted of an attempt to work out an integrated theory for all the electrical and radiation phenomena accompanying consciousness, and to duplicate the electrical functions of mind without the use of animal material.

The range of potential products was immense. The first product Stalin had asked for was a receiver, if possible, capable of tuning in the thoughts of a human mind and of translating those thoughts into either a punch-tape machine, an adapted German Hellschreiber machine, or phonetic speech. If the grids could be turned around and the brain-equivalent machine could serve not as a receiver but as a transmitter, it might be able to send out stunning forces which would paralyze or kill the process of thought.

At its best, Rogov's machine would be designed to confuse human thought over great distances, to select human targets to be confused, and to maintain an electronic jamming system which would jam straight into the human mind without the requirement of tubes or receivers.

He had succeeded—in part. He had given himself a violent headache in the first year of work.

In the third year he had killed mice at a distance of ten kilometers. In the seventh year he had brought on mass hallucinations and a wave, of suicides in a neighboring village. It was this which impressed Bulganin.

Rogov was now working on the receiver end. No one had ever explored the infinitely narrow, infinitely subtle bands of radiation which distinguished one human mind from another, but Rogov was trying, as it were, to tune in on minds far away.

He had tried to develop a telepathic helmet of some kind, but it did not work. He had then turned away from the reception of pure thought to the reception of visual and auditory images. Where the nerve ends reached the brain itself, he had managed over the years to distinguish whole pockets of micro-phenomena, and on some of these he had managed to get a fix.

With infinitely delicate tuning he had succeeded one day in picking up the eyesight of their second chauffeur and had managed, thanks to a needle thrust in just below his own right eyelid, to "see" through the other man's eyes as the other man, all unaware, washed their Zis limousine 1,600 meters away.

Cherpas had surpassed his feat later that winter and had managed to bring in an entire family having dinner over in a nearby city. She had invited B. Gauck to have a needle inserted into his cheekbone so that he could see with the eyes of an unsuspecting spied-on stranger. Gauck had refused any kind of needles, but Gausgofer had joined in the work.

The espionage machine was beginning to take form.

Two more steps remained. The first step consisted of tuning in on some remote target, such as the White House in Washington or the NATO Headquarters outside of Paris. The machine itself could obtain perfect intelligence by eavesdropping on the living minds of people far away.

The second problem consisted of finding a method of jamming those minds at a distance, stunning them so that the subject personnel fell into tears, confusion, or sheer insanity.

Rogov had tried, but he had never gotten more than thirty kilometers from the nameless village of Ya. Ch.

One November there had been seventy cases of hysteria, most of them ending in suicide, down in the city of Kharkov several hundred kilometers away, but Rogov was not sure that his own machine was doing it.

Comrade Gausgofer dared to stroke his sleeve. Her white lips smiled and her watery eyes grew happy as she said in her high, cruel voice, "*You* can do it, Comrade. You can do it."

Cherpas looked on with contempt. Gauck said nothing.

The female agent Gausgofer saw Cherpas's eyes upon her, and for a moment an arc of living hatred leapt between the two women.

The three of them went back to work on the machine.

Gauck sat on his stool and watched them.

The laboratory workers never talked very much and the room was quiet.

∾ IV ∾

It was the year in which Eristratov died that the
machine made a breakthrough. Eristratov died after the
Soviet and People's democracies had tried to end the cold
war with the Americans.

It was May. Outside the laboratory the squirrels ran
among the trees. The leftovers from the night's rain
dripped on the ground and kept the earth moist. It was
comfortable to leave a few windows open and to let the
smell of the forest into the workshop.

The smell of their oil-burning heaters and the stale
smell of insulation, of ozone, and of the heated electronic
gear was something with which all of them were much too
familiar.

Rogov had found that his eyesight was beginning to
suffer because he had to get the receiver needle somewhere
near his optic nerve in order to obtain visual impressions
from the machine. After months of experimentation with
both animal and human subjects he had decided to copy
one of their last experiments, successfully performed on a
prisoner boy fifteen years of age, by having the needle
slipped directly through the skull, up and behind the eye.
Rogov had disliked using prisoners, because Gauck,
speaking on behalf of security, always insisted that a
prisoner used in experiments had to be destroyed in not
less than five days from the beginning of the experiment.
Rogov had satisfied himself that the skull-and-needle
technique was safe, but he was very tired of trying to get

frightened, unscientific people to carry the load of intense, scientific attentiveness required by the machine.

Rogov recapitulated the situation to his wife and to their two strange colleagues.

Somewhat ill-humored, he shouted at Gauck, "Have you ever known what this is all about? You've been here years. Do you know what we're trying to do? Don't you ever want to take part in the experiments yourself? Do you realize how many years of mathematics have gone into the making of these grids and the calculation of these wave patterns? Are you good for anything?"

Gauck said, tonelessly and without anger, "Comrade Professor, I am obeying orders. You are obeying orders, too. I've never impeded you."

Rogov almost raved. "I know you never got in my way. We're all good servants of the Soviet State. It's not a question of loyalty. It's a question of enthusiasm. Don't you ever want to glimpse the science we're making? We are a hundred years or a thousand years ahead of the capitalist Americans. Doesn't that excite you? Aren't you a human being? Why don't you take part? Will you understand me when I explain it?"

Gauck said nothing: he looked at Rogov with his beady eyes. His dirty-gray face did not change expression. Gausgofer exhaled loudly in a grotesquely feminine sigh of relief, but she too said nothing. Cherpas, her winning smile and her friendly eyes looking at her husband and two colleagues, said, "Go ahead, Nikolai. The comrade can follow if he wants to."

Gausgofer looked enviously at Cherpas. She seemed

inclined to keep quiet, but then had to speak. She said, "Do go ahead, Comrade Professor."

Said Rogov, "*Kharosho*, I'll do what I can. The machine is now ready to receive minds over immense distances." He wrinkled his lip in amused scorn. "We may even spy into the brain of the chief rascal himself and find out what Eisenhower is planning to do today against the Soviet people. Wouldn't it be wonderful if our machine could stun him and leave him sitting addled at his desk?"

Gauck commented, "Don't try it. Not without orders."

Rogov ignored the interruption and went on. "First I receive. I don't know what I will get, who I will get, or where they will be. All I know is that this machine will reach out across all the minds of men and beasts now living and it will bring the eyes and ears of a single mind directly into mine. With the new needle going directly into the brain it will be possible for me to get a very sharp fixation of position. The trouble with that boy last week was that even though we knew he was seeing something outside of this room, he appeared to be getting sounds in a foreign language and did not know enough English or German to realize where or what the machine had taken him to see."

Cherpas laughed. "I'm not worried. I saw then it was safe. You go first, my husband. If our comrades don't mind—?"

Gauck nodded.

Gausgofer lifted her bony hand breathlessly up to her skinny throat and said, "Of course, Comrade Rogov, of course. You did *all* the work. You *must* be the first."

Rogov sat down.

A white-smocked technician brought the machine over to him. It was mounted on three rubber-tired wheels and it resembled the small X-ray units used by dentists. In place of the cone at the head of the X-ray machine there was a long, incredibly tough needle. It had been made for them by the best surgical-steel craftsmen in Prague.

Another technician came up with a shaving bowl, a brush, and a straight razor. Under the gaze of Gauck's deadly eyes he shaved an area four centimeters square on the top of Rogov's head.

Cherpas herself then took over. She set her husband's head in the clamp and used a micrometer to get the skullfittings so tight and so clear that the needle would push through the dura mater at exactly the right point.

All this work she did deftly with kind, very strong fingers. She was gentle, but she was firm. She was his wife, but she was also his fellow scientist and his fellow colleague in the Soviet State.

She stepped back and looked at her work. She gave him one of their own very special smiles, the secret gay smiles which they usually exchanged with each other only when they were alone. "You won't want to do this every day. We're going to have to find some way of getting into the brain without using this needle. But it won't hurt you."

"Does it matter if it does hurt?" said Rogov. "This is the triumph of all our work. *Bring it down.*"

Gausgofer looked as though she would like to be invited to take part in the experiment, but she dared not interrupt Cherpas. Cherpas, her eyes gleaming with attention, reached over and pulled down the handle, which brought the tough needle to within a tenth of a millimeter of the right place.

Rogov spoke very carefully. "All I felt was a little sting. You can turn the power on now."

Gausgofer could not contain herself. Timidly she addressed Cherpas. "May *I* turn on the power?"

Cherpas nodded. Gauck watched. Rogov waited. Gausgofer pulled down the bayonet switch.

The power went on.

With an impatient twist of her hand, Anastasia Cherpas ordered the laboratory attendants to the other end of the room. Two or three of them had stopped working and were staring at Rogov, staring like dull sheep. They looked embarrassed and then they huddled in a white-smocked herd at the other end of the laboratory.

The wet May wind blew in on all of them. The scent of forest and leaves was about them.

The three watched Rogov.

Rogov's complexion began to change. His face became flushed. His breathing was so loud and heavy they could hear it several meters away. Cherpas fell on her knees in front of him, eyebrows lifted in mute inquiry.

Rogov did not dare nod, not with a needle in his brain. He said through flushed lips, speaking thickly and heavily, "Do—not—stop—now."

Rogov himself did not know what was happening. He thought he might see an American room, or a Russian room, or a tropical colony. He might see palm trees, or forests, or desks. He might see guns or buildings, wash-rooms or beds, hospitals, homes, churches. He might see with the eyes of a child, a woman, a man, a soldier, a philosopher, a slave, a worker, a savage, a religious one, a Communist, a reactionary, a governor, a policeman. He might hear voices; he might hear English, or French, or Russian, Swahili, Hindu, Malay, Chinese, Ukrainian, Armenian, Turkish, Greek. He did not know.

Something strange was happening.

It *seemed* to him that he had left the world, that he had left time. The hours and the centuries shrank up as the meters and the machine, unchecked, reached out for the most powerful signal which any humankind had transmitted. Rogov did not know it, but the machine had conquered time.

The machine reached the dance, the human challenger, and the dance festival of the year that was not A.D. 13,582, but which might have been.

Before Rogov's eyes the golden shape and the golden steps shook and fluttered in a ritual a thousand times more compelling than hypnotism. The rhythms meant nothing and everything to him. This was Russia, this was Communism. This was his life—indeed it was his soul acted out before his very eyes.

For a second, the last second of his ordinary life, he looked through flesh-and-blood eyes and saw the shabby woman whom he had once thought beautiful. He saw Anastasia Cherpas, and he did not care.

His vision concentrated once again on the dancing image, this woman, those postures, that dance!

Then the sound came in—music which would have made a Tchaikovsky weep, orchestras which would have silenced Shostakovich or Khachaturian forever, so much did it surpass the music of the twentieth century.

The people-who-were-not-people between the stars had taught mankind many arts. Rogov's mind was the best of its time, but his time was far, far behind the time of the great dance. With that one vision Rogov went firmly and completely mad. He became blind to the sight of Cherpas, Gausgofer, and Gauck. He forgot the village of Ya. Ch. He forgot himself. He was like a fish, bred in stale fresh water, which is thrown for the first time into a living stream. He was like an insect emerging from the chrysalis. His twentieth-century mind could not hold the imagery and the impact of the music and the dance.

But the needle was there and the needle transmitted into his mind more than his mind could stand.

The synapses of his brain flicked like switches. The future flooded into him.

He fainted. Cherpas leapt forward and lifted the needle. Rogov fell out of the chair.

∽ V ∽

It was Gauck who got the doctors. By nightfall they had Rogov resting comfortably and under heavy sedation. There were two doctors, both from the military headquarters. Gauck had obtained authorization for their services by dint of a direct telephone call to Moscow.

Both the doctors were annoyed. The senior one never stopped grumbling at Cherpas.

"You should not have done it, Comrade Cherpas. Comrade Rogov should not have done it either. You can't go around sticking things into brains. That's a medical problem. None of you people are doctors of medicine. It's all right for you to contrive devices with the prisoners, but you can't inflict things like this on Soviet scientific personnel. I'm going to get blamed because I can't bring Rogov back. You heard what he was saying. All he did was mutter, 'That golden shape on the golden steps, that music, that me is a true me, that golden shape, that golden shape, I want to be with that golden shape,' and rubbish like that. Maybe you've ruined a first-class brain forever—" He stopped himself short as though he had said too much. After all, the problem was a security problem and apparently both Gauck and Gausgofer represented the security agencies.

Gausgofer turned her watery eyes on the doctor and said in a low, even, unbelievably poisonous voice, "Could *she* have done it, Comrade Doctor?"

The doctor looked at Cherpas, answering Gausgofer. "How? You were there. I wasn't. *How* could she have done it? *Why* should she do it? You were there."

Cherpas said nothing. Her lips were compressed tight with grief. Her yellow hair gleamed, but her hair was all that remained, at that moment, of her beauty. She was frightened and she was getting ready to be sad. She had no time to hate foolish women or to worry about security; she was concerned with her colleague, her lover, her husband, Rogov.

There was nothing much for them to do except to wait. They went into a large room and tried to eat.

The servants had laid out immense dishes of cold sliced meat, pots of caviar, and an assortment of sliced breads, pure butter genuine coffee, and liquors.

None of them ate much.

They were all waiting.

At 9:15 the sound of rotors beat against the house.

The big helicopter had arrived from Moscow.

Higher authorities took over.

∽ VI ∽

The higher authority was a deputy minister, a man by the name of V. Karper.

Karper was accompanied by two or three uniformed colonels, by an engineer civilian, by a man from the headquarters of the Communist Party of the Soviet Union, and by two doctors.

They dispensed with the courtesies. Karper merely said, "You are Cherpas. I have met you. You are Gausgofer. I have seen your reports. You are Gauck."

The delegation went into Rogov's bedroom. Karper snapped, "Wake him."

The military doctor who had given him sedatives said "Comrade, you mustn't—"

Karper cut him off. "Shut up." He turned to his own physician, pointed at Rogov. "Wake him up."

The doctor from Moscow talked briefly with the senior military doctor. He too began shaking his head. He gave Karper a disturbed look. Karper guessed what he might hear. He said, "Go ahead. I know there is some danger to the patient, but I've got to get back to Moscow with a report."

The two doctors worked over Rogov. One of them

asked for his bag and gave Rogov an injection. Then all of them stood back from the bed.

Rogov writhed in his bed. He squirmed. His eyes opened, but he did not see them. With childishly clear and simple words Rogov began to talk: ". . . that golden shape, the golden stairs, the music, take me back to the music, I want to be with the music, I really am the music . . ." and so on in an endless monotone.

Cherpas leaned over him so that her face was directly in his line of vision. "My darling! My darling, wake up. This is serious."

It was evident to all of them that Rogov did not hear her, because he went on muttering about golden shapes.

For the first time in many years Gauck took the initiative. He spoke directly to the man from Moscow, Karper. "Comrade, may I make a suggestion?"

Karper looked at him. Gauck nodded at Gausgofer. "We were both sent here by orders of Comrade Stalin. She is senior. She bears the responsibility. All I do is double-check."

The deputy minister turned to Gausgofer. Gausgofer had been staring at Rogov on the bed; her blue, watery eyes were tearless and her face was drawn into an expression of extreme tension.

Karper ignored that and said to her firmly, clearly, commandingly, "What do you recommend?"

Gausgofer looked at him very directly and said in a measured voice, "I do not think that the case is one of brain damage. I believe that he has obtained a communication which he must share with another human being and that unless one of us follows him there may be no answer."

Karper barked, "Very well. But what do we do?"

"Let *me* follow—into the machine."

Anastasia Cherpas began to laugh slyly and frantically. She seized Karper's arm and pointed her finger at Gausgofer. Karper stared at her.

Cherpas slowed down her laughter and shouted at Karper, "The woman's mad. She has loved my husband for many years. She has hated my presence, and now she thinks that she can save him. She thinks that she can follow. She thinks that he wants to communicate with her. That's ridiculous. I will go myself!"

Karper looked about. He selected two of his staff and stepped over into a corner of the room. They could hear him talking, but they could not distinguish the words. After a conference of six or seven minutes he returned.

"You people have been making serious security charges against each other. I find that one of our finest weapons, the mind of Rogov, is damaged. Rogov's not just a man. He is a Soviet project." Scorn entered his voice. "I find that the senior security officer, a policewoman with a notable record, is charged by another Soviet scientist with a silly infatuation. I disregard such charges. The development of the Soviet State and the work of Soviet science cannot be impeded by personalities. Comrade Gausgofer will follow. I am acting tonight because my own staff physician says that Rogov may not live and it is very important for us to find out just what has happened to him and why."

He turned his baneful gaze on Cherpas. "You will not protest, Comrade. Your mind is the property of the Russian State. Your life and your education have been paid for by the workers. You cannot throw these things away because of personal sentiment. If there is anything to be found Comrade Gausgofer will find it for both of us."

The whole group of them went back into the laboratory. The frightened technicians were brought over from the barracks. The lights were turned on and the windows were closed. The May wind had become chilly.

The needle was sterilized.

The electronic grids were warmed up.

Gausgofer's face was an impassive mask of triumph as she sat in the receiving chair. She smiled at Gauck as an attendant brought the soap and the razor to shave a clean patch on her scalp.

Gauck did not smile back. His black eyes stared at her. He said nothing. He did nothing. He watched.

Karper walked to and fro, glancing from time to time at the hasty but orderly preparation of the experiment.

Anastasia Cherpas sat down at a laboratory table about five meters away from the group. She watched the back of Gausgofer's head as the needle was lowered. She buried her face in her hands. Some of the others thought they heard her weeping, but no one heeded Cherpas very much. They were too intent on watching Gausgofer.

Gausgofer's face became red. Perspiration poured down the flabby cheeks. Her fingers tightened on the arm of her chair.

Suddenly she shouted at them, *"That golden shape on the golden steps."*

She leapt to her feet, dragging the apparatus with her. No one had expected this. The chair fell to the floor.

The needle holder, lifted from the floor, swung its weight sidewise. The needle twisted like a scythe in Gausgofer's brain. Neither Rogov nor Cherpas had ever expected a struggle within the chair. *They did not know that they were going to tune in on* A.D. *13,582.*

The body of Gausgofer lay on the floor, surrounded by excited officials.

Karper was acute enough to look around at Cherpas.

She stood up from the laboratory table and walked toward him. A thin line of blood flowed down from her cheekbone. Another line of blood dripped down from a position on her cheek, one and a half centimeters forward of the opening of her left ear.

With tremendous composure, her face as white as fresh snow, she smiled at him. "I eavesdropped."

Karper said, "What?"

"I eavesdropped, eavesdropped," repeated Anastasia Cherpas. "I found out where my husband has gone. It is not somewhere in this world. It is something hypnotic beyond all the limitations of our science. We have made a great gun, but the gun has fired upon us before we could fire it. You may think you will change my mind, Comrade Deputy Minister, but you will not.

"I know what has happened. My husband is never coming back. And I am not going any further forward without him.

"Project Telescope is finished. You may try to get someone else to finish it, but you will not."

Karper stared at her and then turned aside.

Gauck stood in his way.

"What do you want?" snapped Karper.

"To tell you," said Gauck very softly, "to tell you, Comrade Deputy Minister, that Rogov is gone as she says he is gone, that she is finished if she says she is finished, that all this is true. I know."

Karper glared at him. "How do you know?"

Gauck remained utterly impassive. With superhuman assurance and perfect calm he said to Karper, "Comrade, I do not dispute the matter. I know these people, though I do not know their science. Rogov is done for."

At last Karper believed him. Karper sat down in a chair beside a table. He looked up at his staff. "Is it possible?"

No one answered.

"I ask you, is it possible?"

They all looked at Anastasia Cherpas, at her beautiful hair, her determined blue eyes, and the two thin lines of blood where she had eavesdropped with small needles.

Karper turned to her. "What do we do now?"

For an answer she dropped to her knees and began sobbing, "No, no, not Rogov! No, no, not Rogov!"

And that was all that they could get out of her. Gauck looked on.

On the golden steps in the golden light, a golden shape danced a dream beyond the limits of all imagination, danced and drew the music to herself until a sigh of yearning, yearning which became a hope and a torment, went through the hearts of living things on a thousand worlds.

Edges of the golden scene faded raggedly and unevenly into black. The gold dimmed down to a pale gold-silver sheen and then to silver, last of all to white. The dancer who had been golden was now a forlorn white-pink figure standing, quiet and fatigued, on the immense white steps. The applause of a thousand worlds roared in upon her.

She looked blindly at them. The dance had overwhelmed her, too. Their applause could mean nothing. The dance was an end in itself. She would have to live, somehow, until she danced again.

War No. 81-Q
(Rewritten Version)

For a few brief happy centuries, war was made into an enormous game. Then the world population passed the thirty-billion point, Acting Chief Minister Chatterji presented the "Rightful Proportions" formula to the world authorities, and war turned from a game into realities. When it was over, hideous new creepers covered the wreckage of cities, saints and morons camped in the overpasses of disused highways, and a few man-hunting machines scoured the world in search of surviving weapons.

∾ | ∾

Long before real war set mankind back a thousand ages, the nations played with their formulae of "safe war." Wars were easily declared, safely fought, won or lost with noblesse oblige, and accepted as decisive. Wars were rare enough to sweep all other events from the television screens, beautiful enough to warrant the utmost in scenic decoration, and tough enough to call for champions with perfect eyesight and no nerves at all. The weapons were dirigibles armed with missiles, countermissiles, and feinting screens; they had been revived because they were slow enough to show well on the viewscreens, hard enough to demand a skillful fight. A whole class of warriors developed to manage these—men who trained on the ski-slopes and underwater beaches of the world's resorts and who then, tanned and fit, sat in control rooms and managed the ships from their own home bases. The kinescopes were paired up so that pictures of the battle alternated with scenes of the warriors sitting in their controls, the foreheads wrinkled with worry, their gasps of dismay or smiles of triumph showing plainly, and the whole drama of human emotion revealed in their performance of a licensed war.

War came near between Tibet and America.

Tibet had been liberated from the Goonhogo, the central Chinese government, only with generous American help and with the threat (was it bluff? was it death?) trembling in the rocket pits around Lake Erie. No one ever found out whether the Americans would have risked real war, because the Chinese did not force a show of strength. The Americans had been supported by the Reunion of India and the Federated Congos on the floor of the world assembly, and there were political debts to be settled when the Tibetan liberation came true. The Congo asked for support on Saharan claims, which was easy enough, since this was a matter of voting in the assembly,

but the Reunion of India asked for the largest solar
power-collector, to reach eighty miles along the southern
crest of the Himalayas. The Americans hesitated, and
then built it under lease from Tibet, keeping title in their
own hands. Just before the first surges of power were due
to pour down into the Bengal plains, Tibetan soldiers
entered the control rooms with a warrant from the
Tibetan ministry of the interior seizing the plant, Tibetan
technicians hooked in new cables which had been flown
from the Goonhogo base at Teli in Yunnan, and the
Tibetans announced they had leased the entire power output to their recent enemies, the Goonhogo of China.

Even in politics, where gratitude is seldom expected,
such bleak ingratitude was hard to bear. The Americans
had just freed the Tibetans from the Chinese, and now the
Tibetans seized the reward which America had built for
Indian help on Tibetan territory. Legally, the deal was
tight. The solar accumulators were on Tibetan soil, and
under the system of "sovereignty" which prevailed at
that time, any nation could do what it pleased on its own
territory and get off scot-free.

Some Americans were so furious that they clamored
for a real war against the Goonhogo of China. The president
himself remarked mildly that it did not seem right to fight
an antagonist merely because he showed himself cleverer
than we.

Congress voted a licensed war.

The president had no further choice. He had to
declare war on Tibet. He put a request for the permit in
to the world secretariat. The license came back for "War
No. 81-Q," since someone in the world secretariat figured

that Tibet should not pay for any but the smallest-size war. The Americans had asked for a class-A war, which would have lasted up to four full days. The world secretariat refused a review of the case.

There was nothing left to do.

America was at war.

The president sent for Jack Reardon.

≈ II ≈

Reardon was the best licensed warrior America had.

"Morning, Jack," said the president. "You haven't fought for two years, when Iceland beat us. Do you feel up to it now?"

"Fitter than ever, sir," said Jack. He hesitated and then went on, "Please don't mention Iceland, sir. Nobody has ever beaten Sigurd Sigurdssen. Lucky for us that he's retired."

"I wouldn't have called you if I just meant to reproach you. I know you did the best that anyone could do short of the great Sigurd himself. That's why you're here. How do you think we should run it?"

"There's not much choice on ships, not with a class-Q war. They had better all five be the new Mark Zeros. Since we challenged, I think the Tibetans will choose the cheapest war they can. They don't want to run up a big bill on themselves. The Goonhogo would help them, but the Chinese would be around two days later, asking for payment."

"I didn't know," said the President with a gentle

smile, "that you were also an expert on international affairs."

Reardon looked uncomfortable. "Sorry, sir," he muttered.

"That's all right," said the president. "I had it figured the same way. They will take the Kerguelen islands then?"

"Probably," said Reardon, "and our picture people are going to be furious. But the French keep those islands cheap. It's the only way they can hold it in the market as a war zone."

The president's manner changed completely. Instead of being a civilized old gentleman who had recently had his breakfast, he acted like the shrewd, selfish politician who had beaten all his competitors for the job and who had then found that his country needed a president much more than he had ever needed a presidency. He looked Reardon in the face, staring sharply and deeply into his eyes, and then asked, in a formal, solemn tone:

"Jack, this may be the biggest question of your life. How do you want to fight it?"

Reardon stiffened. "I thought it would be out of place to make up a list of team mates, sir. I thought perhaps you would have a list—"

"I don't mean that at all," said the president. "Do you prefer to fight it alone?"

"Alone, sir?"

"Don't play modest with me, Reardon," said the president. "You're the best man we have. As a matter of fact, you're the only first-class man we have. There are some youngsters coming up, but there aren't any more in your class—"

Reardon forgot himself, so technical was the subject, and interrupted the president: "Boggs is good, sir. He's had six fights as a mercenary in these little African wars."

"Reardon," said the president, "you interrupted me."

"I beg your pardon, sir," stammered Reardon.

"Boggs has nothing to do with it. I've seen him too, you know. Even if I add him, that only makes two pilots who are first-class."

Reardon looked straight at the president, his face begging for permission to speak.

The president smiled faintly: "Okay, what is it?"

"How about filling in the team with mercenaries, sir?"

"Mercenaries!" shouted the president. "Good lord, no! That would be the worst possible thing we could do. We'd look like fools all over the world. I played with real war to get Tibet free, and the Goonhogo of China gave in just because some of the people in the Goonhogo thought that Americans were still tough. Hire one mercenary and it's all gone. We have the posture of America to preserve. Will you or won't you?"

Reardon looked genuinely puzzled, "Will I what, sir?"

"You fool," said the president, "can you fight the war alone or can't you? You know the rules."

Reardon knew them. For using a single pilot, the nation obtained a tremendous advantage. Two enemy ships down and his nation won, no matter how many ships he himself lost. There hadn't been a one-pilot war since the great Sigurd Sigurdssen defeated Federated Europe, Morocco, Japan, and Brazil in one-two-three-four order, thirty-two years ago. After that no one had challenged

Iceland to a class-Q war. Iceland went on declaring licensed wars on the slightest provocation; the Icelanders had accumulated enough credit to fight a hundred wars. The challenged powers all chose the largest, most complicated wars they could, trying to swamp Sigurd in a maze of teamwork.

Reardon stared out of the window. The president let him think. At last he spoke, and his voice was heavy with conviction,

"I can try it, sir. They've given us the chance by demanding a class-Q war. But I'm no Sigurd and you know it, sir."

"I know it, Reardon," said the president seriously, "but perhaps none of us—not even you yourself—know what your very best performance can be. Will you do it, Reardon, for the country, for me, for yourself?"

Reardon nodded. Fame and victory looked very bleak to him at that moment.

∾ III ∾

The formalities came through with no trouble.

Tibet and America both claimed the Himalayan Escarpment Solar Banks. They agreed that the title should yield through war.

The Universal War Board granted a war permit, subject to strict and clear conditions:

1. The war was to be fought only at the times and places specified.

2. No human being was to be killed or injured, directly

or indirectly, by any performance of the machines of war. Emotional injury was not to be considered.

3. An appropriate territory was to be leased and cleared. Provisions should be made for the maximum removal of wildlife, particularly birds, which might be hurt by the battle.

4. The weapons were to be winged dirigibles with a maximum weight of 22,000 tons, propelled by non-nuclear engines.

5. All radio channels were to be strictly monitored by the U.W.B. and by both parties. At any complaint of jamming or interference the war was to be brought to a halt.

6. Each dirigible should have six non-explosive missiles and thirty non-explosive countermissiles.

7. The U.W.B. was to intercept and to destroy all stray missiles and real weapons before the missiles left the war zone, and each party, regardless of the outcome of the war, was to pay the U.W.B. directly for the interception and destruction of stray missiles.

8. No living human beings were to be allowed on the ships, in the war zone, or on the communications equipment which relayed the war to the world's televisions. (The last remembered casualties of "safe war" had been video crews who had ridden their multicopter into the blazing guns of a combat dirigible before the pilot, thousands of miles away, could see them and stop his guns.)

9. The "stipulated territory" was to be the War Territory of Kerguelen, to be leased by both parties from the Fourteenth French Republic, as agent for

Federated Europe, at the price of four million gold
livres the hour.

10. Seating for the war, apart from video rights
belonging to the combatants, should remain the sole
property of the lessor of the War Territory of Kerguelen.

With these arrangements, the French off-lifted their
sheep from the island ranges of Kerguelen—the weary
sheep were getting thoroughly used to being lifted from
their grazing land to Antarctic lighters every time a war
occurred—and the scene was ready.

Reardon planned to work from Omaha; he supposed
that his Tibetan counterparts would be stationed in Lhasa,
but since Tibet had not been an independent power for
many generations, he wondered what mercenaries they
might obtain. They might get Sung from Peking; he had
six battles more than Reardon and was a dependable
fighter.

∾ IV ∾

The French sold out their seats and view-spots around
Kerguelen very easily. The usual smugglers sold telescopes
which would allegedly give perfect non-copyright views
of the war and, as usual, most of them did not work; the
purchasers merely had a cruise out of Durban, Madras, or
Perth in vain.

The warships were ready. The American ones were
gold in color, stubby wings sticking out from the sides of
their cigar-shaped bodies, the ancient American eagle
surrounded by red, white and blue circles on their sides.

The five Tibetan ships turned out to be old Chinese Goonhogo models on rental. The emblem of China had been painted out and the prayer-wheel of Tibet shone fresh with new paint. The Chinese mechanics were expert to the point of trickiness; the American member of the umpire team insisted on inspection of all ten ships before he signed for the entry into the War Territory of Kerguelen.

The minute of opening was noon, local time. Reardon started with a real advantage. Positions had been chosen at random by the umpires and he was facing into a strong west wind, while the enemy ships had to hold back lest they be blown out of the territory.

Some fool in a swivel chair had named the American airships for characters out of Shakespeare, so that Reardon found himself managing the *Prospero*, the *Ariel*, the *Oberon*, the *Caliban*, and the *Titania*. The Tibetans had not taken the time to re-name the Chinese ships, which had the titles of old dynasties: the *Han*, the *Yuan*, the *Ch'ing*, the *Chin*, and the *Ming*.

Reardon kept his ships lined up close to the spectators, so that the Tibetans could not fire missiles at him without shooting out of the Territory and being penalized. He glanced up at the board in Omaha to see his antagonists, who had come on the telescreen. Sung was there, all right; so, too, was Baartek, a famous mercenary who flew under the flag of Liechtenstein and looked for quarrels wherever he could find them. The other three were strangers. One of them, wearing Tibetan clothes, was a girl. "That's a good Chinese propaganda trick," thought Reardon. "Trust the Goonhogo never to miss a bet!"

The Chinese got the displeasure of the spectators by casting a smoke screen. There really wasn't much else they could do, with their dirigibles pumping awkwardly in reverse against the wind. When the smoke screen neared his ships, Reardon jumped. He put the *Prospero* on manual, made three wild guesses, and sprang.

The *Prospero* came ruined out of the other side of the smoke wall. Two missiles had pierced her and Reardon doubted that the salvage crew would get much of her by the time the war ended.

But he had almost won the war. He had rammed both the *Han* and the *Ming*. He used the eyes of the *Ariel* to watch them. The crippled *Ming* fought for position over the cold, cold waters of the deep South Indian Ocean. Reardon suspected that Baartek had taken over. She fired suddenly; he twisted the *Ariel*. Sheets of flame behind his ship told him that the U.W.B. had intercepted the missiles with live weapons, to keep them from harming the massed spectators. The flashes went on for so long that his viewscreens shone with a quivering, milky white. There were going to be a lot of headaches among those spectators who watched those interception flashes too long, thought he. Baartek obviously did not care what his Tibetan employers paid in penalty money. Yet the *Ariel* had gotten away so easily!

The *Han*, meanwhile, though falling, had attacked the *Caliban*, which lost its left wing and began drifting downward. Reardon shot a reproachful glance at the robot who had been managing the ship for him, and decided not to take time to curse the robot programmers who had guessed events so poorly.

The face and voice of the U.W.B. umpire appeared on all screens. "The *Caliban*, American. The *Han*, Tibetan. Take both of them off the field. Suspend fire and remove."

Under the scoring system, Reardon had just lost the winning of the war. All he needed to do was to down two enemy ships and keep one of his own in the air for the period of the war, and he had won. But the *Ming*, now on the whitecaps and breaking up, was the first of his victories; the *Han* was to have been the other. Now he had to start over again.

He put the *Ariel* on robot and took over the *Titania* himself.

One of the enemy ships began creeping toward him along the line of the spectators. It could not fire at him, because the Territory was rectangular and the *Titania* was too close to a corner. He could not fire at it unless he got the *Titania* down with her belly almost in the water; then his stray shots would escape into space.

He and the enemy started their dive at the same time.

His command screen blanked out. The face of the president appeared on the screen. Only the president had that kind of overriding priority.

"How's it going, my boy? Doesn't look too good, does it?"

Reardon wanted to scream, "Get off, you fool!"

But it was the president; one does not scream at presidents.

He forced himself to speak politely, though he knew his face had gone white with rage. "Please, sir, get off the screen. It's all right, sir. Thank you."

The president got off the screen and Reardon found

himself back on the *Titania* just as the enemy cut her in
two.

In a wild rage, but a controlled rage, he took over the
Ariel, letting the ruined *Titania* go to the waves below.

He spat a smoke screen himself, and it rushed toward
him. He rose to the top of it just in time to see two
Chinese ships go looking for him. He dived back in. The
smoke was thinning. He struck for the lever which fired a
time-on-target, all missiles reaching for the same instant.
But he thought of that fool of a president and he struck
the wrong lever: DESTRUCT.

The *Ariel* blew up in a pretty show of fireworks.
There were two other orange clouds near her. The video
eye on the foredeck of the *Ariel* showed him that he had
technically won the war. The other two ships went down
with him.

He switched to the *Oberon*, his last remaining ship.
There were still two Chinese to his one. They were the
Ch'ing and the *Yuan*.

The umpire came on, "You hit 'destruct.' That is not
allowed as a weapon in a licensed war."

"It was an error," snapped Reardon. "You can look at
your tape of me. You can see that I was reaching for 'time-
on-target'."

There was a moment of silence while the blank
screens buzzed. Then the umpire came back on, speaking
to Baartek and Sung but letting Reardon listen in. "The
rules don't really cover this," said the umpire. "It was a
mistake, but your ships were taking a chance in getting
that close to him. He was coming after you from the top.
I rule it a net gain."

Now all he had to do was to stay alive for the next sixty-seven minutes—alive meaning with a ship in the field.

He began creeping along the line of the spectators, so close that some of them backed up. Many voices called for the umpire, but Reardon made sure that he had his hundred meters' tolerance.

The *Ch'ing* and the *Yuan* both lined up on him. He had to use emergency jets to dip in order to escape their missiles. He thought that the *Ch'ing* had four left and the *Yuan* three, but the battle had gone so fast, with so much in smoke, that he could not be absolutely sure. It was like some of the old card games: sometimes even the best players lost command of a complete recollection of the cards.

He dived again.

The Chinese ships followed.

A missile clipped the elevator vane of his right wing.

Reardon took advantage of it. He turned the *Oberon* sideways, like a crippled ship, and let it drop toward the water.

The *Yuan* followed for a look and he gave it to her. He cut a hole in her that he could see daylight through. She drifted toward the spectators, out of control. There was a bright flash from the protective weapons of the U.W.B. and she was gone.

The *Oberon* touched water and as she touched, Reardon rammed the engines into full reverse. He fired two of his precious missiles directly into the water itself. An enormous cloud of steam arose and the *Oberon* rose faster than an airship had ever risen before. He could not see where he was going, because his video was still looking at the waves and he was rising in reverse, but he watched his damage-control screen and he set his audio on HIGH.

The impact came.

The *Oberon* crunched into something that could only be the *Ch'ing*.

Reardon increased the thrust, cutting his ship in a sharp turn, still in reverse. He fired backwards into the ship he had rammed and pushed it inexorably back toward the water. The two ships, in collision, had not yet burst into flame.

Damage control suddenly lit up like a Christmas tree. The whole back of his ship was gone.

Using his fingertips and stroking the controls as lightly as he possibly could, he called for ASCEND. All he could see was the open sky above and the spectator craft, looking odd since they seemed to sit sidewise in the air, on the left of his pattern. The *Oberon* came loose from something.

He had sunk the *Ch'ing* without ever seeing it.

The umpire came on the board. "Your ship's clear of the water. The other one is out. War is over, sixty-one minutes ahead of time. Victory is declared for America. Tibet has lost."

In a different tone, the umpire said, "Congratulations, my boy. The enemy pilots wish to congratulate you, too. May they?"

∾ V ∾

Before Reardon could say yes or no, his screen blanked out.

The president had used his priority again.

Reardon saw with amusement that the old gentleman was weeping. "You've done it, lad, you've done it. I always knew you would."

Reardon forced his face into a smile of approval and sat waiting for the screen to show him the faces of his friendly enemies. Baartek was sure to insist on a dinner; he always did.

Mark Elf

The years rolled by; the Earth lived on, even when a stricken and haunted mankind crept through the glorious ruins of an immense past.

∞ I ∞
Descent of a Lady

Stars wheeled silently over an early summer sky, even though men had long ago forgotten to call such nights by the name of June.

Laird tried to watch the stars with his eyes closed. It was a ticklish and terrifying game for a telepath: at any moment he might feel the heavens opening up and might, as his mind touched the image of the nearer stars, plunge himself into a nightmare of perpetual falling. Whenever he had this sickening, shocking, ghastly, suffocating feeling of limitless fall, he had to close his mind against telepathy long enough to let his powers heal.

He was reaching with his mind for objects just above

the Earth, burnt-out space stations which flitted in their multiplex orbits, spinning forever, left over from the wreckage of ancient atomic wars.

He found one.

Found one so ancient it had no surviving cryotronic controls. Its design was archaic beyond belief; chemical tubes had apparently once lifted it out of Earth's atmosphere.

He opened his eyes and promptly lost it.

Closing his eyes he groped again with his seeking mind until he found the ancient derelict. As his mind reached for it again the muscles of his jaw tightened. He sensed life within it, life as old as the archaic machine itself.

In an instant, he made contact with his friend Tong Computer.

He poured his knowledge into Tong's mind. Keenly interested, Tong shot back at him an orbit which would cut the mildly parabolic pattern of the old device and bring it back down into Earth's atmosphere.

Laird made a supreme effort.

Calling on his unseen friends to aid him, he searched once more through the rubbish that raced and twinkled unseen just above the sky. Finding the ancient machine, he managed to give it a push.

In this fashion, about sixteen thousand years after she left Hitler's Reich, Carlotta vom Acht began her return to the Earth of men.

In all those years, she had not changed.

Earth had.

The ancient rocket tipped. Four hours later it had begun to graze the stratosphere, and its ancient controls,

preserved by cold and time against all change, went back
into effect. As they thawed, they became activated.

The course flattened out.

Fifteen hours later, the rocket was seeking a destination.

Electronic controls which had really been dead for
thousands of years, out in the changeless time of space
itself, began to look for German territory, seeking the
territory by feedbacks which selected characteristic Nazi
patterns of electronic communications scramblers.

There were none.

How could the machine know this? The machine had
left the town of Pardubice, on April 2, 1945, just as the last
German hideouts were being mopped up by the Red
Army. How could the machine know that there was no
Hitler, no Reich, no Europe, no America, no nations? The
machine was keyed to German codes. Only German codes.

This did not affect the feedback mechanisms.

They looked for German codes anyway. There were
none. The electronic computer in the rocket began to go
mildly neurotic. It chattered to itself like an angry monkey,
rested, chattered again, and then headed the rocket for
something which seemed to be vaguely electrical. The
rocket descended and the girl awoke.

She knew she was in the box in which her daddy had
placed her. She knew that she was not a cowardly swine
like the Nazis whom her father despised. She was a good
Prussian girl of noble military family. She had been
ordered to stay in the box by her father. What daddy told
her to do she had always done. That was the first kind of
rule for her kind of girl, a sixteen-year-old of the Junker
class. The noise increased.

The electronic chattering flared up into a wild medley of clicks.

She could smell something perfectly dreadful burning, something awful and rotten like flesh. She was afraid that it was herself, but she felt no pain.

"*Vadi, Vadi,* what is happening to me?" she cried to her father.

(Her father had been dead sixteen thousand and more years. Obviously enough, he did not answer.)

The rocket began to spin. The ancient leather harness holding her broke loose. Even though her section of the rocket was no bigger than a coffin, she was cruelly bruised.

She began to cry.

She vomited, even though very little came up. Then she slid in her own vomit and felt nasty and ashamed because of something which was a terribly simple human reaction.

The noises all met in a screaming, shrieking climax. The last thing she remembered was the firing of the forward decelerators. The metal had become fatigued so that the tubes not only fired forward; they blew themselves to pieces sidewise as well.

She was unconscious when the rocket crashed. Perhaps that saved her life, since the least muscular tension would have led to the ripping of muscle and the crack of bone.

∽ II ∽
A Moron Found Her

His metals and plumes beamed in the moonlight as he

scampered about the dark forest in his gorgeous uniform. The government of the world had long since been left to the Morons by the True Men, who had no interest in such things as politics or administration.

Carlotta's weight, not her conscious will, had tripped the escape handle.

Her body lay half in, half out of the rocket.

She had gotten a bad burn on her left arm where her skin touched the hot outer surface of the rocket.

The Moron parted the bushes and approached.

"I am the Lord High Administrator of Area Seventy-three," he said, identifying himself according to the rules.

The unconscious girl did not answer. He rose up close to the rocket, crouching low lest the dangers of the night devour him, and listened intently to the radiation counter built in under the skin of his skull behind his left ear. He lifted the girl dextrously, flung her gently over his shoulder, turned about, ran back into the bushes, made a right-angle turn, ran a few paces, looked about him undecidedly, and then ran (still uncertain, still rabbit-like) down to the brook.

He reached into his pocket and found a burn-balm. He applied a thick coating to the burn on her arm. It would stay, killing the pain and protecting the skin, until the burn was healed.

He splashed cool water on her face. She awakened.

"*Wo bin ich?*" said she in German.

On the other side of the world, Laird, the telepath, had forgotten for the moment about the rocket. He might have understood her, but he was not there. The forest was around her and the forest was full of life, fear, hate, and pitiless destruction.

The Moron babbled in his own language.

She looked at him and thought that he was a Russian.

Said she in German, "Are you a Russian? Are you a German? Are you part of General Vlasov's army? How far are we from Prague? You must treat me courteously. I am an important girl . . ."

The Moron stared at her.

His face began to grin with innocent and consummate lust. (The True Men had never felt it necessary to inhibit the breeding habits of Morons. It was hard for any kind of human being to stay alive between the Beasts, the Unforgiven, and the Menschenjägers. The True Men wanted the Morons to go on breeding, to carry reports, to gather up a few necessaries, and to distract the other inhabitants of the world enough to let the True Men have the quiet and contemplation which their exalted but weary temperaments demanded.)

This Moron was typical of his kind. To him food meant eat, water meant drink, woman meant lust.

He did not discriminate.

Weary, confused, and bruised though she was, Carlotta still recognized his expression.

Sixteen thousand years ago she had expected to be raped or murdered by the Russians. This soldier was a fantastic little man, plump and grinning, with enough medals for a Soviet colonel general. From what she could see in the moonlight, he was clean-shaven and pleasant, but he looked innocent and stupid to be so high-ranking an officer. Perhaps the Russians were all like that, she thought.

He reached for her.

Tired as she was, she slapped him.

The Moron was mixed up in his thoughts. He knew that he had the right to capture any Moron woman whom he might find. Yet he also knew that it was worse than death to touch any woman of the True Men. Which was this—this thing—this power—this entity who had descended from the stars?

Pity is as old and emotional as lust. As his lust receded, his elemental human pity took over. He reached in his jerkin pocket for a few scraps of food.

He held them out to her.

She ate, looking at him trustfully, very much the child.

Suddenly there was a crashing in the woods.

Carlotta wondered what had happened.

When she first saw him, his face had been full of concern. Then he had grinned and had talked. Later he had become lustful. Finally he had acted very much the gentleman. Now he looked blank, brain and bone and skin all concentrated into the act of listening—listening for something else, beyond the crashing, which she could not hear. He turned back to her.

"You must run. You must run. Get up and run. I tell you, run!"

She listened to his babble without comprehension.

Once again he crouched to listen.

He looked at her with blank horror on his face. Carlotta tried to understand what was the matter, but she could not riddle his meaning.

Three more strange little men dressed exactly like him came crashing out of the woods.

They ran like elk or deer before a forest fire. Their faces were blank with the exertion of running. Their eyes looked straight ahead so that they seemed almost blind. It was a wonder that they evaded the trees. They came crashing down the slope, scattering leaves as they ran. They splashed the waters of the brook as they stomped recklessly through it. With a half-animal cry Carlotta's Moron joined them.

The last she saw of him, he was running away into the woods, his plumes grinning ridiculously as his head nodded with the exertion of running.

From the direction from which the Morons had come, an unearthly creepy sound whistled through the woods. It was whistling, stealthy and low, accompanied by the very quiet sound of machinery.

The noise sounded like all the tanks in the world compressed into the living ghost of a tank, into the heart of a machine which survived its own destruction and, spiritlike, haunted the scenes of old battles.

As the sound approached Carlotta turned toward it. She tried to stand up and could not. She faced the danger. (All Prussian girls, destined to be the mothers of officers, were taught to face danger and never to turn their backs on it.) As the noise came close to her she could hear the high crazy inquiry of soft electronic chatter. It resembled the sonar she had once heard in her father's laboratory at the Reich's secret office's project Nordnacht.

The machine came out of the woods.

And it did look like a ghost.

∾ III ∾
The Death of All Men

Carlotta stared at the machine. It had legs like a grasshopper, a body like a ten-foot turtle, and three heads which moved restlessly in the moonlight.

From the forward edge of the top shell a hidden arm leapt forth, seeming to strike at her, deadlier than a cobra, quicker than a jaguar, more silent than a bat flitting across the face of the moon.

"Don't!" Carlotta screamed in German. The arm stopped suddenly in the moonlight.

The stop was so sudden that the metal twanged like the string of a bow.

The heads of the machine all turned toward her.

Something like surprise seemed to overtake the machine. The whistling dropped down to a soothing purr. The electronic chatter burst up to a crescendo and then stopped. The machine dropped to its knees.

Carlotta crawled over to it.

Said she in German, "What are you?"

"I am the death of all men who oppose the Sixth German Reich," said the machine in fluted singsong German. "If the Reichsangehöriger wishes to identify me, my model and number are written on my carapace."

The machine knelt at a height so low that Carlotta could seize one of the heads and look in the moonlight at the edge of the top shell. The head and neck, though made of metal, felt much more weak and brittle than she expected. There was about the machine an air of immense age.

"I can't see," wailed Carlotta. "I need a light."

There was the ache and grind of long-unused machinery. Another mechanical arm appeared, dropping flakes of near-crystallized dirt as it moved. The tip of the arm exuded light, blue, penetrating, and strange.

Brook, forest, small valley, machine, even herself, were all lit up by the soft penetrating blue light which did not hurt her eyes. The light even gave her a sense of well-being. With the light she could read. Traced on the carapace just above the three heads was this inscription:

WAFFENAMT DES SECHSTEN
DEUTSCHEN REICHES
BURG EISENHOWER, A.D. 2495

And then below it in much larger Latin letters:

MENSCHENJÄGER MARK ELF

"What does 'Man-hunter, Model Eleven' mean?"

"That's me," whistled the machine. "How is it you don't know me if you are a German?"

"Of course, I'm a German, you fool!" said Carlotta. "Do I look like a Russian?"

"What is a Russian?" said the machine.

Carlotta stood in the blue light wondering, dreaming, dreading—dreading the unknown which had materialized around her.

When her father, Heinz Horst Ritter vom Acht, professor and doctor of mathematical physics at project Nordnacht, had fired her into the sky before he himself awaited a gruesome death at the hands of the Soviet soldiery, he had told her nothing about the Sixth Reich, nothing about what she might meet, nothing about the future. It came to her mind that perhaps the world was dead, that the strange little men were not near Prague, that she was in Heaven or Hell, herself being dead, or if herself alive, was in some other world, or her own world in the future, or things beyond all human ken, or problems which no mind could solve . . .

She fainted again.

The Menschenjäger could not know that she was unconscious and addressed her in serious high-pitched singsong German. "German citizen, have confidence that I will protect you. I am built to identify German thoughts and to kill all men who do not have true German thoughts."

The machine hesitated. A loud chatter of electronic clicks echoed across the silent woods while the machine tried to compute its own mind. It was not easy to select from the long-unused store of words for so ancient and so new a situation. The machine stood in its own blue light. The only sound was the sound of the brook moving irresistibly about its gentle and unliving business. Even the birds in the trees and the insects round about were hushed into silence by the presence of the dreaded whistling machine.

To the sound-receptors of the Menschenjäger, the running of the Morons, by now some two miles distant, came as a very faint pitter-patter.

The machine was torn between two duties, the long-current and familiar duty of killing all men who were not German, and the ancient and forgotten duty of succoring all Germans, whoever they might be. After another period of electronic chatter, the machine began to speak again. Beneath the grind of its singsong German there was a curious warning, a reminder of the whistle which it made as it moved, a sound of immense mechanical and electronic effort.

Said the machine, "You are German. It has been long since there has been any German anywhere. I have gone around the world two thousand three hundred and twenty-eight times. I have killed seventeen thousand four hundred and sixty-nine enemies of the Sixth German Reich for sure, and I have probably killed forty-two thousand and seven additional ones. I have been back to the automatic restoration center eleven times. The enemies who call themselves the True Men always elude me. One of them I have not killed for more than three thousand years. The ordinary men whom some call the Unforgiven are the ones I kill most of all, but frequently I catch Morons and kill them, too. I am fighting for Germany, but I cannot find Germany anywhere. There are no Germans in Germany. There are no Germans anywhere. I accept orders from no one but a German. Yet there have been no Germans anywhere, no Germans anywhere, no Germans anywhere . . ."

The machine seemed to get a catch in its electronic brain because it went on repeating *no Germans anywhere* three or four hundred times.

Carlotta came to as the machine was dreamily talking

to itself, repeating with sad and lunatic intensity, *no Germans anywhere*.

Said she, "I'm a German."

". . . no Germans anywhere, no Germans anywhere, except you, except you, except you."

The mechanical voice ended in a thin screech.

Carlotta tried to come to her feet.

At last the machine found words again. "What—do—I—do—now?"

"Help me," said Carlotta firmly.

This command seemed to tap an operable feedback in the ancient cybernetic assembly. "I cannot help you, member of the Sixth German Reich. For that you need a rescue machine. I am not a rescue machine. I am a hunter of men, designed to kill all the enemies of the German Reich."

"Get me a rescue machine then," said Carlotta.

The blue light went off, leaving Carlotta standing blinded in the dark. She was shaky on her legs. The voice of the Menschenjäger came to her.

"I am not a rescue machine. There are no rescue machines. There are no rescue machines anywhere. There is no Germany anywhere. There are no Germans anywhere, no Germans anywhere, no Germans anywhere, except you. You must ask a rescue machine. Now I go. I must kill men. Men who are enemies of the Sixth German Reich. That is all I can do. I can fight forever. I shall find a man and kill him. Then I shall find another man and kill him. I depart on the work of the Sixth German Reich."

The whistling and clicking resumed.

With incredible daintiness, the machine stepped as

lightly as a cat across the brook. Carlotta listened intently in the darkness. Even the dry leaves of last year did not stir as the Menschenjäger moved through the shadow of the fresh leafy trees.

Abruptly there was silence.

Carlotta could hear the agonized clickety-clack of the computers in the Menschenjäger. The forest became a weird silhouette as the blue light went back on.

The machine returned.

Standing on the far side of the brook, it spoke to her in the dry, high-fluted singing German voice.

"Now that I have found a German I will report to you once every hundred years. That is correct. Perhaps that is correct. I do not know. I was built to report to officers. You are not an officer. Nevertheless you are a German. So I will report every hundred years. Meanwhile, watch out for the Kaskaskia Effect."

Carlotta, sitting again, was chewing some of the dry cubic food scraps which the Moron had left behind. They tasted like a mockery of chocolate. With her mouth full, she tried to shout to the Menschenjäger, *"Was ist das?"*

Apparently the machine understood, because it answered, "The Kaskaskia Effect is an American weapon. The Americans are all gone. There are no Americans anywhere, no Americans anywhere, no Americans anywhere—"

"Stop repeating yourself," said Carlotta. "What is that effect you are talking about?"

"The Kaskaskia Effect stops the Menschenjägers, stops the True Men, stops the Beasts. It can be sensed, but it cannot be seen or measured. It moves like a cloud.

Only simple men with clean thoughts and happy lives can live inside it. Birds and ordinary beasts can live inside it, too. The Kaskaskia Effect moves about like clouds. There are more than twenty-one and less than thirty-four Kaskaskia Effects moving slowly about this planet Earth. I have carried other Menschenjägers back for restoration and rebuilding, but the restoration center can find no fault. The Kaskaskia Effect ruins us. Therefore, we run away . . . even though the officers told us to run from nothing. If we did not run away, we would cease to exist. You are a German. I think the Kaskaskia Effect would kill you. Now I go to hunt a man. When I find him I will kill him."

The blue light went off.

The machine whistled and clicked its way into the dark silence of the wooded night.

∽ IV ∽
Conversation with the Middle-Sized Bear

Carlotta was completely adult.

She had left the screaming uproar of Hitler Germany as it fell to ruins in its Bohemian outposts. She had obeyed her father, the Ritter vom Acht, as he passed her and her sisters into missiles which had been designed as personnel and supply carriers for the First German National Socialist Moon Base.

He and his medical brother, Professor Doctor Joachim vom Acht, had harnessed the girls securely in their missiles.

Their uncle the Doctor had given them shots.

Karla had gone first, then Juli, and then Carlotta.

Then the barbed-wire fortress of Pardubice and the monotonous grind of Wehrmacht trucks trying to escape the air strikes of the Red Air Force and the American fighter-bombers died in the one night, and this mysterious "forest in the middle of nothing-at-all" was born in the next night.

Carlotta was completely dazed.

She found a smooth-looking place at the edge of the brook. The old leaves were heaped high here. Without regard for further danger, she slept.

She had not been asleep more than a few minutes before the bushes parted again.

This time it was a bear. The bear stood at the edge of the darkness and looked into the moonlit valley with the brook running through it. He could hear no sound of Morons, no whistle of manshonyagger, as he and his kind called the hunting machines. When he was sure all was safe, he twitched his claws and reached delicately into a leather bag which was hanging from his neck by a thong. Gently he took out a pair of spectacles and fitted them slowly and carefully in front of his tired old eyes.

He then sat down next to the girl and waited for her to wake up.

She did not wake until dawn.

Sunlight and birdsong awakened her.

(Could it have been the probing of Laird's mind, whose far-reaching senses told him that a woman had magically and mysteriously emerged from the archaic rocket and that there was a human being unlike all the

other kinds of mankind waking at a brookside in a place
which had once been called Maryland?)

Carlotta awoke, but she was sick.

She had a fever.

Her back ached.

Her eyelids were almost stuck together with foam. The world had had time to develop all sorts of new allergenic substances since she had last walked on the surface of the Earth. Four civilizations had come and vanished. They and their weapons were sure to leave membrane-inflaming residue behind.

Her skin itched.

Her stomach felt upset.

Her arm was numb and covered with some kind of sticky black. She did not know it was a burn covered by the salve which the Moron had given her the previous night.

Her clothes were dry and seemed to be falling off her in shreds.

She felt so bad that when she noticed the bear, she did not even have strength to run.

She just closed her eyes again.

Lying there with her eyes closed she wondered all over again where she was.

Said the bear in perfect German, "You are at the edge of the Unselfing Zone. You have been rescued by a Moron. You have stopped a Menschenjäger very mysteriously. For the first time in my own life I can see into a German mind and see that the word manshonyagger should really be Menschenjäger, a hunter of men. Allow me to introduce myself. I am the Middle-Sized Bear who lives in these woods."

The voice not only spoke German, but it spoke exactly the right kind of German. The voice sounded like the German which Carlotta had heard throughout her life from her father. It was a masculine voice, confident, serious, reassuring. With her eyes still closed she realized that it was a bear who was doing the talking. With a start, she recalled that the bear had been wearing spectacles.

Said she, sitting up, "What do *you* want?"

"Nothing," said the bear mildly.

They looked at each other for a while.

Then said Carlotta, "Who are you? Where did you learn German? What's going to happen to me?"

"Does the Fräulein," asked the bear, "wish me to answer the questions in order?"

"Don't be silly," said Carlotta. "I don't care what order. Anyhow, I'm hungry. Do you have anything I could eat?"

The bear responded gently, "You wouldn't like hunting for insect grubs. I have learned German by reading your mind. Bears like me are friends of the True Men and we are good telepaths. The Morons are afraid of us, but we are afraid of the manshonyaggers. Anyhow, you don't have to worry very much because your husband is coming soon."

Carlotta had been walking down toward the brook to get a drink. His last words stopped her in her tracks.

"My husband?" she gasped.

"So probably that it is certain. There is a True Man named Laird who has brought you down. He already knows what you are thinking, and I can see his pleasure in finding a human being who is wild and strange, but not really wild and not really strange. At this moment he is thinking that you may have left the centuries to bring the gift of vitality back among mankind. He is thinking that you and he will have wonderful children. Now he is telling me not to tell you what I think he thinks, for fear that you will run away." The bear chuckled.

Carlotta stood, her mouth agape.

"You may sit in my chair," said the Middle-Sized Bear, "or you can wait here until Laird comes to get you. Either way you will be taken care of. Your sickness will heal. Your ailments will go away. You will be happy again. I know this because I am one of the wisest of all known bears."

Carlotta was angry, confused, frightened, and sick again. She started to run.

Something as solid as a blow hit her.

She knew without being told that it was the bear's mind reaching out and encompassing hers.

It hit—boom!—and that was all.

She had never before stopped to think of how comfortable a bear's mind was. It was like lying in a great big bed and having mother take care of one when one was a very little girl, glad to be petted and sure of getting well.

The anger poured out of her. The fear left her. The sickness began to lighten. The morning seemed beautiful.

She herself felt beautiful as she turned—

Out of the blue sky, dropping swiftly but gracefully, came the figure of a bronze young man. A happy thought pulsed against her mind. *That is Laird, my beloved. He is coming. He is coming. I shall be happy forever after.*

It *was* Laird.

And so she was.

The Queen of the Afternoon

Above all, as she began to awaken, she wished for her family. She called to them, "Mutti, Vati, Carlotta, Karla! Where are you?" But of course she cried it in German since she was a good Prussian girl. Then she remembered.

How long had it been since her father had put her and her two sisters into the space capsules? She had no idea. Even her father, the Ritter vom Acht, and her uncle, Professor Doctor Joachim vom Acht—who had administered the shots in Parbudice, Germany, on April 2, 1945— could not have imagined that the girls would remain in suspended animation for thousands of years. But so it was.

Afternoon sunlight gleamed orange and gold on the rich purple shades of the Fighting Trees. Charls looked at the trees, knowing that as the sunset moved from orange to red and as darkness crept over the eastern horizon, they would once again glow with quiet fire.

How long was it since the trees were planted—Fighting Trees, the True Men called them—for the express purpose of sending their immense roots down into the earth, seeking out the radioactives in the soil and the waters beneath, concentrating the poisonous wastes into their hard pods, then dropping the waxy pods until, at some later time, the waters which came from above the earth, and those yet in the earth, would once more be clean? Charls did not know.

One thing he did know. To touch one of the trees, to touch it directly, was certain death.

He wanted very much to break a twig but he did not dare. Not only was it *tambu*, but he feared the sickness. His people had made much progress in the last few generations, enough so that at times they did not fear to face True Men and to argue with them. But the sickness was not something with which one could argue.

At the thought of a True Man, an unaccountable thickness gripped him in the throat. He felt sentimental, tender, fearful; the yearning that gripped him was a kind of love, and yet he knew that it could not be love since he had never seen a True Man except at a distance.

Why, Charls wondered, was he thinking so much about True Men? Was there, perhaps, one nearby?

He looked at the setting sun, which was by now red enough to be looked at safely. Something in the atmosphere was making him uneasy. He called to his sister.

"Oda, Oda!"

She did not answer.

Again he called. "Oda, Oda!"

This time he heard her coming, plowing recklessly

through the underbrush. He hoped she would remember to avoid the Fighting Trees. Oda was sometimes too impatient.

Suddenly there she was before him.

"You called me, Charls? You called me? You've found something? Shall we go somewhere together? What do you want? Where are mother and father?"

Charls could not help laughing. Oda was always like that.

"One question at a time, little sister. Weren't you afraid you would die the burning death, going through the trees like that? I know you don't want to believe in the *tambu*, but the sickness is real."

"It isn't," she said. She shook her head. "Maybe it was once . . . I guess it really was once"—granting him a concession—"but do you, yourself, know of anybody who has died from the trees for a thousand years?"

"Of course not, silly. I haven't been alive a thousand years."

Oda's impatience returned. "*You* know what I mean. And anyway, I decided the whole thing is silly. We all accidentally brush against the trees. So one day I *ate* a pod. And nothing happened."

He was appalled. "You *ate* a pod?"

"That's what I said. And nothing happened."

"Oda, one of these days you're going to go too far."

She smiled at him. "And now I suppose you are going to say that the oceans' beds were not always filled with grass."

He was indignant. "No, of course I know better than that. I know that the grass was put into the oceans for the same reason that the Fighting Trees were planted—to eat up all the poisons that the Old Ones left in the days of the Ancient Wars."

How long they would have bickered he did not know, but just then his ears caught an unfamiliar noise. He knew the sound the True Men made as they sped on their mysterious errands in the upper air. He knew the ominous buzz that the Cities gave off should he approach them too closely. He knew also the clicking noises that the few remaining manshonyaggers made as they crept through the Wild, alert for any non-German to kill. Poor blind machines, they were so easy to outsmart.

But this noise, this noise was different. It was nothing he had ever heard before.

The whistling sound rose and throbbed against the upper reaches of his hearing. It had a curiously spiral quality about it as though it approached and receded, all the while veering toward him. Charls was filled with terror, feeling threatened beyond all understanding.

Now Oda heard it too. Their quarrel forgotten, she seized his arm. "What is it, Charls? What could it be?"

His voice was hesitant and full of wonder. "I don't know."

"Are the True Men doing something, something new that we never heard before? Do they want to hurt us, or enslave us? Do they want to catch us? Do we want to be caught? Charls, tell me, do we want to be caught? Could it be the True Men coming? I seem to smell True Man. They *did* come once before and caught some of us and took them away and did strange things to them, so that they looked like True Men, didn't they, Charls? Could it be the True Men again?"

In spite of his fear, Charls had a certain amount of impatience with Oda. She talked so much.

The noise persisted and intensified. Charls sensed that it was directly over his head, but he could see nothing.

Oda said, "Charls, I think I see it. Do you see it, Charls?"

Suddenly he too saw the circle—a dim whiteness, a vapor train that increased in size and volume. Concomitantly the sound increased, until he felt his eardrums would burst. It was nothing ever before seen in his world. . . .

A thought struck him. It was as hard as a physical blow; it sapped his courage and manhood as nothing before had ever done; he did not feel young and strong any more. He could hardly frame his words.

"Oda, could that be—"

"Be what?"

"Could it be one of the old, old weapons from the Ancient Past? Could it be coming back to destroy us all, as the legends have always foretold? People have always said they would come back. . . ." His voice trailed off.

Whatever the danger, he knew that he was completely helpless, helpless to protect himself, helpless to protect Oda.

Against the ancient weapons there was no defense. This place was no safer than that place, that place no better than this. People still had to live their lives under the threat of weapons from long, long ago. This was the first time that he personally had met the threat, but he had heard of it. He reached for Oda's hand.

Oda, singularly courageous now that there was real

danger, drew him over onto the bank, away from the *cenote*. With half his mind he wondered why she seemed to want to move away from the water. She tugged at his arm, and he sat down beside her.

Already, he knew, it was too late to go looking for their parents or others of their pack. Sometimes it took a whole day to round up the entire family—the *thing* was coming down relentlessly, and Charls felt so drained of energy that he stopped talking. He thought at her: *Let's just wait it out here,* and she squeezed his hand as she thought back: *Yes, my brother.*

The long box in the circle of light continued to descend, inexorable.

It was odd. Charls could feel a human presence, but the mind was strangely closed to him. He felt a quality of mind that he had never felt before. He had read the minds of True Men as they flew far overhead; he knew the minds of his own people; he could distinguish the thoughts of most of the birds and beasts; it was no trouble to detect the crude electronic hunger of the mechanical mind of a manshonyagger.

But this—this being had a mind that was raw, elemental, hot. And closed.

Now the box was very near. Would it crash in this valley or the next? The screams from within it were extremely shrill. Charls's ears hurt and his eyes smarted from the intensity of heat and noise. Oda held his hand tightly.

The object crashed into the ground.

It ripped the hillside just across the *cenote*. Had Oda not instinctively moved away from the *cenote*, the box would have hit *them*, Charls realized.

Charls and Oda stood up cautiously.

Somehow the box must have decelerated: It was hot, but not hot enough to make the broken trees around it burst into flame. Steam rose from the crushed leaves.

The noise was gone.

Charls and Oda moved to within ten man-lengths of the object. Charls framed his clearest thought and flung it at the box: *Who are you?*

The being within obviously did not perceive him as he was. There came forth a wild thought, directed at living beings in general.

Fools, fools, help me! Get me out of here!

Oda caught the thought, as did Charls. She stepped in mentally and Charls was astonished at the clarity and force of her inquiry. It was simple but beautifully strong and hard. She thought the one idea:

How?

From the box there came again the frantic babble of demand: *The handles, you fools. The handles on the outside. Take the handles and let me out!*

Charls and Oda looked at each other. Charls was not sure that he really wanted to let this creature "out." Then he thought further. Maybe the unpleasantness that radiated from the box was simply the result of imprisonment. He knew that he himself would hate to be encased like that.

Together Charls and Oda risked the broken leaves, walking gingerly up to the box itself. It was black and old; it looked like something the elders called "iron"—and never touched. They saw the handles, pitted and scarred.

With the ghost of a smile, Charls nodded to his sister. Each took a handle and lifted.

The sides of the box crackled. The iron was hot but not unbearably so. With a rusty shriek, the ancient door flew open.

They looked into the box.

There lay a young woman.

She had no fur, only long hair on her head.

Instead of fur, she had strange, soft objects on her body but as she sat up, these objects began to disintegrate.

At first the girl looked frightened; then, as she glanced at Oda and Charls, she began to laugh. Her thought came through, clearly and rather cruelly: *I guess I don't have to worry about modesty in front of puppy dogs.*

Oda did not seem to mind the thought but Charls's feelings were hurt. The girl said words with her mouth but they could not understand them. Each of them took an elbow and led her to the ground.

They reached the edge of the *cenote* and Oda gestured to the strange girl to sit down. She did, and made more words.

Oda was as puzzled as Charls, but then she began to smile. Spieking had worked before, when the girl was in the box. Why not now? The only thing was, this odd girl did not seem to know how to control her thoughts. Everything she thought was directed at the world at large—at the valley, at the sunset sky, at the *cenote*. She did not seem to realize that she was shouting every thought aloud.

Oda put her question to the young woman: *Who are you?*

The hot, strange mind flung back quickly: *Juli, of course.*

At this point Charls intervened. *There's no "of course" about it,* he spieked.

What am I doing? the girl's thoughts ran. *I'm in mental telepathy with puppy-dog people.*

Embarrassed, Charls and Oda watched her as her thoughts splashed out.

"Doesn't she know how to close off her thoughts?" Charls wondered. And why had her mind seemed so closed when she was in the box?

Puppy-dog people. Where can I be if I'm mixed up with puppy-dog people? Can this be Earth? Where have I been? How long have I been gone? Where is Germany? Where are Carlotta and Karla? Where are Daddy and Mother and Uncle Joachim? Puppy-dog people!

Charls and Oda felt the sharp edge of the mind that was so recklessly flinging all these thoughts. There was a kind of laughter that was cruel each time she thought *puppy-dog people.* They could feel that this mind was as bright as the brightest minds of the True Men—but this mind was different. It did not have the singleness of devotion or the wary wisdom that saturated the minds of the True Men.

Then Charls remembered something. His parents had once told him of a mind that was something like this one.

Juli continued to pour out her thoughts like sparks from a fire, like raindrops from a big splash. Charls was frightened and did not know what to do; and Oda began to turn away from the strange girl.

Then Charls perceived it. Juli was frightened. She was calling them *puppy-dog people* to cover her fear. She really did not know where she was.

He mused, not directing his thought at Juli: *Just because she's frightened, it doesn't mean she has the right to think sharp, bright things at us.*

Perhaps it was his posture that betrayed his attitude; Juli seemed to catch the thought.

Suddenly she burst into words again, words that they could not understand. It sounded as though she were begging, asking, pleading, expostulating. She seemed to be calling for specific persons or things. Words poured forth, and these were names that the True Men used. Was it her parents? Her lover? Her siblings? It had to be someone she had known before entering that screaming box, where she had been captive in the blue of the sky for . . . for how long?

Suddenly she was quiet. Her attention had shifted.

She pointed to the Fighting Trees.

The sunset had so darkened that the trees were beginning to light up. The soft fire was coming to life as it had during all the years of Charls's life and those of his forefathers.

As she pointed, Juli made words again. She kept repeating them. It sounded like *v-a-s-i-s-d-a-s.*

Charls could not help being a little irritated. *Why doesn't she just think?* It was odd that they could not read her mind when she was using the words.

Again, although Charls had not aimed the question at her, Juli seemed to catch it. From her there came a flame of thought, a single idea, that leapt like a fountain of fire from that tired little female head:

What is this world?

Then the thought shifted focus slightly. *Vati, Vati,*

where am I? Where are you? What has become of me?
There was something forlorn and desolate to it.

Oda put out a soft hand toward the girl. Juli looked at
her and some of the harsh, fearful thoughts returned.
Then the sheer compassion of Oda's posture seemed to
catch Juli's attention, and with relaxation came complete
collapse. The great and terrifying thought disappeared.
Juli burst into tears. She put her long arms about Oda.
Oda patted her back and Juli sobbed even harder.

Out of the sobbing came a funny, friendly thought,
loving and no longer contemptuous: *Dear little puppy
dogs, dear little puppy dogs, please help me. You are
supposed to be our best friends . . . do help me now. . . .*

Charls perked up his ears. Something—or someone—
was coming over the top of the hill.

Certainly a thought as big and as sharp as Juli's could
attract all living forms within kilometers. It might even
catch the attention of the aloof but ominous True Men.

A moment later Charls relaxed. He recognized the
stride of his parents. He turned to Oda.

"Hear that?"

She smiled. "It's father and mother. They must have
heard that big thought the girl had."

Charls watched with pride as his parents approached.
It was a well-justified pride. Bil and Kae both appeared, as
they were, sensitive and intelligent. In addition, their fur
was well-matched. Bil's beautiful caramel coat had spots
of white and black only along his cheekbones and nose
and at the tip of his tail; Kae was a uniform fawn-beige
with which her beautiful green eyes made a striking
contrast.

"Are you both all right?" Bil asked as they approached. "Who is that? She looks like a True Man. Is she friendly? Has she hurt you? Was she the one who was doing all that violent thinking? We could feel it clear across the hillside."

Oda burst into a giggle. "You ask as many questions as I do, Daddy."

Charls said, "All we know is that a box came from the sky and that she was in it. You heard that shrieking noise as it came down first, didn't you?"

Kae laughed. "Who didn't hear it?"

"The box hit right over there. You can see where it hurt the hillside."

The area where the box had landed was black and forbidding. Around it the fallen Fighting Trees gleamed in tangled confusion on the ground.

Bil looked at Juli and shook his head. "I don't see why she wasn't killed if it hit that hard."

Juli began to speak in words again, but at last she seemed to understand. Shouting her language would not help any. Instead, she thought: *Please, dear little puppy dogs. Please help me. Please understand me.*

Bil kept his dignity but he noticed with dismay that his tail was wagging of its own accord. He realized that the urge was uncontrollable. He felt both resentful and happy as he thought back at her: *Of course we understand you and we'll try to help you; but please don't think your thoughts so hard or so recklessly. They hurt our minds when they are so bright and sharp.*

Juli tried to turn down the intensity of her thought. She pleaded: *Take me to Germany.*

The four Unauthorized Men—mother, father, daughter, and son—looked at each other. They had no idea of what a Germany might be.

It was Oda who turned to Juli, girl to girl, and spieked: *Think some Germany at us so we can know what it is.*

There came forth from the strange girl images of unbelievable beauty. Picture after clear picture emerged until the little family was almost blinded by the magnificence of the display. They saw the whole ancient world come to life. Cities stood bright in a green-encircled world. There were no aloof and languid True Men; instead, all the people they saw in Juli's mind resembled Juli herself. They were vital, sometimes fierce, forceful; they were tall, erect, long-fingered; and of course they did not have the tails of the Unauthorized Men. The children were pretty beyond belief.

The most amazing thing about this world was the tremendous number of people in it. The people were thicker than the birds of passage, more crowded than the salmon at running time.

Charls had thought himself a well-traveled young man. He had met at least four dozen other persons besides his own family, and he had seen True Men in the skies above him hundreds of times. He had often witnessed the intolerable brightness of Cities and had walked around them more than once until, each time, he had been firmly assured that there was no way for him to enter. He thought his valley a good one. In a few more years he would be old enough to visit the nearby valleys and to look for a wife for himself.

But this vision that came from Juli's mind . . . he could

not imagine how so many people could live together. How could they all greet each other in the mornings? How could they all agree on anything? How could they all ever become still enough to be aware of each other's presence, each other's needs?

There came a particularly strong, bright image. Small-wheeled boxes were hurtling people at insensate speed up and down smooth, smooth roads.

"So that's what *roads* were for," he gasped to himself.

Among the people he saw many dogs. They were nothing like the creatures of Charls's world. They were not the long, otter-like animals whom the Unauthorized Men despised as lowly kindred; nor were they like the Unauthorized Men themselves, and they were certainly not like those modified animals who in appearance were almost indistinguishable from True Men. No, these dogs of Juli's world were bounding, happy creatures with few responsibilities. There seemed to be an affectionate relationship between them and the people there. They shared laughter and sorrow.

Juli had closed her eyes as she tried to bring Germany to them. Concentrating hard, now she brought into the picture of beauty and happiness something else—fearful flying things that dropped fire; thunder and noise; a most unpleasant face, a screaming face with a dab of black fur above the mouth; a licking of flame in the night; a thunder of death machines. Across this thunder there was the image of Juli and two other girls who resembled her; they were moving with a man, obviously their father, toward three iron boxes that looked like the one Juli had landed in. Then there was darkness.

That was Germany.

Juli slumped to the ground.

Gently the four of them probed at her mind. To them it was like a diamond, as clear and transparent as a sunlit pool in the forest, but the light it shot back to them was not a reflection. It was rich and bright and dazzling. Now that it was at rest, they could see deeply into it. They saw hunger, hurt, and loneliness. They saw a loneliness so great that each of them in turn tried to think of a way to assuage it. *Love,* they thought, *what she needs is love, and her own kind.* But where would they find an Ancient One? Would a True Man answer?

Bil said, "There's only one thing to do. We've got to take her to the house of the Wise Old Bear. He has communications with the True Men."

Oda cried out, "But she hasn't done anything wrong!"

Her father looked at her. "Darling, we don't know what this is. She's an Ancient One come back to this world after a sleep in space itself. It's been thousands of years since her world lived; I think she's beginning to realize that, and that's what put her into shock. We need help. Our people may once have been dogs, and that's what she thinks we are. We can't let that bother us. But she needs a house, and the only unauthorized house that I know of belongs to the Wise Old Bear."

Charls looked at his parents. His eyes were troubled. "What is this business about dogs? Is that why we feel so mixed up when we think about True Men? I'm confused about her too. Do you suppose I really want to belong to her?"

"Not really," his father said. "That's just a feeling left

over from long, long ago. We lead our own lives now. But this girl, she's too big a problem for us. We will take her to the Bear. At least he has a house."

Juli was still unconscious, and to them she was so big. Each took a limb and with difficulty they managed to carry her. Within less than a tenth of a night they had reached the house of the Wise Old Bear. Fortunately they had not met any manshonyaggers or other dangers of the forest.

At the door of the house of the Wise Old Bear they gently laid the girl on the ground.

Bil shouted, "Bear, Bear, come out, come out!"

"Who is there?" a voice boomed from within.

"Bil and his family. We have an Ancient with us. Come out. We need your help."

The light that had been streaming from the doorway with a yellow glare was suddenly reduced to endurable proportions as the immense bulk of the Bear loomed in the doorway before them.

He pulled his spectacles from a case attached to his belt, put them on his nose, and squinted at Juli.

"Bless my soul," he said. "Another one. Where on earth did you get an ancient girl?"

Pompous but happy, Charls spoke up. "She came out of the sky in a screaming box."

The Bear nodded wisely.

Then Bil spoke up. "You said 'another one.' What did you mean?"

The Bear winced slightly. "Forget I said that," he told them. "I forgot for a moment that you are not True Men. Please forget it."

Bil said, "You mean it's something Unauthorized Men are not supposed to know about?"

The Bear nodded unhappily.

Understanding, Bil said, "Well, if you *can* ever tell us about it, will you, please?"

"Of course," the Bear replied. "And now I think I'd better call my housekeeper to take care of her. Herkie, Herkie, come here."

A blonde woman appeared, peering anxiously. Obviously there was something the matter with her blue eyes but she seemed to be functioning adequately.

Bil backed away from the door. "That's an Experimental person," he said. "That's a cat!"

The Bear was completely uninterested. "So it is, but you can see that her eyes are imperfect. That's why she is allowed to be my housekeeper and why her name isn't prefaced by a C'."

Bil understood. The errors True Men made in trying to breed Underpersons were often destroyed but occasionally one was allowed to live if it seemed able to function at some necessary task. The Bear had connections with True Men. If he needed a housekeeper, an imperfect modified animal provided an ideal solution.

Herkie bent over Juli's still form. She peered in puzzlement at Juli's face. Then she looked up at the Bear. "I don't understand," she said. "I don't see how it could be."

"Later," the Bear said. "When we are alone."

Herkie strained to see into the darkness and perceived the dog family. "Oh, I see," she said.

Bil and Charls were embarrassed. Oda and Kae did not seem to notice the slight.

Bil waved his hand. "Well, good-bye. I hope you can take care of her all right."

"Thank you for bringing her," the Bear said. "The True Men will probably give you a reward."

In spite of himself, Bil felt his tail beginning to wag again.

"Will we ever see her again?" Oda asked. "Do you think we'll ever see her again? I love her, I love her. . . ."

"Perhaps," her father answered. "She will know who saved her, and I think she will seek us out."

Juli awoke slowly. *Where am I? What is this place?* She had a partial return of memory. *The puppy-dog people. Where are they?* She felt conscious of someone at her bedside. She looked up into clouded blue eyes staring anxiously into hers.

"I'm Herkie," the woman said. "I'm the Bear's house-keeper."

Juli felt as though she had awakened in a mental hospital. It was all so impossible. Puppy-dog people and now a *bear*? And surely the blonde woman with the bad eyes was not a human?

Herkie patted her hand. "Of course you're confused," she said.

Juli was taken aback. "You're *talking*! You're talking and I understand you. You're talking German. We're not just communicating telepathically."

"Of course," Herkie said. "I speak true Doych. It's one of the Bear's favorite languages."

"One of . . ." Juli broke off. "It's all so confusing."

Again Herkie patted her hand. "Of course it is."

Juli lay back and looked at the ceiling. *I must be in some other world.*

No, Herkie thought at her, *but you've been gone a long time.*

The Bear came into the room. "Feeling better?" he asked.

Juli merely nodded.

"In the morning we will decide what to do," he said. "I have some connections with the True Men, and I think that we had best take you to the Vomact."

Juli sat up as if hit by a bolt of lightning. "What do you mean, 'the Vomacht'? That is my name, vom Acht!"

"I thought it might be," the Bear said. Herkie, peering at her from the bedside, nodded wisely.

"I was sure of it," she said. Then, "I think you need some good hot soup and a rest. In the morning it will all straighten itself out."

The tiredness of years seemed to settle in Juli's bones. *I do need to rest,* she thought. *I need to get things sorted out in my mind.* So suddenly that she did not even have a chance to be startled by it, she was asleep.

Herkie and the Bear studied her face. "There's a remarkable resemblance," the Bear said. Herkie nodded in agreement. "It's the time differential I'm worried about. Do you think that will be important?"

"I don't know," Herkie replied. "Since I'm not human, I don't know what bothers people." She straightened and stretched to her full length. "I know!" she said. "I *do* know! She must have been sent here to help us with the rebellion!"

"No," the Bear said. "She has been too long in Time

for her arrival to have been intentional. It is true that she may help us, she may very well help us, but I think that her arrival at this particular time and place is fortuitous rather than planned."

"Sometimes I think I understand a particular human mind," Herkie said, "but I'm sure you're correct. I can hardly wait for them to meet each other!"

"Yes," he said, "although I'm afraid that it's going to be rather traumatic. In more than one way."

When Juli awoke after her deep sleep, she found a thoughtful Herkie awaiting her.

Juli stretched and her mind, still uncontrolled, asked: *Are you really a cat?*

Yes, Herkie thought back at her. *But you are going to have to discipline that thought process of yours. Everyone can read your thoughts.*

I'm sorry, Juli spieked, *but I'm just not used to all this telepathy.*

"I know." Herkie had switched to German.

"I still don't understand how you know German," Juli said.

"It's rather a long story. I learned it from the Bear. I think, perhaps, you had better ask him how he learned it."

"Wait a minute. I'm beginning to remember what happened before I fell asleep. The Bear mentioned my name, my family name, vom Acht."

Herkie switched the subject. "We've made you some clothes. We tried to copy the style of those you had on, but they were coming to pieces so badly that we are not sure we got the new ones right."

She looked so anxious to please that Juli reassured her immediately. *If they fit, I'm sure they'll be just fine.*

Oh, they fit, Herkie spieked. *We measured you. Now, after your bath and meal, you will dress and the Bear and I will take you to the City. Underpersons like me are not ordinarily allowed in the City, but this time I think that an exception will be made.*

There was something sweet and wise in the face with the clouded blue eyes. Juli felt that Herkie was her friend. *I am,* Herkie spieked, and Juli was once more made aware that she must learn to control her thoughts, or at least the broadcasting of them.

You'll learn, Herkie spieked. *It just takes some practice.*

They approached the City on foot, the Bear leading the way, Juli behind him, and Herkie bringing up the rear. They encountered two manshonyaggers along the road but the Bear spoke true Doych to them from some distance and they turned silently and slunk away.

Juli was fascinated. "What *are* they?" she asked.

"Their real name is 'Menschenjäger' and they were invented to kill people whose ideas did not accord with those of the Sixth German Reich. But there are very few of them still functional, and so many of us have learned Doych since . . . since . . ."

"Yes?"

"Since an event you'll find out about in the City. Now let's get on with it."

They neared the City wall and Juli became conscious of a buzzing sound, and of a powerful force that excluded them. Her hair stood on end and she felt a tingling sensation of mild electrical shock. Obviously there was a force field around the City.

"What is it?" she cried out.

"Just a static charge to keep back the Wild," the Bear said soothingly. "Don't worry, I have a damper for it."

He held up a small device in his right paw, pushed a button on it, and immediately a corridor opened before them.

When they reached the City wall, the Bear felt carefully along the upper ridge. At a certain point he paused, then reached for a strange-looking key that hung from a cord around his neck.

Juli could see no difference between this section of the wall and any other but the Bear inserted his key into a notch he had located and a section of the barrier swung up. The three passed through and silently the wall fell back into position.

The Bear hurried them along dusty streets. Juli saw a number of people but most of them seemed to her aloof, austere, uncaring. They bore little resemblance to the lusty Prussians she remembered.

Eventually they arrived at the door of a large building that looked old and imposing. Beside the door there was an inscription. The Bear was hurrying them through the entryway.

Oh, please, Mr. Bear, may I stop to read it?

Just plain Bear is all right. And yes, of course you may. It may even help you to understand some of the things that you are going to learn today.

The inscription was in German, and it was in the form of a poem. It looked as though it had been carved hundreds of years earlier (as indeed it had. Juli could not know that at this time).

Herkie looked up. "Oh, the first . . ."

"Hush," said the Bear.

Juli read the poem to herself silently.

> *Youth*
> *Fading, fading, going*
> *Flowing*
> *Like life blood from our veins. . . .*
> *Little remains.*
> *The glorious face*
> *Erased,*
> *Replaced*
> *By one which mirrors tears,*
> *The years*
> *Gone by.*
> *Oh, Youth,*
> *Linger yet a while!*
> *Smile*
> *Still upon us*
> *The wretched few*
> *Who worship*
> *You. . . .*

"I don't understand it," said Juli.

"You will," the Bear said. "Unfortunately, you will."

An official in a bright green robe trimmed with gold approached. "We have not had the honor of your presence for some time," he said respectfully to the Bear.

"I've been rather busy," the Bear replied. "But how is she?"

Juli realized with a start that the conversation was not telepathic but was in German. *How do all these people know German?* She unthinkingly flung her thought abroad.

Hush came back the simultaneous warnings from Herkie and the Bear.

Juli felt thoroughly admonished. "I'm sorry," she almost whispered. "I don't know how I'll ever learn the trick."

Herkie was immediately sympathetic. "It *is* a trick," she said, "but you're already better at it than you were when you arrived. You just have to be careful. You can't fling your thoughts everywhere."

"Never mind that now," the Bear said and he turned to the green-uniformed official. "Is it possible to have an audience? I think it's important."

"You may have to wait a little while," the official said, "but I'm sure she will always grant audience to *you.*"

The Bear looked a little smug at that, Juli noticed.

They sat down to wait and from time to time Herkie patted Juli's arm reassuringly.

It was actually not long before the official reappeared. "She will see you now," he said.

He led them through a long corridor to a large room at the end of which was a dais with a chair. "Not quite a throne," Juli thought to herself. Behind the chair stood a young and handsome male, a True Man. In the chair sat a woman, old, old beyond imagining; her wrinkled hands were claws, but in the haggard, wrinkled face one could still detect some trace of beauty.

Juli's sense of bewilderment grew. She *knew* this person, but she did not. Her sense of orientation, already splintered by the events of the past "day," almost disintegrated. She grabbed Herkie's hand as if it were the only familiar element in a world she could not understand.

The woman spoke. Her voice was old and weak, but she spoke in German.

"So, Juli, you have come. Laird told me he was bringing you in. I am so happy to see you, and to know that you are all right."

Juli's senses reeled. She *knew*, she *knew*, but she could not believe. Too much had changed, too much had happened, in the short time that she had returned to life.

Gasping, tentatively, she whispered, "Carlotta?"

Her sister nodded. "Yes, Juli, it is I. And this is my husband, Laird." She nodded her head toward the handsome young man behind her. "He brought me in about two hundred years ago, but unfortunately as an Ancient I cannot undergo the rejuvenation process that has been developed since we left the Earth."

Juli began to sob. "Oh, Carlotta, it's all so hard to believe. And you're so old! You were only two years older than I."

"Darling, I've had two hundred years of bliss. They couldn't rejuvenate me but they could at least prolong my life. Now, it is not from purely altruistic purposes that I have had Laird bring you in. Karla is still out there, but since she was only sixteen when she was suspended, we thought that you would be better suited to the task.

"In fact, we really didn't do you any favor in bringing you in because now you too will begin to age. But to be forever in suspended animation is not any life either."

"Of course not," Juli said. "And anyway, if I had lived a normal life, I would have aged."

Carlotta leaned over to kiss her.

"At least we're together at last," Juli sighed.

"Darling," Carlotta said, "it is wonderful to have even this little time together. You see, I'm dying. There comes a point when, with all technology, the scientists cannot keep a body alive. And we need help, help with the rebellion."

"The rebellion?"

"Yes. Against the Jwindz. They were Chinesians, philosophers. Now they are the true rulers of the Earth, and we—so they believe—are merely their Instrumentality, their police force. Their power is not over the body of man but over the *soul*. That is almost a forgotten word here now. Say 'mind' instead. They call themselves the Perfect Ones and have sought to remake man in their own image. But they are remote, removed, bloodless.

"They have recruited persons of all races, but man has not responded well. Only a handful aspire to the kind of esthetic perfection the Jwindz have as their goal. So the Jwindz have resorted to their knowledge of drugs and opiates to turn True Man into a tranquilized, indifferent people—to make it easy to govern them, to control everything that they do. Unfortunately some of our"—she nodded toward Laird—"descendants have joined them.

"We need you, Juli. Since I came back from the ancient world, Laird and I have done what we could to free True Men from this form of slavery, because it *is* slavery. It is a lack of vitality, a lack of meaning to life. We used to have a word for it in the old days. Remember? 'Zombie.'"

"What do you want me to do?"

During the entire conversation between the sisters, Herkie, the Bear, and Laird had remained silent.

Now Laird spoke. "Until Carlotta came to us, we were drifting along, uncaring, in the power of the Jwindz. We did not know what it was, really, to be a human being. We felt that our only purpose in life was to serve the Jwindz: If they were perfect, what other function could we perform? It was our duty to serve their needs—to maintain and guard the cities, to keep out the Wild, to administer the drugs. Some of the Instrumentality even preyed upon the Unauthorized Men, the Unforgiven, and, as a last resort, the True Men, to supply their laboratories.

"But now many of us no longer believe in the perfection of the Jwindz—or perhaps we have come to believe in something more than human perfection. We have been serving men. We should have been serving *mankind*.

"Now we feel that the time has come to put an end to this tyranny. Carlotta and I have allies among some of our descendants and among some of the Unforgiven and, as you have seen, even among the Unauthorized Men and other animal-derived persons. I think there must still be a connection from the time that human beings had 'pets' in the old days."

Juli looked about her and realized that Herkie was quietly purring. "Yes," she said, "I see what you mean."

Laird continued, "What we want to do is to set up a *real* Instrumentality—not a force for the service of the

Jwindz, but one for the service of man. We are determined that never again shall man betray his own image. We will establish the Instrumentality of Mankind, one benevolent but not manipulative."

Carlotta nodded slowly. Her aged face showed concern. "I will die in a few days and you will marry Laird. You will be the new Vomact. With any luck by the time you are as old as I am, your descendants and some of mine should have freed the Earth from the power of the Jwindz."

Juli again felt completely disoriented. "I'm to marry your husband?"

Again Laird spoke. "I have loved your sister well for more than two hundred years. I shall love you too, because you are so much like her. Do not think that I am being disloyal. She and I have discussed this for some time before I brought you in. If she were not dying, I should continue to be faithful to her. But now we need you."

Carlotta concurred. "It is true. He has made me very happy, and he will make you happy too, through all the years of your life. Juli, I could not have had you brought in had I not had some plan for your future. You could never be happy with one of those drugged, tranquilized True Men. Trust me in this, please. It is the only thing to do."

Tears formed in Juli's eyes. "To have found you at last and then to lose you after such a short time . . ."

Herkie patted her hand and Juli looked up to see sympathetic tears in her clouded blue eyes.

It was three days later that Carlotta died. She died with a smile on her face and Laird and Juli each holding one of her hands. She spoke at the last and pressed their hands. "I'll see you later. Out among the stars."

Juli wept uncontrollably.

They postponed the wedding ceremony for seven days of mourning. For once the City gates were opened and the static fields of electricity cut off because even the Jwindz could not control the feelings of the animal-derived persons, the Unauthorized Men, even some of the True Men, toward this woman who had come to them from an ancient world.

The Bear was particularly mournful. "I was the one who found her, you know, after you brought her in," he said to Laird.

"I remember."

So that's what the Bear meant when he said 'another one,' Bil said.

Charls and Oda, Bil and Kae were among the mourners. Juli saw them and thought, *My dear little puppy-dog people,* but this time the thought was loving and not contemptuous.

Oda's tail wagged. *I've thought of something,* she spieked at Juli. *Can you meet me down by the* cenote *in two days' time?*

Yes, thought Juli, proud of herself at being sure, for the first time, that her thought had gone only to the person for whom it was meant. She knew that she had been successful when she glanced at Laird's face and saw that he had not read her thought.

When she met Oda at the *cenote,* Juli did not know what was expected of her—nor what she herself expected.

You must be very careful in directing your thoughts,

Oda spieked. *We never know when some of the Jwindz are overhead.*

I think I'm learning, Juli spieked. Oda nodded.

What my idea was, it was to make use of the Fighting Trees. The True Men are still afraid of the sickness. But, you see, I know that the sickness is gone. I got so tired of brushing past the trees and always worrying about it that I decided to test it out, and I ate a pod from one of the Fighting Trees—and nothing happened. I've never been afraid of them since. So if we met there, we rebels, in a grove of the Fighting Trees, the officials of the Jwindz would never find us. They'd be afraid to hunt for us there.

Juli's face lightened. *That's a very good idea. May I consult with Laird?*

Certainly. He has always been one of us. And your sister was too.

Juli was sad again. *I feel so alone.*

No. You have Laird, and you have us, and the Bear, and his housekeeper. And in time there will be others. Now we must part.

Juli returned from her meeting with Oda at the *cenote* to find Laird deep in conference with the Bear and a young man who bore a singular resemblance to Laird— and to the youthful Carlotta that Juli remembered.

Laird smiled at her. "This is your great-nephew," he said, "my grandson."

Juli's perspective of time and age received another jolt. Laird appeared to be no older than his grandson. *How do I fit in to this?* she wondered, and accidentally broadcast the thought.

"I know that all of this must be difficult for you to

comprehend," Laird said, taking her hand. "Carlotta had some difficulty in adjusting too. But try, please try, my dear, because we need you so desperately and I, I particularly, have already become dependent on you. I could not face Carlotta's loss without you."

Juli felt a vague sense of embarrassment. "What is my"—she could not say it—"what is his name?"

"I beg your pardon. He is named Joachim for your uncle."

Joachim smiled and then gave her a brief hug. "You see," he said, "the reason we need your help with the rebellion is the cult that was built up around your sister, my grandmother. When she returned to earth as an Ancient One, there was a kind of cult set up about her. That is why she was 'The Vomact' and why you must also be. It is a rallying point for those of us who oppose the power of the Jwindz. Grandmother Carlotta had a minikingdom here, and even the Jwindz could not keep people from coming to pay her court. You must have realized that at the mourning session for her."

"Yes, I could see that she had a great deal of respect from many kinds of people. If she was in favor of a rebellion, I am sure she must have been correct. Carlotta was always a most upright person. And now I must tell you about the plan that Oda proposes." She proceeded to do so.

"It might work," the Bear said. "True Men have been very careful about observing the *tambu* of the Fighting Trees. In fact, I may even have an improvement on Oda's idea." He began to get excited and dropped his spectacles. Joachim picked them up.

"Bear," he said, "you always do that when you're excited."

"I think it means I have a good idea," the Bear said. "Look, why don't we use the manshonyaggers?"

The others looked at him in bewilderment and Laird said slowly, "I think I may see what you're getting at. The manshonyaggers, although there are not many of them left, respond only to German and—"

"And the leaders of the Jwindz are Chinesian, too proud to have learned another language," the Bear broke in, smiling.

"Yes. So if we establish headquarters in the Fighting Trees and let it be known that the new Vomact is there—"

"And surround the grove with manshonyaggers—"

They were breaking in upon each other as the idea began to take shape. The excitement grew.

"I think it will work," Laird said.

"I think so too," Joachim reassured him. "I will get together the Band of Cousins and after you're established in the Fighting Trees, we'll make a raid on the drug center and bring the tranquilizers to the grove, where we can destroy them."

"The Band of Cousins?" Juli asked.

"Carlotta's and my descendants who have not joined the Instrumentality of the Jwindz," Laird told her.

"Why would *any* of them have joined?"

Laird shrugged. "Greed, power, all kinds of very human motives. Even an illusion of physical immortality. We tried to give our children ideals but the corruption of power is very great. You must know that."

Remembering a howling, hateful face with a black mustache above the mouth, a face from her own time and place, Juli nodded.

Herkie and the Bear, Charls and Oda, Bil and Kae accompanied Juli into the grove of Fighting Trees. At first Bil and Kae were reluctant. It was only after Oda's confession of having eaten a pod that they agreed to go, and then Bil's reaction was that of a typical father.

"How *could* you take such a chance?" he asked Oda.

Her eyes were bright and her tail wagged furiously. "I just had to," she said.

He glanced at Herkie. "Now if *she* had done it . . ."

Herkie drew herself up to her full height. "I think that the relationship of curiosity and cats has, perhaps, been a little exaggerated," she said. "Actually, we're generally rather careful."

"I didn't mean to be disrespectful," Bil said hastily, and Herkie saw his tail droop.

"It's a common misconception," she said kindly, and Bil's tail straightened.

When they reached the center of the grove, they spread a picnic and gathered around. Juli was hungry. In the City she had been offered synthetic food, no doubt healthful and full of vitamins but not satisfying to the appetite of an Ancient Prussian girl. The animal-derived persons had brought real *food* and Juli ate happily.

The Bear, in particular, noticed her enjoyment. "You see," he said, "that's how they did it."

"Did what?" asked Juli, her mouth full of bread.

"How they drugged the majority of True Men. True Men were so accustomed to living on synthetic foodstuffs that when the Jwindz introduced tranquilizers into the synthetics, True Men never knew the difference. I hope that if the Band of Cousins succeeds in capturing the drug supply, the withdrawal symptoms for the True Men will not be too severe."

Bil looked up. "That's something we should consider," he said. "If there *are* severe withdrawal symptoms, a number of the True Men may be tempted to join the Jwindz in an attempt to recover the drugs."

The Bear nodded. "That's what I was thinking," he said.

It was several days before Laird, Joachim, and the Band of Cousins joined them. By this time Juli had become almost accustomed to the daylight darkness under the thick leaves and branches of the Fighting Trees, and the soft-glowing illumination at night.

Laird greeted her affectionately. "I have missed you," he said simply. "Already I have grown very attached to you."

Juli blushed and changed the subject. "Did you—or, rather, the Band of Cousins—succeed?"

"Oh, yes. There was very little difficulty. The officials of the Jwindz had grown quite careless since they have had the minds of most True Men under their control for generations. It was only a matter of Joachim's pretending to be tranquilized, and he had free access to the drug room. Over a period of days he managed to transfer the entire supply to the Cousins and to substitute placebos. I wonder when *that* will be discovered."

"As soon as the first withdrawal symptoms occur, I should think," Joachim ventured.

Something that had been nagging at the back of Juli's mind surfaced. "You have your *grandson* here, and the

Band of Cousins. But where are your and Carlotta's own children? Obviously you had some."

His face saddened. "Of course. But since they were half-Ancient, they could not only not be rejuvenated, but the combination of the chemistry made it such that their lives could not even be prolonged. They all died in their seventies and eighties. It was a great sadness to Carlotta and me. You too, my dear, if we have children, must be prepared for that. By the time of the next generation, however, the Ancient blood is sufficiently diluted that rejuvenation may take place. Joachim is a hundred and fifty years old."

"And you? And you?" she said.

He looked at her. "This is very hard on you, isn't it? I'm over three hundred years old."

Juli could not disbelieve but neither could she quite comprehend. Laird was so handsome and youthful; Carlotta had been so old.

She tried to shake the cobwebs from her mind. "What do we do with the tranquilizers now that we have them?"

Oda had approached at the latter part of the conversation. Her eyes sparkled and her tail wagged madly. "I have an idea," she announced.

"I hope it's as good as your last one," Laird said.

"I hope so too. Look, why don't we just feed the tranquilizers back to the officials? The Jwindz probably will never notice. Then we won't have to worry about fighting them. They could just gradually die off or maybe . . . do you think . . . we could send them out into space? To another planet?"

Laird nodded slowly. "You do have good ideas. Yes, to feed the tranquilizers back to them . . . but how?"

"We work well together," the Bear said, indicating Oda. "She has an idea and it triggers another one in my mind." Carefully he put on his spectacles. "I have here a map of the terrain in this vicinity. Except for the *cenote* there is no water for many kilometers in any direction. If we dropped the tranquilizers—all of them—into the *cenote*, and then if one of the Cousins could prepare the synthetic food of the Jwindz's officials so it was very spicy—I think that the problem would be solved."

Laird said, "We do have one of the Cousins who has infiltrated the Jwindz. But what would induce them to drink the water?"

Charls had joined the group. "I have heard," he said, "of an ancient spice people used to like which eventually produced thirst. It used to be found in the oceans, before they were filled with grass. But some of it remains on the banks of the sea. I believe that it was called 'salt.'"

"Now that you mention it, I've heard of that too." The Bear nodded wisely. "So that is what we need to do. 'Salt.' We introduce it into their food, then we entice them to the grove with the knowledge that the new Vomact is here together with the heart of a rebellion. It's risky but I think it's the best idea, or combination of ideas, yet."

Laird agreed. "It's as you say, risky, but it may work, and they're not likely to execute any of us if it doesn't. They'll just tranquilize us. I think that we have a better than even chance of winning. And if True Man is not revitalized, not freed from this bondage of tranquility and apathy, I believe that the entire breed will be extinguished within a few hundred years. They have come to the point that they care about nothing."

All worlds know how the plan was carried out. It was exactly as the Bear had foretold. The thirsty officials of the Jwindz, their food highly salted, drank eagerly from the water of the *cenote* and were quickly tranquilized. They put up no opposition to the members of the rebellion who soon thereafter emerged from the shelter of the Fighting Trees.

Joachim was sad. "One of my brothers had joined them," he said.

Laird laid a comforting arm across his shoulder. "Well, he's only tranquilized. We may be able to help him as he comes out of it."

"Perhaps, but it violates all my principles."

"Don't be too high-minded, Joachim. Principles are fine, but there is such a thing as rehabilitation."

And this was the way that the Instrumentality of Mankind was established. In time it would govern many worlds. Juli, by virtue of being the Vomact, became one of the first Ladies of the Instrumentality. Laird, as her husband, was one of the first Lords.

Juli lived to see some of her descendants among the first great Scanners in Space. She was very proud of them, and she was very old. Laird, of course, was as young as ever. All of her animal-descended friends had long since died. She missed them, although Laird was ever faithful.

At last, so old that she had difficulty in moving, Juli called Laird to her. She looked up into his handsome face. "My darling, you have made me very happy, just as you did Carlotta. But now I am old and, I think, dying. You are still so young and vital. I wish it were possible for me to undergo the rejuvenation, but since it isn't possible, I think we should call in Karla."

He responded so rapidly that her feelings were somewhat hurt. "Yes, I think that we should call in Karla."

He turned away from her momentarily.

She said, with a hint of tears in her voice, "I know that you will make her happy and love her very much."

His silence continued for a moment before he turned back to her.

She saw suddenly that there were lines in his face, lines she had never seen before.

"What is happening to you?" she asked.

"My darling and last love," he said, "I will be losing you twice. I cannot bear it. I have asked the physician for medicine to counteract the rejuvenation. In an hour I shall be as old as you. We are going together. And somewhere out there we will meet Carlotta and we will hold hands, the three of us, among the stars. Karla will find her own man and her own fate."

Together they sat and watched the descent of Karla's spacecraft.

Scanners Live in Vain

Martel was angry. He did not even adjust his blood away from anger. He stamped across the room by judgment, not by sight. When he saw the table hit the floor, and could tell by the expression on Luĉi's face that the table must have made a loud crash, he looked down to see if his leg were broken. It was not. Scanner to the core, he had to scan himself. The action was reflex and automatic. The inventory included his legs, abdomen, Chestbox of instruments, hands, arms, face, and back with the mirror. Only then did Martel go back to being angry. He talked with his voice, even though he knew that his wife hated its blare and preferred to have him write.

"I tell you, I must cranch. I have to cranch. It's my worry, isn't it?"

When Luĉi answered, he saw only a part of her words as he read her lips: "Darling . . . you're my husband . . . right to love you . . . dangerous . . . do it . . . dangerous . . . wait. . . ."

He faced her, but put sound in his voice, letting the blare hurt her again: "I tell you, I am going to cranch."

Catching her expression, he became rueful and a little tender: "Can't you understand what it means to me? To get out of this horrible prison in my own head? To be a man again—hearing your voice, smelling smoke? To *feel* again—to feel my feet on the ground, to feel the air move against my face? Don't you know what it means?"

Her wide-eyed worrisome concern thrust him back into pure annoyance. He read only a few of the words as her lips moved: ". . . love you . . . your own good . . . don't you think I want you to be human? . . . your own good . . . too much . . . he said . . . they said . . ."

When he roared at her, he realized that his voice must be particularly bad. He knew that the sound hurt her no less than did the words: "Do you think I wanted you to marry a Scanner? Didn't I tell you we're almost as low as the habermans? We're dead, I tell you. We've got to be dead to do our work. How can anybody go to the Up-and-Out? Can you dream what raw Space is? I warned you. But you married me. All right, you married a man. Please, darling, let me be a man. Let me hear your voice, let me feel the warmth of being alive, of being human. Let me!"

He saw by her look of stricken assent that he had won the argument. He did not use his voice again. Instead, he pulled his tablet up from where it hung against his chest. He wrote on it, using the pointed fingernail of his right forefinger—the talking nail of a Scanner—in quick clean-cut script: *Pls, drlng, whrs crnching wire?*

She pulled the long gold-sheathed wire out of the pocket of her apron. She let its field sphere fall to the carpeted floor. Swiftly, dutifully, with the deft obedience of a Scanner's wife, she wound the Cranching Wire around his head, spirally around his neck and chest. She avoided the instruments set in his chest. She even avoided the radiating scars around the instruments, the stigmata of men who had gone Up and into the Out. Mechanically he lifted a foot as she slipped the wire between his feet. She drew the wire taut. She snapped the small plug into the High-Burden control next to his Heart-Reader. She helped him to sit down, arranging his hands for him, pushing his head back into the cup at the top of the chair. She turned then, full-face toward him, so that he could read her lips easily. Her expression was composed:

"Ready, darling?"

She knelt, scooped up the sphere at the other end of the wire, stood erect calmly, her back to him. He scanned her, and saw nothing in her posture but grief which would have escaped the eye of anyone but a Scanner. She spoke: he could see her chest-muscles moving. She realized that she was not facing him, and turned so that he could see her lips:

"Ready at last?"

He smiled a *yes*.

She turned her back to him again. (Luêi could never bear to watch him go Under-the-Wire.) She tossed the wire-sphere into the air. It caught in the force-field, and hung there. Suddenly it glowed. That was all. All—except for the sudden red stinking roar of coming back to his senses. Coming back, across the wild threshold of pain—

∽|∾

When he awakened under the wire, he did not feel as

though he had just cranched. Even though it was the second cranching within the week, he felt fit. He lay in the chair. His ears drank in the sound of air touching things in the room. He heard Luci breathing in the next room, where she was hanging up the wire to cool. He smelt the thousand-and-one smells that are in anybody's room: the crisp freshness of the germ-burner, the sour-sweet tang of the humidifier, the odor of the dinner they had just eaten, the smells of clothes, furniture, of people themselves. All these were pure delight. He sang a phrase or two of his favorite song:

> *Here's to the haberman, Up and Out!*
> *Up—oh!—and Out—oh!—Up and Out! . . .*

He heard Luci chuckle in the next room. He gloated over the sounds of her dress as she swished to the doorway.

She gave him her crooked little smile. "You sound all right. Are you all right, really?"

Even with this luxury of senses, he scanned. He took the flash-quick inventory which constituted his professional skill. His eyes swept in the news of the instruments. Nothing showed off scale, beyond the Nerve Compression hanging in the edge of *Danger*. But he could not worry about the Nerve-box. That always came through cranching. You couldn't get under the wire without having it show on the Nerve-box. Some day the box would go to *Overload* and drop back down to *Dead*. That was the way a haberman ended. But you couldn't have everything. People who went to the Up-and-Out had to pay the price for Space.

Anyhow, he should worry! He was a Scanner. A good one, and he knew it. If he couldn't scan himself, who could? This cranching wasn't too dangerous. Dangerous, but not too dangerous.

Luĉi put out her hand and ruffled his hair as if she had been reading his thoughts, instead of just following them: "But you know you shouldn't have! You shouldn't!"

"But I did!" He grinned at her.

Her gaiety still forced, she said: "Come on, darling, let's have a good time. I have almost everything there is in the icebox—all your favorite tastes. And I have two new records just full of smells. I tried them out myself, and even I liked them. And you know me—"

"Which?"

"Which what, you old darling?"

He slipped his hand over her shoulders as he limped out of the room. (He could never go back to feeling the floor beneath his feet, feeling the air against his face, without being bewildered and clumsy. As if cranching was real, and being a haberman was a bad dream. But he *was* a haberman, and a Scanner.) "You know what I meant, Luĉi . . . the smells, which you have. Which one did you like, on the record?"

"Well-l-l," said she, judiciously, "there were some lamb chops that were the strangest things—"

He interrupted: "What are lambtchots?"

"Wait till you smell them. Then guess. I'll tell you this much. It's a smell hundreds and hundreds of years old. They found about it in the old books."

"Is a lambtchot a Beast?"

"I won't tell you. You've got to wait," she laughed, as

she helped him sit down and spread out his tasting dishes before him. He wanted to go back over the dinner first, sampling all the pretty things he had eaten, and savoring them this time with his now-living lips and tongue.

When Luĉi had found the Music Wire and had thrown its sphere up into the force-field, he reminded her of the new smells. She took out the long glass records and set the first one into a transmitter.

"Now sniff!"

A queer, frightening, exciting smell came over the room. It seemed like nothing in this world, nor like anything from the Up-and-Out. Yet it was familiar. His mouth watered. His pulse beat a little faster; he scanned his Heartbox. (Faster, sure enough.) But that smell, what was it? In mock perplexity, he grabbed her hands, looked into her eyes, and growled:

"Tell me, darling! Tell me, or I'll eat you up!"

"That's just right!"

"What?"

"You're right. It should make you want to eat me. It's meat."

"Meat. Who?"

"Not a person," said she, knowledgeably, "a Beast. A Beast which people used to eat. A lamb was a small sheep—you've seen sheep out in the Wild, haven't you?— and a chop is part of its middle—here!" She pointed at her chest.

Martel did not hear her. All his boxes had swung over toward *Alarm*, some to *Danger*. He fought against the roar of his own mind, forcing his body into excess excitement. How easy it was to be a Scanner when you really stood outside your own body, haberman-fashion, and looked back into it with your eyes alone. Then you could manage the body, rule it coldly even in the enduring agony of Space. But to realize that you *were* a body, that this thing was ruling you, that the mind could kick the flesh and send it roaring off into panic! That was bad.

He tried to remember the days before he had gone into the Haberman Device, before he had been cut apart for the Up-and-Out. Had he always been subject to the rush of his emotions from his mind to his body, from his body back to his mind, confounding him so that he couldn't scan? But he hadn't been a Scanner then.

He knew what had hit him. Amid the roar of his own pulse, he knew. In the nightmare of the Up-and-Out, that smell had forced its way through to him, while their ship burned off Venus and the habermans fought the collapsing metal with their bare hands. He had scanned them: all were in *Danger*. Chestboxes went up to *Overload* and dropped to *Dead* all around him as he had moved from man to man, shoving the drifting corpses out of his way as he fought to scan each man in turn, to clamp vises on unnoticed broken legs, to snap the Sleeping Valve on men whose instruments showed that they were hopelessly near *Overload*. With men trying to work and cursing him for a Scanner while he, professional zeal aroused, fought to do his job and keep them alive in the Great Pain of Space, he had smelled that smell. It had fought its way along his rebuilt nerves, past the Haberman cuts, past all the safeguards of physical and mental discipline. In the wildest hour of tragedy, he had smelled aloud. He remembered it was like a bad cranching, connected with the fury and nightmare all around him. He had even stopped his work to scan himself, fearful that the First Effect might come, breaking past all haberman cuts and ruining him with the Pain of Space. But he had come through. His own instruments stayed and stayed at *Danger*, without nearing *Overload*. He had done his job, and won a commendation for it. He had even forgotten the burning ship.

All except the smell.

And here the smell was all over again—the smell of meat-with-fire . . .

Luĉi looked at him with wifely concern. She obviously thought he had cranched too much, and was about to haberman back. She tried to be cheerful: "You'd better rest, honey."

He whispered to her: "Cut—off—that—smell."

She did not question his word. She cut the transmitter. She even crossed the room and stepped up the room controls until a small breeze flitted across the floor and drove the smells up to the ceiling.

He rose, tired and stiff. (His instruments were normal, except that Heart was fast and Nerves still hanging on the edge of Danger.) He spoke sadly:

"Forgive me, Luĉi. I suppose I shouldn't have cranched. Not so soon again. But darling, I have to get out from being a haberman. How can I ever be near you? How can I be a man—not hearing my own voice, not even feeling my own life as it goes through my veins? I love you, darling. Can't I ever be near you?"

Her pride was disciplined and automatic: "But you're a Scanner!"

"I know I'm a Scanner. But so what?"

She went over the words, like a tale told a thousand times to reassure herself: "You are the bravest of the brave, the most skillful of the skilled. All Mankind owes most honor to the Scanner, who unites the Earths of mankind. Scanners are the protectors of the habermans. They are the judges in the Up-and-Out. They make men live in the place where men need desperately to die. They are the most honored of Mankind, and even the Chiefs of the Instrumentality are delighted to pay them homage!"

With obstinate sorrow he demurred: "Luĉi, we've heard that all before. But does it pay us back—"

"'Scanners work for more than pay. They are the strong guards of Mankind.' Don't you remember that?"

"But our lives, Luĉi. What can you get out of being the wife of a Scanner? Why did you marry me? I'm human only when I cranch. The rest of the time—you know what I am. A machine. A man turned into a machine. A man who has been killed and kept alive for duty. Don't you realize what I miss?"

"Of course, darling, of course—"

He went on: "Don't you think I remember my childhood? Don't you think I remember what it is to be a man and not a haberman? To walk and feel my feet on the ground? To feel decent clean pain instead of watching my body every minute to see if I'm alive? How will I know if I'm dead? Did you ever think of that, Luĉi? How will I know if I'm dead?"

She ignored the unreasonableness of his outburst. Pacifyingly, she said: "Sit down, darling. Let me make you some kind of a drink. You're over-wrought."

Automatically he scanned. "No, I'm not! Listen to me. How do you think it feels to be in the Up-and-Out with the crew tied-for-Space all around you? How do you think it feels to watch them sleep? How do you think I like scanning, scanning, scanning month after month, when I can feel the Pain-of-Space beating against every part of my body, trying to get past my Haberman blocks? How do you think I like to wake the men when I have to, and have them hate me for it? Have you ever seen habermans fight—strong men fighting, and neither knowing pain, fighting until one touches *Overload*? Do you think about that, Luĉi?" Triumphantly he added: "Can you blame me if I cranch, and come back to being a man, just two days a month?"

"I'm not blaming you, darling. Let's enjoy your cranch. Sit down now, and have a drink."

He was sitting down, resting his face in his hands, while she fixed the drink, using natural fruits out of bottles in addition to the secure alkaloids. He watched her restlessly and pitied her for marrying a Scanner; and then, though it was unjust, resented having to pity her.

Just as she turned to hand him the drink, they both jumped a little when the phone rang. It should not have rung. They had turned it off. It rang again, obviously on the emergency circuit. Stepping ahead of Luĉi, Martel strode over to the phone and looked into it. Vomact was looking at him.

The custom of Scanners entitled him to be brusque, even with a Senior Scanner, on certain given occasions. This was one.

Before Vomact could speak, Martel spoke two words

into the plate, not caring whether the old man could read lips or not:

"Cranching. Busy."

He cut the switch and went back to Luĉi.

The phone rang again.

Luĉi said, gently, "I can find out what it is, darling. Here, take your drink and sit down."

"Leave it alone," said her husband. "No one has a right to call when I'm cranching. He knows that. He ought to know that."

The phone rang again. In a fury, Martel rose and went to the plate. He cut it back on. Vomact was on the screen. Before Martel could speak, Vomact held up his Talking Nail in line with his Heartbox. Martel reverted to discipline:

"Scanner Martel present and waiting, sir."

The lips moved solemnly: "Top emergency."

"Sir, I am under the wire."

"Top emergency."

"Sir, don't you understand?" Martel mouthed his words, so he could be sure that Vomact followed. "I . . . am . . . under . . . the . . . wire. Unfit . . . for . . . Space!"

Vomact repeated: "Top emergency. Report to your central Tie-in."

"But, sir, no emergency like this—"

"Right, Martel. No emergency like this, ever before. Report to Tie-in." With a faint glint of kindliness, Vomact added: "No need to de-cranch. Report as you are."

This time it was Martel whose phone was cut out. The screen went gray.

He turned to Luĉi. The temper had gone out of his

voice. She came to him. She kissed him, and rumpled his hair. All she could say was,

"I'm sorry."

She kissed him again, knowing his disappointment. "Take good care of yourself, darling. I'll wait."

He scanned, and slipped into his transparent aircoat. At the window he paused, and waved. She called, "Good luck!" As the air flowed past him he said to himself,

"This is the first time I've felt flight in—in eleven years. Lord, but it's easy to fly if you can feel yourself live!"

Central Tie-in glowed white and austere far ahead. Martel peered. He saw no glare of incoming ships from the Up-and-Out, no shuddering flare of Space-fire out of control. Everything was quiet, as it should be on an off-duty night.

And yet Vomact had called. He had called an emergency higher than Space. There was no such thing. But Vomact had called it.

∾ II ∾

When Martel got there, he found about half the Scanners present, two dozen or so of them. He lifted the Talking Finger. Most of the Scanners were standing face to face, talking in pairs as they read lips. A few of the old, impatient ones were scribbling on their Tablets and then thrusting the Tablets into other people's faces. All the faces wore the dull dead relaxed look of a haberman. When Martel entered the room, he knew that most of the others laughed in the deep isolated privacy of their own minds, each thinking things it would be useless to express in formal words. It had been a long time since a Scanner showed up at a meeting cranched.

Vomact was not there: probably, thought Martel, he was still on the phone calling others. The light of the phone flashed on and off; the bell rang. Martel felt odd when he realized that of all those present, he was the only one to hear that loud bell. It made him realize why ordinary people did not like to be around groups of habermans or Scanners. Martel looked around for company.

His friend Chang was there, but was busy explaining to some old and testy Scanner that he did not know why Vomact had called. Martel looked further and saw Parizianski. He walked over, threading his way past the others with a dexterity that showed he could feel his feet from the inside, and did not have to watch them. Several of the others stared at him with their dead faces, and tried to smile. But they lacked full muscular control and their faces twisted into horrid masks. (Scanners knew better than to show expression on faces which they could no longer govern. Martel added to himself, *I swear* I'll *never smile unless I'm cranched*.)

Parizianski gave him the sign of the talking finger. Looking face to face, he spoke:

"You come here cranched?"

Parizianski could not hear his own voice, so the words roared like the words on a broken and screeching phone; Martel was startled, but knew that the inquiry was well meant. No one could be better-natured than the burly Pole.

"Vomact called. Top emergency."

"You told him you were cranched?"

"Yes."

"He still made you come?"

"Yes."

"Then all this—it is not for Space? You could not go Up-and-Out? You are like ordinary men."

"That's right."

"Then why did he call us?" Some pre-Haberman habit made Parizianski wave his arms in inquiry. The hand struck the back of the old man behind them. The slap could be heard throughout the room, but only Martel heard it. Instinctively, he scanned Parizianski and the old Scanner: they scanned him back. Only then did the old man ask why Martel had scanned him. When Martel explained that he was Under-the-Wire, the old man moved swiftly away to pass on the news that there was a cranched Scanner present at the Tie-in.

Even this minor sensation could not keep the attention of most of the Scanners from the worry about the Top Emergency. One young man, who had scanned his first transit just the year before, dramatically interposed himself between Parizianski and Martel. He dramatically flashed his Tablet at them:

Is Vmct mad?

The older men shook their heads. Martel, remembering that it had not been too long that the young man had been haberman, mitigated the dead solemnity of the denial with a friendly smile. He spoke in a normal voice, saying:

"Vomact is the Senior of Scanners. I am sure that he could not go mad. Would he not see it on his boxes first?"

Martel had to repeat the question, speaking slowly and

mouthing his words, before the young Scanner could understand the comment. The young man tried to make his face smile, and twisted it into a comic mask. But he took up his Tablet and scribbled:

Yr rght.

Chang broke away from his friend and came over, his half-Chinese face gleaming in the warm evening. (It's strange, thought Martel, that more Chinese don't become Scanners. Or not so strange, perhaps, if you think that they never fill their quota of habermans. Chinese love good living too much. The ones who do scan are all good ones.) Chang saw that Martel was cranched, and spoke with voice:

"You break precedents. Luĉi must be angry to lose you?"

"She took it well. Chang, that's strange."

"What?"

"I'm cranched, and I can hear. Your voice sounds all right. How did you learn to talk like—like an ordinary person?"

"I practiced with soundtracks. Funny you noticed it. I think I am the only Scanner in or between the Earths who can pass for an Ordinary Man. Mirrors and soundtracks. I found out how to act."

"But you don't . . . ?"

"No. I don't feel, or taste, or hear, or smell things, any more than you do. Talking doesn't do me much good. But I notice that it cheers up the people around me."

"It would make a difference in the life of Luĉi."

Chang nodded sagely. "My father insisted on it. He said, 'You may be proud of being a Scanner. I am sorry

you are not a Man. Conceal your defects.' So I tried. I
wanted to tell the old boy about the Up-and-Out, and
what we did there, but it did not matter. He said,
'Airplanes were good enough for Confucius, and they are
for me too.' The old humbug! He tries so hard to be a
Chinese when he can't even read Old Chinese. But he's
got wonderful good sense, and for somebody going on two
hundred he certainly gets around."

Martel smiled at the thought: "In his airplane?"

Chang smiled back. This discipline of his facial muscles
was amazing; a bystander would not think that Chang was
a haberman, controlling his eyes, cheeks, and lips by cold
intellectual control. The expression had the spontaneity of
life. Martel felt a flash of envy for Chang when he looked
at the dead cold faces of Parizianski and the others. He
knew that he himself looked fine: but why shouldn't he?
He was cranched. Turning to Parizianski he said,

"Did you see what Chang said about his father? The
old boy uses an airplane."

Parizianski made motions with his mouth, but the
sounds meant nothing. He took up his Tablet and showed
it to Martel and Chang:

Bzz bzz. Ha ha. Gd ol' boy.

At that moment, Martel heard steps out in the corridor.
He could not help looking toward the door. Other eyes
followed the direction of his glance.

Vomact came in.

The group shuffled to attention in four parallel
lines. They scanned one another. Numerous hands
reached across to adjust the electrochemical controls on
Chestboxes which had begun to load up. One Scanner

held out a broken finger which his counter-scanner had discovered, and submitted it for treatment and splinting.

Vomact had taken out his Staff of Office. The cube at the top flashed red light through the room, the lines reformed, and all Scanners gave the sign meaning, *Present and ready!*

Vomact countered with the stance signifying, *I am the Senior and take Command.*

Talking fingers rose in the counter-gesture, *We concur and commit ourselves.*

Vomact raised his right arm, dropped the wrist as though it were broken, in a queer searching gesture, meaning: *Any men around? Any habermans not tied? All clear for the Scanners?*

Alone of all those present, the cranched Martel heard the queer rustle of feet as they all turned completely around without leaving position, looking sharply at one another and flashing their beltlights into the dark corners of the great room. When again they faced Vomact, he made a further sign:

All clear. Follow my words.

Martel noticed that he alone relaxed. The others could not know the meaning of relaxation with the minds blocked off up there in their skulls, connected only with the eyes, and the rest of the body connected with the mind only by controlling non-sensory nerves and the instrument boxes on their chests. Martel realized that, cranched as he was, he expected to hear Vomact's voice: the Senior had been talking for some time. No sound escaped his lips. (Vomact never bothered with sound.)

". . . and when the first men to go Up and Out went to the Moon, what did they find?"

"Nothing," responded the silent chorus of lips.

"Therefore they went further, to Mars and to Venus. The ships went out year by year, but they did not come back until the Year One of Space. Then did a ship come back with the First Effect. Scanners, I ask you, what is the First Effect?"

"No one knows. No one knows."

"No one will ever know. Too many are the variables. By what do we know the First Effect?"

"By the Great Pain of Space," came the chorus.

"And by what further sign?"

"By the need, oh the need for death."

Vomact again: "And who stopped the need for death?"

"Henry Haberman conquered the first effect, in the Year 3 of Space."

"And, Scanners, I ask you, what did he do?"

"He made the habermans."

"How, O Scanners, are habermans made?"

"They are made with the cuts. The brain is cut from the heart, the lungs. The brain is cut from the ears, the nose. The brain is cut from the mouth, the belly. The brain is cut from desire, and pain. The brain is cut from the world. Save for the eyes. Save for the control of the living flesh."

"And how, O Scanners, is flesh controlled?"

"By the boxes set in the flesh, the controls set in the chest, the signs made to rule the living body, the signs by which the body lives."

"How does a haberman live and live?"

"The haberman lives by control of the boxes."

"Whence come the habermans?"

Martel felt in the coming response a great roar of broken voices echoing through the room as the Scanners, habermans themselves, put sound behind their mouthings:

"Habermans are the scum of Mankind. Habermans are the weak, the cruel, the credulous, and the unfit. Habermans are the sentenced-to-more-than-death. Habermans live in the mind alone. They are killed for Space but they live for Space. They master the ships that connect the Earths. They live in the Great Pain while ordinary men sleep in the cold cold sleep of the transit."

"Brothers and Scanners, I ask you now: are we habermans or are we not?"

"We are habermans in the flesh. We are cut apart, brain and flesh. We are ready to go to the Up-and-Out. All of us have gone through the Haberman Device."

"We are habermans then?" Vomact's eyes flashed and glittered as he asked the ritual question.

Again the chorused answer was accompanied by a roar of voices heard only by Martel: "Habermans we are, and more, and more. We are the Chosen who are habermans by our own free will. We are the Agents of the Instrumentality of Mankind."

"What must the others say to us?"

"They must say to us, 'You are the bravest of the brave, the most skillful of the skilled. All Mankind owes most honor to the Scanner, who unites the Earths of Mankind. Scanners are the protectors of the habermans. They are the judges in the Up-and-Out. They make men live in the place where men need desperately to die. They are the most honored of mankind, and even the Chiefs of the Instrumentality are delighted to pay them homage!'"

Vomact stood more erect: "What is the secret duty of the Scanner?"

"To obey the Instrumentality only in accordance with Scanner Law."

"What is the second secret duty of the Scanner?"

"To keep secret our law, and to destroy the acquirers thereof."

"How to destroy?"

"Twice to the *Overload*, back and *Dead*."

"If habermans die, what the duty then?"

The Scanners all compressed their lips for answer. (Silence was the code.) Martel, who—long familiar with the Code—was a little bored with the proceedings, noticed that Chang was breathing too heavily; he reached over and adjusted Chang's Lung-control and received the thanks of Chang's eyes. Vomact observed the interruption and glared at them both. Martel relaxed, trying to imitate the dead cold stillness of the others. It was so hard to do, when you were cranched.

"If others die, what the duty then?" asked Vomact.

"Scanners together inform the Instrumentality. Scanners together accept the punishment. Scanners together settle the case."

"And if the punishment be severe?"

"Then no ships go."

"And if Scanners not be honored?"

"Then no ships go."

"And if a Scanner goes unpaid?"

"Then no ships go."

"And if the Others and the Instrumentality are not in all ways at all times mindful of their proper obligation to the Scanners?"

"Then no ships go."

"And what, O Scanners, if no ships go?"

"The Earths fall apart. The Wild comes back in. The Old Machines and the Beasts return."

"What is the known duty of a Scanner?"

"Not to sleep in the Up-and-Out."

"What is the second duty of a Scanner?"

"To keep forgotten the name of fear."

"What is the third duty of a Scanner?"

"To use the wire of Eustace Cranch only with care, only with moderation." Several pair of eyes looked quickly at Martel before the mouthed chorus went on. "To cranch only at home, only among friends, only for the purpose of remembering, of relaxing, or of begetting."

"What is the word of the Scanner?"

"Faithful though surrounded by death."

"What is the motto of the Scanner?"

"Awake though surrounded by silence."

"What is the work of the Scanner?"

"Labor even in the heights of the Up-and-Out, loyalty even in the depths of the Earths."

"How do you know a Scanner?"

"We know ourselves. We are dead though we live. And we Talk with the Tablet and the Nail."

"What is this Code?"

"This code is the friendly ancient wisdom of Scanners, briefly put that we may be mindful and be cheered by our loyalty to one another."

At this point the formula should have run: "We complete the Code. Is there work or word for the Scanners?" But Vomact said, and he repeated:

"Top Emergency. Top Emergency."

They gave him the sign, *Present and ready!*

He said, with every eye straining to follow his lips:

"Some of you know the work of Adam Stone?"

Martel saw lips move, saying: "The Red Asteroid. The Other who lives at the edge of Space."

"Adam Stone has gone to the Instrumentality, claiming success for his work. He says that he has found how to Screen Out the Pain of Space. He says that the Up-and-Out can be made safe for ordinary men to work in, to stay awake in. He says that there need be no more Scanners."

Beltlights flashed on all over the room as Scanners sought the right to speak. Vomact nodded to one of the older men. "Scanner Smith will speak."

Smith stepped slowly up into the light, watching his own feet. He turned so that they could see his face. He spoke: "I say that this is a lie. I say that Stone is a liar. I say that the Instrumentality must not be deceived."

He paused. Then, in answer to some question from the audience which most of the others did not see, he said:

"I invoke the secret duty of the Scanners."

Smith raised his right hand for Emergency Attention:

"I say that Stone must die."

∽ III ∽

Martel, still cranched, shuddered as he heard the boos,

groans, shouts, squeaks, grunts, and moans which came from the Scanners who forgot noise in their excitement and strove to make their dead bodies talk to one another's deaf ears. Beltlights flashed wildly all over the room. There was a rush for the rostrum and Scanners milled around at the top, vying for attention until Parizianski—by sheer bulk—shoved the others aside and down, and turned to mouth at the group.

"Brother Scanners, I want your eyes."

The people on the floor kept moving, with their numb bodies jostling one another. Finally Vomact stepped up in front of Parizianski, faced the others, and said:

"Scanners, be Scanners! Give him your eyes."

Parizianski was not good at public speaking. His lips moved too fast. He waved his hands, which took the eyes of the others away from his lips. Nevertheless, Martel was able to follow most of the message:

". . . can't do this. Stone may have succeeded. If he has succeeded, it means the end of Scanners. It means the end of habermans, too. None of us will have to fight in the Up-and-Out. We won't have anybody else going Under-the-Wire for a few hours or days of being human. Everybody will be Other. Nobody will have to cranch, never again. Men can be men. The habermans can be killed decently and properly, the way men were killed in the Old Days, without anybody keeping them alive. They won't have to work in the Up-and-Out! There will be no more Great Pain—think of it! No . . . more . . . Great . . . Pain! How do we know that Stone is a liar—" Lights began flashing directly into his eyes. (The rudest insult of Scanner to Scanner was this.)

Vomact again exercised authority. He stepped in front of Parizianski and said something which the others could not see. Parizianski stepped down from the rostrum. Vomact again spoke:

"I think that some of the Scanners disagree with our Brother Parizianski. I say that the use of the rostrum be suspended till we have had a chance for private discussion. In fifteen minutes I will call the meeting back to order."

Martel looked around for Vomact when the Senior had rejoined the group on the floor. Finding the Senior, Martel wrote swift script on his Tablet, waiting for a chance to thrust the tablet before the senior's eyes. He had written:

Am crnchd. Rspctfly requst prmissn lv now, stnd by fr orders.

Being cranched did strange things to Martel. Most meetings that he attended seemed formal, hearteningly ceremonial, lighting up the dark inward eternities of habermanhood. When he was not cranched, he noticed his body no more than a marble bust notices its marble pedestal. He had stood with them before. He had stood with them effortless hours, while the long-winded ritual broke through the terrible loneliness behind his eyes, and made him feel that the Scanners, though a confraternity of the damned, were none the less forever honored by the professional requirements of their mutilation.

This time, it was different. Coming cranched, and in full possession of smell-sound-taste-feeling, he reacted more or less as a normal man would. He saw his friends and colleagues as a lot of cruelly driven ghosts, posturing out the meaningless ritual of their indefeasible damnation.

What difference did anything make, once you were a haberman? Why all this talk about habermans and Scanners? Habermans were criminals or heretics, and Scanners were gentlemen-volunteers, but they were all in the same fix—except that Scanners were deemed worthy of the short-time return of the Cranching Wire, while habermans were simply disconnected while the ships lay in port and were left suspended until they should be awakened, in some hour of emergency or trouble, to work out another spell of their damnation. It was a rare haberman that you saw on the street—someone of special merit or bravery, allowed to look at mankind from the terrible prison of his own mechanified body. And yet, what Scanner ever pitied a haberman? What Scanner ever honored a haberman except perfunctorily in the line of duty? What had the Scanners, as a guild and a class, ever done for the habermans, except to murder them with a twist of the wrist whenever a haberman, too long beside a Scanner, picked up the tricks of the Scanning trade and learned how to live at his own will, not the will the Scanners imposed? What could the Others, the ordinary men, know of what went on inside the ships? The Others slept in their cylinders, mercifully unconscious until they woke up on whatever other Earth they had consigned themselves to. What could the Others know of the men who had to stay alive within the ship?

What could any Other know of the Up-and-Out? What Other could look at the biting acid beauty of the stars in open Space? What could they tell of the Great Pain, which started quietly in the marrow, like an ache, and proceeded by the fatigue and nausea of each separate nerve cell, brain cell, touchpoint in the body, until life itself became a terrible aching hunger for silence and for death?

He was a Scanner. All right, he *was* a Scanner. He had been a Scanner from the moment when, wholly normal, he had stood in the sunlight before a Subchief of the Instrumentality, and had sworn:

"I pledge my honor and my life to Mankind. I sacrifice myself willingly for the welfare of Mankind. In accepting the perilous austere Honor, I yield all my rights without exception to the Honorable Chiefs of the Instrumentality and to the Honored Confraternity of Scanners."

He had pledged.

He had gone into the Haberman Device.

He remembered his Hell. He had not had such a bad one, even though it had seemed to last a hundred-million years, all of them without sleep. He had learned to feel with his eyes. He had learned to see despite the heavy eyeplates set back of his eyeballs to insulate his eyes from the rest of him. He had learned to watch his skin. He still remembered the time he had noticed dampness on his shirt, and had pulled out his scanning mirror only to discover that he had worn a hole in his side by leaning against a vibrating machine. (A thing like that could not happen to him now; he was too adept at reading his own instruments.) He remembered the way that he had gone Up-and-Out, and the way that the Great Pain beat into him, despite the fact that his touch, smell, feeling, and hearing were gone for all ordinary purposes. He remembered killing habermans, and keeping others alive, and standing for months beside the Honorable Scanner-Pilot while neither of them slept. He remembered going ashore on

Earth Four, and remembered that he had not enjoyed it, and had realized on that day that there was no reward.

Martel stood among the other Scanners. He hated their awkwardness when they moved, their immobility when they stood still. He hated the queer assortment of smells which their bodies yielded unnoticed. He hated the grunts and groans and squawks which they emitted from their deafness. He hated them, and himself.

How could Luĉi stand him? He had kept his chestbox reading *Danger* for weeks while he courted her, carrying the Cranching Wire about with him most illegally, and going direct from one cranch to the other without worrying about the fact that his indicators all crept to the edge of *Overload*. He had wooed her without thinking of what would happen if she did say, "Yes." She had.

"And they lived happily ever after." In Old Books they did, but how could they, in life? He had had eighteen days under-the-wire in the whole of the past year! Yet she had loved him. She still loved him. He knew it. She fretted about him through the long months that he was in the Up-and-Out. She tried to make home mean something to him even when he was haberman, make food pretty when it could not be tasted, make herself lovable when she could not be kissed—or might as well not, since a haberman body meant no more than furniture. Luĉi was patient.

And now, Adam Stone! (He let his Tablet fade: how could he leave, now?)

God bless Adam Stone!

Martel could not help feeling a little sorry for himself. No longer would the high keen call of duty carry him through two hundred or so years of the Others' time, two million private eternities of his own. He could slouch and relax. He could forget High Space, and let the Up-and-Out be tended by Others. He could cranch as much as he dared. He could be almost normal—almost—for one year or five years or no years. But at least he could stay with Luĉi. He could go with her into the Wild, where there were Beasts and Old Machines still roving the dark places. Perhaps he would die in the excitement of the hunt, throwing spears at an ancient steel Manshonjagger as it leapt from its lair, or tossing hot spheres at the tribesmen of the Unforgiven who still roamed the Wild. There was still life to live, still a good normal death to die, not the moving of a needle out in the silence and pain of Space!

He had been walking about restlessly. His ears were attuned to the sounds of normal speech, so that he did not feel like watching the mouthings of his brethren. Now they seemed to have come to a decision. Vomact was moving to the rostrum. Martel looked about for Chang, and went to stand beside him. Chang whispered,

"You're as restless as water in mid-air! What's the matter? Decranching?"

They both scanned Martel, but the instruments held steady and showed no sign of the cranch giving out.

The great light flared in its call to attention. Again they formed ranks. Vomact thrust his lean old face into the glare, and spoke:

"Scanners and Brothers, I call for a vote." He held himself in the stance which meant: *I am the Senior and take Command.*

A beltlight flashed in protest.

It was old Henderson. He moved to the rostrum,

spoke to Vomact, and—with Vomact's nod of approval—turned full-face to repeat his question:

"Who speaks for the Scanners Out in Space?"

No beltlight or hand answered.

Henderson and Vomact, face to face, conferred for a few moments. Then Henderson faced them again:

"I yield to the Senior in Command. But I do not yield to a Meeting of the Confraternity. There are sixty-eight Scanners, and only forty-seven present, of whom one is cranched and U.D. I have therefore proposed that the Senior in Command assume authority only over an Emergency Committee of the Confraternity, not over a Meeting. Is that agreed and understood by the Honorable Scanners?"

Hands rose in assent.

Chang murmured in Martel's ear, "Lot of difference that makes! Who can tell the difference between a Meeting and a Committee?" Martel agreed with the words, but was even more impressed with the way that Chang, while haberman, could control his own voice.

Vomact resumed chairmanship: "We now vote on the question of Adam Stone.

"First, we can assume that he has not succeeded, and that his claims are lies. We know that from our practical experience as Scanners. The Pain of Space is only part of scanning," (*But the essential part, the basis of it all,* thought Martel.) "and we can rest assured that Stone cannot solve the problem of Space Discipline."

"That tripe again," whispered Chang, unheard save by Martel.

"The Space Discipline of our Confraternity has

kept High Space clean of war and dispute. Sixty-eight disciplined men control all High Space. We are removed by our oath and our haberman status from all Earthly passions.

"Therefore, if Adam Stone has conquered the Pain of Space, so that Others can wreck our confraternity and bring to Space the trouble and ruin which afflicts Earths, I say that Adam Stone is wrong. If Adam Stone succeeds, Scanners live in vain!

"Secondly, if Adam Stone has not conquered the Pain of Space, he will cause great trouble in all the Earths. The Instrumentality and the Subchiefs may not give us as many habermans as we need to operate the ships of Mankind. There will be wild stories, and fewer recruits, and, worst of all, the discipline of the Confraternity may relax if this kind of nonsensical heresy is spread around.

"Therefore, if Adam Stone has succeeded, he threatens the ruin of the Confraternity and should die.

"Therefore, if Adam Stone has not succeeded, he is a liar and a heretic, and should die."

"I move the death of Adam Stone."

And Vomact made the sign, *The Honorable Scanners are pleased to vote.*

∾ IV ∾

Martel grabbed wildly for his beltlight. Chang, guessing ahead, had his light out and ready; its bright beam, voting *No*, shone straight up at the ceiling. Martel got his light out and threw its beam upward in dissent. Then he looked around. Out of the forty-seven present, he could see only five or six glittering.

Two more lights went on. Vomact stood as erect as a frozen corpse. Vomact's eyes flashed as he stared back and forth over the group, looking for lights. Several more went on. Finally Vomact took the closing stance: *May it please the Scanners to count the vote.*

Three of the older men went up on the rostrum with Vomact. They looked over the room. (Martel thought: *These damned ghosts are voting on the life of a real man, a live man! They have no right to do it. I'll tell the Instrumentality!* But he knew that he would not. He thought of Luĉi and what she might gain by the triumph of Adam Stone: the heart-breaking folly of the vote was then almost too much for Martel to bear.)

All three of the tellers held up their hands in unanimous agreement on the sign of the number: *Fifteen against.*

Vomact dismissed them with a bow of courtesy. He turned and again took the stance: *I am the Senior and take Command.*

Marveling at his own daring, Martel flashed his beltlight on. He knew that any one of the bystanders might reach over and twist his Heartbox to *Overload* for such an act. He felt Chang's hand reaching to catch him by the aircoat. But he eluded Chang's grasp and ran, faster than a Scanner should, to the platform. As he ran, he wondered what appeal to make. He wouldn't get time to say much, and wouldn't be seen by all of them. It was no use talking common sense. Not now. It had to be law.

He jumped up on the rostrum beside Vomact, and took the stance: *Scanners, an Illegality!*

He violated good custom while speaking, still in the stance: "A Committee has no right to vote death by a majority vote. It takes two-thirds of a full Meeting."

He felt Vomact's body lunge behind him, felt himself falling from the rostrum, hitting the floor, hurting his knees and his touch-aware hands. He was helped to his feet. He was scanned. Some Scanner he scarcely knew took his instruments and toned him down.

Immediately Martel felt more calm, more detached, and hated himself for feeling so.

He looked up at the rostrum. Vomact maintained the stance signifying: *Order!*

The Scanners adjusted their ranks. The two Scanners next to Martel took his arms. He shouted at them, but they looked away, and cut themselves off from communication altogether.

Vomact spoke again when he saw the room was quiet: "A Scanner came here cranched. Honorable Scanners, I apologize for this. It is not the fault of our great and worthy Scanner and friend, Martel. He came here under orders. I told him not to de-cranch. I hoped to spare him an unnecessary haberman. We all know how happily Martel is married, and we wish his brave experiment well. I like Martel. I respect his judgment. I wanted him here. I knew you wanted him here. But he is cranched. He is in no mood to share in the lofty business of the Scanners. I therefore propose a solution which will meet all the requirements of fairness. I propose that we rule Scanner Martel out of order for his violation of rules. This violation would be inexcusable if Martel were not cranched.

"But at the same time, in all fairness to Martel, I

further propose that we deal with the points raised so
improperly by our worthy but disqualified brother."

Vomact gave the sign, *The Honorable Scanners are
pleased to vote.* Martel tried to reach his own beltlight; the
dead strong hands held him tightly and he struggled in
vain. One lone light shone high: Chang's, no doubt.

Vomact thrust his face into the light again: "Having the
approval of our worthy Scanners and present company for
the general proposal, I now move that this Committee
declare itself to have the full authority of a Meeting, and
that this Committee further make me responsible for all
misdeeds which this Committee may enact, to be held
answerable before the next full Meeting, but not before
any other authority beyond the closed and secret ranks of
Scanners."

Flamboyantly this time, his triumph evident, Vomact
assumed the *vote* stance.

Only a few lights shone: far less, patently, than a
minority of one-fourth.

Vomact spoke again. The light shone on his high calm
forehead, on his dead relaxed cheekbones. His lean
cheeks and chin were half-shadowed, save where the
lower light picked up and spotlighted his mouth, cruel
even in repose. (Vomact was said to be a descendant of
some Ancient Lady who had traversed, in an illegitimate
and inexplicable fashion, some hundreds of years of time
in a single night. Her name, the Lady Vomact, had passed
into legend; but her blood and her archaic lust for mastery
lived on in the mute masterful body of her descendant.
Martel could believe the old tales as he stared at the
rostrum, wondering what untraceable mutation had left

the Vomact kith as predators among mankind.) Calling loudly with the movement of his lips, but still without sound, Vomact appealed:

"The Honorable Committee is now pleased to reaffirm the sentence of death issued against the heretic and enemy, Adam Stone." Again the *vote* stance.

Again Chang's light shone lonely in its isolated protest.

Vomact then made his final move:

"I call for the designation of the Senior Scanner present as the manager of the sentence. I call for authorization to him to appoint executioners, one or many, who shall make evident the will and majesty of Scanners. I ask that I be accountable for the deed, and not for the means. The deed is a noble deed, for the protection of Mankind and for the honor of the Scanners; but of the means it must be said that they are to be the best at hand, and no more. Who knows the true way to kill an Other, here on a crowded and watchful Earth? This is no mere matter of discharging a cylindered sleeper, no mere question of upgrading the needle of a haberman. When people die down here, it is not like the Up-and-Out. They die reluctantly. Killing within the Earth is not our usual business, O Brothers and Scanners, as you know well. You must choose me to choose my agent as I see fit. Otherwise the common knowledge will become the common betrayal whereas if I alone know the responsibility, I alone could betray us, and you will not have far to look in case the Instrumentality comes searching." (*What about the killer you choose?* thought Martel. *He too will know unless—unless* you *silence him forever.*)

Vomact went into the stance: *The Honorable Scanners are pleased to vote.*

One light of protest shone; Chang's, again.

Martel imagined that he could see a cruel joyful smile on Vomact's dead face—the smile of a man who knew himself righteous and who found his righteousness upheld and affirmed by militant authority.

Martel tried one last time to come free.

The dead hands held. They were locked like vises until their owners' eyes unlocked them: how else could they hold the piloting month by month?

Martel then shouted: "Honorable Scanners, this is judicial murder."

No ear heard him. He was cranched, and alone.

Nonetheless, he shouted again: "You endanger the Confraternity."

Nothing happened.

The echo of his voice sounded from one end of the room to the other. No head turned. No eyes met his.

Martel realized that as they paired for talk, the eyes of the Scanners avoided him. He saw that no one desired to watch his speech. He knew that behind the cold faces of his friends there lay compassion or amusement. He knew that they knew him to be cranched—absurd, normal, man-like, temporarily no Scanner. But he knew that in this matter the wisdom of Scanners was nothing. He knew that only a cranched Scanner could feel with his very blood the outrage and anger which deliberate murder would provoke among the Others. He knew that the Confraternity endangered itself, and knew that the most ancient prerogative of law was the monopoly of death. Even the Ancient Nations, in the times of the Wars, before the Wild Machines, before the Beasts, before men went into the Up-and-Out—even the Ancients had known this. How did they say it? *Only the State shall kill.* The States were gone but the Instrumentality remained, and the Instrumentality could not pardon things which occurred within the Earths but beyond its authority. Death in Space was the business, the right of the Scanners: how could the Instrumentality enforce its law in a place where all men who wakened, wakened only to die in the Great Pain? Wisely did the Instrumentality leave Space to the Scanners, wisely had the Confraternity not meddled inside the Earths. And now the Confraternity itself was going to step forth as an outlaw band, as a gang of rogues as stupid and reckless as the tribes of the Unforgiven!

Martel knew this because he was cranched. Had he been haberman, he would have thought only with his mind, not with his heart and guts and blood. How could the other Scanners know?

Vomact returned for the last time to the Rostrum: *The Committee has met and its will shall be done.* Verbally he added: "Senior among you, I ask your loyalty and your silence."

At that point, the two Scanners let his arms go. Martel rubbed his numb hands, shaking his fingers to get the circulation back into the cold fingertips. With real freedom, he began to think of what he might still do. He scanned himself: the cranching held. He might have an hour, he might have a day. Well, he could go on even if haberman, but it would be inconvenient, having to talk with Finger and Tablet. He looked about for Chang. He saw his friend standing patient and immobile in a quiet corner. Martel moved slowly, so as not to attract any more attention to himself than could be helped. He faced Chang, moved until his face was in the light, and then articulated:

"What are we going to do? You're not going to let them kill Adam Stone, are you? Don't you realize what Stone's work will mean to us, if it succeeds? No more scanning. No more Scanners. No more habermans. No more Pain in the Up-and-Out. I tell you, if the others were all cranched, as I am, they would see it in a human way, not with the narrow crazy logic which they used in the meeting. We've got to stop them. How can we do it? What are we going to do? What does Parizianski think? Who has been chosen?"

"Which question do you want me to answer?"

Martel laughed. (It felt good to laugh, even then; it felt like being a man.) "Will you help me?"

Chang's eyes flashed across Martel's face as Chang answered: "No. No. No."

"You won't help?"

"No."

"Why not, Chang? Why not?"

"I am a Scanner. The vote has been taken. You would do the same if you were not in this unusual condition."

"I'm not in an unusual condition. I'm cranched. That merely means that I see things the way that the Others would. I see the stupidity. The recklessness. The selfishness. It is murder."

"What is murder? Have you not killed? You are not one of the Others. You are a Scanner. You will be sorry for what you are about to do, if you do not watch out."

"But why did you vote against Vomact then? Didn't

you too see what Adam Stone means to all of us? Scanners will live in vain. Thank God for that! Can't you see it?"

"No."

"But you talk to me, Chang. You are my friend?"

"I talk to you. I am your friend. Why not?"

"But what are you going to do?"

"Nothing, Martel. Nothing."

"Will you help me?"

"No."

"Not even to save Stone?"

"Then I will go to Parizianski for help."

"It will do no good."

"Why not? He's more human than you, right now."

"He will not help you, because he has the job. Vomact designated him to kill Adam Stone."

Martel stopped speaking in mid-movement. He suddenly took the stance: *I thank you, Brother, and I depart.*

At the window he turned and faced the room. He saw that Vomact's eyes were upon him. He gave the stance, *I thank you, Brother, and I depart,* and added the flourish of respect which is shown when Seniors are present. Vomact caught the sign, and Martel could see the cruel lips move. He thought he saw the words ". . . take good care of yourself . . ." but did not wait to inquire. He stepped backward and dropped out the window.

Once below the window and out of sight, he adjusted his aircoat to maximum speed. He swam lazily in the air, scanning himself thoroughly, and adjusting his adrenal intake down. He then made the movement of release, and felt the cold air rush past his face like running water.

Adam Stone had to be at Chief Downport.

Adam Stone had to be there.

Wouldn't Adam Stone be surprised in the night? Surprised to meet the strangest of beings, the first renegade among Scanners. (Martel suddenly appreciated that it was himself of whom he was thinking. Martel the Traitor to Scanners! That sounded strange and bad. But what of Martel, the Loyal to Mankind? Was that not compensation? And if he won, he won Luĉi. If he lost, he lost nothing—an unconsidered and expendable haberman. It happened to be himself. But in contrast to the immense reward, to Mankind, to the Confraternity, to Luĉi, what did that matter?)

Martel thought to himself: "Adam Stone will have two visitors tonight. Two Scanners, who are the friends of one another." He hoped that Parizianski was still his friend.

"And the world," he added, "depends on which of us gets there first."

Multifaceted in their brightness, the lights of Chief Downport began to shine through the mist ahead. Martel could see the outer towers of the city and glimpsed the phosphorescent periphery which kept back the Wild, whether Beasts, Machines, or the Unforgiven.

Once more Martel invoked the lords of his chance: "Help me to pass for an Other!"

∞ V ∞

Within the Downport, Martel had less trouble than he thought. He draped his aircoat over his shoulder so that it concealed the instruments. He took up his scanning mirror, and made up his face from the inside, by adding tone and animation to his blood and nerves until the muscles of his face glowed and the skin gave out a healthy sweat. That way he looked like an ordinary man who had just completed a long night flight.

After straightening out his clothing, and hiding his Tablet within his jacket, he faced the problem of what to do about the Talking Finger. If he kept the nail, it would show him to be a Scanner. He would be respected, but he would be identified. He might be stopped by the guards whom the Instrumentality had undoubtedly set around the person of Adam Stone. If he broke the nail—but he couldn't! No Scanner in the history of the Confraternity had ever willingly broken his nail. That would be Resignation, and there was no such thing. The only way *out*, was in the Up-and-Out! Martel put his finger to his mouth and bit off the nail. He looked at the now-queer finger, and sighed to himself.

He stepped toward the city gate, slipping his hand into his jacket and running up his muscular strength to four times normal. He started to scan, and then realized that his instruments were masked. *Might as well take all the chances at once,* he thought.

The watcher stopped him with a searching Wire. The sphere thumped suddenly against Martel's chest.

"Are you a Man?" said the unseen voice. (Martel knew that as a Scanner in haberman condition, his own field-charge would have illuminated the sphere.)

"I am a Man." Martel knew that the timbre of his voice had been good; he hoped that it would not be taken for that of a Manshonjagger or a Beast or an Unforgiven one, who with mimicry sought to enter the cities and ports of Mankind.

"Name, number, rank, purpose, function, time departed."

"Martel." He had to remember his old number, not Scanner 34. "Sunward 4234, 182nd Year of Space. Rank, rising Subchief." That was no lie, but his substantive rank. "Purpose, personal and lawful within the limits of this city. No function of the Instrumentality. Departed Chief Outport 2019 hours." Everything now depended on whether he was believed, or would be checked against Chief Outport.

The voice was flat and routine: "Time desired within the city."

Martel used the standard phrase: "Your Honorable sufferance is requested."

He stood in the cool night air, waiting. Far above him, through a gap in the mist, he could see the poisonous glittering in the sky of Scanners. *The stars are my enemies,* he thought: *I have mastered the stars but they hate me. Ho, that sounds Ancient! Like a Book. Too much cranching.*

The voice returned: "Sunward 4234 dash 182 rising Subchief Martel, enter the lawful gates of the city. Welcome. Do you desire food, raiment, money, or companionship?" The voice had no hospitality in it, just business. This was certainly different from entering a city in a Scanner's role! Then the petty officers came out, and threw their beltlights on their fretful faces, and mouthed their words with preposterous deference, shouting against the stone deafness of a Scanner's ears. So that was the way that a Subchief was treated: matter of fact, but not bad. Not bad.

Martel replied: "I have that which I need, but beg of the city a favor. My friend Adam Stone is here. I desire to see him, on urgent and personal lawful affairs."

The voice replied: "Did you have an appointment with Adam Stone?"

"No."

"The city will find him. What is his number?"

"I have forgotten it."

"You have forgotten it? Is not Adam Stone a Magnate of the Instrumentality? Are you truly his friend?"

"Truly." Martel let a little annoyance creep into his voice. "Watcher, doubt me and call your Subchief."

"No doubt implied. Why do you not know the number? This must go into the record," added the voice.

"We were friends in childhood. He has crossed the—" Martel started to say "the Up-and-Out" and remembered that the phrase was current only among Scanners. "He has leapt from Earth to Earth, and has just now returned. I knew him well and I seek him out. I have word of his kith. May the Instrumentality protect us!"

"Heard and believed. Adam Stone will be searched."

At a risk, though a slight one, of having the sphere sound an alarm for *non-Man*, Martel cut in on his Scanner speaker within his jacket. He saw the trembling needle of light await his words and he started to write on it with his blunt finger. *That won't work*, he thought, and had a moment's panic until he found his comb, which had a sharp enough tooth to write. He wrote: "Emergency none. Martel Scanner calling Parizianski Scanner."

The needle quivered and the reply glowed and faded out: "Parizianski Scanner on duty and D.C. Calls taken by Scanner Relay."

Martel cut off his speaker.

Parizianski was somewhere around. Could he have crossed the direct way, right over the city wall, setting off the alert, and invoking official business when the petty officers overtook him in mid-air? Scarcely. That meant that a number of other Scanners must have come in with Parizianski, all of them pretending to be in search of a few of the tenuous pleasures which could be enjoyed by a haberman, such as the sight of the newspictures or the viewing of beautiful women in the Pleasure Gallery. Parizianski was around, but he could not have moved privately, because Scanner Central registered him on duty and recorded his movements city by city.

The voice returned. Puzzlement was expressed in it. "Adam Stone is found and awakened. He has asked pardon of the Honorable, and says he knows no Martel. Will you see Adam Stone in the morning? The city will bid you welcome."

Martel ran out of resources. It was hard enough mimicking a man without having to tell lies in the guise of one. Martel could only repeat: "Tell him I am Martel. The husband of Luĉi."

"It will be done."

Again the silence, and the hostile stars, and the sense that Parizianski was somewhere near and getting nearer; Martel felt his heart beating faster. He stole a glimpse at his chestbox and set his heart down a point. He felt calmer, even though he had not been able to scan with care.

The voice this time was cheerful, as though an

annoyance had been settled: "Adam Stone consents to see you. Enter Chief Downport, and welcome."

The little sphere dropped noiselessly to the ground and the wire whispered away into the darkness. A bright arc of narrow light rose from the ground in front of Martel and swept through the city to one of the higher towers— apparently a hostel, which Martel had never entered. Martel plucked his aircoat to his chest for ballast, stepped heel-and-toe on the beam, and felt himself whistle through the air to an entrance window which sprang up before him as suddenly as a devouring mouth.

A tower guard stood in the doorway. "You are awaited, sir. Do you bear weapons, sir?"

"None," said Martel, grateful that he was relying on his own strength.

The guard led him past the check-screen. Martel noticed the quick flight of a warning across the screen as his instruments registered and identified him as a Scanner. But the guard had not noticed it.

The guard stopped at a door. "Adam Stone is armed. He is lawfully armed by authority of the Instrumentality and by the liberty of this city. All those who enter are given warning."

Martel nodded in understanding at the man, and went in.

Adam Stone was a short man, stout and benign. His gray hair rose stiffly from a low forehead. His whole face was red and merry-looking. He looked like a jolly guide from the Pleasure Gallery, not like a man who had been at the edge of the Up-and-Out, fighting the Great Pain without haberman protection.

He stared at Martel. His look was puzzled, perhaps a little annoyed, but not hostile.

Martel came to the point. "You do not know me. I lied. My name is Martel, and I mean you no harm. But I lied. I beg the Honorable gift of your hospitality. Remain armed. Direct your weapon against me—"

Stone smiled: "I am doing so," and Martel noticed the small Wirepoint in Stone's capable, plump hand.

"Good. Keep on guard against me. It will give you confidence in what I shall say. But do, I beg you, give us a screen of privacy. I want no casual lookers. This is a matter of life and death."

"First: whose life and death?" Stone's face remained calm, his voice even.

"Yours and mine, and the worlds'."

"You are cryptic but I agree." Stone called through the doorway: "Privacy, please." There was a sudden hum, and all the little noises of the night quickly vanished from the air of the room.

Said Adam Stone: "Sir, who are you? What brings you here?"

"I am Scanner Thirty-four."

"You a Scanner? I don't believe it."

For answer, Martel pulled his jacket open, showing his chestbox. Stone looked up at him, amazed. Martel explained:

"I am cranched. Have you never seen it before?"

"*Not with men.* On animals. Amazing! But—what do you want?"

"The truth. Do you fear me?"

"Not with this," said Stone, grasping the Wirepoint. "But I shall tell you the truth."

"Is it true that you have conquered the Great Pain?"

Stone hesitated, seeking words for an answer.

"Quick, can you tell me how you have done it, so that I may believe you?"

"I have loaded ships with life."

"Life?"

"Life. I don't know what the Great Pain is, but I did find that in the experiments, when I sent out masses of animals or plants, the life in the center of the mass lived longest. I built ships—small ones, of course—and sent them out with rabbits, with monkeys—"

"Those are Beasts?"

"Yes. With small Beasts. And the Beasts came back unhurt. They came back because the walls of the ships were filled with life. I tried many kinds, and finally found a sort of life which lives in the waters. Oysters. Oysterbeds. The outermost oysters died in the great pain. The inner ones lived. The passengers were unhurt."

"But they were Beasts?"

"Not only Beasts. Myself."

"You!"

"I came through Space alone. Through what you call the Up-and-Out, alone. Awake and sleeping. I am unhurt. If you do not believe me, ask your brother Scanners. Come and see my ship in the morning. I will be glad to see you then, along with your brother Scanners. I am going to demonstrate before the Chiefs of the Instrumentality."

Martel repeated his question: "You came here alone?"

Adam Stone grew testy: "Yes, alone. Go back and check your Scanners' register if you do not believe me. You never put me in a bottle to cross Space."

Martel's face was radiant. "I believe you now. It is true. No more Scanners. No more habermans. No more cranching."

Stone looked significantly toward the door.

Martel did not take the hint. "I must tell you that—"

"Sir, tell me in the morning. Go enjoy your cranch. Isn't it supposed to be pleasure? Medically I know it well. But not in practice."

"It is pleasure. It's normality—for a while. But listen. The Scanners have sworn to destroy you, and your work."

"What!"

"They have met and have voted and sworn. You will make Scanners unnecessary, they say. You will bring the Ancient Wars back to the world, if Scanning is lost and the Scanners live in vain!"

Adam Stone was nervous but kept his wits about him: "You're a Scanner. Are you going to kill me—or try?"

"No, you fool. I have betrayed the Confraternity. Call guards the moment I escape. Keep guards around you. I will try to intercept the killer."

Martel saw a blur in the window. Before Stone could turn, the Wirepoint was whipped out of his hand. The blur solidified and took form as Parizianski.

Martel recognized what Parizianski was doing: *High speed.*

Without thinking of his cranch, he thrust his hand to his chest, set himself up to *High speed* too. Waves of fire, like the Great Pain, but hotter, flooded over him. He fought to keep his face readable as he stepped in front of Parizianski and gave the sign,

Top Emergency.

Parizianski spoke, while the normally moving body of Stone stepped away from them as slowly as a drifting cloud: "Get out of my way. I am on a mission."

"I know it. I stop you here and now. Stop. Stop. Stop. Stone is right."

Parizianski's lips were barely readable in the haze of pain which flooded Martel. (He thought: *God, God, God of the Ancients! Let me hold on! Let me live under* Overload *just long enough!*) Parizianski was saying: "Get out of my way. By order of the Confraternity, get out of my way!" And Parizianski gave the sign, *Help I demand in the name of my Duty!*

Martel choked for breath in the syrup-like air. He tried one last time: "Parizianski, friend, friend, my friend. Stop. Stop." (No Scanner had ever murdered Scanner before.)

Parizianski made the sign: *You are unfit for duty, and I will take over.*

Martel thought, *For the first time in the world!* as he reached over and twisted Parizianski's Brainbox up to *Overload.* Parizianski's eyes glittered in terror and understanding. His body began to drift down toward the floor.

Martel had just strength enough to reach his own Chestbox. As he faded into Haberman or death, he knew not which, he felt his fingers turning on the control of speed, turning down. He tried to speak, to say, "Get a Scanner, I need help, get a Scanner . . ."

But the darkness rose about him, and the numb silence clasped him.

Martel awakened to see the face of Luĉi near his own.

He opened his eyes wider, and found that he was hearing—hearing the sound of her happy weeping, the sound of her chest as she caught the air back into her throat.

He spoke weakly: "Still cranched? Alive?"

Another face swam into the blur beside Luĉi's. It was Adam Stone. His deep voice rang across immensities of Space before coming to Martel's hearing. Martel tried to read Stone's lips, but could not make them out. He went back to listening to the voice:

". . . not cranched. Do you understand me? Not cranched!"

Martel tried to say: "But I can hear! I can feel!" The others got his sense if not his words.

Adam Stone spoke again:

"You have gone back through the Haberman. I put you back first. I didn't know how it would work in practice, but I had the theory all worked out. You don't think the Instrumentality would waste the Scanners, do you? You go back to normality. We are letting the habermans die as fast as the ships come in. They don't need to live any more. But we are restoring the Scanners. You are the first. Do you understand me? You are the first. Take it easy, now."

Adam Stone smiled. Dimly behind Stone, Martel thought that he saw the face of one of the Chiefs of the Instrumentality. That face, too, smiled at him, and then both faces disappeared upward and away.

Martel tried to lift his head, to scan himself. He could not. Luĉi stared at him, calming herself, but with an expression of loving perplexity. She said,

"My darling husband! You're back again, to stay!"

Still, Martel tried to see his box. Finally he swept his hand across his chest with a clumsy motion. There was nothing there. The instruments were gone. He was back to normality but still alive.

In the deep weak peacefulness of his mind, another troubling thought took shape. He tried to write with his finger, the way that Luĉi wanted him to, but he had neither pointed fingernail nor Scanner's Tablet. He had to use his voice. He summoned up his strength and whispered:

"Scanners?"

"Yes, darling? What is it?"

"Scanners?"

"Scanners. Oh, yes, darling, they're all right. They had to arrest some of them for going into *High speed* and running away. But the Instrumentality caught them all— all those on the ground—and they're happy now. Do you know, darling," she laughed, "some of them didn't want to be restored to normality. But Stone and the Chiefs persuaded them."

"Vomact?"

"He's fine, too. He's staying cranched until he can be restored. Do you know, he has arranged for Scanners to take new jobs. You're all Deputy Chiefs for Space. Isn't that nice? But he got himself made Chief for Space. You're all going to be pilots, so that your fraternity and guild can go on. And Chang's getting changed back right now. You'll see him soon."

Her face turned sad. She looked at him earnestly and said: "I might as well tell you now. You'll worry otherwise.

There has been one accident. Only one. When you and your friend called on Adam Stone, your friend was so happy that he forgot to scan, and he let himself die of *Overload*."

"Called on Stone?"

"Yes. Don't you remember? Your friend."

He still looked surprised, so she said:

"Parizianski."

The Lady Who Sailed *The Soul*

∿ I ∿

The story ran—how did the story run? Everyone knew the reference to Helen America and Mr. Grey-no-more, but no one knew exactly how it happened. Their names were welded to the glittering timeless jewelry of romance. Sometimes they were compared to Heloise and Abelard, whose story had been found among books in a long-buried library. Other ages were to compare their life with the weird, ugly-lovely story of the Go-Captain Taliano and the Lady Dolores Oh.

Out of it all, two things stood forth—their love and the image of the great sails, tissue-metal wings with which the bodies of people finally fluttered out among the stars.

Mention him, and others knew her. Mention her, and they knew him. He was the first of the inbound sailors, and she was the lady who sailed *The Soul*.

It was lucky that people lost their pictures. The romantic hero was a very young-looking man, prematurely old and still quite sick when the romance came. And

Helen America, she was a freak, but a nice one: a grim, solemn, sad, little brunette who had been born amid the laughter of humanity. She was not the tall, confident heroine of the actresses who later played her.

She was, however, a wonderful sailor. That much was true. And with her body and mind she loved Mr. Grey-no-more, showing a devotion which the ages can neither surpass nor forget. History may scrape off the patina of their names and appearances, but even history can do no more than brighten the love of Helen America and Mr. Grey-no-more.

Both of them, one must remember, were sailors.

∽ II ∽

The child was playing with a spieltier. She got tired of letting it be a chicken, so she reversed it into the fur-bearing position. When she extended the ears to the optimum development, the little animal looked odd indeed. A light breeze blew the animal-toy on its side, but the spieltier good-naturedly righted itself and munched contentedly on the carpet.

The little girl suddenly clapped her hands and broke forth with the question,

"Mamma, what's a sailor?"

"There used to be sailors, darling, a long time ago. They were brave men who took the ships out to the stars, the very first ships that took people away from our sun. And they had big sails. I don't know how it worked, but somehow, the light pushed them, and it took them a quarter

of a life to make a single one-way trip. People only lived a hundred and sixty years at that time, darling, and it was forty years each way, but we don't need sailors any more."

"Of course not," said the child, "we can go right away. You've taken me to Mars and you've taken me to New Earth as well, haven't you, mamma? And we can go anywhere else soon, but that only takes one afternoon."

"That's planoforming, honey. But it was a long time before the people knew how to planoform. And they could not travel the way we could, so they made great big sails. They made sails so big that they could not build them on Earth. They had to hang them out, halfway between Earth and Mars. And you know, a funny thing happened . . . Did you ever hear about the time the world froze?"

"No, mamma, what was that?"

"Well, a long time ago, one of these sails drifted and people tried to save it because it took a lot of work to build it. But the sail was so large that it got between the Earth and the sun. And there was no more sunshine, just night all the time. And it got very cold on Earth. All the atomic power plants were busy, and all the air began to smell funny. And the people were worried and in a few days they pulled the sail back out of the way. And the sunshine came again."

"Mamma, were there ever any girl sailors?"

A curious expression crossed over the mother's face. "There was one. You'll hear about her later on when you are older. Her name was Helen America and she sailed The Soul out to the stars. She was the only woman that ever did it. And that is a wonderful story."

The mother dabbed at her eyes with a handkerchief.

The child said: "Mamma, tell me now. What's the story all about?"

At this point the mother became very firm and she said: "Honey, there are some things that you are not old enough to hear yet. But when you are a big girl, I'll tell you all about them."

The mother was an honest woman. She reflected a moment, and then she added, ". . . unless you read about it yourself first."

∽ III ∽

Helen America was to make her place in the history of mankind, but she started badly. The name itself was a misfortune.

No one ever knew who her father was. The officials agreed to keep the matter quiet.

Her mother was not in doubt. Her mother was the celebrated she-man Mona Muggeridge, a woman who had campaigned a hundred times for the lost cause of complete identity of the two genders. She had been a feminist beyond all limits, and when Mona Muggeridge, the one and only *Miss* Muggeridge, announced to the press that she was going to have a baby, that was first-class news.

Mona Muggeridge went further. She announced her firm conviction that fathers should not be identified. She proclaimed that no woman should have consecutive children with the same man, that women should be advised to pick different fathers for their children, so as to diversify and beautify the race. She capped it all by announcing that she, Miss Muggeridge, had selected the perfect father and would inevitably produce the only perfect child.

Miss Muggeridge, a bony, pompous blonde, stated that she would avoid the nonsense of marriage and family names, and that therefore the child, if a boy, would be named John America, and if a girl, Helen America.

Thus it happened that little Helen America was born with the correspondents in the press services waiting outside the delivery room. News-screens flashed the picture of a pretty three-kilogram baby. "It's a girl." "The perfect child." "Who's the dad?"

That was just the beginning. Mona Muggeridge was belligerent. She insisted, even after the baby had been photographed for the thousandth time, that this was the finest child ever born. She pointed to the child's perfections. She demonstrated all the foolish fondness of a doting mother, but felt that she, the great crusader, had discovered this fondness for the first time.

To say that this background was difficult for the child would be an understatement.

Helen America was a wonderful example of raw human material triumphing over its tormentors. By the time she was four years old, she spoke six languages, and was beginning to decipher some of the old Martian texts. At the age of five she was sent to school. Her fellow schoolchildren immediately developed a rhyme:

> *Helen, Helen*
> *Fat and dumb*

Doesn't know where
Her daddy's from!

Helen took all this and perhaps it was an accident of
genetics that she grew to become a compact little
person—deadly serious little brunette. Challenged by
lessons, haunted by publicity, she became careful and
reserved about friendships and desperately lonely in an
inner world.

When Helen America was sixteen her mother came to
a bad end. Mona Muggeridge eloped with a man she
announced to be the perfect husband for the perfect
marriage hitherto overlooked by mankind. The perfect
husband was a skilled machine polisher. He already had a
wife and four children. He drank beer and his interest in
Miss Muggeridge seems to have been a mixture of good-
natured comradeship and a sensible awareness of her
motherly bankroll. The planetary yacht on which they
eloped broke the regulations with an off-schedule flight.
The bridegroom's wife and children had alerted the
police. The result was a collision with a robotic barge
which left both bodies identifiable.

At sixteen Helen was already famous, and at seventeen
already forgotten, and very much alone.

∽ IV ∽

This was the age of sailors. The thousands of photo-
reconnaissance and measuring missiles had begun to
come back with their harvest from the stars. Planet after

planet swam into the ken of mankind. The new worlds became known as the interstellar search missiles brought back photographs, samples of atmosphere, measurements of gravity, cloud coverage, chemical make-up, and the like. Of the very numerous missiles which returned from their two- or three-hundred-year voyages, three brought back reports of New Earth, an earth so much like Terra itself that it could be settled.

The first sailors had gone out almost a hundred years before. They had started with small sails not over two thousand miles square. Gradually the size of the sails increased. The technique of adiabatic packing and the carrying of passengers in individual pods reduced the damage done to the human cargo. It was great news when a sailor returned to Earth, a man born and reared under the light of another star. He was a man who had spent a month of agony and pain, bringing a few sleep-frozen settlers, guiding the immense light-pushed sailing craft which had managed the trip through the great interstellar deeps in an objective time-period of forty years.

Mankind got to know the look of a sailor. There was a plantigrade walk to the way he put his body on the ground. There was a sharp, stiff, mechanical swing to his neck. The man was neither young nor old. He had been awake and conscious for forty years, thanks to the drug which made possible a kind of limited awareness. By the time the psychologists interrogated him, first for the proper authorities of the Instrumentality and later for the news releases, it was plain enough that he thought the forty years were about a month. He never volunteered to sail back, because he had actually aged forty years. He was a young man, young in his hopes and wishes, but a man who had burnt up a quarter of a human lifetime in a single agonizing experience.

At this time Helen America went to Cambridge. Lady Joan's College was the finest woman's college in the Atlantic world. Cambridge had reconstructed its protohistoric traditions and the neo-British had recaptured that fine edge of engineering which reconnected their traditions with the earliest antiquity.

Naturally enough the language was cosmopolite Earth and not archaic English, but the students were proud to live at a reconstructed university very much like the archaeological evidence showed it to have been before the period of darkness and troubles came upon the Earth. Helen shone a little in this renaissance.

The news-release services watched Helen in the crudest possible fashion. They revived her name and the story of her mother. Then they forgot her again. She had put in for six professions, and her last choice was "sailor." It happened that she was the first woman to make the application—first because she was the only woman young enough to qualify who had also passed the scientific requirements.

Her picture was beside his on the screens before they ever met each other.

Actually, she was not anything like that at all. She had suffered so much in her childhood from *Helen, Helen, fat and dumb,* that she was competitive only on a coldly professional basis. She hated and loved and missed the tremendous mother whom she had lost, and she resolved so fiercely not to be like her mother that she became an embodied antithesis of Mona.

The mother had been horsy, blonde, big—the kind of woman who is a feminist because she is not very feminine. Helen never thought about her own femininity. She just worried about herself. Her face would have been round if it had been plump, but she was not plump. Black-haired, dark-eyed, broad-bodied but thin, she was a genetic demonstration of her unknown father. Her teachers often feared her. She was a pale, quiet girl, and she always knew her subject.

Her fellow students had joked about her for a few weeks and then most of them had banded together against the indecency of the press. When a news-frame came out with something ridiculous about the long-dead Mona, the whisper went through Lady Joan's:

"Keep Helen away . . . those people are at it again."

"Don't let Helen look at the frames now. She's the best person we have in the non-collateral sciences and we can't have her upset just before the tripos . . ."

They protected her, and it was only by chance that she saw her own face in a news-frame. There was the face of a man beside her. He looked like a little old monkey, she thought. Then she read, "PERFECT GIRL WANTS TO BE SAILOR. SHOULD SAILOR HIMSELF DATE PERFECT GIRL?" Her cheeks burned with helpless, unavoidable embarrassment and rage, but she had grown too expert at being herself to do what she might have done in her teens—hate the man. She knew it wasn't his fault either. It wasn't even the fault of the silly pushing men and women from the news services. It was time, it was custom, it was man himself. But she had only to be herself, if she could ever find out what that really meant.

∽ **V** ∽

Their dates, when they came, had the properties of nightmares.

A news service sent a woman to tell her she had been awarded a week's holiday in New Madrid.

With the sailor from the stars.

Helen refused.

Then *he* refused too, and he was a little too prompt for her liking. She became curious about him.

Two weeks passed, and in the office of the news service a treasurer brought two slips of paper to the director. They were the vouchers for Helen America and Mr. Grey-no-more to obtain the utmost in preferential luxury at New Madrid. The treasurer said, "These have been issued and registered as gifts with the Instrumentality, sir. Should they be cancelled?" The executive had his fill of stories that day, and he felt humane. On an impulse he commanded the treasurer, "Tell you what. Give those tickets to the young people. No publicity. We'll keep out of it. If they don't want us, they don't have to have us. Push it along. That's all. Go."

The tickets went back out to Helen. She had made the highest record ever reported at the university, and she needed a rest. When the newsservice woman gave her the ticket, she said,

"Is this a trick?"

Assured that it was not, she then asked,

"Is that man coming?"

She couldn't say "*the* sailor"—it sounded too much

like the way people had always talked about herself—and she honestly didn't remember his other name at the moment.

The woman did not know.

"Do I have to see him?" said Helen.

"Of course not," said the woman. The gift was unconditional.

Helen laughed, almost grimly. "All right, I'll take it and say thanks. But one picturemaker, mind you, just one, and I walk out. Or I may walk out for no reason at all. Is that all right?"

It was.

Four days later Helen was in the pleasure world of New Madrid, and a master of the dances was presenting her to an odd, intense old man whose hair was black.

"Junior scientist Helen America—Sailor of the stars Mr. Grey-no-more. "

He looked at them shrewdly and smiled a kindly, experienced smile. He added the empty phrase of his profession, "I have had the honor and I withdraw."

They were alone together on the edge of the dining room. The sailor looked at her very sharply indeed, and then said:

"Who are you? Are you somebody I have already met? Should I remember you? There are too many people here on Earth. What do we do next? What are we supposed to do? Would you like to sit down?"

Helen said one "Yes" to all those questions and never dreamed that the single *yes* would be articulated by hundreds of great actresses, each one in the actress's own special way, across the centuries to come.

They did sit down.

How the rest of it happened, neither one was ever quite sure.

She had had to quiet him almost as though he were a hurt person in the House of Recovery. She explained the dishes to him and when he still could not choose, she gave the robot selections for him. She warned him, kindly enough, about manners when he forgot the simple ceremonies of eating which everyone knew, such as standing up to unfold the napkin or putting the scraps into the solvent tray and the silverware into the transfer.

At last he relaxed and did not look so old.

Momentarily forgetting the thousand times she had been asked silly questions herself, she asked him,

"Why did *you* become a sailor?"

He stared at her in open-eyed inquiry as though she had spoken to him in an unknown language and expected a reply. Finally he mumbled the answer, "Are you—you, too—saying that—that I shouldn't have done it?"

Her hand went to her mouth in instinctive apology.

"No, no, no. You see, I myself have put in to be a sailor."

He merely looked at her, his young-old eyes open with observativeness. He did not stare, but merely seemed to be trying to understand words, each one of which he could comprehend individually but which in sum amounted to sheer madness. She did not turn away from his look, odd though it was. Once again, she had the chance to note the indescribable peculiarity of this man who had managed enormous sails out in the blind empty black between untwinkling stars. He was young as a boy. The hair which gave him his name was glossy black. His beard must have been removed permanently, because his skin was that of a middle-aged woman—well-kept, pleasant, but showing the unmistakable wrinkles of age and betraying no sign of the normal stubble which the males in her culture preferred to leave on their faces. The skin had age without experience. The muscles had grown older, but they did not show *how* the person had grown.

Helen had learned to be an acute observer of people as her mother took up with one fanatic after another; she knew full well that people carry their secret biographies written in the muscles of their faces, and that a stranger passing on the street tells us (whether he wishes to or not) all his inmost intimacies. If we but look sharply enough, and in the right light, we know whether fear or hope or amusement has tallied the hours of his days, we divine the sources and outcome of his most secret sensuous pleasures, we catch the dim but persistent reflections of those other people who have left the imprints of their personalities on him in turn.

All this was absent from Mr. Grey-no-more: he had age but not the stigmata of age; he had growth without the normal markings of growth; he had lived without living, in a time and world in which most people stayed young while living too much.

He was the uttermost opposite of her mother that Helen had ever seen, and with a pang of undirected apprehension Helen realized that this man meant a great deal to her future life, whether she wished him to or not. She saw in him a young bachelor, prematurely old, a man whose love had been given to emptiness and horror, not to the tangible rewards and disappointments of human life. He had had all space for his mistress, and space had used him harshly. Still young, he was old; already old, he was young.

The mixture was one which she knew that she had never seen before, and which she suspected that no one else had ever seen, either. He had in the beginning of life the sorrow, compassion, and wisdom which most people find only at the end.

It was he who broke the silence. "You did say, didn't you, that you yourself had put in to be a sailor?"

Even to herself, her answer sounded silly and girlish. "I'm the first woman ever to qualify with the necessary scientific subjects while still young enough to pass the physical . . ."

"You must be an unusual girl," said he mildly. Helen realized, with a thrill, a sweet and bitterly real hope that this young-old man from the stars had never heard of the "perfect child" who had been laughed at in the moments of being born, the girl who had all America for a father, who was famous and unusual and alone so terribly much that she could not even imagine being ordinary, happy, decent, or simple.

She thought to herself, *It would take a wise freak who sails in from the stars to overlook who I am,* but to him she simply said, "It's no use talking about being 'unusual.' I'm tired of this Earth, and since I don't have to die to leave it, I think I would like to sail to the stars. I've got less to lose than you may think . . ." She started to tell him about Mona Muggeridge but she stopped in time.

The compassionate gray eyes were upon her, and at

this point it was he, not she, who was in control of the situation. She looked at the eyes themselves. They had stayed open for forty years, in the blackness near to pitch-darkness of the tiny cabin. The dim dials had shone like blazing suns upon his tired retinas before he was able to turn his eyes away. From time to time he had looked out at the black nothing to see the silhouettes of his sails, almost-blackness against total blackness, as the miles of their sweep sucked up the push of light itself and accelerated him and his frozen cargo at almost immeasurable speeds across an ocean of unfathomable silence. Yet, what he had done, she had asked to do.

The stare of his gray eyes yielded to a smile of his lips. In the young-old face, masculine in structure and feminine in texture, the smile had a connotation of tremendous kindness. She felt singularly much like weeping when she saw him smile in that particular way at her. Was that what people learned between the stars? To care for other people very much indeed and to spring upon them only to reveal love and not devouring to their prey?

In a measured voice he said, "I believe you. You're the first one that I have believed. All these people have said that they wanted to be sailors too, even when they looked at me. They could not know what it means, but they said it anyhow, and I hated them for saying it. You, though— you're different. Perhaps you will sail among the stars, but I hope that you will not."

As though waking from a dream, he looked around the luxurious room, with the gilt-and-enamel robot-waiters standing aside with negligent elegance. They were designed to be always present and never obtrusive: this was a difficult esthetic effect to achieve, but their designer had achieved it.

The rest of the evening moved with the inevitability of good music. He went with her to the forever-lonely beach which the architects of New Madrid had built beside the hotel. They talked a little, they looked at each other, and they made love with an affirmative certainty which seemed outside themselves. He was very tender, and he did not realize that in a genitally sophisticated society, he was the first lover she had ever wanted or had ever had. (How could the daughter of Mona Muggeridge want a lover or a mate or a child?)

On the next afternoon, she exercised the freedom of her times and asked him to marry her. They had gone back to their private beach, which, through miracles of ultra-fine mini-weather adjustments, brought a Polynesian afternoon to the high chilly plateau of central Spain.

She asked him, *she* did, to marry her, and he refused, as tenderly and as kindly as a man of sixty-five can refuse a girl of eighteen. She did not press him; they continued the bittersweet love affair.

They sat on the artificial sand of the artificial beach and dabbled their toes in the man-warmed water of the ocean. Then they lay down against an artificial sand dune which hid New Madrid from view.

"Tell me," Helen said, "can I ask again, why did you become a sailor?"

"Not so easily answered," he said. "Adventure, maybe. That, at least in part. And I wanted to see Earth. Couldn't afford to come in a pod. Now—well, I've enough to keep me the rest of my life. I can go back to New Earth as a passenger in a month instead of forty years—be frozen in no more time than the wink of an eye, put in my adiabatic pod, linked in to the next sailing ship, and wake up home again while some other fool does the sailing."

Helen nodded. She did not bother to tell him that she knew all this. She had been investigating sailing ships since meeting the sailor.

"Out where you sail among the stars," she said, "can you tell me—can you possibly tell me anything of what it's like out there?"

His face looked inward on his soul and afterward his voice came as from an immense distance.

"There are moments—or is it weeks—you can't really tell in the sail ship—when it seems worthwhile. You feel . . . your nerve endings reach out until they touch the stars. You feel enormous, somehow." Gradually he came back to her. "It's trite to say, of course, but you're never the same afterward. I don't mean just the obvious physical thing, but—you find yourself—or maybe you lose yourself. That's why," he continued, gesturing toward New Madrid, out of sight behind the sand dune, "I can't stand this. New Earth, well, it's like Earth must have been in the old days, I guess. There's something fresh about it. Here . . ."

"I know," said Helen America, and she did. The slightly decadent, slightly corrupt, too comfortable air of Earth must have had a stifling effect on the man from beyond the stars.

"There," he said, "you won't believe this, but sometimes the ocean's too cold to swim in. We have music that doesn't come from machines, and pleasures that come

from inside our own bodies without being put there. I
have to get back to New Earth."

Helen said nothing for a little while, concentrating on
stilling the pain in her heart.

"I . . . I . . ." she began.

"I know," he said fiercely, almost savagely turning on
her. "But I can't take you. I can't! You're too young, you've
got a life to live and I've thrown away a quarter of mine.
No, that's not right. I didn't throw it away. I wouldn't
trade it back because it's given me something inside I
never had before. And it's given me you."

"But if—"she started again to argue.

"No. Don't spoil it. I'm going next week to be frozen
in my pod to wait for the next sail ship. I can't stand much
more of this, and I might weaken. That would be a terrible
mistake. But we have this time together now, and we have
our separate lifetimes to remember in. Don't think of anything else. There's nothing, nothing we can do."

Helen did not tell him—then or ever—of the child she
had started to hope for, the child they would now never
have. Oh, she could have used the child. She could have
tied him to her, for he was an honorable man and would
have married her had she told him. But Helen's love, even
then in her youth, was such that she could not use this
means. She wanted him to come to her of his own free
will, marrying her because he could not live without her.
To that marriage their child would have been an additional
blessing.

There was the other alternative, of course. She could
have borne the child without naming the father. But *she*
was no Mona Muggeridge. She knew too well the terrors

and insecurity and loneliness of being Helen America ever to be responsible for the creation of another. And for the course she had laid out there was no place for a child. So she did the only thing she could. At the end of their time in New Madrid, she let him say a real goodbye. Wordless and without tears, she left. Then she went up to an arctic city, a pleasure city where such things are well-known, and amidst shame, worry, and a driving sense of regret she appealed to a confidential medical service which eliminated the unborn child. Then she went back to Cambridge and confirmed her place as the first woman to sail a ship to the stars.

∽ VI ∾

The presiding Lord of the Instrumentality at that time was a man named Wait. Wait was not cruel but he was never noted for tenderness of spirit or for a high regard for the adventuresome proclivities of young people. His aide said to him, "This girl wants to sail a ship to New Earth. Are you going to let her?"

"Why not?" said Wait. "A person is a person. She is well-bred, well-educated. If she fails, we will find out something eighty years from now when the ship comes back. If she succeeds, it will shut up some of these women who have been complaining." The Lord leaned over his desk: "If she qualifies, and if she goes, though, don't give her any convicts. Convicts are too good and too valuable as settlers to be sent along on a fool trip like that. You can send her on something of a gamble. Give her all religious fanatics. We have more than enough. Don't you have twenty or thirty thousand who are waiting?"

He said, "Yes, sir, twenty-six thousand two hundred. Not counting recent additions."

"Very well," said the Lord of the Instrumentality. "Give her the whole lot of them and give her that new ship. Have we named it?"

"No, sir," said the aide.

"Name it then."

The aide looked blank.

A contemptuous wise smile crossed the face of the senior bureaucrat. He said, "Take that ship now and name it. Name it *The Soul* and let *The Soul* fly to the stars. And let Helen America be an angel if she wants to. Poor thing, she has not got much of a life to live on this Earth, not the way she was born, and the way she was brought up. And it's no use to try and reform her, to transform her personality, when it's a lively, rich personality. It does not do any good. We don't have to punish her for being herself. Let her go. Let her have it."

Wait sat up and stared at his aide and then repeated very firmly:

"Let her have it, *only if she qualifies.*"

∽ VII ∽

Helen America did qualify.

The doctors and the experts tried to warn her against it.

One technician said: "Don't you realize what this is

going to mean? Forty years will pour out of your life in a single month. You leave here a girl. You will get there a woman of sixty. Well, you will probably still have a hundred years to live after that. And it's painful. You will have all these people, thousands and thousands of them. You will have some Earth cargo. There will be about thirty thousand pods strung on sixteen lines behind you. Then you will have the control cabin to live in. We will give you as many robots as you need, probably a dozen. You will have a mainsail and a foresail and you will have to keep the two of them."

"I know. I have read the book," said Helen America. "And I sail the ship with light, and if the infrared touches that sail—I go. If I get radio interference, I pull the sails in. And if the sails fail, I wait as long as I live."

The technician looked a little cross. "There is no call for you to get tragic about it. Tragedy is easy enough to contrive. And if you want to be tragic, you can be tragic without destroying thirty thousand other people or without wasting a large amount of Earth property. You can drown in water right here, or jump into a volcano like the Japanese in the old books. Tragedy is not the hard part. The hard part is when you don't quite succeed and you have to keep on fighting. When you must keep going on and on and on in the face of really hopeless odds, of real temptations to despair.

"Now this is the way that the foresail works. That sail will be twenty thousand miles at the wide part. It tapers down and the total length will be just under eighty-thousand miles. It will be retracted or extended by small servo-robots. The servo-robots are radio-controlled.

You had better use your radio sparingly, because after all these batteries, even though they are atomic, have to last forty years. They have got to keep you alive."

"Yes, sir," said Helen America very contritely.

"You've got to remember what your job is. You're going because you are cheap. You are going because a sailor takes a lot less weight than a machine. There is no all-purpose computer built that weighs as little as a hundred and fifty pounds. You do. You go simply because you are expendable. Anyone that goes out to the stars takes one chance in three of never getting there. But you are not going because you are a leader, you are going because you are young. You have a life to give and a life to spare. Because your nerves are good. You understand that?"

"Yes, sir, I knew that."

"Furthermore, you are going because you'll make the trip in forty years. If we send automatic devices and have them manage the sails, they would get there—possibly. But it would take them from a hundred years to a hundred-and-twenty or more, and by that time the adiabatic pods would have spoiled, most of the human cargo would not be fit for revival, and the leakage of heat, no matter how we face it, would be enough to ruin the entire expedition. So remember that the tragedy and the trouble you face is mostly work. Work, and that's all it is. That is your big job."

Helen smiled. She was a short girl with rich dark hair, brown eyes, and very pronounced eyebrows, but when Helen smiled she was almost a child again, and a rather charming one. She said: "My job is work. I understand that, sir."

∽ VIII ∽

In the preparation area, the make-ready was fast but not hurried. Twice the technicians urged her to take a holiday before she reported for final training. She did not accept their advice. She wanted to go forth; she knew that they knew she wanted to leave Earth forever, and she also knew they knew she was not merely her mother's daughter. She was trying, somehow, to be herself. She knew the world did not believe, but the world did not matter.

The third time they suggested a vacation, the suggestion was mandatory. She had a gloomy two months which she ended up enjoying a little bit on the wonderful islands of the Hesperides, islands which were raised when the weight of the Earthports caused a new group of small archipelagos to form below Bermuda.

She reported back, fit, healthy, and ready to go.

The senior medical officer was very blunt.

"Do you really know what we are going to do to you? We are going to make you live forty years out of your life in one month."

She nodded, white of face, and he went on, "Now to give you those forty years we've got to slow down your bodily processes. After all, the sheer biological task of breathing forty years' worth of air in one month involves a factor of about five hundred to one. No lungs could stand it. Your body must circulate water. It must take in food. Most of this is going to be protein. There will be some kind of a hydrate. You'll need vitamins.

"Now, what we are going to do is to slow the brain down, very much indeed, so that the brain will be working at about that five-hundred-to-one ratio. We don't want you incapable of working. Somebody has got to manage the sails.

"Therefore, if you hesitate or you start to think, a thought or two is going to take several weeks. Meanwhile your body can be slowed down some. But the different parts can't be slowed down at the same rate. Water, for example, we brought down to about eighty to one. Food, to about three hundred to one.

"You won't have time to drink forty years' worth of water. We circulate it, get it through, purify it, and get it back in your system, unless you break your link-up.

"So what you face is a month of being absolutely wide awake, on an operating table and *being operated on without anesthetic,* while doing some of the hardest work that mankind has ever found.

"You'll have to take observations, you'll have to watch your lines with the pods of people and cargo behind you, you'll have to adjust the sails. If there is anybody surviving at destination point, they will come out and meet you.

"At least that happens most of the times.

"I am not going to assure you you will get the ship in. If they don't meet you, take an orbit beyond the farthest planet and either let yourself die or try to save yourself. You can't get thirty thousand people down on a planet single-handedly.

"Meanwhile, though, you've got a real job. We are going to have to build these controls right into your body. We'll start by putting valves in your chest arteries. Then we go on, catheterizing your water. We are going to make an artificial colostomy that will go forward here just in front of your hip joint. Your water intake has a certain psychological value so that about one five-hundredth of your water we are going to leave you to drink out of a cup. The rest of it is going to go directly into your bloodstream. Again about a tenth of your food will go that way. You understand that?"

"You mean," said Helen, "I eat one-tenth, and the rest goes in intravenously?"

"That's right," said the medical technician. "We will pump it into you. The concentrates are there. The reconstitutor is there. Now these lines have a double connection. One set of connections runs into the maintenance machine. That will become the logistic support for your body. And these lines are the umbilical cord for a human being alone among the stars. They are your life.

"And now if they should break or if you should fall, you might faint for a year or two. If that happens, your local system takes over: that's the pack on your back.

"On Earth, it weighs as much as you do. You have already been drilled with the model pack. You know how easy it is to handle in space. That'll keep you going for a subjective period of about two hours. No one has ever worked out a clock yet that would match the human mind, so instead of giving you a clock we are giving you an odometer attached to your own pulse and we mark it off in grades. If you watch it in terms of tens of thousands of pulse beats, you may get some information out of it.

"I don't know what kind of information, but you may find it helpful somehow." He looked at her sharply and then turned back to his tools, picking up a shining needle with a disk on the end.

"Now, let's get back to this. We are going to have to get right into your mind. That's chemical too."

Helen interrupted. "You said you were not going to operate on my head."

"Only the needle. That's the only way we can get to the mind. Slow it down enough so that you will have this subjective mind operating at a rate that will make the forty years pass in a month." He smiled grimly, but the grimness changed to momentary tenderness as he took in her brave obstinate stance, her girlish, admirable, pitiable determination.

"I won't argue it," she said. "This is as bad as a marriage and the stars are my bridegroom." The image of the sailor went across her mind, but she said nothing of him.

The technician went on. "Now, we have already built in psychotic elements. You can't even expect to remain sane. So you'd better not worry about it. You'll have to be insane to manage the sails and to survive utterly alone and be out there even a month. And the trouble is, in that month you are going to know it's really forty years. There is not a mirror in the place, but you'll probably find shiny surfaces to look at yourself.

"You won't look so good. You will see yourself aging, every time you slow down to look. I don't know what the problem is going to be on that score. It's been bad enough on men.

"Your hair problem is going to be easier than men's. The sailors we sent out, we simply had to kill all the hair roots. Otherwise the men would have been swamped in their own beards. And a tremendous amount of the nutrient would be wasted if it went into raising of hair on the face which no machine in the world could cut off fast enough to keep a man working. I think what we will do is inhibit hair on the top of your head. Whether it comes out in the same color or not is something you will find for yourself later. Did you ever meet the sailor that came in?"

The doctor knew she had met him. He did not know that it was the sailor from beyond the stars who called her. Helen managed to remain composed as she smiled at him to say: "Yes, you gave him new hair. Your technician planted a new scalp on his head, remember. Somebody on your staff did. The hair came out black and he got the nickname of Mr. Grey-no-more."

"If you are ready next Tuesday, we'll be ready too. Do you think you can make it by then, my lady?"

Helen felt odd seeing this old, serious man refer to her as "lady," but she knew he was paying respect to a profession and not just to an individual.

"Tuesday is time enough." She felt complimented that he was an old-fashioned enough person to know the ancient names of the days of the week and to use them. That was a sign that he had not only learned the essentials at the University but that he had picked up the elegant inconsequentialities as well.

∾ IX ∾

Two weeks later was twenty-one years later by the

chronometers in the cabin. Helen turned for the ten-thousand-times-ten-thousandth time to scan the sails.

Her back ached with a violent throb.

She could feel the steady roar of her heart like a fast vibrator as it ticked against the time-span of her awareness. She could look down at the meter on her wrist and see the hands on the watchlike dials indicate tens of thousands of pulses very slowly.

She heard the steady whistle of air in her throat as her lungs seemed shuddering with sheer speed.

And she felt the throbbing pain of a large tube feeding an immense quantity of mushy water directly into the artery of her neck.

On her abdomen, she felt as if someone had built a fire. The evacuation tube operated automatically but it burnt as if a coal had been held to her skin, and a catheter, which connected her bladder to another tube, stung as savagely as the prod of a scalding-hot needle. Her head ached and her vision blurred.

But she could still see the instruments and she still could watch the sails. Now and then she could glimpse, faint as a tracery of dust, the immense skein of people and cargo that lay behind them.

She could not sit down. It hurt too much.

The only way that she could be comfortable for resting was to lean against the instrument panel, her lower ribs against the panel, her tired forehead against the meters.

Once she rested that way and realized that it was two and a half months before she got up. She knew that rest had no meaning, and she could see her face moving, a distorted image of her own face growing old in the reflections from the glass face of the "apparent weight" dial. She could look at her arms with blurring vision, note the skin tightening, loosening, and tightening again, as changes in temperatures affected it.

She looked out one more time at the sails and decided to take in the foresail. Wearily she dragged herself over the control panel with a servo-robot. She selected the right control and opened it for a week or so. She waited there, her heart buzzing, her throat whistling air, her fingernails breaking off gently as they grew. Finally she checked to see if it really had been the right one, pushed again, and nothing happened.

She pushed a third time. There was no response.

Now she went back to the master panel, re-read, checked the light direction, found a certain amount of infrared pressure which she should have been picking up. The sails had very gradually risen to something not far from the speed of light itself because they moved fast with the one side dulled; the pods behind, sealed against time and eternity, swam obediently in an almost perfect weightlessness.

She scanned; her reading had been correct.

The sail *was* wrong.

She went back to the emergency panel and pressed. Nothing happened.

She broke out a repair robot and sent it out to effect repairs, punching the papers as rapidly as she could to give instructions. The robot went out and an instant (three days) later it replied. The panel on the repair robot rang forth, "Does not conform."

She sent a second repair robot. That had no effect either.

She sent a third, the last. Three bright lights, "Does not conform," stared at her. She moved the servo-robots to the other side of the sails and pulled hard.

The sail was still not at the right angle.

She stood there wearied and lost in space, and she prayed: "Not for me, God, I am running away from a life that I did not want. But for this ship's souls and for the poor foolish people that I am taking who are brave enough to want to worship their own way and need the light of another star, I ask you, God, help me now." She thought she had prayed very fervently and she hoped that she would get an answer to her prayer.

It did not work out that way. She was bewildered, alone.

There was no sun. There was nothing, except the tiny cabin and herself more alone than any woman had ever been before. She sensed the thrill and ripple of her muscles as they went through days of adjustment while her mind noticed only the matter of minutes. She leaned forward, forced herself not to relax, and finally she remembered that one of the official busybodies had included a weapon.

What she would use a weapon for she did not know.

It pointed. It had a range of two hundred thousand miles. The target could be selected automatically.

She got down on her knees trailing the abdominal tube and the feeding tube and the catheter tubes and the helmet wires, each one running back to the panel. She crawled underneath the panel for the servo-robots and she pulled out a written manual. She finally found the right frequency for the weapon's controls. She set the weapon up and went to the window.

At the last moment she thought, "Perhaps the fools are going to make me shoot the window out. It ought to have been designed to shoot through the window without hurting it. That's the way they should have done it."

She wondered about the matter for a week or two.

Just before she fired it she turned and there, next to her, stood her sailor, the sailor from the stars, Mr. Grey-no-more. He said: "It won't work that way."

He stood clear and handsome, the way she had seen him in New Madrid. He had no tubes, he did not tremble, she could see the normal rise and fall of his chest as he took one breath every hour or so. One part of her mind knew that he was a hallucination. Another part of her mind believed that he was real. She was mad, and she was very happy to be mad at this time, and she let the hallucination give her advice. She re-set the gun so that it would fire through the cabin wall, and it fired a low charge at the repair mechanism out beyond the distorted and immovable sail.

The low charge did the trick. The interference had been something beyond all technical anticipation. The weapon had cleaned out the forever-unidentifiable obstruction, leaving the servo-robots free to attack their tasks like a tribe of maddened ants. They worked again. They had had defenses built in against the minor impediments of space. All of them scurried and skipped about.

With a sense of bewilderment close to religion, she perceived the wind of starlight blowing against the immense sails. The sails snapped into position. She got a momentary touch of gravity as she sensed a little weight. *The Soul* was back on her course.

∽ **X** ∽

"It's a girl," they said to him on New Earth. "It's a girl. She must have been eighteen herself."

Mr. Grey-no-more did not believe it.

But he went to the hospital and there in the hospital he saw Helen America.

"Here I am, sailor," said she. "I sailed too." Her face was white as chalk, her expression was that of a girl of about twenty. Her body was that of a well-preserved woman of sixty.

As for him, he had not changed again, since he had returned home inside a pod.

He looked at her. His eyes narrowed, and then, in a sudden reversal of roles, it was he who was kneeling beside her bed and covering her hands with his tears.

Half-coherently, he babbled at her: "I ran away from you because I loved you so. I came back here where you would never follow, or if you did follow, you'd still be a young woman, and I'd still be too old. But you have sailed *The Soul* in here and you wanted me."

The nurse of New Earth did not know about the rules which should be applied to the sailors from the stars. Very quietly she went out of the room, smiling in tenderness and human pity at the love which she had seen. But she was a practical woman and she had a sense of her own advancement. She called a friend of hers at the news service and said: "I think I have got the biggest romance in history. If you get here soon enough you can get the first telling of the story of Helen America and Mr. Grey-no-more. They just met like that. I guess they'd seen each other somewhere. They just met like that and fell in love."

The nurse did not know that they had forsworn a love on Earth. The nurse did not know that Helen America had made a lonely trip with an icy purpose, and the nurse did not know that the crazy image of Mr. Grey-no-more, the sailor himself, had stood beside Helen twenty years out from nothing-at-all in the depth and blackness of space between the stars.

∽ XI ∾

The little girl had grown up, had married, and now had a little girl of her own. The mother was unchanged, but the spieltier was very, very old. It had outlived all its marvelous tricks of adaptability, and for some years had stayed frozen in the role of a yellow-haired, blue-eyed girl doll. Out of sentimental sense of the fitness of things, she had dressed the spieltier in a bright blue jumper with matching panties. The little animal crept softly across the floor on its tiny human hands, using its knees for hind feet. The mock-human face looked up blindly and squeaked for milk.

The young mother said, "Mom, you ought to get rid of that thing. It's all used up and it looks horrible with your nice period furniture."

"I thought you loved it," said the older woman.

"Of course," said the daughter. "It was cute, when I was a child. But I'm not a child any more, and it doesn't even work."

The spieltier had struggled to its feet and clutched its
mistress's ankle. The older woman took it away gently, and
put down a saucer of milk and a cup the size of a thimble.
The spieltier tried to curtsey, as it had been motivated to
do at the beginning, slipped, fell, and whimpered. The
mother righted it and the little old animal-toy began dipping milk with its thimble and sucking the milk into its
tiny toothless old mouth.

"You remember, Mom—"said the younger woman and
stopped.

"Remember what, dear?"

"You told me about Helen America and Mr. Grey-no-
more when that was brand new."

"Yes, darling, maybe I did."

"You didn't tell me everything," said the younger
woman accusingly.

"Of course not. You were a child."

"But it was awful. Those messy people, and the horrible
way sailors lived. I don't see how you idealized it and
called it a romance—"

"But it was. It is," insisted the other.

"Romance, my foot," said the daughter. "It's as bad as
you and the worn-out spieltier." She pointed at the tiny,
living, aged doll who had fallen asleep beside its milk. "I
think it's horrible. You ought to get rid of it. And the world
ought to get rid of sailors."

"Don't be harsh, darling," said the mother.

"Don't be a sentimental old slob," said the daughter.

"Perhaps we are," said the mother with a loving sort of
laugh. Unobtrusively she put the sleeping spieltier on a
padded chair where it would not be stepped on or hurt.

∽ XII ∽

Outsiders never knew the real end of the story.

More than a century after their wedding, Helen lay dying: she was dying happily, because her beloved sailor was beside her. She believed that if they could conquer space, they might conquer death as well.

Her loving, happy, weary dying mind blurred over and she picked up an argument they hadn't touched upon for decades.

"You did *so* come to *The Soul*," she said. "You did so stand beside me when I was lost and did not know how to handle the weapon."

"If I came then, darling, I'll come again, wherever you are. You're my darling, my heart, my own true love. You're my bravest of ladies, my boldest of people. You're my own. You sailed for me. You're my lady who sailed *The Soul*."

His voice broke, but his features stayed calm. He had never before seen anyone die so confident and so happy.

When the People Fell

"Can you imagine a rain of people through an acid fog? Can you imagine thousands and thousands of human bodies, without weapons, overwhelming the unconquerable monsters? Can you—"

"Look, sir," interrupted the reporter.

"Don't interrupt me! You ask me silly questions. I tell you I saw the Goonhogo itself. I saw it take Venus. Now ask me about that!"

The reporter had called to get an old man's reminiscences about bygone ages. He did not expect Dobyns Bennett to flare up at him.

Dobyns Bennett thrust home the psychological advantage he had gotten by taking the initiative. "Can you imagine showhices in their parachutes, a lot of them dead, floating out of a green sky? Can you imagine mothers crying as they fell? Can you imagine people pouring down on the poor helpless monsters?"

Mildly, the reporter asked what showhices were.

"That's old Chinesian for children," said Dobyns Bennett. "I saw the last of the nations burst and die, and you want to ask me about fashionable clothes and things. Real history never gets into the books. It's too shocking. I suppose you were going to ask me what I thought of the new striped pantaloons for women!"

"No," said the reporter, but he blushed. The question was in his notebook and he hated blushing.

"Do you know what the Goonhogo did?"

"What?" asked the reporter, struggling to remember just what a Goonhogo might be.

"It took Venus," said the old man, somewhat more calmly.

Very mildly, the reporter murmured, "It *did*?"

"You bet it did!" said Dobyns Bennett belligerently.

"Were you there?" asked the reporter.

"You bet I was there when the Goonhogo took Venus," said the old man. "I was there and it's the damnedest thing I've ever seen. You know who I am. I've seen more worlds than you can count, boy, and yet when the nondies and the needies and the showhices came pouring out of the sky, that was the worst thing that any man could ever see. Down on the ground, there were the loudies the way they'd always been—"

The reporter interrupted, very gently. Bennett might as well have been speaking a foreign language. All of this had happened three hundred years before. The reporter's job was to get a feature from him and to put it into a language which people of the present time could understand.

Respectfully he said, "Can't you start at the beginning of the story?"

"You bet. That's when I married Terza. Terza was the prettiest girl you ever saw. She was one of the Vomacts, a great family of scanners, and her father was a very important man. You see, I was thirty-two, and when a man is thirty-two, he thinks he is pretty old, but I wasn't really old, I just thought so, and he wanted Terza to marry me because she was such a complicated girl that she needed a man's help. The Court back home had found her unstable and the Instrumentality had ordered her left in her father's care until she married a man who then could take on proper custodial authority. I suppose those are old customs to you, boy—"

The reporter interrupted again. "I am sorry, old man," said he. "I know you are over four hundred years old and you're the only person who remembers the time the Goonhogo took Venus. Now the Goonhogo was a government, wasn't it?"

"Anyone knows that," snapped the old man. "The Goonhogo was a sort of separate Chinesian government. Seventeen billion of them all crowded in one small part of Earth. Most of them spoke English the way you and I do, but they spoke their own language, too, with all those funny words that have come on down to us. They hadn't mixed in with anybody else yet. Then, you see, the Waywanjong himself gave the order and that is when the people started raining. They just fell right out of the sky. You never saw anything like it—"

The reporter had to interrupt him again and again to get the story bit by bit. The old man kept using terms that he couldn't seem to realize were lost in history and that had to be explained to be intelligible to anyone of this era. But his memory was excellent and his descriptive powers as sharp and alert as ever. . . .

✧✧✧

Young Dobyns Bennett had not been at Experimental Area A very long, before he realized that the most beautiful female he had ever seen was Terza Vomact. At the age of fourteen, she was fully mature. Some of the Vomacts did mature that way. It may have had something to do with their being descended from unregistered, illegal people centuries back in the past. They were even said to have mysterious connections with the lost world back in the age of nations when people could still put numbers on the years.

He fell in love with her and felt like a fool for doing it.

She was so beautiful, it was hard to realize that she was the daughter of Scanner Vomact himself. The scanner was a powerful man.

Sometimes romance moves too fast and it did with Dobyns Bennett because Scanner Vomact himself called in the young man and said, "I'd like to have you marry my daughter Terza, but I'm not sure she'll approve of you. If you can get her, boy, you have my blessing."

Dobyns was suspicious. He wanted to know why a senior scanner was willing to take a junior technician.

All that the scanner did was to smile. He said, "I'm a lot older than you, and with this new santaclara drug coming in that may give people hundreds of years, you may think that I died in my prime if I die at a hundred and twenty. You may live to four or five hundred. But I know my time's coming up. My wife has been dead for a long time and we have no other children and I know that Terza needs a father in a very special kind of way. The psychologist found her to be unstable. Why don't you take her outside the area? You can get a pass through the dome anytime. You can go out and play with the loudies."

Dobyns Bennett was almost as insulted as if someone had given him a pail and told him to go play in the sandpile. And yet he realized that the elements of play in courtship were fitted together and that the old man meant well.

The day that it all happened, he and Terza were outside the dome. They had been pushing loudies around.

Loudies were not dangerous unless you killed them. You could knock them down, push them out of the way, or tie them up; after a while, they slipped away and went about their business. It took a very special kind of ecologist to figure out what their business was. They floated two meters high, ninety centimeters in diameter, gently just above the land of Venus, eating microscopically. For a long time, people thought there was radiation on which they subsisted. They simply multiplied in tremendous numbers. In a silly sort of way, it was fun to push them around, but that was about all there was to do.

They never responded with intelligence.

Once, long before, a loudie taken into the laboratory for experimental purposes had typed a perfectly clear message on the typewriter. The message had read, "Why don't you Earth people go back to Earth and leave us alone? We are getting along all—"

And that was all the message that anybody had ever got out of them in three hundred years. The best laboratory conclusion was that they had very high intelligence if they ever chose to use it, but that their volitional mechanism was so profoundly different from the psychology of human beings that it was impossible to force a loudie to respond to stress as people did on Earth.

The name *loudie* was some kind of word in the old Chinesian language. It meant the "ancient ones." Since it was the Chinesians who had set up the first outposts on Venus, under the orders of their supreme boss the Waywonjong, their term lingered on.

Dobyns and Terza pushed loudies, climbed over the hills, and looked down into the valleys where it was impossible to tell a river from a swamp. They got thoroughly wet, their air converters stuck, and perspiration itched and tickled along their cheeks. Since they could not eat or drink while outside—at least not with any reasonable degree of safety—the excursion could not be called a picnic. There was something mildly refreshing about playing child with a very pretty girl-child—but Dobyns wearied of the whole thing.

Terza sensed his rejection of her. Quick as a sensitive animal, she became angry and petulant. "You didn't have to come out with me!"

"I wanted to," he said, "but now I'm tired and want to go home."

"You treat me like a child. All right, play with me. Or you treat me like a woman. All right, be a gentleman. But don't seesaw all the time yourself. I just got to be a little bit happy and you have to get middle-aged and condescending. I won't take it."

"Your father—" he said, realizing the moment he said it that it was a mistake.

"My father this, my father that. If you're thinking

about marrying me, do it yourself." She glared at him, stuck her tongue out, ran over a dune, and disappeared.

Dobyns Bennett was baffled. He did not know what to do. She was safe enough. The loudies never hurt anyone. He decided to teach her a lesson and to go on back himself, letting her find her way home when she pleased. The Area Search Team could find her easily if she really got lost.

He walked back to the gate.

When he saw the gates locked and the emergency lights on, he realized that he had made the worst mistake of his life.

His heart sinking within him, he ran the last few meters of the way, and beat the ceramic gate with his bare hands until it opened only just enough to let him in.

"What's wrong?" he asked the doortender.

The doortender muttered something which Dobyns could not understand.

"Speak up, man!" shouted Dobyns. "What's wrong?"

"The Goonhogo is coming back and they're taking over."

"That's impossible," said Dobyns. "They couldn't—" He checked himself. *Could* they?

"The Goonhogo's taken over," the gatekeeper insisted. "They've been given the whole thing. The Earth Authority has voted it to them. The Waywonjong has decided to send people right away. They're sending them."

"What do the Chinesians want with Venus? You can't kill a loudie without contaminating a thousand acres of land. You can't push them away without them drifting back. You can't scoop them up. Nobody can live here until we solve the problem of these things. We're a long way from having solved it," said Dobyns in angry bewilderment.

The gatekeeper shook his head. "Don't ask me. That's all I hear on the radio. Everybody else is excited too."

Within an hour, the rain of people began.

Dobyns went up to the radar room, saw the skies above. The radar man himself was drumming his fingers against the desk. He said, "Nothing like this has been seen for a thousand years or more. You know what there is up there? Those are warships, the warships left over from the last of the old dirty wars. I knew the Chinesians were inside them. Everybody knew about it. It was sort of like a museum. Now they don't have any weapons in them. But do you know—there are millions of people hanging up there over Venus and I don't know what they are going to do!"

He stopped and pointed at one of the screens. "Look, you can see them running in patches. They're behind each other, so they cluster up solid. We've never had a screen look like that."

Dobyns looked at the screen. It was, as the operator said, full of blips.

As they watched, one of the men exclaimed, "What's that milky stuff down there in the lower left? See, it's—it's pouring," he said. "It's pouring somehow out of those dots. How can you pour things into a radar? It doesn't really show, does it?"

The radar man looked at his screen. He said, "Search me. I don't know what it is, either. You'll have to find out. Let's just see what happens."

Scanner Vomact came into the room. He said, once he

had taken a quick, experienced glance at the screens, "This may be the strangest thing we'll ever see, but I have a feeling they're dropping people. Lots of them. Dropping them by the thousands, or by the hundreds of thousands, or even by the millions. But people are coming down there. Come along with me, you two. We'll go out and see it. There may be somebody that we can help."

By this time, Dobyns's conscience was hurting him badly. He wanted to tell Vomact that he had left Terza out there, but he had hesitated—not only because he was ashamed of leaving her, but because he did not want to tattle on the child to her father. Now he spoke.

"Your daughter's still outside."

Vomact turned on him solemnly. The immense eyes looked very tranquil and very threatening, but the silky voice was controlled.

"You may find her." The scanner added, in a tone which sent the thrill of menace up Dobyns's back, "And everything will be well if you bring her back."

Dobyns nodded as though receiving an order.

"I shall," said Vomact, "go out myself, to see what I can do, but I leave the finding of my daughter to you."

They went down, put on the extra-long-period converters, carried their miniaturized survey equipment so that they could find their way back through the fog, and went out. Just as they were at the gate, the gatekeeper said, "Wait a moment, sir and excellency. I have a message for you here on the phone. Please call Control."

Scanner Vomact was not to be called lightly and he knew it. He picked up the connection unit and spoke harshly.

The radar man came on the phone screen in the gate-keeper's wall. "They're overhead now, sir."

"Who's overhead?"

"The Chinesians are. They're coming down. I don't know how many there are. There must be two thousand warships over our heads right here and there are more thousands over the rest of Venus. They're down now. If you want to see them hit ground, you'd better get outside quick."

Vomact and Dobyns went out.

Down came the Chinesians. People's bodies were raining right out of the milk-cloudy sky. Thousands upon thousands of them with plastic parachutes that looked like bubbles. Down they came.

Dobyns and Vomact saw a headless man drift down. The parachute cords had decapitated him.

A woman fell near them. The drop had torn her breathing tube loose from her crudely bandaged throat and she was choking in her own blood. She staggered toward them, tried to babble but only drooled blood with mute choking sounds, and then fell face forward into the mud.

Two babies dropped. The adult accompanying them had been blown off course. Vomact ran, picked them up, and handed them to a Chinesian man who had just landed. The man looked at the babies in his arms, sent Vomact a look of contemptuous inquiry, put the weeping children down in the cold slush of Venus, gave them a last imper-sonal glance, and ran off on some mysterious errand of his own.

Vomact kept Bennett from picking up the children.

"Come on, let's keep looking. We can't take care of all of them."

The world had known that the Chinesians had a lot of unpredictable public habits; but they never suspected that the nondies and the needies and the showhices could pour down out of a poisoned sky. Only the Goonhogo itself would make such a reckless use of human life. *Nondies* were men and *needies* were women and *showhices* were the little children. And the *Goonhogo* was a name left over from the old days of nations. It meant something like republic or state or government. Whatever it was, it was the organization that ran the Chinesians in the Chinesian manner, under the Earth Authority.

And the ruler of the Goonhogo was the Waywonjong.

The Waywonjong didn't come to Venus. He just sent his people. He sent them floating down into Venus, to tackle the Venusian ecology with the only weapons which could make a settlement of that planet possible—people themselves. Human arms could tackle the loudies, the loudies who had been called "old ones" by the first Chinesian scouts to cover Venus.

The loudies had to be gathered together so gently that they would not die and, in dying, each contaminate a thousand acres. They had to be kept together by human bodies and arms in a gigantic living corral.

Scanner Vomact rushed forward.

A wounded Chinesian man hit the ground and his parachute collapsed behind him. He was clad in a pair of shorts, had a knife at his belt, canteen at his waist. He had an air converter attached next to his ear, with a tube running into his throat. He shouted something unintelligible at them and limped rapidly away.

People kept on hitting the ground all around Vomact and Dobyns.

The self-disposing parachutes were bursting like bubbles in the misty air, a moment or two after they touched the ground. Someone had done a tricky, efficient job with the chemical consequences of static electricity.

And as the two watched, the air was heavy with people. One time, Vomact was knocked down by a person. He found that it was two Chinesian children tied together.

Dobyns asked, "What are you doing? Where are you going? Do you have any leaders?"

He got cries and shouts in an unintelligible language. Here and there someone shouted in English, "This way!" or "Leave us alone!" or "Keep going . . ." but that was all.

The experiment worked.

Eighty-two million people were dropped in that one day.

After four hours which seemed barely short of endless, Dobyns found Terza in a corner of the cold hell. Though Venus was warm, the suffering of the almost-naked Chinesians had chilled his blood.

Terza ran toward him.

She could not speak.

She put her head on his chest and sobbed. Finally she managed to say, "I've—I've—I've tried to help, but they're too many, too many, too many!" And the sentence ended as shrill as a scream.

Dobyns led her back to the experimental area.

They did not have to talk. Her whole body told him that she wanted his love and the comfort of his presence, and that she had chosen that course of life which would keep them together.

As they left the drop area, which seemed to cover all of Venus so far as they could tell, a pattern was beginning to form. The Chinesians were beginning to round up the loudies.

Terza kissed him mutely after the gatekeeper had let them through. She did not need to speak. Then she fled to her room.

The next day, the people from Experimental Area A tried to see if they could go out and lend a hand to the settlers. It wasn't possible to lend a hand; there were too many settlers. People by the millions were scattered all over the hills and valleys of Venus, sludging through the mud and water with their human toes, crushing the alien mud, crushing the strange plants. They didn't know what to eat. They didn't know where to go. They had no leaders.

All they had were orders to gather the loudies together in large herds and hold them there with human arms.

The loudies didn't resist.

After a time-lapse of several Earth days the Goonhogo sent small scout cars. They brought a very different kind of Chinesian—these late arrivals were uniformed, educated, cruel, smug men. They knew what they were doing. And they were willing to pay any sacrifice of their own people to get it done.

They brought instructions. They put the people together in gangs. It did not matter where the nondies and needies had come from on Earth; it didn't matter whether they found their own showhices or somebody else's. They were shown the jobs to do and they got to work. Human bodies accomplished what machines could not have done—they kept the loudies firmly but gently encircled until every last one of the creatures was starved into nothingness.

Rice fields began to appear miraculously.

Scanner Vomact couldn't believe it. The Goonhogo biochemists had managed to adapt rice to the soil of Venus. And yet the seedlings came out of boxes in the scout cars and weeping people walked over the bodies of their own dead to keep the crop moving toward the planting.

Venusian bacteria could not kill human beings, nor could they dispose of human bodies after death. A problem arose and was solved. Immense sleds carried dead men, women, and children—those who had fallen wrong, or drowned as they fell, or had been trampled by others—to an undisclosed destination. Dobyns suspected the material was to be used to add Earth-type organic waste to the soil of Venus, but he did not tell Terza.

The work went on.

The nondies and needies kept working in shifts. When they could not see in the darkness, they proceeded without seeing—keeping in line by touch or by shout. Foremen, newly trained, screeched commands. Workers lined up, touching fingertips. The job of building the fields kept on.

"That's a big story," said the old man. "Eighty-two million people dropped in a single day. And later I heard that the Waywonjong said it wouldn't have mattered if seventy million of them had died. Twelve million survivors would have been enough to make a spacehead for the Goonhogo. The Chinesians got Venus, all of it.

"But I'll never forget the nondies and the needies and the showhices falling out of the sky, men and women and children with their poor scared Chinesian faces. That funny Venusian air made them look green instead of tan. There they were, falling all around.

"You know something, young man?" said Dobyns Bennett, approaching his fifth century of age.

"What?" said the reporter.

"There won't be things like that happening on any world again. Because now, after all, there isn't any separate Goonhogo left. There's only one Instrumentality and they don't care what a man's race may have been in the ancient years. Those were the rough old days, the ones I lived in. Those were the days *men* still tried to do things."

Dobyns almost seemed to doze off, but he roused himself sharply and said, "I tell you, the sky was full of people. They fell like water. They fell like rain. I've seen the awful ants in Africa, and there's not a thing among the stars to beat them for prowling horror. Mind you, they're worse than anything the stars contain. I've seen the crazy worlds near Alpha Centauri, but I never saw anything like the time the people fell on Venus. More than eighty-two million in one day and my own little Terza lost among them.

"But the rice did sprout. And the loudies died as the walls of people held them in with human arms. Walls of people, I tell you, with volunteers jumping in to take the places of the falling ones.

"They were people still, even when they shouted in the darkness. They tried to help each other even while they fought a fight that had to be fought without violence. They were people still. And they did so win. It was crazy and impossible, but they won. Mere human beings did what machines and science would have taken another thousand years to do . . .

"The funniest thing of all was the first house that I saw a nondie put up, there in the rain of Venus. I was out there with Vomact and with a pale sad Terza. It wasn't much of a house, shaped out of twisted Venusian wood. There it was. *He* built it, the smiling half-naked Chinesian nondie. We went to the door and said to him in English, 'What are you building here, a shelter or a hospital?'

"The Chinesian grinned at us. 'No,' he said, 'gambling.'

"Vomact wouldn't believe it: 'Gambling?'

"'Sure,' said the nondie. 'Gambling is the first thing a man needs in a strange place. It can take the worry out of his soul.'"

"Is that all?" said the reporter.

Dobyns Bennett muttered that the personal part did not count. He added, "Some of my great-great-great-great-great-grandsons may come along. You count those greats. Their faces will show you easily enough that I married into the Vomact line. Terza saw what happened. She saw how people build worlds. This was the hard way to build them. She never forgot the night with the dead Chinesian babies lying in the half-illuminated mud, or the parachute ropes dissolving slowly. She heard the needies weeping and the helpless nondies comforting them and leading them off to nowhere. She remembered the cruel, neat officers coming out of the scout cars. She got home and saw the rice come up, and saw how the Goonhogo made Venus a Chinesian place."

"What happened to you personally?" asked the reporter.

"Nothing much. There wasn't any more work for us, so we closed down Experimental Area A. I married Terza.

"Any time later, when I said to her, 'You're not such a bad girl!' she was able to admit the truth and tell me she was not. That night in the rain of people would test anybody's soul and it tested hers. She had met a big test and passed it. She used to say to me, 'I saw it once. I saw the people fall, and I never want to see another person suffer again. Keep me with you, Dobyns, keep me with you forever.'

"And," said Dobyns Bennett, "it wasn't forever, but it was a happy and sweet three hundred years. She died after our fourth diamond anniversary. Wasn't that a wonderful thing, young man?"

The reporter said it was. And yet, when he took the story back to his editor, he was told to put it into the archives. It wasn't the right kind of story for entertainment and the public would not appreciate it any more.

Think Blue, Count Two

∽ | ∽

Before the great ships whispered between the stars by means of planoforming, people had to fly from star to star with immense sails—huge films assorted in space on long, rigid, coldproof rigging. A small spaceboat provided room for a sailor to handle the sails, check the course, and watch the passengers who were sealed, like knots in immense threads, in their little adiabatic pods which trailed behind the ship. The passengers knew nothing, except for going to sleep on Earth and waking up on a strange new world forty, fifty, or two hundred years later.

This was a primitive way to do it. But it worked.

On such a ship Helen America had followed Mr. Grey-no-more. On such ships, the Scanners retained their ancient authority over space. Two hundred planets and more were settled in this fashion, including Old North Australia, destined to be the treasure house of them all.

The Emigration Port was a series of low, square buildings—nothing like Earthport, which towers above the clouds like a frozen nuclear explosion.

Emigration Port is dour, drab, dreary, and efficient. The walls are black-red like old blood merely because they are cheaper to heat that way. The rockets are ugly and simple; the rocket pits, as inglorious as machine shops. Earth has a few showplaces to tell visitors about. Emigration Port is not one of them. The people who work there get the privilege of real work and secure professional honors. The people who *go* there become unconscious very soon. What they remember about Earth is a little room like a hospital room, a little bed, some music, some talk, the sleep, and (perhaps) the cold.

From Emigration Port they go to their pods, sealed in. The pods go to the rockets and these to the sailing ship. That's the old way of doing it.

The new way is better. All a person does now is visit a pleasant lounge, or play a game of cards, or eat a meal or two. All he needs is half the wealth of a planet, or a couple hundred years' seniority marked "excellent" without a single break.

The photonic sails were different. Everyone took chances.

A young man, bright of skin and hair, merry at heart, set out for a new world. An older man, his hair touched with gray, went with him. So, too, did thirty thousand others. And also, the most beautiful girl on Earth.

Earth could have kept her, but the new worlds needed her.

She had to go.

She went by light-sail ship. And she had to cross space—space, where the danger always waits.

Space sometimes commands strange tools to its

uses—the screams of a beautiful child, the laminated brain of a long-dead mouse, the heartbroken weeping of a computer. Most space offers no respite, no relay, no rescue, no repair. All dangers must be anticipated; otherwise they become mortal. And the greatest of all hazards is the risk of man himself.

"She's beautiful," said the first technician.

"She's just a child," said the second.

"She won't look like much of a child when they're two hundred years out," said the first.

"But she *is* a child," said the second, smiling, "a beautiful doll with blue eyes, just going tiptoe into the beginnings of grown-up life." He sighed.

"She'll be frozen," said the first.

"Not all the time," said the second. "Sometimes they wake up. They have to wake up. The machines defreeze them. You remember the crimes on the *Old Twenty-two*. Nice people, but the wrong combinations. And everything went wrong, dirtily, brutally wrong."

They both remembered *Old Twenty-two*. The hell-ship had drifted between the stars for a long time before its beacon brought rescue. Rescue was much too late.

The ship was in immaculate condition. The sails were set at a correct angle. The thousands of frozen sleepers, strung out behind the ship in their one-body adiabatic pods, would have been in excellent condition, but they had merely been left in open space too long and most of them had spoiled. The inside of the ship—there was the trouble. The sailor had failed or died. The reserve passengers had been awakened. They did not get on well with one another. Or else they got on too horribly well, in the wrong way. Out between the stars, encased only by a frail limited cabin, they had invented new crimes and committed them upon each other—crimes which a million years of Earth's old wickedness had never brought to the surface of man before.

The investigators of *Old Twenty-two* had become very sick, reconstructing the events that followed the awakening of the reserve crew; two of them had asked for blanking and had obviously retired from service.

The two technicians knew all about *Old Twenty-two* as they watched the fifteen-year-old woman sleeping on the table. Was she a woman? Was she a girl? What would happen to her if she did wake up on the flight?

She breathed delicately.

The two technicians looked across her figure at one another and then the first one said:

"We'd better call the psychological guard. It's a job for him."

"He can try," said the second.

The psychological guard, a man whose number-name ended in the digits Tiga-belas, came cheerfully into the room a half-hour later. He was a dreamy-looking old man, sharp and alert, probably in his fourth rejuvenation. He looked at the beautiful girl on the table and inhaled sharply,

"What's this for—a ship?"

"No," said the first technician, "it's a beauty contest."

"Don't be a fool," said the psychological guard. "You mean they are really sending that beautiful child into the Up-and-Out?"

"It's stock," said the second technician. "The people out on Wereld Schemering are running dreadfully ugly, and they flashed a sign to the Big Blink that they had to have better-looking people. The Instrumentality is doing right by them. All the people on this ship are handsome or beautiful."

"If she's that precious, why don't they freeze her and put her in a pod? That way she would either get there or she would not. A face as pretty as that," said Tiga-belas, "could start trouble anywhere. Let alone a ship. What's her name-number?"

"On the board there," said the first technician. "It's all on the board there. You'll want the others too. They're listed, too, and ready to go on the board."

"Veesey-koosey," read the psychological guard, saying the words aloud, "or five-six. That's a silly name, but it's rather cute." With one last look back at the sleeping girl, he bent to his work of reading the case histories of the people added to the reserve crew. Within ten lines, he saw why the girl was being kept ready for emergencies, instead of sleeping the whole trip through. She had a Daughter Potential of 999.999, meaning that any normal adult of either sex could *and would* accept her as a daughter after a few minutes of relationship. She had no skill in herself, no learning, no trained capacities. But she could remotivate almost anyone older than herself, and she showed a probability of making that remotivated person put up a gigantic fight for life. For her sake. And secondarily the adopter's.

That was all, but it was special enough to put her in the cabin. She had tested out into the literal truth of the ancient poetic scrap, "the fairest of the daughters of old, old Earth."

When Tiga-belas finished taking his notes from the records, the working time was almost over. The technicians had not interrupted him. He turned around to look one last time at the lovely girl. She was gone. The second technician had left and the first was cleaning his hands.

"You haven't frozen her?" cried Tiga-belas. "I'll have to fix her too, if the safeguard is to work."

"Of course you do," said the first technician. "We've left you two minutes for it."

"You give me two minutes," said Tiga-belas, "to protect a trip of four hundred and fifty years!"

"Do you need more," said the technician, and it was not even a question, except in form.

"Do I?" said Tiga-belas. He broke into a smile. "No, I don't. That girl will be safe long after I am dead."

"When do you die?" said the technician, socially.

"Seventy-three years, two months, four days," said Tiga-belas agreeably. "I'm a fourth-and-last."

"I thought so," said the technician. "You're smart. Nobody starts off that way. We all learn. I'm sure you'll take care of that girl."

They left the laboratory together and ascended to the surface and the cool restful night of Earth.

∾ II ∾

Late the next day, Tiga-belas came in, very cheerful indeed. In his left hand he held a drama spool, full commercial size. In his right hand there was a black plastic cube with shimmering silver contact-points gleaming on its sides. The two technicians greeted him politely.

The psychological guard could not hide his excitement and his pleasure.

"I've got that beautiful child taken care of. The way she is going to be fixed, she'll keep her Daughter Potential, but it's going to be a lot closer to one thousand point double zero than it was with all those nines. I've used a mouse-brain."

"If it's frozen," said the first technician, "we won't be able to put it in the computer. It will have to go forward with the emergency stores."

"This brain isn't frozen," said Tiga-belas indignantly. "It's been laminated. We stiffened it with celluprime and then we veneered it down, about seven thousand layers. Each one has plastic of at least two molecular thicknesses. This mouse can't spoil. As a matter of fact, this mouse is going to go on thinking forever. He won't think much, unless we put the voltage on him, but he'll think. And he can't spoil. This is ceramic plastic, and it would take a major weapon to break it."

"The contacts . . . ?" said the second technician.

"They don't go through," said Tiga-belas. "This mouse is tuned into that girl's personality, up to a thousand meters. You can put him anywhere in the ship. The case has been hardened. The contacts are just attached on the outside. They feed to nickel-steel counterpart contacts on the inside. I told you, this mouse is going to be thinking when the last human being on the last known planet is dead. And it's going to be thinking about that girl. Forever."

"Forever is an awfully long time," said the first technician, with a shiver. "We only need a safety period of two thousand years. The girl herself would spoil in less than a thousand years, if anything did go wrong."

"Never you mind," said Tiga-belas, "that girl is going to be guarded whether she is spoiled or not." He spoke to the cube. "You're going along with Veesey, fellow, and if she is an *Old Twenty-two* you'll turn the whole thing into a toddle-garden frolic complete with ice cream and hymns to the West Wind." Tiga-belas looked up at the other men and said, quite unnecessarily, "He can't hear me."

"Of course not," said the first technician, very dryly.

They all looked at the cube. It was a beautiful piece of engineering. The psychological guard had reason to be proud of it.

"Do you need the mouse any more?" said the first technician.

"Yes," said Tiga-belas. "One-third of a millisecond at forty megadynes. I want him to get her whole life printed on his left cortical lobe. Particularly her screams. She screamed badly at ten months. Something she got in her mouth. She screamed at ten when she thought the air had stopped in her drop-shaft. It hadn't, or she wouldn't be here. They're in her record. I want the mouse to have those screams. And she had a pair of red shoes for her fourth birthday. Give me the full two minutes with her. I've printed the key on the complete series of *Marcia and the Moon Men*—that was the best box drama for teen-age girls that they ran last year. Veesey saw it. This time she'll see it again, but the mouse will be tied in. She won't have the chance of a snowball in hell of forgetting it."

Said the first technician, "What was that?"

"Huh?" said Tiga-belas.

"What was that you just said, that, at the end?"

"Are you deaf?"

"No," said the technician huffily. "I just didn't understand what you meant."

"I said that she would not have the chance of a snowball in hell of forgetting it."

"That's what I thought you said," replied the technician. "What is a snowball? What is hell? What sort of chances do they make?"

The second technician interrupted eagerly. "I know," he explained. "Snowballs are ice formations on Neptune. Hell is a planet out near Khufu VII. I don't know how anybody would get them together."

Tiga-belas looked at them with the weary amazement of the very old. He did not feel like explaining, so he said gently:

"Let's leave the literature till another time. All I meant was, Veesey will be safe when she's cued into this mouse. The mouse will outlast her and everybody else, and no teen-age girl is going to forget *Marcia and the Moon Men.* Not when she saw every single episode twice over. This girl did."

"She's not going to render the other passengers ineffectual? That wouldn't help," said the first technician.

"Not a bit," said Tiga-belas.

"Give me those strengths again," said the first technician.

"Mouse—one-third millisecond at forty megadynes."

"They'll hear that way beyond the moon," said the technician. "You can't put that sort of stuff into people's heads without a permit. Do you want us to get a special permit from the Instrumentality?"

"For one-third of a millisecond?"

The two men faced each other for a moment; then the technician began creasing his forehead, his mouth began to smile, and they both laughed. The second technician did not understand it and Tiga-belas said to him:

"I'm putting the girl's whole lifetime into one-third of a millisecond at top power. It will drain over into the mouse-brain inside this cube. What is the normal human reaction within one-third millisecond?"

"Fifteen milliseconds—" The second technician started to speak and stopped himself.

"That's right," said Tiga-belas. "People don't get anything at all in less than fifteen milliseconds. This mouse isn't only veneered and laminated; *he's fast*. The lamination is faster than his own synapses ever were. Bring on the girl."

The first technician had already gone to get her.

The second technician turned back for one more question. "Is the mouse dead?"

"No. Yes. Of course not. What do you mean? Who knows?" said Tiga-belas all in one breath.

The younger man stared but the couch with the beautiful girl had already rolled into the room. Her skin had chilled down from pink to ivory and her respiration was no longer visible to the naked eye, but she was still beautiful. The deep freezing had not yet begun.

The first technician began to whistle. "Mouse—forty megadynes, one-third of a millisecond. Girl, output maximum, same time. Girl input, two minutes, what volume?"

"Anything," said Tiga-belas. "Anything. Whatever you use for deep personality engraving."

"Set," said the technician.

"Take the cube," said Tiga-belas.

The technician took it and fitted it into the coffinlike box near the girl's head.

"Good-bye, immortal mouse," said Tiga-belas. "Think about the beautiful girl when I am dead and don't get too tired of *Marcia and the Moon Men* when you've seen it for a million years . . ."

"Record," said the second technician. He took it from Tiga-belas and put it into a standard drama-shower, but one with output cables heavier than any home had ever installed.

"Do you have a code word?" said the first technician.

"It's a little poem," said Tiga-belas. He reached in his pocket. "Don't read it aloud. If any of us misspoke a word, there is a chance she might hear it and it would heterodyne the relationship between her and the laminated mouse."

The two looked at a scrap of paper. In clear, archaic writing there appeared the lines:

> *Lady if a man*
> *Tries to bother you, you can*
> *Think blue,*
> *Count two,*
> *And look for a red shoe.*

The technicians laughed warmly. "That'll do it," said the first technician.

Tiga-belas gave them an embarrassed smile of thanks.

"Turn them both on," he said. "Good-bye, girl," he murmured to himself. "Good-bye, mouse. Maybe I'll see you in seventy-four years."

The room flashed with a kind of invisible light inside their heads. In moon orbit a navigator wondered about his mother's red shoes. Two million people on Earth started to count "one-two" and then wondered why they had done so.

A bright young parakeet, in an orbital ship, began reciting the whole verse and baffled the crew as to what the meaning might be.

Apart from this, there were no side-effects.

The girl in the coffin arched her body with terrible strain. The electrodes had scorched the skin at her temples. The scars stood bright red against the chilled fresh skin of the girl.

The cube showed no sign from the dead-live live-dead mouse.

While the second technician put ointment on Veesey's scars, Tiga-belas put on a headset and touched the terminals of the cube very gently without moving it from the snap-in position it held in the coffin-shaped box.

He nodded, satisfied. He stepped back.

"You're sure the girl got it?"

"We'll read it back before she goes to deep-freeze."

"*Marcia and the Moon Men,* what?"

"Can't miss it," said the first technician. "I'll let you know if there's anything missing. There won't be."

Tiga-belas took one last look at the lovely, lovely girl. Seventy-three years, two months, three days, he thought to himself. And she, beyond Earth rules, may be awarded a thousand years. And the mouse-brain has got a million years.

Veesey never knew any of them—neither the first technician, nor the second technician, nor Tiga-belas, the psychological guard.

To the day of her death, she knew that *Marcia and the Moon Men* had included the most wonderful blue lights, the hypnotic count of "one-two, one-two" and the prettiest red shoes that any girl had seen on or off Earth.

∽ III ∾

Three hundred and twenty-six years later she had to wake up.

Her box had opened.

Her body ached in every muscle and nerve.

The ship was screaming emergency and she had to get up.

She wanted to sleep, to sleep, or to die.

The ship kept screaming.

She had to get up.

She lifted an arm to the edge of her coffin-bed. She had practiced getting in and out of the bed in the long training period before they sent her underground to be hypnotized and frozen. She knew just what to reach for, just what to expect. She pulled herself over on her side. She opened her eyes.

The lights were yellow and strong. She closed her eyes again.

This time a voice sounded from somewhere near her. It seemed to be saying, "Take the straw in your mouth."

Veesey groaned.

The voice kept on saying things.

Something scratchy pressed against her mouth.

She opened her eyes.

The outline of a human head had come between her and the light.

She squinted, trying to see if it might be one more of the doctors. No, this was the ship.

The face came into focus.

It was the face of a very handsome and very young man. His eyes looked into hers. She had never seen any-one who was both handsome and sympathetic, quite the way that he was. She tried to see him clearly, and found herself beginning to smile.

The drinking-tube thrust past her lips and teeth. Automatically she sucked at it. The fluid was something like soup, but it had a medicinal taste too.

The face had a voice. "Wake up," he said, "wake up. It doesn't do any good to hold back now. You need some exercise as soon as you can manage it."

She let the tube slip from her mouth and gasped, "Who are you?"

"Trece," he said, "and that's Talatashar over there. We've been up for two months, rescuing the robots. We need your help."

"Help," she murmured, "my help?"

Trece's face wrinkled and crinkled in a delightful grin. "Well, we sort of needed you. We really do need a third mind to watch the robots when we think we've fixed them. And besides, we're lonely. Talatashar and I aren't much company to each other. We looked over the list of reserve crew and we decided to wake you." He reached out a friendly hand to her.

When she sat up she saw the other man, Talatashar. She immediately recoiled: she had never seen anyone so ugly. His hair was gray and cropped. Piggy little eyes peered out of eye-sockets which looked flooded with fat. His cheeks hung down in monstrous jowls on either side. On top of all that, his face was lopsided. One side seemed wide awake but the other was twisted in an endless spasm which looked like agony. She could not help putting her hand to her mouth. And it was with the back of her hand against her lips that she spoke.

"I thought—I thought everybody on this ship was supposed to be handsome."

One side of Talatashar's face smiled at her while the other half stayed with its expression of frozen hurt.

"We were," his voice rumbled, and it was not of itself an unpleasant voice, "we all were. Some of us always get spoiled in the freezing. It will take you a while to get used to me." He laughed grimly. "It took *me* a while to get used to me. In two months, I've managed. Pleased to meet you. Maybe you'll be pleased to meet me, after a while. What do you think of that, eh, Trece?"

"What?" said Trece, who had watched them both with friendly worry.

"The girl. So tactful. The direct diplomacy of the very

young. Was I handsome, she said. No, say I. What is she, anyhow?"

Trece turned to her. "Let me help you sit," he said.

She sat up on the edge of her box.

Wordlessly he passed the skin of fluid to her with its drinking tube, and she went back to sucking her broth. Her eyes peered up at the two men like the eyes of a small child. They were as innocent and troubled as the eyes of a kitten which has met worry for the first time.

"What are you?" said Trece.

She took her lips away from the tube for a moment. "A girl," she said.

Half of Talatashar's face smiled a sophisticated smile. The other half moved a little with muscular drag, but expressed nothing. "We see that," said he, grimly.

"He means," said Trece conciliatorily, "what have you been trained for?"

She took her mouth away again. "Nothing," said she.

The men laughed—both of them. First, Trece laughed with all the evil in the world in his voice. Then Talatashar laughed, and he was too young to laugh his own way. His laughter, too, was cruel. There was something masculine, mysterious, threatening, and secret in it, as though he knew all about things which girls could find out only at the cost of pain and humiliation. He was as alien, for the moment, as men have always been from women: filled with secret motives and concealed desires, driven by bright sharp thoughts which women neither had nor wished to have. Perhaps more than his body had spoiled.

There was nothing in Veesey's own life to make her

fear that laugh, but the instinctive reaction of a million years of womanhood behind her was to disregard the evil, go on the alert for more trouble, and hope for the best at the moment. She knew, from books and tapes, all about sex. This laugh had nothing to do with babies or with love. There was contempt and power and cruelty in it—the cruelty of men who are cruel merely because they are men. For an instant she hated both of them, but she was not alarmed enough to set off the trigger of the protective devices which the psychological guard had built into her mind itself. Instead, she looked down the cabin, ten meters long and four meters wide.

This was home now, perhaps forever. There were sleepers somewhere, but she did not see their boxes. All she had was this small space and the two men—Trece with his warm smile, his nice voice, his interesting gray-blue eyes; and Talatashar, with his ruined face. And their laughter. That wretchedly mysterious masculine laughter, hostile and laughing-at in its undertones.

Life's life, she thought, and I must live it. Here.

Talatashar, who had finished laughing, now spoke in a very different voice.

"There will be time for the fun and games later. First, we have to get the work done. The photonic sails aren't picking up enough starlight to get us anywhere. The mainsail is ripped by a meteor. We can't repair it, not when it's twenty miles across. So we have to jury-rig the ship—that's the right old word."

"How does it work?" asked Veesey sadly, not much interested in her own question. The aches and pains of the long freeze were beginning to bedevil her.

Talatashar said, "It's simple. The sails are coated. We were put into orbit by rockets. The pressure of light is bigger on one side than on the other. With some pressure on one side and virtually no pressure on the other, the ship has to go somewhere. Interstellar matter is very fine and does not give us enough drag to slow us down. The sails pull away from the brightest source of light at any time. For the first eighty years it was the sun. Then we began trying to get both the sun and some bright patches of light behind it. Now we have more light coming at us than we want, and we will be pulled away from our destination if we do not point the blind side of the sails at the goal and the pushing sides at the next best source. The sailor died, for some reason we can't figure out. The ship's automatic mechanism woke us up and the navigation board explained the situation to us. Here we are. We have to fix the robots."

"But what's the matter with them? Why don't they do it themselves? Why did they have to wake up people? They're supposed to be so smart." She particularly wondered, Why did they have to wake up *me*? But she suspected the answer—that the men had done it, not the robots—and she did not want to make them say it. She still remembered how their masculine laughter had turned ugly.

"The robots weren't programmed to tear up sails—only to fix them. We've got to condition them to accept the damage that we want to leave, and to go ahead with the new work which we are adding."

"Could I have something to eat?" asked Veesey.

"Let me get it!" cried Trece.

"Why not?" said Talatashar.

While she ate, they went over the proposed work in detail, the three of them talking it out calmly. Veesey felt more relaxed. She had the sensation that they were taking her in as a partner.

By the time they completed their work schedules, they were sure it would take between thirty-five and forty-two normal days to get the sails stiffened and re-hung. The robots did the outside work, but the sails were seventy thousand miles long by twenty thousand miles wide.

Forty-two days!

The work was not forty-two days at all.

It was one year and three days before they finished.

The relationships in the cabin had not changed much. Talatashar left her alone except to make ugly remarks. Nothing he had found in the medicine cabinet had made him look any better, but some of the things drugged him so that he slept long and well.

Trece had long since become her sweetheart, but it was such an innocent romance that it might have been conducted on grass, under elms, at the edge of an Earthside silky river.

Once she had found them fighting and had exclaimed: "Stop it! Stop it! You can't!"

When they did stop hitting each other, she said wonderingly:

"I thought you *couldn't*. Those boxes. Those safeguards. Those things they put in with us."

And Talatashar said, in a voice of infinite ugliness and finality, "That's what *they* thought. I threw those things out of the ship months ago. Don't want them around."

The effect on Trece was dramatic, as bad as if he had walked into one of the Ancient Unselfing Grounds unaware. He stood utterly still, his eyes wide and his voice filled with fear when, at last, he did speak.

"So—that's—why—we—fought!"

"You mean the boxes? They're gone, all right."

"But," gasped Trece, "each was protected by each one's box. We were all protected—from ourselves. God help us all!"

"What is God?" said Talatashar.

"Never mind. It's an old word. I heard it from a robot. But what are we going to do? What are *you* going to do?" said he accusingly to Talatashar.

"Me," said Talatashar,. "I'm doing nothing. Nothing has happened." The working side of his face twisted in a hideous smile.

Veesey watched both of them.

She did not understand it, but she feared it, that unspecific danger.

Talatashar gave them his ugly, masculine laugh, but this time Trece did not join him. He stared open-mouthed at the other man.

Talatashar put on a show of courage and indifference. "Shift's up," he said, "and I'm turning in."

Veesey nodded and tried to say good night but no words came. She was frightened and inquisitive. Of the two, feeling inquisitive was worse. There were thirty-odd thousand people all around her, but only these two were alive and present. They knew something which she did not know.

Talatashar made a brave show of it by bidding her,

"Mix up something special for the big eating tomorrow. Mind you do it, girl."

He climbed into the wall.

When Veesey turned toward Trece, it was he who fell into her arms.

"I'm frightened," he said. "We can face anything in space, but we can't face us. I'm beginning to think that the sailor killed himself. *His* psychological guard broke down too. And now we're all alone with just us."

Veesey looked instinctively around the cabin. "It's all the same as before. Just the three of us, and this little room, and the Up-and-Out outside."

"Don't you see it, darling?" He grabbed her by the shoulders. "The little boxes protected us from ourselves. And now there aren't any. We are helpless. There isn't anything here to protect us from us. What hurts man like man? What kills people like people? What danger to us could be more terrible than ourselves?"

She tried to pull away. "It's not that bad."

Without answering he pulled her to him. He began tearing at her clothes. The jacket and shorts, like his own, were omni-textile and fitted tight. She fought him off but she was not the least bit frightened. She was sorry for him, and at this moment the only thing that worried her was that Talatashar might wake up and try to help her. That would be too much.

Trece was not hard to stop.

She got him to sit down and they drifted into the big chair together.

His face was as tear-stained as her own.

That night, they did not make love.

In whispers, in gasps, he told her the story of *Old Twenty-two*. He told her that people poured out among the stars and that the ancient things inside people woke up, so that the deeps of their minds were more terrible than the blackest depth of space. Space never committed crimes. It just killed. Nature could transmit death, but only man could carry crime from world to world. Without the boxes, they looked into the bottomless depths of their own unknown selves.

She did not really understand, but she tried as well as she possibly could.

He went to sleep—it was long after his shift should have ended—murmuring over and over again:

"Veesey, Veesey, protect me from me! What can I do now, now, now, so that I won't do something terrible later on? What *can* I do? *Now* I'm afraid of me, Veesey, and afraid of *Old Twenty-two*. Veesey, Veesey, you've got to save me from me. What can I do now, now, now . . . ?"

She had no answer and after he slept, she slept. The yellow lights burned brightly on them both. The robot-board, reading that no human being was in the "on" position, assumed complete control of the ship and sails.

Talatashar woke them in the morning.

No one that day, nor any of the succeeding days, said anything about the boxes. There was nothing to say.

But the two men watched each other like unrelated beasts and Veesey herself began watching them in turn. Something wrong and vital had come into the room, some exuberance of life which she had never known existed. It did not smell; she could not see it; she could not reach it with her fingers. It was something real, nevertheless. Perhaps it was what people once called *danger*.

She tried to be particularly friendly to both the men. It made the feeling diminish within her. But Trece became surly and jealous and Talatashar smiled his untruthful lopsided smile.

∞ IV ∞

Danger came to them by surprise.

Talatashar's hands were on her, pulling her out of her own sleeping-box.

She tried to fight but he was as remorseless as an engine.

He pulled her free, turned her around, and let her float in the air. She would not touch the floor for a minute or two, and he obviously counted on getting control of her again. As she twisted in the air, wondering what had happened, she saw Trece's eyes rolling as they followed her movement. Only a fraction of a second later did she realize that she saw Trece too. He was tied up with emergency wire, and the wire which bound him was tied to one of the stanchions in the wall. He was more helpless than she.

A cold deep fear came upon her.

"Is this a crime?" she whispered to the empty air. "Is this what crime is, what you are doing to me?"

Talatashar did not answer her, but his hands took a firm terrible grip on her shoulders. He turned her around. She slapped at him. He slapped her back, hitting so hard that her jaw felt like a wound.

She had hurt herself accidentally a few times; the doctor-robots had always hurried to her aid. But no other human being had ever hurt her. Hurting people—why, that wasn't done, except for the games of men! It wasn't done. It couldn't happen. It did.

All in a rush she remembered what Trece had told her about *Old Twenty-two*, and about what happened to people when they lost their own outsides in space and began making up evil from the people-insides which, after a million and more years of becoming human, still followed them everywhere—even into space itself.

This was crime come back to man.

She managed to say it to Talatashar. "You are going to commit crimes? On this ship? With me?"

His expression was hard to read, with half of his face frozen in a perpetual rictus of unfulfilled laughter. They were facing each other now. Her face was feverish from the pain of his slap, but the good side of his face showed no corresponding imprint of pain from having been struck by her. It showed nothing but strength, alertness, and a kind of attunement which was utterly and unimaginably wrong.

At last he answered her, and it was as if he wandered among the wonders of his own soul.

"I'm going to do what I please. What *I* please. Do you understand?"

"Why don't you just ask us?" she managed to say. "Trece and I will do anything you want. We're all alone in this little ship, millions of miles from nowhere. Why shouldn't we do what you want? Let him go. And talk to me. We'll do what you want. Anything. You have rights too."

His laugh was close to a crazy scream.

He put his face close to her and hissed at her so sharply that droplets of his spittle sprayed against her cheek and ear.

"I don't want rights!" he shouted at her. "I don't want what's mine. I don't want to do right. Do you think I haven't heard the two of you, night after night, making soft loving sounds when the cabin has gone dark? Why do you think I threw the cubes out of the ship? Why do you think I needed power?"

"I don't know," she said, sadly and meekly. She had not given up hope. As long as he was talking he might talk himself out and become reasonable again. She had heard of robots blowing their circuits, so that they had to be hunted down by other robots. But she had never thought that it might happen to people too.

Talatashar groaned. The history of man was in his groan—the anger at life, which promises so much and gives so little, and despair about time, which tricks man while it shapes him. He sat back on the air and let himself drift toward the floor of the cabin, where the magnetic carpeting drew the silky iron filaments in their clothing.

"You're thinking he'll get over this, aren't you?" said he, speaking of himself.

She nodded.

"You're thinking he'll get reasonable and let both of us alone, aren't you?"

She nodded again.

"You're thinking—Talatashar, he'll get well when we arrive at Wereld Schemering, and the doctors will fix his face, and then we'll all be happy again. That's what you're thinking, isn't it?"

She still nodded. Behind her she heard Trece give a loud groan against his gag, but she did not dare take her eyes off Talatashar and his spoiled, horrible face.

"Well, it won't be that way, Veesey," he said. The finality in his voice was almost calm.

"Veesey, you're not going to get there. I'm going to do what I have to do. I'm going to do things to you that no one ever did in space before, and then I'm going to throw your body out the disposal door. But I'll let Trece watch it all before I kill him too. And then, do you know what I'll do?"

Some strange emotion—it was probably fear—began tightening the muscles in her throat. Her mouth had become dry. She barely managed to croak, "No, I don't know what you'll do then . . ."

Talatashar looked as though he were staring inward.

"I don't either," said he, "except that it's not something I want to do. I don't want to do it at all. It's cruel and messy and when I get through I won't have you and him to talk to. But this is something I have to do. It's justice, in a strange way. You've got to die because you're bad. And I'm bad too; but if you die, I won't be so bad."

He looked up at her brightly, almost as though he were normal. "Do you know what I'm talking about? Do you understand any of it?"

"No. No. No," Veesey stammered, but she could not help it.

Talatashar stared not at her but at the invisible face of his crime-to-come and said, almost cheerfully:

"You might as well understand. It's you who will die for it, and then him. Long ago you did me a wrong, a dirty, intolerable wrong. It wasn't the you who's sitting here. You're not big enough or smart enough to do anything as awful as the things that were done to me. It wasn't this you who did it, it was the real, true you instead. And now you are going to be cut and burned and choked and brought back with medicines and cut and choked and hurt again, as long as your body can stand it. And when your body stops, I'm going to put on an emergency suit and shove your dead body out into space with him. He can go out alive, for all I care. Without a suit, he'll last two gasps. And then part of my justice will be done. That's what people have called crime. It's just justice, private justice that comes out of the deep insides of man. Do you understand, Veesey?"

She nodded. She shook her head. She nodded again. She didn't know how to respond.

"And then there are more things which I'll have to do," he went on, with a sort of purr. "Do you know what there is outside this ship, waiting for my crime?"

She shook her head, and so he answered himself.

"There are thirty thousand people following in their pods behind this ship. I'll pull them in by two and two and I will get young girls. The others I'll throw loose in space. And with the girls I'll find out what it is—what it is I've always had to do, and never knew. Never knew, Veesey, till I found myself out in space with you."

His voice almost went dreamy as he lost himself in his own thoughts. The twisted side of his face showed its endless laugh, but the mobile side looked thoughtful and melancholy, so that she felt there was something inside him which might be understood, if only she had the quickness and the imagination to think of it.

Her throat still dry, she managed to half-whisper at him:

"Do you hate me? Why do you want to hurt me? Do you hate girls?"

"I don't hate girls," he blazed, "I hate *me*. Out here in space I found it out. You're not a person. Girls aren't people. They are soft and pretty and cute and cuddly and warm, but they have no feelings. I was handsome before my face spoiled, but that didn't matter. I always knew that girls weren't people. They're something like robots. They have all the power in the world and none of the worry. Men have to obey, men have to beg, men have to suffer, because they are built to suffer and to be sorry and to obey. All a girl has to do is to smile her pretty smile or to cross her pretty legs, and the man gives up everything he has ever wanted and fought for, just to be her slave. And then the girl"—and at this point he got to screaming again, in a high shrill shout—"and then the girl gets to be a woman and she has children, more girls to pester men, more men to be the victims of girls, more cruelty and more slaves. You're so cruel to me, Veesey! You're so cruel that you don't even know you're cruel. If you'd known how I wanted you, you'd have suffered like a person. But you didn't suffer. You're a girl. Well, you're going to find out now. You will suffer and then you will die. But you won't die until you know how men feel about women."

"Tala," she said, using the nickname they had so rarely used to him, "Tala, that's not so. I never meant you to suffer."

"Of course you didn't," he snapped. "Girls don't know what they do. That's what makes them girls. They're worse than snakes, worse than machines." He was mad, crazy-mad, in the outer deep of space. He stood up so suddenly that he shot through the air and had to catch himself on the ceiling.

A noise in the side of the cabin made them both turn for a moment. Trece was trying to break loose from his bonds. It did no good. Veesey flung herself toward Trece, but Talatashar caught her by the shoulder. He twisted her around. His eyes blazed at her out of his poor, misshapen face.

Veesey had sometime wondered what death would be like. She thought:

This is it.

Her body still fought Talatashar, there in the spaceboat cabin. Trece groaned behind his shackles and his gag. She tried to scratch at Talatashar's eyes, but the thought of death made her seem far away. Far away, inside herself.

Inside herself, where other people could not reach, ever—no matter what happened.

Out of that deep nearby remoteness, words came into her head:

> *Lady if a man*
> *Tries to bother you, you can*
> > *Think blue,*
> > *Count two,*
> *And look for a red shoe.*

Thinking blue was not hard. She just imagined the yellow cabin lights turning blue. Counting "one-two" was the simplest thing in the world. And even with Talatashar straining to catch her free hand, she managed to remember the beautiful, beautiful red shoes which she had seen in *Marcia and the Moon Men*.

The lights dimmed momentarily and a huge voice roared at them from the control board.

"Emergency, top emergency! People! People out of repair!"

Talatashar was so astonished that he let her go.

The board whined at them like a siren. It sounded as though the computer had become flooded with weeping.

In an utterly different voice from his impassioned talkative rage, Talatashar looked directly at her and asked, very soberly, "Your cube. Didn't I get your cube too?"

There was a knocking on the wall. A knocking from the millions of miles of emptiness outside. A knocking out of nowhere.

A person they had never seen before stepped into the ship, walking through the double wall as though it had been nothing more than a streamer of mist.

It was a man. A middle-aged man, sharp of face, strong in torso and limbs, clad in very old-style clothes. In his belt he had a whole collection of weapons, and in his hand a whip.

"You there," said the stranger to Talatashar, "untie that man."

He gestured with the whip-butt toward Trece, still bound and gagged.

Talatashar got over his surprise.

"You're a cube-ghost. You're not real!"

The whip hissed in the air and a long red welt appeared on Talatashar's wrist. The drops of blood began to float beside him in the air before he could speak again.

Veesey could say nothing; her mind and body seemed to be blanking out.

As she sank to the floor, she saw Talatashar shake himself, walk over to Trece, and begin untying the knots.

When Talatashar got the gag out of Trece's mouth, Trece spoke—not to him, but to the stranger:

"Who are you?"

"I do not exist," said the stranger, "but I can kill you, any of you, if I wish. You had better do as I say. Listen carefully. You too," he added, turning halfway around and looking at Veesey. "You listen too, because it's you who called me."

All three listened. The fight was gone out of them. Trece rubbed his wrists and shook his hands to get the circulation going in them again.

The stranger turned, in courtly and elegant fashion, so that he spoke most directly to Talatashar.

"I derive from the young lady's cube. Did you notice the lights dim? Tiga-belas left a false cube in her freeze-box but he hid me in the ship. When she thought the key notions at me, there was a fraction of a microvolt which called for more power at my terminals. I am made from the brain of some small animal, but I bear the personality and the strength of Tiga-belas. I shall last a billion years. When the current came on full power, I became operative as a distortion in your minds. I do not exist," said he, specifically addressing himself to Talatashar, "but if I needed to take out my imaginary pistol and to shoot you in the head with it, my control is so strong that your bone would comply with my command. The hole would appear in your head and your blood and your brains would pour out, just as much as blood is pouring from your hand just now. Look at your hand and believe me, if you wish."

Talatashar refused to look.

The stranger went on in a very deliberate tone. "No bullet would come from my pistol, no ray, no blast, nothing. Nothing at all. But your flesh would believe me, even if your thoughts did not. Your bone structure would believe me, whether you thought so or not. I am communicating to every separate single cell in your body, to everything which I feel to be alive. If I think *bullet* at you, your bone will pull aside for the imaginary wound. Your skin will part, your blood will pour out, your brains will splash. They will not do it by physical force but by communication from me. Communication direct, you fool. That may not be real violence, but it serves my purpose just as well. Now do you understand me? Look at your wrist."

Talatashar did not avert his eyes from the stranger. In an odd cold voice he said, "I believe you. I guess I am crazy. Are you going to kill me?"

"I don't know," said the stranger.

Trece said, "Please, are you a person or machine?"

"I don't know," said the stranger to him too.

"What's your name?" asked Veesey. "Did you get a name when they made you and sent you with us?"

"My name," said the stranger, with a bow to her, "is Sh'san."

"Glad to meet you, Sh'san," said Trece, holding out his own hand.

They shook hands.

"I felt your hand," said Trece. He looked at the other

two in amazement. "I felt his hand, I really did. What were you doing out in space all this time?"

The stranger smiled. "I have work to do, not talk to make."

"What do you want us to do," said Talatashar, "now that you've taken over?"

"I haven't taken over," said Sh'san, "and you will do what you have to do. Isn't that the nature of people?"

"But, please—" said Veesey.

The stranger had vanished and the three of them were alone in the spaceboat cabin again. Trece's gag and bindings had finally drifted down to the carpet but Tala's blood hung gently in the air beside him.

Very heavily, Talatashar spoke. "Well, we're through that. Would you say I was crazy?"

"Crazy?" said Veesey. "I don't know the word."

"Damaged in the thinking," explained Trece to her. Turning to Talatashar he began to speak seriously. "I think that—" He was interrupted by the control board. Little bells rang and a sign lighted up. They all saw it. *Visitors expected,* said the glowing sign.

The storage door opened and a beautiful woman came into the cabin with them. She looked at them as though she knew them all. Veesey and Trece were inquisitive and startled, but Talatashar turned white, dead white.

∾ **V** ∾

Veesey saw that the woman wore a dress of the style which had vanished a generation ago—a style now seen only in the story-boxes. There was no back to it. The lady had a bold cosmetic design fanning out from her spinal column. In front, the dress hung from the usual magnet tabs which had been inserted into the shallow fatty area of the chest, but in her case the tabs were above the clavicles, so that the dress rose high, with an air of old-fashioned prudishness. Magnet tabs were at the usual place just below the ribcage, holding the half-skirt, which was very full, in a wide sweep of unpressed pleats. The lady wore a necklace and matching bracelet of off-world coral. The lady did not even look at Veesey. She went straight to Talatashar and spoke to him with peremptory love.

"Tal, be a good boy. You've been bad."

"Mama," gasped Talatashar. "Mama, you're dead!"

"Don't argue with me," she snapped. "Be a good boy. Take care of the little girl. Where is the little girl?" She looked around and saw Veesey. "That little girl," she added, "be a good boy to *that* little girl. If you don't, you will break your mother's heart, you will ruin your mother's life, you will break your mother's heart, just like your father did. Don't make me tell you twice."

She leaned over and kissed him on the forehead, and it seemed to Veesey that both sides of the man's face were equally twisted, for that moment.

She stood up, looked around, nodded politely at Trece and Veesey, and walked back into the storage room, closing the door after her.

Talatashar plunged after her, opening the door with a bang and shutting it with a slam. Trece called after him:

"Don't stay in there too long. You'll freeze."

Trece added, speaking to Veesey, "This is something

your cube is doing. That Sh'san, he's the most powerful warden I ever saw. Your psychological guard must have been a genius. And you know what's the matter with *him*?" He nodded at the closed door. "He told me once, just in general. His own mother raised him. He was born in the asteroid belt and she didn't turn him in."

"You mean, his very own mother?" said Veesey.

"Yes, his genealogical mother," said Trece.

"How *dirty!*" said Veesey. "I never heard of anything like it."

Talatashar came back into the room and said nothing to either of them.

The mother did not reappear.

But Sh'san, the eidetic man imprinted in the cube, continued to assert his authority over all three of them.

Three days later Marcia herself appeared, talked to Veesey for half an hour about her adventures with the Moon Men, and then disappeared again. Marcia never pretended that she was real. She was too pretty to be real. A thick cascade of yellow hair crowned a well-formed head; dark eyebrows arched over vivid brown eyes; and an enchantingly mischievous smile pleased Veesey, Trece, and Talatashar. Marcia admitted that she was the imaginary heroine of a dramatic series from the story-boxes. Talatashar had calmed down completely after the apparition of Sh'san followed by that of his mother. He seemed anxious to get to the bottom of the phenomena. He tried to do it by asking Marcia.

She answered his questions willingly.

"What are you?" he demanded. The friendly smile on

the good side of his face was more frightening than a
scowl would have been.

"I'm a little girl, silly," said Marcia.

"But you're not real," he insisted.

"No," she admitted, "but are you?" She laughed a happy
girlish laugh—the teen-ager tying up the bewildered adult
in his own paradox.

"Look," he persisted, "you know what I mean. You're
just something that Veesey saw in the story-boxes and
you've come to give her imaginary red shoes."

"You can feel the shoes after I've left," said Marcia.

"That means the cube has made them out of something on this ship," said Talatashar, very triumphantly.

"Why not?" said Marcia. "I don't know about ships. I
guess he does."

"But even if the shoes are real, you're not," said
Talatashar. "Where do you go when you 'leave' us?"

"I don't know," said Marcia. "I came here to visit
Veesey. When I go away I suppose that I·will be where I
was before I came."

"And where was that?"

"Nowhere," said Marcia, looking solid and real.

"Nowhere? So you admit you're nothing?"

"I will if you want me to," said Marcia, "but this conversation doesn't make much sense to me. Where were
you before you were here?"

"Here? You mean in this boat? I was on Earth," said
Talatashar.

"Before you were in this universe, where were you?"

"I wasn't born, so I didn't exist."

"Well," said Marcia, "it's the same with me, only a

little bit different. Before I existed I didn't exist. When I exist, I'm here. I'm an echo out of Veesey's personality and I'm helping her to remember that she is a pretty young girl. I feel as real as you feel. So there!"

Marcia went back to talking about her adventures with the Moon Men and Veesey was fascinated to hear all the things they had had to leave out of the story-box version. When Marcia was through, she shook hands with the two men, gave Veesey a little peck of a kiss on her left cheek, and walked through the hull into the gnawing emptiness of space, marked only by the starless rhomboids of the sails which cut off part of the heavens from view.

Talatashar pounded his fist in his other, open hand. "Science has gone too far. They will kill us with their precautions."

Trece said, deadly calm, "And what might you have done?"

Talatashar fell into a gloomy silence.

And on the tenth day after the apparitions began, they ended. The power of the cube drew itself into a whole thunderbolt of decision. Apparently the cube and the ship's computers had somehow filled in each other's data.

The person who came in this time was a space captain, gray, wrinkled, erect, tanned by the radiation of a thousand worlds.

"You know who I am," he said.

"Yes, sir, a captain," said Veesey.

"I don't know you," said Talatashar, "and I'm not sure I believe in you."

"Has your hand healed?" asked the captain, grimly.

Talatashar fell silent.

The captain called them to attention. "Listen. You are not going to live long enough to get to the stars on your present course. I want Trece to set the macro-chronography for intervals of ninety-five years, and then I want to watch while he gives two of you at a time five years on watch. That will do to set the sails, check the tangling of the pod lines, and send out report beacons. This ship should have a sailor, but there is not enough equipment to turn one of you into a sailor, so we'll have to take a chance on the robot controls while all three of you sleep in your freeze-beds. Your sailor died of a blood clot and the robots pushed him out of the cabin before they woke you—"

Trece winced. "I thought he had committed suicide."

"Not a bit," said the captain. "Now listen. You'll get through in about three sleeps if you obey orders. If you don't, you'll never get there."

"It doesn't matter about me," said Talatashar, "but this little girl has got to get to Wereld Schemering while she still has some life. One of your blasted apparitions told me to take care of her, but the idea is a good one, anyhow."

"Me too," said Trece. "I didn't realize that she was just a kid until I saw her talking to that other kid Marcia. Maybe I'll have a daughter like her some day."

The captain said nothing to these comments but gave them the full, happy smile of an old, wise man.

An hour later they were through with the checkup of the boat. The three were ready to go to their separate freeze-beds. The captain was getting ready to make his farewell.

Talatashar spoke up. "Sir, I can't help asking it, but who are you?"

"A captain," said the captain promptly.

"You know what I mean," said Tala wearily.

The captain seemed to be looking inside himself. "I am a temporary, artificial personality created out of your minds by the personality which you call Sh'san. Sh'san is on the ship, but hidden from you, so that you will do him no harm. Sh'san was imprinted with the personality of a man, a real man, by the name of Tiga-belas. Sh'san was also imprinted with the personalities of five or six good space officers, just in case those skills might be needed. A small amount of static electricity keeps Sh'san on the alert, and when he is in the right position, he has a triggering mechanism which can call for more current from the ship's supply."

"But what *is* he? What *are* you?" Talatashar kept on, almost pleading. "I was about to commit a terrible crime and you ghosts came in and saved me. Are you imaginary? Are you real?"

"That's philosophy. I'm made by science. I wouldn't know," said the captain.

"Please," said Veesey, "could you tell us what it seems like to you? Not what it is. What it seems like."

The captain sagged, as though the discipline had gone out of him—as though he suddenly felt terribly old. "When I'm talking and doing things, I suppose that I feel about like any other space captain. If I stop to think about it, I find myself pretty upsetting. I know that I'm just an echo in your minds, combined with the experience and wisdom which has gone into the cube. So I guess that I do what real people do. I just don't think about it very much. I mind my business." He stiffened and straightened and was himself again. "My own business," he repeated.

"And Sh'san," said Trece, "how do you feel about him?"

A look of awe—almost a look of terror—came upon the captain's face. "He? Oh, him." The tone of wonder enriched his voice and made it echo in the small cabin of the spaceboat. "Sh'san. He is the thinker of all thinking, the 'to be' of being, the doer of doings. He is powerful beyond your strongest imagination. He makes me come living out of your living minds. In fact," said the captain with a final snarl, "he is a dead mouse-brain laminated with plastic and I have no idea at all of who *I* am. Good night to you all!"

The captain set his cap on his head and walked straight through the hull. Veesey ran to a viewpoint but there was nothing outside the ship. Nothing. Certainly no captain.

"What can we do," said Talatashar, "but obey?"

They obeyed. They climbed into their freeze-beds. Talatashar attached the correct electrodes to Veesey and to Trece before he went to his bed and attached his own. They called to each other pleasantly as the lids came down.

They slept.

∽ VI ∽

At destination, the people of Wereld Schemering did the ingathering of pods, sails, and ship themselves. They did not wake the sleepers till they had them all assured of safety on the ground.

They woke the three cabinmates together. Veesey, Trece, and Talatashar were so busy answering questions about the dead sailor, about the repaired sails, and about their problems on the trip that they did not have time to talk to each other. Veesey saw that Talatashar seemed to be very handsome. The port doctors had done something to restore his face, so that he seemed a strangely dignified young-old man. At last Trece had a chance to talk to her.

"Good-bye, kid," he said. "Go to school for a while here and then find yourself a good man. I'm sorry."

"Sorry for what?" she said, a terrible fear rising within her.

"For smooching around with you before that trouble came. You're just a kid. But you're a good kid." He ran his fingers through her hair, turned on his heel, and was gone.

She stood, utterly forlorn, in the middle of the room. She wished that she could weep. What use had she been on the trip?

Talatashar had come up to her unnoticed.

He held out his hand. She took it.

"Give it time, child," said he.

Is it *child* again? she thought to herself. To him she said, politely, "Maybe we'll see each other again. This is a pretty small world."

His face lit up in an oddly agreeable smile. It made such a wonderful difference for the paralysis to be gone from one side. He did not look old at all, not really old.

His voice took on urgency. "Veesey, remember that I remember. I remember what almost happened. I remember what we thought we saw. Maybe we did see all those things. We won't see them on the ground. But I want you to remember this. You saved us all. Me too. And Trece, and the thirty thousand out behind."

"Me?" she said. "What did I do?"

"You tuned in help. You let Sh'san work. It all came through you. If you hadn't been honest and kind and friendly, if you hadn't been terribly intelligent, no cube could have worked. That wasn't any dead mouse working miracles on us. It was your mind and your own goodness that saved us. The cube just added the sound effects. I tell you, if you hadn't been along, two dead men would be sailing off into the Big Nothing with thirty thousand spoiling bodies trailing along behind. You saved us all. You may not know how you did it, but you did."

An official tapped him on the arm; Tala said, firmly but politely, to him, "Just a moment."

"That's it, I guess," he said to her.

A contrary spirit seized her; she had to speak, though she risked unhappiness by talking. "And what you said about girls . . . then . . . that time?"

"I remember it." His face twisted almost back to its old ugliness for a moment. "I remember it. But I was wrong. Wrong."

She looked at him and she thought in her own mind about the *blue* sky, about the *two* doors behind them, and about the *red* shoes in her luggage. Nothing miraculous happened. No Sh'san, no voices, no magic cubes.

Except that he turned around, came back to her, and said, "Look. Let's make sure that we see each other next week. These people at the desk can tell us where we are going to be, so that we'll find each other. Let's pester them."

Together they went to the immigration desk.

The Colonel Came Back from the Nothing-at-All

∾ I ∾
The Naked and Alone

We looked through the peephole of the hospital door.

Colonel Harkening had torn off his pajamas again and lay naked face down on the floor.

His body was rigid.

His face was turned sharply to the left so that the neck muscles showed. His right arm stuck out straight from the body. The elbow formed a right angle, with the forearm and hand pointing straight upward. The left arm also pointed straight out, but in this case the hand and forearm pointed downward in line with the body.

The legs were in the grotesque parody of a running position.

Except that Colonel Harkening wasn't running.

He was lying flat on the floor.

Flat, as though he were trying to squeeze himself out

of the third dimension and to lie in two planes only. Grosbeck stood back and gave Timofeyev his turn at the peephole.

"I still say he needs a naked woman," said Grosbeck. Grosbeck always went in for the elementals.

We had atropine, surgital, a whole family of the digitalinids, assorted narcotics, electrotherapy, hydrotherapy, subsonictherapy, temperature shock, audiovisual shock, mechanical hypnosis, and gas hypnosis.

None of these had had the least effect on Colonel Harkening.

When we picked the colonel up he tried to lie down.

When we put clothes on him he tore them off.

We had already brought his wife to see him. She had wept because the world had acclaimed her husband a hero, dead in the vast, frightening emptiness of space. His miraculous return had astonished seven continents on Earth and the settlements on Venus and Mars.

Harkening had been test pilot for the new device which had been developed by a team at the Research Office of the Instrumentality.

They called it a chronoplast, though a minority held out for the term planoform.

The theory of it was completely beyond me, though the purpose was simple enough. Crudely stated, the theory sought to compress living, material bodies into a two-dimensional frame while skipping the living body and its material adjuncts through two dimensions only to some inconceivably remote point in space. As our technology now stood it would have taken us a century at the least to reach Alpha Centauri, the nearest star.

Desmond, the Harkening, who held the titular rank of colonel under the Chiefs of the Instrumentality, was one of the best space navigators we had. His eyes were perfect, his mind cool, his body superb, his experience first-rate: What more could we ask?

Humanity had sent him out in a minute spaceship not much larger than the elevator in an ordinary private home. Somewhere between Earth and the Moon with millions of televideo watchers following his course, he had disappeared.

Presumably he had turned on the chronoplast and had been the first man to planoform.

We never saw his craft again.

But we found the colonel, all right.

He lay naked in the middle of Central Park in New York, which lay about a hundred miles west of the Ancient Ruins.

He lay in the grotesque position in which we had just observed him in the hospital cell, forming a sort of human starfish.

Four months had passed and we had made very little progress with the colonel.

It was not much trouble keeping him alive since we fed him by massive rectal and intravenous administrations of the requisites of medical survival. He did not oppose us. He did not fight except when we put clothes on him or tried to keep him too long out of the horizontal plane.

When kept upright too long he would awaken just enough to go into a mad, silent, gloating rage, fighting the attendants, the straitjacket, and anything else that got in his way.

We had had one hellish time in which the poor man suffered for an entire week, bound firmly in canvas and struggling every minute of the week to get free and to resume his nightmarish position.

The wife's visit last week had done no more good than I expected Grosbeck's suggestion to do this week.

The colonel paid no more attention to her than he paid to us doctors.

If he had come back from the stars, come back from the cold beyond the Moon, come back from all the terrors of the Up-and-Out, come back by means unknown to any man living, come back in a form not himself and nevertheless himself, how could we expect the crude stimuli of previous human knowledge to awaken him?

When Timofeyev and Grosbeck turned back to me after looking at him for the some-thousandth time, I told them I did not think we could make any progress with the case by ordinary means.

"Let's start all over again. This man is here. He can't be here because nobody can come back from the stars, mother-naked in his own skin, and land from outer space in Central Park so gently that he shows not the slightest abrasion from a fall. Therefore, he isn't in that room, you and I aren't talking about anything, and there isn't any problem. Is that right?"

"No," they chorused simultaneously.

I turned on Grosbeck as the more obdurate of the two. "Have it your way then. He is there, major premise. He can't be there, minor premise. We don't exist. Q.E.D. That suit you any better?"

"No, sir and doctor, Chief and Leader," said Grosbeck,

sticking to the courtesies even though he was angry. "You are trying to destroy the entire context of this case, and, by doing so, are trying to lead us even further into unorthodox methods of treatment. Lord and Heaven, sir! We can't go any further that way. This man is crazy. It doesn't matter how he got into Central Park. That's a problem for the engineers. It's not a medical problem. His craziness *is* a medical problem. We can try to cure it, or we can try not to cure it. But we won't get anywhere if we mix the medicine with the engineering—"

"It's not that bad," interjected Timofeyev gently.

As the older of my associates he had the right to address me by my short title. He turned to me. "I agree with you, sir and doctor Anderson, that the engineering is mixed up with this man's mental and physical state. After all, he is the first person to go out in a chronoplast and neither we nor the engineers nor anybody else has the faintest idea of what happened to him. The engineers can't find the machine, and we can't find his consciousness. Let's leave the machine to the engineers, but let's persevere on the medical side of the case."

I said nothing, waiting for them to let off steam until they were prepared to reason with me and not just shout at me in their desperation.

They looked at me, keeping their silence grudgingly, and trying to make me take the initiative in the unpleasant case.

"Open the cell door," I said. "He's not going to run away in that position. All he wants to do is be flat."

"Flatter than a Scotch pancake in a Chinese hell," said Grosbeck, "and you're not going to get anywhere by leaving him in his flatness. He was a human being once and the only way to make a human being be a human being is to appeal to the human being side of him, not to some imaginary flat side that got thrown into him while he was out—wherever he was."

Grosbeck himself smiled a lopsided grin; he was capable of seeing the humor of his own vehemence at times. "Shall we say he was out *underneath space,* sir and doctor, Chief and Leader?"

"That's a good way to put it," I said. "You can try your naked woman idea later on, but I frankly don't think it's going to do any good. That man isn't corticating at a level above that of the simplest invertebrates except when he's in that grotesque position. If he's not thinking, he's not seeing. If he's not seeing, he won't see a woman any more than anything else. There's nothing wrong with the body. The trouble lies in the brain. I still see it as a problem of getting into the brain."

"Or the soul," breathed Timofeyev, whose full name was Herbert Hoover Timofeyev, and who came from the most religious part of Russia. "You can't leave the soul out sometimes, doctor . . ."

We had entered the cell and stood there looking helplessly at the naked man.

The patient breathed very quietly. His eyes were open; we had not been able to make the eyes blink, even with a photoflash. The patient acquired a grotesque and elementary humanity when he was taken out of his flat position. His mind reached, intellectually speaking, a high point no higher than that of a terrorized, panicked, momentarily deranged squirrel. When clothed or out of position he fought madly, hitting indiscriminately at objects and persons.

Poor Colonel Harkening! We three were supposed to be the best doctors on Earth, and we could do nothing for him.

We had even tried to study his way of fighting to see whether the muscular and eye movements involved in the struggle revealed where he had been or what experiences he had undergone. Even that was fruitless. He fought something after the fashion of a nine-month-old infant, using his adult strength, but using it indiscriminately.

We never got a sound out of him.

He breathed hard as he fought. His sputum bubbled. Froth appeared on his lips. His hands made clumsy movements to tear away the shirts and robes and walkers which we put on him. Sometimes his fingernails or toenails tore his own skin as he got free of gloves or shoes.

He always went back to the same position:

On the floor.

Face down.

Arms and legs in swastika form.

There he was back from outer space. He was the first man to return, and yet he had not really returned.

As we stood there helpless, Timofeyev made the first serious suggestion we had gotten that day.

"Do you dare to try a secondary telepath?"

Grosbeck looked shocked.

I dared to give the subject thought. Secondary telepaths were in bad repute because they were supposed to come into the hospitals and have their telepathic capacities removed once it had been proved that they were not true telepaths with a real capacity for complete interchange.

Under the Ancient Law many of them could and did elude us.

With their dangerous part-telepathic capacities they took up charlatanism and fakery of the worst kind, pretending to talk with the dead, precipitating neurotics into psychotics, healing a few sick people and bungling ten other cases for each case that they did heal, and, in general, disturbing the good order of society.

And yet, if everything else had failed . . .

∽ II ∽
The Secondary Telepath

A day later we were back in Harkening's hospital cell, almost in the same position.

The three of us stood around the naked body on the floor.

There was a fourth person with us, a girl.

Timofeyev had found her. She was a member of his own religious group, the Post-Soviet Orthodox Eastern Quakers. You could tell when they spoke Anglic because they used the word "thou" from the Ancient English Language instead of the word "thee."

Timofeyev looked at me.

I nodded at him very quietly.

He turned to the girl. "Canst thou help him, sister?"

The child was scarcely more than twelve. She was a little girl with a long, lean face, a soft, mobile mouth, quick gray-green eyes, a mop of tan hair that fell over her shoulders. She had expressive, tapering hands. She showed no shock at all at the sight of the naked man lost in the depths of his insanity.

She knelt down on the floor and spoke gently directly into the ear of Colonel Harkening.

"Canst thou hear me, brother? I have come to help thee. I am thy sister Liana. I am thy sister under the love of God. I am thy sister born of the flesh of man. I am thy sister under the sky. I am thy sister come to help thee. I am thy sister, brother. I am thy sister. Waken a little and I can help thee. Waken a little to the words of thy sister. Waken a little for the love and the hope. Waken to let the love come in. Waken to let the love awaken thee further. Waken to let mankind get thee. Waken to return again, return again to the realm of man. The realm of man is a friendly realm. The friendship of man is a friendly thing. Thy friend is thy sister, by the name of Liana. Thy friend is here. Waken a little to the words of thy friend . . ."

As she talked on I saw that she made a gentle movement with her left hand, motioning us out of the room.

I nodded to my two colleagues, jerking my head to indicate that we should step out in the corridor. We stepped just beyond the door so that we could still look in.

The child went on with her endless chant.

Grosbeck stood rigid, glaring at her as though she were an intrusion into the field of regular medicine. Timofeyev tried to look sweet, benevolent, and spiritual; he forgot and, instead, just looked excited. I got very tired and began to wonder when I could interrupt the child. It did not seem to me that she was getting anywhere.

She herself settled the matter.

She burst into tears.

She went on talking as she wept, her voice broken with sobs, the tears from her eyes pouring down her cheeks and dropping on the face of the colonel just below her face.

The colonel might as well have been made of porcelainized concrete.

I could see his breathing, but the pupils of his eyes did not move. He was no more alive than he had been all these weeks. No more alive, and no less alive.

No change. At last the girl gave up her weeping and talking and came out to the corridor to us.

She spoke to me directly. "Art thou a brave man, Anderson, sir and doctor, Chief and Leader?"

It was a silly question. How does anybody answer a question like that? All I could say was "I suppose so. What do you want to do?"

"I want you three," said she as solemnly as a witch. "I want you three to wear the helmet of the pinlighters and ride with me into hell itself. That soul is lost. It is frozen by a force I do not know, frozen out beyond the stars, where the stars caught it and made it their own, so that the poor man and brother that thou seest is truly among us, but his soul weeps in the unholy pleasure between the stars where it is lost to the mercy of God and to the friendship of mankind. Wilt thou, O brave man, sir and doctor, Chief and Leader, ride with me to hell itself?"

What could I say but yes?

◦◦ III ◦◦
The Return

Late that night we made the return from the Nothing-at-All. There were five pinlighters' helmets, crude things, mechanical correctives to natural telepathy, devices to throw the synapses of one mind into another so that all five of us could think the same thoughts.

It was the first time that I had been in contact with the minds of Grosbeck and Timofeyev. They surprised me.

Timofeyev really was clean all the way through, as clean and simple as washed linen. He was really a very simple man. The urgencies and pressures of his everyday life did not go down to the insides.

Grosbeck was very different. He was as alive, as cackling, and as violent as a whole barnyard full of fowl: His mind was dirty in spots, clean in others. It was bright, smelly, alive, vivid, moving.

I caught an echo of my own mind from them. To Timofeyev I seemed cold, high, icy, and mysterious; to Grosbeck I looked like a solid lump of coal. He couldn't see into my mind very much and he didn't even want to.

We all sensed out toward Liana, and in reaching for the sense-of-the-mind of Liana we encountered the mind of the colonel . . .

Never have I encountered something so terrible.

It was raw pleasure.

As a doctor I have seen pleasure—the pleasure of morphine which destroys, the pleasure of fennine which kills and ruins, even the pleasure of the electrode buried in the living brain.

As a doctor I had been required to see the wickedest of men kill themselves under the law. It was a simple thing we did. We put a thin wire directly into the pleasure center of the brain. The bad man then put his head near an electric field of the right phase and voltage. It was simple enough. He died of pleasure in a few hours.

This was worse.

This pleasure was not in human form.

Liana was somewhere near and I caught her thoughts as she said, "We must go there, sirs and doctors, Chiefs and Leaders.

"We must go there together, the four of us, go to where no man was, go to the Nothing-at-All, go to the hope and the heart of the pain, go to the pain which return may this man, go to the power which is greater than space, go to the power which has sent him home, go to the place which is not a place, find the force which is not a force, force the force which is not a force to give this heart and spare it back to us.

"Come with me if you come at all. Come with me to the end of things. Come with me—"

Suddenly there was a flash as of sheet lightning in our minds.

It was bright lightning, bright, delicate, multicolored, gentle. Suffusing everything, it was like a cascade of pure color, pastel in hue, but intense in its brightness. The light came.

The light came, I say.

Strange.

And it was gone.

That was all.

The experience was so quick that it could hardly be called instantaneous. It seemed to happen less than instantaneously, if you can imagine that. We all five felt that we had been befriended, looked at. *We felt that we had been made the toys or the pets of some gigantic form of life immensely beyond the limits of human imagination, and that that life in looking at the four of us—the three doctors and Liana—had seen us and the colonel and had realized that the colonel needed to go back to his own kind.*

Because it was five, not four, who stood up.

The colonel was trembling, but he was sane. He was alive. He was human again. He said very weakly:

"Where am I? Is this an Earth hospital?"

And then he fell into Timofeyev's arms.

Liana was already gliding out the door.

I followed her out.

She turned on me. "Sir and doctor, Chief and Leader, all I ask is no thanks, and no money, no notice and no word of what has happened. My powers come from the goodness of the Lord's grace and from the friendliness of mankind. I should not intrude into the field of medicine. I should not have come if thy friend Timofeyev had not asked me as a matter of common mercy. Claim the credit for thy hospital, sir and doctor, Chief and Leader, but thou and thy friends should forget me."

I stammered at her, "But the reports? . . ."

"Write the reports any way thou wishes, but mention me not."

"But our patient. He is our patient, too, Liana."

She smiled a smile of great sweetness, of girlish and childish friendliness. "If he need me, I shall come to him . . ."

The world was better, but not much the wiser.

The chronoplast spaceship was never found. The colonel's return was never explained. The colonel never left Earth again. All he knew was that he had pushed a button out somewhere near the Moon and that he had then awakened in a hospital after four months had been unaccountably lost.

And all the world knew was that he and his wife had unaccountably adopted a strange but beautiful little girl, poor in family, but rich in the mild generosity of her own spirit.

The Game of Rat and Dragon

The Table

Pinlighting is a hell of a way to earn a living. Underhill was furious as he closed the door behind himself. It didn't make much sense to wear a uniform and look like a soldier if people didn't appreciate what you did.

He sat down in his chair, laid his head back in the headrest, and pulled the helmet down over his forehead.

As he waited for the pin-set to warm up, he remembered the girl in the outer corridor. She had looked at it, then looked at him scornfully.

"Meow." That was all she had said. Yet it had cut him like a knife.

What did she think he was—a fool, a loafer, a uniformed nonentity? Didn't she know that for every half-hour of pinlighting, he got a minimum of two months' recuperation in the hospital?

By now the set was warm. He felt the squares of space around him, sensed himself at the middle of an immense grid, a cubic grid, full of nothing. Out in that nothingness, he could sense the hollow aching horror of space itself and could feel the terrible anxiety which his mind encountered whenever it met the faintest trace of inert dust.

As he relaxed, the comforting solidity of the Sun, the clockwork of the familiar planets and the Moon rang in on him. Our own solar system was as charming and as simple as an ancient cuckoo clock filled with familiar ticking and with reassuring noises. The odd little moons of Mars swung around their planet like frantic mice, yet their regularity was itself an assurance that all was well. Far above the plane of the ecliptic, he could feel half a ton of dust more or less drifting outside the lanes of human travel.

Here there was nothing to fight, nothing to challenge the mind, to tear the living soul out of a body with its roots dripping in effluvium as tangible as blood.

Nothing ever moved in on the solar system. He could wear the pin-set forever and be nothing more than a sort of telepathic astronomer, a man who could feel the hot, warm protection of the Sun throbbing and burning against his living mind.

Woodley came in.

"Same old ticking world," said Underhill. "Nothing to report. No wonder they didn't develop the pin-set until they began to planoform. Down here with the hot Sun around us, it feels so good and so quiet. You can feel everything spinning and turning. It's nice and sharp and compact. It's sort of like sitting around home."

Woodley grunted. He was not much given to flights of fantasy.

Undeterred, Underhill went on, "It must have been

pretty good to have been an ancient man. I wonder why they burned up their world with war. They didn't have to planoform. They didn't have to go out to earn their livings among the stars. They didn't have to dodge the Rats or play the Game. They couldn't have invented pinlighting because they didn't have any need of it, did they, Woodley?"

Woodley grunted, "Uh-huh." Woodley was twenty-six years old and due to retire in one more year. He already had a farm picked out. He had gotten through ten years of hard work pinlighting with the best of them. He had kept his sanity by not thinking very much about his job, meeting the strains of the task whenever he had to meet them, and thinking nothing more about his duties until the next emergency arose.

Woodley never made a point of getting popular among the Partners. None of the Partners liked him very much. Some of them even resented him. He was suspected of thinking ugly thoughts of the Partners on occasion, but since none of the Partners ever thought a complaint in articulate form, the other pinlighters and the Chiefs of the Instrumentality left him alone.

Underhill was still full of the wonder of their job. Happily he babbled on, "What does happen to us when we planoform? Do you think it's sort of like dying? Did you ever see anybody who had his soul pulled out?"

"Pulling souls is just a way of talking about it," said Woodley. "After all these years, nobody knows whether we have souls or not."

"But I saw one once. I saw what Dogwood looked like when he came apart. There was something funny. It looked wet and sort of sticky as if it were bleeding and it went out of him—and you know what they did to Dogwood? They took him away, up in that part of the hospital where you and I never go—way up at the top part where the others are, where the others always have to go if they are alive after the Rats of the Up-and-Out have gotten them."

Woodley sat down and lit an ancient pipe. He was burning something called tobacco in it. It was a dirty sort of habit, but it made him look very dashing and adventurous.

"Look here, youngster. You don't have to worry about that stuff. Pinlighting is getting better all the time. The Partners are getting better. I've seen them pinlight two Rats forty-six million miles apart in one and a half milliseconds. As long as people had to try to work the pin-sets themselves, there was always the chance that with a minimum of four-hundred milliseconds for the human mind to set a pinlight, we wouldn't light the Rats up fast enough to protect our planoforming ships. The Partners have changed all that. Once they get going, they're faster than Rats. And they always will be. I know it's not easy, letting a Partner share your mind—"

"It's not easy for them, either," said Underhill.

"Don't worry about them. They're not human. Let them take care of themselves. I've seen more pinlighters go crazy from monkeying around with Partners than I have ever seen caught by the Rats. How many of them do you actually know of that got grabbed by Rats?"

Underhill looked down at his fingers, which shone green and purple in the vivid light thrown by the tuned-in pin-set, and counted ships. The thumb for the *Andromeda*, lost with crew and passengers, the index finger and the middle finger for *Release Ships 43* and *56*, found with their pin-sets burned out and every man, woman, and child on board dead or insane. The ring finger, the little finger, and the thumb of the other hand were the first three battleships to be lost to the Rats—lost as people realized that there was something out there *underneath space itself* which was alive, capricious, and malevolent.

Planoforming was sort of funny. It felt like—

Like nothing much.

Like the twinge of a mild electric shock.

Like the ache of a sore tooth bitten on for the first time.

Like a slightly painful flash of light against the eyes.

Yet in that time, a forty-thousand-ton ship lifting free above Earth disappeared somehow or other into two dimensions and appeared half a light-year or fifty light-years off.

At one moment, he would be sitting in the Fighting Room, the pin-set ready and the familiar solar system ticking around inside his head. For a second or a year (he could never tell how long it really was, subjectively), the funny little flash went through him and then he was loose in the Up-and-Out, the terrible open spaces between the stars, where the stars themselves felt like pimples on his telepathic mind and the planets were too far away to be sensed or read.

Somewhere in this outer space, a gruesome death awaited, death and horror of a kind which Man had never encountered until he reached out for interstellar space itself. Apparently the light of the suns kept the Dragons away.

Dragons. That was what people called them. To ordinary people, there was nothing, nothing except the shiver of planoforming and the hammer blow of sudden death or the dark spastic note of lunacy descending into their minds.

But to the telepaths, they were Dragons.

In the fraction of a second between the telepaths' awareness of a hostile something out in the black, hollow nothingness of space and the impact of a ferocious, ruinous psychic blow against all living things within the ship, the telepaths had sensed entities something like the Dragons of ancient human lore, beasts more clever than beasts, demons more tangible than demons, hungry vortices of aliveness and hate compounded by unknown means out of the thin, tenuous matter between the stars.

It took a surviving ship to bring back the news—a ship in which, by sheer chance, a telepath had a light-beam ready, turning it out at the innocent dust so that, within the panorama of his mind, the Dragon dissolved into nothing at all and the other passengers, themselves non-telepathic, went about their way not realizing that their own immediate deaths had been averted.

From then on, it was easy—almost.

Planoforming ships always carried telepaths. Telepaths had their sensitiveness enlarged to an immense range by the pin-sets, which were telepathic amplifiers adapted to the mammal mind. The pin-sets in turn were electronically geared into small dirigible light bombs. Light did it.

Light broke up the Dragons, allowed the ships to

reform three-dimensionally, skip, skip, skip, as they moved from star to star.

The odds suddenly moved down from a hundred to one against mankind to sixty to forty in mankind's favor.

This was not enough. The telepaths were trained to become ultrasensitive, trained to become aware of the Dragons in less than a millisecond.

But it was found that the Dragons could move a million miles in just under two milliseconds and that this was not enough for the human mind to activate the light beams.

Attempts had been made to sheathe the ships in light at all times.

This defense wore out.

As mankind learned about the Dragons, so too, apparently, the Dragons learned about mankind. Somehow they flattened their own bulk and came in on extremely flat trajectories very quickly.

Intense light was needed, light of sunlike intensity. This could be provided only by light bombs. Pinlighting came into existence.

Pinlighting consisted of the detonation of ultra-vivid miniature photo-nuclear bombs, which converted a few ounces of a magnesium isotope into pure visible radiance.

The odds kept coming down in mankind's favor, yet ships were being lost.

It became so bad that people didn't even want to find the ships because the rescuers knew what they would see. It was sad to bring back to Earth three hundred bodies ready for burial and two hundred or three hundred lunatics, damaged beyond repair, to be wakened, and fed,

and cleaned, and put to sleep, wakened and fed again
until their lives were ended.

Telepaths tried to reach into the minds of the psychotics
who had been damaged by the Dragons, but they found
nothing there beyond vivid spouting columns of fiery
terror bursting from the primordial id itself, the volcanic
source of life.

Then came the Partners.

Man and Partner could do together what man could
not do alone. Men had the intellect. Partners had the
speed.

The Partners rode their tiny craft, no larger than
footballs, outside the spaceships. They planoformed with
the ships. They rode beside them in their six-pound craft
ready to attack.

The tiny ships of the Partners were swift. Each carried
a dozen pinlights, bombs no bigger than thimbles.

The pinlighters threw the Partners—quite literally
threw—by means of mind-to-firing relays directly at the
Dragons.

What seemed to be Dragons to the human mind
appeared in the form of gigantic Rats in the minds of the
Partners.

Out in the pitiless nothingness of space, the Partners'
minds responded to an instinct as old as life. The Partners
attacked, striking with a speed faster than man's, going
from attack to attack until the Rats or themselves were
destroyed. Almost all the time it was the Partners who
won.

With the safety of the interstellar skip, skip, skip of the
ships, commerce increased immensely, the population of

all the colonies went up, and the demand for trained Partners increased.

Underhill and Woodley were a part of the third generation of pinlighters and yet, to them, it seemed as though their craft had endured forever.

Gearing space into minds by means of the pin-set, adding the Partners to those minds, keying up the minds for the tension of a fight on which all depended—this was more than human synapses could stand for long. Underhill needed his two months' rest after half an hour of fighting. Woodley needed his retirement after ten years of service. They were young. They were good. But they had limitations.

So much depended on the choice of Partners, so much on the sheer luck of who drew whom.

∽ II ∽
The Shuffle

Father Moontree and the little girl named West entered the room. They were the other two pinlighters. The human complement of the Fighting Room was now complete.

Father Moontree was a red-faced man of forty-five who had lived the peaceful life of a farmer until he reached his fortieth year. Only then, belatedly, did the authorities find he was telepathic and agree to let him late in life enter upon the career of pinlighter. He did well at it, but he was fantastically old for this kind of business.

Father Moontree looked at the glum Woodley and the

musing Underhill. "How're the youngsters today? Ready for a good fight?"

"Father always wants a fight," giggled the little girl named West. She was such a little little girl. Her giggle was high and childish. She looked like the last person in the world one would expect to find in the rough, sharp dueling of pinlighting.

Underhill had been amused one time when he found one of the most sluggish of the Partners coming away happy from contact with the mind of the girl named West.

Usually the Partners didn't care much about the human minds with which they were paired for the journey. The Partners seemed to take the attitude that human minds were complex and fouled up beyond belief, anyhow. No Partner ever questioned the superiority of the human mind, though very few of the Partners were much impressed by that superiority.

The Partners liked people. They were willing to fight with them. They were even willing to die for them. But when a Partner liked an individual the way, for example, that Captain Wow or the Lady May liked Underhill, the liking had nothing to do with intellect. It was a matter of temperament, of feel.

Underhill knew perfectly well that Captain Wow regarded his, Underhill's, brains as silly. What Captain Wow liked was Underhill's friendly emotional structure, the cheerfulness and glint of wicked amusement that shot through Underhill's unconscious thought patterns, and the gaiety with which Underhill faced danger. The words, the history books, the ideas, the science—Underhill could sense all that in his own mind, reflected back from Captain Wow's mind, as so much rubbish.

Miss West looked at Underhill. "I bet you've put stickum on the stones."

"I did not!"

Underhill felt his ears grow red with embarrassment. During his novitiate, he had tried to cheat in the lottery because he got particularly fond of a special Partner, a lovely young mother named Murr. It was so much easier to operate with Murr and she was so affectionate toward him that he forgot pinlighting was hard work and that he was not instructed to have a good time with his Partner. They were both designed and prepared to go into deadly battle together.

One cheating had been enough. They had found him out and he had been laughed at for years.

Father Moontree picked up the imitation-leather cup and shook the stone dice which assigned them their Partners for the trip. By senior rights he took first draw.

He grimaced. He had drawn a greedy old character, a tough old male whose mind was full of slobbering thoughts of food, veritable oceans full of half-spoiled fish. Father Moontree had once said that he burped cod liver oil for weeks after drawing that particular glutton, so strongly had the telepathic image of fish impressed itself upon his mind. Yet the glutton was a glutton for danger as well as for fish. He had killed sixty-three Dragons, more than any other Partner in the service, and was quite literally worth his weight in gold.

The little girl West came next. She drew Captain Wow. When she saw who it was, she smiled.

"I *like* him," she said. "He's such fun to fight with. He feels so nice and cuddly in my mind."

"Cuddly, hell," said Woodley. "I've been in his mind, too. It's the most leering mind in this ship, bar none."

"Nasty man," said the little girl. She said it decoratively, without reproach.

Underhill, looking at her, shivered.

He didn't see how she could take Captain Wow so calmly. Captain Wow's mind *did* leer. When Captain Wow got excited in the middle of a battle, confused images of Dragons, deadly Rats, luscious beds, the smell of fish, and the shock of space all scrambled together in his mind as he and Captain Wow, their consciousnesses linked together through the pin-set, became a fantastic composite of human being and Persian cat.

That's the trouble with working with cats, thought Underhill. It's a pity that nothing else anywhere will serve as Partner. Cats were all right once you got in touch with them telepathically. They were smart enough to meet the needs of the flight, but their motives and desires were certainly different from those of humans.

They were companionable enough as long as you thought tangible images at them, but their minds just closed up and went to sleep when you recited Shakespeare or Colegrove, or if you tried to tell them what space was.

It was sort of funny realizing that the Partners who were so grim and mature out here in space were the same cute little animals that people had used as pets for thousands of years back on Earth. He had embarrassed himself more than once while on the ground saluting perfectly ordinary non-telepathic cats because he had forgotten for the moment that they were not Partners.

He picked up the cup and shook out his stone dice.

He was lucky—he drew the Lady May.

The Lady May was the most thoughtful Partner he had ever met. In her, the finely bred pedigree mind of a Persian cat had reached one of its highest peaks of development. She was more complex than any human woman, but the complexity was all one of emotions, memory, hope, and discriminated experience—experience sorted through without benefit of words.

When he had first come into contact with her mind, he was astonished at its clarity. With her he remembered her kittenhood. He remembered every mating experience she had ever had. He saw in a half-recognizable gallery all the other pinlighters with whom she had been paired for the fight. And he saw himself radiant, cheerful, and desirable.

He even thought he caught the edge of a longing—

A very flattering and yearning thought: *What a pity he is not a cat.*

Woodley picked up the last stone. He drew what he deserved—a sullen, scarred old tomcat with none of the verve of Captain Wow. Woodley's Partner was the most animal of all the cats on the ship, a low, brutish type with a dull mind. Even telepathy had not refined his character. His ears were half chewed off from the first fights in which he had engaged. He was a serviceable fighter, nothing more.

Woodley grunted.

Underhill glanced at him oddly. Didn't Woodley ever do anything but grunt?

Father Moontree looked at the other three. "You might as well get your Partners now. I'll let the Go-Captain know we're ready to go into the Up-and-Out."

∽ III ∽
The Deal

Underhill spun the combination lock on the Lady May's cage. He woke her gently and took her into his arms. She humped her back luxuriously, stretched her claws, started to purr, thought better of it, and licked him on the wrist instead. He did not have the pin-set on, so their minds were closed to each other, but in the angle of her mustache and in the movement of her ears, he caught some sense of the gratification she experienced in finding him as her Partner.

He talked to her in human speech, even though speech meant nothing to a cat when the pin-set was not on.

"It's a damn shame, sending a sweet little thing like you whirling around in the coldness of nothing to hunt for Rats that are bigger and deadlier than all of us put together. You didn't ask for this kind of fight, did you?"

For answer, she licked his hand, purred, tickled his cheek with her long fluffy tail, turned around and faced him, golden eyes shining.

For a moment, they stared at each other, man squatting, cat standing erect on her hind legs, front claws digging into his knee. Human eyes and cat eyes looked across an immensity which no words could meet, but which affection spanned in a single glance.

"Time to get in," he said.

She walked docilely to her spheroid carrier. She climbed in. He saw to it that her miniature pin-set rested firmly and comfortably against the base of her brain. He made sure that her claws were padded so that she could not tear herself in the excitement of battle.

Softly he said to her, "Ready?"

For answer, she preened her back as much as her harness would permit and purred softly within the confines of the frame that held her.

He slapped down the lid and watched the sealant ooze around the seam. For a few hours, she was welded into her projectile until a workman with a short cutting arc would remove her after she had done her duty.

He picked up the entire projectile and slipped it into the ejection tube. He closed the door of the tube, spun the lock, seated himself in his chair, and put his own pin-set on.

Once again he flung the switch.

He sat in a small room, *small, small, warm, warm,* the bodies of the other three people moving close around him, the tangible lights in the ceiling bright and heavy against his closed eyelids.

As the pin-set warmed, the room fell away. The other people ceased to be people and became small glowing heaps of fire, embers, dark red fire, with the consciousness of life burning like old red coals in a country fireplace.

As the pin-set warmed a little more, he felt Earth just below him, felt the ship slipping away, felt the turning Moon as it swung on the far side of the world, felt the planets and the hot, clear goodness of the sun which kept the Dragons so far from mankind's native ground.

Finally, he reached complete awareness.

He was telepathically alive to a range of millions of miles. He felt the dust which he had noticed earlier high above the ecliptic. With a thrill of warmth and tenderness, he felt the consciousness of the Lady May pouring over into his own. Her consciousness was as gentle and clear and yet sharp to the taste of his mind as if it were scented oil. It felt relaxing and reassuring. He could sense her welcome of him. It was scarcely a thought, just a raw emotion of greeting.

At last they were one again.

In a tiny remote corner of his mind, as tiny as the smallest toy he had ever seen in his childhood, he was still aware of the room and the ship, and of Father Moontree picking up a telephone and speaking to a Go-Captain in charge of the ship.

His telepathic mind caught the idea long before his ears could frame the words. The actual sound followed the idea the way that thunder on an ocean beach follows the lightning inward from far out over the seas.

"The Fighting Room is ready. Clear to planoform, sir."

∾ IV ∾
The Play

Underhill was always a little exasperated the way that Lady May experienced things before he did.

He was braced for the quick vinegar thrill of planoforming, but he caught her report of it before his own nerves could register what happened.

Earth had fallen so far away that he groped for several

milliseconds before he found the Sun in the upper rear right-hand corner of his telepathic mind.

That was a good jump, he thought. *This way we'll get there in four or five skips.*

A few hundred miles outside the ship, the Lady May thought back at him, "O warm, O generous, O gigantic man! O brave, O friendly, O tender and huge Partner! O wonderful with you, with you so good, good, good, warm, warm, now to fight, now to go, good with you . . ."

He knew that she was not thinking words, that his mind took the clear amiable babble of her cat intellect and translated it into images which his own thinking could record and understand.

Neither one of them was absorbed in the game of mutual greetings. He reached out far beyond her range of perception to see if there was anything near the ship. It was funny how it was possible to do two things at once. He could scan space with his pin-set mind and yet at the same time catch a vagrant thought of hers, a lovely, affectionate thought about a son who had had a golden face and a chest covered with soft, incredibly downy white fur.

While he was still searching, he caught the warning from her.

We jump again!

And so they had. The ship had moved to a second planoform. The stars were different. The sun was immeasurably far behind. Even the nearest stars were barely in contact. This was good Dragon country, this open, nasty, hollow kind of space. He reached farther, faster, sensing and looking for danger, ready to fling the Lady May at danger wherever he found it.

Terror blazed up in his mind, so sharp, so clear, that it came through as a physical wrench.

The little girl named West had found something— something immense, long, black, sharp, greedy, horrific. She flung Captain Wow at it.

Underhill tried to keep his own mind clear. "Watch out!" he shouted telepathically at the others, trying to move the Lady May around.

At one corner of the battle, he felt the lustful rage of Captain Wow as the big Persian tomcat detonated lights while he approached the streak of dust which threatened the ship and the people within.

The lights scored near misses.

The dust flattened itself, changing from the shape of a sting ray into the shape of a spear.

Not three milliseconds had elapsed.

Father Moontree was talking human words and was saying in a voice that moved like cold molasses out of a heavy jar, "C-a-p-t-a-i-n." Underhill knew that the sentence was going to be "Captain, move fast!"

The battle would be fought and finished before Father Moontree got through talking.

Now, fractions of a millisecond later, the Lady May was directly in line.

Here was where the skill and speed of the Partners came in. She could react faster than he. She could see the threat as an immense Rat coming directly at her.

She could fire the light-bombs with a discrimination which he might miss.

He was connected with her mind, but he could not follow it.

His consciousness absorbed the tearing wound inflicted by the alien enemy. It was like no wound on Earth—raw, crazy pain which started like a burn at his navel. He began to writhe in his chair.

Actually he had not yet had time to move a muscle when the Lady May struck back at their enemy.

Five evenly spaced photonuclear bombs blazed out across a hundred-thousand miles.

The pain in his mind and body vanished.

He felt a moment of fierce, terrible, feral elation running through the mind of the Lady May as she finished her kill. It was always disappointing to the cats to find out that their enemies disappeared at the moment of destruction.

Then he felt her hurt, the pain and the fear that swept over both of them as the battle, quicker than the movement of an eyelid, had come and gone. In the same instant there came the sharp and acid twinge of planoform.

Once more the ship went skip.

He could hear Woodley thinking at him. "You don't have to bother much. This old son-of-a-gun and I will take over for a while."

Twice again the twinge, the skip.

He had no idea where he was until the lights of the Caledonia space port shone below.

With a weariness that lay almost beyond the limits of thought, he threw his mind back into rapport with the pin-set, fixing the Lady May's projectile gently and neatly in its launching tube.

She was half dead with fatigue, but he could feel the beat of her heart, could listen to her panting, and he grasped the grateful edge of a "Thanks" reaching from her mind to his.

∽ V ∽
The Score

They put him in the hospital at Caledonia.

The doctor was friendly but firm. "You actually got touched by that Dragon. That's as close a shave as I've ever seen. It's all so quick that it'll be a long time before we know what happened scientifically, but I suppose you'd be ready for the insane asylum now if the contact had lasted several tenths of a millisecond longer. What kind of cat did you have out in front of you?"

Underhill felt the words coming out of him slowly. Words were such a lot of trouble compared with the speed and the joy of thinking, fast and sharp and clear, mind to mind! But words were all that could reach ordinary people like this doctor.

His mouth moved heavily as he articulated words. "Don't call our Partners cats. The right thing to call them is Partners. They fight for us in a team. You ought to know we call them Partners, not cats. How is mine?"

"I don't know," said the doctor contritely. "We'll find out for you. Meanwhile, old man, you take it easy. There's nothing but rest that can help you. Can you make yourself sleep, or would you like us to give you some kind of sedative?"

"I can sleep," said Underhill. "I just want to know about the Lady May."

The nurse joined in. She was a little antagonistic. "Don't you want to know about the other people?"

"They're okay," said Underhill. "I knew that before I came in here."

He stretched his arms and sighed and grinned at them. He could see they were relaxing and were beginning to treat him as a person instead of a patient.

"I'm all right," he said. "Just let me know when I can go see my Partner."

A new thought struck him. He looked wildly at the doctor. "They didn't send her off with the ship, did they?"

"I'll find out right away," said the doctor. He gave Underhill a reassuring squeeze of the shoulder and left the room.

The nurse took a napkin off a goblet of chilled fruit juice.

Underhill tried to smile at her. There seemed to be something wrong with the girl. He wished she would go away. First she had started to be friendly and now she was distant again. *It's a nuisance being telepathic,* he thought. *You keep trying to reach even when you are not making contact.*

Suddenly she swung around on him.

"You pinlighters! You and your damn cats!"

Just as she stamped out, he burst into her mind. He saw himself a radiant hero, clad in his smooth suede uniform, the pin-set crown shining like ancient royal jewels around his head. He saw his own face, handsome and masculine, shining out of her mind. He saw himself very far away and he saw himself as she hated him.

She hated him in the secrecy of her own mind. She

hated him because he was—she thought—proud and strange and rich, better and more beautiful than people like her.

He cut off the sight of her mind and, as he buried his face in the pillow, he caught an image of the Lady May.

"She *is* a cat," he thought. "That's all she is—a *cat!*"

But that was not how his mind saw her—quick beyond all dreams of speed, sharp, clever, unbelievably graceful, beautiful, wordless, and undemanding.

Where would he ever find a woman who could compare with her?

The Burning of the Brain

Dolores Oh

I tell you, it is sad, it is more than sad, it is fearful—for it is a dreadful thing to go into the Up-and-Out, to fly without flying, to move between the stars as a moth may drift among the leaves on a summer night.

Of all the men who took the great ships into planoform none was braver, none stronger, than Captain Magno Taliano.

Scanners had been gone for centuries and the jonasoidal effect had become so simple, so manageable, that the traversing of light-years was no more difficult to most of the passengers of the great ships than to go from one room to the other.

Passengers moved easily.

Not the crew.

Least of all the captain.

The captain of a jonasoidal ship which had embarked on an interstellar journey was a man subject to rare and overwhelming strains. The art of getting past all the complications of space was far more like the piloting of turbulent waters in ancient days than like the smooth seas which legendary men once traversed with sails alone.

Go-Captain on the *Wu-Feinstein*, finest ship of its class, was Magno Taliano.

Of him it was said, "He could sail through hell with the muscles of his left eye alone. He could plow space with his living brain if the instruments failed . . ."

Wife to the Go-Captain was Dolores Oh. The name was Japonical, from some nation of the ancient days. Dolores Oh had been once beautiful, so beautiful that she took men's breath away, made wise men into fools, made young men into nightmares of lust and yearning. Wherever she went men had quarreled and fought over her.

But Dolores Oh was proud beyond all common limits of pride. She refused to go through the ordinary rejuvenescence. A terrible yearning a hundred or so years back must have come over her. Perhaps she said to herself, before that hope and terror which a mirror in a quiet room becomes to anyone: "Surely I am me. There must be a *me* more than the beauty of my face, there must be a something other than the delicacy of skin and the accidental lines of my jaw and my cheekbone.

"What have men loved if it wasn't me? Can I ever find out who I am or what I am if I don't let beauty perish and live on in whatever flesh age gives me?"

She had met the Go-Captain and had married him in a romance that left forty planets talking and half the ship lines stunned.

Magno Taliano was at the very beginning of his genius. Space, we can tell you, is rough—rough like the wildest of storm-driven waters, filled with perils which only the most sensitive, the quickest, the most daring of men can surmount.

Best of them all, class for class, age for age, out of class, beating the best of his seniors, was Magno Taliano.

For him to marry the most beautiful beauty of forty worlds was a wedding like Heloise and Abelard's or like the unforgettable romance of Helen America and Mr. Grey-no-more.

The ships of the Go-Captain Magno Taliano became more beautiful year by year, century by century.

As ships became better he always obtained the best. He maintained his lead over the other Go-Captains so overwhelmingly that it was unthinkable for the finest ship of mankind to sail out amid the roughnesses and uncertainties of two-dimensional space without himself at the helm.

Stop-Captains were proud to sail space beside him. (Though the Stop-Captains had nothing more to do than to check the maintenance of the ship, its loading and unloading when it was in normal space, they were still more than ordinary men in their own kind of world, a world far below the more majestic and adventurous universe of the Go-Captains.)

Magno Taliano had a niece who in the modern style used a place instead of a name: she was called "Dita from the Great South House."

When Dita came aboard the *Wu-Feinstein* she had heard much of Dolores Oh, her aunt by marriage who had once captivated the men in many worlds. Dita was wholly unprepared for what she found.

Dolores greeted her civilly enough, but the civility was a sucking pump of hideous anxiety, the friendliness was the driest of mockeries, the greeting itself an attack.

What's the matter with the woman? thought Dita.

As if to answer her thought, Dolores said aloud and in words: "It's nice to meet a woman who's not trying to take Taliano from me. I love him. Can you believe that? Can you?"

"Of course," said Dita. She looked at the ruined face of Dolores Oh, at the dreaming terror in Dolores's eyes, and she realized that Dolores had passed all limits of nightmare and had become a veritable demon of regret, a possessive ghost who sucked the vitality from her husband, who dreaded companionship, hated friendship, rejected even the most casual of acquaintances, because she feared forever and without limit that there was really nothing to herself, and feared that without Magno Taliano she would be more lost than the blackest of whirlpools in the nothing between the stars.

Magno Taliano came in.

He saw his wife and niece together.

He must have been used to Dolores Oh. In Dita's eyes Dolores was more frightening than a mud-caked reptile raising its wounded and venomous head with blind hunger and blind rage. To Magno Taliano the ghastly woman who stood like a witch beside him was somehow the beautiful girl he had wooed and had married one-hundred-sixty-four years before.

He kissed the withered cheek, he stroked the dried

and stringy hair, he looked into the greedy, terror-haunted eyes as though they were the eyes of a child he loved. He said, lightly and gently,

"Be good to Dita, my dear."

He went on through the lobby of the ship to the inner sanctum of the planoforming room.

The Stop-Captain waited for him. Outside on the world of Sherman the scented breezes of that pleasant planet blew in through the open windows of the ship.

Wu-Feinstein, finest ship of its class, had no need for metal walls. It was built to resemble an ancient, prehistoric estate named Mount Vernon, and when it sailed between the stars it was encased in its own rigid and self-renewing field of force.

The passengers went through a few pleasant hours of strolling on the grass, enjoying the spacious rooms, chatting beneath a marvelous simulacrum of an atmosphere-filled sky.

Only in the planoforming room did the Go-Captain know what happened. The Go-Captain, his pinlighters sitting beside him, took the ship from one compression to another, leaping hotly and frantically through space, sometimes one light-year, sometimes a hundred light-years, jump, jump, jump, jump until the ship, the light touches of the captain's mind guiding it, passed the perils of millions upon millions of worlds, came out at its appointed destination, and settled as lightly as one feather resting upon others, settled into an embroidered and decorated countryside where the passengers could move as easily away from their journey as if they had done nothing more than to pass an afternoon in a pleasant old house by the side of a river.

∞ II ∞
The Lost Locksheet

Magno Taliano nodded to his pinlighters. The Stop-Captain bowed obsequiously from the doorway of the planoforming room. Taliano looked at him sternly, but with robust friendliness. With formal and austere courtesy he asked,

"Sir and Colleague, is everything ready for the jonasoidal effect?"

The Stop-Captain bowed even more formally. "Truly ready, Sir and Master."

"The locksheets in place?"

"Truly in place, Sir and Master."

"The passengers secure?"

"The passengers are secure, numbered, happy and ready, Sir and Master."

Then came the last and the most serious of questions. "Are my pinlighters warmed with their pin-sets and ready for combat?"

"Ready for combat, Sir and Master." With these words the Stop-Captain withdrew. Magno Taliano smiled to his pinlighters. Through the minds of all of them there passed the same thought.

How could a man that pleasant stay married all those years to a hag like Dolores Oh? How could that witch, that horror, have ever been a beauty? How could that beast have ever been a woman, particularly the divine and glamorous Dolores Oh whose image we still see in four-di every now and then?

Yet pleasant he was, though long he may have been married to Dolores Oh. Her loneliness and greed might suck at him like a nightmare, but his strength was more than enough strength for two.

Was he not the captain of the greatest ship to sail between the stars?

Even as the pinlighters smiled their greetings back to him, his right hand depressed the golden ceremonial lever of the ship. This instrument alone was mechanical. All other controls in the ship had long since been formed telepathically or electronically.

Within the planoforming room the black skies became visible and the tissue of space shot up around them like boiling water at the base of a waterfall. Outside that one room the passengers still walked sedately on scented lawns.

From the wall facing him, as he sat rigid in his Go-Captain's chair, Magno Taliano sensed the forming of a pattern which in three or four hundred milliseconds would tell him where he was and would give him the next clue as to how to move.

He moved the ship with the impulses of his own brain, to which the wall was a superlative complement.

The wall was a living brickwork of locksheets, laminated charts, one-hundred-thousand charts to the inch, the wall preselected and preassembled for all imaginable contingencies of the journey which, each time afresh, took the ship across half-unknown immensities of time and space. The ship leapt, as it had before.

The new star focused.

Magno Taliano waited for the wall to show him where

he was, expecting (in partnership with the wall) to flick the ship back into the pattern of stellar space, moving it by immense skips from source to destination.

This time nothing happened.

Nothing?

For the first time in a hundred years his mind knew panic.

It couldn't be nothing. Not *nothing*. Something had to focus. The locksheets always focused.

His mind reached into the locksheets and he realized with a devastation beyond all limits of ordinary human grief that they were lost as no ship had ever been lost before. By some error never before committed in the history of mankind, the entire wall was made of duplicates of the same locksheet.

Worst of all, the Emergency Return sheet was lost. They were amid stars none of them had ever seen before, perhaps as near as five-hundred-million miles, perhaps as far as forty parsecs.

And the locksheet was lost.

And they would die.

As the ship's power failed coldness and blackness and death would crush in on them in a few hours at the most. That then would be all, all of the *Wu-Feinstein,* all of Dolores Oh.

∞ III ∞
The Secret of the Old Dark Brain

Outside of the planoforming room of the *Wu-Feinstein*

the passengers had no reason to understand that they were marooned in the nothing-at-all.

Dolores Oh rocked back and forth in an ancient rocking chair. Her haggard face looked without pleasure at the imaginary river that ran past the edge of the lawn. Dita from the Great South House sat on a hassock by her aunt's knees.

Dolores was talking about a trip she had made when she was young and vibrant with beauty, a beauty which brought trouble and hate wherever it went.

". . . so the guardsman killed the captain and then came to my cabin and said to me, 'You've got to marry me now. I've given up everything for your sake,' and I said to him, 'I never said that I loved you. It was sweet of you to get into a fight, and in a way I suppose it is a compliment to my beauty, but it doesn't mean that I belong to you the rest of my life. What do you think I am, anyhow?'"

Dolores Oh sighed a dry, ugly sigh, like the crackling of sub-zero winds through frozen twigs. "So you see, Dita, being beautiful the way you are is no answer to anything. A woman has got to be herself before she finds out what she is. I know that my lord and husband, the Go-Captain, loves me because my beauty is gone, and with my beauty gone there is nothing but *me* to love, is there?"

An odd figure came out on the verandah. It was a pinlighter in full fighting costume. Pinlighters were never supposed to leave the planoforming room, and it was most extraordinary for one of them to appear among the passengers.

He bowed to the two ladies and said with the utmost courtesy,

"Ladies, will you please come into the planoforming room? We have need that you should see the Go-Captain now."

Dolores's hand leapt to her mouth. Her gesture of grief was as automatic as the striking of a snake. Dita sensed that her aunt had been waiting a hundred years and more for disaster, that her aunt had craved ruin for her husband the way that some people crave love and others crave death.

Dita said nothing. Neither did Dolores, apparently at second thought, utter a word.

They followed the pinlighter silently into the planoforming room.

The heavy door closed behind them.

Magno Taliano was still rigid in his Captain's chair.

He spoke very slowly, his voice sounding like a record played too slowly on an ancient parlophone.

"*We are lost in space, my dear,*" said the frigid, ghostly voice of the Captain, still in his Go-Captain's trance. "*We are lost in space and I thought that perhaps if your mind aided mine we might think of a way back.*"

Dita started to speak.

A pinlighter told her: "Go ahead and speak, my dear. Do you have any suggestion?"

"Why don't we just go back? It would be humiliating, wouldn't it? Still it would be better than dying. Let's use the Emergency Return Locksheet and go on right back. The world will forgive Magno Taliano for a single failure after thousands of brilliant and successful trips." The pinlighter, a pleasant enough young man, was as friendly and calm as a doctor informing someone of a death or of a mutilation. "The impossible has happened, Dita from the Great South House. All the locksheets are wrong. They are all the same one. And not one of them is good for emergency return."

With that the two women knew where they were. They knew that space would tear into them like threads being pulled out of a fiber so that they would either die bit by bit as the hours passed and as the material of their bodies faded away a few molecules here and a few there. Or, alternatively, they could die all at once in a flash if the Go-Captain chose to kill himself and the ship rather than to wait for a slow death. Or, if they believed in religion, they could pray.

The pinlighter said to the rigid Go-Captain, "We think we see a familiar pattern at the edge of your own brain. May we look in?"

Taliano nodded very slowly, very gravely.

The pinlighter stood still.

The two women watched. Nothing visible happened, but they knew that beyond the limits of vision and yet before their eyes a great drama was being played out. The minds of the pinlighters probed deep into the mind of the frozen Go-Captain, searching amid the synapses for the secret of the faintest clue to their possible rescue.

Minutes passed. They seemed like hours.

At last the pinlighter spoke. "We can see into your midbrain, Captain. At the edge of your paleocortex there is a star pattern which resembles the upper left rear of our present location."

The pinlighter laughed nervously. "We want to know, can you fly the ship home on your brain?"

Magno Taliano looked with deep tragic eyes at the inquirer. His slow voice came out at them once again since he dared not leave the half-trance which held the entire ship in stasis. *"Do you mean can I fly the ship on a brain alone? It would burn out my brain and the ship would be lost anyhow . . ."*

"But we're lost, lost, lost," screamed Dolores Oh. Her face was alive with hideous hope, with a hunger for ruin, with a greedy welcome of disaster. She screamed at her husband, "Wake up, my darling, and let us die together. At least we can belong to each other that much, that long, forever!"

"Why die?" said the pinlighter softly. "You tell him, Dita."

Said Dita, "Why not try, Sir and Uncle?"

Slowly Magno Taliano turned his face toward his niece. Again his hollow voice sounded. *"If I do this I shall be a fool or a child or a dead man, but I will do it for you."*

Dita had studied the work of the Go-Captains and she knew well enough that if the paleocortex was lost the personality became intellectually sane, but emotionally crazed. With the most ancient part of the brain gone the fundamental controls of hostility, hunger, and sex disappeared. The most ferocious of animals and the most brilliant of men were reduced to a common level—a level of infantile friendliness in which lust and playfulness and gentle, unappeasable hunger became the eternity of their days.

Magno Taliano did not wait.

He reached out a slow hand and squeezed the hand of Dolores Oh. *"As I die you shall at last be sure I love you."*

Once again the women saw nothing. They realized they had been called in simply to give Magno Taliano a last glimpse of his own life.

A quiet pinlighter thrust a beam-electrode so that it reached square into the paleocortex of Captain Magno Taliano.

The planoforming room came to life. Strange heavens swirled about them like milk being churned in a bowl.

Dita realized that her partial capacity of telepathy was functioning even without the aid of a machine. With her mind she could feel the dead wall of the locksheets. She was aware of the rocking of the *Wu-Feinstein* as it leapt from space to space, as uncertain as a man crossing a river by leaping from one ice-covered rock to the other.

In a strange way she even knew that the paleocortical part of her uncle's brain was burning out at last and forever, that the star patterns which had been frozen in the locksheets lived on in the infinitely complex pattern of his own memories, and that with the help of his own telepathic pinlighters he was burning out his brain cell by cell in order for them to find a way to the ship's destination. This indeed was his last trip.

Dolores Oh watched her husband with a hungry greed surpassing all expression.

Little by little his face became relaxed and stupid.

Dita could see the midbrain being burned blank, as the ship's controls with the help of the pinlighters searched through the most magnificent intellect of its time for a last course into harbor.

Suddenly Dolores Oh was on her knees, sobbing by the hand of her husband.

A pinlighter took Dita by the arm.

"We have reached destination," he said.

"And my uncle?"

The pinlighter looked at her strangely.

She realized he was speaking to her without moving his lips—speaking mind-to-mind with pure telepathy.

"Can't you see it?"

She shook her head dazedly.

The pinlighter thought his emphatic statement at her once again.

"As your uncle burned out his brain, you picked up his skills. Can't you sense it? You are a Go-Captain yourself and one of the greatest of us."

"And he?"

The pinlighter thought a merciful comment at her.

Magno Taliano had risen from the chair and was being led from the room by his wife and consort, Dolores Oh. He had the amiable smile of an idiot, and his face for the first time in more than a hundred years trembled with shy and silly love.

From Gustible's Planet

Shortly after the celebration of the four thousandth anniversary of the opening of space, Angary J. Gustible discovered Gustible's planet. The discovery turned out to be a tragic mistake.

Gustible's planet was inhabited by highly intelligent life forms. They had moderate telepathic powers. They immediately mind-read Angary J. Gustible's entire mind and life history, and embarrassed him very deeply by making up an opera concerning his recent divorce.

The climax of the opera portrayed his wife throwing a teacup at him. This created an unfavorable impression concerning Earth culture, and Angary J. Gustible, who held a reserve commission as a Subchief of the Instrumentality, was profoundly embarrassed to find that it was not the higher realities of Earth which he had conveyed to these people, but the unpleasant intimate facts.

As negotiations proceeded, other embarrassments developed.

In physical appearance the inhabitants of Gustible's planet, who called themselves Apicians, resembled nothing more than oversize ducks, ducks four feet to four feet six in height. At their wing tips, they had developed juxtaposed thumbs. They were paddle-shaped and sufficed to feed the Apicians.

Gustible's planet matched Earth in several respects: in the dishonesty of the inhabitants, in their enthusiasm for good food, in their instant capacity to understand the human mind. Before Gustible began to get ready to go back to Earth, he discovered that the Apicians had copied his ship. There was no use hiding this fact. They had copied it in such detail that the discovery of Gustible's planet meant the simultaneous discovery of Earth . . .

By the Apicians.

The implications of this tragic development did not show up until the Apicians followed him home. They had a planoforming ship capable of traveling in non-space just as readily as his.

The most important feature of Gustible's planet was its singularly close match to the biochemistry of Earth. The Apicians were the first intelligent life forms ever met by human beings who were at once capable of smelling and enjoying everything which human beings smelled and enjoyed, capable of following any human music with forthright pleasure, and capable of eating and drinking everything in sight.

The very first Apicians on Earth were greeted by somewhat alarmed ambassadors who discovered that an appetite for Munich beer, Camembert cheese, tortillas, and enchiladas, as well as the better grades of chow mein, far transcended any serious cultural, political, or strategic interests which the new visitors might have.

Arthur Djohn, a Lord of the Instrumentality who was acting for this particular matter, delegated an Instrumentality agent named Calvin Dredd as the chief diplomatic officer of Earth to handle the matter.

Dredd approached one Schmeckst, who seemed to be the Apician leader. The interview was an unfortunate one.

Dredd began by saying, "Your Exalted Highness, we are delighted to welcome you to Earth—"

Schmeckst said, "Are those edible?" and proceeded to eat the plastic buttons from Calvin Dredd's formal coat, even before Dredd could say though not edible they were attractive.

Schmeckst said, "Don't try to eat those, they are really not very good."

Dredd, looking at his coat sagging wide open, said, "May I offer you some food?"

Schmeckst said, "Indeed, yes."

And while Schmeckst ate an Italian dinner, a Peking dinner, a red-hot peppery Szechuanese dinner, a Japanese sukiyaki dinner, two British breakfasts, a smorgasbord, and four complete servings of diplomatic-level Russian zakouska, he listened to the propositions of the Instrumentality of Earth.

These did not impress him. Schmeckst was intelligent despite his gross and offensive eating habits. He pointed out: "We two worlds are equal in weapons. We can't fight. Look," said he to Calvin Dredd in a threatening tone.

Calvin Dredd braced himself, as he had learned to do. Schmeckst also braced him.

For an instant Dredd did not know what had happened. Then he realized that in putting his body into a rigid and controlled posture he had played along with the low-grade but manipulable telepathic powers of the visitors. He was frozen rigid till Schmeckst laughed and released him.

Schmeckst said, "You see, we are well matched. I can freeze you. Nothing short of utter desperation could get you out of it. If you try to fight us, we'll lick you. We are going to move in here and live with you. We have enough room on our planet. You can come and live with us too. We would like to hire a lot of those cooks of yours. You'll simply have to divide space with us, and that's all there is to it."

That really was all there was to it. Arthur Djohn reported back to the Lords of the Instrumentality that, for the time being, nothing could be done about the disgusting people from Gustible's planet.

They kept their greed within bounds—by their standards. A mere seventy-two thousand of them swept the Earth, hitting every wine shop, dining hall, snack bar, soda bar, and pleasure center in the world. They ate popcorn, alfalfa, raw fruit, live fish, birds on the wing, prepared foods, cooked and canned foods, food concentrates, and assorted medicines.

Outside of an enormous capacity to hold many times what the human body could tolerate in the way of food, they showed very much the same effects as persons. Thousands of them got various local diseases, sometimes called by such undignified names as the Yangtze rapids, Delhi belly, the Roman groanin', or the like. Other thousands became ill and had to relieve themselves in the fashion of ancient emperors. Still they came.

Nobody liked them. Nobody disliked them enough to wish a disastrous war.

Actual trade was minimal. They bought large quantities of foodstuffs, paying in rare metals. But their economy on their own planet produced very little which the world itself wanted. The cities of mankind had long since developed to a point of comfort and corruption where a relatively monocultural being, such as the citizens of Gustible's planet, could not make much impression. The word "Apician" came to have unpleasant connotations of bad manners, greediness, and prompt payment. Prompt payment was considered rude in a credit society, but after all it was better than not being paid at all.

The tragedy of the relationship of the two groups came from the unfortunate picnic of the lady Ch'ao, who prided herself on having ancient Chinesian blood. She decided that it would be possible to satiate Schmeckst and the other Apicians to a point at which they would be able to listen to reason. She arranged a feast which, for quality and quantity, had not been seen since previous historic times, long before the many interruptions of war, collapse, and rebuilding of culture. She searched the museums of the world for recipes.

The dinner was set forth on the telescreens of the entire world. It was held in a pavilion built in the old Chinesian style. A soaring dream of dry bamboo and paper walls, the festival building had a thatched roof in the true ancient fashion. Paper lanterns with real candles illuminated the scene. The fifty selected Apician guests gleamed like ancient idols. Their feathers shone in the light and they clicked their paddlelike thumbs readily as they spoke, telepathically and fluently, in any Earth language which they happened to pick out of the heads of their hearers.

The tragedy was fire. Fire struck the pavilion, wrecked the dinner. The lady Ch'ao was rescued by Calvin Dredd. The Apicians fled. All of them escaped, all but one. Schmeckst himself. Schmeckst suffocated.

He let out a telepathic scream which was echoed in the living voices of all the human beings, other Apicians, and animals within reach, so that the television viewers of the world caught a sudden cacophony of birds shrilling, dogs barking, cats yowling, otters screeching, and one lone panda letting out a singularly high grunt. Then Schmeckst perished. The pity of it . . .

The Earth leaders stood about, wondering how to solve the tragedy. On the other side of the world, the Lords of the Instrumentality watched the scene. What they saw was amazing and horrible. Calvin Dredd, cold, disciplined agent that he was, approached the ruins of the pavilion. His face was twisted in an expression which they had difficulty in understanding. It was only after he licked his lips for the fourth time and they saw a ribbon of drool running down his chin that they realized he had gone mad with appetite. The lady Ch'ao followed close behind, drawn by some remorseless force.

She was out of her mind. Her eyes gleamed. She stalked like a cat. In her left hand she held a bowl and chopsticks.

The viewers all over the world watching the screen could not understand the scene. Two alarmed and dazed

Apicians followed the humans, wondering what was going to happen.

Calvin Dredd made a sudden reach. He pulled out the body of Schmeckst.

The fire had finished Schmeckst. Not a feather remained on him. And then the flash fire, because of the peculiar dryness of the bamboo and the paper and the thousands upon thousands of candles, had baked him. The television operator had an inspiration. He turned on the smell-control.

Throughout the planet Earth, where people had gathered to watch this unexpected and singularly interesting tragedy, there swept a smell which mankind had forgotten. It was an essence of roast duck.

Beyond all imagining, it was the most delicious smell that any human being had ever smelled. Millions upon millions of human mouths watered. Throughout the world people looked away from their sets to see if there were any Apicians in the neighborhood. Just as the Lords of the Instrumentality ordered the disgusting scene cut off, Calvin Dredd and the lady Ch'ao began eating the roast Apician, Schmeckst.

Within twenty-four hours most of the Apicians on Earth had been served, some with cranberry sauce, others baked, some fried Southern style. The serious leaders of Earth dreaded the consequences of such uncivilized conduct. Even as they wiped their lips and asked for one more duck sandwich, they felt that this behavior was difficult beyond all imagination.

The blocks that the Apicians had been able to put on

human action did not operate when they were applied to human beings who, looking at an Apician, went deep into the recesses of their personality and were animated by a mad hunger which transcended all civilization.

The Lords of the Instrumentality managed to round up Schmeckst's deputy and a few other Apicians and to send them back to their ship.

The soldiers watching them licked their lips. The captain tried to see if he could contrive an accident as he escorted his state visitors. Unfortunately, tripping Apicians did not break their necks, and the Apicians kept throwing violent mind-blocks at human beings in an attempt to save themselves.

One of the Apicians was so undiplomatic as to ask for a chicken salad sandwich and almost lost a wing, raw and alive, to a soldier whose appetite had been restimulated by reference to food.

The Apicians went back, the few survivors. They liked Earth well enough and Earth food was delicious, but it was a horrible place when they considered the cannibalistic human beings who lived there—so cannibalistic that they ate ducks!

The Lords of the Instrumentality were relieved to note that when the Apicians left they closed the space lane behind them. No one quite knows how they closed it, or what defenses they had. Mankind, salivating and ashamed, did not push the pursuit hotly. Instead, people tried to make up chicken, duck, goose, Cornish hen, pigeon, sea-gull, and other sandwiches to duplicate the incomparable taste of a genuine inhabitant of Gustible's planet. None were quite authentic and people, in their right minds, were not uncivilized enough to invade another world solely for getting the inhabitants as tidbits.

The Lords of the Instrumentality were happy to report to one another and to the rest of the world at their next meeting that the Apicians had managed to close Gustible's planet altogether, had had no further interest in dealing with Earth, and appeared to possess just enough of a technological edge on human beings to stay concealed from the eyes and the appetites of men.

Save for that, the Apicians were almost forgotten. A confidential secretary of the Office of Interstellar Trade was astonished when the frozen intelligences of a methane planet ordered forty thousand cases of Munich beer. He suspected them of being jobbers, not consumers. But on the instructions of his superiors he kept the matter confidential and allowed the beer to be shipped.

It undoubtedly went to Gustible's planet, but they did not offer any of their own citizens in exchange.

The matter was closed. The napkins were folded. Trade and diplomacy were at an end.

Himself in Anachron

And Time there is
And Time there was
And Time goes on, before—
But what is the Knot
That binds the time
That holds it here, and more—
Oh, the Knot in Time
Is a secret place
They sought in times of yore—
Somewhere in Space
They seek it still
But Tasco hunts no more . . .
HE FOUND IT
      from "Mad Dita's Song"

First they threw out every bit of machinery which was not vital to their lives or the function of the ship. Then went Dita's treasured honeymoon items (foolishly and typically she had valued these over the instruments). Next they ejected every bit of nutrient except the minimum for survival for two persons. Tasco knew then. It was not enough. The ship still had to be lightened.

He remembered that the Subchief had said, bitterly enough: "So you got leave to time-travel together! You fool! I don't know whether it was your idea or hers to have a 'honeymoon in time,' but with everyone watching your marriage you've got the sentimental mob behind you. 'Honeymoon in time,' indeed. Why? Is it that your woman is jealous of your time trips? Don't be an idiot, Tasco. You know that ship's not built for two. You don't even have to go at all; we can send Vomact. He's single." Tasco remembered, too, the quick warmth of his jealousy at the mention of Vomact. If anything had been needed to steel his determination, that name had done it. How could he possibly have backed out after the publicity over his proposed flight to find the Knot. The Subchief must have realized from the expression on his face something of his feelings; he had said with a knowledgeable grin: "Well, if anybody can find the Knot, it'll be you. But listen, leave her here. Take her later if you like but go first alone." But Tasco could remember, too, Dita's kitten-soft body as she nestled up to him holding his eyes with her own and murmuring, "But, darling, you promised . . ."

Yes, he had been warned, but that didn't make the tragedy any easier. Yes, he could have left her behind, but what kind of marriage would they have had with the blot of her bitterness on the first days of their married life? And how could he have lived with himself if he had let Vomact go in his place? How, even, would Dita have regarded him? He could not deceive himself; he knew that Dita loved him, loved him dearly, but he had been a hero ever since she had known him and how much would she have loved him without the hero image? He loved her enough not to want to find out.

And now, one of them must go, be lost in space and time forever. Tasco looked at her, his beloved. He thought, *I have loved you forever, but in our case forever was only three earth days. Shall I love you there in space and timelessness?* To postpone, if only for minutes, the eternal parting, he pretended to find some other instrument which could be disposed of, and sent through the hatch one person's share of the remaining nutrient. Now the decision was made. Dita came over to stand beside him.

"Does that do it, Tasco? Is the ship light enough now for us to get out of the Knot?" Instead of answering he held her tightly against him. *I've done what I had to,* he thought . . . *Dita, Dita, not to hold you ever again . . .*

Softly, not to disturb the moon-pale curve of her hair, he passed his hand over her head. Then he released her.

"Get ready to take over, Dita. I could not murder you, oh my darling, and unless the ship is lightened by the weight of one of us we will both die here in the Knot. You must take it back, you have to take back the ship and all the instrument-gathered data. It's not you or me or us now. We're the servants of the Instrumentality. You must understand . . ."

Still within his arms, she backed away enough to look at his face. She was dewy-eyed, loving, frightened, her lips trembling with affection. She was adorable, and Cranch! how incompetent. But she'd make it; she had to. She said nothing at first, trying to hold her lips steady, and then she said the thing that would annoy him most. "Don't, darling, don't. I couldn't stand it. . . . Please don't leave me."

His reaction was completely spontaneous: His open hand caught her across the cheek, hard. A reciprocal anger flashed across her eyes and mouth, but she gained control of herself. She returned to pleading.

"Tasco, Tasco, don't be bad to me. If we have to die together, I can face it. Don't leave me, please don't leave me. I don't blame you . . ." *I don't blame you!* he thought. *By the Forgotten One, that's really rather good!*

He said, as quietly as he could, "I've told you. Somebody has got to take this ship back to our own time and place. We've found the Knot. This is the Knot in Time. Look."

He pointed. The Merochron swung slightly back and forth, from + 1,000,000:1 to -500,000:1. "Look hard— twenty-years-a-minute-plus to ten-years-a-minute-minus. The ship has a chance of getting out if the load is lightened. We've thrown everything else we could out. Now I'm going. I love you; you love me. It will be as hard for me to leave you as for you to see me go. A lifetime with you would not have been enough. But, Dita, you owe me this . . . to take the ship back safely. Don't make it harder for me. If you can hold it on Left Subformal Probability, do it. If not, keep on trying to slow down in backtime."

"But, darling . . ."

He wanted to be tender. Words caught in his throat. But *their* time had run out. Their honeymoon had been a gamble, their own gamble, and now it and their life together were over. Three earth days! The Instrumentality remained; the Chiefs and Lords waited; a million lives would be a cheap price for a fix on the Knot in Time. Dita could do it. Even she could do it if the ship were lighter by a man.

His farewell kiss was not one she would remember. He was in a hurry now to finish it; the sooner he left, the better her chances were of getting back. And still she looked at him as if she expected him to stay and talk. Something in her eyes made him suspicious that she would try to hinder him. He cut in his helmet speaker and said:

"Goodbye. I love you. I have to go now, quickly. Please do as I ask and don't get in my way."

She was weeping now. "Tasco, you're going to die . . ."

"Maybe," he said.

She reached for him, tried to hold him. "Darling, don't. Don't go. Don't hurry so."

Roughly he pushed her back into the control seat. He tried to hold his anger that she would not let him do even this right, to die for her. She would make it a scene. "Sweetheart," he said, "don't make me say it all over again. Anyhow, I may not die. I'll aim for a planet full of nymphs and I'll live a thousand years."

He had half expected to stir her to jealousy or anger . . . at least some other emotion, but she disregarded his poor joke and went on quietly weeping. A wisp of smoke rising in the hot moving air of the cabin made them look to the control panel. The Probability Selector was glowing. Tasco kept his face immobile, glad that she did not realize the significance of the reading. *Now no one will ever find me, even if I live,* he thought. *But go, go, go!*

He smiled at her through his shimmering suit. He

touched her arm with his metal claw. Then, before she could stop him he backed into the escape hatch, slammed the door on himself, fumbled for the ejector gun, pressed the button. Pressed it hard.

Thunder, and a wash like water. There went his world, his wife, his time, himself . . . He floated free in anachron. Others had gone astray between the Probabilities; none had come back. They had borne it, he supposed. If they could, he could too. And then it caught him. The others, had they left wives and sweethearts? Was it for them too a personal tragedy? *Himself and Dita, they had not had to come. Vanity, pride, jealousy, stubbornness. They had come. And now: himself in anachron.*

He felt himself leaping from Probability to Probability like a pebble bouncing down a corrugated plastic roof. He couldn't even tell whether he was going toward Formal or Resolved. Perhaps he was still somewhere in Left Subformal.

The clatter ceased. He waited for more blows.

One more came. Only one, and sharp.

He felt tension go out of him. He felt the Probabilities firming around him, listened to the selector working in his helmet as it coded him into a time-space combination fit for human life. The thing had a murmur in it which he had never heard in a practice jump, but then, this wasn't practice. He had never before gotten out between the Probabilities, never floated free in anachron.

A feeling of weight and direction made him realize that he was coming back to common space. His feet were touching ground. He stood still, attempting to relax while a world took shape around him. There was something very strange about the whole business. The grey color of the space around him resembled the grey of fast backtiming, the blind blur which he had so often seen from the cabin window when, having chosen a Probability, he had coursed it down until the Selectors had given him an opening he could land in. *But how could he be backtiming with no ship, no power?*

Unless—

Unless the Knot in Time in flinging him out had imparted to him a time-momentum in his own body. But even if that were so he should decelerate. Was he coming down in ratio? This still felt like hightiming, 10,000:1 or higher.

He tried briefly to think of Dita but his personal situation outweighed everything else. A new worry hit him. What was his own personal consumption of time? With time so high outside his unit was it also rising inside? How long would his nutrients last? He tried to be aware of his own body, to feel hunger, to catch a glimpse of himself. Was the automatic nutrition keeping up with the changing time? On inspiration, he rubbed his face against the mask to see if his whiskers had grown since he left the ship.

He had a beard. Plenty.

Before he could figure that one out, there was one last *Snap!* and he fainted.

When he recovered, he was still erect. Some kind of frame supported him. Who had put it there, and how? By the continued greyness he could tell that his physiological time and external time had not yet met. He felt a violent impatience. There should be some way to slow down. His helmet felt heavy. Disregarding the risks, he clawed at the mask until it came off.

The air was sweet but thick, thick. He had to fight to breathe it in. It was hardly worth the struggle.

He was still hightiming, more so than he had thought anybody could with an exposed body. He looked down and saw his beard tremble as it grew. He felt the stab of fingernails growing against his palms; there should have been an automatic cut-off but time was going too fast. Clenching his hand, he broke off the nails roughly. His boots had apparently broken off his toenails, and although his feet were uncomfortable the pressure was bearable. Anyway there was nothing he could do about it.

His immense tiredness warned him that the automatic nutrient system was not keeping up with his bodily time. With effort he fitted his claw to his belt and twisted until the supplementary food vial was released. He felt the needle pierce the skin of his belly; he twisted again until the hot surge of nourishment told him that the food-injector had reached a vein. Almost immediately his strength began to rise.

He watched the blur of buildings flashing into instantaneous shape around him, standing a moment, and then melting slowly away. Now he could see a little more of his surroundings. He seemed to be standing in the mouth of a cave or in a great doorway. It was curious, that, about the buildings. All the other buildings he had seen in time had worked the other way. First the slow upthrust as they were built, then the greying evenness of age, then the flash of removal. But, he reminded himself tiredly, he was backtiming and he thought it probable that no other human being had ever backtimed so hard and fast or for so long a time.

He seemed now to be rapidly decelerating. A building appeared around him, then he was outside of it, then back in again. Suddenly a great light shone in front of him.

Now he was inside a large palace. He seemed to be placed on a pedestal, high up at the center of things. Shimmering masses began to take form around him at rhythmic intervals: people? There was something wrong about the way they moved; why did they move with that strange awkwardness?

As the light persisted and this building seemed solid, he made an effort to squint to try to see more. His eyeballs were the only part of his anatomy that seemed to move freely. His breaking growing breaking fingernails and toenails and the growing beard reminded him to break off another food needle in his vein. His skin itched intolerably. As he realized the increasing immobility of his arms he felt panic and while there was still time pushed the continuous-flow button on the supplementary nutrients. Despite the food, enough to keep him alive in the cold of space, he could no longer move his hands and fingers. And still, it seemed only minutes since he had left the ship. (*Dita, Dita, are you out of the Knot? Did you manage it in time? If only I calculated the weight load right . . .*)

The building continued stable around him. He rolled his eyes to try to see where he was, when he was.

I'm still alive, he thought. *Nobody else ever got out of anachron. That's something. Nobody else ever stepped out of time to be seen again.*

Deceleration continued. The bright light before him remained even and he found he could see better. In front of him was a sort of picture, high and large. What was it? Panels, a series of panels, paintings from some remote past.

He peered harder and recognized that the panel at the top left was himself, Tasco Magnon. There he was: shimmering space suit, marble armrests, pedestal below him. But they had given him wings like the wings of angels of the Old Strong Religion. Great white wings. And they had put a halo around his head. The next panel showed him as he felt: suit shimmering but his face old and tired.

The panels on the lower level were equally curious. The first showed a bed of grass or moss with luminescence glowing above it. The second showed a skeleton standing in a frame.

His tired mind sought to make sense of the panels.

People became plainer in the blur around him. Sometimes he could almost see individuals. The colors of the paintings brightened, brightened, until they flashed gay and bold, then disappeared.

Disappeared completely, flatly.

His brain, so old and tired now, struggled with immense effort to reach the truth. Physiological time was utterly deranged. Each minute seemed years. His thoughts became old memories while he thought them. But the truth came through to him:

He was still backtiming.

He had passed the time of his arrival and resurrection in this world. The resurrection was wisely prophesied by the beings who built the palace, painted the wings and halo around him.

He would die soon, in the remote past of this civilization.

Long afterwards, centuries before his own death, his alien remains would fade into the system of this time-space locus; and in fading, they would seem to glow and to assemble. They must have been untouchable and beyond manipulation. The people who had built the palace and their forefathers had watched dust turn to skeleton, skeleton heave upright, skeleton become mummy, mummy become corpse, corpse become old man, old man become young—himself as he had left the spaceship. He had landed in his own tomb, his own temple.

He had yet to fulfil the things which these people had seen him do, and had recorded in the panels of his temple.

Across his fatigue he felt a thrill of weary remote pride: he knew that he was sure to fulfil the godhood which these people had so faithfully recorded. He knew he would become young and glorious, only to disappear. He'd done it, a few minutes or millennia ago.

The clash of time within his body tore at him with peculiar pain. The food needle seemed to have no further effect. His vitals felt dry.

The building glowed as it seemed to come nearer.

The ages thrust against him. He thought, "I am Tasco Magnon and have been a god. I will become one again."

But his last conscious thought was nothing grandiose. A glimpse of moon-pale hair, a half-turned cheek. In the aching lost silence of his own mind he called,

Dita! Dita!

❖❖❖

The twisted timeship took form at the Dateport of the Instrumentality. Officials and engineers rushed up, opened the door. The young woman who sat at the controls staring blindly was white-faced beyond all weeping. They tried to rouse her from her trance-like state but she clung desperately to the controls, repeating like a chant:

"He jumped out. Tasco jumped out. He jumped out. Alone, alone in anachron . . ."

Gravely and gently the officials lifted her from the controls so that they could remove the now-priceless instruments.

The Crime and the Glory
of Commander Suzdal

*Do not read this story; turn the page quickly. The story
may upset you. Anyhow, you probably know it already. It
is a very disturbing story. Everyone knows it. The glory
and the crime of Commander Suzdal have been told in a
thousand different ways. Don't let yourself realize that the
story is the truth.*

*It isn't. Not at all. There's not a bit of truth to it. There
is no such planet as Arachosia, no such people as klopts,
no such world as Catland. These are all just imaginary,
they didn't happen, forget about it, go away and read
something else.*

∾ *The Beginning* ∾

Commander Suzdal was sent forth in a shell-ship to

explore the outermost reaches of our galaxy. His ship was called a cruiser, but he was the only man in it. He was equipped with hypnotics and cubes to provide him the semblance of company, a large crowd of friendly people who could be convoked out of his own hallucinations.

The Instrumentality even offered him some choice in his imaginary companions, each of whom was embodied in a small ceramic cube containing the brain of a small animal but imprinted with the personality of an actual human being.

Suzdal, a short, stocky man with a jolly smile, was blunt about his needs:

"Give me two good security officers. I can manage the ship, but if I'm going into the unknown, I'll need help in meeting the strange problems which might show up."

The loading official smiled at him, "I never heard of a cruiser commander who *asked* for security officers. Most people regard them as an utter nuisance."

"That's all right," said Suzdal. "I don't."

"Don't you want some chess players?"

"I can play chess," said Suzdal, "all I want to, using the spare computers. All I have to do is set the power down and they start losing. On full power, they always beat me."

The official then gave Suzdal an odd look. He did not exactly leer, but his expression became both intimate and a little unpleasant. "What about other companions?" he asked, with a funny little edge to his voice.

"I've got books," said Suzdal, "a couple of thousand. I'm going to be gone only a couple of years Earth time."

"Local-subjective, it might be several thousand years," said the official, "though the time will wind back up again as you re-approach Earth. And I wasn't talking about books," he repeated, with the same funny, prying lilt to his voice.

Suzdal shook his head with momentary worry, ran his hand through his sandy hair. His blue eyes were forthright and he looked straightforwardly into the official's eyes. "What do you mean, then, if not books? Navigators? I've got them, not to mention the turtle-men. They're good company, if you just talk to them slowly enough and then give them plenty of time to answer. Don't forget, I've been out before . . ."

The official spat out his offer: "Dancing girls. WOMEN. Concubines. Don't you want any of those? We could even cube your own wife for you and print her mind on a cube for you. That way she could be with you every week that you were awake."

Suzdal looked as though he would spit on the floor in sheer disgust. "Alice? You mean, you want me to travel around with a ghost of her? How would the real Alice feel when I came back? Don't tell me that you're going to put my wife on a mousebrain. You're just offering me delirium. I've got to keep my wits out there with space and time rolling in big waves around me. I'm going to be crazy enough, just as it is. Don't forget, I've been out there before. Getting back to a real Alice is going to be one of my biggest reality factors. It will help me to get home." At this point, Suzdal's own voice took on the note of intimate inquiry, as he added, "Don't tell me that a lot of cruiser commanders ask to go flying around with imaginary wives. That would be pretty nasty, in my opinion. Do many of them do it?"

"We're here to get you loaded on board ship, not to discuss what other officers do or do not do. Sometimes we think it good to have a female companion on the ship with the commander, even if she is imaginary. If you ever found anything among the stars which took on female form, you'd be mighty vulnerable to it."

"Females, among the stars? Bosh!" said Suzdal.

"Strange things have happened," said the official.

"Not that," said Suzdal. "Pain, craziness, distortion, panic without end, a craze for food—yes, those I can look for and face. They will be there. But females, no. There aren't any. I love my wife. I won't make females up out of my own mind. After all, I'll have the turtle-people aboard, and they will be bringing up their young. I'll have plenty of family to watch and to take part in. I can even give Christmas parties for the young ones."

"What kind of parties are those?" asked the official.

"Just a funny little ancient ritual that I heard about from an outer pilot. You give all the young things presents, once every local-subjective year."

"It sounds nice," said the official, his voice growing tired and final. "You still refuse to have a cube-woman on board. You wouldn't have to activate her unless you really needed her."

"You haven't flown, yourself, have you?" asked Suzdal.

It was the official's turn to flush. "No," he said, flatly.

"Anything that's in that ship, I'm going to think about. I'm a cheerful sort of man, and very friendly. Let me just get along with my turtle-people. They're not lively, but they are considerate and restful. Two thousand or more years, local-subjective, is a lot of time. Don't give me additional decisions to make. It's work enough, running the ship. Just leave me alone with my turtle-people. I've gotten along with them before."

"You, Suzdal, are the commander," said the loading official. "We'll do as you say."

"Fine," smiled Suzdal. "You may get a lot of queer types on this run, but I'm not one of them."

The two men smiled agreement at one another and the loading of the ship was completed.

The ship itself was managed by turtle-men, who aged very slowly, so that while Suzdal coursed the outer rim of the galaxy and let the thousands of years—local count—go past while he slept in his frozen bed, the turtle-men rose generation by generation, trained their young to work the ship, taught the stories of the Earth that they would never see again, and read the computers correctly, to awaken Suzdal only when there was a need for human intervention and for human intelligence. Suzdal awakened from time to time, did his work and then went back. He felt that he had been gone from Earth only a few months.

Months indeed! He had been gone more than a subjective ten thousand years, when he met the siren capsule.

It looked like an ordinary distress capsule. The kind of thing that was often shot through space to indicate some complication of the destiny of man among the stars. This capsule had apparently been flung across an immense distance, and from the capsule Suzdal got the story of Arachosia.

The story was false. The brains of a whole planet—the wild genius of a malevolent, unhappy race—had been dedicated to the problem of ensnaring and attracting a normal pilot from Old Earth. The story which the capsule sang conveyed the rich personality of a wonderful woman with a contralto voice. The story was true, in part. The appeals were real, in part. Suzdal listened to the story and it sank, like a wonderfully orchestrated piece of grand opera, right into the fibers of his brain. It would have been different if he had known the real story.

Everybody now knows the real story of Arachosia, the bitter terrible story of the planet which was a paradise, which turned into a hell. The story of how people got to be something different from people. The story of what happened way out there in the most dreadful place among the stars.

He would have fled if he knew the real story. He couldn't understand what we now know:

Mankind could not meet the terrible people of Arachosia without the people of Arachosia following them home and bringing to mankind a grief greater than grief, a craziness worse than mere insanity, a plague surpassing all imaginable plagues. The Arachosians had become unpeople, and yet, in their innermost imprinting of their personalities, they remained people. They sang songs which exalted their own deformity and which praised themselves for what they had so horribly become, and yet, in their own songs, in their own ballads, the organ tones of the refrain rang out:

And I mourn Man!

They knew what they were and they hated themselves. Hating themselves, they pursued mankind.

Perhaps they are still pursuing mankind.

The Instrumentality has by now taken good pains that the Arachosians will never find us again, has flung networks of deception out along the edge of the galaxy to make sure that those lost ruined people cannot find us. The Instrumentality knows and guards our world and all the other worlds of mankind against the deformity which has become Arachosia. We want nothing to do with Arachosia. Let them hunt for us. They won't find us.

How could Suzdal know that?

This was the first time someone had met the Arachosians, and he met them only with a message in which an elfin voice sang the elfin song of ruin, using perfectly clear words in the old common tongue to tell a story so sad, so abominable, that mankind has not forgotten it yet. In its essence the story was very simple. This is what Suzdal heard, and what people have learned ever since then.

The Arachosians were settlers. Settlers could go out by sail-ship, trailing behind them the pods. That was the first way.

Or they could go out by planoform ship, ships piloted by skillful men, who went into Space^2 and came out again and found man.

Or for very long distances indeed, they could go out in the new combination. Individual pods packed into an enormous shell-ship, a gigantic version of Suzdal's own ship. The sleepers frozen, the machines waking, the ship fired to and beyond the speed of light, flung below space, coming out at random and homing on a suitable target. It was a gamble, but brave men took it. If no target was found, their machines might course space forever, while the bodies, protected by freezing as they were, spoiled bit by bit, and while the dim light of life went out in the individual frozen brains.

The shell-ships were the answers of mankind to an overpopulation which neither the old planet Earth nor its daughter planets could quite respond to. The shell-ships took the bold, the reckless, the romantic, the willful, sometimes the criminals out among the stars. Mankind lost track of these ships, over and over again. The advance explorers, the organized Instrumentality, would stumble upon human beings, cities and cultures, high or low, tribes or families, where the shell-ships had gone on, far, far beyond the outermost limits of mankind, where the instruments of search had found an Earthlike planet, and the shell-ship, like some great dying insect, had dropped to the planet, awakened its people, broken open, and destroyed itself with its delivery of newly reborn men and women, to settle a world.

Arachosia looked like a good world to the men and women who came to it. Beautiful beaches, with cliffs like endless rivieras rising above. Two bright big moons in the sky, a sun not too far away. The machines had pretested the atmosphere and sampled the water, had already scattered the forms of Old Earth life into the atmosphere and in the seas so that as the people awakened they heard the singing of Earth birds and they knew that Earth fish had already been adapted to the oceans and flung in, there to multiply. It seemed a good life, a rich life. Things went well.

Things went very, very well for the Arachosians.

This is the truth.

This was, thus far, the story told by the capsule.

But here they diverged.

The capsule did not tell the dreadful, pitiable truth about Arachosia. It invented a set of plausible lies. The voice which came telepathically out of the capsule was that of a mature, warm happy female—some woman of early middle age with a superb speaking contralto.

Suzdal almost fancied that he talked to it, so real was the personality. How could he know that he was being beguiled, trapped?

It sounded right, *really* right.

"And then," said the voice, "the Arachosian sickness has been hitting us. Do not land. Stand off. Talk to us. Tell us about medicine. Our young die, without reason. Our farms are rich, and the wheat here is more golden than it was on Earth, the plums more purple, the flowers whiter. Everything does well—except people.

"Our young die . . ." said the womanly voice, ending in a sob.

"Are there any symptoms?" thought Suzdal, and almost as though it had heard his question, the capsule went on.

"They die of nothing. Nothing which our medicine can test, nothing which our science can show. They die. Our population is dropping. People, do not forget us! Man, whoever you are, come quickly, come now, bring help! But for your own sake, do not land. Stand off-planet and view us through screens so that you can take word back to the home of man about the lost children of mankind among the strange and outermost stars!"

Strange, indeed!

The truth was far stranger, and very ugly indeed.

Suzdal was convinced of the truth of the message. He had been selected for the trip because he was good-natured, intelligent, and brave; this appeal touched all three of his qualities.

Later, much later, when he was arrested, Suzdal was asked, "Suzdal, you fool, why didn't you test the message? You've risked the safety of all the mankinds for a foolish appeal!"

"It wasn't foolish!" snapped Suzdal. "That distress capsule had a sad, wonderful womanly voice and the story checked out true."

"With whom?" said the investigator, flatly and dully.

Suzdal sounded weary and sad when he replied to the point. "It checked out with my books. With my knowledge." Reluctantly he added, "And with my own judgment . . ."

"Was your judgment good?" said the investigator.

"No," said Suzdal, and let the single word hang on the air as though it might be the last word he would ever speak.

But it was Suzdal himself who broke the silence when he added, "Before I set course and went to sleep, I activated my security officers in cubes and had them check the story. They got the real story of Arachosia, all right. They cross-ciphered it out of patterns in the distress capsule and they told me the whole real story very quickly, just as I was waking up."

"And what did you do?"

"I did what I did. I did that for which I expect to be punished. The Arachosians were already walking around the outside of my hull by then. They had caught my ship. They had caught me. How was I to know that the wonderful, sad story was true only for the first twenty full years that the woman told about. And she wasn't even a woman. Just a klopt. Only the first twenty years . . ."

Things had gone well for the Arachosians for the first twenty years. Then came disaster, but it was not the tale told in the distress capsule.

They couldn't understand it. They didn't know why it had to happen to them. They didn't know why it waited twenty years, three months, and four days. But their time came.

We think it must have been something in the radiation of their sun. Or perhaps a combination of that particular sun's radiation and the chemistry, which even the wise machines in the shell-ship had not fully analyzed, which reached out and was spread from within. The disaster hit. It was a simple one and utterly unstoppable.

They had doctors. They had hospitals. They even had a limited capacity for research.

But they could not research fast enough. Not enough to meet this disaster. It was simple, monstrous, enormous.

Femininity became carcinogenic.

Every woman on the planet began developing cancer at the same time, on her lips, in her breasts, in her groin, sometimes along the edge of her jaw, the edge of her lip, the tender portions of her body. The cancer had many forms, and yet it was always the same. There was something about the radiation which reached through, which reached into the human body, and which made a particular form of desoxycorticosterone turn into a sub-form—unknown on earth—of pregnandiol, which infallibly caused cancer. The advance was rapid.

The little baby girls began to die first. The women clung weeping to their fathers, their husbands. The mothers tried to say goodbye to their sons.

One of the doctors, herself, was a woman, a strong woman.

Remorselessly, she cut live tissue from her living body, put it under the microscope, took samples of her own urine, her blood, her spit, and she came up with the answer: *There is no answer.* And yet there was something better and worse than an answer.

If the sun of Arachosia killed everything which was female, if the female fish floated upside down on the surface of the sea, if the female birds sang a shriller, wilder song as they died above the eggs which would never hatch, if the female animals grunted and growled in the lairs where they hid away with pain, female human beings did not have to accept death so tamely. The doctor's name was Astarte Kraus.

∾ *The Magic of the Klopts* ∾

The human female could do what the animal female could not. She could turn male. With the help of equipment from the ship, tremendous quantities of testosterone were manufactured, and every single girl and woman still surviving was turned into a man. Massive injections were administered to all of them. Their faces grew heavy, they all returned to growing a little bit, their chests flattened out, their muscles grew stronger, and in less than three months they were indeed men.

Some lower forms of life had survived because they were not polarized clearly enough to the forms of male and female, which depended on that particular organic chemistry for survival. With the fish gone, plants clotted the oceans, the birds were gone but the insects survived; dragonflies, butterflies, mutated versions of grasshoppers, beetles, and other insects swarmed over the planet. The men who had lost women worked side by side with the men who had been made out of the bodies of women.

When they knew each other, it was unutterably sad for them to meet. Husband and wife, both bearded, strong, quarrelsome, desperate, and busy. The little boys somehow realizing that they would never grow up to have sweethearts, to have wives, to get married, to have daughters.

But what was a mere world to stop the driving brain and the burning intellect of Dr. Astarte Kraus? She became the leader of her people, the men and the men-women. She drove them forward, she made them survive, she used cold brains on all of them.

(Perhaps, if she had been a sympathetic person, she would have let them die. But it was the nature of Dr. Kraus not to be sympathetic—just brilliant, remorseless, implacable against the universe which had tried to destroy her.)

Before she died, Dr. Kraus had worked out a carefully programmed genetic system. Little bits of the men's tissues could be implanted by a surgical routine in the abdomens, just inside the peritoneal wall, crowding a little bit against the intestines, an artificial womb and artificial chemistry and artificial insemination by radiation, by heat made it possible for men to bear boy children.

What was the use of having girl children if they all died? The people of Arachosia went on. The first generation lived through the tragedy, half insane with the grief and disappointment. They sent out message capsules and they knew that their messages would reach Earth in six million years.

As new explorers, they had gambled on going further than other ships went. They had found a good world, but they were not quite sure where they were. Were they still within the familiar galaxy, or had they jumped beyond to one of the nearby galaxies? They couldn't quite tell. It was a part of the policy of Old Earth not to over-equip the exploring parties for fear that some of them, taking violent cultural change or becoming aggressive empires, might turn back on Earth and destroy it. Earth always made sure that it had the advantages.

The third and fourth and fifth generations of Arachosians were still people. All of them were male. They had the human memory, they had human books, they knew the words *mama, sister, sweetheart,* but they no longer really understood what these terms referred to.

The human body, which had taken four million years on Earth to grow, has immense resources within it, resources greater than the brain, or the personality, or the hopes of the individual. And the bodies of the Arachosians decided things for them. Since the chemistry of femininity meant instant death, and since an occasional girl baby was born dead and buried casually, the bodies made the adjustment. The men of Arachosia became both men and women. They gave themselves the ugly nickname "klopt." Since they did not have the rewards of family life, they became strutting cockerels, who mixed their love with murder, who blended their songs with duels, who sharpened their weapons, and who earned the right to reproduce within a strange family system which no decent Earth-man would find comprehensible.

But they did survive.

And the method of their survival was so sharp, so fierce, that it was indeed a difficult thing to understand.

In less than four hundred years the Arachosians had civilized into groups of fighting clans. They still had just one planet, around just one sun. They lived in just one place. They had a few spacecraft they had built themselves. Their science, their art, and their music moved forward with strange lurches of inspired neurotic genius, because they lacked the fundamentals in the human personality itself, the balance of male and female, the family, the operations of love, of hope, of reproduction. They survived, but they themselves had become monsters and did not know it.

Out of their memory of old mankind they created a legend of Old Earth. Women in that memory were deformities, who should be killed. Misshapen beings, who should be erased. The family, as they recalled it, was filth and abomination which they were resolved to wipe out if they should ever meet it.

They, themselves, were bearded homosexuals, with rouged lips, ornate earrings, fine heads of hair, and very few old men among them. They killed off their men before they became old; the things they could not get from love or relaxation or comfort, they purchased with battle and death. They made up songs proclaiming themselves to be the last of the old men and the first of the new, and they sang their hate to mankind when they should meet, and they sang, "Woe is Earth that we should find it," and yet something inside them made them add to almost every song a refrain which troubled even them:

And I mourn Man!

They mourned mankind and yet they plotted to attack all of humanity.

∽ *The Trap* ∽

Suzdal had been deceived by the message capsule. He put himself back in the sleeping compartment and he directed the turtle-men to take the cruiser to Arachosia, wherever it might be. He did not do this crazily or wantonly. He did it as a matter of deliberate judgment. A judgment for which he was later heard, tried, judged fairly, and then put to something worse than death.

He deserved it.

He sought for Arachosia without stopping to think of the most fundamental rule: How could he keep the Arachosians, singing monsters that they were, from following him home to the eventual ruin of Earth? Might not their condition be a disease which could be contagious, or might not their fierce society destroy the other societies of men and leave Earth and all of men's other worlds in ruin? He did not think of this, so he was heard, and tried and punished much later. We will come to that.

∽ *The Arrival* ∽

Suzdal awakened in orbit off Arachosia. And he awakened knowing he had made a mistake. Strange ships clung to his shell-ship like evil barnacles from an unknown ocean, attached to a familiar water craft. He called to his turtle-men to press the controls and the controls did not work.

The outsiders, whoever they were, man or woman or beast or god, had enough technology to immobilize his ship. Suzdal immediately realized his mistake. Naturally, he thought of destroying himself and the ship, but he was afraid that if he destroyed himself and missed destroying the ship completely there was a chance that his cruiser, a late model with recent weapons, would fall into the hands of whoever it was walking on the outer dome of his own cruiser. He could not afford the risk of mere individual suicide. He had to take a more drastic step. This was not time for obeying Earth rules.

His security officer—a cube ghost wakened to human form—whispered the whole story to him in quick intelligent gasps:

"They are people, sir.

"More people than I am.

"I'm a ghost, an echo working out of a dead brain.

"These are real people, Commander Suzdal, but they

are the worst people ever to get loose among the stars. You must destroy them, sir!"

"I can't," said Suzdal, still trying to come fully awake. *"They're people."*

"Then you've got to beat them off. By any means, sir. By any means whatever. Save Earth. Stop them. Warn Earth."

"And I?" asked Suzdal, and was immediately sorry that he had asked the selfish, personal question.

"You will die or you will be punished," said the security officer sympathetically, "and I do not know which one will be worse."

"Now?"

"Right now. There is no time left for you. No time at all."

"But the rules . . . ?"

"You have already strayed far outside of rules."

There were rules, but Suzdal left them all behind.

Rules, rules for ordinary times, for ordinary places, for understandable dangers.

This was a nightmare cooked up by the flesh of man, motivated by the brains of man. Already his monitors were bringing him news of who these people were, these seeming maniacs, these men who had never known women, these boys who had grown to lust and battle, who had a family structure which the normal human brain could not accept, could not believe, could not tolerate. The things on the outside were people, and they weren't. The things on the outside had the human brain, the human imagination, and the human capacity for revenge, and yet Suzdal, a brave officer, was so frightened by the mere nature of them that he did not respond to their efforts to communicate.

He could feel the turtle-women among his crew aching with fright itself, as they realized who was pounding on their ship and who it was that sang through loud announcing machines that they wanted *in, in, in.*

Suzdal committed a crime. It is the pride of the Instrumentality that the Instrumentality allows its officers to commit crimes or mistakes or suicide. The Instrumentality does the things for mankind that a computer can not do. The Instrumentality leaves the human brain, the human choice in action.

The Instrumentality passes dark knowledge to its staff, things not usually understood in the inhabited world, things prohibited to ordinary men and women because the officers of the Instrumentality, the captains and the subchiefs and the chiefs, must know their jobs. If they do not, all mankind might perish.

Suzdal reached into his arsenal. He knew what he was doing. The larger moon of Arachosia was habitable. He could see that there were earth plants already on it, and earth insects. His monitors showed him that the Arachosian men-women had not bothered to settle on the planet. He threw an agonized inquiry at his computers and cried out:

"Read me the age it's in!"

The machine sang back, "More than thirty million years."

Suzdal had strange resources. He had twins or quadruplets of almost every Earth animal. The earth animals were carried in tiny capsules no larger than a medicine capsule and they consisted of the sperm and the ovum of the higher animals, ready to be matched for sowing, ready to be imprinted; he also had small life-bombs which could surround any form of life with at least a chance of survival.

He went to the bank and he got cats, eight pairs, sixteen earth cats, *Felis domesticus,* the kind of cat that you and I know, the kind of cat which is bred, sometimes for telepathic uses, sometimes to go along on the ships and serve as auxiliary weapons when the minds of the pin-lighters direct the cats to fight off dangers.

He coded these cats. He coded them with messages just as monstrous as the messages which had made the men-women of Arachosia into monsters. This is what he coded:

> *Do not breed true.*
> *Invent new chemistry.*
> *You will serve man.*
> *Become civilized.*
> *Learn speech.*
> *You will serve man.*
> *When man calls you will serve man.*
> *Go back, and come forth.*
> *Serve man.*

These instructions were no mere verbal instructions. They were imprints on the actual molecular structure of the animals. They were changes in the genetic and biological coding which went with these cats. And then Suzdal committed his offense against the laws of mankind. He had a chronopathic device on board the ship. A time distorter, usually to be used for a moment or a second or two to bring the ship away from utter destruction.

The men-women of Arachosia were already cutting through the hull.

He could hear their high, hooting voices screaming delirious pleasure at one another as they regarded him as the first of their promised enemies that they had ever met, the first of the monsters from Old Earth who had finally overtaken them. The true, evil people on whom they, the men-women of Arachosia, would be revenged.

Suzdal remained calm. He coded the genetic cats. He loaded them into life-bombs. He adjusted the controls of his chronopathic machine illegally, so that instead of reaching one second for a ship of eighty thousand tons, they reached two million years for a load of less than four kilos. He flung the cats into the nameless moon of Arachosia.

And he flung them back in time,

And he knew he did not have to wait.

He didn't.

∽ *The Catland Suzdal Made* ∽

The cats came. Their ships glittered in the naked sky above Arachosia. Their little combat craft attacked. The cats who had not existed a moment before, but who had then had two million years in which to follow a destiny printed into their brains, printed down their spinal cords, etched into the chemistry of their bodies and personalities. The cats had turned into people of a kind, with speech, intelligence, hope, and a mission. Their mission was to reach Suzdal, to rescue him, to obey him, and to damage Arachosia.

The cat ships screamed their battle warnings.

"This is the day of the year of the promised age. *And now come cats!*"

The Arachosians had waited for battle for four thousand years and now they got it. The cats attacked them. Two of the cat craft recognized Suzdal, and the cats reported,

"Oh Lord, oh God, oh Maker of all things, oh Commander of Time, oh Beginner of Life, we have waited since Everything began to serve You, to serve Your Name, to obey Your Glory! May we live for You, may we die for You. We are Your people."

Suzdal cried and threw his message to all the cats.

"Harry the klopts but don't kill them all!"

He repeated, "Harry them and stop them until I escape." He flung his cruiser into nonspace and escaped.

Neither cat nor Arachosian followed him.

And that's the story, but the tragedy is that Suzdal got back. And the Arachosians are still there and the cats are still there. Perhaps the Instrumentality knows where they are, perhaps the Instrumentality does not. Mankind does not really want to find out. It is against all law to bring up a form of life superior to man. Perhaps the cats are. Perhaps somebody knows whether the Arachosians won and killed the cats and added the cat science to their own and are now looking for us somewhere, probing like blind men through the stars for us true human beings to meet, to hate, to kill. Or perhaps the cats won.

Perhaps the cats are imprinted by a strange mission, by weird hopes of serving men they don't recognize. Perhaps they think we are all Arachosians and should be saved only for some particular cruiser commander, whom they will never see again. They won't see Suzdal, because we know what happened to him.

∾ *The Trial of Suzdal* ∾

Suzdal was brought to trial on a great stage in the open world. His trial was recorded. He had gone in when he should not have gone in. He had searched for the Arachosians without waiting and asking for advice and reinforcements. What business was it of his to relieve a distress ages old? What business indeed?

And then the cats. We had the records of the ship to show that something came out of that moon. Spacecraft, things with voices, things that could communicate with the human brain. We're not even sure, since they transmitted directly into the receiver computers, that they spoke an Earth language. Perhaps they did it with some sort of direct telepathy. But the crime was, *Suzdal had succeeded.*

By throwing the cats back two million years, by coding them to survive, coding them to develop civilization, coding them to come to his rescue, he had created a whole new world in less than one second of objective time.

His chronopathic device had flung the little life-bombs back to the wet earth of the big moon over Arachosia and in less time than it takes to record this, the bombs came back in the form of a fleet built by a race, an Earth race, though of cat origin, two million years old.

The court stripped Suzdal of his name and said, "You will not be named Suzdal any longer."

The court stripped Suzdal of his rank.

"You will not be a commander of this or any other navy, neither imperial nor of the Instrumentality."

The court stripped Suzdal of his life. "You will not live longer, former commander, and former Suzdal."

And then the court stripped Suzdal of death.

"You will go to the planet Shayol, the place of uttermost shame from which no one ever returns. You will go there with the contempt and hatred of mankind. We will not punish you. We do not wish to know about you any more. You will live on, but for us you will have ceased to exist."

That's the story. It's a sad, wonderful story. The Instrumentality tries to cheer up all the different kinds of mankind by telling them it isn't true, it's just a ballad.

Perhaps the records do exist. Perhaps somewhere the crazy klopts of Arachosia breed their boyish young, deliver their babies, always by Caesarean, feed them always by bottle, generations of men who have known fathers and who have no idea of what the word *mother* might be. And perhaps the Arachosians spend their crazy lives in endless battle with intelligent cats who are serving a mankind that may never come back.

That's the story.

Furthermore, it isn't true.

Golden the Ship Was—Oh! Oh! Oh!

Aggression started very far away.

War with Raumsog came about twenty years after the great cat scandal which, for a while, threatened to cut the entire planet Earth from the desperately essential santaclara drug. It was a short war and a bitter one.

Corrupt, wise, weary old Earth fought with masked weapons, since only hidden weapons could maintain so ancient a sovereignty—sovereignty which had long since lapsed into a titular paramountcy among the communities of mankind. Earth won and the others lost, because the leaders of Earth never put other considerations ahead of survival. And this time, they thought, they were finally and really threatened.

The Raumsog war was never known to the general public except for the revival of wild old legends about golden ships.

∽|∽

On Earth the Lords of the Instrumentality met. The

357

presiding chairman looked about and said, "Well, gentlemen, all of us have been bribed by Raumsog. We have all been paid off individually. I myself received six ounces of stroon in pure form. Will the rest of you show better bargains?"

Around the room, the councilors announced the amounts of their bribes.

The chairman turned to the secretary. "Enter the bribes in the record and then mark the record off-the-record."

The others nodded gravely.

"Now we must fight. Bribery is not enough. Raumsog has been threatening to attack Earth. It's been cheap enough to let him threaten, but obviously we don't mean to let him do it."

"How are you going to stop him, Lord Chairman?" growled a gloomy old member. "Get out the golden ships?"

"Exactly that." The chairman looked deadly serious.

There was a murmurous sigh around the room. The golden ships had been used against an inhuman life-form many centuries before. They were hidden somewhere in nonspace and only a few officials of Earth knew how much reality there was to them. Even at the level of the Lords of the Instrumentality the council did not know precisely what they were.

"One ship," said the chairman of the Lords of the Instrumentality, "will be enough."

It was.

∽ II ∽

The dictator Lord Raumsog on his planet knew the difference some weeks later.

"You can't mean that," he said. "You can't mean it. There is no such ship that size. The golden ships are just a story. No one ever saw a picture of one."

"Here is a picture, my Lord," said the subordinate.

Raumsog looked at it. "It's a trick. Some piece of trick photography. They distorted the size. The dimensions are wrong. Nobody has a ship that size. You could not build it, or if you did build it, you could not operate it. There just is not any such thing—" He babbled on for a few more sentences before he realized that his men were looking at the picture and not at him.

He calmed down.

The boldest of the officers resumed speaking. "That one ship is ninety million miles long, Your Highness. It shimmers like fire, but moves so fast that we cannot approach it. But it came into the center of our fleet almost touching our ships, stayed there twenty or thirty thousandths of a second. There it was, we thought. We saw the evidence of life on board: light beams waved; they examined us and then, of course, it lapsed back into nonspace. Ninety million miles, Your Highness. Old Earth has some stings yet and we do not know what the ship is doing."

The officers stared with anxious confidence at their overlord.

Raumsog sighed. "If we must fight, we'll fight. We can destroy that too. After all, what is size in the spaces between the stars? What difference does it make whether it is nine miles or nine million or ninety million?" He sighed again. "Yet I must say ninety million miles is an awful big size for a ship. I don't know what they are going to do with it."

He did not.

∾ III ∾

It is strange—strange and even fearful—what the love of Earth can do to men. Tedesco, for example.

Tedesco's reputation was far-flung. Even among the Go-Captains, whose thoughts were rarely on such matters, Tedesco was known for his raiment, the foppish arrangement of his mantle of office, and his bejeweled badges of authority. Tedesco was known too for his languid manner and his luxurious sybaritic living. When the message came, it found Tedesco in his usual character.

He was lying on the air-draft with his brain pleasure centers plugged into the triggering current. So deeply lost in pleasure was he that the food, the women, the clothing, the books of his apartments were completely neglected and forgotten. All pleasure save the pleasure of electricity acting on the brain was forgotten.

So great was the pleasure that Tedesco had been plugged into the current for twenty hours without interruption—a manifest disobedience of the rule which set six hours as maximum pleasure.

And yet, when the message came—relayed to Tedesco's brain by the infinitesimal crystal set there for the transmittal of messages so secret that even thought was too vulnerable to interception—when the message came Tedesco struggled through layer after layer of bliss and unconsciousness.

The ships of gold—the golden ships—for Earth is in danger.

Tedesco struggled. *Earth is in danger.* With a sigh of bliss he made the effort to press the button which turned off the current. And with a sigh of cold reality he took a look at the world about him and turned to the job at hand. Quickly he prepared to wait upon the Lords of the Instrumentality.

The chairman of the Lords of the Instrumentality sent out the Lord Admiral Tedesco to command the golden ship. The ship itself, larger than most stars, was an incredible monstrosity. Centuries before it had frightened away nonhuman aggressors from a forgotten corner of the galaxies.

The Lord Admiral walked back and forth on his bridge. The cabin was small, twenty feet by thirty. The control area of the ship measured nothing over a hundred feet. All the rest was a golden bubble of the feinting ship, nothing more than thin and incredibly rigid foam with tiny wires cast across it so as to give the illusion of a hard metal and strong defenses.

The ninety million miles of length were right. Nothing else was.

The ship was a gigantic dummy, the largest scarecrow ever conceived by the human mind.

Century after century it had rested in nonspace between the stars, waiting for use. Now it proceeded helpless and defenseless against a militant and crazy dictator Raumsog and his horde of hard-fighting and very real ships. Raumsog had broken the disciplines of space. He had killed the pinlighters. He had imprisoned the Go-captains. He had used renegades and apprentices to pillage the immense interstellar ships and had armed the captive vessels to the teeth. In a system which had not known real war, and least of all war against Earth, he had planned well.

He had bribed, he had swindled, he had propagandized. He expected Earth to fall before the threat itself. Then he launched his attack.

With the launching of the attack, Earth itself changed. Corrupt rascals became what they were in title: the leaders and the defenders of mankind.

Tedesco himself had been an elegant fop. War changed him into an aggressive captain, swinging the largest vessel of all time as though it were a tennis bat.

He cut in on the Raumsog fleet hard and fast.

Tedesco shifted his ship right, north, up, over.

He appeared before the enemy and eluded them— down, forward, right, over.

He appeared before the enemy again. One successful shot from them could destroy an illusion on which the safety of mankind itself depended. It was his business not to allow them that shot.

Tedesco was not a fool. He was fighting his own strange kind of war, but he could not help wondering where the real war was proceeding.

∾ IV ∾

Prince Lovaduck had obtained his odd name because he had had a Chinesian ancestor who did love ducks, ducks in their Peking form—succulent duck skins brought forth to him ancestral dreams of culinary ecstasy.

His ancestress, an English lady, had said, "Lord Lovaduck, that fits you!"—and the name had been proudly taken as a family name. Lord Lovaduck had a small ship. The ship was tiny and had a very simple and threatening name: *Anybody*.

The ship was not listed in the space register and he himself was not in the Ministry of Space Defense. The craft was attached only to the Office of Statistics and Investigation—under the listing, "vehicle" 3/4 for the Earth treasury. He had very elementary defenses. With him on the ship went one chronopathic idiot essential to his final and vital maneuvers.

With him also went a monitor. The monitor, as always, sat rigid, catatonic, unthinking, unaware—except for the tape recorder of his living mind which unconsciously noted every imminent mechanical movement of the ship and was prepared to destroy Lovaduck, the chronopathic idiot, and the ship itself should they attempt to escape the authority of Earth or should they turn against Earth. The life of a monitor was a difficult one but was far better than execution for crime, its usual alternative. The monitor made no trouble. Lovaduck also had a very small collection of weapons, weapons selected with exquisite care for the atmosphere, the climate, and the precise conditions of Raumsog's planet.

He also had a psionic talent, a poor crazy little girl who wept, and whom the Lords of the Instrumentality had cruelly refused to heal, because her talents were better in unshielded form than they would have been had she been brought into the full community of mankind. She was a class-three etiological interference.

∾ V ∾

Lovaduck brought his tiny ship near the atmosphere of Raumsog's planet. He had paid good money for his captaincy to this ship and he meant to recover it. Recover it he would, and handsomely, if he succeeded in his adventurous mission.

The Lords of the Instrumentality were the corrupt rulers of a corrupt world, but they had learned to make corruption serve their civil and military ends, and they were in no mind to put up with failures. If Lovaduck failed he might as well not come back at all. No bribery could save him from this condition. No monitor could let him escape. If he succeeded, he might be almost as rich as an Old North Australian or a stroon merchant.

Lovaduck materialized his ship just long enough to hit the planet by radio. He walked across the cabin and slapped the girl. The girl became frantically excited. At the height of her excitement he slapped a helmet on her head, plugged in the ship's communication system, and flung her own peculiar emotional psionic radiations over the entire planet.

She was a luck-changer. She succeeded: for a few moments, at every place on that planet, under the water and on it, in the sky and in the air, luck went wrong just a little. Quarrels did occur, accidents did happen, mischances moved just within the limits of sheer probability. They all occurred within the same minute. The uproar was reported just as Lovaduck moved his ship to another position. This was the most critical time of all. He dropped down into the atmosphere. He was immediately detected. Ravening weapons reached for him, weapons sharp enough to scorch the very air and to bring every living being on the planet into a condition of screaming alert.

No weapons possessed by Earth could defend against such an attack.

Lovaduck did not defend. He seized the shoulders of his chronopathic idiot. He pinched the poor defective; the idiot fled, taking the ship with him. The ship moved back three, four seconds in time to a period slightly earlier than the first detection. All the instruments on Raumsog's planet went off. There was nothing on which they could act.

Lovaduck was ready. He discharged the weapons. The weapons were not noble.

The Lords of the Instrumentality played at being chivalrous and did love money, but when life and death were at stake, they no longer cared much about money, or credit, or even about honor. They fought like the animals of Earth's ancient past—they fought to kill. Lovaduck had discharged a combination of organic and inorganic poisons with a high dispersion rate. Seventeen million people, nine hundred and fifty thousandths of the entire population, were to die within that night.

He slapped the chronopathic idiot again. The poor freak whimpered. The ship moved back two more seconds in time.

As he unloaded more poison, he could feel the mechanical relays reach for him.

He moved to the other side of the planet, moving

backward one last time, dropped a final discharge of virulent carcinogens, and snapped his ship into nonspace, into the outer reaches of nothing. Here he was far beyond the reach of Raumsog.

∽ VI ∽

Tedesco's golden ship moved serenely toward the dying planet, Raumsog's fighters closing on it. They fired—it evaded, surprisingly agile for so immense a craft, a ship larger than any sun seen in the heavens of that part of space. But while the ships closed in their radios reported:

"The capital has blanked out."

"Raumsog himself is dead."

"There is no response from the north."

"People are dying in the relay stations."

The fleet moved, intercommunicated, and began to surrender. The golden ship appeared once more and then it disappeared, apparently forever.

∽ VII ∽

The Lord Tedesco returned to his apartments and to the current for plugging into the centers of pleasure in his brain. But as he arranged himself on the air-jet his hand stopped on its mission to press the button which would start the current. He realized, suddenly, that he had pleasure. The contemplation of the golden ship and of what he had accomplished—alone, deceptive, without the praise of all the worlds for his solitary daring—gave even greater pleasure than that of the electric current. And he sank back on the jet of air and thought of the golden ship, and his pleasure was greater than any he had ever experienced before.

∾ VIII ∾

On Earth, the Lords of the Instrumentality gracefully acknowledged that the golden ship had destroyed all life on Raumsog's planet. Homage was paid to them by the many worlds of mankind. Lovaduck, his idiot, his little girl, and the monitor were taken to hospitals. Their minds were erased of all recollection of their accomplishments.

Lovaduck himself appeared before the Lords of the Instrumentality. He felt that he had served on the golden ship and he did not remember what he had done. He knew nothing of a chronopathic idiot. And he remembered nothing of his little "vehicle." Tears poured down his face when the Lords of the Instrumentality gave him their highest decorations and paid him an immense sum of money. They said: "You have served well and you are discharged. The blessings and the thanks of mankind will forever rest upon you . . ."

Lovaduck went back to his estates wondering that his service should have been so great. He wondered, too, in the centuries of the rest of his life, how any man—such as himself—could be so tremendous a hero and never quite remember how it was accomplished.

∾ IX ∾

On a very remote planet, the survivors of a Raumsog cruiser were released from internment. By special orders, direct from Earth, their memories had been discoordinated so that they would not reveal the pattern of defeat. An obstinate reporter kept after one spaceman. After many hours of hard drinking the survivor's answer was still the same:

"Golden the ship was—oh! oh! oh! Golden the ship was—oh! oh! oh!"

Drunkboat

Perhaps it is the saddest, maddest, wildest story in the whole long history of space. It is true that no one else had ever done anything like it before, to travel at such a distance, and at such speeds, and by such means. The hero looked like such an ordinary man—when people looked at him for the first time. The second time, ah! that was different.

And the heroine. Small she was, and ash-blonde, intelligent, perky, and hurt. Hurt—yes, that's the right word. She looked as though she needed comforting or helping, even when she was perfectly all right. Men felt more like men when she was near. Her name was Elizabeth.

Who would have thought that her name would ring loud and clear in the wild vomiting nothing which made up Space[3]?

He took an old, old rocket, of an ancient design. With it he outflew, outfled, outjumped all the machines which had ever existed before. You might almost think that he went so fast that he shocked the great vaults of the sky, so that the ancient poem might have been written for him alone. "All the stars threw down their spears and watered heaven with their tears."

Go he did, so fast, so far that people simply did not believe it at first. They thought it was a joke told by men, a farce spun forth by rumor, a wild story to while away the summer afternoon.

We know his name now.

And our children and their children will know it for always.

Rambo. Artyr Rambo of Earth Four.

But he followed his Elizabeth where no space was. He went where men could not go, had not been, did not dare, would not think.

He did all this of his own free will.

Of course people thought it was a joke at first, and got to making up silly songs about the reported trip.

"Dig me a hole for that reeling feeling! . . ." sang one.

"Push me the call for the umber number! . . ." sang another.

"Where is the ship of the ochre joker? . . ." sang a third.

Then people everywhere found it was true. Some stood stock still and got gooseflesh. Others turned quickly to everyday things. Space[3] had been found, and it had been pierced. Their world would never be the same again. The solid rock had become an open door.

Space itself, so clean, so empty, so tidy, now looked like a million million light-years of tapioca pudding— gummy, mushy, sticky, not fit to breathe, not fit to swim in.

How did it happen?

Everybody took the credit, each in his own different way.

∽ I ∽

"He came for me," said Elizabeth. "I died and he came for me because the machines were making a mess of my life when they tried to heal my terrible, useless death."

∽ II ∽

"I went myself," said Rambo. "They tricked me and lied to me and fooled me, but I took the boat and I became the boat and I got there. Nobody made me do it. I was angry, but I went. And I came back, didn't I?"

He too was right, even when he twisted and whined on the green grass of Earth, his ship lost in a space so terribly far and strange that it might have been beneath his living hand, or might have been half a galaxy away.

How can anybody tell, with Space^3?

It was Rambo who got back, looking for his Elizabeth. He loved her. So the trip was his, and the credit his.

∽ III ∽

But the Lord Crudelta said, many years later, when he spoke in a soft voice and talked confidentially among friends, "The experiment was mine. I designed it. I picked

Rambo. I drove the selectors mad, trying to find a man who would meet those specifications. And I had that rocket built to the old, old plans. It was the sort of thing which human beings first used when they jumped out of the air a little bit, leaping like flying fish from one wave to the next and already thinking that they were eagles. If I had used one of the regular planoform ships, it would have disappeared with a sort of reverse gurgle, leaving space milky for a little bit while it faded into nastiness and obliteration. But I did not risk that. I put the rocket on a launching pad. *And the launching pad itself was an interstellar ship!* Since we were using an ancient rocket, we did it up right, with the old, old writing, mysterious letters printed all over the machine. We even had the name of our Organization—I and O and M, for 'the Instrumentality of Mankind'—written on it good and sharp.

"How would I know," went on the Lord Crudelta, "that we would succeed more than we wanted to succeed, that Rambo would tear space itself loose from its hinges and leave that ship behind, just because he loved Elizabeth so sharply much, so fiercely much?"

Crudelta sighed.

"I know it and I don't know it. I'm like that ancient man who tried to take a water boat the wrong way around the planet Earth and found a new world instead. Columbus, he was called. And the land, that was Australia or America or something like that. That's what I did. I sent Rambo out in that ancient rocket and he found a way through space-three. Now none of us will ever know who might come bulking through the floor or take shape out of the air in front of us."

Crudelta added, almost wistfully, "What's the use of telling the story? Everybody knows it, anyhow. My part in it isn't very glorious. Now the end of it, that's pretty. The bungalow by the waterfall and all the wonderful children that other people gave to them, you could write a poem about that. But the next to the end, how he showed up at the hospital helpless and insane, looking for his own Elizabeth. That was sad and eerie, that was frightening. I'm glad it all came to the happy ending with the bungalow by the waterfall, but it took a crashing long time to get there. And there are parts of it that we will never quite understand, the naked skin against naked space, the eyeballs riding something much faster than light ever was. Do you know what an *aoudad* is? It's an ancient sheep that used to live on Old Earth, and here we are, thousands of years later, with a children's nonsense rhyme about it. The animals are gone but the rhyme remains. It'll be like that with Rambo someday. Everybody will know his name and all about his drunkboat, but they will forget the scientific milestone that he crossed, hunting for Elizabeth in an ancient rocket that couldn't fly from peetle to pootle.... Oh, the rhyme? Don't you know that? It's a silly thing. It goes:

Point your gun at a murky lurky.
(Now you're talking ham or turkey!)
Shoot a shot at a dying aoudad.
(Don't ask the lady why or how, dad!)

Don't ask me what 'ham' and 'turkey' are. Probably parts of ancient animals, like beefsteak or sirloin. But the children still say the words. They'll do that with Rambo and his drunken boat some day. They may even tell the story of Elizabeth. But they will never tell the part about how he got to the hospital. That part is too terrible, too real, too sad and wonderful at the end. They found him on the grass. Mind you, naked on the grass, and nobody knew where he had come from!"

∽ IV ∽

They found him naked on the grass and nobody knew where he had come from. They did not even know about the ancient rocket which the Lord Crudelta had sent beyond the end of nowhere with the letters I, O, and M written on it. They did not know that this was Rambo, who had gone through Space[3]. The robots noticed him first and brought him in, photographing everything that they did. They had been programmed that way, to make sure that anything unusual was kept in the records.

Then the nurses found him in an outside room.

They assumed that he was alive, since he was not dead, but they could not prove that he was alive, either.

That heightened the puzzle.

The doctors were called in. Real doctors, not machines. They were very important men. Citizen Doctor Timofeyev, Citizen Doctor Grosbeck, and the director himself, Sir and Doctor Vomact. They took the case.

(Over on the other side of the hospital Elizabeth waited, unconscious, and nobody knew it at all. Elizabeth, for whom he had jumped space, and pierced the stars, but nobody knew it yet!)

The young man could not speak. When they ran eye-prints and fingerprints through the Population Machine, they found that he had been bred on Earth itself, but had been shipped out as a frozen and unborn baby to Earth Four. At tremendous cost, they queried Earth Four with an "instant message," only to discover that the young man who lay before them in the hospital had been lost from an experimental ship on an intergalactic trip.

Lost.

No ship and no sign of ship.

And here he was.

They stood at the edge of space, and did not know what they were looking at. They were doctors and it was their business to repair or rebuild people, not to ship them around. How should such men know about Space^3 when they did not even know about Space^2 except for the fact that people got on the planoform ships and made trips through it? They were looking for sickness when their eyes saw engineering. They treated him when he was well.

All he needed was time, to get over the shock of the most tremendous trip ever made by a human being, but the doctors did not know that and they tried to rush his recovery.

When they put clothes on him, he moved from coma to a kind of mechanical spasm and tore the clothing off. Once again stripped, he lay himself roughly on the floor and refused food or speech.

They fed him with needles while the whole energy of space, had they only known it, was radiating out of his body in new forms.

They put him all by himself in a locked room and watched him through the peephole.

He was a nice-looking young man, even though his mind was blank and his body was rigid and unconscious. His hair was very fair and his eyes were light blue but his face showed character—a square chin; a handsome, resolute, sullen mouth; old lines in the face which looked as though, when conscious, he must have lived many days or months on the edge of rage.

When they studied him the third day in the hospital, their patient had not changed at all.

He had torn off his pajamas again and lay naked, face down, on the floor.

His body was as immobile and tense as it had been on the day before.

(One year later, this room was going to be a museum with a bronze sign reading, "Here lay Rambo after he left the Old Rocket for Space Three," but the doctors still had no idea of what they were dealing with.)

His face was turned so sharply to the left that the neck muscles showed. His right arm stuck out straight from the body. The left arm formed an exact right angle from the body, with the left forearm and hand pointing rigidly upward at 90° from the upper arm. The legs were in the grotesque parody of a running position.

Doctor Grosbeck said, "It looks to me like he's swimming. Let's drop him in a tank of water and see if he moves." Grosbeck sometimes went in for drastic solutions to problems.

Timofeyev took his place at the peephole. "Spasm, still," he murmured. "I hope the poor fellow is not feeling pain when his cortical defenses are down. How can a man fight pain if he does not even know what he is experiencing?"

"And you, Sir and Doctor," said Grosbeck to Vomact, "what do you see?"

Vomact did not need to look. He had come early and had looked long and quietly at the patient through the peephole before the other doctors arrived. Vomact was a wise man, with good insight and rich intuitions. He could guess in an hour more than a machine could diagnose in a year; he was already beginning to understand that this was a sickness which no man had ever had before. Still, there were remedies waiting.

The three doctors tried them.

They tried hypnosis, electrotherapy, massage, subsonics, atropine, surgital, a whole family of the digitalinids, and some quasi-narcotic viruses which had been grown in orbit where they mutated fast. They got the beginning of a response when they tried gas hypnosis combined with an electronically amplified telepath; this showed that something still went on inside the patient's mind. Otherwise the brain might have seemed to be mere fatty tissue, without a nerve in it. The other attempts had shown nothing. The gas showed a faint stirring away from fear and pain. The telepath reported glimpses of unknown skies. (The doctors turned the telepath over to the Space Police promptly, so they could try to code the star patterns which he had seen in the patient's mind, but the patterns did not fit. The telepath, though a keen-witted man, could not remember them in enough detail for them to be scanned against the samples of piloting sheets.)

The doctors went back to their drugs and tried ancient, simple remedies—morphine and caffeine to counteract each other, and a rough massage to make him dream again, so that the telepath could pick it up.

There was no further result that day, or the next.

Meanwhile the Earth authorities were getting restless. They thought, quite rightly, that the hospital had done a good job of proving that the patient had not been on Earth until a few moments before the robots found him on the grass. How had he gotten on the grass?

The airspace of Earth reported no intrusion at all, no vehicle marking a blazing arc of air incandescing against metal, no whisper of the great forces which drove a planoform ship through Space[2].

(Crudelta, using faster-than-light ships, was creeping slow as a snail back toward Earth, racing his best to see if Rambo had gotten there first.)

On the fifth day, there was the beginning of a break-through.

∽ **V** ∽

Elizabeth had passed.

This was found out only much later, by a careful check of the hospital records.

The doctors only knew this much:

Patients had been moved down the corridor, sheet-covered figures immobile on wheeled beds.

Suddenly the beds stopped rolling.

A nurse screamed.

The heavy steel-and-plastic wall was bending inward. Some slow, silent force was pushing the wall into the corridor itself.

The wall ripped.

A human hand emerged.

One of the quick-witted nurses screamed, "*Push* those beds! *Push* them out of the way."

The nurses and robots obeyed.

The beds rocked like a group of boats crossing a wave when they came to the place where the floor, bonded to the wall, had bent upward to meet the wall as it tore inward. The peach-colored glow of the lights flicked. Robots appeared.

A second human hand came through the wall. Pushing in opposite directions, the hands tore the wall as though it had been wet paper.

The patient from the grass put his head through.

He looked blindly up and down the corridor, his eyes not quite focusing, his skin glowing a strange red-brown from the burns of open space.

"No," he said. Just that one word.

But that "No" was heard. Though the volume was not loud, it carried through the hospital. The internal telecommunications system relayed it. Every switch in the place went negative. Frantic nurses and robots, with even the doctors helping them, rushed to turn all the machines back on—the pumps, the ventilators, the artificial kidneys, the brain re-recorders, even the simple air engines which kept the atmosphere clean.

Far overhead an aircraft spun giddily. Its "off" switch, surrounded by triple safeguards, had suddenly been thrown into the negative position. Fortunately the robot-pilot got it going again before crashing into earth.

The patient did not seem to know that his word had this effect.

(Later the world knew that this was part of the "drunkboat effect." The man himself had developed the capacity for using his neurophysical system as a machine control.)

In the corridor, the machine-robot who served as policeman arrived. He wore sterile, padded velvet gloves with a grip of sixty metric tons inside his hands. He approached the patient. The robot had been carefully trained to recognize all kinds of danger from delirious or psychotic humans; later he reported that he had an input of "danger, extreme" on every band of sensation. He had been expecting to seize the prisoner with irreversible firmness and to return him to his bed, but with this kind of danger sizzling in the air, the robot took no chances. His wrist itself contained a hypodermic pistol which operated on compressed argon.

He reached out toward the unknown, naked man who stood in the big torn gap of the wall. The wrist-weapon hissed and a sizable injection of condamine, the most powerful narcotic in the known universe, spat its way through the skin of Rambo's neck. The patient collapsed.

The robot picked him up gently and tenderly, lifted him through the torn wall, pushed the door open with a kick which broke the lock, and put the patient back on his bed. The robot could hear doctors coming, so he used his enormous hands to pat the steel wall back into its proper shape. Work-robots or underpeople could finish the job later, but meanwhile it looked better to have that part of the building set at right angles again.

Doctor Vomact arrived, followed closely by Grosbeck.

"What happened?" he yelled, shaken out of a lifelong calm. The robot pointed at the ripped wall.

"He tore it open. I put it back," said the robot.

The doctors turned to look at the patient. He had crawled off his bed again and was on the floor, but his breathing was light and natural.

"What did you give him?" cried Vomact to the robot.

"Condamine," said the robot, "according to rule forty-seven-B. The drug is not to be mentioned outside the hospital."

"I know that," said Vomact absentmindedly and a little crossly. "You can go along now. Thank you."

"It is not usual to thank robots," said the robot, "but you can read a commendation into my record if you want to."

"Get the blazes out of here!" shouted Vomact at the officious robot.

The robot blinked. "There are no blazes but I have the impression you mean me. I shall leave, with your permission." He jumped with odd gracefulness around the two doctors, fingered the broken doorlock absentmindedly, as though he might have wished to repair it, and then, seeing Vomact glare at him, left the room completely.

A moment later soft muted thuds began. Both doctors listened a moment and then gave up. The robot was out in the corridor, gently patting the steel floor back into shape. He was a tidy robot, probably animated by an amplified chicken-brain, and when he got tidy he became obstinate.

"Two questions, Grosbeck," said the Sir and Doctor Vomact.

"Your service, sir!"

"Where was the patient standing when he pushed the wall into the corridor, and how did he get the leverage to do it?"

Grosbeck narrowed his eyes in puzzlement. "Now that you mention it, I have no idea of how he did it. In fact, he could not have done it. But he has. And the other question?"

"What do you think of condamine?"

"Dangerous, of course, as always. Addiction can—"

"Can you have addiction with no cortical activity?" interrupted Vomact.

"Of course," said Grosbeck promptly. "Tissue addiction."

"Look for it, then," said Vomact.

Grosbeck knelt beside the patient and felt with his fingertips for the muscle endings. He felt where they knotted themselves into the base of the skull, the tips of the shoulders, the striped area of the back.

When he stood up there was a look of puzzlement on his face. "I never felt a human body like this one before. I am not even sure that it *is* human any longer."

Vomact said nothing. The two doctors confronted one another. Grosbeck fidgeted under the calm stare of the senior man. Finally he blurted out:

"Sir and Doctor, I know what we *could* do."

"And that," said Vomact levelly, without the faintest hint of encouragement or of warning, "is what?"

"It wouldn't be the first time that it's been done in a hospital."

"What?" said Vomact, his eyes—those dreaded eyes!—making Grosbeck say what he did not want to say.

Grosbeck flushed. He leaned toward Vomact so as to whisper, even though there was no one standing near them. His words, when they came, had the hasty indecency of a lover's improper suggestion,

"Kill the patient, Sir and Doctor. Kill him. We have plenty of records of him. We can get a cadaver out of the basement and make it into a good simulacrum. Who knows what we will turn loose among mankind if we let him get well?"

"Who knows?" said Vomact without tone or quality to his voice. "But Citizen and Doctor, what is the twelfth duty of a physician?"

"'Not to take the law into his own hands, keeping healing for the healers and giving to the state or the Instrumentality whatever properly belongs to the state or the Instrumentality.'" Grosbeck sighed as he retracted his own suggestion. "Sir and Doctor, I take it back. It wasn't medicine which I was talking about. It was government and politics which were really in my mind."

"And now . . . ?" asked Vomact.

"Heal him, or let him be until he heals himself."

"And which would you do?"

"I'd try to heal him."

"How?" said Vomact.

"Sir and Doctor," cried Grosbeck, "do not ride my weaknesses in this case! I know that you like me because I am a bold, confident sort of man. Do not ask me to be myself when we do not even know where this body came from. If I were bold as usual, I would give him typhoid and condamine, stationing telepaths nearby. But this is something new in the history of man. We are people and perhaps he is not a person any more. Perhaps he represents the combination of people with some kind of a new force. How did he get here from the far side of nowhere? How many million times has he been enlarged or reduced? We do not know what he is or what has happened to him. How can we treat a man when we are treating the cold of space, the heat of suns, the frigidity of distance? We know what to do with flesh, but this is not quite flesh any more. Feel him yourself, Sir and Doctor! You will touch something which nobody has ever touched before."

"I have," Vomact declared, "already felt him. You are right. We will try typhoid and condamine for half a day. Twelve hours from now let us meet each other at this place. I will tell the nurses and the robots what to do in the interim."

They both gave the red-tanned spread-eagled figure on the floor a parting glance. Grosbeck looked at the body with something like distaste mingled with fear; Vomact was expressionless, save for a wry wan smile of pity.

At the door the head nurse awaited them. Grosbeck was surprised at his chief's orders.

"Ma'am and Nurse, do you have a weaponproof vault in this hospital?"

"Yes, sir," she said. "We used to keep our records in it until we telemetered all our records into Computer Orbit. Now it is dirty and empty."

"Clean it out. Run a ventilator tube into it. Who is your military protector?"

"My what?" she cried, in surprise.

"Everyone on Earth has military protection. Where are the forces, the soldiers, who protect this hospital of yours?"

"My Sir and Doctor!" she called out. "My Sir and Doctor! I'm an old woman and I have been allowed to work here for three hundred years. But I never thought of that idea before. Why would I need soldiers?"

"Find who they are and ask them to stand by. They are specialists too, with a different kind of art from ours. Let them stand by. They may be needed before this day is out. Give my name as authority to their lieutenant or sergeant. Now here is the medication which I want you to apply to this patient."

Her eyes widened as he went on talking, but she was a disciplined woman and she nodded as she heard him out, point by point. Her eyes looked very sad and weary at the end but she was a trained expert herself and she had enormous respect for the skill and wisdom of the Sir and Doctor Vomact. She also had a warm, feminine pity for the motionless young male figure on the floor, swimming forever on the heavy floor, swimming between archipelagoes which no man living had ever dreamed before.

∞ VI ∞

Crisis came that night.

The patient had worn handprints into the inner wall of the vault, but he had not escaped.

The soldiers, looking oddly alert with their weapons gleaming in the bright corridor of the hospital, were really very bored, as soldiers always become when they are on duty with no action.

Their lieutenant was keyed up. The wirepoint in his hand buzzed like a dangerous insect. Sir and Doctor Vomact, who knew more about weapons than the soldiers thought he knew, saw that the wirepoint was set to HIGH, with a capacity of paralyzing people five stories up, five stories down, or a kilometer sideways. He said nothing. He merely thanked the lieutenant and entered the vault, closely followed by Grosbeck and Timofeyev.

The patient swam here too.

He had changed to an arm-over-arm motion, kicking his legs against the floor. It was as though he had swum on the other floor with the sole purpose of staying afloat, and had now discovered some direction in which to go, albeit very slowly. His motions were deliberate, tense, rigid, and so reduced in time that it seemed as though he hardly moved at all. The ripped pajamas lay on the floor beside him.

Vomact glanced around, wondering what forces the man could have used to make those handprints on the steel wall. He remembered Grosbeck's warning that the patient should die, rather than subject all mankind to new and unthought risks, but though he shared the feeling, he could not condone the recommendation.

Almost irritably, the great doctor thought to himself—where could the man be going?

(To Elizabeth, the truth was, to Elizabeth, now only sixty meters away. Not till much later did people understand what Rambo had been trying to do—crossing sixty mere meters to reach his Elizabeth when he had already jumped an uncount of light-years to return to her. To his own, his dear, his well-beloved who needed him!)

The condamine did not leave its characteristic mark of deep lassitude and glowing skin: perhaps the typhoid was successfully contradicting it. Rambo did seem more lively than before. The name had come through on the regular message system, but it still did not mean anything to the Sir and Doctor Vomact. It would. It would.

Meanwhile the other two doctors, briefed ahead of time, got busy with the apparatus which the robots and the nurses had installed.

Vomact murmured to the others, "I think he's better off. Looser all around. I'll try shouting."

So busy were they that they just nodded.

Vomact screamed at the patient, "Who are you? What are you? Where do you come from?"

The sad blue eyes of the man on the floor glanced at him with a surprisingly quick glance, but there was no other real sign of communication. The limbs kept up their swim against the rough concrete floor of the vault. Two of the bandages which the hospital staff had put on him had worn off again. The right knee, scraped and bruised, deposited a sixty-centimeter trail of blood—some old and black and coagulated, some fresh, new and liquid—on the floor as it moved back and forth.

Vomact stood up and spoke to Grosbeck and Timofeyev. "Now," he said, "let us see what happens when we apply the pain."

The two stepped back without being told to do so.

Timofeyev waved his hand at a small white-enameled orderly-robot who stood in the doorway.

The pain net, a fragile cage of wires, dropped down from the ceiling.

It was Vomact's duty, as senior doctor, to take the greatest risk. The patient was wholly encased by the net of wires, but Vomact dropped to his hands and knees, lifted the net at one corner with his right hand, thrust his own head into it next to the head of the patient. Doctor Vomact's robe trailed on the clean concrete, touching the black old stains of blood left from the patient's "swim" throughout the night.

Now Vomact's mouth was centimeters from the patient's ear.

Said Vomact, "Oh."

The net hummed.

The patient stopped his slow motion, arched his back, looked steadfastly at the doctor.

Doctor Grosbeck and Timofeyev could see Vomact's face go white with the impact of the pain machine, but Vomact kept his voice under control and said evenly and loudly to the patient:

"*Who—are—you?*"

The patient said flatly, "Elizabeth."

The answer was foolish but the tone was rational.

Vomact pulled his head out from under the net, shouting again at the patient, "*Who—are—you?*"

The naked man replied, speaking very clearly:

"Chwinkle, chwinkle, little chweeble,
I am feeling very feeble!"

Vomact frowned and murmured to the robot, "More pain. Turn it up to pain ultimate."

The body threshed under the net, trying to resume its swim on the concrete.

A loud wild braying cry came from the victim under the net. It sounded like a screamed distortion of the name Elizabeth, echoing out from endless remoteness.

It did not make sense.

Vomact screamed back, *"Who—are—you?"*

With unexpected clarity and resonance, the voice came back to the three doctors from the twisting body under the net of pain:

"I'm the shipped man, the ripped man, the gypped man, the dipped man, the hipped man, the tripped man, the tipped man, the slipped man, the flipped man, the nipped man, the ripped man, the clipped man—aah!" His voice choked off with a cry and he went back to swimming on the floor, despite the intensity of the pain net immediately above him.

The doctor lifted his hand. The pain net stopped buzzing and lifted high into the air.

He felt the patient's pulse. It was quick. He lifted an eyelid. The reactions were much closer to normal.

"Stand back," he said to the others.

"Pain on both of us," he said to the robot.

The net came down on the two of them.

"Who are you?" shrieked Vomact, right into the patient's ear, holding the man halfway off the floor and not quite knowing whether the body which tore steel walls might not, somehow, tear both of them apart as they stood.

The man babbled back at him: "I'm the most man, the post man, the host man, the ghost man, the coast man, the boast man, the dosed man, the grossed man, the toast man, the roast man, no! no! no!"

He struggled in Vomact's arms. Grosbeck and Timofeyev stepped forward to rescue their chief when the patient added, very calmly and clearly:

"Your procedure is all right, Doctor, whoever you are. More fever, please. More pain, please. Some of that dope to fight the pain. You're pulling me back. I know I am on Earth. Elizabeth is near. For the love of God, get me Elizabeth! But don't rush me. I need days and days to get well."

The rationality was so startling that Grosbeck, without waiting for orders from Vomact, as chief doctor, ordered the pain net lifted.

The patient began babbling again: "I'm the three man, the he man, the tree man, the me man, the three man, the three man. . . ." His voice faded and he slumped unconscious.

Vomact walked out of the vault. He was a little unsteady.

His colleagues took him by the elbows.

He smiled wanly at them. "I wish it were lawful. . . . I could use some of that condamine myself. No wonder the pain nets wake the patients up and even make dead people do twitches! Get me some liquor. My heart is old."

Grosbeck sat him down while Timofeyev ran down the corridor in search of medicinal liquor.

Vomact murmured, "How are we going to find *his* Elizabeth? There must be millions of them. And he's from Earth Four too."

"Sir and Doctor, you have worked wonders," said Grosbeck. "To go under the net. To take those chances. To bring him to speech. I will never see anything like it again. It's enough for any one lifetime, to have seen this day."

"But what do we do next?" asked Vomact wearily, almost in confusion.

That particular question needed no answer.

∾ VII ∾

The Lord Crudelta had reached Earth.

His pilot landed the craft and fainted at the controls with sheer exhaustion.

Of the escort cats, who had ridden alongside the space craft in the miniature spaceships, three were dead, one was comatose, and the fifth was spitting and raving.

When the port authorities tried to slow the Lord Crudelta down to ascertain his authority, he invoked Top Emergency, took over the command of troops in the name of the Instrumentality, arrested everyone in sight but the troop commander, and requisitioned the troop commander to take him to the hospital. The computers at the port had told him that one Rambo, "sans origine," had arrived mysteriously on the grass of a designated hospital.

Outside the hospital, the Lord Crudelta invoked Top Emergency again, placed all armed men under his own command, ordered a recording monitor to cover all his actions if he should later be channeled into a court-martial, and arrested everyone in sight.

The tramp of heavily armed men, marching in combat order, overtook Timofeyev as he hurried back to Vomact with a drink. The men were jogging along on the double. All of them had live helmets and their wirepoints were buzzing.

Nurses ran forward to drive the intruders out, ran backward when the sting of the stun-rays brushed cruelly over them. The whole hospital was in an uproar.

The Lord Crudelta later admitted that he had made a serious mistake.

The Two Minutes' War broke out immediately.

You have to understand the pattern of the Instrumentality to see how it happened. The Instrumentality was a self-perpetuating body of men with enormous powers and a strict code. Each was a plenum of the low, the middle, and the high justice. Each could do anything he found necessary or proper to maintain the Instrumentality and to keep the peace between the worlds. But if he made a mistake or committed a wrong—ah, then, it was suddenly different. Any Lord could put another Lord to death in an emergency, but he was assured of death and disgrace himself if he assumed this responsibility. The only difference between ratification and repudiation came in the fact that Lords who killed in an emergency and were proved wrong were marked down on a very shameful list, while those who killed other Lords rightly (as later examination might prove) were listed on a very honorable list, but still killed.

With three Lords, the situation was different. Three Lords made an emergency court; if they acted together, acted in good faith, and reported to the computers of the Instrumentality, they were exempt from punishment, though not from blame or even reduction to citizen status. Seven Lords, or all the Lords on a given planet at a given moment, were beyond any criticism except that of a dignified reversal of their actions should a later ruling prove them wrong.

This was all the business of the Instrumentality. The Instrumentality had the perpetual slogan: "Watch, but do not govern; stop war, but do not wage it; protect, but do not control; and first, survive!"

The Lord Crudelta had seized the troops—not his troops, but the light regular troops of Manhome Government—because he feared that the greatest danger in the history of man might come from the person whom he himself had sent through Space[3].

He never expected that the troops would be plucked out from his command—an overriding power reinforced by robotic telepathy and the incomparable communications net, both open and secret, reinforced by thousands of years in trickery, defeat, secrecy, victory, and sheer experience, which the Instrumentality had perfected since it emerged from the Ancient Wars.

Overriding, overridden!

These were the commands which the Instrumentality had used before recorded time began. Sometimes they suspended their antagonists on points of law, sometimes by the deft and deadly insertion of weapons, most often by cutting in on other people's mechanical and social controls and doing their will, only to drop the controls as suddenly as they had taken them.

But not Crudelta's hastily called troops.

∽ VIII ∾

The war broke out with a change of pace.

Two squads of men were moving into that part of the

hospital where Elizabeth lay, waiting the endless returns to the jelly-baths which would rebuild her poor ruined body.

The squads changed pace.

The survivors could not account for what happened

They all admitted to great mental confusion—afterward.

At the time it seemed that they had received a clear, logical command to turn and to defend the women's section by counterattacking their own main battalion right in their rear.

The hospital was a very strong building. Otherwise it would have melted to the ground or shot up in flame.

The leading soldiers suddenly turned around, dropped for cover, and blazed their wirepoints at the comrades who followed them. The wirepoints were cued to organic material, though fairly harmless to inorganic. They were powered by the power relays which every soldier wore on his back.

In the first ten seconds of the turnaround, twenty-seven soldiers, two nurses, three patients, and one orderly were killed. One hundred and nine other people were wounded in that first exchange of fire.

The troop commander had never seen battle, but he had been well trained. He immediately deployed his reserves around the external exits of the building and sent his favorite squad, commanded by a Sergeant Lansdale whom he trusted well, down into the basement, so that it could rise vertically from the basement into the women's quarters and find out who the enemy was.

As yet, he had no idea that it was his own leading troops turning and fighting their comrades.

He testified later, at the trial, that he personally had no

sensations of eerie interference with his own mind. He merely knew that his men had unexpectedly come upon armed resistance from antagonists—identity unknown!— who had weapons identical with theirs. Since the Lord Crudelta had brought them along in case there might be a fight with unspecified antagonists, he felt right in assuming that a Lord of the Instrumentality knew what he was doing. This was the enemy, all right.

In less than a minute, the two sides had balanced out. The line of fire had moved right into his own force. The lead men, some of whom were wounded, simply turned around and began defending themselves against the men immediately behind them. It was as though an invisible line, moving rapidly, had parted the two sections of the military force.

The oily black smoke of dissolving bodies began to glut the ventilators.

Patients were screaming, doctors cursing, robots stamping around, and nurses trying to call each other.

The war ended when the troop commander saw Sergeant Lansdale, whom he himself had sent upstairs, leading a charge out of the women's quarters—directly at his own commander!

The officer kept his head.

He dropped to the floor and rolled sidewise as the air chittered at him, the emanations of Lansdale's wirepoint killing all the tiny bacteria in the air. On his helmet phone he pushed the manual controls to TOP VOLUME and to NONCOMS ONLY and he commanded, with a sudden flash of brilliant mother-wit:

"Good job, Lansdale!"

Lansdale's voice came back as weak as if it had been off-planet. "We'll keep them out of this section yet, sir!"

The troop commander called back very loudly but calmly, not letting on that he thought his sergeant was psychotic, "Easy now. Hold on. I'll be with you."

He changed to the other channel and said to his nearby men, "Cease fire. Take cover and wait."

A wild scream came to him from the phones.

It was Lansdale. "Sir! Sir! I'm fighting *you*, sir. I just caught on. It's getting me again. Watch out."

The buzz and burr of the weapons suddenly stopped.

The wild human uproar of the hospital continued.

A tall doctor, with the insignia of high seniority, came gently to the troop commander and said, "You can stand up and take your soldiers out now, young fellow. The fight was a mistake."

"I'm not under your orders," snapped the young officer. "I'm under the Lord Crudelta. He requisitioned this force from the Manhome Government. Who are you?"

"You may salute me, captain," said the doctor. "I am Colonel General Vomact of the Earth Medical Reserve. But you had better not wait for the Lord Crudelta."

"But *where* is he?"

"In my bed," said Vomact.

"Your *bed?*" cried the young officer in complete amazement.

"In bed. Doped to the teeth. I fixed him up. He was excited. Take your men out. We'll treat the wounded on the lawn. You can see the dead in the refrigerators downstairs in a few minutes, except for the ones that went smoky from direct hits."

"But the fight? . . ."

"A mistake, young man, or else—"

"Or else what?" shouted the young officer, horrified at the utter mess of his own combat experience.

"Or else a weapon no man has ever seen before. Your troops fought each other. Your command was intercepted."

"I could see that," snapped the officer, "as soon as I saw Lansdale coming at me."

"But do you know what took him over?" said Vomact gently, while taking the officer by the arm and beginning to lead him out of the hospital. The captain went willingly, not noticing where he was going, so eagerly did he watch for the other man's words.

"I think I know," said Vomact. "Another man's dreams. Dreams which have learned how to turn themselves into electricity or plastic or stone. Or anything else. Dreams coming to us out of space-three."

The young officer nodded dumbly. This was too much. "Space-three?" he murmured. It was like being told that the really alien invaders, whom men had been expecting for fourteen thousand years and had never met, were waiting for him on the grass. Until now Space^3 had been a mathematical idea, a romancer's daydream, but not a fact.

The Sir and Doctor Vomact did not even ask the young officer. He brushed the young man gently at the nape of the neck and shot him through with tranquilizer. Vomact then led him out to the grass. The young captain stood alone and whistled happily at the stars in the sky. Behind him, his sergeants and corporals were sorting out the survivors and getting treatment for the wounded.

The Two Minutes' War was over.

Rambo had stopped dreaming that his Elizabeth was in danger. He had recognized, even in his deep sick sleep, that the tramping in the corridor was the movement of armed men. His mind had set up defenses to protect Elizabeth. He took over command of the forward troops and set them to stopping the main body. The powers which Space³ had worked into him made this easy for him to do, even though he did not know that he was doing it.

∽ IX ∽

"How many dead?" said Vomact to Grosbeck and Timofeyev.

"About two hundred."

"And how many irrecoverable dead?"

"The ones that got turned into smoke. A dozen, maybe fourteen. The other dead can be fixed up, but most of them will have to get new personality prints."

"Do you know what happened?" asked Vomact.

"No, Sir and Doctor," they both chorused.

"I do. I think I do. No, I *know* I do. It's the wildest story in the history of man. Our patient did it—Rambo. He took over the troops and set them against each other. That Lord of the Instrumentality who came charging in—Crudelta. I've known him for a long long time. He's behind this case. He thought that troops would help, not sensing that troops would invite attack upon themselves. And there is something else."

"Yes?" they said, in unison.

"Rambo's woman—the one he's looking for. She must be here."

"Why?" said Timofeyev.

"Because *he's* here."

"You're assuming that he came here because of his own will, Sir and Doctor."

Vomact smiled the wise crafty smile of his family; it was almost a trademark of the Vomact house.

"I am assuming all the things which I cannot otherwise prove.

"First, I assume that he came here naked out of space itself, driven by some kind of force which we cannot even guess.

"Second, I assume he came *here* because he wanted something. A woman named Elizabeth, who must already be here. In a moment we can go inventory all our Elizabeths.

"Third, I assume that the Lord Crudelta knew something about it. He has led troops into the building. He began raving when he saw me. I know hysterical fatigue, as do you, my brothers, so I condamined him for a night's sleep.

"Fourth, let's leave our man alone. There'll be hearings and trials enough, Space knows, when all these events get scrambled out."

Vomact was right.
He usually was.
Trials did follow.

It was lucky that Old Earth no longer permitted

newspapers or television news. The population would have been frothed up to riot and terror if they had ever found out what happened at the Old Main Hospital just to the west of Meeya Meefla.

~ X ~

Twenty-one days later, Vomact, Timofeyev, and Grosbeck were summoned to the trial of the Lord Crudelta. A full panel of seven Lords of the Instrumentality was there to give Crudelta an ample hearing and, if required, a sudden death. The doctors were present both as doctors for Elizabeth and Rambo and as witnesses for the Investigating Lord.

Elizabeth, fresh up from being dead, was as beautiful as a newborn baby in exquisite, adult feminine form. Rambo could not take his eyes off her, but a look of bewilderment went over his face every time she gave him a friendly, calm, remote little smile. (She had been told that she was his girl, and she was prepared to believe it, but she had no memory of him or of anything else more than sixty hours back, when speech had been reinstalled in her mind; and he, for his part, was still thick of speech and subject to strains which the doctors could not quite figure out.)

The Investigating Lord was a man named Starmount.

He asked the panel to rise.

They did so.

He faced the Lord Crudelta with great solemnity. "You are obliged, my Lord Crudelta, to speak quickly and clearly to this court."

"Yes, my Lord," he answered.

"We have the summary power."

"You have the summary power. I recognize it."

"You will tell the truth or else you will lie."

"I shall tell the truth or I will lie."

"You may lie, if you wish, about matters of fact and opinion, but you will in no case lie about human relationships. If you do lie, nevertheless, you will ask that your name be entered in the Roster of Dishonor."

"I understand the panel and the rights of this panel. I will lie if I wish—though I don't think I will need to do so"—and here Crudelta flashed a weary intelligent smile at all of them—"but I will not lie about matters of relationship. If I do, I will ask for dishonor."

"You have yourself been well trained as a Lord of the Instrumentality?"

"I have been so trained and I love the Instrumentality well. In fact, I am myself the Instrumentality, as are you, and as are the honorable Lords beside you. I shall behave well, for as long as I live this afternoon."

"Do you credit him, my Lords?" asked Starmount.

The members of the panel nodded their mitred heads. They had dressed ceremonially for the occasion.

"Do you have a relationship to the woman Elizabeth?"

The members of the trial panel caught their breath as they saw Crudelta turn white. "My Lords!" he cried, and answered no further.

"It is the custom," said Starmount firmly, "that you answer promptly or that you die."

The Lord Crudelta got control of himself. "I am answering. I did not know who she was, except for the fact

that Rambo loved her. I sent her to Earth from Earth
Four, where I then was. Then I told Rambo that she had
been murdered and hung desperately at the edge of
death, wanting only his help to return to the green fields
of life."

Said Starmount, "Was that the truth?"

"My Lord and Lords, it was a lie."

"Why did you tell it?"

"To induce rage in Rambo and to give him an overriding
reason for wanting to come to Earth faster than any man
has ever come before."

"A-a-ah! A-a-ah!" Two wild cries came from Rambo,
more like the call of an animal than like the sound of a
man.

Vomact looked at his patient, felt himself beginning
to growl with a deep internal rage. Rambo's powers,
generated in the depths of Space[3], had begun to operate
again. Vomact made a sign. The robot behind Rambo had
been coded to keep Rambo calm. Though the robot had
been enameled to look like a white gleaming hospital
orderly, he was actually a police-robot of high powers,
built up with an electronic cortex based on the frozen
midbrain of an old wolf. (A wolf was a rare animal, something like a dog.) The robot touched Rambo, who dropped
off to sleep. Doctor Vomact felt the anger in his own mind
fade away. He lifted his hand gently; the robot caught the
signal and stopped applying the narcoleptic radiation.
Rambo slept normally; Elizabeth looked worriedly at the
man who she had been told was her own.

The Lords turned back from the glances at Rambo.

Said Starmount, icily, "And why did you do that?"

"Because I wanted him to travel through space-three."

"Why?"

"To show it could be done."

"And do you, my Lord Crudelta, affirm that this man has in fact traveled through space-three?"

"I do."

"Are you lying?"

"I have the right to lie, but I have no wish to do so. In the name of the Instrumentality itself, I tell you that this is the truth."

The panel members gasped. Now there was no way out. Either the Lord Crudelta was telling the truth, *which meant that all former times had come to an end and that a new age had begun for all the kinds of mankind,* or else he was lying in the face of the most powerful form of affirmation which any of them knew.

Even Starmount himself took a different tone. His teasing, restless, intelligent voice took on a new timbre of kindness.

"You do therefore assert that this man has come back from outside our galaxy with nothing more than his own natural skin to cover him? No instruments? No power?"

"I did not say that," said Crudelta. "Other people have begun to pretend I used such words. I tell you, my Lords, that I planoformed for twelve consecutive Earth days and nights. Some of you may remember where Outpost Baiter Gator is. Well, I had a good Go-Captain, and he took me four long jumps beyond there, out into intergalactic space. I left this man there. When I reached Earth, he had been here twelve days, more or less. I have assumed, therefore, that his trip was more or less instantaneous. I was on my way back to Baiter Gator, counting by Earth time, when the doctor here found this man on the grass outside the hospital."

Vomact raised his hand. The Lord Starmount gave him the right to speak. "My Sirs and Lords, we did not find this man on the grass. The robots did, and made a record. But even the robots did not see or photograph his arrival."

"We know that," said Starmount angrily, "and we know that we have been told that nothing came to Earth by any means whatever, in that particular quarter hour. Go on, my Lord Crudelta. What relation are you to Rambo?"

"He is my victim."

"Explain yourself!"

"I computed him out. I asked the machines where I would be most apt to find a man with a tremendous lot of rage in him, and was informed that on Earth Four the rage level had been left high because that particular planet had a considerable need for explorers and adventurers, in whom rage was a strong survival trait. When I got to Earth Four, I commanded the authorities to find out which border cases had exceeded the limits of allowable rage. They gave me four men. One was much too large. Two were old. This man was the only candidate for my experiment. I chose him."

"What did you tell him?"

"Tell him? I told him his sweetheart was dead or dying."

"No, no," said Starmount. "Not at the moment of crisis. What did you tell him to make him cooperate in the first place?"

"I told him," said the Lord Crudelta evenly, "that I was

myself a Lord of the Instrumentality and that I would kill him myself if he did not obey, and obey promptly."

"And under what custom or law did you act?"

"Reserved material," said the Lord Crudelta promptly. "There are telepaths here who are not a part of the Instrumentality. I beg leave to defer until we have a shielded place."

Several members of the panel nodded and Starmount agreed with them. He changed the line of questioning.

"You forced this man, therefore, to do something which he did not wish to do?"

"That is right," said the Lord Crudelta.

"Why didn't you go yourself, if it is that dangerous?"

"My Lords and Honorables, it was the nature of the experiment that the experimenter himself should not be expended in the first try. Artyr Rambo has indeed traveled through space-three. I shall follow him myself, in due course." (How the Lord Crudelta did do so is another tale, told about another time.) "If I had gone and if I had been lost, that would have been the end of the space-three trials. At least for our time."

"Tell us the exact circumstances under which you last saw Artyr Rambo before you met after the battle in the Old Main Hospital."

"We had put him in a rocket of the most ancient style. We also wrote writing on the outside of it, just the way the Ancients did when they first ventured into space. Ah, that was a beautiful piece of engineering and archeology! We copied everything right down to the correct models of fifteen thousand years ago, when the Paroskii and Murkins were racing each other into space. The rocket was white, with a red and white gantry beside it. The letters IOM were on the rocket, not that the words mattered. The rocket has gone into nowhere, but the passenger sits here. It rose on a stool of fire. The stool became a column. Then the landing field disappeared."

"And the landing field," said Starmount quietly, "what was that?"

"A modified planoform ship. We have had ships go milky in space because they faded molecule by molecule. We have had others disappear utterly. The engineers had changed this around. We took out all the machinery needed for circumnavigation, for survival, or for comfort. The landing field was to last three or four seconds, no more. Instead, we put in fourteen planoform devices, all operating in tandem, so that the ship would do what other ships do when they planoform—namely, drop one of our familiar dimensions and pick up a new dimension from some unknown category of space—but do it with such force as to get out of what people call space-two and move over into space-three."

"And space-three, what did you expect of that?"

"I thought that it was universal and instantaneous, in relation to our universe. That everything was equally distant from everything else. That Rambo, wanting to see his girl again, would move in a thousandth of a second from the empty space beyond Outpost Baiter Gator into the hospital where she was."

"And, my Lord Crudelta, what made you think so?"

"A hunch, my Lord, for which you are welcome to kill me."

Starmount turned to the panel. "I suspect, my Lords,

that you are more likely to doom him to long life, great responsibility, immense rewards, and the fatigue of being his own difficult and complicated self."

The mitres moved gently and the members of the panel rose.

"You, my Lord Crudelta, will sleep till the trial is finished."

A robot stroked him and he fell asleep.

"Next witness," said the Lord Starmount, "in five minutes."

∽ XI ∽

Vomact tried to keep Rambo from being heard as a witness. He argued fiercely with the Lord Starmount in the intermission. "You Lords have shot up my hospital, abducted two of my patients, and now you are going to torment both Rambo and Elizabeth. Can't you leave them alone? Rambo is in no condition to give coherent answers and Elizabeth may be damaged if she sees him suffer."

The Lord Starmount said to him, "You have your rules, Doctor, and we have ours. This trial is being recorded, inch by inch and moment by moment. Nothing is going to be done to Rambo unless we find that he has planet-killing powers. If that is true, of course, we will ask you to take him back to the hospital and to put him to death very pleasantly. But I don't think it will happen. We want his story so that we can judge my colleague Crudelta. Do you think that the Instrumentality would survive if it did not have fierce internal discipline?"

Vomact nodded sadly; he went back to Grosbeck and

Timofeyev, murmuring sadly to them, "Rambo's in for it. There's nothing we could do."

The panel reassembled. They put on their judicial mitres. The lights of the room darkened and the weird blue light of justice was turned on.

The robot orderly helped Rambo to the witness chair.

"You are obliged," said Starmount, "to speak quickly and clearly to this court."

"You're not Elizabeth," said Rambo.

"I am the Lord Starmount," said the investigating Lord, quickly deciding to dispense with the formalities. "Do you know me?"

"No," said Rambo.

"Do you know where you are?"

"Earth," said Rambo.

"Do you wish to lie or to tell the truth?"

"A lie," said Rambo, "is the only truth which men can share with each other, so I will tell you lies, the way we always do."

"Can you report your trip?"

"No."

"Why not, citizen Rambo?"

"Words won't describe it."

"Do you remember your trip?"

"Do you remember your pulse of two minutes ago?" countered Rambo.

"I am not playing with you," said Starmount. "We think you have been in space-three and we want you to testify about the Lord Crudelta."

"Oh!" said Rambo. "I don't like him. I never did like him."

"Will you nevertheless try to tell us what happened also to you?"

"Should I, Elizabeth?" asked Rambo of the girl, who sat in the audience.

She did not stammer. "Yes," she said, in a clear voice which rang through the big room. "Tell them, so that we can find our lives again."

"I will tell you," said Rambo.

"When did you last see the Lord Crudelta?"

"When I was stripped and fitted to the rocket, four jumps out beyond Outpost Baiter Gator. He was on the ground. He waved good-bye to me."

"And then what happened?"

"The rocket rose. It felt very strange, like no craft I had ever been in before. I weighed many, many gravities."

"And then?"

"The engines went on. I was thrown out of space itself."

"What did it seem like?"

"Behind me I left the working ships, the cloth and the food which goes through space. I went down rivers which did not exist. I felt people around me though I could not see them, red people shooting arrows at live bodies."

"*Where* were you?" asked a panel member.

"In the wintertime where there is no summer. In an emptiness like a child's mind. In peninsulas which had torn loose from the land. And I *was* the ship."

"You were what?" asked the same panel member.

"The rocket nose. The cone. The boat. I was drunk. It was drunk. I was the drunkboat myself," said Rambo.

"And where did you go?" resumed Starmount.

"Where crazy lanterns stared with idiot eyes. Where the waves washed back and forth with the dead of all the ages. Where the stars became a pool and I swam in it. Where blue turns to liquor, stronger than alcohol, wilder than music, fermented with the *red red reds* of love. I saw all the things that men have ever thought they saw, but it was me who really saw them. I've heard phosphorescence singing and tides that seemed like crazy cattle clawing their way out of the ocean, their hooves beating the reefs. You will not believe me, but I found Floridas wilder than this, where the flowers had human skins and eyes like big cats."

"What are you talking about?" asked the Lord Starmount.

"What I found in space-three," snapped Artyr Rambo. "Believe it or not. This is what I now remember. Maybe it's a dream, but it's all I have. It was years and years and it was the blink of an eye. I dreamed green nights. I felt places where the whole horizon became one big waterfall. The boat that was me met children and I showed them El Dorado, where the gold men live. The people drowned in space washed gently past me. I was a boat where all the lost spaceships lay ruined and still. Seahorses which were not real ran beside me. The summer months came and hammered down the sun. I went past archipelagoes of stars, where the delirious skies opened up for wanderers. I cried for me. I wept for man. I wanted to be the drunk-boat sinking. I sank. I fell. It seemed to me that the grass was a lake, where a sad child, on hands and knees, sailed a toy boat as fragile as a butterfly in spring. I can't forget the pride of unremembered flags, the arrogance of prisons which I suspected, the swimming of the businessmen! Then I was on the grass."

"This may have scientific value," said the Lord Starmount, "but it is not of judicial importance. Do you have any comment on what you did during the battle in the hospital?"

Rambo was quick and looked sane. "What I did, I did not do. What I did not do, I cannot tell. Let me go, because I am tired of you and space, big men and big things. Let me sleep and let me get well."

Starmount lifted his hand for silence.

The panel members stared at him.

Only the few telepaths present knew that they had all said, "Aye. Let the man go. Let the girl go. Let the doctors go. But bring back the Lord Crudelta later on. He has many troubles ahead of him, and we wish to add to them."

∾ XII ∾

Between the Instrumentality, the Manhome Government, and the authorities at the Old Main Hospital, everyone wished to give Rambo and Elizabeth happiness.

As Rambo got well, much of his Earth Four memory returned. The trip faded from his mind.

When he came to know Elizabeth, he hated the girl.

This was not his girl—his bold, saucy Elizabeth of the markets and the valleys, of the snowy hills and the long boat rides. This was somebody meek, sweet, sad, and hopelessly loving.

Vomact cured that.

He sent Rambo to the Pleasure City of the Hesperides, where bold and talkative women pursued him because he was rich and famous.

In a few weeks—a very few indeed—he wanted *his* Elizabeth, this strange shy girl who had been cooked back from the dead while he rode space with his own fragile bones.

"Tell the truth, darling." He spoke to her once gravely and seriously. "The Lord Crudelta did not arrange the accident which killed you?"

"They say he wasn't there," said Elizabeth. "They say it was an actual accident. I don't know. I will never know."

"It doesn't matter now," said Rambo. "Crudelta's off among the stars, looking for trouble and finding it. We have our bungalow, and our waterfall and each other."

"Yes, my darling," she said, "each other. And no fantastic Floridas for us."

He blinked at this reference to the past, but he said nothing. A man who has been through Space³ needs very little in life, outside of *not* going back to Space³. Sometimes he dreamed he was the rocket again, the old rocket taking off on an impossible trip. Let other men follow! he thought. Let other men go! I have Elizabeth and I am here.

A Planet Named Shayol

∾|∾

There was a tremendous difference between the liner and the ferry in Mercer's treatment. On the liner, the attendants made gibes when they brought him his food.

"Scream good and loud," said one rat-faced steward, "and then we'll know it's you when they broadcast the sounds of punishment on the Emperor's birthday."

The other, fat steward ran the tip of his wet, red tongue over his thick, purple-red lips one time and said, "Stands to reason, man. If you hurt all the time, the whole lot of you would die. Something pretty good must happen, along with the—whatchamacallit. Maybe you turn into a woman. Maybe you turn into two people. Listen, cousin, if it's real crazy fun, let me know . . ." Mercer said nothing. Mercer had enough troubles of his own not to wonder about the daydreams of nasty men.

At the ferry it was different. The biopharmaceutical staff was deft, impersonal, quick in removing his shackles. They took off all his prison clothes and left them on the liner. When he boarded the ferry, naked, they looked him over as if he were a rare plant or a body on the operating table. They were almost kind in the clinical deftness of their touch. They did not treat him as a criminal, but as a specimen.

Men and women, clad in their medical smocks, they looked at him as though he were already dead.

He tried to speak. A man, older and more authoritative than the others, said firmly and clearly, "Do not worry about talking. I will talk to you myself in a very little time. What we are having now are the preliminaries, to determine your physical condition. Turn around, please."

Mercer turned around. An orderly rubbed his back with a very strong antiseptic.

"This is going to sting," said one of the technicians, "but it is nothing serious or painful. We are determining the toughness of the different layers of your skin."

Mercer, annoyed by this impersonal approach, spoke up just as a sharp little sting burned him above the sixth lumbar vertebra. "Don't you know who I am?"

"Of course we know who you are," said a woman's voice. "We have it all in a file in the corner. The chief doctor will talk about your crime later, if you want to talk about it. Keep quiet now. We are making a skin test, and you will feel much better if you do not make us prolong it."

Honesty forced her to add another sentence: "And we will get better results as well."

They had lost no time at all in getting to work.

He peered at them sidewise to look at them. There was nothing about them to indicate that they were human devils in the antechambers of hell itself. Nothing was there to indicate that this was the satellite of Shayol, the final and uttermost place of chastisement and shame. They looked like medical people from his life before he committed the crime without a name.

They changed from one routine to another. A woman, wearing a surgical mask, waved her hand at a white table.

"Climb up on that, please."

No one had said "please" to Mercer since the guards had seized him at the edge of the palace. He started to obey her and then he saw that there were padded handcuffs at the head of the table. He stopped.

"Get along, please," she demanded. Two or three of the others turned around to look at both of them.

The second "please" shook him. He had to speak. These were people, and he was a person again. He felt his voice rising, almost cracking into shrillness as he asked her, "Please, Ma'am, is the punishment going to begin?"

"There's no punishment here," said the woman. "This is the satellite. Get on the table. We're going to give you your first skin-toughening before you talk to the head doctor. Then you can tell him all about your crime—"

"You know my crime?" he said, greeting it almost like a neighbor.

"Of course not," said she, "but all the people who come through here are believed to have committed crimes. Somebody thinks so or they wouldn't be here. Most of them want to talk about their personal crimes. But don't slow me down. I'm a skin technician, and down on the surface of Shayol you're going to need the very best work that any of us can do for you. Now get on that table. And when you are ready to talk to the chief you'll have something to talk about besides your crime."

He complied.

Another masked person, probably a girl, took his hands in cool, gentle fingers and fitted them to the padded cuffs in a way he had never sensed before. By now he thought he knew every interrogation machine in the whole empire, but this was nothing like any of them.

The orderly stepped back. "All clear, Sir and Doctor."

"Which do you prefer?" said the skin technician. "A great deal of pain or a couple of hours' unconsciousness?"

"Why should I want pain?" said Mercer.

"Some specimens do," said the technician, "by the time they arrive here. I suppose it depends on what people have done to them before they got here. I take it you did not get any of the dream-punishments."

"No," said Mercer. "I missed those." He thought to himself, I didn't know that I missed anything at all.

He remembered his last trial, himself wired and plugged in to the witness stand. The room had been high and dark. Bright blue light shone on the panel of judges, their judicial caps a fantastic parody of the episcopal mitres of long, long ago. The judges were talking, but he could not hear them. Momentarily the insulation slipped and he heard one of them say, "Look at that white, devilish face. A man like that is guilty of everything. I vote for Pain Terminal." "Not Planet Shayol?" said a second voice. "The dromozoa place," said a third voice. "That should suit him," said the first voice. One of the judicial engineers must then have noticed that the prisoner was listening illegally. He was cut off. Mercer then thought that he had gone through everything which the cruelty and intelligence of mankind could devise.

But this woman said he had missed the dream-punishments. Could there be people in the universe even worse off than himself? There must be a lot of people down on Shayol. They never came back.

He was going to be one of them; would they boast to him of what they had done, before they were made to come to this place?

"You asked for it," said the woman technician. "It is just an ordinary anesthetic. Don't panic when you awaken. Your skin is going to be thickened and strengthened chemically and biologically."

"Does it hurt?"

"Of course," said she. "But get this out of your head. We're not punishing you. The pain here is just ordinary medical pain. Anybody might get it if they needed a lot of surgery. The punishment, if that's what you want to call it, is down on Shayol. Our only job is to make sure that you are fit to survive after you are landed. In a way, we are saving your life ahead of time. You can be grateful for that if you want to be. Meanwhile, you will save yourself a lot of trouble if you realize that your nerve endings will respond to the change in the skin. You had better expect to be very uncomfortable when you recover. But then, we can help that, too." She brought down an enormous lever and Mercer blacked out.

When he came to, he was in an ordinary hospital room, but he did not notice it. He seemed bedded in fire. He lifted his hand to see if there were flames on it. It looked the way it always had, except that it was a little red and a little swollen. He tried to turn in the bed. The fire became a scorching blast which stopped him in mid-turn. Uncontrollably, he moaned.

A voice spoke, "You are ready for some pain-killer."

It was a girl nurse. "Hold your head still," she said, "and I will give you half an amp of pleasure. Your skin won't bother you then."

She slipped a soft cap on his head. It looked like metal but it felt like silk.

He had to dig his fingernails into his palms to keep from threshing about on the bed.

"Scream if you want to," she said. "A lot of them do. It will just be a minute or two before the cap finds the right lobe in your brain."

She stepped to the corner and did something which he could not see.

There was the flick of a switch.

The fire did not vanish from his skin. He still felt it; but suddenly it did not matter. His mind was full of delicious pleasure which throbbed outward from his head and seemed to pulse down through his nerves. He had visited the pleasure palaces, but he had never felt anything like this before.

He wanted to thank the girl, and he twisted around in the bed to see her. He could feel his whole body flash with pain as he did so, but the pain was far away. And the pulsating pleasure which coursed out of his head, down his spinal cord, and into his nerves was so intense that the pain got through only as a remote, unimportant signal.

She was standing very still in the corner.

"Thank you, nurse," said he.

She said nothing.

He looked more closely, though it was hard to look while enormous pleasure pulsed through his body like a symphony written in nerve-messages. He focused his eyes on her and saw that she too wore a soft metallic cap.

He pointed at it.

She blushed all the way down to her throat.

She spoke dreamily, "You looked like a nice man to me. I didn't think you'd tell on me . . ."

He gave her what he thought was a friendly smile, but with the pain in his skin and the pleasure bursting out of his head, he really had no idea of what his actual expression might be. "It's against the law," he said. "It's terribly against the law. But it is nice."

"How do you think *we* stand it here?" said the nurse. "You specimens come in here talking like ordinary people and then you go down to Shayol. Terrible things happen to you on Shayol. Then the surface station sends up parts of you, over and over again. I may see your head ten times, quick-frozen and ready for cutting up, before my two years are up. You prisoners ought to know how we suffer," she crooned, the pleasure-charge still keeping her relaxed and happy. "You ought to die as soon as you get down there and not pester us with your torments. We can hear you screaming, you know. You keep on sounding like people even after Shayol begins to work on you. Why do you do it, Mr. Specimen?" She giggled sillily. "You hurt our feelings so. No wonder a girl like me has to have a little jolt now and then. It's real, real dreamy and I don't mind getting you ready to go down on Shayol." She staggered over to his bed. "Pull this cap off me, will you? I haven't got enough will power left to raise my hands."

Mercer saw his hand tremble as he reached for the cap.

His fingers touched the girl's soft hair through the cap. As he tried to get his thumb under the edge of the cap, in order to pull it off, he realized this was the loveliest girl he had ever touched. He felt that he had always loved her, that he always would. Her cap came off. She stood erect, staggering a little before she found a chair to hold to. She closed her eyes and breathed deeply.

"Just a minute," she said in her normal voice. "I'll be with you in just a minute. The only time I can get a jolt of this is when one of you visitors gets a dose to get over the skin trouble."

She turned to the room mirror to adjust her hair. Speaking with her back to him, she said, "I hope I didn't say anything about downstairs."

Mercer still had the cap on. He loved this beautiful girl who had put it on him. He was ready to weep at the thought that she had had the same kind of pleasure which he still enjoyed. Not for the world would he say anything which could hurt her feelings. He was sure she wanted to be told that she had not said anything about "downstairs"— probably shop talk for the surface of Shayol—so he assured her warmly, "You said nothing. Nothing at all."

She came over to the bed, leaned, kissed him on the lips. The kiss was as far away as the pain; he felt nothing; the Niagara of throbbing pleasure which poured through his head left no room for more sensation. But he liked the friendliness of it. A grim, sane corner of his mind whispered to him that this was probably the last time he would ever kiss a woman, but it did not seem to matter.

With skilled fingers she adjusted the cap on his head. "There, now. You're a sweet guy. I'm going to pretend-forget and leave the cap on you till the doctor comes."

With a bright smile she squeezed his shoulder.

She hastened out of the room.

The white of her skirt flashed prettily as she went out the door. He saw that she had very shapely legs indeed.

She was nice, but the cap . . . ah, it was the cap that mattered! He closed his eyes and let the cap go on stimulating the pleasure centers of his brain. The pain in his skin was still there, but it did not matter any more than did the chair standing in the corner. The pain was just something that happened to be in the room.

A firm touch on his arm made him open his eyes.

The older, authoritative-looking man was standing beside the bed, looking down at him with a quizzical smile.

"She did it again," said the old man.

Mercer shook his head, trying to indicate that the young nurse had done nothing wrong.

"I'm Doctor Vomact," said the older man, "and I am going to take this cap off you. You will then experience the pain again, but I think it will not be so bad. You can have the cap several more times before you leave here."

With a swift, firm gesture he snatched the cap off Mercer's head.

Mercer promptly doubled up with the inrush of fire from his skin. He started to scream and then saw that Doctor Vomact was watching him calmly.

Mercer gasped, "It is—easier now."

"I knew it would be," said the doctor. "I had to take the cap off to talk to you. You have a few choices to make."

"Yes, Doctor," gasped Mercer.

"You have committed a serious crime and you are going down to the surface of Shayol."

"Yes," said Mercer.

"Do you want to tell me your crime?"

Mercer thought of the white palace walls in perpetual sunlight, and the soft mewing of the little things when he reached them. He tightened his arms, legs, back, and jaw. "No," he said, "I don't want to talk about it. It's the crime without a name. Against the Imperial family . . ."

"Fine," said the doctor, "that's a healthy attitude. The crime is past. Your future is ahead. Now, I can destroy your mind before you go down—if you want me to."

"That's against the law," said Mercer.

Doctor Vomact smiled warmly and confidently. "Of course it is. A lot of things are against human law. But there are laws of science, too. Your body, down on Shayol, is going to serve science. It doesn't matter to me whether the body has Mercer's mind or the mind of a low-grade shellfish. I have to leave enough mind in you to keep the body going, but I can wipe out the historic you and give your body a better chance of being happy. It's your choice, Mercer. Do you want to be you or not?"

Mercer shook his head back and forth, "I don't know."

"I'm taking a chance," said Doctor Vomact, "in giving you this much leeway. I'd have it done if I were in your position. It's pretty bad down there."

Mercer looked at the full, broad face. He did not

trust the comfortable smile. Perhaps this was a trick to increase his punishment. The cruelty of the Emperor was proverbial. Look at what he had done to the widow of his predecessor, the Dowager Lady Da. She was younger than the Emperor himself, and he had sent her to a place worse than death. If he had been sentenced to Shayol, why was this doctor trying to interfere with the rules? Maybe the doctor himself had been conditioned, and did not know what he was offering.

Doctor Vomact read Mercer's face. "All right. You refuse. You want to take your mind down with you. It's all right with me. I don't have you on my conscience. I suppose you'll refuse the next offer too. Do you want me to take your eyes out before you go down? You'll be much more comfortable without vision. I *know* that, from the voices that we record for the warning broadcasts. I can sear the optic nerves so that there will be no chance of your getting vision again."

Mercer rocked back and forth. The fiery pain had become a universal itch, but the soreness of his spirit was greater than the discomfort of his skin.

"You refuse that, too?" said the doctor.

"I suppose so," said Mercer.

"Then all I have to do is to get ready. You can have the cap for a while, if you want."

Mercer said, "Before I put the cap on, can you tell me what happens down there?"

"Some of it," said the doctor. "There is an attendant. He is a man, but not a human being. He is a homunculus fashioned out of cattle material. He is intelligent and very conscientious. You specimens are turned loose on the surface of Shayol. The dromozoa are a special lifeform there. When they settle in your body, B'dikkat—that's the attendant—carves them out with an anesthetic and sends them up here. We freeze the tissue cultures, and they are compatible with almost any kind of oxygen-based life. Half the surgical repair you see in the whole universe comes out of buds that we ship from here. Shayol is a very healthy place, so far as survival is concerned. You won't die."

"You mean," said Mercer, "that I am getting perpetual punishment."

"I didn't say that," said Doctor Vomact. "Or if I did, I was wrong. You won't die soon. I don't know how long you will live down there. Remember, no matter how uncomfortable you get, the samples which B'dikkat sends up will help thousands of people in all the inhabited worlds. Now take the cap."

"I'd rather talk," said Mercer. "It may be my last chance."

The doctor looked at him strangely. "If you can stand that pain, go ahead and talk."

"Can I commit suicide down there?"

"I don't know," said the doctor. "It's never happened. And to judge by the voices, you'd think they wanted to."

"Has anybody ever come back from Shayol?"

"Not since it was put off limits about four hundred years ago."

"Can I talk to other people down there?"

"Yes," said the doctor.

"Who punishes me down there?"

"Nobody does, you fool," cried Doctor Vomact. "It's

not punishment. People don't like it down on Shayol, and it's better, I guess, to get convicts instead of volunteers. But there isn't anybody *against* you at all."

"No jailers?" asked Mercer, with a whine in his voice.

"No jailers, no rules, no prohibitions. Just Shayol, and B'dikkat to take care of you. Do you still want your mind and your eyes?"

"I'll keep them," said Mercer. "I've gone this far and I might as well go the rest of the way."

"Then let me put the cap on you for your second dose," said Doctor Vomact.

The doctor adjusted the cap just as lightly and delicately as had the nurse; he was quicker about it. There was no sign of his picking out another cap for himself. The inrush of pleasure was like a wild intoxication. His burning skin receded into distance. The doctor was near in space, but even the doctor did not matter. Mercer was not afraid of Shayol. The pulsation of happiness out of his brain was too great to leave room for fear or pain.

Doctor Vomact was holding out his hand.

Mercer wondered why, and then realized that the wonderful, kindly cap-giving man was offering to shake hands. He lifted his own. It was heavy, but his arm was happy, too.

They shook hands. It was curious, thought Mercer, to feel the handshake beyond the double level of cerebral pleasure and dermal pain.

"Goodbye, Mr. Mercer," said the doctor. "Goodbye and a good night . . ."

∼ II ∼

The ferry satellite was a hospitable place. The hundreds of hours that followed were like a long, weird dream.

Twice again the young nurse sneaked into his bedroom with him when he was being given the cap and had a cap with him. There were baths which calloused his whole body. Under strong local anesthetics, his teeth were taken out and stainless steel took their place. There were irradiations under blazing lights which took away the pain of his skin. There were special treatments for his fingernails and toe-nails. Gradually they changed into formidable claws; he found himself stropping them on the aluminum bed one night and saw that they left deep marks.

His mind never became completely clear.

Sometimes he thought he was home with his mother, that he was little again, and in pain. Other times, under the cap, he laughed in his bed to think that people were sent to this place for punishment when it was all so terribly much fun. There were no trials, no questions, no judges. Food was good, but he did not think about it much; the cap was better. Even when he was awake, he was drowsy.

At last, with the cap on him, they put him into an adiabatic pod—a one-body missile which could be dropped from the ferry to the planet below. He was all closed in, except for his face.

Doctor Vomact seemed to swim into the room. "You are strong, Mercer," the doctor shouted, "you are very strong! Can you hear me?"

Mercer nodded.

"We wish you well, Mercer. No matter what happens, remember you are helping other people up here."

"Can I take the cap with me?" said Mercer.

For an answer, Doctor Vomact removed the cap himself. Two men closed the lid of the pod, leaving Mercer in total darkness. His mind started to clear, and he panicked against his wrappings.

There was the roar of thunder and the taste of blood.

The next thing that Mercer knew, he was in a cool, cool room, much chillier than the bedrooms and operating rooms of the satellite. Someone was lifting him gently onto a table.

He opened his eyes.

An enormous face, four times the size of any human face Mercer had ever seen, was looking down at him. Huge brown eyes, cowlike in their gentle inoffensiveness, moved back and forth as the big face examined Mercer's wrappings. The face was that of a handsome man of middle years, clean-shaven, hair chestnut-brown, with sensual, full lips and gigantic but healthy yellow teeth exposed in a half-smile. The face saw Mercer's eyes open, and spoke with a deep friendly roar.

"I'm your best friend. My name is B'dikkat, but you don't have to use that here. Just call me Friend, and I will always help you."

"I hurt," said Mercer.

"Of course you do. You hurt all over. That's a big drop," said B'dikkat.

"Can I have a cap, please," begged Mercer. It was not

a question; it was a demand; Mercer felt that his private inward eternity depended on it.

B'dikkat laughed. "I haven't any caps down here. I might use them myself. Or so they think. I have other things, much better. No fear, fellow, I'll fix you up."

Mercer looked doubtful. If the cap had brought him happiness on the ferry, it would take at least electrical stimulation of the brain to undo whatever torments the surface of Shayol had to offer.

B'dikkat's laughter filled the room like a bursting pillow.

"Have you ever heard of condamine?"

"No," said Mercer.

"It's a narcotic so powerful that the pharmacopoeias are not allowed to mention it."

"You have that?" said Mercer hopefully.

"Something better. I have super-condamine. It's named after the New French town where they developed it. The chemists hooked in one more hydrogen molecule. That gave it a real jolt. If you took it in your present shape, you'd be dead in three minutes, but those three minutes would seem like ten thousand years of happiness to the inside of your mind." B'dikkat rolled his brown cow eyes expressively and smacked his rich red lips with a tongue of enormous extent.

"What's the use of it, then?"

"*You* can take it," said B'dikkat. "You can take it after you have been exposed to the dromozoa outside this cabin. You get all the good effects and none of the bad. You want to see something?"

What answer is there except *yes*, thought Mercer

grimly; does he think I have an urgent invitation to a tea party?

"Look out the window," said B'dikkat, "and tell me what you see."

The atmosphere was clear. The surface was like a desert, ginger-yellow with streaks of green where lichen and low shrubs grew, obviously stunted and tormented by high, dry winds. The landscape was monotonous. Two or three hundred yards away there was a herd of bright pink objects which seemed alive, but Mercer could not see them well enough to describe them clearly. Further away, on the extreme right of his frame of vision, there was the statue of an enormous human foot, the height of a six-story building. Mercer could not see what the foot was connected to. "I see a big foot," said he, "but—"

"But what?" said B'dikkat, like an enormous child hiding the denouement of a hugely private joke. Large as he was, he would have been dwarfed by any one of the toes on that tremendous foot.

"But it can't be a real foot," said Mercer.

"It is," said B'dikkat. "That's Go-Captain Alvarez, the man who found this planet. After six hundred years he's still in fine shape. Of course, he's mostly dromozootic by now, but I think there is some human consciousness inside him. You know what I do?"

"What?" said Mercer.

"I give him six cubic centimeters of super-condamine and he snorts for me. Real happy little snorts. A stranger might think it was a volcano. That's what super-condamine can do. And you're going to get plenty of it. You're a lucky, lucky man, Mercer. You have me for a friend, and you have my needle for a treat. I do all the work and you get all the fun. Isn't that a nice surprise?"

Mercer thought, You're lying! Lying! Where do the screams come from that we have all heard broadcast as a warning on Punishment Day? Why did the doctor offer to cancel my brain or to take out my eyes?

The cow-man watched him sadly, a hurt expression on his face. "You don't believe me," he said, very sadly.

"It's not quite that," said Mercer, with an attempt at heartiness, "but I think you're leaving something out."

"Nothing much," said B'dikkat. "You jump when the dromozoa hit you. You'll be upset when you start growing new parts—heads, kidneys, hands. I had one fellow in here who grew thirty-eight hands in a single session outside. I took them all off, froze them, and sent them upstairs. I take good care of everybody. You'll probably yell for a while. But remember, just call me Friend, and I have the nicest treat in the universe waiting for you. Now, would you like some fried eggs? I don't eat eggs myself, but most true men like them."

"Eggs?" said Mercer. "What have eggs got to do with it?"

"Nothing much. It's just a treat for you people. Get something in your stomach before you go outside. You'll get through the first day better."

Mercer, unbelieving, watched as the big man took two precious eggs from a cold chest, expertly broke them into a little pan, and put the pan in the heat-field at the center of the table Mercer had awakened on.

"Friend, eh?" B'dikkat grinned. "You'll see I'm a good friend. When you go outside, remember that."

An hour later, Mercer did go outside.

Strangely at peace with himself, he stood at the door. B'dikkat pushed him in a brotherly way, giving him a shove which was gentle enough to be an encouragement.

"Don't make me put on my lead suit, fellow." Mercer had seen a suit, fully the size of an ordinary space-ship cabin, hanging on the wall of an adjacent room. "When I close this door, the outer one will open. Just walk on out."

"But what will happen?" said Mercer, the fear turning around in his stomach and making little grabs at his throat from the inside.

"Don't start that again," said B'dikkat. For an hour he had fended off Mercer's questions about the outside. A map? B'dikkat had laughed at the thought. Food? He said not to worry. Other people? They'd be there. Weapons? What for, B'dikkat had replied. Over and over again, B'dikkat had insisted that he was Mercer's friend. What would happen to Mercer? The same that happened to everybody else.

Mercer stepped out.

Nothing happened. The day was cool. The wind moved gently against his toughened skin.

Mercer looked around apprehensively.

The mountainous body of Captain Alvarez occupied a good part of the landscape to the right. Mercer had no wish to get mixed up with that. He glanced back at the cabin. B'dikkat was not looking out the window.

Mercer walked slowly, straight ahead.

There was a flash on the ground, no brighter than the glitter of sunlight on a fragment of glass. Mercer felt a sting in the thigh, as though a sharp instrument had touched him lightly. He brushed the place with his hand.

It was as though the sky fell in.

A pain—it was more than a pain; it was a living throb—ran from his hip to his foot on the right side. The throb reached up to his chest, robbing him of breath. He fell, and the ground hurt him. Nothing in the hospital-satellite had been like this. He lay in the open air, trying not to breathe, but he did breathe anyhow. Each time he breathed, the throb moved with his thorax. He lay on his back, looking at the sun. At last he noticed that the sun was violet-white.

It was no use even thinking of calling. He had no voice. Tendrils of discomfort twisted within him. Since he could not stop breathing, he concentrated on taking air in the way that hurt him least. Gasps were too much work. Little tiny sips of air hurt him least.

The desert around him was empty. He could not turn his head to look at the cabin. Is this it? he thought. Is an eternity of this the punishment of Shayol?

There were voices near him.

Two faces, grotesquely pink, looked down at him. They might have been human. The man looked normal enough, except for having two noses side by side. The woman was a caricature beyond belief. She had grown a breast on each cheek and a cluster of naked baby-like fingers hung limp from her forehead.

"It's a beauty," said the woman, "a new one."

"Come along," said the man.

They lifted him to his feet. He did not have strength enough to resist. When he tried to speak to them a harsh cawing sound, like the cry of an ugly bird, came from his mouth.

They moved with him efficiently. He saw that he was being dragged to the herd of pink things.

As they approached, he saw that they were people. Better, he saw that they had once been people. A man with the beak of a flamingo was picking at his own body. A woman lay on the ground; she had a single head, but beside what seemed to be her original body, she had a boy's naked body growing sidewise from her neck. The boy-body, clean, new, paralytically helpless, made no movement other than shallow breathing. Mercer looked around. The only one of the group who was wearing clothing was a man with his overcoat on sidewise. Mercer stared at him, finally realizing that the man had two—or was it three?—stomachs growing on the outside of his abdomen. The coat held them in place. The transparent peritoneal wall looked fragile.

"New one," said his female captor. She and the two-nosed man put him down.

The group lay scattered on the ground.

Mercer lay in a state of stupor among them.

An old man's voice said, "I'm afraid they're going to feed us pretty soon."

"Oh, no!" "It's too early!" "Not again!" Protests echoed from the group.

The old man's voice went on, "Look, near the big toe of the mountain!"

The desolate murmur in the group attested their confirmation of what he had seen.

Mercer tried to ask what it was all about, but produced only a caw.

A woman—was it a woman?—crawled over to him on

her hands and knees. Besides her ordinary hands, she was covered with hands all over her trunk and halfway down her thighs. Some of the hands looked old and withered. Others were as fresh and pink as the baby-fingers on his captress's face. The woman shouted at him, though it was not necessary to shout.

"The dromozoa are coming. This time it hurts. When you get used to the place, you can dig in—"

She waved at a group of mounds which surrounded the herd of people.

"They're dug in," she said.

Mercer cawed again.

"Don't you worry," said the hand-covered woman, and gasped as a flash of light touched her.

The lights reached Mercer too. The pain was like the first contact but more probing. Mercer felt his eyes widen as odd sensations within his body led to an inescapable conclusion: these lights, these things, these whatever they were, were feeding him and building him up.

Their intelligence, if they had it, was not human, but their motives were clear. In between the stabs of pain he felt them fill his stomach, put water in his blood, draw water from his kidneys and bladder, massage his heart, move his lungs for him.

Every single thing they did was well meant and beneficent in intent.

And every single action hurt.

Abruptly, like the lifting of a cloud of insects, they were gone. Mercer was aware of a noise somewhere outside—a brainless, bawling cascade of ugly noise. He started to look around. And the noise stopped.

It had been himself, screaming. Screaming the ugly screams of a psychotic, a terrified drunk, an animal driven out of understanding or reason.

When he stopped, he found he had his speaking voice again.

A man came to him, naked like the others. There was a spike sticking through his head. The skin had healed around it on both sides. "Hello, fellow," said the man with the spike.

"Hello," said Mercer. It was a foolishly commonplace thing to say in a place like this.

"You can't kill yourself," said the man with the spike through his head.

"Yes, you can," said the woman covered with hands.

Mercer found that his first pain had disappeared. "What's happening to me?"

"You got a part," said the man with the spike. "They're always putting parts on us. After a while B'dikkat comes and cuts most of them off, except for the ones that ought to grow a little more. Like her," he added, nodding at the woman who lay with the boy-body growing from her neck.

"And that's all?" said Mercer. "The stabs for the new parts and the stinging for the feeding?"

"No," said the man. "Sometimes they think we're too cold and they fill our insides with fire. Or they think we're too hot and they freeze us, nerve by nerve."

The woman with the boy-body called over, "And sometimes they think we're unhappy, so they try to force us to be happy. *I* think that's the worst of all."

Mercer stammered, "Are you people—I mean—are you the only herd?"

The man with the spike coughed instead of laughing.

"Herd! That's funny. The land is full of people. Most of them dig in. We're the ones who can still talk. We stay together for company. We get more turns with B'dikkat that way."

Mercer started to ask another question, but he felt the strength run out of him. The day had been too much.

The ground rocked like a ship on water. The sky turned black. He felt someone catch him as he fell. He felt himself being stretched out on the ground. And then, mercifully and magically, he slept.

∾ III ∾

Within a week, he came to know the group well. They were an absentminded bunch of people. Not one of them ever knew when a dromozoon might flash by and add another part. Mercer was not stung again, but the incision he had obtained just outside the cabin was hardening. Spike-head looked at it when Mercer modestly undid his belt and lowered the edge of his trouser-top so they could see the wound.

"You've got a head," he said. "A whole baby head. They'll be glad to get that one upstairs when B'dikkat cuts it off you."

The group even tried to arrange his social life. They introduced him to the girl of the herd. She had grown one body after another, pelvis turning into shoulders and the pelvis below that turning into shoulders again until she was five people long. Her face was unmarred. She tried to be friendly to Mercer.

He was so shocked by her that he dug himself into the

soft dry crumbly earth and stayed there for what seemed like a hundred years. He found later that it was less than a full day. When he came out, the long many-bodied girl was waiting for him.

"You didn't have to come out just for me," said she.

Mercer shook the dirt off himself.

He looked around. The violet sun was going down, and the sky was streaked with blues, deeper blues, and trails of orange sunset.

He looked back at her. "I didn't get up for you. It's no use lying there, waiting for the next time."

"I want to show you something," she said. She pointed to a low hummock. "Dig that up."

Mercer looked at her. She seemed friendly. He shrugged and attacked the soil with his powerful claws. With tough skin and heavy digging-nails on the ends of his fingers, he found it was easy to dig like a dog. The earth cascaded beneath his busy hands. Something pink appeared down in the hole he had dug. He proceeded more carefully.

He knew what it would be.

It was. It was a man, sleeping. Extra arms grew down one side of his body in an orderly series. The other side looked normal.

Mercer turned back to the many-bodied girl, who had writhed closer.

"That's what I think it is, isn't it?"

"Yes," she said. "Doctor Vomact burned his brain out for him. And took his eyes out, too."

Mercer sat back on the ground and looked at the girl. "You told me to do it. Now tell me what for."

"To let you see. To let you know. To let you think."

"That's all?" said Mercer.

The girl twisted with startling suddenness. All the way down her series of bodies, her chests heaved. Mercer wondered how the air got into all of them. He did not feel sorry for her; he did not feel sorry for anyone except himself. When the spasm passed the girl smiled at him apologetically.

"They just gave me a new plant."

Mercer nodded grimly.

"What now, a hand? It seems you have enough."

"Oh, those," she said, looking back at her many torsos. "I promised B'dikkat that I'd let them grow. He's *good*. But that man, stranger. Look at that man you dug up. Who's better off, he or we?"

Mercer stared at her. "Is that what you had me dig him up for?"

"Yes," said the girl.

"Do you expect me to answer?"

"No," said the girl, "not now."

"Who are you?" said Mercer.

"We never ask that here. It doesn't matter. But since you're new, I'll tell you. I used to be the Lady Da—the Emperor's stepmother."

"You!" he exclaimed.

She smiled, ruefully. "You're still so fresh you think it matters! But I have something more important to tell you." She stopped and bit her lip.

"What?" he urged. "Better tell me before I get another bite. I won't be able to think or talk then, not for a long time. Tell me now."

She brought her face close to his. It was still a lovely face, even in the dying orange of this violet-sunned sunset. "People never live forever."

"Yes," said Mercer. "I knew that."

"*Believe* it," ordered the Lady Da.

Lights flashed across the dark plain, still in the distance. Said she, "Dig in, dig in for the night. They may miss you."

Mercer started digging. He glanced over at the man he had dug up. The brainless body, with motions as soft as those of a starfish under water, was pushing its way back into the earth.

Five or seven days later, there was a shouting through the herd.

Mercer had come to know a half-man, the lower part of whose body was gone and whose viscera were kept in place with what resembled a translucent plastic bandage. The half-man had shown him how to lie still when the dromozoa came with their inescapable errands of doing good.

Said the half-man, "You can't fight them. They made Alvarez as big as a mountain, so that he never stirs. Now they're trying to make us happy. They feed us and clean us and sweeten us up. Lie still. Don't worry about screaming. We all do."

"When do we get the drug?" said Mercer.

"When B'dikkat comes."

B'dikkat came that day, pushing a sort of wheeled sled ahead of him. The runners carried it over the hillocks; the wheels worked on the surface.

Even before he arrived, the herd sprang into furious action. Everywhere, people were digging up the sleepers.

By the time B'dikkat reached their waiting place, the herd must have uncovered twice their own number of sleeping pink bodies—men and women, young and old. The sleepers looked no better and no worse than the waking ones.

"Hurry!" said the Lady Da. "He never gives any of us a shot until we're all ready."

B'dikkat wore his heavy lead suit.

He lifted an arm in friendly greeting, like a father returning home with treats for his children. The herd clustered around him but did not crowd him.

He reached into the sled. There was a harnessed bottle which he threw over his shoulders. He snapped the locks on the straps. From the bottle there hung a tube. Midway down the tube there was a small pressure-pump. At the end of the tube there was a glistening hypodermic needle.

When ready, B'dikkat gestured for them to come closer. They approached him with radiant happiness. He stepped through their ranks and past them, to the girl who had the boy growing from her neck. His mechanical voice boomed through the loudspeaker set in the top of his suit.

"Good girl. Good, good girl. You get a big, big present." He thrust the hypodermic into her so long that Mercer could see an air bubble travel from the pump up to the bottle.

Then he moved back to the others, booming a word now and then, moving with improbable grace and speed amid the people. His needle flashed as he gave them hypodermics under pressure. The people dropped to sitting positions or lay down on the ground as though half-asleep.

He knew Mercer. "Hello, fellow. Now you can have the fun. It would have killed you in the cabin. Do you have anything for me?"

Mercer stammered, not knowing what B'dikkat meant, and the two-nosed man answered for him. "I think he has a nice baby head, but it isn't big enough for you to take yet."

Mercer never noticed the needle touch his arm.

B'dikkat had turned to the next knot of people when the super-condamine hit Mercer.

He tried to run after B'dikkat, to hug the lead space suit, to tell B'dikkat that he loved him. He stumbled and fell, but it did not hurt.

The many-bodied girl lay near him. Mercer spoke to her.

"Isn't it wonderful? You're beautiful, beautiful, beautiful. I'm so happy to be here."

The woman covered with growing hands came and sat beside them. She radiated warmth and good fellowship. Mercer thought that she looked very distinguished and charming. He struggled out of his clothes. It was foolish and snobbish to wear clothing when none of these nice people did.

The two women babbled and crooned at him.

With one corner of his mind he knew that they were saying nothing, just expressing the euphoria of a drug so powerful that the known universe had forbidden it. With most of his mind he was happy. He wondered how anyone could have the good luck to visit a planet as nice as this. He tried to tell the Lady Da, but the words weren't quite straight.

A painful stab hit him in the abdomen. The drug went after the pain and swallowed it. It was like the cap in the hospital, only a thousand times better. The pain was gone, though it had been crippling the first time.

He forced himself to be deliberate. He rammed his mind into focus and said to the two ladies who lay pinkly nude beside him in the desert. "That was a good bite. Maybe I will grow another head. That would make B'dikkat happy!"

The Lady Da forced the foremost of her bodies into an upright position. Said she, "I'm strong, too. I can talk. Remember, man, remember. People never live forever. We can die, too, we can die like real people. I do so believe in death!"

Mercer smiled at her through his happiness.

"Of course you can. But isn't this nice . . ."

With this he felt his lips thicken and his mind go slack. He was wide awake, but he did not feel like doing anything. In that beautiful place, among all those companionable and attractive people, he sat and smiled.

B'dikkat was sterilizing his knives.

Mercer wondered how long the super-condamine had lasted him. He endured the ministrations of the dromozoa without screams or movement. The agonies of nerves and itching of skin were phenomena which happened somewhere near him, but meant nothing. He watched his own body with remote, casual interest. The Lady Da and the hand-covered woman stayed near him. After a long time the half-man dragged himself over to the group with his powerful arms. Having arrived, he blinked sleepily and friendlily at them, and lapsed back into the restful stupor from which he had emerged. Mercer saw the sun rise on occasion, closed his eyes briefly, and opened them to see stars shining. Time had no meaning. The dromozoa fed him in their mysterious way; the drug canceled out his needs for cycles of the body.

At last he noticed a return of the inwardness of pain.

The pains themselves had not changed; he had.

He knew all the events which could take place on Shayol. He remembered them well from his happy period. Formerly he had noticed them—now he felt them.

He tried to ask the Lady Da how long they had had the drug, and how much longer they would have to wait before they had it again. She smiled at him with benign, remote happiness; apparently her many torsos, stretched out along the ground, had a greater capacity for retaining the drug than did his body. She meant him well, but was in no condition for articulate speech.

The half-man lay on the ground, arteries pulsating prettily behind the half-transparent film which protected his abdominal cavity.

Mercer squeezed the man's shoulder.

The half-man woke, recognized Mercer, and gave him a healthily sleepy grin.

"'A good morrow to you, my boy.' That's out of a play. Did you ever see a play?"

"You mean a game with cards?"

"No," said the half-man, "a sort of eye-machine with real people doing the figures."

"I never saw that," said Mercer, "but I—"

"But you want to ask me when B'dikkat is going to come back with the needle."

"Yes," said Mercer, a little ashamed of his obviousness.

"Soon," said the half-man. "That's why I think of plays. We all know what is going to happen. We all know when it is going to happen. We all know what the dummies will do"—he gestured at the hummocks in which the decorticated men were cradled—"and we all know what the new people will ask. But we never know how long a scene is going to take."

"What's a 'scene'?" asked Mercer. "Is that the name for the needle?"

The half-man laughed with something close to real humor. "No, no, no. You've got the lovelies on the brain. A scene is just part of a play. I mean we know the order in which things happen, but we have no clocks and nobody cares enough to count days or to make calendars and there's not much climate here, so none of us know how long anything takes. The pain seems short and the pleasure seems long. I'm inclined to think that they are about two Earth-weeks each."

Mercer did not know what an "Earth-week" was, since he had not been a well-read man before his conviction, but he got nothing more from the half-man at that time. The half-man received a dromozootic implant, turned red in the face, shouted senselessly at Mercer, "Take it out, you fool! Take it out of me!"

While Mercer looked on helplessly, the half-man twisted over on his side, his pink dusty back turned to Mercer, and wept hoarsely and quietly to himself.

Mercer himself could not tell how long it was before B'dikkat came back. It might have been several days. It might have been several months.

Once again B'dikkat moved among them like a father; once again they clustered like children. This time B'dikkat smiled pleasantly at the little head which had grown out of Mercer's thigh—a sleeping child's head, covered with light hair on top and with dainty eyebrows over the resting eyes. Mercer got the blissful needle.

When B'dikkat cut the head from Mercer's thigh, he felt the knife grinding against the cartilage which held the head to his own body. He saw the child-face grimace as the head was cut; he felt the far, cool flash of unimportant pain, as B'dikkat dabbed the wound with a corrosive antiseptic which stopped all bleeding immediately.

The next time it was two legs growing from his chest.

Then there had been another head beside his own.

Or was that after the torso and legs, waist to toe-tips, of the little girl which had grown from his side?

He forgot the order.

He did not count time.

Lady Da smiled at him often, but there was no love in this place. She had lost the extra torsos. In between teratologies, she was a pretty and shapely woman; but the nicest thing about their relationship was her whisper to him, repeated some thousands of times, repeated with smiles and hope, "People never live forever."

She found this immensely comforting, even though Mercer did not make much sense out of it.

Thus events occurred, and victims changed in appearance, and new ones arrived. Sometimes B'dikkat took the new ones, resting in the everlasting sleep of their burned-out brains, in a ground-truck to be added to other herds. The bodies in the truck threshed and bawled without human speech when the dromozoa struck them.

Finally, Mercer did manage to follow B'dikkat to the door of the cabin. He had to fight the bliss of super-condamine to do it. Only the memory of previous hurt, bewilderment, and perplexity made him sure that if he did not ask B'dikkat when he, Mercer, was happy, the answer would no longer be available when he needed it. Fighting pleasure itself, he begged B'dikkat to check the records and to tell him how long he had been there.

B'dikkat grudgingly agreed, but he did not come out of the doorway. He spoke through the public address box built into the cabin, and his gigantic voice roared out over the empty plain, so that the pink herd of talking people stirred gently in their happiness and wondered what their friend B'dikkat might be wanting to tell them. When he said it, they thought it exceedingly profound, though none of them understood it, since it was simply the amount of time that Mercer had been on Shayol:

"Standard years—eighty-four years, seven months, three days, two hours, eleven and one half minutes. Good luck, fellow."

Mercer turned away.

The secret little corner of his mind, which stayed sane through happiness and pain, made him wonder about B'dikkat. What persuaded the cow-man to remain on Shayol? What kept him happy without super-condamine? Was B'dikkat a crazy slave to his own duty or was he a man who had hopes of going back to his own planet some day, surrounded by a family of little cow-people resembling himself? Mercer, despite his happiness, wept a little at the strange fate of B'dikkat. His own fate he accepted.

He remembered the last time he had eaten—actual eggs from an actual pan. The dromozoa kept him alive, but he did not know how they did it.

He staggered back to the group. The Lady Da, naked in the dusty plain, waved a hospitable hand and showed that there was a place for him to sit beside her. There were unclaimed square miles of seating space around them, but he appreciated the kindliness of her gesture none the less.

∽ IV ∽

The years, if they were years, went by. The land of Shayol did not change.

Sometimes the bubbling sound of geysers came faintly across the plain to the herd of men; those who could talk declared it to be the breathing of Captain Alvarez. There was night and day, but no setting of crops, no change of season, no generations of men. Time stood still for these people, and their load of pleasure was so commingled with the shocks and pains of the dromozoa that the words of the Lady Da took on very remote meaning.

"People never live forever."

Her statement was a hope, not a truth in which they could believe. They did not have the wit to follow the stars in their courses, to exchange names with each other, to harvest the experience of each for the wisdom of all. There was no dream of escape for these people. Though they saw the old-style chemical rockets lift up from the field beyond B'dikkat's cabin, they did not make plans to hide among the frozen crop of transmuted flesh.

Far long ago, some other prisoner than one of these had tried to write a letter. His handwriting was on a rock. Mercer read it, and so had a few of the others, but they could not tell which man had done it. Nor did they care.

The letter, scraped on stone, had been a message home. They could still read the opening: "Once, I was like you, stepping out of my window at the end of day, and letting the winds blow me gently toward the place I lived in. Once, like you, I had one head, two hands, ten fingers on my hands. The front part of my head was called a face, and I could talk with it. Now I can only write, and that only when I get out of pain. Once, like you, I ate foods, drank liquid, had a name. I cannot remember the name I had. You can stand up, you who get this letter. I cannot even stand up. I just wait for the lights to put my food in me molecule by molecule, and to take it out again. Don't think that I am punished any more. This place is not a punishment. It is something else."

Among the pink herd, none of them ever decided what was "something else."

Curiosity had died among them long ago.

Then came the day of the little people.

It was a time—not an hour, not a year: a duration somewhere between them—when the Lady Da and Mercer sat wordless with happiness and filled with the joy of super-condamine. They had nothing to say to one another; the drug said all things for them.

A disagreeable roar from B'dikkat's cabin made them stir mildly.

Those two, and one or two others, looked toward the speaker of the public address system.

The Lady Da brought herself to speak, though the matter was unimportant beyond words. "I do believe," said she, "that we used to call that the War Alarm."

They drowsed back into their happiness.

A man with two rudimentary heads growing beside his own crawled over to them. All three heads looked very happy, and Mercer thought it delightful of him to appear in such a whimsical shape. Under the pulsing glow of super-condamine, Mercer regretted that he had not used times when his mind was clear to ask him who he had once been. He answered it for them. Forcing his eyelids open by sheer will power, he gave the Lady Da and Mercer the lazy ghost of a military salute and said, "Suzdal, Ma'am and Sir, former cruiser commander. They are sounding the alert. Wish to report that I am . . . I am . . . I am not quite ready for battle."

He dropped off to sleep.

The gentle peremptorinesses of the Lady Da brought his eyes open again.

"Commander, why are they sounding it here? Why did you come to us?"

"You, Ma'am, and the gentleman with the ears seem to think best of our group. I thought you might have orders."

Mercer looked around for the gentleman with the ears. It was himself. In that time his face was almost wholly obscured with a crop of fresh little ears, but he paid no attention to them, other than expecting that B'dikkat would cut them all off in due course and that the dromozoa would give him something else.

The noise from the cabin rose to a higher, ear-splitting intensity.

Among the herd, many people stirred.

Some opened their eyes, looked around, murmured, "It's a noise," and went back to the happy drowsing with super-condamine.

The cabin door opened.

B'dikkat rushed out, *without his suit.* They had never seen him on the outside without his protective metal suit.

He rushed up to them, looked wildly around, recognized the Lady Da and Mercer, picked them up, one under each arm, and raced with them back to the cabin. He flung them into the double door. They landed with bone-splitting crashes, and found it amusing to hit the ground so hard. The floor tilted them into the room. Moments later, B'dikkat followed.

He roared at them, "You're people, or you were. You understand people; I only obey them. But this I will not obey. Look at that!"

Four beautiful human children lay on the floor. The two smallest seemed to be twins, about two years of age. There was a girl of five and a boy of seven or so. All of them had slack eyelids. All of them had thin red lines around their temples and their hair, shaved away, showed how their brains had been removed.

B'dikkat, heedless of danger from dromozoa, stood beside the Lady Da and Mercer, shouting.

"You're real people. I'm just a cow. I do my duty. My duty does not include this. These are *children*."

The wise, surviving recess of Mercer's mind registered shock and disbelief. It was hard to sustain the emotion, because the super-condamine washed at his consciousness like a great tide, making everything seem lovely. The forefront of his mind, rich with the drug, told him, "Won't it be nice to have some children with us!" But the undestroyed interior of his mind, keeping the honor he knew before he came to Shayol, whispered, "This is a crime worse than any crime we have committed! *And the Empire has done it.*"

"What have you done?" said the Lady Da. "What can we do?"

"I tried to call the satellite. When they knew what I was talking about, they cut me off. After all, I'm not people. The head doctor told me to do my work."

"Was it Doctor Vomact?" Mercer asked.

"Vomact?" said B'dikkat. "He died a hundred years ago, of old age. No, a new doctor cut me off. I don't have people-feeling, but I am Earth-born, of Earth blood. I have emotions myself. Pure cattle emotions! *This* I cannot permit."

"What have you done?"

B'dikkat lifted his eyes to the window. His face was illuminated by a determination which, even beyond the edges of the drug which made them love him, made him seem like the father of this world—responsible, honorable, unselfish.

He smiled. "They will kill me for it, I think. But I have put in the Galactic Alert—*all ships here.*"

The Lady Da, sitting back on the floor, declared, "But that's only for new invaders! It is a false alarm." She pulled herself together and rose to her feet. "Can you cut these things off me, right now, in case people come? And get

me a dress. And do you have anything which will counteract the effect of the super-condamine?"

"That's what I wanted!" cried B'dikkat. "I will not take
these children. You give me leadership."

There and then, on the floor of the cabin, he trimmed
her down to the normal proportions of mankind.

The corrosive antiseptic rose like smoke in the air of the
cabin. Mercer thought it all very dramatic and pleasant,
and dropped off in catnaps part of the time. Then he felt
B'dikkat trimming him too. B'dikkat opened a long, long
drawer and put the specimens in; from the cold in the
room it must have been a refrigerated locker.

He sat them both up against the wall.

"I've been thinking," he said. "There is no antidote for
super-condamine. Who would want one? But I can give
you the hypos from my rescue boat. They are supposed to
bring a person back, no matter what has happened to that
person out in space."

There was a whining over the cabin roof. B'dikkat
knocked a window out with his fist, stuck his head out of
the window and looked up.

"Come on in," he shouted.

There was the thud of a landing craft touching ground
quickly. Doors whirred. Mercer wondered, mildly, why
people dared to land on Shayol. When they came in he
saw that they were not people; they were Customs
Robots, who could travel at velocities which people could
never match. One wore the insigne of an inspector.

"Where are the invaders?"

"There are no—" began B'dikkat.

The Lady Da, imperial in her posture though she was

completely nude, said in a voice of complete clarity, "I am a former Empress, the Lady Da. Do you know me?"

"No, Ma'am," said the robot inspector. He looked as uncomfortable as a robot could look. The drug made Mercer think that it would be nice to have robots for company, out on the surface of Shayol.

"I declare this Top Emergency, in the ancient words. Do you understand? Connect me with the Instrumentality."

"We can't—" said the inspector.

"You can ask," said the Lady Da.

The inspector complied.

The Lady Da turned to B'dikkat. "Give Mercer and me those shots now. Then put us outside the door so the dromozoa can repair these scars. Bring us in as soon as a connection is made. Wrap us in cloth if you do not have clothes for us. Mercer can stand the pain."

"Yes," said B'dikkat, keeping his eyes away from the four soft children and their collapsed eyes.

The injection burned like no fire ever had. It must have been capable of fighting the super-condamine, because B'dikkat put them through the open window, so as to save time going through the door. The dromozoa, sensing that they needed repair, flashed upon them. This time the super-condamine had something else fighting it.

Mercer did not scream but he lay against the wall and wept for ten thousand years; in objective time, it must have been several hours.

The Customs Robots were taking pictures. The dromozoa were flashing against them too, sometimes in whole swarms, but nothing happened.

Mercer heard the voice of the communicator inside the cabin calling loudly for B'dikkat. "Surgery Satellite calling Shayol. B'dikkat, get on the line!"

He obviously was not replying.

There were soft cries coming from the other communicator, the one which the customs officials had brought into the room. Mercer was sure that the eye-machine was on and that people in other worlds were looking at Shayol for the first time.

B'dikkat came through the door. He had torn navigation charts out of his lifeboat. With these he cloaked them.

Mercer noted that the Lady Da changed the arrangement of the cloak in a few minor ways and suddenly looked like a person of great importance.

They re-entered the cabin door.

B'dikkat whispered, as if filled with awe, "The Instrumentality has been reached, and a Lord of the Instrumentality is about to talk to you."

There was nothing for Mercer to do, so he sat back in a corner of the room and watched. The Lady Da, her skin healed, stood pale and nervous in the middle of the floor.

The room filled with an odorless intangible smoke. The smoke clouded. The full communicator was on.

A human figure appeared.

A woman, dressed in a uniform of radically conservative cut, faced the Lady Da.

"This is Shayol. You are the Lady Da. You called me."

The Lady Da pointed to the children on the floor. "This must not happen," she said. "This is a place of punishments, agreed upon between the Instrumentality and the Empire. No one said anything about children."

The woman on the screen looked down at the children.

"This is the work of insane people!" she cried.

She looked accusingly at the Lady Da. "Are you imperial?"

"I was an Empress, Madam," said the Lady Da.

"And you permit this!"

"Permit it?" cried the Lady Da. "I had nothing to do with it." Her eyes widened. "I am a prisoner here myself. Don't you understand?"

The image-woman snapped, "No, I don't."

"I," said the Lady Da, "am a specimen. Look at the herd out there. I came from them a few hours ago."

"Adjust me," said the image-woman to B'dikkat. "Let me see that herd."

Her body, standing upright, soared through the wall in a flashing arc and was placed in the very center of the herd.

The Lady Da and Mercer watched her. They saw even the image lose its stiffness and dignity. The image-woman waved an arm to show that she should be brought back into the cabin. B'dikkat tuned her back into the room.

"I owe you an apology," said the image. "I am the Lady Johanna Gnade, one of the Lords of the Instrumentality."

Mercer bowed, lost his balance, and had to scramble up from the floor. The Lady Da acknowledged the introduction with a royal nod.

The two women looked at each other.

"You will investigate," said the Lady Da, "and when you have investigated, please put us all to death. You know about the drug?"

"Don't mention it," said B'dikkat. "Don't even say

the name into a communicator. It is a secret of the Instrumentality!"

"I am the Instrumentality," said the Lady Johanna. "Are you in pain? I did not think that any of you were alive. I had heard of the surgery banks on your off-limits planet, but I thought that robots tended parts of people and sent up the new grafts by rocket. Are there any people with you? Who is in charge? Who did this to the children?"

B'dikkat stepped in front of the image. He did not bow. "I'm in charge."

"You're underpeople!" cried the Lady Johanna. "You're a cow!"

"A bull, Ma'am. My family is frozen back on Earth itself, and with a thousand years' service I am earning their freedom and my own. Your other questions, Ma'am. I do all the work. The dromozoa do not affect me much, though I have to cut a part off myself now and then. I throw those away. They don't go into the bank. Do you know the secret of this place?"

The Lady Johanna talked to someone behind her on another world. Then she looked at B'dikkat and commanded, "Just don't name the drug or talk too much about it. Tell me the rest."

"We have," said B'dikkat very formally, "thirteen hundred and twenty-one people who can still be counted on to supply parts when the dromozoa implant them. There are about seven hundred more, including Go-Captain Alvarez, who have been so thoroughly absorbed by the planet that it is no use trimming them. The Empire set up this place as a point of uttermost punishment. But the Instrumentality gave secret orders for *medicine*"—he accented the word strangely, meaning super-condamine—"to be issued so that the punishment would be counteracted. The Empire supplies our convicts. The Instrumentality distributes the surgical material."

The Lady Johanna lifted her right hand in a gesture of silence and compassion. She looked around the room. Her eyes came back to the Lady Da. Perhaps she guessed what effort the Lady Da had made in order to remain standing erect while the two drugs, the super-condamine and the lifeboat drug, fought within her veins.

"You people can rest. I will tell you now that all things possible will be done for you. The Empire is finished. The Fundamental Agreement, by which the Instrumentality surrendered the Empire a thousand years ago, has been set aside. We did not know that you people existed. We would have found out in time, but I am sorry we did not find out sooner. Is there anything we can do for you right away?"

"Time is what we all have," said the Lady Da. "Perhaps we cannot ever leave Shayol, because of the dromozoa and the *medicine*. The one could be dangerous. The other must never be permitted to be known."

The Lady Johanna Gnade looked around the room. When her glance reached him, B'dikkat fell to his knees and lifted his enormous hands in complete supplication.

"What do you want?" said she.

"These," said B'dikkat, pointing to the mutilated children. "Order a stop on children. Stop it now!" He commanded her with the last cry, and she accepted his command. "And, Lady—" he stopped as if shy.

"Yes? Go on."

"Lady, I am unable to kill. It is not in my nature. To work, to help, but not to kill. What do I do with these?" He gestured at the four motionless children on the floor.

"Keep them," she said. "Just keep them."

"I can't," he said. "There's no way to get off this planet alive. I do not have food for them in the cabin. They will die in a few hours. And governments," he added wisely, "take a long, long time to do things."

"Can you give them the *medicine?*"

"No, it would kill them if I give them that stuff first before the dromozoa have fortified their bodily processes."

The Lady Johanna Gnade filled the room with tinkling laughter that was very close to weeping. "Fools, poor fools, and the more fool I! If super-condamine works only *after* the dromozoa, what is the purpose of the secret?"

B'dikkat rose to his feet, offended. He frowned, but he could not get the words with which to defend himself.

The Lady Da, ex-empress of a fallen empire, addressed the other Lady with ceremony and force: "Put them outside, so they will be touched. They will hurt. Have B'dikkat give them the drug as soon as he thinks it safe. I beg your leave, my Lady . . ."

Mercer had to catch her before she fell.

"You've all had enough," said the Lady Johanna. "A storm ship with heavily armed troops is on its way to your ferry satellite. They will seize the medical personnel and find out who committed this crime against children."

Mercer dared to speak. "Will you punish the guilty doctor?"

"*You* speak of punishment." she cried. "You!"

"It's fair. I was punished for doing wrong. Why shouldn't he be?"

"Punish—punish!" she said to him. "We will cure that doctor. And we will cure you too, if we can."

Mercer began to weep. He thought of the oceans of happiness which super-condamine had brought him, forgetting the hideous pain and the deformities on Shayol. Would there be no next needle? He could not guess what life would be like off Shayol. Was there to be no more tender, fatherly B'dikkat coming with his knives?

He lifted his tear-stained face to the Lady Johanna Gnade and choked out the words. "Lady, we are all insane in this place. I do not think we want to leave."

She turned her face away, moved by enormous compassion. Her next words were to B'dikkat. "You are wise and good, even if you are not a human being. Give them all of the drug they can take. The Instrumentality will decide what to do with all of you. I will survey your planet with robot soldiers. Will the robots be safe, cowman?"

B'dikkat did not like the thoughtless name she called him, but he held no offense. "The robots will be all right, Ma'am, but the dromozoa will be excited if they cannot feed them and heal them. Send as few as you can. We do not know how the dromozoa live or die."

"As few as I can," she murmured. She lifted her hand in command to some technician unimaginable distances away. The odorless smoke rose about her and the image was gone.

A shrill cheerful voice spoke up. "I fixed your window," said the Customs Robot. B'dikkat thanked him absent-mindedly. He helped Mercer and the Lady Da into the doorway. When they had gotten outside, they were promptly stung by the dromozoa. It did not matter.

B'dikkat himself emerged, carrying the four children in his two gigantic, tender hands. He lay the slack bodies on the ground near the cabin. He watched as the bodies went into spasm with the onset of the dromozoa. Mercer and the Lady Da saw that his brown cow eyes were rimmed with red and that his huge cheeks were dampened by tears.

Hours or centuries.

Who could tell them apart?

The herd went back to its usual life, except that the intervals between needles were much shorter. The once-commander, Suzdal, refused the needle when he heard the news. Whenever he could walk, he followed the Customs Robots around as they photographed, took soil samples, and made a count of the bodies. They were particularly interested in the mountain of Go-Captain Alvarez and professed themselves uncertain as to whether there was organic life there or not. The mountain did appear to react to super-condamine, but they could find no blood, no heart-beat. Moisture, moved by the dromozoa, seemed to have replaced the once-human bodily processes.

∽ V ∽

And then, early one morning, the sky opened.

Ship after ship landed. People emerged, wearing clothes.

The dromozoa ignored the newcomers. Mercer, who

was in a state of bliss, confusedly tried to think this through until he realized that the ships were loaded to their skins with communications machines; the "people" were either robots or images of persons in other places.

The robots swiftly gathered together the herd. Using wheelbarrows, they brought the hundreds of mindless people to the landing area.

Mercer heard a voice he knew. It was the Lady Johanna Gnade. "Set me high," she commanded.

Her form rose until she seemed one-fourth the size of Alvarez. Her voice took on more volume.

"Wake them all," she commanded.

Robots moved among them, spraying them with a gas which was both sickening and sweet. Mercer felt his mind go clear. The super-condamine still operated in his nerves and veins, but his cortical area was free of it. He thought clearly.

"I bring you," cried the compassionate feminine voice of the gigantic Lady Johanna, "the judgment of the Instrumentality on the planet Shayol.

"Item: the surgical supplies will be maintained and the dromozoa will not be molested. Portions of human bodies will be left here to grow, and the grafts will be collected by robots. Neither man nor homunculus will live here again.

"Item: the underman B'dikkat, of cattle extraction, will be rewarded by an immediate return to Earth. He will be paid twice his expected thousand years of earnings."

The voice of B'dikkat, without amplification, was almost as loud as hers through the amplifier. He shouted his protest, "Lady, Lady!"

She looked down at him, his enormous body reaching to ankle height on her swirling gown, and said in a very informal tone, "What do you want?"

"Let me finish my work first," he cried, so that all could hear. "Let me finish taking care of these people."

The specimens who had minds all listened attentively. The brainless ones were trying to dig themselves back into the soft earth of Shayol, using their powerful claws for the purpose. Whenever one began to disappear, a robot seized him by a limb and pulled him out again.

"Item: cephalectomies will be performed on all persons with irrecoverable minds. Their bodies will be left here. Their heads will be taken away and killed as pleasantly as we can manage, probably by an overdosage of super-condamine."

"The last big jolt," murmured Commander Suzdal, who stood near Mercer. "That's fair enough."

"Item: the children have been found to be the last heirs of the Empire. An over-zealous official sent them here to prevent their committing treason when they grew up. The doctor obeyed orders without questioning them. Both the official and the doctor have been cured and their memories of this have been erased, so that they need have no shame or grief for what they have done."

"It's unfair," cried the half-man. "They should be punished as we were!"

The Lady Johanna Gnade looked down at him. "Punishment is ended. We will give you anything you wish, but not the pain of another. I shall continue.

"Item: since none of you wish to resume the lives which you led previously, we are moving you to another planet nearby. It is similar to Shayol, but much more beautiful. There are no dromozoa."

At this an uproar seized the herd. They shouted, wept, cursed, appealed. They all wanted the needle, and if they had to stay on Shayol to get it, they would stay.

"Item," said the gigantic image of the lady, overriding their babble with her great but feminine voice, "you will not have super-condamine on the new planet, since without dromozoa it would kill you. But there will be caps. *Remember the caps.* We will try to cure you and to make people of you again. But if you give up, we will not force you. Caps are very powerful; with medical help you can live under them many years."

A hush fell on the group. In their various ways, they were trying to compare the electrical caps which had stimulated their pleasure-lobes with the drug which had drowned them a thousand times in pleasure. Their murmur sounded like assent.

"Do you have any questions?" said the Lady Johanna.

"When do we get the caps?" said several. They were human enough that they laughed at their own impatience.

"Soon," said she reassuringly. "Very soon."

"Very soon," echoed B'dikkat, reassuring his charges even though he was no longer in control.

"Question," cried the Lady Da.

"My Lady . . . ?" said the Lady Johanna, giving the ex-empress her due courtesy.

"Will we be permitted marriage?"

The Lady Johanna looked astonished. "I don't know." She smiled. "I don't know any reason why not—"

"I claim this man Mercer," said the Lady Da. "When

the drugs were deepest, and the pain was greatest, he was the one who always tried to think. May I have him?"

Mercer thought the procedure arbitrary but he was so happy that he said nothing. The Lady Johanna scrutinized him and then she nodded. She lifted her arms in a gesture of blessing and farewell.

The robots began to gather the pink herd into two groups. One group was to whisper in a ship over to a new world, new problems and new lives. The other group, no matter how much its members tried to scuttle into the dirt, was gathered for the last honor which humanity could pay their manhood.

B'dikkat, leaving everyone else, jogged with his bottle across the plain to give the mountain-man Alvarez an especially large gift of delight.

On the Gem Planet

Consider the horse. He climbed up through the crevasses of a cliff of gems; the force which drove him was the love of man.

Consider Mizzer, the resort planet, where the dictator Colonel Wedder reformed the culture so violently that whatever had been slovenly now became atrocious.

Consider Genevieve, so rich that she was the prisoner of her own wealth, so beautiful that she was the victim of her own beauty, so intelligent that she knew there was nothing, nothing to be done about her fate.

Consider Casher O'Neill, a wanderer among the planets, thirsting for justice and yet hoping in his innermost thoughts that "justice" was not just another word for revenge.

Consider Pontoppidan, that literal gem of a planet, where the people were too rich and busy to have good food, open air, or much fun. All they had were diamonds, rubies, tourmalines, and emeralds.

Add these together and you have one of the strangest stories ever told from world to world.

∽|∽

When Casher O'Neill came to Pontoppidan, he found that the capital city was appropriately called Andersen.

This was the second century of the Rediscovery of Man. People everywhere had taken up old names, old languages, old customs, as fast as the robots and the underpeople could retrieve the data from the rubbish of forgotten starlanes or the subsurface ruins of Manhome itself.

Casher knew this very well, to his bitter cost. Re-acculturation had brought him revolution and exile. He came from the dry, beautiful planet of Mizzer. He was himself the nephew of the ruined ex-ruler, Kuraf, whose collection of objectionable books had at one time been unmatched in the settled galaxy; he had stood aside, half-assenting, when the colonels Gibna and Wedder took over the planet in the name of reform; he had implored the Instrumentality, vainly, for help when Wedder became a tyrant; and now he traveled among the stars, looking for men or weapons who might destroy Wedder and make Kaheer again the luxurious, happy city which it once had been.

He felt that his cause was hopeless when he landed on Pontoppidan. The people were warm-hearted, friendly, intelligent, but they had no motives to fight for, no weapons to fight with, no enemies to fight against. They had little public spirit, such as Casher O'Neill had seen back on his native planet of Mizzer. They were concerned about little things.

Indeed, at the time of his arrival, the Pontoppidans were wildly excited about a horse.

A horse! Who worries about one horse?

Casher O'Neill himself said so. "Why bother about a horse? We have lots of them on Mizzer. They are four-handed beings, eight times the weight of a man, with only one finger on each of the four hands. The fingernail is very heavy and permits them to run fast. That's why our people have them, for running."

"Why run?" said the Hereditary Dictator of Pontoppidan. "Why run, when you can fly? Don't you have ornithopters?"

"We don't run with them," said Casher indignantly. "We make them run against each other and then we pay prizes to the one which runs fastest."

"But then," said Philip Vincent, the Hereditary Dictator, "you get a very illogical situation. When you have tried out these four-fingered beings, you know how fast each one goes. So what? Why bother?"

His niece interrupted. She was a fragile little thing, smaller than Casher O'Neill liked women to be. She had clear gray eyes, well-marked eyebrows, a very artificial coiffure of silver-blonde hair, and the most sensitive little mouth he had ever seen. She conformed to the local fashion by wearing some kind of powder or face cream which was flesh-pink in color but which had overtones of lilac. On a woman as old as twenty-two, such a coloration would have made the wearer look like an old hag, but on Genevieve it was pleasant, if rather startling. It gave the effect of a

happy child playing grown-up and doing the job joyfully
and well. Casher knew that it was hard to tell ages in these
off-trail planets. Genevieve might be a grande dame in
her third or fourth rejuvenation.

He doubted it, on second glance. What she said was
sensible, young, and pert:

"But uncle, they're *animals*!"

"I know that," he rumbled.

"But uncle, don't you see it?"

"Stop saying 'but uncle' and tell me what you mean,"
growled the Dictator, very fondly.

"Animals are always *uncertain.*"

"Of course," said the uncle.

"That makes it a game, uncle," said Genevieve.
"They're never sure that any one of them would do the
same thing twice. Imagine the excitement—the beautiful
big beings from earth running around and around on their
four middle fingers, the big fingernails making the gems
jump loose from the ground!"

"I'm not at all sure it's that way. Besides, Mizzer may
be covered with something valuable, such as earth or
sand, instead of gemstones like the ones we have here on
Pontoppidan. You know, your flower-pots with their rich,
warm, wet, soft earth?"

"Of course I do, uncle. And I know what you paid for
them. You were very generous. And still are," she added
diplomatically, glancing quickly at Casher O'Neill to see
how the familial piety went across with the visitor.

"We're not that rich on Mizzer. It's mostly sand, with
farmland along the Twelve Niles, our big rivers."

"I've seen pictures of rivers," said Genevieve.

"Imagine living on a whole world full of flower-pot stuff!"

"You're getting off the subject, darling. We were wondering why anyone would bring one horse, just one horse, to Pontoppidan. I suppose you could race a horse against himself, if you had a stopwatch. But would it be fun? Would you do that, young man?"

Casher O'Neill tried to be respectful. "In my home we used to have a lot of horses. I've seen my uncle time them one by one."

"Your uncle?" said the Dictator interestedly. "Who was your uncle that he had all these four-fingered 'horses' running around? They're all Earth animals and very expensive."

Casher felt the coming of the low, slow blow he had met so many times before, right from the whole outside world into the pit of his stomach. "My uncle"—he stammered—"my uncle—I thought you knew—was the old Dictator of Mizzer, Kuraf."

Philip Vincent jumped to his feet, very lightly for so well-fleshed a man. The young mistress, Genevieve, clutched at the throat of her dress.

"Kuraf!" cried the old Dictator. "Kuraf! We know about him, even here. But you were supposed to be a Mizzer patriot, not one of Kuraf's people."

"He doesn't have any children—" Casher began to explain.

"I should think not, not with those habits!" snapped the old man.

"—so I'm his nephew and his heir. But I'm not trying to put the Dictatorship back, even though I should be dictator. I just want to get rid of Colonel Wedder. He has ruined my people, and I am looking for money or weapons or help to make my home-world free." This was the point, Casher O'Neill knew, at which people either started believing him or did not. If they did not, there was not much he could do about it. If they did, he was sure to get some sympathy. So far, no help. Just sympathy.

But the Instrumentality, while refusing to take action against Colonel Wedder, had given young Casher O'Neill an all-world travel pass—something which a hundred lifetimes of savings could not have purchased for the ordinary man. (His obscene old uncle had gone off to Sunvale, on Ttiollé, the resort planet, to live out his years between the casino and the beach.) Casher O'Neill held the conscience of Mizzer in his hand. Only he, among the star travelers, cared enough to fight for the freedom of the Twelve Niles. Here, now, in this room, there was a turning point.

"I won't give you anything," said the Hereditary Dictator, but he said it in a friendly voice. His niece started tugging at his sleeve.

The older man went on. "Stop it, girl. I won't give you anything, not if you're part of that rotten lot of Kuraf's, not unless—"

"Anything, sir, anything, just so that I get help or weapons to go home to the Twelve Niles!"

"All right, then. Unless you open your mind to me. I'm a good telepath myself."

"Open my mind! Whatever for?" The incongruous indecency of it shocked Casher O'Neill. He'd had men and women and governments ask a lot of strange things from him, but no one before had had the cold impudence to ask him to open his mind. "And why you?" he went on, "What would you get out of it? There's nothing much in my mind."

"To make sure," said the Hereditary Dictator, "that you are not too honest and sharp in your beliefs. If you're positive that you know what to do, you might be another Colonel Wedder, putting your people through a dozen torments for a Utopia which never quite comes true. If you don't care at all, you might be like your uncle. He did no real harm. He just stole his planet blind and he had some extraordinary habits which got him talked about between the stars. He never killed a man in his life, did he?"

"No, sir," said Casher O'Neill, "he never did." It relieved him to tell the one little good thing about his uncle; there was so very, very little which could be said in Kuraf's favor.

"I don't like slobbering old libertines like your uncle," said Philip Vincent, "but I don't hate them either. They don't hurt other people much. As a matter of actual fact, they don't hurt anyone but themselves. They waste property, though. Like these horses you have on Mizzer. We'd never bring living beings to this world of Pontoppidan, just to play games with. And you know we're not poor. We're no Old North Australia, but we have a good income here."

That, thought Casher O'Neill, is the understatement of the year, but he was a careful young man with a great deal at stake, so he said nothing.

The Dictator looked at him shrewdly. He appreciated the value of Casher's tactful silence. Genevieve tugged at his sleeve, but he frowned her interruption away.

"If," said the Hereditary Dictator, *"if,"* he repeated, "you pass two tests, I will give you a green ruby as big as my head. If my Committee will allow me to do so. But I think I can talk them around. One test is that you let me peep all over your mind, to make sure that I am not dealing with one more honest fool. If you're too honest, you're a fool and a danger to mankind. I'll give you a dinner and ship you off-planet as fast as I can. And the other test is—solve the puzzle of this horse. The one horse on Pontoppidan. Why is the animal here? What should we do with it? If it's good to eat, how should we cook it? Or can we trade to some other world, like your planet Mizzer, which seems to set a value on horses?"

"Thank you, sir—" said Casher O'Neill.

"But, uncle," said Genevieve.

"Keep quiet, my darling, and let the young man speak," said the Dictator.

"—all I was going to ask, is," said Casher O'Neill, "what's a green ruby good for? I didn't even know they came green."

"That, young man, is a Pontoppidan specialty. We have a geology based on ultra-heavy chemistry. This planet was once a fragment from a giant planet which imploded. The use is simple. With a green ruby you can make a laser beam which will boil away your city of Kaheer in a single sweep. We don't have weapons here and we don't believe in them, so I won't give you a weapon. You'll have to travel further to find a ship and to get the apparatus for mounting your green ruby. *If I* give it to you. But you will be one more step along in your fight with Colonel Wedder."

"Thank you, thank you, most honorable sir!" cried Casher O'Neill.

"But uncle," said Genevieve, "you shouldn't have picked those two things because I know the answers."

"You know all about *him*" said the Hereditary Dictator, "by some means of your own?"

Genevieve flushed under her lilac-hued foundation cream. "I know enough for us to know."

"How do you know it, my darling?"

"I just know," said Genevieve.

Her uncle made no comment, but he smiled widely and indulgently as if he had heard that particular phrase before.

She stamped her foot. "And I know about the horse, too. *All* about it."

"Have you seen it?"

"No."

"Have you talked to it?"

"Horses don't talk, uncle."

"Most underpeople do," he said.

"This isn't an underperson, uncle. It's a plain unmodified Old Earth animal. It never did talk."

"Then what do you know, my honey?" The uncle was affectionate, but there was the crackle of impatience under his voice.

"I taped it. The whole thing. The story of the horse of Pontoppidan. And I've edited it, too. I was going to show it to you this morning, but your staff sent that young man in."

Casher O'Neill looked his apologies at Genevieve.

She did not notice him. Her eyes were on her uncle.

"Since you've done this much, we might as well see it." He turned to the attendants. "Bring chairs. And drinks. You know mine. The young lady will take tea with lemon. Real tea. Will you have coffee, young man?"

"You have coffee!" cried Casher O'Neill. As soon as he said it, he felt like a fool. Pontoppidan was a *rich* planet. On most worlds' exchanges, coffee came out to about two man-years per kilo. Here halftracks crunched their way through gems as they went to load up the frequent trading vessels.

The chairs were put in place. The drinks arrived. The Hereditary Dictator had been momentarily lost in a brown study, as though he were wondering about his promise to Casher O'Neill. He had even murmured to the young man, "Our bargain stands? Never mind what my niece says." Casher had nodded vigorously. The old man had gone back to frowning at the servants and did not relax until a tiger-man bounded into the room, carrying a tray with acrobatic precision. The chairs were already in place.

The uncle held his niece's chair for her as a command that she sit down. He nodded Casher O'Neill into a chair on the other side of himself.

He commanded, "Dim the lights . . ."

The room plunged into semi-darkness.

Without being told, the people took their places immediately behind the three main seats and the under-people perched or sat on benches and tables behind them. Very little was spoken. Casher O'Neill could sense that Pontoppidan was a well-run place. He began to wonder if the Hereditary Dictator had much real work left to do, if he could fuss that much over a single horse. Perhaps all he did was boss his niece and watch the robots load truckloads of gems into sacks while the underpeople weighed them, listed them, and wrote out the bills for the customers.

∾ II ∾

There was no screen; this was a good machine.

The planet Pontoppidan came into view, its airless brightness giving strong hints of the mineral riches which might be found.

Here and there enormous domes, such as the one in which this palace was located, came into view.

Genevieve's own voice, girlish, impulsive, and yet didactic, rang out with the story of her planet. It was as though she had prepared the picture not only for her own uncle but for off-world visitors as well. *By Joan, that's it!* thought Casher O'Neill. *If they don't raise much food here, outside of the hydroponics, and don't have any real People Places, they* have *to trade: that does mean visitors and many, many of them.*

The story was interesting, but the girl herself was more interesting. Her face shone in the shifting light which the images—a meter, perhaps a little more, from the floor—reflected across the room. Casher O'Neill thought that he had never before seen a woman who so peculiarly combined intelligence and charm. She was girl, girl, girl, all the way through; but she was also very smart and pleased with being smart. It betokened a happy life. He found himself glancing covertly at her. Once he caught her glancing, equally covertly, at him. The darkness of the scene enabled them both to pass it off as an accident without embarrassment.

Her viewtape had come to the story of the *dipsies*, enormous canyons which lay like deep gashes on the surface of the planet. Some of the color views were spectacular beyond belief. Casher O'Neill, as the "appointed one" of Mizzer, had had plenty of time to wander through the non-salacious parts of his uncle's collections, and he had seen pictures of the most notable worlds.

Never had he seen anything like this. One view showed a sunset against a six-kilometer cliff of a material which looked like solid emerald. The peculiar bright sunshine of Pontoppidan's small, penetrating, lilac-hued sun ran like living water over the precipice of gems. Even the reduced image, one meter by one meter, was enough to make him catch his breath.

The bottom of the dipsy had vapor emerging in curious cylindrical columns which seemed to erode as they reached two or three times the height of a man. The recorded voice of Genevieve was explaining that the very thin atmosphere of Pontoppidan would not be breathable for another 2,520 years, since the settlers did not wish to squander their resources on a luxury like breathing when the whole planet only had 60,000 inhabitants; they would rather go on with masks and use their wealth in other ways. After all, it was not as though they did not have their domed cities, some of them many kilometers in radius. Besides the usual hydroponics, they had even imported 7.2 hectares of garden soil, 5.5 centimeters deep, together with enough water to make the gardens rich and fruitful.

They had bought worms, too, at the price of eight carats of diamond per living worm, in order to keep the soil of the gardens loose and living.

Genevieve's transcribed voice rang out with pride as she listed these accomplishments of her people, but a note of sadness came in which she returned to the subject of the dipsies. ". . . and though we would like to live in them and develop their atmospheres, we dare not. There is too much escape of radioactivity. The geysers themselves may or may not be contaminated from one hour to the next. So we just look at them. Not one of them has ever been settled, except for the Hippy Dipsy, where the horse came from. Watch this next picture."

The camera sheered up, up, up from the surface of the planet. Where it had wandered among mountains of diamonds and valleys of tourmalines, it now took to the blue-black of near, inner space. One of the canyons showed (from high altitude) the grotesque pattern of a human woman's hips and legs, though what might have been the upper body was lost in a confusion of broken hills which ended in a bright almost-iridescent plain to the North.

"That," said the real Genevieve, overriding her own voice on the screen, "is the Hippy Dipsy. There, see the blue? That's the only lake on all of Pontoppidan. And here we drop to the hermit's house."

Casher O'Neill almost felt vertigo as the camera plummeted from off-planet into the depths of that immense canyon. The edges of the canyon almost seemed to move like lips with the plunge, opening and folding inward to swallow him up.

Suddenly they were beside a beautiful little lake.

A small hut stood beside the shore.

In the doorway there sat a man, dead.

His body had been there a long time; it was already mummified.

Genevieve's recorded voice explained the matter: ". . . in Norstrilian law and custom, they told him that his time had come. They told him to go to the Dying House, since he was no longer fit to live. In Old North Australia, they are so rich that they let everyone live as long as he wants, unless the old person can't take rejuvenation any more, even with stroon, and unless he or she gets to be a real pest to the living. If that happens, they are invited to go to the Dying House, where they shriek and pant with delirious joy for weeks or days until they finally die of an overload of sheer happiness and excitement. . . ." There was a hesitation, even in the recording. "We never knew why this man refused. He stood off-planet and said that he had seen views of the Hippy Dipsy. He said it was the most beautiful place on all the worlds, and that he wanted to build a cabin there, to live alone, except for his non-human friend. We thought it was some small pet. When we told him that the Hippy Dipsy was very dangerous, he said that this did not matter in the least to him, since he was old and dying anyhow. Then he offered to pay us twelve times our planetary income if we would lease him twelve hectares on the condition of absolute privacy. No pictures, no scanners, no help, no visitors. Just solitude and scenery. His name was Perinō. My great-grandfather asked for nothing more, except the written transfer of credit. When he paid it, Perinō even asked that he be left alone after he was dead. Not even a vault rocket so that he could either orbit Pontoppidan forever or start a very slow journey to nowhere, the way so many people like it. So this is our first picture of him. We took it when the light went off in the People Room and one of the tiger-men told us that he was sure a human consciousness had come to an end in the Hippy Dipsy.

"And we never even thought of the pet. After all, we had never made a picture of him. This is the way he arrived from Perinõ's shack."

A robot was shown in a control room, calling excitedly in the old Common Tongue.

"People, people! Judgment needed! Moving object coming out of the Hippy Dipsy. Object has improper shape. Not a correct object. Should not rise. Does so anyhow. People, tell me, people, tell me! Destroy or not destroy? This is an improper object. It should fall, not rise. Coming out of the Hippy Dipsy."

A firm click shut off the robot's chatter. A well-shaped woman took over. From the nature of her work and the lithe, smooth tread with which she walked, Casher O'Neill suspected that she was of cat origin, but there was nothing in her dress or in her manner to show that she was underpeople.

The woman in the picture lighted a screen.

She moved her hands in the air in front of her, like a blind person feeling his way through open day.

The picture on the inner screen came to resolution.

A face showed in it.

What a face! thought Casher O'Neill, and he heard the other people around him in the viewing room.

The horse!

Imagine a face like that of a newborn cat, thought Casher. Mizzer is full of cats. But imagine the face with a huge mouth, with big yellow teeth—a nose long beyond imagination. Imagine eyes which look friendly. In the picture they were rolling back and forth with exertion, but even there—when they did not feel observed—there was nothing hostile about the set of the eyes. They were tame, companionable eyes. Two ridiculous ears stood high, and a little tuft of golden hair showed on the crest of the head between the ears.

The viewed scene was comical, too. The cat-woman was as astonished as the viewers. It was lucky that she had touched the emergency switch, so that she not only saw the horse, but had recorded herself and her own actions while bringing him into view.

Genevieve whispered across the chest of the Hereditary Dictator: "Later we found he was a palomino pony. That's a very special kind of horse. And Perinō had made him immortal, or almost immortal."

"Sh-h!" said her uncle.

The screen-within-the-screen showed the cat-woman waving her hands in the air some more. The view broadened.

The horse had four hands and no legs, or four legs and no hands, whichever way you want to count them.

The horse was fighting his way up a narrow cleft of rubies which led out of the Hippy Dipsy. He panted heavily. The oxygen bottles on his sides swung wildly as he clambered. He must have seen something, perhaps the image of the cat-woman, because he said a word:

Whay-yay-yay-yay-whay-yay!

The cat-woman in the nearer picture spoke very distinctly:

"Give your name, age, species, and authority for being on this planet." She spoke clearly and with the utmost possible authority.

The horse obviously heard her. His ears tipped forward. But his reply was the same as before:

Whay-yay-yay!

Casher O'Neill realized that he had followed the mood of the picture and had seen the horse the way that the people on Pontoppidan would have seen him. On second thought, the horse was nothing special, by the standards of the Twelve Niles or the Little Horse Market in the city of Kaheer. It was an old pony stallion, no longer fit for breeding and probably not for riding either. The hair had whitened among the gold; the teeth were worn. The animal showed many injuries and burns. Its only use was to be killed, cut up, and fed to the racing dogs. But he said nothing to the people around him. They were still spell-bound by the picture.

The cat-woman repeated:

"Your name isn't Whayayay. Identify yourself properly; name first."

The horse answered her with the same word in a higher key.

Apparently forgetting that she had recorded herself as well as the emergency screen, the cat-woman said, "I'll call real people if you don't answer! They'll be annoyed at being bothered."

The horse rolled his eyes at her and said nothing.

The cat-woman pressed an emergency button on the side of the room. One could not see the other communication screen which lighted up, but her end of the conversation was plain.

"I want an ornithopter. Big one. Emergency."

A mumble from the side screen.

"To go to the Hippy Dipsy. There's an underperson there, and he's in so much trouble that he won't talk." From the screen beside her, the horse seemed to have understood the sense of the message, if not the words, because he repeated:

Whay-yay-whay-yay-yay!

"See," said the cat-woman to the person in the other screen, "that's what he's doing. It's obviously an emergency."

The voice from the other screen came through, tinny and remote by double recording:

"Fool, yourself, cat-woman! Nobody can fly an ornithopter into a dipsy. Tell your silly friend to go back to the floor of the dipsy and we'll pick him up by space rocket."

Whay-yay-yay! said the horse impatiently.

"He's not *my friend*," said the cat-woman with brisk annoyance. "I just discovered him a couple of minutes ago. He's asking for help. Any idiot can see that, even if we don't know his language."

The picture snapped off.

The next scene showed tiny human figures working with searchlights at the top of an immeasurably high cliff. Here and there, the beam of the searchlight caught the cliff face; the translucent faceted material of the cliff looked almost like rows of eerie windows, their lights snapping on and off, as the searchlight moved.

Far down there was a red glow. Fire came from inside the mountain.

Even with telescopic lenses the cameraman could not get the close-up of the glow. On one side there was the figure of the horse, his four arms stretched at impossible angles as he held himself firm in the crevasse; on the other side of the fire there were the even tinier figures of men, laboring to fit some sort of sling to reach the horse.

For some odd reason having to do with the techniques of recording, the voices came through very plainly, even the heavy, tired breathing of the old horse. Now and then he uttered one of the special horse-words which seemed to be the limit of his vocabulary. He was obviously watching the men, and was firmly persuaded of their friendliness to him. His large, tame, yellow eyes rolled wildly in the light of the searchlight and every time the horse looked down, he seemed to shudder.

Casher O'Neill found this entirely understandable. The bottom of the Hippy Dipsy was nowhere in sight; the horse, even with nothing more than the enlarged finger-nails of his middle fingers to help him climb, had managed to get about four of the six kilometers' height of the cliff face behind him.

The voice of a tiger-man sounded clearly from among the shift of men, underpeople, and robots who were struggling on the face of the cliff.

"It's a gamble, but not much of a gamble. I weigh six hundred kilos myself, and, do you know, I don't think I've ever had to use my full strength since I was a kitten. I *know* that I can jump across the fire and help that thing be more comfortable. I can even tie a rope around him so that he won't slip and fall after all the work we've done. And the work he's done, too," added the tiger-man grimly. "*Perhaps* I can just take him in my arms and jump back with him. It will be perfectly safe if you have a safety rope around each of us. After all, I never saw a less prehensile creature in my life. You can't call those fingers of his 'fingers.' They look like little boxes of bone, designed for running around and not much good for anything else."

There was a murmur of other voices and then the command of the supervisor. "Go ahead."

No one was prepared for what happened next.

The cameraman got the tiger-man right in the middle of his frame, showing the attachment of one rope around the tiger-man's broad waist. The tiger-man was a modified type whom the authorities had not bothered to put into human cosmetic form. He still had his ears on top of his head, yellow and black fur over his face, huge incisors overlapping his lower jaw, and enormous antenna-like whiskers sticking out from his moustache. He must have been thoroughly modified inside, however, because his temperament was calm, friendly, and even a little humorous; he must have had a carefully re-done mouth, because the utterance of human speech came to him clearly and without distortion.

He jumped—a mighty jump, right through the top edges of the flame.

The horse saw him.

The horse jumped too, almost in the same moment, also through the top of the flame, going the other way.

The horse had feared the tiger-man more than he did the cliff.

The horse landed right in the group of workers. He tried not to hurt them with his flailing limbs, but he did knock one man—a true man, at that—off the cliff. The man's scream faded as he crashed into the impenetrable darkness below.

The robots were quick. Having no emotions except *on*, *off*, and *high*, they did not get excited. They had the horse trussed and, before the true men and underpeople had ensured their footing, they had signaled the crane operator at the top of the cliff. The horse, his four arms swinging limply, disappeared upward.

The tiger-man jumped back through the flames to the nearer ledge. The picture went off.

In the viewing room, the Hereditary Dictator Philip Vincent stood up. He stretched, looking around.

Genevieve looked at Casher O'Neill expectantly.

"That's the story," said the Dictator mildly. "Now you solve it."

"Where is the horse now?" said Casher O'Neill.

"In the hospital, of course. My niece can take you to see him."

∽ III ∽

After a short, painful, and very thorough peeping of his own mind by the Hereditary Dictator, Casher O'Neill and Genevieve set off for the hospital in which the horse was being kept in bed. The people of Pontoppidan had not known what else to do with him, so they had placed him under strong sedation and were trying to feed him with sugar-water compounds going directly into his veins. Genevieve told Casher that the horse was wasting away.

They walked to the hospital over amethyst pebbles.

Instead of wearing his spacesuit, Casher wore a surface helmet which enriched his oxygen. His hosts had not counted on his getting spells of uncontrollable itching from the sharply reduced atmospheric pressure. He did not dare mention the matter, because he was still hoping to get the green ruby as a weapon in his private war for the liberation of the Twelve Niles from the rule of Colonel Wedder. Whenever the itching became less than excruciating, he enjoyed the walk and the company of the slight, beautiful girl who accompanied him across the fields of jewels to the hospital. (In later years, he sometimes wondered what might have happened. Was the itching a part of his destiny, which saved him for the freedom of the city of Kaheer and the planet Mizzer? Might not the innocent brilliant loveliness of the girl have otherwise tempted him to forswear his duty and stay forever on Pontoppidan?)

The girl wore a new kind of cosmetic for outdoor walking—a warm peach-hued powder which let the natural pink of her cheeks show through. Her eyes, he saw, were a living, deep gray; her eyelashes, long; her smile, innocently provocative beyond all ordinary belief. It was a wonder that the Hereditary Dictator had not had to stop duels and murders between young men vying for her favor.

They finally reached the hospital, just as Casher O'Neill thought he could stand it no longer and would have to ask Genevieve for some kind of help or carriage to get indoors and away from the frightful itching.

The building was underground.

The entrance was sumptuous. Diamonds and rubies, the size of building-bricks on Mizzer, had been set to frame the doorway, which was apparently enameled steel. Kuraf at his most lavish had never wasted money on anything like this door-frame. Genevieve saw his glance.

"It did cost a lot of credits. We had to bring a blind artist all the way from Olympia to paint that enamel-work. The poor man. He spent most of his time trying to steal extra gem-stones when he should have known that we pay justly and never allowed anyone to get away with stealing."

"What do you do?" asked Casher O'Neill.

"We cut thieves up in space, just at the edge of the atmosphere. We have more manned boats in orbit than any other planet I know of. Maybe Old North Australia has more, but, then, nobody ever gets close enough to Old North Australia to come back alive and tell."

They went on into the hospital.

A respectful chief surgeon insisted on keeping them in the office and entertaining them with tea and confectionery, when they both wanted to go see the horse; common politeness prohibited their pushing through. Finally they got past the ceremony and into the room in which the horse was kept.

Close up, they could see how much he had suffered. There were cuts and abrasions over almost all of his body. One of his *hooves*—the doctor told them that was the correct name, *hoof*, for the big middle fingernail on which he walked—was split; the doctor had put a cadmium-silver bar through it. The horse lifted his head when they entered, but he saw that they were just more people, not horsey people, so he put his head down, very patiently.

"What's the prospect, doctor?" asked Casher O'Neill, turning away from the animal.

"Could I ask you, sir, a foolish question first?"

Surprised, Casher could only say yes.

"You're an O'Neill. Your uncle is Kuraf. How do you happen to be called 'Casher'?"

"That's simple," laughed Casher. "This is my young-man-name. On Mizzer, everybody gets a baby name, which nobody uses. Then he gets a nickname. Then he gets a young-man-name, based on some characteristic or some friendly joke, until he picks out his career. When he enters his profession, he picks out his own career name. If I liberate Mizzer and overthrow Colonel Wedder, I'll have to think up a suitable career name for myself."

"But why 'Casher,' sir?" persisted the doctor.

"When I was a little boy and people asked me what I wanted, I always asked for cash. I guess that contrasted with my uncle's wastefulness, so they called me Casher."

"But what is cash? One of your crops?"

It was Casher's time to look amazed. "Cash is money. Paper credits. People pass them back and forth when they buy things."

"Here on Pontoppidan, all the money belongs to me. All of it," said Genevieve. "My uncle is trustee for me. But I have never been allowed to touch it or to spend it. It's all just planet business."

The doctor blinked respectfully. "Now this horse, sir, if you will pardon my asking about your name, is a very strange case. Physiologically he is a pure Earth type. He is suited only for a vegetable diet, but otherwise he is a very close relative of man. He has a single stomach and a very large cone-shaped heart. That's where the trouble is. The heart is in bad condition. He is dying."

"Dying?" cried Genevieve.

"That's the sad, horrible part," said the doctor. "He is dying but he cannot die. He could go on like this for many years. Perinõ wasted enough stroon on this animal to make a planet immortal. Now the animal is worn out but cannot die."

Casher O'Neill let out a long, low, ululating whistle. Everybody in the room jumped. He disregarded them. It was the whistle he had used near the stables, back among the Twelve Niles, when he wanted to call a horse.

The horse knew it. The large head lifted. The eyes rolled at him so imploringly that he expected tears to fall from them, even though he was pretty sure that horses could not lachrymate.

He squatted on the floor, close to the horse's head, with a hand on its mane.

"Quick," he murmured to the surgeon. "Get me a piece of sugar and an underperson-telepath. The underperson-telepath must not be of carnivorous origin."

The doctor looked stupid. He snapped "Sugar" at an assistant, but he squatted down next to Casher O'Neill and said, "You will have to repeat that about an underperson. This is not an underperson hospital at all. We have very few of them here. The horse is here only by command of His Excellency Philip Vincent, who said that the horse of Perinõ should be given the best of all possible care. He even told me," said the doctor, "that if anything wrong happened to this horse, I would ride patrol for it for the next eighty years. So I'll do what I can. Do you find me too talkative? Some people do. What kind of an underperson do you want?"

"I need," said Casher, very calmly, "a telepathic underperson, both to find out what this horse wants and to tell the horse that I am here to help him. Horses are vegetarians and they do not like meat-eaters. Do you have a vegetarian underperson around the hospital?"

"We used to have some squirrel-men," said the chief surgeon, "but when we changed the air circulating system the squirrel-men went away with the old equipment. I think they went to a mine. We have tiger-men, cat-men, and my secretary is a wolf."

"Oh, no!" said Casher O'Neill. "Can you imagine a sick horse confiding in a wolf?"

"It's no more than you are doing," said the surgeon, very softly, glancing up to see if Genevieve were in hearing range, and apparently judging that she was not. "The Hereditary Dictators here sometimes cut suspicious guests to pieces on their way off the planet. That is, unless the guests are licensed, regular traders. You are not. You might be a spy, planning to rob us. How do I know? I wouldn't give a diamond chip for your chances of being alive next week. What do you want to do about the horse? That might please the Dictator. And *you* might live."

Casher O'Neill was so staggered by the confidence of the surgeon that he squatted there thinking about himself, not about the patient. The horse licked him, seemingly sensing that he needed solace.

The surgeon had an idea. "Horses and dogs used to go

together, didn't they, back in the old days of Manhome, when all the people lived on planet Earth?"

"Of course," said Casher. "We still run them together in hunts on Mizzer, but under these new laws of the Instrumentality we've run out of underpeople-criminals to hunt."

"I have a good dog," said the chief surgeon. "She talks pretty well, but she is so sympathetic that she upsets the patients by loving them too much. I have her down in the second underbasement tending the dish-sterilizing machinery."

"Bring her up," said Casher in a whisper.

He remembered that he did not need to whisper about this, so he stood up and spoke to Genevieve:

"They have found a good dog-telepath who may reach through to the mind of the horse. It may give us the answer."

She put her hand on his forearm gently, with the approbatory gesture of a princess. Her fingers dug into his flesh. Was she wishing him well against her uncle's habitual treachery, or was this merely the impulse of a kind young girl who knew nothing of the way the world was run?

∽ IV ∽

The interview went extremely well.

The dog-woman was almost perfectly humaniform. She looked like a tired, cheerful, worn-out old woman, not valuable enough to be given the life-prolonging santaclara drug called *stroon*. Work had been her life and she had had plenty of it. Casher O'Neill felt a twinge of envy when he realized that happiness goes by the petty chances of life and not by the large destiny. This dog-woman, with her haggard face and her stringy gray hair, had more love, happiness, and sympathy than Kuraf had found with his pleasures, Colonel Wedder with his powers, or himself with his crusade. Why did life do that? Was there no justice, ever? Why should a worn-out worthless old underwoman be happy when he was not?

"Never mind," she said, "you'll get over it and then you will be happy."

"Over what?" he said. "I didn't say anything."

"I'm not going to say it," she retorted, meaning that she was telepathic. "You're a prisoner of yourself. Some day you will escape to unimportance and happiness. You're a good man. You're trying to save yourself, but you really *like* this horse."

"Of course I do," said Casher O'Neill. "He's a brave old horse, climbing out of that hell to get back to people."

When he said the word *hell* her eyes widened, but she said nothing. In his mind, he saw the sign of a fish scrawled on a dark wall and he felt her think at him, *So you too know something of the "dark wonderful knowledge" which is not yet to be revealed to all mankind?*

He thought a *cross* back at her and then turned his thinking to the horse, lest their telepathy be monitored and strange punishments await them both.

She spoke in words, "Shall we link?"

"Link," he said.

Genevieve stepped up. Her clear-cut, pretty, sensitive face was alight with excitement. "Could I—could I be cut in?"

"Why not?" said the dog-woman, glancing at him. He nodded. The three of them linked hands and then the dog-woman put her left hand on the forehead of the old horse.

The sand splashed beneath their feet as they ran toward Kaheer. The delicious pressure of a man's body was on their backs. The red sky of Mizzer gleamed over them. There came the shout:

"I'm a horse, I'm a horse, I'm a horse!"

"You're from Mizzer," thought Casher O'Neill, "from Kaheer itself!"

"I don't know names," thought the horse, "but you're from my land. The land, the good land."

"What are you doing here?"

"Dying," thought the horse. "Dying for hundreds and thousands of sundowns. The old one brought me. No riding, no running, no people. Just the old one and the small ground. I have been dying since I came here."

Casher O'Neill got a glimpse of Perinō sitting and watching the horse, unconscious of the cruelty and loneliness which he had inflicted on his large pet by making it immortal and then giving it no work to do.

"Do you know what dying is?"

Thought the horse promptly: "Certainly. No-horse."

"Do you know what life is?"

"Yes. Being a horse."

"I'm not a horse," thought Casher O'Neill, "but I am alive."

"Don't complicate things," thought the horse at him, though Casher realized it was his own mind and not the horse's which supplied the words.

"Do you want to die?"

"To no-horse? Yes, if this room, forever, is the end of things."

"What would you like better?" thought Genevieve, and her thoughts were like a cascade of newly-minted silver coins falling into all their minds: brilliant, clean, bright, innocent.

The answer was quick: "Dirt beneath my hooves, and wet air again, and a man on my back."

The dog-woman interrupted: "Dear horse, you know me?"

"You're a dog," thought the horse. "Goo-oo-oo-ood dog!"

"Right," thought the happy old slattern, "and I can tell these people how to take care of you. Sleep now, and when you waken you will be on the way to happiness."

She thought the command *sleep* so powerfully at the old horse that Casher O'Neill and Genevieve both started to fall unconscious and had to be caught by the hospital attendants.

As they re-gathered their wits, she was finishing her commands to the surgeon. "—and put about 40% supplementary oxygen into the air. He'll have to have a real person to ride him, but some of your orbiting sentries would rather ride a horse up there than do nothing. You can't repair the heart. Don't try it. Hypnosis will take care of the sand of Mizzer. Just load his mind with one or two of the drama-cubes packed full of desert adventure. Now, don't you worry about me. I'm not going to give you any more suggestions. People-man, you!" She laughed. "You can forgive us dogs anything, except for being right. It makes you feel inferior for a few minutes. Never mind. I'm going back downstairs to my dishes. I love them, I really do. Good-bye, you pretty thing," she said to Genevieve. "And good-bye, wanderer! Good luck to you," she said to Casher O'Neill. "You will remain miserable as long as you seek justice, but when you give up, righteousness will come to you and you will be happy. Don't worry. You're young and it won't hurt you to suffer a few more years. Youth is an extremely curable disease, isn't it?"

She gave them a full curtsy, like one Lady of the Instrumentality saying good-bye to another. Her wrinkled old face was lit up with smiles, in which happiness was mixed with a tiniest bit of playful mockery.

"Don't mind me, boss," she said to the surgeon. "Dishes, here I come." She swept out of the room.

"See what I mean?" said the surgeon. "She's so horribly *happy*! How can anyone run a hospital if a dishwasher gets all over the place, making people happy? We'd be out of jobs. Her ideas were good, though."

They were. They worked. Down to the last letter of the dog-woman's instructions.

There was argument from the council. Casher O'Neill went along to see them in session.

One councillor, Bashnack, was particularly vociferous in objecting to any action concerning the horse. "Sire," he cried, "sire! We don't even know the name of the animal! I must protest this action, when we don't know—"

"That we don't," assented Philip Vincent. "But what does a name have to do with it?"

"The horse has no identity, not even the identity of an

animal. It is just a pile of meat left over from the estate of Perinō. We should kill the horse and eat the meat ourselves. Or, if we do not want to eat the meat, then we should sell it off-planet. There are plenty of peoples around here who would pay a pretty price for genuine Earth meat. Pay no attention to me, sire! You are the Hereditary Dictator and I am nothing. I have no power, no property, nothing. I am at your mercy. All I can tell you is to follow your own best interests. I have only a voice. You cannot reproach me for using my voice when I am trying to help you, sire, can you? That's all I am doing, helping you. If you spend any credits at all on this animal you will be doing wrong, wrong, wrong. We are not a rich planet. We have to pay for expensive defenses just in order to stay alive. We cannot even afford to pay for air that our children can go out and play. And you want to spend money on a horse which cannot even talk! I tell you, sire, this council is going to vote against you, just to protect your own interests and the interests of the Honorable Genevieve as Eventual Title-holder of all Pontoppidan. You are not going to get away with this, sire! We are helpless before your power, but we will insist on advising you—"

"Hear! Hear!" cried several of the councillors, not the least dismayed by the slight frown of the Hereditary Dictator.

"I will take the word," said Philip Vincent himself.

Several had had their hands raised, asking for the floor. One obstinate man kept his hand up even when the Dictator announced his intention to speak. Philip Vincent took note of him, too:

"You can talk when I am through, if you want to."

He looked calmly around the room, smiled imperceptibly at his niece, gave Casher O'Neill the briefest of nods, and then announced:

"Gentlemen, it's not the horse which is on trial. It's Pontoppidan. It's we who are trying ourselves. And before whom are we trying ourselves, gentlemen? Each of us is before that most awful of courts, his own conscience.

"If we kill that horse, gentlemen, we will not be doing the horse a great wrong. He is an old animal, and I do not think that he will mind dying very much, now that he is away from the ordeal of loneliness which he feared more than death. After all, he has already had his great triumph— the climb up the cliff of gems, the jump across the volcanic vent, the rescue by people whom he wanted to find. The horse has done so well that he is really beyond us. We can help him, a little, or we can hurt him, a little; beside the immensity of his accomplishment, we cannot really do very much either way.

"No, gentlemen, we are not judging the case of the horse. We are judging space. What happens to a man when he moves out into the Big Nothing? Do we leave Old Earth behind? Why did civilization fall? Will it fall again? Is civilization a gun or a blaster or a laser or a rocket? Is it even a planoforming ship or a pinlighter at his work? You know as well as I do, gentlemen, that civilization is not what we can do. If it had been, there would have been no fall of Ancient Man. Even in the Dark Ages they had a few fusion bombs, they could make some small guided missiles, and they even had weapons like the Kaskaskas Effect, which we have never been able to rediscover. The Dark Ages weren't dark because people lost techniques or science. They were dark *because people lost people*. It's a lot of work to be human, and it's work which must be kept up, or it begins to fade. Gentlemen, the horse judges us.

"Take the word, gentlemen. 'Civilization' is itself a lady's word. There were female writers in a country called France who made that word popular in the third century before space travel. To be 'civilized' meant for people to be tame, to be kind, to be polished. If we kill this horse, we are wild. If we treat the horse gently, we are tame. Gentlemen, I have only one witness and that witness will utter only one word. Then you shall vote and vote freely."

There was a murmur around the table at this announcement. Philip Vincent obviously enjoyed the excitement he had created. He let them murmur on for a full minute or two before he slapped the table gently and said, "Gentlemen, the witness. Are you ready?"

There was a murmur of assent. Bashnack tried to say "It's still a question of public funds!" but his neighbors shushed him. The table became quiet. All faces turned toward the Hereditary Dictator.

"Gentlemen, the testimony. Genevieve, is that what you yourself told me to say? Is civilization always a woman's choice first, and only later a man's?"

"Yes," said Genevieve, with a happy, open smile.

The meeting broke up amid laughter and applause.

∽ V ∽

A month later Casher O'Neill sat in a room in a medium-size planoforming liner. They were out of reach of Pontoppidan. The Hereditary Dictator had not changed his mind and cut him down with green beams. Casher had strange memories, not bad ones for a young man.

He remembered Genevieve weeping in the garden.

"I'm romantic," she cried, and wiped her eyes on the sleeve of his cape. "Legally I'm the owner of this planet, rich, powerful, free. But I can't leave here. I'm too important. I can't marry whom I want to marry. I'm too important. My uncle can't do what *he* wants to do—he's Hereditary Dictator and he always must do what the Council decides after weeks of chatter. I can't love you. You're a prince and a wanderer, with travels and battles and justice and strange things ahead of you. I can't go. I'm too important. I'm too sweet! I'm too nice; I hate, hate, hate myself sometimes. Please, Casher, could you take a flier and run away with me into space."

"Your uncle's lasers could cut us to pieces before we got out."

He held her hands and looked gently down into her face. At this moment he did not feel the fierce, aggressive, happy glow which an able young man feels in the presence of a beautiful and tender young woman. He felt something much stranger, softer, quieter—an emotion very sweet to the mind and restful to the nerves. It was the simple, clear compassion of one person for another. He took a chance for her sake, because the "dark knowledge" was wonderful but very dangerous in the wrong hands.

He took both her beautiful little hands in his, so that she looked up at him and realized that he was not going to kiss her. Something about his stance made her realize that she was being offered a more precious gift than a sky-lit romantic kiss in a garden. Besides, it was just touching helmets.

He said to her, with passion and kindness in his voice:

"You remember that dog-woman, the one who works with the dishes in the hospital?"

"Of course. She was good and bright and happy, and helped us all."

"Go work with her, now and then. Ask her nothing. Tell her nothing. Just work with her at her machines. Tell her I said so. Happiness is catching. You might catch it. I think I did myself, a little."

"I think I understand you," said Genevieve softly. "Casher, good-bye and good, good luck to you. My uncle expects us."

Together they went back into the palace.

Another memory was the farewell to Philip Vincent, the Hereditary Dictator of Pontoppidan. The calm, clean-shaven, ruddy, well-fleshed face looked at him with benign regard. Casher O'Neill felt more respect for this man when he realized that ruthlessness is often the price of peace, and vigilance the price of wealth.

"You're a clever young man. A very clever young man. You may win back the power of your Uncle Kuraf."

"I don't want *that* power!" cried Casher O'Neill.

"I have advice for you," said the Hereditary Dictator, "and it is good advice or I would not be here to give it. I have learned the political arts well: otherwise I would not be alive. Do not refuse power. Just take it and use it wisely. Do not hide from your wicked uncle's name. Obliterate it.

Take the name yourself and rule so well that, in a few decades, no one will remember your uncle. Just you. You are young. You can't win now. But it is in your fate to grow and to triumph. I know it. I am good at these things. I have given you your weapon. I am not tricking you. It is packed safely and you may leave with it."

Casher O'Neill was breathing softly, believing it all, and trying to think of words to thank the stout, powerful older man when the dictator added, with a little laugh in his voice:

"Thank you, too, for saving me money. You've lived up to your name, Casher."

"Saved you money?"

"The alfalfa. The horse wanted alfalfa."

"Oh, that idea!" said Casher O'Neill. "It was obvious. I don't deserve much credit for that."

"*I* didn't think of it," said the Hereditary Dictator, "and my staff didn't either. We're not stupid. That shows you are bright. You realized that Perinō must have had a food converter to keep the horse alive in the Hippy Dipsy. All we did was set it to alfalfa and we saved ourselves the cost of a shipload of horse food twice a year. We're glad to save that credit. We're well off here, but we don't like to waste things. You may bow to me now, and leave."

Casher O'Neill had done so, with one last glance at the lovely Genevieve, standing fragile and beautiful beside her uncle's chair.

His last memory was very recent.

He had paid two hundred thousand credits for it, right on this liner. He had found the Stop-Captain, bored now that the ship was in flight and the Go-Captain had taken over.

"Can you get me a telepathic fix on a horse?"

"What's a horse?" said the Stop-Captain. "Where is it? Do you want to pay for it?"

"A horse," said Casher O'Neill patiently, "is an unmodified earth animal. Not underpeople. A big one, but quite intelligent. This one is in orbit right around Pontoppidan. And I will pay the usual price."

"A million Earth credits," said the Stop-Captain.

"Ridiculous!" cried Casher O'Neill.

They settled on two hundred thousand credits for a good fix and ten thousand for the use of the ship's equipment even if there were failure. It was not a failure. The technician was a snake-man: he was deft, cool, and superb at his job. In only a few minutes he passed the headset to Casher O'Neill, saying politely, "This is it, I think."

It was. He had reached right into the horse's mind.

The endless sands of Mizzer swam before Casher O'Neill. The long lines of the Twelve Niles converged in the distance. He galloped steadily and powerfully. There were other horses nearby, other riders, other things, but he himself was conscious only of the beat of the hooves against the strong moist sand, the firmness of the appreciative rider upon his back. Dimly, as in a hallucination, Casher O'Neill could also see the little orbital ship in which the old horse cantered in mid-air, with an amused cadet sitting on his back. Up there, with no weight, the old worn-out heart would be good for many, many years. Then he saw the horse's paradise again. The flash of hooves threatened to overtake him, but he outran them all. There was the expectation of a stable at the end, a rubdown, good succulent green food, and the glimpse of a filly in the morning.

The horse of Pontoppidan felt extremely wise. He had trusted *people*—people, the source of all kindness, all cruelty, all power among the stars. And the people had been good. The horse felt very much horse again. Casher felt the old body course along the river's edge like a dream of power, like a completion of service, like an ultimate fulfillment of companionship.

On the Storm Planet

∾|∾

"At two seventy-five in the morning," said the Administrator to Casher O'Neill, "you will kill this girl with a knife. At two seventy-seven, a fast groundcar will pick you up and bring you back here. Then the power cruiser will be yours. Is that a deal?"

He held out his hand as if he wanted Casher O'Neill to shake it then and there, making some kind of an oath or bargain.

Casher did not want to slight the man, so he picked up his glass and said, "Let's drink to the deal, first!"

The Administrator's quick, restless, darting eyes looked Casher up and down very suspiciously. The warm sea-wet air blew through the room. The Administrator seemed wary, suspicious, alert, but underneath his slight hostility there was another emotion, of which Casher could perceive just the edge. Fatigue with its roots in bottomless despair: despair set deep in irrecoverable fatigue?

That other emotion, which Casher could barely discern, was very strange indeed. On all his voyages back and forth through the inhabited worlds, Casher had met many odd types of men and women. He had never seen anything like this Administrator before—brilliant, erratic, boastful. His title was "Mr. Commissioner" and he was an ex-Lord of the Instrumentality on this planet of Henriada, where the population had dropped from six hundred million persons down to some forty thousand. Indeed, local government had disappeared into limbo, and this odd man, with the title of "Administrator," was the only law and civil authority which the planet knew.

Nevertheless, he had a surplus power cruiser and Casher O'Neill was determined to get that cruiser as a part of his long plot to return to his home planet of Mizzer and to unseat the usurper, Colonel Wedder.

The Administrator stared sharply, wearily at Casher and then he, too, lifted his glass. The green twilight colored his liquor and made it seem like some strange poison. It was only Earth-byegarr, though a little on the strong side.

With a sip, only a sip, the older man relaxed a little. "You may be out to trick me, young man. You may think that I am an old fool running an abandoned planet. You may even be thinking that killing this girl is some kind of a crime. It is not a crime at all. I am the Administrator of Henriada and I have ordered that girl killed every year for the last eighty years. She isn't even a girl, to start with. Just an underperson. Some kind of an animal turned into a domestic servant. I can even appoint you a deputy sheriff. Or chief of detectives. That might be better. I haven't had a chief of detectives for a hundred years and more. You are my chief of detectives. Go in tomorrow. The house is not hard to find. It's the biggest and best house left on this planet. Go in tomorrow morning. Ask for her master and be sure that you use the correct title, 'Mister and Owner Murray Madigan.' The robots will tell you to keep out. If you persist, she will come to the door. That's when you will stab her through the heart, right there in the doorway. My groundcar will race up one metric minute later. You jump in and come back here. We've been through this before. Why don't you agree? Don't you know who I am?"

"I know perfectly well"—Casher O'Neill smiled—"who you are, Mr. Commissioner and Administrator. You are the honorable Rankin Meiklejohn, once of Earth Two. After all, the Instrumentality itself gave me a permit to land on this planet on private business. They knew who *I* was, too, and what I wanted. There's something funny about all this. Why should you give me a power cruiser— the best ship, you yourself say, in your whole fleet—just for killing one modified animal which looks and talks like a girl? Why me? Why the visitor? Why the man from off-world? Why should you care whether this particular underperson is killed or not? If you've given the order for her death eighty times in eighty years, why hasn't it been carried out long ago? Mind you, Mr. Administrator, I'm not saying no. I want that cruiser. I want it very much indeed. But what's the deal? What's the trick? Is it the house you want?"

"Beauregard? No, I don't want Beauregard. Old Madigan can rot in it for all that I care. It's between Ambiloxi and Mottile, on the Gulf of Esperanza. You can't miss it. The road is good. You could drive yourself there."

"What is it, then?" Casher's voice had an edge of persistence to it.

The Administrator's response was singular indeed. He filled his huge inhaler-glass with the potent byegarr. He stared over the full glass at Casher O'Neill as if he were an enemy. He drained the glass. Casher knew that that much liquor, taken suddenly, could kill the normal human being.

The Administrator did not fall over dead.

He did not even become noticeably more drunk.

His face turned red and his eyes almost popped out, as the harsh 160-proof liquor took effect, but he still did not say anything. He just stared at Casher. Casher, who had learned in his long exile to play many games, just stared back.

The Administrator broke first.

He leaned forward and burst into a bird-like shriek of laughter. The laughter went on and on until it seemed that the man had hogged all the merriment in the galaxy. Casher snorted a little laugh along with the man, more out of nervous reflex than anything else, but he waited for the Administrator to stop laughing.

The Administrator finally got control of himself. With a broad grin and a wink at Casher, he poured himself four fingers more of the byegarr into his glass, drank it down as if he had had a sip of cream, and then—only very slightly unsteady—stood up, came over, and patted Casher on the shoulder.

"You're a smart boy, my lad. I'm cheating you. I don't care whether the power cruiser is there or not. I'm giving you something which has no value at all to me. Who's ever going to take a power cruiser off this planet? It's ruined. It's abandoned. And so am I. Go ahead. You can have the cruiser. For nothing. Just take it. Free. Unconditionally."

This time it was Casher who leaped to his feet and stared down into the face of the feverish, wanton little man.

"Thank you, Mr. Administrator!" he cried, trying to catch the hand of the Administrator so as to seal the deal.

Rankin Meiklejohn looked awfully sober for a man with that much liquor in him. He held his right hand behind his back and would not shake.

"You can have the cruiser all right. No terms. No conditions. No deal. It's yours. *But kill that girl first!* Just as a favor to me. I've been a good host. I like you. I want to do you a favor. Do me one. Kill that girl. At two seventy-five in the morning. Tomorrow."

"Why?" asked Casher, his voice loud and cold, trying to wring some sense out of the chattering man.

"Just—just—just because I say so. . . ." stammered the Administrator.

"Why?" asked Casher, cold and loud again.

The liquor suddenly took over inside the Administrator. He groped back for the arm of his chair, sat down suddenly, and then looked up at Casher. He was very drunk indeed. The strange emotion, the elusive fatigue-despair, had vanished from his face. He spoke straightforwardly. Only the excessive care of his articulation would have shown a passer-by that he was drunk.

"Because, you fool," said Meiklejohn, "those people, more than eighty in eighty years, that I have sent to Beauregard with orders to kill the girl. Those people—"

he repeated, and stopped speaking, clamping his lips together.

"What happened to them?" asked Casher calmly and persuasively.

The Administrator grinned again and seemed to be on the edge of one of his wild laughs.

"What happened?" shouted Casher at him.

"I don't know," said the Administrator. "For the life of me, I don't know. Not one of them ever came back."

"What happened to them? Did she kill them?" cried Casher.

"How would I know?" said the drunken man, getting visibly more sleepy.

"Why didn't you report it?"

This seemed to rouse the Administrator. "Report that one little girl had stopped me, the planetary Administrator? Just one little girl, and not even a human being! They would have sent help, and laughed at me. By the Bell, young man, I've been laughed at enough! I need no help from outside. You're going in there tomorrow morning. At two seventy-five, with a knife. And a ground-car waiting."

He stared fixedly at Casher and then suddenly fell asleep in his chair. Casher called to the robots to show him to his room; they tended to the master as well.

∾ II ∾

The next morning at two seventy-five sharp, nothing happened. Casher walked down the baroque corridor, looking into beautiful barren rooms. All the doors were open.

Through one door he heard a sick, deep bubbling snore.

It was the Administrator, sure enough. He lay twisted on his bed. A small nursing machine was beside him, her white enameled body only slightly rusty. She held up a mechanical hand for silence and somehow managed to make the gesture seem light, delicate, and pretty, even from a machine.

Casher walked lightly back to his own room, where he ordered hotcakes, bacon, and coffee. He studied a tornado through the armored glass of his window, while the robots prepared his food. The elastic trees clung to the earth with a fury which matched the fury of the wind. The trunk of the tornado reached like the nose of a mad elephant down into the gardens, but the flora fought back. A few animals whipped upward and out of sight. The tornado then came straight for the house, but did not damage it outside of making a lot of noise.

"We have two or three hundred of those a day," said a butler robot. "That is why we store all space-craft underground and have no weather machines. It would cost more, the people said, to make this planet livable than the planet could possibly yield. The radio and news are in the library, sir. I do not think that the honorable Rankin Meiklejohn will wake until evening, say seven-fifty or eight o'clock."

"Can I go out?"

"Why not, sir? You are a true man. You can do what you wish."

"I mean, is it safe for me to go out?"

"Oh, no, sir! The wind would tear you apart or carry you away."

"Don't people ever go out?"

"Yes, sir. With groundcars or with automatic body armor. I have been told that if it weighs fifty tons or better, the person inside is safe. I would not know, sir. As you see, I am a robot. I was made here, though my brain was formed on Earth Two, and I have never been outside this house."

Casher looked at the robot. This one seemed unusually talkative. He chanced the opportunity of getting some more information.

"Have you ever heard of Beauregard?"

"Yes, sir. It is the best house on this planet. I have heard people say that it is the most solid building on Henriada. It belongs to the Mister and Owner Murray Madigan. He is an Old North Australian, a renunciant who left his home planet and came here when Henriada was a busy world. He brought all his wealth with him. The underpeople and robots say that it is a wonderful place on the inside."

"Have you seen it?"

"Oh, no, sir, I have never left this building."

"Does the man Madigan ever come here?"

The robot seemed to be trying to laugh, but did not succeed. He answered, very unevenly, "Oh, no, sir. He never goes anywhere."

"Can you tell me anything about the female who lives with him?"

"No, sir," said the robot.

"Do you know anything about her?"

"Sir, it is not that. I know a great deal about her."

"Why can't you talk about her, then?"

"I have been commanded not to, sir."

"I am," said Casher O'Neill, "a true human being. I herewith countermand those orders. Tell me about her."

The robot's voice became formal and cold. "The orders cannot be countermanded, sir."

"Why not?" snapped Casher. "Are they the Administrator's?"

"No, sir."

"Whose, then?"

"Hers," said the robot softly, and left the room.

$$\sim \text{III} \sim$$

Casher O'Neill spent the rest of the day trying to get information; he obtained very little.

The Deputy Administrator was a young man who hated his chief.

When Casher, who dined with him—the two of them having a poorly-cooked state luncheon in a dining room which would have seated five hundred people—tried to come to the point by asking bluntly, "What do you know about Murray Madigan?" he got an answer which was blunt to the point of incivility.

"Nothing."

"You never heard of him?" cried Casher.

"Keep your troubles to yourself, mister visitor," said the Deputy Administrator. "I've got to stay on this planet long enough to get promoted off. You can leave. You shouldn't have come."

"I have," said Casher, "an all-world pass from the Instrumentality."

"All right," said the young man, "that shows that you are more important than I am. Let's not discuss the matter. Do you like your lunch?"

Casher had learned diplomacy in his childhood, when he was the heir apparent to the Dictatorship of Mizzer. When his horrible uncle, Kuraf, lost the rulership, Casher had approved of the coup by the Colonels Wedder and Gibna; but now Wedder was supreme and enforcing a period of terror and virtue. Casher thus knew courts and ceremony, big talk and small talk, and on this occasion, he let the small talk do. The young Deputy Administrator had only one ambition, to get off the planet Henriada and never to see or hear of Rankin Meiklejohn again.

Casher could understand the point.

Only one curious thing happened during dinner.

Toward the end, Casher slipped in the question, very informally: "Can underpeople give orders to robots?"

"Of course," said the young man. "That's one of the reasons we use underpeople. They have more initiative. They amplify our orders to robots on many occasions."

Casher smiled. "I didn't mean it quite that way. Could an underperson give an order to a robot which a real human being could not then countermand?"

The young man started to answer, even though his mouth was full of food. He was not a very polished young man. Suddenly he stopped chewing and his eyes grew wide. Then, with his mouth half full, he said: "You are trying to talk about this planet, I guess. You can't help it. You're on the track. Stay on the track, then. Maybe you will get out of it alive. I refuse to get mixed up with it, with you, with him and his hateful schemes. All I want to do is to leave when my time comes."

The young man resumed chewing, his eyes fixed steadfastly on his plate.

Before Casher could pass off the matter by making some casual remark, the butler-robot stopped behind him and leaned over.

"Honorable sir, I heard your question. May I answer it?"

"Of course," said Casher, softly.

"The answer, sir," said the butler-robot, softly but clearly, "to your question is *no, no, never.* That is the general rule of the civilized worlds. But on this planet of Henriada, sir, the answer is *yes.*"

"Why?" asked Casher.

"It is my duty, sir," said the robot butler, "to recommend to you this dish of fresh artichokes. I am not authorized to deal with other matters."

"Thank you," said Casher, straining a little to keep himself looking imperturbable.

Nothing much happened that night, except that Meiklejohn got up long enough to get drunk all over again. Though he invited Casher to come and drink with him, he never seriously discussed the girl except for one outburst.

"Leave it till tomorrow. Fair and square. Open and above-board. Frank and honest. That's me. I'll take you around Beauregard myself. You'll see it's easy. A knife, eh? A traveled young man like you would know what to do with a knife. And a little girl, too. Not very big. Easy job. Don't give it another thought. Would you like some apple juice in your byegarr?"

Casher had taken three contraintoxicant pills before going to drink with the ex-Lord, but even at that, he could not keep up with Meiklejohn. He accepted the dilution of apple juice gravely, gracefully, and gratefully.

The little tornadoes stamped around the house. Meiklejohn, now launched into some drunken story of ancient injustices which had been done to him on other worlds, paid no attention to them. In the middle of the night, past nine-fifty in the evening, Casher woke alone in his chair, very stiff and uncomfortable. The robots must have had standing instructions concerning the Administrator, and had apparently taken him off to bed. Casher walked wearily to his own room, cursed the thundering ceiling, and went to sleep again.

∽ IV ∽

The next day was very different indeed.

The Administrator was as sober, brisk, and charming as if he had never taken a drink in his life.

He had the robots call Casher to join him at breakfast and said, by way of greeting, "I'll wager you thought I was drunk last night."

"Well . . ." said Casher.

"Planet fever. That's what it was. Planet fever. A bit of

alcohol keeps it from developing too far. Let's see. It's three-sixty now. Could you be ready to leave by four?"

Casher frowned at his watch, which had the conventional twenty-four hours.

The Administrator saw the glance and apologized. "Sorry! My fault, a thousand times. I'll get you a metric watch right away. Ten hours a day, a hundred minutes an hour. We're very progressive here on Henriada."

He clapped his hands and ordered that a watch be taken to Casher's room, along with the watch-repairing robot to adjust it to Casher's body rhythms.

"Four, then," he said, rising briskly from the table. "Dress for a trip by groundcar. The servants will show you how."

There was a man already waiting in Casher's room. He looked like a plump, wise ancient Hindu, as shown in the archaeology books. He bowed pleasantly and said, "My name is Gosigo. I am a forgetty, settled on this planet, but for this day I am your guide and driver from this place to the mansion of Beauregard."

Forgetties were barely above underpeople in status. They were persons convicted of various major crimes, to whom the courts of the worlds, or the Instrumentality, had allowed total amnesia instead of death or some punishment worse than death, such as the planet Shayol.

Casher looked at him seriously. The man did not carry with him the permanent air of bewilderment which Casher had noticed in many forgetties. Gosigo saw the glance and interpreted it.

"I'm well enough, now, sir. And I am strong enough to break your back if I had the orders to do it."

"You mean, damage my spine? What a hostile, unpleasant thing to do!" said Casher. "Anyhow, I rather think I could kill you first if you tried it. Whatever gave you such an idea?"

"The Administrator is always threatening people that he will have me do it to them."

"Have you ever really broken anybody's back?" asked Casher, looking Gosigo over very carefully and re-judging him. The man, though shorter than Casher, was luxuriously muscled; like many plump men, he looked pleasant on the outside but could be very formidable to an enemy.

Gosigo smiled briefly, almost happily. "Well, no, not exactly."

"Why haven't you? Does the Administrator always countermand his own orders? I should think that he would sometimes be too drunk to remember to do it?"

"It's not that . . ." said Gosigo.

"Why don't you, then?"

"I have other orders," said Gosigo, rather hesitantly. "Like the orders I have today. One set from the Administrator, one set from the Deputy Administrator, and a third set from an outside source."

"Who's the outside source?"

"She has told me not to explain just yet."

Casher stood stock still. "Do you mean who I think you mean?"

Gosigo nodded very slowly, pointing at the ventilator as though it might have a microphone in it.

"Can you tell me what your orders are?"

"Oh, certainly. The Administrator has told me to drive both himself and you to Beauregard, to take you to the door, to watch you stab the undergirl, and to call the second groundcar to your rescue. The Deputy Administrator has told me to take you to Beauregard and to let you do as you please, bringing you back here by way of Ambiloxi if you happen to come out of Mister Murray's house alive."

"And the other orders?"

"To close the door upon you when you enter and to think of you no more in this life, because you will be very happy."

"Are you crazy?" cried Casher.

"I am a forgetty," said Gosigo, with some dignity, "but I am not insane."

"Whose orders are you going to obey, then?"

Gosigo smiled a warmly human smile at him. "Doesn't that depend on you, sir, and not on me? Do I look like a man who is going to kill you soon?"

"No, you don't," said Casher.

"Do you think what you look like to me?" went on Gosigo, with a purr. "Do you really think that I would help you if I thought that you would kill a small girl?"

"You know it!" cried Casher, feeling his face go white.

"Who doesn't?" said Gosigo. "What else have we got to talk about, here on Henriada? Let me help you on with these clothes, so that you will at least survive the ride." With this he handed shoulder padding and padded helmet to Casher, who began to put on the garments, very clumsily.

Gosigo helped him.

When Casher was fully dressed, he thought that he had never dressed this elaborately for space itself. The world of Henriada must be a tumultuous place if people needed this kind of clothing to make a short trip.

Gosigo had put on the same kind of clothes.

He looked at Casher in a friendly manner, with an arch smile which came close to humor. "Look at me, honorable visitor. Do I remind you of anybody?"

Casher looked honestly and carefully, and then said, "No, you don't."

The man's face fell. "It's a game," he said. "I can't help trying to find out who I really am. Am I a Lord of the Instrumentality who has betrayed his trust? Am I a scientist who twisted knowledge into unimaginable wrong? Am I a dictator so foul that even the Instrumentality, which usually leaves things alone, had to step in and wipe me out? Here I am, healthy, wise, alert. I have the name Gosigo on this planet. Perhaps I am a mere native of this planet, who has committed a local crime. I am triggered. If anyone ever did tell me my true name or my actual past, I have been conditioned to shriek loud, fall unconscious, and forget anything which might be said on such an occasion. People told me that I must have chosen this instead of death. Maybe. Death sometimes looks tidy to a forgetty."

"Have you ever screamed and fainted?"

"I don't even know *that*," said Gosigo, "no more than you know where you are going this very day."

Casher was tied to the man's mystifications, so he did not let himself be provoked into a useless show of curiosity. Inquisitive about the forgetty himself, he asked:

"Does it hurt . . . does it hurt to be a forgetty?"

"No," said Gosigo, "it doesn't hurt, no more than you will."

Gosigo stared suddenly at Casher. His voice changed tone and became at least one octave higher. He clapped his hands to his face and panted through his hands as if he would never speak again.

"But—Oh! The fear—the eerie, dreary fear of *being me* . . . !"

He still stared at Casher.

Quieting down at last, he pulled his hands away from his face, as if by sheer force, and said in an almost-normal voice, "Shall we get on with our trip?"

Gosigo led the way out into the bare bleak corridor. A perceptible wind was blowing through it, though there was no sign of an open window or door. They followed a majestic staircase, with steps so broad that Casher had to keep changing pace on them, all the way down to the bottom of the building. This must, at some time, have been a formal reception hall. Now it was full of cars.

Curious cars.

Land vehicles of a kind which Casher had never seen before. They looked a little bit like the ancient "fighting tanks" which he had seen in pictures. They also looked a little like submarines of a singularly short and ugly shape. They had high spiked wheels, but their most complicated feature was a set of giant corkscrews, four on each side, attached to the car by intricate yet operational apparatus. Since Casher had been landed right into the palace by planoform, he had never had occasion to go outside among the tornadoes of Henriada.

The Administrator was waiting, wearing a coverall on which was stenciled his insignia of rank.

Casher gave him a polite bow. He glanced down at the

handsome metric wristwatch which Gosigo had strapped on his wrist, outside the coverall. It read: 3:95.

Casher bowed to Rankin Meiklejohn and said, "I'm ready, sir, if you are."

"Watch him!" whispered Gosigo, half a step behind Casher.

The Administrator said, "Might as well be going." The man's voice trembled.

Casher stood polite, alert, immobile. Was this danger? Was this foolishness? Could the Administrator already be drunk again?

Casher watched the Administrator carefully but quietly, waiting for the older man to precede him into the nearest groundcar, which had its door standing opened.

Nothing happened, except that the Administrator began to turn pale.

There must have been six or eight people present. The others must have seen the same sort of thing before, because they showed no sign of curiosity or bewilderment. The Administrator began to tremble. Casher could see it, even through the bulk of the travelwear. The man's hands shook.

The Administrator said, in a high nervous voice: "Your knife. You have it with you?"

Casher nodded.

"Let me see it," said the Administrator.

Casher reached down to his boot and brought out the beautiful, superbly-balanced knife. Before he could stand erect, he felt the clamp of Gosigo's heavy fingers on his shoulder.

"Master," said Gosigo to Meiklejohn, "tell your visitor to put his weapon away. It is not allowed for any of us to show weapons in your presence."

Casher tried to squirm out of the heavy grip without losing his balance or his dignity. He found that Gosigo was knowledgeable about karate too. The forgetty held ground, even when the two men waged an immobile, invisible sort of wrestling match, the leverage of Casher's shoulder working its way hither and yon against the strong grip of Gosigo's powerful hand.

The Administrator ended it. He said, "Put away your knife. . . ." in that high funny voice of his.

The watch had almost reached 4:00, but no one had yet gotten into the car.

Gosigo spoke again, and when he did there was a contemptuous laugh from the Deputy Administrator, who had stood by in ordinary indoor clothes.

"Master, isn't it time for 'one for the road'?"

"Of course, of course," chattered the Administrator. He began breathing almost normally again.

"Join me," he said to Casher. "It's a local custom."

Casher had let his knife slip back into his bootsheath. When the knife dropped out of sight, Gosigo released his shoulder; he now stood facing the Administrator and rubbed his bruised shoulder. He said nothing, but shook his head gently, showing that he did not want a drink.

One of the robots brought the Administrator a glass, which appeared to contain at least a liter and a half of water. The Administrator said, very politely, "Sure you won't share it?"

This close, Casher could smell the reek of it. It was

pure byegarr, and at least 160-proof. He shook his head again, firmly but also politely.

The Administrator lifted the glass.

Casher could see the muscles of the man's throat work as the liquid went down. He could hear the man breathing heavily between swallows. The clear liquid went lower and lower in the gigantic glass.

At last it was all gone.

The Administrator cocked his head sidewise and said to Casher in a parrot-like voice, "Well, toodle-oo!"

"What do you mean, sir?" asked Casher.

The Administrator had a pleasant glow on his face. Casher was surprised that the man was not dead after that big and sudden a drink.

"I just mean, g'bye. I'm—not—feeling—well."

With that he fell straight forward, as stiff as a rock tower. One of the servants, perhaps another forgetty, caught him before he hit the ground.

"Does he always do this?" asked Casher of the miserable and contemptuous Deputy Administrator.

"Oh, no," said the Deputy. "Only at times like these."

"What do you mean, 'like these'?"

"When he sends one more armed man against the girl at Beauregard. They never come back. You won't come back, either. You could have left earlier, but you can't now. Go along and try to kill the girl. I'll see you here about 5:25 if you succeed. As a matter of fact, if you come back at all, I'll try to wake *him* up. But you won't come back. Good luck. I suppose that's what you need. Good luck."

Casher shook hands with the man without removing his gloves. Gosigo had already climbed into the driver's seat of the machine and was testing the electric engines. The big corkscrews began to plunge down, but before they touched the floor, Gosigo had reversed them and thrown them back into the "up" position.

The people in the room ran for cover as Casher entered the machine, though there was no immediate danger in sight. Two of the human servants dragged the Administrator up the stairs, the Deputy Administrator following them rapidly.

"Seat belt," said Gosigo.

Casher found it and snapped it closed.

"Head belt," said Gosigo.

Casher stared at him. He had never heard of a head belt.

"Pull it down from the roof, sir. Put the net under your chin."

Casher glanced up.

There was a net fitted snug against the roof of the vehicle, just above his head. He started to pull it down, but it did not yield. Angrily, he pulled harder, and it moved slowly downward. *By the Bell and Bank, do they want to hang me in this!* he thought to himself as he dragged the net down. There was a strong fibre belt attached to each end of the net, while the net itself was only fifteen to twenty centimeters wide. He ended up in a foolish position, holding the head belt with both hands lest it snap back into the ceiling and not knowing what to do with it. Gosigo leaned over and, half-impatiently, helped him adjust the web under his chin. It pinched for a moment and Casher felt as though his head were being dragged by a heavy weight.

"Don't fight it," said Gosigo. "Relax."

Casher did. His head was lifted several centimeters into a foam pocket, which he had not previously noticed, in the back of the seat. After a second or two, he realized that the position was odd but comfortable.

Gosigo had adjusted his own head belt and had turned on the lights of the vehicle. They blazed so bright that Casher almost thought they might be a laser, capable of charring the inner doors of the big room.

The lights must have keyed the door.

$$\infty\, V \,\infty$$

Two panels slid open and a wild uproar of wind and vegetation rushed in. It was rough and stormy but far below hurricane velocity.

The machine rolled forward clumsily and was out of the house and on the road very quickly.

The sky was brown, bright luminous brown, shot through with streaks of yellow. Casher had never seen a sky of that color on any other world he had visited, and in his long exile he had seen many planets.

Gosigo, staring straight ahead, was preoccupied with keeping the vehicle right in the middle of the black, soft, tarry road.

"Watch it!" said a voice speaking right into his head.

It was Gosigo, using an intercom which must have been built into the helmets.

Casher watched, though there was nothing to see except for the rush of mad wind. Suddenly the groundcar turned dark, spun upside down, and was violently shaken. An oily, pungent stench of pure fetor immediately drenched the whole car.

Gosigo pulled out a panel with a console of buttons. Light and fire, intolerably bright, burned in on them through the windshield and the portholes on the side.

The battle was over before it began.

The groundcar lay in a sort of swamp. The road was visible thirty or thirty-five meters away.

There was a grinding sound inside the machine and the groundcar righted itself. A singular sucking noise followed, then the grinding sound stopped. Casher could glimpse the big corkscrews on the side of the car eating their way into the ground.

At last the machine was steady, pelted only by branches, leaves, and what seemed like kelp.

A small tornado was passing over them.

Gosigo took time to twist his head sidewise and to talk to Casher.

"An air-whale swallowed us and I had to burn our way out."

"A what?" cried Casher.

"An air-whale," repeated Gosigo calmly on the intercom. "There are no indigenous forms of life on this planet, but the imported Earth forms have changed wildly since we brought them in. The tornadoes lifted the whales around enough so that some of them got adapted to flying. They were the meat-eating kind, so they like to crack our groundcars open and eat the goodies inside. We're safe enough from them for the time being, provided we can make it back to the road. There are a few wild men who live in the wind, but they would not become dangerous to us unless we found ourselves really helpless. Pretty soon I can unscrew us from the ground and try to get back on the road. It's not really too far from here to Ambiloxi."

The trip to the road was a long one, even though they could see the road itself all the time that they tried various approaches.

The first time, the groundcar tipped ominously forward. Red lights showed on the panel and buzzers buzzed. The great spiked wheels spun in vain as they chewed their way into a bottomless quagmire.

Gosigo, calling back to his passenger, cried, "Hold steady! We're going to have to shoot ourselves out of this one backward!"

Casher did not know how he could be any steadier, belted, hooded, and strapped as he was, but he clutched the arms of his seat.

The world went red with fire as the front of the car spat flame in rocket-like quantities. The swamp ahead of them boiled into steam, so that they could see nothing. Gosigo changed the windshield over from visual to radar, and even with radar there was not much to be seen— nothing but a gray swirl of formless wraiths, and the weird lurching sensation as the machine fought its way back to solid ground. The console suddenly showed green and Gosigo cut the controls. They were back where they had been, with the repulsive burnt entrails of the air-whale scattered among the coral trees.

"Try again," said Gosigo, as though Casher had something to do with the matter.

He fiddled with the controls and the groundcar rose

several feet. The spikes on the wheels had been hydrauli-
cally extended until they were each at least 150 centimeters
long. In sensation, the car felt like a large enclosed bicycle
as it teetered on its big wheels. The wind was strong and
capricious but there was no tornado in sight.

"Here we go," said Gosigo redundantly. The groundcar
pressed forward in a mad rush, hastening obliquely
through the vegetation and making for the highway on
Casher's right.

A bone-jarring crash told them that they had not
made it. For a moment he was too dizzy to see where
they were.

He was glad of his helmet and happy about the web
brace which held his neck. That crash would have killed
him if he had not had full protection.

Gosigo seemed to think the trip normal. His classic
Hindu features relaxed in a wise smile as he said, "Hit a
boulder. Fell on our side. Try again."

Casher managed to gasp, "Is the machine unbreakable?"

There was a laugh in Gosigo's voice when he answered,
"Almost. We're the most vulnerable items in it."

Again fire spat at the ground, this time from the side
of the groundcar. It balanced itself precariously on the
four high wheels. Gosigo turned on the radar screen to
look through the steam which their own jets had called up.

There the road was, plain and near.

"Try again!" he shouted, as the machine lunged forward
and then performed a veritable ballet on the surface of the
marsh. It rushed, slowed, turned around on a hummock,
gave itself an assist with the jets, and then scrambled
through the water.

Casher saw the inverted cone of a tornado, half a kilometer or less away, veering toward them.

Gosigo sensed his unspoken thought, because he answered, "Problem: who gets to the road first, that or we?"

The machine bucked, lurched, twisted, spun.

Casher could see nothing any more from the wind screen in front, but it was obvious that Gosigo knew what he was doing.

There was the sickening, stomach-wrenching twist of a big drop and then a new sound was heard—a grinding as of knives.

Gosigo, unworried, took his head out of the headnet and looked over at Casher with a smile. "The twister will probably hit us in a minute or two, but it doesn't matter now. We're on the road and I've bolted us to the surface."

"Bolted?" gasped Casher.

"You know, those big screws on the outside of the car. They were made to go right into the road. All the roads here are neo-asphaltum and self-repairing. There will be traces of them here when the last known person on the last known planet is dead. These are *good* roads." He stopped for the sudden hush. "Storm's going over us . . ."

It began again before he could finish his sentence. Wild raving winds tore at the machine, which sat so solid that it seemed bedded in permastone.

Gosigo pushed two buttons and then calibrated a dial. He squinted at his instruments and then pressed a button mounted on the edge of his navigator's seat. There was a sharp explosion, like a blasting of rock by chemical methods.

Casher started to speak but Gosigo held out a warning hand for silence.

He tuned his dials quickly. The windscreen faded out, radar came on and then went off, and at last a bright map—bright red in background with sharp gold lines—appeared across the whole width of the screen. There were a dozen or more bright points on the map. Gosigo watched these intently.

The map blurred, faded, dissolved into red chaos.

Gosigo pushed another button and then could see out of the front glass screen again.

"What was that?" asked Casher.

"Miniaturized radar rocket. I sent it up twelve kilometers for a look around. It transmitted a map of what it saw and I put it on our radar screen. The tornadoes are heavier than usual, but I think we can make it. Did you notice the top right of the map?"

"The top right?" asked Casher.

"Yes, the top right. Did you see what was there?"

"Why, nothing," said Casher. "Nothing was there."

"You're utterly right," said Gosigo. "What does that mean to you?"

"I don't understand you," said Casher. "I suppose it means that there is nothing there."

"Right again. But let me tell you something. There never is."

"Never is what?"

"Anything," said Gosigo. "There never is anything on the maps at that point. That's east of Ambiloxi. That's Beauregard. It never shows on the maps. Nothing happens there."

"No bad weather—ever?" asked Casher.

"Never," said Gosigo.

"Why not?" asked Casher.

"*She* will not permit it," said Gosigo firmly, as though his words made sense.

"You mean, her weather machines work?" said Casher, grasping for the only rational explanation possible.

"Yes," said Gosigo.

"Why?"

"She pays for them."

"How can she?" exclaimed Casher. "Your whole world of Henriada is bankrupt!"

"Her part isn't."

"Stop mystifying me," said Casher. "Tell me who she is and what this is all about."

"Put your head in the net," said Gosigo. "I'm not making puzzles because I want to do so. I have been commanded not to talk."

"Because you are a forgetty?"

"What's that got to do with it? Don't talk to me that way. Remember, I am not an animal or an underperson. I may be your servant for a few hours, but I am a *man*. You'll find out, soon enough. *Hold tight!*"

The groundcar came to a panic stop, the spiked teeth eating into the resilient firm neo-asphaltum of the road. At the instant they stopped, the outside corkscrews began chewing their way into the ground. First Casher felt as though his eyes were popping out, because of the suddenness of the deceleration; now he felt like holding the arms of his seat as the tornado reached directly for their car, plucking at it again and again. The enormous outside screws held and he could feel the car straining to meet the gigantic suction of the storm.

"Don't worry," shouted Gosigo over the noise of the storm. "I always pin us down a little bit more by firing the quick-rockets straight up. These cars don't often go off the road."

Casher tried to relax.

The funnel of the tornado, which seemed almost like a living being, plucked after them once or twice more and then was gone.

This time, Casher had seen no sign of the air-whales which rode the storms. He had seen nothing but rain and wind and desolation.

The tornado was gone in a moment. Ghostlike shapes trailed after it in enormous prancing leaps.

"Wind-men," said Gosigo, glancing at them incuriously. "Wild people who have learned to live on Henriada. They aren't much more than animals. We are close to the territory of the lady. They would not dare attack us here."

Casher O'Neill was too stunned to query the man or to challenge him.

Once more the car picked itself up and coursed along the smooth, narrow, winding neo-asphaltum road, almost as though the machine itself were glad to function and to function well.

∽ VI ∽

Casher could never quite remember when they went from the howling wildness of Henriada into the stillness and beauty of the domains of Mister Murray Madigan. He could recall the feeling but not the facts.

The town of Ambiloxi eluded him completely. It was so normal a town, so old-fashioned a little town that he could not think of it very much. Old people sat on the wooden boardwalk taking their afternoon look at the strangers who passed through. Horses were tethered in a row along the main street, between the parked machines. It looked like a peaceful picture from the ancient ages.

Of tornadoes there was no sign, nor of the hurt and ruin which showed around the house of Rankin Meiklejohn. There were few underpeople or robots about, unless they were so cleverly contrived as to look almost exactly like real people. How can you remember something which is pleasant and non-memorable? Even the buildings did not show signs of being fortified against the frightful storms which had brought the prosperous planet of Henriada to a condition of abandonment and ruin.

Gosigo, who had a remarkable talent for stating the obvious, said tonelessly, "The weather machines are working here. There is no need for special precaution."

But he did not stop in the town for rest, refreshments, conversation, or fuel. He went through deftly and quietly, the gigantic armored groundcar looking out of place among the peaceful and defenseless vehicles. He went as though he had been on the same route many times before, and knew the routine well.

Once beyond Ambiloxi he speeded up, though at a moderate pace, compared to the frantic elusive action he had taken against storms in the earlier part of the trip. The landscape was earthlike . . . wet . . . and most of the ground was covered with vegetation.

Old radar countermissile towers stood along the road. Casher could not imagine their possible use, even though he was sure, from the looks of them, that they were long obsolete.

"What's the countermissile radar for?" he asked, speaking comfortably now that his head was out of the head net.

Gosigo turned around and gave him a tortured glance in which pain and bewilderment were mixed. "Countermissile radar? Countermissile radar? I don't know that word, though it seems as though I should. . . ."

"Radar is what you were using to see with, back in the storm, when the ceiling and visibility were zero."

Gosigo turned back to his driving, narrowly missing a tree. "That? That's just artificial vision. Why did you use the word 'countermissile radar'? There isn't any of that stuff here except what we have on our machine, though the mistress may be watching us if her set is on."

"Those towers," said Casher. "They look like counter-missile towers from the ancient times."

"Towers. There aren't any towers here," snapped Gosigo.

"Look," cried Casher. "Here are two more of them."

"No man made those. They aren't buildings. It's just air coral. Some of the coral which people brought from earth mutated and got so it could live in the air. People used to plant it for windbreaks, before they decided to give up Henriada and move out. They didn't do much good, but they are pretty to look at."

They rode along a few minutes without asking
questions. Tall trees had Spanish moss trailing over them.
They were close to a sea. Small marshes appeared to
the right and left of the road; here, where the endless
tornadoes were kept out, everything had a park-like
effect. The domains of the estate of Beauregard were
unlike anything else on Henriada—an area of peaceful
wildness in a world which was rushing otherwise toward
uninhabitability and ruin. Even Gosigo seemed more
relaxed, more cheerful as he steered the groundcar along
the pleasant elevated road.

Gosigo sighed, leaned forward, managed the controls,
and brought the car to a stop.

He turned around calmly and looked full-face at
Casher O'Neill.

"You have your knife?"

Casher automatically felt for it. It was there, safe
enough in his boot-sheath. He simply nodded.

"You have your orders."

"You mean, killing the girl?"

"Yes," said Gosigo, "killing the girl."

"I remember that. You didn't have to stop the car to
tell me that."

"I'm telling you now," said Gosigo, his wise Hindu face
showing neither humor nor outrage. "Do it."

"You mean, kill her? Right at first sight?"

"Do it," said Gosigo. "You have your orders."

"I'm the judge of that," said Casher. "It will be on my
conscience. Are you watching me for the Administrator?"

"That drunken fool?" said Gosigo. "I don't care about
him, except that I am a forgetty and I belong to him.

We're in *her* territory now. You are going to do whatever she wants. You have orders to kill her. All right. Kill her."

"You mean—she wants to be murdered?"

"Of course not!" said Gosigo, with the irritation of an adult who has to explain too many things to an inquisitive child.

"Then how can I kill her without finding out what this is all about?"

"She knows. She knows herself. She knows her master. She knows this planet. She knows me and she knows something about you. Go ahead and kill her, since those are your orders. If she wants to die, that's not for you or me to decide. It's her business. If she does not want to die, you will not succeed."

"I'd like to see the person," said Casher, "who could stop me in a sudden knife attack. Have *you* told her that I am coming?"

"I've told her nothing, but she knows we are coming and she is pretty sure what you have been sent for. Don't think about it. Just do what you are told. Jump for her with the knife. She will take care of the matter."

"But—" cried Casher.

"Stop asking questions," said Gosigo. "Just follow orders and remember that she will take care of you. Even you." He started up the groundcar.

Within less than a kilometer they had crossed a low ridge of land and there before them lay Beauregard—the mansion at the edge of the waters, its white pillars shining, its pergolas glistening in the bright air, its yards and palmettos tidy.

Casher was a brave man, but he felt the palms of his

hands go wet when he realized that in a minute or two he would have to commit a murder.

∾ VII ∾

The groundcar swung up the drive. It stopped. Without a word, Gosigo activated the door. The air smelled calm, sea-wet, salt and yet coolly fresh.

Casher jumped out and ran to the door.

He was surprised to feel that his legs trembled as he ran.

He had killed before, real men in real quarrels. Why should a mere animal matter to him?

The door stopped him.

Without thinking, he tried to wrench it open.

The knob did not yield and there was no automatic control in sight. This was indeed a very antique sort of house. He struck the door with his hands. The thuds sounded around him. He could not tell whether they resounded in the house. No sound or echo came from beyond the door.

He began rehearsing the phrase, "I want to see Mister and Owner Madigan. . . ."

The door did open.

A little girl stood there.

He knew her. He had always known her. She was his sweetheart, come back out of his childhood. She was the sister he had never had. She was his own mother, when young. She was at the marvelous age, somewhere between ten and thirteen, where the child—as the phrase goes—

"becomes an old child and not a raw grown-up." She was kind, calm, intelligent, expectant, quiet, inviting, unafraid. She felt like someone he had never left behind: yet, at the same moment, he knew he had never seen her before.

He heard his voice asking for the Mister and Owner Madigan while he wondered, at the back of his mind, who the girl might be. Madigan's daughter? Neither Rankin Meiklejohn nor the deputy had said anything about a human family.

The child looked at him levelly.

He must have finished braying his question at her.

"Mister and Owner Madigan," said the child, "sees no one this day, but you are seeing me." She looked at him levelly and calmly. There was an odd hint of humor, of fearlessness, in her stance.

"Who are you?" he blurted out.

"I am the housekeeper of this house."

"You?" he cried, wild alarm beginning in his throat.

"My name," she said, "is T'ruth."

His knife was in his hand before he knew how it had gotten there. He remembered the advice of the Administrator: *plunge, plunge, stab, stab, run!*

She saw the knife but her eyes did not waver from his face.

He looked at her uncertainly.

If this was an underperson, it was the most remarkable one he had ever seen. But even Gosigo had told him to do his duty, to stab, to kill the woman named T'ruth. Here she was. He could not do it.

He spun the knife in the air, caught it by its tip, and held it out to her, handle first.

"I was sent to kill you," he said, "but I find I cannot do it. I have lost a cruiser."

"Kill me if you wish," she said, "because I have no fear of you."

Her calm words were so far outside his experience that he took the knife in his left hand and lifted his arm as if to stab toward her.

He dropped his arm.

"I cannot do it," he whined. "What have you done to me?"

"I have done nothing to you. You do not wish to kill a child and I look to you like a child. Besides, I think you love me. If this is so, it must be very uncomfortable for you."

Casher heard his knife clatter to the floor as he dropped it. He had never dropped it before.

"Who are you," he gasped, "that you should do this to me?"

"I am me," she said, her voice as tranquil and happy as that of any girl, provided that the girl was caught at a moment of great happiness and poise. "I am the house-keeper of this house." She smiled almost impishly and added, "It seems that I must almost be the ruler of this planet as well." Her voice turned serious. "*Man,*" she said, "can't you see it, man? I am an animal, a turtle. I am incapable of disobeying the word of man. When I was little I was trained and I was given orders. I shall carry out those orders as long as I live. When I look at you, I feel strange. You look as though you loved me already, but you do not know what to do. Wait a moment. I must let Gosigo go."

The shining knife on the floor of the doorway, she saw; she stepped over it.

Gosigo had gotten out of the groundcar and was giving her a formal, low bow.

"Tell me," she cried, "what have you just seen?" There was friendliness in her call, as though the routine were an old game.

"I saw Casher O'Neill bound up the steps. You yourself opened the door. He thrust his dagger into your throat and the blood spat out in a big stream, rich and dark and red. You died in the doorway. For some reason Casher O'Neill went on into the house without saying anything to me. I became frightened and I fled."

He did not look frightened at all.

"If I am dead," she said, "how can I be talking to you?"

"Don't ask me," cried Gosigo. "I am just a forgetty. I always go back to the Honorable Rankin Meiklejohn, each time that you are murdered, and I tell him the truth of what I saw. Then he gives me the medicine and I tell him something else. At that point he will get drunk and gloomy again, the way that he always does."

"It's a pity," said the child. "I wish I could help him, but I can't. He won't come to Beauregard."

"Him?" Gosigo laughed. "Oh, no, not him! Never! He just sends other people to kill you."

"And he's never satisfied," said the child sadly, "no matter how many times he kills me!"

"Never," said Gosigo cheerfully, climbing back into the groundcar. "Bye now."

"Wait a moment," she called. "Wouldn't you like something to eat or drink before you drive back? There's a bad clutch of storms on the road."

"Not me," said Gosigo. "He might punish me and

make me a forgetty all over again. Say, maybe that's already happened. Maybe I'm a forgetty who's been put through it several times, not just once." Hope surged into his voice. "T'ruth! T'ruth! Can *you* tell me?"

"Suppose I did tell you," said she. "What would happen?"

His face became sad. "I'd have a convulsion and forget what I told you. Well, good-bye anyhow. I'll take a chance on the storms. If you ever see that Casher O'Neill again," called Gosigo, looking right through Casher O'Neill, "tell him I liked him but that we'll never meet again."

"I'll tell him," said the girl gently. She watched as the heavy brown man climbed nimbly into the car. The top crammed shut with no sound. The wheels turned and in a moment the car had disappeared behind the palmettoes in the drive.

While she had talked to Gosigo in her clear warm high girlish voice, Casher had watched her. He could see the thin shape of her shoulders under the light blue shift that she wore. There was the suggestion of a pair of panties under the dress, so light was the material. Her hips had not begun to fill. When he glanced at her in one-quarter profile, he could see that her cheek was smooth, her hair well-combed, her little breasts just beginning to bud on her chest. Who was this child who acted like an empress?

She turned back to him and gave him a warm, apologetic smile.

"Gosigo and I always talk over the story together. Then he goes back and Meiklejohn does not believe it and spends unhappy months planning my murder all over again. I suppose, since I am just an animal, that I should not call it a 'murder' when somebody tries to kill me, but I resist, of course. I do not care about me, but I have orders, strong orders, to keep my master and his house safe from harm."

"How old are you?" asked Casher. He added, "—if you can tell the truth."

"I can tell nothing but the truth. I am conditioned. I am nine hundred and six Earth-years old."

"Nine hundred?" he cried. "But you look like a child. . . ."

"I am a child," said the girl, "and not a child. I am an Earth turtle, changed into human form by the convenience of man. My life expectancy was increased three hundred times when I was modified. They tell me that my normal life span should have been three hundred years. Now it is ninety thousand years, and sometimes I am afraid. You will be dead of happy old age, Casher O'Neill, while I am still opening the drapes in this house to let the sunlight in. But let's not stand in the door and talk. Come on in and get some refreshments. You're not going anywhere, you know."

Casher followed her into the house but he put his worry into words. "You mean I am your prisoner."

"Not my prisoner, Casher. Yours. How could you cross that ground which you traveled in the groundcar? You could get to the ends of my estate all right, but then the storms would pick you up and whirl you away to a death which nobody would even see."

She turned into a big old room, bright with light-colored wooden furniture.

Casher stood there, awkwardly. He had returned his

knife to its boot-sheath when they left the vestibule. Now he felt very odd, sitting with his victim on a sun-porch.

T'ruth was untroubled. She rang a brass bell which stood on an old-fashioned round table. Feminine footsteps clattered in the hall. A female servant entered the room, dressed in a black dress with a white apron. Casher had seen such servants in the old drama cubes, but he had never expected to meet one in the flesh.

"We'll have high tea," said T'ruth. "Which do you prefer, tea or coffee, Casher? Or I have beer and wines. Even two bottles of whiskey brought all the way from Earth."

"Coffee would be fine for me," said Casher.

"And you know what I want, Eunice," said T'ruth to the servant.

"Yes, *ma'am*," said the maid, disappearing.

Casher leaned forward.

"That servant—is she human?"

"Certainly," said T'ruth.

"Then why is she working for an underperson like you? I mean—I don't mean to be unpleasant or anything—but I mean—that's against all laws."

"Not here, on Henriada, it isn't."

"And why not?" persisted Casher.

"Because, on Henriada, I am myself the law."

"But the government—?"

"It's gone."

"The Instrumentality?"

T'ruth frowned. She looked like a wise, puzzled child. "Maybe you know that part better than I do. They leave an Administrator here, probably because they do not have any other place to put him and because he needs some kind of work to keep him alive. Yet they do not give him enough real power to arrest my master or to kill me. They ignore me. It seems to me that if I do not challenge them, they leave me alone."

"But their rules—?" insisted Casher.

"They don't enforce them, neither here in Beauregard nor over in the town of Ambiloxi. They leave it up to me to keep these places going. I do the best I can."

"That servant, then? Did they lease her to you?"

"Oh, no," laughed the girl-woman. "She came to kill me twenty years ago, but she was a forgetty and she had no place else to go, so I trained her as a maid. She has a contract with my master, and her wages are paid every month into the satellite above the planet. She can leave if she ever wants to. I don't think she will."

Casher sighed. "This is all too hard to believe. You are a child, but you are almost a thousand years old. You're an underperson, but you command a whole planet—"

"Only when I need to!" she interrupted him.

"You are wiser than most of the people I have ever known and yet you look young. How old do you feel?"

"I feel like a child," she said, "a child one thousand years old. And I have had the education and the memory and the experience of a wise lady stamped right into my brain."

"Who was the lady?" asked Casher.

"The Owner and Citizen Agatha Madigan. The wife of my master. As she was dying they transcribed her brain on mine. That's why I speak so well and know so much."

"But that's illegal!" cried Casher.

"I suppose it was," said T'ruth, "but my master had it done, anyhow."

Casher leaned forward in his chair. He looked earnestly at the person. One part of him still loved her for the wonderful little girl that he had thought she was, but another part was in awe of a being more powerful than anyone he had seen before. She returned his gaze with that composed half-smile which was wholly feminine and completely self-possessed; she looked tenderly upon him as their faces were reflected by the yellow morning light of Henriada. "I begin to understand," he said, "that you are what you have to be. It is very strange, here in this forgotten world."

"Henriada is strange," she said, "and I suppose that I must seem strange to you. You are right, though, about each of us being what she has to be. Isn't that liberty itself? If we each one *must* be something, isn't liberty the business of finding it out and then doing it—that one job, that uttermost mission compatible with our natures? How terrible it would be, to be something and never know what!"

"Like who?" said Casher.

"Like Gosigo, perhaps. He was a great king and he was a good king, on some faraway world where they still need kings. But he committed an intolerable mistake and the Instrumentality made him into a forgetty and sent him here."

"So that's the mystery!" said Casher. "And what am I?"

She looked at him calmly and steadfastly before she answered. "You are a killer, too. It must make your life very hard in many ways. You keep having to justify yourself."

This was so close to the truth—so close to Casher's long worries as to whether justice might not just be a cover name for "revenge"—that it was his turn to gasp and be silent.

"And I have work for you," added the amazing child.

"Work? Here?"

"Yes. Something much worse than killing. And you must do it, Casher, if you want to go away from here before I die, eighty-nine thousand years from now." She looked around. "Hush!" she added. "Eunice is coming and I do not want to frighten her by letting her know the terrible things that you are going to have to do."

"Here?" he whispered urgently. "Right here, in this house?"

"Right here in this house," she said in a normal voice, as Eunice entered the room bearing a huge tray covered with plates of food and two pots of beverage.

Casher stared at the human woman who worked so cheerfully for an animal; but neither Eunice, who was busy setting things out on the table, nor T'ruth, who, turtle and woman that she was, could not help rearranging the dishes with gentle peremptories, paid the least attention to him.

The words rang in his head. "In this house . . . something worse than killing." They made no sense. Neither did it make sense to have high tea before five hours, decimal time.

He sighed and they both glanced at him, Eunice with amused curiosity, T'ruth with affectionate concern.

"He's taking it better than most of them do, ma'am," said Eunice. "Most of them who come here to kill you are very upset when they find out that they cannot do it."

"He's a killer, Eunice, a real killer, so I think he wasn't too bothered."

Eunice turned to him very pleasantly and said, "A killer, sir. It's a pleasure to have you here. Most of them are terrible amateurs and then the lady has to heal them before we can find something for them to do."

Casher couldn't resist a spot inquiry. "Are all the other would-be killers still here?"

"Most of them, sir. The ones that nothing happened to. Like me. Where else would we go? Back to the Administrator, Rankin Meiklejohn?" She said the last with heavy scorn indeed, curtsied to him, bowed deeply to the woman-girl T'ruth, and left the room.

T'ruth looked friendlily at Casher O'Neill. "I can tell that you will not digest your food if you sit here waiting for bad news. When I said you had to do something worse than killing, I suppose I was speaking from a woman's point of view. We have a homicidal maniac in the house. He is a house guest and he is covered by Old North Australian law. That means we cannot kill him or expel him, though he is almost as immortal as I am. I hope that you and I can frighten him away from molesting my master. I cannot cure him or love him. He is too crazy to be reached through his emotions. Pure, utter awful fright might do it, and it takes a man for that job. If you do this, I will reward you richly."

"And if I don't?" said Casher.

Again she stared at him as though she were trying to see through his eyes all the way down to the bottom of his soul; again he felt for her that tremor of compassion, ever so slightly tinged with male desire, which he had experienced when he first met her in the doorway of Beauregard.

Their locked glances broke apart.

T'ruth looked at the floor. "I cannot lie," she said, as though it were a handicap. "If you do not help me I shall have to do the things which it is in my power to do. The chief thing is nothing. To let you live here, to let you sleep and eat in this house until you get bored and ask me for some kind of routine work around the estate. I could make you work," she went on, looking up at him and blushing all the way to the top of her bodice, "by having you fall in love with me, but that would not be kind. I will not do it that way. Either you make a deal with me or you do not. It's up to you. Anyhow, let's eat first. I've been up since dawn, expecting one more killer. I even wondered if you might be the one who would succeed. That would be terrible, to leave my master all alone!"

"But you—wouldn't you yourself mind being killed?"

"Me? When I've already lived a thousand years and have eighty-nine thousand more to go! It couldn't matter less to me. Have some coffee."

And she poured his coffee.

∽ VIII ∽

Two or three times Casher tried to get the conversation back to the work at hand, but T'ruth diverted him with trivialities. She even made him walk to the enormous window, where they could see far across the marshes and the bay. The sky in the remote distance was dark and full of worms. Those were tornadoes, beyond the reach of her weather machines, which coursed around the rest of

Henriada but stopped short at the boundaries of Ambiloxi and Beauregard. She made him admire the weird coral castles which had built themselves up from the bay bottom, hundreds of feet into the air. She tried to make him see a family of wild windpeople who were slyly and gently stealing apples from her orchard, but either his eyes were not used to the landscape or T'ruth could see much further than he could.

This was a world rich in water. If it had not been located within a series of bad pockets of space, the water itself could have become an export. Mankind had done the best it could, raising kelp to provide the iron and phosphorus so often lacking in off-world diets, controlling the weather at great expense. Finally the Instrumentality recommended that they give up. The exports of Henriada never quite balanced the imports. The subsidies had gone far beyond the usual times. The Earth life had adapted with a vigor which was much too great. Ordinary forms rapidly found new shapes, challenged by the winds, the rains, the novel chemistry, and the odd radiation patterns of Henriada. Killer whales became airborne, coral took to the air, human babies lost in the wind sometimes survived to become subhuman and wild, jellyfish became sky-sweepers. The former inhabitants of Henriada had chosen a planet at a reasonable price—not cheap, but reasonable—from the owner who had in turn bought it from a post-Soviet settling cooperative. They had leased the new planet, had worked out an ecology, had emigrated, and were now doing well.

Henriada kept the wild weather, the lost hopes, and the ruins.

And of these ruins, the greatest was Murray Madigan.

Once a prime landholder and host, a gentleman among gentlemen, the richest man on the whole world, Madigan had become old, senile, weak. He faced death or catalepsis. The death of his wife made him fear his own death, and with his turtle-girl T'ruth, he had chosen catalepsis. Most of the time he was frozen in a trance, his heartbeat imperceptible, his metabolism very slow. Then, for a few hours or days, he was normal. Sometimes the sleeps were for weeks, sometimes for years. The Instrumentality doctors had looked him over—more out of scientific curiosity than from any judicial right—and had decided that though this was an odd way to live, it was a legal one. They went away and left him alone. He had had the whole personality of his dying wife Agatha Madigan impressed on the turtle-child, though this was illegal; the doctor had, quite simply, been bribed.

All this was told by T'ruth to Casher as they ate and drank their way slowly through an immense repast.

An archaic wood fire roared in a real fireplace.

While she talked, Casher watched the gentle movement of her shoulder blades when she moved forward, the loose movement of her light dress as she moved, the childish face which was so tender, so appealing, and yet so wise.

Knowing as little as he did about the planet of Henriada, Casher tried desperately to fit his own thinking together and to make sense out of the predicament in which he found himself. Even if the girl *were* attractive, this told him nothing of the real challenges which he still faced inside this very house. No longer was his preoccupation with getting the power cruiser his main job on Henriada;

no evidence was at hand to show that the drunken, deranged Administrator, Rankin Meiklejohn, would give him anything at all unless he, Casher, killed the girl.

Even that had become a forgotten mission. Despite the fact that he had come to the estate of Beauregard for the purpose of killing her, he was now on a journey without a destination. Years of sad experience had taught him that when a project went completely to pieces, he still had the mission of personal survival, if his life were to mean anything to his home planet, Mizzer, and if his return, in any way or any fashion, could bring real liberty back to the Twelve Niles.

So he looked at the girl with a new kind of unconcern. How could she help his plans? Or hinder them? The promises she made were too vague to be of any real use in the sad complicated world of politics.

He just tried to enjoy her company and the strange place in which he found himself.

The Gulf of Esperanza lay just within his vision. At the far horizon he could see the helpless tornadoes trying to writhe their way past the weather machines which still functioned, at the expense of Beauregard, all along the coast from Ambiloxi to Mottile. He could see the shoreline choked with kelp, which had once been a cash crop and was now a nuisance. Ruined buildings in the distance were probably the leftovers of processing plants; the artificial-looking coral castles obscured his view of them.

And this house—how much sense did this house make?

An undergirl, eerily wise, who herself admitted that she had obtained an unlawful amount of conditioning; a master who was a living corpse; a threat which could not even be mentioned freely within the house; a household which seemed to have displaced the planetary government; a planetary government which the Instrumentality, for unfathomable reasons of its own, had let fall into ruin. Why? Why? And why again?

The turtle-girl was looking at him. If he had been an art student, he would have said that she was giving him the tender, feminine, and irrecoverably remote smile of a Madonna, but he did not know the motifs of the ancient pictures; he just knew that it was a smile characteristic of T'ruth herself.

"You are wondering . . . ?" she said.

He nodded, suddenly feeling miserable that mere words had come between them.

"You are wondering why the Instrumentality let you come here . . . ?"

He nodded again.

"I don't know either," said she, reaching out and taking his hand. His hand felt and looked like the hairy paw of a giant as she held his right hand with her two pretty, well-kept little-girl hands; but the strength of her eyes and the steadfastness of her voice showed that it was she who was giving the reassurance, not he.

The child was helping *him*!

The idea was outrageous, impossible, true.

It was enough to alarm him, to make him begin to pull his hand again. She clutched him with tender softness, with weak strength, and he could not resist her. Again he had the feeling, which had gripped him so strongly when he first met her at the door of Beauregard and failed to kill her, that he had always known her and had always loved her. (Was there not some planet on which eccentric people believed a weird cult, thinking that human beings were endlessly reborn with fragmentary recollections of their own previous human lives? It was almost like that. Here. Now. He did not know the girl but he had always known her. He did not love the girl and yet he had loved her from the beginning of time.)

Said she, so softly that it was almost a whisper: "Wait. . . . Wait. . . . Your death may come through that door pretty soon and I will tell you how to meet it. But before that, even, I have to show you the most beautiful thing in the world."

Despite her little hand lying tenderly and firmly on his, Casher spoke irritably: "I'm tired of talking riddles here on Henriada. The Administrator gives me the mission of killing you and I fail in it. Then you promise me a battle and give me a good meal instead. Now you talk about the battle and start off with some other irrelevance. You're going to make me angry if you keep on and, and, and"— he stammered at last—"and I get pretty useless if I'm angry. If you want me to do a fight for you, let me know the fight and let me go do it now. I'm willing enough."

Her remote, kind half-smile did not waver. "Casher," she said, "what I am going to show you is your most important weapon in the fight."

With her free left hand she tugged at the fine chain of a thin gold necklace. Some kind of a piece of jewelry came out of the top of her shift dress, where she had kept it hidden. It was the image of two pieces of wood with a man nailed to them.

Casher stared and then he burst into hysterical laughter.

"Now you've done it, ma'am," he cried. "I'm no use to you or to anybody else. I know what that is, and up to now I've just suspected it. It's what the robot, rat, and Copt agreed on when they went exploring back in space-three. It's the Old Strong Religion. You've put it in my mind and now the next person who meets me will peep it and will wipe it out. Me too, probably, along with it. That's no weapon. That's a defeat. You've done me in. I knew the Sign of the Fish a long time ago, but I had a chance of getting away with just that little bit."

"Casher!" she cried. "Casher! Get hold of yourself. You will know nothing about this before you leave Beauregard. You will forget. You will be safe."

He stood on his feet, not knowing whether to run away, to laugh out loud, or to sit down and weep at the silly sad misfortune which had befallen him. To think that he himself had become brain-branded as a fanatic—forever denied travel between the stars—just because an under-girl had shown him an odd piece of jewelry!

"It's not as bad as you think," said the little girl, and stood up too. Her face peered lovingly at Casher's. "Do you think, Casher, that I am afraid?"

"No," he admitted.

"You will not remember this, Casher. Not when you leave. I am not just the turtle-girl T'ruth. I am also the imprint of the citizen Agatha. Have you ever heard of her?"

"Agatha Madigan?" He shook his head slowly. "No. I don't see how . . . No, I'm sure that I never heard of her."

"Didn't you ever hear the story of the Hechizera of Gonfalon?"

Casher looked surprised. "Sure I saw it. It's a play. A drama. It is said to be based on some legend out of immemorial time. The 'space-witch' they called her, and she conjured fleets out of nothing by sheer hypnosis. It's an old story."

"Eleven hundred years isn't so long," said the girl. "Eleven hundred years, fourteen local months come tonight."

"You weren't alive eleven hundred years ago," said Casher accusingly.

He stood up from the remains of their meal and wandered over toward the window. That terrible piece of religious jewelry made him uncomfortable. He knew that it was against all laws to ship religion from world to world. What would he do, what could he do, now that he had actually beheld an image of the God Nailed High? That was exactly the kind of contraband which the police and customs robots of hundreds of worlds were looking for.

The Instrumentality was easy about most things, but the transplanting of religion was one of its hostile obsessions. Religions leaked from world to world, anyhow. It was said that sometimes even the underpeople and robots carried bits of religion through space, though this seemed improbable. The Instrumentality left religion alone when it had a settled place on a single planet, but the Lords of the Instrumentality themselves shunned other people's devotional lives and simply took good care that fanaticisms did not once more flare up between the stars, once again bringing wild hope and great death to all the mankinds.

And now, thought Casher, *the Instrumentality has been good to me in its big impersonal collective way, but what will it do when my brain is on fire with forbidden knowledge?*

The girl's voice called him back to himself.

"I have the answer to your problem, Casher," said she, "if you would only listen to me. I *am* the Hechizera of Gonfalon, at least I am as much as any one person can be printed on another."

His jaw dropped as he turned back to her. "You mean that you, child, really are imprinted with this woman Agatha Madigan? Really imprinted?"

"I have all her skills, Casher," said the girl quietly, "and a few more which I have learned on my own."

"But I thought it was just a story. . . ." said Casher. "If you're that terrible woman from Gonfalon, you don't need me. I'm quitting. Now."

Casher walked toward the door. Disgusted, finished, through. She might be a child, she might be charming, she might need help, but if she came from that terrible old story, she did not need him.

"Oh, no, you don't," said she.

∽ IX ∽

Unexpectedly, she took her place in the doorway, barring it.

In her hand was the image of the man on the two pieces of wood.

Ordinarily Casher would not have pushed a lady. Such

was his haste that he did so this time. When he touched her, it was like welded steel; neither her gown nor her body yielded a thousandth of a millimeter to his strong hand and heavy push.

"And now what?" she asked gently.

Looking back, he saw that the real T'ruth, the smiling girl-woman, still stood soft and real in the window.

Deep within, he began to give up; he had heard of hypnotists who could project, but he had never met one as strong as this.

She was doing it. How was she doing it? Or was she doing it? The operation could be subvolitional. There might be some art carried over from her animal past which even her re-formed mind could not explain. Operations too subtle, too primordial for analysis. Or skills which she used without understanding.

"I project," she said.

"I see you do," he replied glumly and flatly.

"I do kinesthetics," she said. His knife whipped out of his bootsheath and floated in the air in front of him.

He snatched it out of the air instinctively. It wormed a little in his grasp, but the force on the knife was nothing more than he had felt when passing big magnetic engines.

"I blind," she said. The room went totally dark for him.

"I hear," he said, and prowled at her like a beast, going by his memory of the room and by the very soft sound of her breathing. He had noticed by now that the simulacrum of herself which she had put in the doorway did not make any sound at all, not even that of breathing.

He knew that he was near her. His fingertips reached out for her shoulder or her throat. He did not mean to hurt her, merely to show her that two could play at tricks.

"I stun," she said, and her voice came at him from all directions. It echoed from the ceiling, came from all five walls of the old odd room, from the open windows, from both the doors. He felt as though he were being lifted into space and turned slowly in a condition of weightlessness. He tried to retain self-control, to listen for the one true sound among the many false sounds, to trap the girl by some outside chance.

"I make you remember," said her multiple echoing voice.

For an instant he did not see how this could be a weapon, even if the turtle-girl had learned all the ugly tricks of the Hechizera of Gonfalon.

But then he knew.

He saw his uncle, Kuraf, again. He saw his old apartments vividly around himself. Kuraf was there. The old man was pitiable, hateful, drunk, horrible; the girl on Kuraf's lap laughed at him, Casher O'Neill, and she laughed at Kuraf, too. Casher had once had a teenager's passionate concern with sex and at the same time had had a teenager's dreadful fear of all the unstated, invisible implications of what the man-woman relationship, gone sour, gone wrong, gone bad, might be. The present-moment Casher remembered the long-ago Casher and as he spun in the web of T'ruth's hypnotic powers he found himself back with the ugliest memory he had.

The killings in the palace at Mizzer.

The colonels had taken Kaheer itself, and they

ultimately let Kuraf run away to the pleasure planet of Ttiollé.

But Kuraf's companions, who had debauched the old republic of the Twelve Niles, those people! They did not go. The soldiers, stung to fury, had cut them down with knives. Casher thought of the blood, blood sticky on the floors, blood gushing purple into the carpets, blood bright red and leaping like a fountain when a white throat ended its last gurgle, blood turning brown where handprints, themselves bloody, had left it on marble tables. The warm palace, long ago, had gotten the sweet sick stench of blood all the way through it. The young Casher had never known that people had so much blood inside them, or that so much could pour out on the perfumed sheets, the tables still set with food and drink, or that blood could creep across the floor in growing pools as the bodies of the dead yielded up their last few nasty sounds and their terminal muscular spasms.

Before that day of butchery had ended, one thousand, three hundred and eleven human bodies, ranging in age from two months to eighty-nine years, had been carried out of the palaces once occupied by Kuraf. Kuraf, under sedation, was waiting for a starship to take him to perpetual exile and Casher—Casher himself O'Neill!—was shaking the hand of Colonel Wedder, whose orders had caused all the blood. The hand was washed and the nails pared and cleaned, but the cuff of the sleeve was still rimmed with the dry blood of some other human being. Colonel Wedder either did not notice his own cuff, or he did not care.

"Touch and yield!" said the girl-voice out of nowhere.

Casher found himself on all fours in the room, his sight suddenly back again, the room unchanged, and T'ruth smiling.

"I fought you," she said.

He nodded. He did not trust himself to speak.

He reached for his water-glass, looking at it closely to see if there were any blood on it.

Of course not. Not here. Not this time, not this place.

He pulled himself to his feet.

The girl had sense enough not to help him.

She stood there in her thin modest shift, looking very much like a wise female child, while he stood up and drank thirstily. He refilled the glass and drank again.

Then, only then, did he turn to her and speak:

"Do you do all that?"

She nodded.

"Alone? Without drugs or machinery?"

She nodded again.

"Child," he cried out, "you're not a person! You're a whole weapons system all by yourself. What are you, really? *Who* are you?"

"I am the turtle-child T'ruth," she said, "and I am the loyal property and loving servant of my good master, the Mister and Owner Murray Madigan."

"Madam," said Casher, "you are almost a thousand years old. I am at your service. I do hope you will let me go free later on. And especially, that you will take that religious picture out of my mind."

As Casher spoke, she picked a locket from the table. He had not noticed it. It was an ancient watch or a little round box, swinging on a thin gold chain.

"Watch this," said the child, "if you trust me, and repeat what I then say."

(Nothing at all happened: nothing—anywhere.)

Casher said to her, "You're making me dizzy, swinging that ornament. Put it back on. Isn't that the one you were wearing?"

"No, Casher, it isn't."

"What were we talking about?" demanded Casher.

"Something," said she. "Don't you remember?"

"No," said Casher brusquely. "Sorry, but I'm hungry again." He wolfed down a sweet roll encrusted with sugar and decorated with fruits. His mouth full, he washed the food down with water. At last he spoke to her. "Now what?"

She had watched with timeless grace.

"There's no hurry, Casher. Minutes or hours, they don't matter."

"Didn't you want me to fight somebody after Gosigo left me here?"

"That's right," she said, with terrible quiet.

"I seem to have had a fight right here in this room." He stared around stupidly.

She looked around the room, very cool. "It doesn't look as though anybody's been fighting here, does it?"

"There's no blood here, no blood at all. Everything is clean," said he.

"Pretty much so."

"Then why," said Casher, "should I think I had a fight?"

"This wild weather on Henriada sometimes upsets off-worlders until they get used to it," said T'ruth mildly.

"If I didn't have a fight in the past, am I going to get into one in the future?"

The old room with the golden-oak furniture swam around him. The world outside was strange with the sunlit marshes and wide bayous trailing off to the forever-thundering storm, just over the horizon, which lay beyond the weather machines. Casher shrugged and shivered. He looked straight at the girl. She stood erect and looked at him with the even regard of a reigning empress. Her young budding breasts barely showed through the thinness of her shift; she wore golden flat-heeled shoes. Around her neck there was a thin gold chain, but the object on the chain hung down inside her dress. It excited him a little to think of her flat chest barely budding into womanhood. He had never been a man who had an improper taste for children, but there was something about this person which was not childlike at all.

"You are a girl and not a girl. . . ." he said in bewilderment.

She nodded gravely.

"You are that woman in the story, the Hechizera of Gonfalon. You are reborn."

She shook her head, equally seriously. "No, I am not reborn. I am a turtle-child, an underperson with a very long life, and I have been imprinted with the personality of the Citizen Agatha. This is all."

"You stun," he said, "but I do not know how you do it."

"I stun," she said flatly and around the edge of his mind there flickered up hot little torments of memory.

"Now I remember," he cried. "You have me here to kill somebody. You are sending me into a fight."

"You are going to a fight, Casher. I wish I could send somebody else, not you, but you are the only person here strong enough to do the job."

Impulsively he took her hand. The moment he touched her, she ceased to be a child or an underperson. She felt tender and exciting, like the most desirable and important person he had ever known. His sister? But he had no sister. He felt that he was himself terribly, unendurably important to her. He did not want to let her hand go, but she withdrew from his touch with an authority which no decent man could resist.

"You must fight to the death, now, Casher," she said, looking at him as evenly as might a troop commander examining a special soldier selected for a risky mission.

He nodded. He was tired of having his mind confused. He knew something had happened to him after the forgetty, Gosigo, had left him at the front door, but he was not at all sure of what it was. They seemed to have had a sort of meal together in this room. He felt himself in love with the child. He knew that she was not even a human being. He remembered something about her living ninety thousand years and he remembered something else about her having gotten the name and the skills of the greatest battle hypnotist of all history, the Hechizera of Gonfalon. There was something strange, something frightening about that chain around her neck: there were things he hoped he would never have to know.

He strained at the thought and it broke like a bubble.

"I'm a fighter," he said. "Give me my fight and let me know."

"*He* can kill you. I hope not. You must not kill him. He

is immortal and insane. But in the law of Old North Australia, from which my master, the Mister and Owner Murray Madigan, is an exile, we must not hurt a house guest, nor may we turn him away in a time of great need."

"What do I *do*?" snapped Casher impatiently.

"You fight him. You frighten him. You make his poor crazy mind fearful that he will meet you again."

"I'm supposed to do this."

"You can," she said very seriously. "I've already tested you. That's where you have the little spot of amnesia about this room."

"But *why*? Why bother? Why not get some of your human servants and have them tie him up or put him in a padded room?"

"They can't deal with him. He is too strong, too big, too clever, even though insane. Besides, they don't dare follow him."

"Where does he go?" said Casher sharply.

"Into the control room," replied T'ruth, as if it were the saddest phrase ever uttered.

"What's wrong with that? Even a place as fine as Beauregard can't have too much of a control room. Put locks on the control."

"It's not that kind of a control room."

Almost angry, he shouted, "What is it, then?"

"The control room," she answered, "is for a planoform ship. This house. These counties, all the way to Mottile on the one side and to Ambiloxi on the other. The sea itself, way out into the Gulf of Esperanza. All this is one ship."

Casher's professional interest took over. "If it's turned off, he can't do any harm."

"It's not turned off," she said. "My master leaves it on a very little bit. That way, he can keep the weather machines going and make this edge of Henriada a very pleasant place."

"You mean," said Casher, "that you'd risk letting a lunatic fly all these estates off into space."

"He doesn't even fly," said T'ruth gloomily.

"What does he *do*, then?" yelled Casher.

"When he gets at the controls, he just hovers."

"He hovers? By the Bell, girl, don't try to fool me. If you hover a place as big as this, you could wipe out the whole planet any moment. There have been only two or three pilots in the history of space who would be able to hover a machine like this one."

"He can, though," insisted the little girl.

"Who is he, anyhow?"

"I thought you knew. Or had heard somewhere about it. His name is John Joy Tree."

"Tree the Go-Captain?" Casher shivered in the warm room. "He died a long time ago after he made that record flight."

"He did not die. He bought immortality and went mad. He came here and he lives under my master's protection."

"Oh," said Casher. There was nothing else he could say. John Joy Tree, the great Norstrilian who took the first of the Long Plunges outside the galaxy: he was like Magno Taliano of ages ago, who could fly space on his living brain alone.

But fight him? How could anybody fight him?

Pilots are for piloting; killers are for killing; women are

for loving or forgetting. When you mix up the purposes, everything goes wrong.

Casher sat down abruptly. "Do you have any more of that coffee?"

"You don't need coffee," she said.

He looked up, inquiringly.

"You're a fighter. You need a war. That's it," she said, pointing with her girlish hand to a small doorway which looked like the entrance to a closet. "Just go in there. He's in there now. Tinkering with the machines again. Making me wait for my master to get blown to bits at any minute! And I've put up with it for over a hundred years."

"Go yourself," he said.

"You've been in a ship's control room," she declared.

"Yes," he nodded.

"You know how people go all naked and frightened inside. You know how much training it takes to make a Go-Captain. What do you think happens to me?" At last, long last, her voice was shrill, angry, excited, childish.

"What happens?" said Casher dully, not caring very much; he felt weary in every bone. Useless battles, murder he had to try, dead people arguing after their ballads had already grown out of fashion. Why didn't the Hechizera of Gonfalon do her own work?

Catching his thought, she screeched at him, "Because I *can't!*"

"All right," said Casher. "Why not?"

"Because I turn into me."

"You what?" said Casher, a little startled.

"I'm a turtle-child. My shape is human. My brain is

big. But I'm a *turtle*. No matter how much my master needs me, I'm just a turtle."

"What's that got to do with it?"

"What do turtles do when they're faced with danger? Not underpeople-turtles, but real turtles, little animals. You must have heard of them somewhere."

"I've even seen them," said Casher, "on some world or other. They pull into their shells."

"That's what I do"—she wept—"when I should be defending my master. I can meet most things. I am not a coward. But in that control room, I forget, forget, forget!"

"Send a robot, then!"

She almost screamed at him. "A robot against John Joy Tree? Are you mad, too?"

Casher admitted, in a mumble, that on second thought it wouldn't do much good to send a robot against the greatest Go-Captain of them all. He concluded, lamely, "I'll go, if you want me to."

"Go now," she shouted, "go right in!"

She pulled at his arm, half-dragging and half-leading him to the little brightened door which looked so innocent.

"But—" he said.

"Keep going," she pleaded. "This is all we ask of you. Don't kill him, but frighten him, fight him, wound him if you must. You can do it. I can't." She sobbed as she tugged at him. "I'd just be *me*."

Before he knew quite what had happened she had opened the door. The light beyond was clear and bright and tinged with blue, the way the skies of Manhome, Mother Earth, were shown in all the viewers.

He let her push him in.

He heard the door click behind him.

Before he even took in the details of the room or noticed the man in the Go-Captain's chair, the flavor and meaning of the room struck him like a blow against his throat.

This room, he thought, *is hell.*

He wasn't even sure that he remembered where he had learned the word "hell." It denoted all good turned to evil, all hope to anxiety, all wishes to greed.

Somehow, this room was it.

And then. . . .

∽ X ∾

And then the chief occupant of hell turned and looked squarely at him.

If this was John Joy Tree, he did not look insane.

He was a handsome, chubby man with a red complexion, bright eyes, dancing-blue in color, and a mouth which was as mobile as the mouth of a temptress.

"Good day," said John Joy Tree.

"How do you do," said Casher inanely.

"I do not know your name," said the ruddy brisk man, speaking in a tone of voice which was not the least bit insane.

"I am Casher O'Neill, from the city of Kaheer on the planet Mizzer."

"Mizzer?" John Joy Tree laughed. "I spent a night there, long, long ago. The entertainment was most unusual. But we have other things to talk about. You have come here to kill the undergirl T'ruth. You received your orders from the honorable Rankin Meiklejohn, may he soak in drink! The child has caught you and now she wants you to kill me, but she does not dare utter those words."

John Joy Tree, as he spoke, shifted the spaceship controls to standby, and got ready to get out of his captain's seat.

Casher protested, "She said nothing about killing you. She said you might kill me."

"I might, at that." The immortal pilot stood on the floor. He was a full head shorter than Casher but he was a strong and formidable man. The blue light of the room made him look clear, sharp, distinct.

The whole flavor of the situation tickled the fear-nerves inside Casher's body. He suddenly felt that he wanted very much to go to a bathroom, but he felt—quite surely—that if he turned his back on this man, in this place, he would die like a felled ox in a stockyard. He *had* to face John Joy Tree.

"Go ahead," said the pilot. "Fight me."

"I didn't say that I would fight you," said Casher. "I am supposed to frighten you and I do not know how to do it."

"This isn't getting us anywhere," said John Joy Tree. "Shall we go into the outer room and let poor little T'ruth give us a drink? You can just tell her that you failed."

"I think," said Casher, "that I am more afraid of her than I am of you."

John Joy Tree flung himself into a comfortable passenger's chair. "All right, then. Do something. Do you want to box? Gloves? Bare fists? Or would you like swords? Or wirepoints? There are some over there in the closet. Or we can each take a pilot ship and have a ship-duel out in space."

"That wouldn't make much sense," said Casher, "me fighting a ship against the greatest Go-Captain of them all. . . ."

John Joy Tree greeted this with an ugly underlaugh, a barely audible sound which made Casher feel that the whole situation was ridiculous.

"But I do have one advantage," said Casher. "I know who you are and you do not know who I am."

"How could I tell," said John Joy Tree, "when people keep on getting born all over the place?"

He gave Casher a scornful, comfortable grin. There was charm in the man's poise. Keeping his eyes focused directly on Casher, he felt for a carafe and poured himself a drink.

He gave Casher an ironic toast and Casher took it, standing frightened and alone. More alone than he had ever been before in his life.

Suddenly John Joy Tree sprang lightly to his feet and stared with a complete change of expression past Casher. Casher did not dare look around. This was some old fight trick.

Tree spat out the words, "*You've* done it then. This time you will violate all the laws and kill me. This fashionable oaf is not just one more trick."

A voice behind Casher called very softly, "I don't know." It was a man's voice, old, slow, and tired.

Casher had heard no one come in.

Casher's years of training stood him in good stead. He skipped sidewise in four or five steps, never taking his eyes off John Joy Tree, until the other man had come into his field of vision.

The man who stood there was tall, thin, yellow-skinned, and yellow-haired. His eyes were an old sick blue. He glanced at Casher and said, "I'm Madigan."

Was this the master? thought Casher. *Was this the being whom that lovely child had been imprinted to adore?*

He had no more time for thought.

Madigan whispered, as if to no one in particular, "You find me waking. You find him sane. Watch out."

Madigan lunged for the pilot's controls, but his tall, thin old body could not move very fast.

John Joy Tree jumped out of his chair and ran for the controls, too.

Casher tripped him.

Tree fell, rolled over, and got halfway up, one knee and one foot on the floor. In his hand there shimmered a knife very much like Casher's own.

Casher felt the flame of his body as some unknown force flung him against the wall. He stared, wild with fear.

Madigan had climbed into the pilot's seat and was fiddling with the controls as though he might blow Henriada out of space at any second. John Joy Tree glanced at his old host and then turned his attention to the man in front of him.

There was another man there.

Casher knew him.

He looked familiar.

It was himself, rising and leaping like a snake, left arm weaving the knife for the neck of John Joy Tree.

The image-Casher hit Tree with a thud that resounded through the room.

Tree's bright blue eyes had turned crazy-mad. His knife caught the image-Casher in the abdomen, thrust hard and deep, and left the young man gasping on the floor, trying to push the bleeding entrails back into his belly. The blood poured from the image-Casher all over the rug.

Blood!

Casher suddenly knew what he had to do and how he could do it—all without anybody telling him.

He created a third Casher on the far side of the room and gave him iron gloves. There was himself, unheeded against the wall; there was the dying Casher on the floor; there was the third, stalking toward John Joy Tree.

"Death is here," screamed the third Casher, with a voice which Casher recognized as a fierce crazy simulation of his own.

Tree whirled around. "You're not real," he said.

Image-Casher stepped around the console and hit Tree with an iron glove. The pilot jumped away, a hand reaching up to his bleeding face.

John Joy Tree screamed at Madigan, who was playing with the dials without even putting on the pinlighter helmet.

"You got her in here," he screamed, "you got her in here with this young man! Get her out!"

"Who?" said Madigan softly and absentmindedly.

"T'ruth. That witch of yours. I claim guest-right by all the ancient laws. *Get her out.*"

The real-Casher, standing at the wall, did not know

how he controlled the image-Casher with the iron gloves, but control him he did. He made him speak, in a voice as frantic as Tree's own voice:

"John Joy Tree, I do not bring you death. I bring you blood. My iron hands will pulp your eyes. Blind sockets will stare in your face. My iron hands will split your teeth and break your jaw a thousand times, so that no doctor, no machine will ever fix you. My iron hands will crush your arms, turn your hands into living rags. My iron hands will break your legs. Look at the blood, John Joy Tree. . . . There will be a lot more blood. You have killed me once. See that young man on the floor."

They both glanced at the first image-Casher, who had finally shuddered into death in the great rug. A pool of blood lay in front of the body of the youth.

John Joy Tree turned to the image-Casher and said to him, "You're the Hechizera of Gonfalon. You can't scare me. You're a turtle-girl and can't really hurt me."

"Look at me," said real-Casher.

John Joy Tree glanced back and forth between the duplicates.

Fright began to show.

Both the Cashers now shouted, in crazy voices which came from the depths of Casher's own mind:

"Blood you shall have! Blood and ruin. But we will not kill you. You will live in ruin, blind, emasculated, armless, legless. You will be fed through tubes. You cannot die and you will weep for death but no one will hear you."

"Why?" screamed Tree. "Why? What have I done to you?"

"You remind me," howled Casher, "of my home. You

remind me of the blood poured by Colonel Wedder when the poor useless victims of my uncle's lust paid with their blood for his revenge. You remind me of myself, John Joy Tree, and I am going to punish you as I myself might be punished."

Lost in the mists of lunacy, John Joy Tree was still a brave man.

He flung his knife unexpectedly at real-Casher. Image-Casher, in a tremendous bound, leaped across the room and caught the knife on an iron glove. It clattered against the iron glove and then fell silent onto the rug.

Casher saw what he had to see.

He saw the place of Kaheer, covered with death, with the intimate sticky silliness of sudden death—the dead men holding little packages they had tried to save, the girls, with their throats cut, lying in their own blood but with the lipstick still even and the eyebrow-pencil still pretty on their dead faces. He saw a dead child, ripped open from groin upward to chest, holding a broken doll while the child itself, now dead, looked like a broken doll itself. He saw these things and he made John Joy Tree see them, too.

"You're a bad man," said John Joy Tree.

"I am very bad," said Casher.

"Will you let me go, if I never enter this room again?"

Image-Casher snapped off, both the body on the floor and the fighter with the iron gloves. Casher did not know how Truth had taught him the lost art of fighter-replication, but he had certainly done it well.

"The lady told me you could go."

"But who are you going to use," said John Joy Tree,

calm, sad, and logical, "for your dreams of blood if you don't use me?"

"I don't know," said Casher. "I follow my fate. Go now, if you do not want my iron gloves to crush you."

John Joy Tree trotted out of the room, beaten.

Only then did Casher, exhausted, grab a curtain to hold himself upright and look around the room freely.

The evil atmosphere had gone.

Madigan, old though he was, had locked all the controls on standby.

He walked over to Casher and spoke. "Thank you. She did not invent you. She found you and put you to my service."

Casher coughed out, "The girl. Yes."

"*My* girl," corrected Madigan.

"Your girl," said Casher, remembering the sight of that slight feminine body, those budding breasts, the sensitive lips, the tender eyes.

"She could not have thought you up. She is my dead wife over again. The citizeness Agatha might have done it. But not T'ruth."

Casher looked at the man as he talked. The host wore the bottoms of some very cheap yellow pajamas and a washable bathrobe which had once been stripes of purple, lavender, and white. Now it was faded, like its wearer. Casher also saw the white clean plastic surgical implants on the man's arms, where the machines and tubes hooked in to keep him alive.

"I sleep a lot," said Murray Madigan, "but I am still the master of Beauregard. I am grateful to you."

The hand was frail, withered, dry, without strength.

The old voice whispered: "Tell her to reward you. You can have anything on my estate. Or you can have anything on Henriada. She manages it all for me." Then the old blue eyes opened wide and sharp and Murray Madigan was once again the man, just momentarily, that he had been hundreds of years ago—a Norstrilian trader, sharp, shrewd, wise, and not unkind. He added sharply: "Enjoy her company. She is a good child. But do not take her. Do not try to take her."

"Why not?" said Casher, surprised at his own bluntness.

"Because if you do, she will die. She is *mine*. Imprinted to me. I had her made and she is mine. Without me she would die in a few days. Do not take her."

Casher saw the old man leave the room by a secret door. He left himself, the way he had come in. He did not see Madigan again for two days, and by that time the old man had gone far back into his cataleptic sleep.

∞ X ∞

Two days later T'ruth took Casher to visit the sleeping Madigan.

"You can't go in there," said Eunice in a shocked voice. "*Nobody* goes in there. That's the master's room."

"I'm taking him in," said T'ruth calmly.

She had pulled a cloth-of-gold curtain aside and she was spinning the combination locks on a massive steel door. It was set in Daimoni material.

The maid went on protesting. "But even you, little ma'am, can't take him in there!"

"Who says I can't?" said T'ruth calmly and challengingly.

The awfulness of the situation sank in on Eunice.

In a small voice she muttered, "If you're taking him in, you're taking him in. But it's never been done before."

"Of course it hasn't, Eunice, not in your time. But Casher O'Neill has already met the mister and owner. He has fought for the mister and owner. Do you think I would take a stray or random guest in to look at the master, just like that?"

"Oh, not at all, no," said Eunice.

"Then go away, woman," said the lady-child. "You don't want to see this door open, do you?"

"Oh, no," shrieked Eunice and fled, putting her hands over her ears as though that would shut out the sight of the door.

When the maid had disappeared, T'ruth pulled with her whole weight against the handle of the heavy door. Casher expected the mustiness of the tomb or the medicinality of a hospital; he was astonished when fresh air and warm sunlight poured out from that heavy, mysterious door. The actual opening was so narrow, so low, that Casher had to step sidewise as he followed T'ruth into the room.

The master's room was enormous. The windows were flooded with perpetual sunlight. The landscape outside must have been the way Henriada looked in its prime, when Mottile was a resort for the carefree millions of vacationers, and Ambiloxi, a port feeding worlds halfway across the galaxy. There was no sign of the ugly snaky storms which worried and pestered Henriada in these later years. Everything was landscape, order, neatness, the triumph of man, as though Poussin had painted it.

The room itself, like the other great living-rooms of the estate of Beauregard, was exuberant neo-baroque in which the architect, himself half-mad, had been given wild license to work out his fantasies in steel, plastic, plaster, wood, and stone. The ceiling was not flat, but vaulted. The four corners of the room were each alcoves, cutting deep into the four sides, so that the room was, in effect, an octagon. The propriety and prettiness of the room had been a little diminished by the shoving of the furniture to one side, sofas, upholstered armchairs, marble tables, and knickknack stands all in an indescribable melange to the left; while the right-hand part of the room—facing the master window with the illusory landscape—was equipped like a surgery with an operating table, hydraulic lifts, bottles of clear and colored fluid hanging from chrome stands, and two large devices which (Casher later surmised) must have been heart-lung and kidney machines. The alcoves, in their turn, were wilder. One was an archaic funeral parlor with an immense coffin, draped in black velvet, resting on a heavy teak stand. The next was a spaceship control cabin of the old kind, with the levers, switches, and controls all in plain sight—the meters actually read the galactically-stable location of this very place, and to do so they had to whirl mightily—as well as a pilot's chair with the usual choice of helmets and the straps and shock absorbers. The third alcove was a simple bedroom done in very old-fashioned taste, the walls a Wedgwood blue with deep wine-colored drapes, coverlets and pillowcases marking a sharp but tolerable contrast. The fourth alcove was the copy of a fortress: it might even be a fortress: the door was heavy and the walls looked as though they might be Daimoni material, indestructible by any imaginable means. Cases of emergency food and water were stacked against the walls. Weapons which looked oiled and primed stood in their racks, together with three different calibers of wirepoint, each with its own fresh-looking battery.

The alcoves had no people in them.

The parlor was deserted.

The Mister and Owner Murray Madigan lay naked on the operating table. Two or three wires led to gauges attached to his body. Casher thought that he could see a faint motion of the chest, as the cataleptic man breathed at a rate one-tenth normal or less.

The girl-lady, T'ruth, was not the least embarrassed.

"I check him four or five times a day. I never let people in here. But you're special, Casher. He's talked with you and fought beside you and he knows that he owes you his life. You're the first human person ever to get into this room."

"I'll wager," said Casher, "that the Administrator of Henriada, the Honorable Rankin Meiklejohn, would give up some of his 'honorable' just to get in here and have one look around. He wonders what Madigan is doing when Madigan is doing nothing. . . ."

"He's not just doing nothing," said T'ruth sharply. "He's sleeping. It's not everybody who can sleep for forty or fifty or sixty thousand years and can wake up a few times a month, just to see how things are going."

Casher started to whistle and then stopped himself, as

though he feared to waken the unconscious, naked old man on the table. "So that's why he chose *you*."

T'ruth corrected him as she washed her hands vigorously in a washbasin. "That's why he had me made. Turtle stock, three hundred years. Multiply that with intensive stroon treatments, three hundred times. Ninety thousand years. Then he had me printed to love him and adore him. He's not my master, you know. He's my god."

"Your what?"

"You heard me. Don't get upset. I'm not going to give you any illegal memories. I worship him. That's what I was printed for, when my little turtle eyes opened and they put me back in the tank to enlarge my brain and to make a woman out of me. That's why they printed every memory of the citizeness Agatha Madigan right into my brain. I'm what he wanted. Just what he wanted. I'm the most wanted being on any planet. No wife, no sweetheart, no mother has ever been wanted as much as he wants me now, when he wakes up and knows that I am still here. You're a smart man. Would you trust any machine—any machine at all—for ninety thousand years?"

"It would be hard," said Casher, "to get batteries of monitors long enough for them to repair each other over that long a time. But that means you have ninety thousand years of it. Four times, five times a day. I can't even multiply the numbers. Don't you ever get tired of it?"

"He's my love, he's my joy, he's my darling little boy," she caroled, as she lifted his eyelids and put colorless drops in each eye. Absentmindedly, she explained. "With this slow metabolism, there's always some danger that his eyelids will stick to his eyeballs. This is part of the check-up."

She tilted the sleeping man's head, looked earnestly into each eye. She then stepped a few paces aside and put her face close to the dial of a gently-humming machine. There was the sound of a shot. Casher almost reached for his gun, which he did not have.

The child turned back to him with a free mischievous smile. "Sorry, I should have warned you. That's my noise-maker. I watch the encephalograph to make sure his brain keeps a little auditory intake. It showed up with the noise. He's asleep, very deeply asleep, but he's not drifting downward into death."

Back at the table she pushed Madigan's chin upward so that the head leaned far back on its neck. Deftly holding the forehead, she took a retractor, opened his mouth with her fingers, depressed the tongue, and looked down into the throat.

"No accumulation there," she muttered, as if to herself.

She pushed the head back into a comfortable position. She seemed on the edge of another set of operations when it was obvious that an idea occurred to her. "Go wash your hands, thoroughly, over there, at the basin. Then push the timer down and be sure you hold your hands under the sterilizer until the timer goes off. You can help me turn him over. I don't have help here. You're the first visitor."

Casher obeyed and while he washed his hands, he saw the girl drench her hands with some flower-scented unguent. She began to massage the unconscious body with professional expertness, even with a degree of roughness. As he stood with his hands under the sterilizer-drier, Casher marveled at the strength of those girlish arms and those little hands. Indefatigably they stroked, rubbed, pummelled, pulled, stretched, and poked the old body. The sleeping man seemed to be utterly unaware of it, but Casher thought that he could see a better skin color and muscle tone appearing.

He walked back to the table and stood facing T'ruth.

A huge peacock walked across the imaginary lawn outside the window, his tail shimmering in a paroxysm of colors.

T'ruth saw the direction of Casher's glance.

"Oh, I program that, too. He likes it when he wakes up. Don't you think he was clever, before he went into catalepsis—to have me made, to have me created to love him and to care for him? It helps that I'm a girl. I can't ever love anybody but him, and it's easy for me to remember that this is the man I love. And it's safer for him. Any man might get bored with these responsibilities. I don't."

"Yet—" said Casher.

"Shh," she said, "wait a bit. This takes care." Her strong little fingers were now plowing deep into the abdomen of the naked old man. She closed her eyes so that she could concentrate all her senses on the one act of tactile impression. She took her hands away and stood erect. "All clear," she said. "I've got to find out what's going on inside him. But I don't dare use X-rays on him. Think of the radiation he'd build up in a hundred years or so. He defecates about twice a month while he's sleeping. I've got to be ready for that. I also have to prime his bladder every week or so. Otherwise he would poison himself just with his own body wastes. Here, now, you can help me turn him over. But watch the wires. Those are the monitor controls. They report his physiological processes, radio a message to me if anything goes wrong, and meanwhile supply the missing neurophysical impulses if any part of the automatic nervous system began to fade out or just simply went off."

"Has that ever happened?"

"Never," she said, "not yet. But I'm ready. Watch that wire. You're turning him too fast. There now, that's right. You can stand back while I massage him on the back."

She went back to her job of being a masseuse. Starting at the muscles joining the skull to the neck, she worked her way down the body, pouring ointment on her hands from time to time. When she got to his legs, she seemed to work particularly hard. She lifted the feet, bent the knees, slapped the calves.

Then she put on a rubber glove, dipped her hand into another jar—one which opened automatically as her hand approached—and came out with her hand greasy. She thrust her fingers into his rectum, probing, thrusting, groping, her brow furrowed.

Her face cleared as she dropped the rubber glove in a disposal can and wiped the sleeping man with a soft linen towel, which also went into a disposal can. "He's all right. He'll get along well for the next two hours. I'll have to give him a little sugar then. All he's getting now is normal saline."

She stood facing him. There was a faint glow in her cheeks from the violent exercise in which she had been indulging, but she still looked both the child and the lady—the child irrecoverably remote, hidden in her own wisdom from the muddled world of adults, and the lady, mistress in her own home, her own estates, her own planet, serving her master with almost-immortal love and zeal.

"I was going to ask you, back there—" said Casher and then stopped.

"You were going to ask me?"

He spoke heavily. "I was going to ask you, what happens to you when he dies? Either at the right time or possibly before his time. What happens to *you*?"

"I couldn't care less," her voice sang out. He could see by the open, honest smile on her face that she meant it. "I'm *his*. I belong to *him*. That's what I'm *for*. They may have programmed something into me, in case he dies. Or they may have forgotten. What matters is his life, not mine. He's going to get every possible hour of life that I can help him get. Don't you think I'm doing a good job?"

"A good job, yes," said Casher. "A strange one, too."

"We can go now," she said.

"What are those alcoves for?"

"Oh, those—they're his make-believes. He picks one of them to go to sleep in—his coffin, his fort, his ship, or his bedroom. It doesn't matter which. I always get him up with the hoist and put him back on his table, where the machines and I can take proper care of him. He doesn't really mind waking up on the table. He has usually forgotten which room he went to sleep in. We can go now."

They walked toward the door.

Suddenly she stopped. "I forgot something. I never forget things, but this is the first time I ever let anybody come in here with me. You were such a *good* friend to him. He'll talk about you for thousands of years. Long, long after you're dead," she added somewhat unnecessarily.

Casher looked at her sharply to see if she might be mocking or deprecating him. There was nothing but the little-girl solemnity, the womanly devotion to an established domestic routine.

"Turn your back," she commanded peremptorily.

"Why?" he asked. "Why—when you have trusted me with all the other secrets."

"He wouldn't want you to see this."

"See what?"

"What I'm going to do. When I was the citizeness Agatha—or when I seemed to be her—I found that men are awfully fussy about some things. This is one of them."

Casher obeyed and stood facing the door.

A different odor filled the room—a strong wild scent, like a geranium pomade. He could hear T'ruth breathing heavily as she worked beside the sleeping man.

She called to him: "You can turn around now."

She was putting away a tube of ointment, standing high to get it into its exact position on a tile shelf.

Casher looked quickly at the body of Madigan. It was still asleep, still breathing very lightly and very slowly.

"What on earth did you *do*?"

T'ruth stopped in mid-step: "You're going to get nosy."

Casher stammered mere sounds.

"You can't help it," she said. "People are inquisitive."

"I suppose they are," he said, flushing at the accusation.

"I gave him his bit of fun. He never remembers it when he wakes up, but the cardiograph sometimes shows increased activity. Nothing happened this time. That was my own idea. I read books and decided that it would be good for his body tone. Sometimes he sleeps through a whole Earth-year, but usually he wakes up several times a month."

She passed Casher, almost pulled herself clear of the floor tugging on the great inside levers of the main door.

She gestured him past. He stooped and stepped through.

"Turn away again," she said. "All I'm going to do is to spin the dials, but they're cued to give any viewer a bad headache so he will forget the combination. Even robots. I'm the only person tuned to these doors."

He heard the dials spinning but did not look around.

She murmured, almost under her breath, "I'm the only one. The only one."

"The only one for what?" asked Casher.

"To love my master, to care for him, to support his planet, to guard his weather. But isn't he beautiful? Isn't he wise? Doesn't his smile win your heart?"

Casher thought of the faded old wreck of a man with the yellow pajama bottoms. Tactfully, he said nothing.

T'ruth babbled on, quite cheerfully, "He is my father, my husband, my baby son, my master, my owner. Think of that, Casher, he owns me! Isn't he lucky—to have me? And aren't I lucky—to belong to him?"

"But what for?" asked Casher, a little crossly, thinking that he was falling in and out of love with this remarkable girl himself.

"For life!" she cried. "In any form, in any way. I am made for ninety thousand years and he will sleep and wake and dream and sleep again, a large part of that."

"What's the use of it?" insisted Casher.

"The use," she said, "the use? What's the use of the

little turtle-egg they took and modified in its memory chains, right down to the molecular level? What's the use of turning me into an undergirl, so that even you have to love me off and on? What's the use of little me, meeting my master for the first time, when I had been manufactured to love him? I can tell you, man, what the use is. Love."

"What did you say?" said Casher.

"I said the use was love. Love is the only end of things. Love on the one side, and death on the other. If you are strong enough to use a real weapon, I can give you a weapon which will put all Mizzer at your mercy. Your cruiser and your laser would just be toys against the weapon of love. You can't fight love. You can't fight me."

They had proceeded down a corridor, forgotten pictures hanging on the walls, unremembered luxuries left untouched by centuries of neglect.

The bright yellow light of Henriada poured in through an open doorway on their right.

From the room came snatches of a man singing while playing a stringed instrument. Later, Casher found that this was a verse of the Henriada Song, the one which went:

> *Don't put your ship in the Boom Lagoon,*
> *Look up North for the raving wave.*
> *Henriada's boiled away*
> *But Ambiloxi's a saving grave.*

They entered the room.

A gentleman stood up to greet them.

It was the great go-pilot, John Joy Tree. His ruddy face smiled, his bright blue eyes lit up, a little condescendingly, as he greeted his small hostess, but then his glance took in Casher O'Neill.

The effect was sudden, and evil.

John Joy Tree looked away from both of them. The phrase which he had started to use stuck in his throat.

He said, in a different voice, very "away" and deeply troubled, "There is blood all over this place. There is a man of blood right here. Excuse me. I am going to be sick."

He trotted past them and out the door which they had entered.

"You have passed a test," said T'ruth. "Your help to my master has solved the problem of the captain and honorable John Joy Tree. He will not go near that control room if he thinks that you are there."

"Do you have more tests for me? Still more? By now, you ought to know me well enough not to need tests."

"I am not a person," she said, "but just a built-up copy of one. I am getting ready to give you your weapon. This is a communications room as well as a music room. Would you like something to eat or drink?"

"Just water," he said.

"At your hand," said T'ruth.

A rock-crystal carafe had been standing on the table beside him, unnoticed. Or had she transported it into the room with one of the tricks of the Hechizera, the dreaded Agatha herself? It didn't matter. He drank. Trouble was coming.

∽ XII ∽

T'ruth had swung open a polished cabinet panel. The

communicator was the kind they mount in planoforming ships right beside the pilot. The rental on one of them was enough to make any planetary government reconsider its annual budget.

"That's *yours*?" cried Casher.

"Why not?" said the little-girl lady. "I have four or five of them."

"But you're *rich*!"

"I'm not. My master is. I belong to my master, too."

"But things like this. He can't handle them. How does he manage?"

"You mean money and things?" The girlish part of her came out. She looked pleased, happy, and mischievous. "I manage them for him. He was the richest man on Henriada when I came here. He had credits of stroon. Now he is about forty times richer."

"He's a Rod McBan!" exclaimed Casher.

"Not even near. Mister McBan had a lot more money than we. But he's rich. Where do you think all the people from Henriada went?"

"I don't know," said Casher.

"To four new planets. They belong to my master and he charges the new settlers a very small land-rent."

"You bought them?" Casher asked.

"For him." T'ruth smiled. "Haven't you heard of planet-brokers?"

"But that's a gambler's business—" said Casher.

"I gambled," she said, "and I won. Now keep quiet and watch me."

She pressed a button. "Instant message."

"Instant message," repeated the machine. "What priority?"

"War news, double A one, subspace penalty."

"Confirmed," said the machine.

"The planet Mizzer. Now. War and peace information. Will fighting end soon?"

The machine clucked to itself.

Casher, knowing the prices of this kind of communication, almost felt that he could see the arterial spurt of money go out of Henriada's budget as the machines reached across the galaxy, found Mizzer, and came back with the answer.

"Skirmishing. Seventh Nile. Ends three local days."

"Close message," said T'ruth.

The machine went off.

T'ruth turned to him. "You're going home soon, Casher, if you can pass a few little tests."

He stared at her.

He blurted, "I need my weapons, my cruiser, and my laser."

"You'll have weapons. Better ones than those. Right now, I want you to go to the front door. When you have opened the door, you will not let anybody in. Close the door. Then please come back to me here, dear Casher, and if you are still alive, I will have some other things for you to do."

Casher turned in bewilderment. It did not occur to him to contradict her. He could end up a forgetty, like the maidservant Eunice or the Administrator's brown man, Gosigo.

Down the halls, he walked. He met no one except

for a few shy cleaning-robots, who bowed their heads politely as he passed.

He found the front door. It stopped him. It looked like wood on the outside, but it was actually a Daimoni door, made of near-indestructible material. There was no sign of a key or dials or controls. Acting like a man in a dream, he took a chance that the door might be keyed to himself. He put his right palm firmly against it, at the left or opening edge.

The door swung in.

Meiklejohn was there. Gosigo held the Administrator upright. It must have been a rough trip. The Administrator's face was bruised and blood trickled from the corner of his mouth. His eyes focused on Casher.

"You're alive. She caught you, too?"

Quite formally, Casher asked, "What do you want in this house?"

"I have come," said the Administrator, "to see her."

"To see whom?" insisted Casher.

The Administrator hung almost slack in Gosigo's arms. By his own standard and in his own way, he was a very brave man, indeed. His eyes looked clear, even though his body was collapsing.

"To see Truth, if she will see me," said Rankin Meiklejohn.

"She cannot," said Casher, "see you now. Gosigo!"

The forgetty turned to Casher and gave him a bow.

"You will forget me. You have not seen me."

"I have not seen you, lord. Give my greetings to your lady. Anything else?"

"Yes. Take your master home, as safely and swiftly as you can."

"My lord!" cried Gosigo, though this was an improper title for Casher. Casher turned around.

"My lord, tell her to extend the weather machines for just a few more kilometers and I will have him home safe in ten minutes. At top speed."

"I can tell her," said Casher, "but I cannot promise she will do it."

"Of course," said Gosigo. He picked up the Administrator and began putting him into the groundcar. Rankin Meiklejohn bawled once, like a man crying in pain. It sounded like a blurred version of the name *Murray Madigan.* No one heard it but Gosigo and Casher; Gosigo busy closing the groundcar, Casher pushing on the big house door.

The door clicked.

There was silence.

The opening of the door was remembered only by the warm sweet salty stink of seaweed, which had disturbed the odor-pattern of the changeless, musty old house.

Casher hurried back with the message about the weather machines.

T'ruth received the message gravely. Without looking at the console, she reached out and controlled it with her extended right hand, not taking her eyes off Casher for a moment. The machine clicked its agreement. T'ruth exhaled.

"Thank you, Casher. Now the Instrumentality and the forgetty are gone."

She stared at him, almost sadly and inquiringly. He wanted to pick her up, to crush her to his chest, to rain his kisses on her face. But he stood stock still. He did not move. This was not just the forever-loving turtle-child; this was the real mistress of Henriada. This was the Hechizera of Gonfalon, whom he had formerly thought about only in terms of a wild, melodic grand opera.

"I think you are seeing me, Casher. It is hard to see people, even when you look at them every day. I think I can see you, too, Casher. It is almost time for us both to do the things which we have to do."

"Which *we* have to do?" he whispered, hoping she might say something else.

"For me, my work here on Henriada. For you, your fate on your homeland of Mizzer. That's what life is, isn't it? Doing what you have to do in the first place. We're lucky people if we find it out. You are ready, Casher. I am about to give you weapons which will make bombs and cruisers and lasers and bombs seem like nothing at all."

"By the Bell, girl! Can't you tell me what those weapons are?"

T'ruth stood in her innocently revealing sheath, the yellow light of the old music room pouring like a halo around her.

"Yes," she said, "I can tell you now. Me."

"You?"

Casher felt a wild surge of erotic attraction for the innocently voluptuous child. He remembered his first insane impulse to crush her with kisses, to sweep her up with hugs, to exhaust her with all the excitement which his masculinity could bring to both of them.

He stared at her.

She stood there, calm.

That sort of an idea did not ring right.

He was going to get her, but he was going to get something far from fun or folly—something, indeed, which he might not even like.

When at last he spoke, it was out of the deep bewilderment of his own thoughts, "What do you mean, you're going to give me yourself? It doesn't sound very romantic to me, nor the tone in which you said it."

The child stepped close to him, reaching up and patting his forehead.

"You're not going to get me for a night's romance, and if you did, you would be sorry. I am the property of my master and of no other man. But I can do something with you which I have never done to anyone else. I can get myself imprinted on you. The technicians are already coming. You will be the turtle-child. You will be the citizeness Agatha Madigan, the Hechizera of Gonfalon herself. You will be many other people. And yourself. You will then win. Accidents may kill you, Casher, but no one will be able to kill you on purpose. Not when you're me. Poor man! Do you know what you will be giving up?"

"What?" he croaked, at the edge of a great fright. He had seen danger before, but never before had danger loomed up from within himself.

"You will not fear death, ever again, Casher. You will have to lead your life minute by minute, second by second, and you will not have the alibi that you are going to die anyhow. You will know that's not special."

He nodded, understanding her words and scrabbling around his mind for a meaning.

"I'm a girl, Casher. . . ."

He looked at her and his eyes widened. She was a

girl—a beautiful, wonderful girl. But she was something more. She was the mistress of Henriada. She was the first of the underpeople really and truly to surpass humanity. To think that he had wanted to grab her poor little body. The body—ah, that was sweet!—but the power within it was the kind of thing that empires and religions are made of.

". . . and if you take the print of me, Casher, you will never lie with a woman without realizing that you know more about her than she does. You will be a seeing man among blind multitudes, a hearing person in the world of the deaf. I don't know how much fun romantic love is going to be to you after this."

Gloomily he said, "If I can free my home planet of Mizzer, it will be worth it. Whatever it is."

"You're not going to turn into a woman!" She laughed. "Nothing that easy. But you are going to get wisdom. And I will tell you the whole story of the Sign of the Fish before you leave here."

"Not that, please," he begged. "That's a religion and the Instrumentality would never let me travel again."

"I'm going to have you scrambled, Casher, so that nobody can read you for a year or two. And the Instrumentality is not going to send you back. *I am.* Through space-three."

"It'll cost you a fine, big ship to do it."

"My master will approve when I tell him, Casher. Now give me that kiss you have been wanting to give me. Perhaps you will remember something of it when you come out of scramble."

She stood there. He did nothing.

"Kiss me!" she commanded.

He put his arm around her. She felt like a big little girl. She lifted her face. She thrust her lips up toward his. She stood on tiptoe.

He kissed her the way a man might kiss a picture or a religious object. The heat and fierceness had gone out of his hopes. He had not kissed a girl, but power—tremendous power and wisdom put into a single slight form.

"Is that the way your master kisses you?"

She gave him a quick smile. "How clever of you! Yes, sometimes. Come along now. We have to shoot some children before the technicians are ready. It will give you a good last chance of seeing what you can do, when you have become what I am. Come along, the guns are in the hall."

∽ XIII ∽

They went down an enormous light-oak staircase to a floor which Casher had never seen before. It must have been the entertainment and hospitality center of Beauregard long ago, when the mister and owner Murray Madigan was himself young.

The robots did a good job of keeping away the dust and the mildew. Casher saw inconspicuous little air-driers placed at strategic places, so that the rich tooled leather on the walls would not spoil, so that the velvet bar-stools would not become slimy with mold, so that the pool tables would not warp nor the golf clubs go out of shape with age and damp. *By the Bell,* he thought, *that man Madigan could have entertained a thousand people at one time in a place this size.*

The gun-cabinet, now, that was functional. The glass shone. The velvet of oil showed on the steel and walnut of the guns. They were old Earth models, very rare and very special. For actual fighting, people used the cheap artillery of the present time or wirepoints for close work. Only the richest and rarest of connoisseurs had the old Earth weapons or could use them.

T'ruth touched the guard-robot and waked him. The robot saluted, looked at her face, and without further inquiry, opened the cabinet.

"Do you know guns?" said T'ruth to Casher.

"Wirepoints," he said. "Never touched a gun in my life."

"Do you mind using a learning-helmet, then? I could teach you hypnotically with the special rules of the Hechizera, but they might give you a headache or upset you emotionally. The helmet is neuro-electric and it has filters."

Casher nodded and saw his reflection nodding in the polished glass doors of the gun-cabinet. He was surprised to see how helpless and lugubrious he looked.

But it was true. Never before in his life had he felt that a situation swept over him, washed him along like a great wave, left him with no choice and no responsibility. Things were her choice now, not his, and yet he felt that her power was benign, self-limited, restricted by factors at which he could no more than guess. He had come for one weapon—the cruiser which he had hoped to get from the Administrator Rankin Meiklejohn. She was offering him something else—psychological weapons in which he had neither experience nor confidence.

She watched him attentively for a long moment and then turned to the gun-watching robot.

"You're little Harry Hadrian, aren't you? The gun-watcher."

"Yes, ma'am," said the silver robot brightly, "and I'm owl-brained too. That makes me very bright."

"Watch this," she said, extending her arms the width of the gun-cabinet and then dropping them after a queer flutter of her hands. "Do you know what that means?"

"Yes, ma'am," said the little robot quickly, the emotion showing in his toneless voice by the speed with which he spoke, not by the intonation, "it-means-you-have-taken-over-and-I-am-off-duty! Can-I-go-sit-in-the-garden-and-look-at-the-live-things?"

"Not quite yet, little Harry Hadrian. There are some wind-people out there now and they might hurt you. I have another errand for you first. Do you remember where the teaching helmets are?"

"Silver hats on the third floor in an open closet with a wire running to each hat. Yes."

"Bring one of those as fast as you can. Pull it loose very carefully from its electrical connection."

The little robot disappeared in a sudden, fast, gentle clatter up the stairs.

T'ruth turned back to Casher. "I have decided what to do with you. I am helping you. You don't have to look so gloomy about it."

"I'm not gloomy. The Administrator sent me here on a crazy errand, killing an unknown underperson. I find out that the person is really a little girl. Then I find out that she is not an underperson, but a frightening old dead woman, still walking around alive. My life gets turned upside down. All my plans are set aside. You propose to send me home to fulfill my life's work on Mizzer. I've struggled for this, so many years! Now you're making it all come through, even though you are going to cook me through space-three to do it, and throw in a lot of illegal religion and hypnotic tricks, that I'm not sure I can handle. Now you tell me to come along—to shoot children with guns. I've never done anything like that in my life and yet I find myself obeying you. I'm tired out, girl, tired out. If you have put me in your power, I don't even know it. I don't even want to know it."

"Here you are, Casher, on the ruined wet world of Henriada. In less than a week you will be recovering among the military casualties of Colonel Wedder's army. You will be under the clear sky of Mizzer, and the Seventh Nile will be near you, and you will be ready at long last to do what you have to do. You will have bits and pieces of memories of me—not enough to make you find your way back here or to tell people all the secrets of Beauregard, but enough for you to remember that you have been loved. You may even"—and she smiled very gently, with a tender wry humor on her face—"marry some Mizzer girl because her body or her face or her manner reminds you to me."

"In a week—?" he gasped.

"Less than that."

"Who are you," he cried out, "that you, an underperson, should run real people and should manipulate their lives?"

"I didn't look for power, Casher. Power doesn't usually work if you look for it. I have eighty-nine thousand years to live, Casher, and as long as my master lives, I shall love him and take care of him. Isn't he handsome? Isn't he wise? Isn't he the most perfect master you ever saw?"

Casher thought of the old ruined-looking body with the plastic knobs set into it; he thought of the faded pajama bottoms; he said nothing.

"You don't have to agree," said T'ruth. "I know I have a special way of looking at him. But they took my turtle brain and raised the IQ to above normal human level. They took me when I was a happy little girl, enchanted by the voice and the glance and the touch of my master— they took me to where this real woman lay dying and they put me into a machine and they put her into one, too. When they were through, they picked me up. I had on a pink dress with pastel blue socks and pink shoes. They carried me out into the corridor, on a rug. They had finished with me. They knew that I wouldn't die. I was healthy. Can't you see it, Casher? I cried myself to sleep, nine hundred years ago."

Casher could not really answer. He nodded sympathetically.

"I was a girl, Casher. Maybe I was a turtle once, but I don't remember that, any more than you remember your mother's womb or your laboratory bottle. In that one hour I was never to be a girl again. I did not need to go to school. I had *her* education, and it was a good one. She spoke twenty or more languages. She was a psychologist and a hypnotist and a strategist. She was also the tyrannical mistress of this house. I cried because my childhood was finished, because I knew what I would have to do. I cried because I knew that I could do it. I *loved* my master so, but I was no longer to be the pretty little servant who brought him his tablets or his sweetmeats or his beer. Now I saw the truth—as she died I had myself become Henriada. The planet was mine to care for, to manage—to protect my master. If I come along and I protect and help you, is that so much for a woman who will just be growing up when your grandchildren will all be dead of old age?"

"No, no," stammered Casher O'Neill. "But your own life? A family, perhaps?"

Anger lashed across her pretty face. Her features were the features of the delicious girl-child T'ruth, but her expression was that of the citizeness Agatha Madigan, perhaps, a worldly woman reborn to the endless world-liness of her own wisdom.

"Should I order a husband from the turtle bank, perhaps? Should I hire out a piece of my master's estate, to be sold to somebody because I'm an underperson, or perhaps put to work somewhere in an industrial ship? I'm *me.* I may be an animal, but I have more civilization in me than all the wind-people on this planet. Poor things! What kind of people are they, if they are only happy when they catch a big mutated duck and tear it to pieces, eating it raw? I'm not going to lose, Casher. I'm going to win. My master will live longer than any person has ever lived before. He gave me that mission when he was strong and wise and well in the prime of his life. I'm going to do what I was made for, Casher, and you're going to go back to Mizzer and make it free, whether you like it or not!"

They both heard a happy scurrying on the staircase.

The small silver robot, little Harry Hadrian, burst upon them; he carried a teaching helmet.

T'ruth said, "Resume your post. You are a good boy, little Harry, and you can have time to sit in the garden later on, when it is safe."

"Can I sit in a tree?" the little robot asked.

"Yes, if it is safe."

Little Harry Hadrian resumed his post by the gun-cabinet. He kept the key in his hand. It was a very strange key, sharp at the end and as long as an awl. Casher supposed that it must be one of the straight magnetic keys, cued to its lock by a series of magnetized patterns.

"Sit on the floor for a minute," said T'ruth to Casher; "you're too tall for me." She slipped the helmet on his head, adjusted the levers on each side so that the helmet sat tight and true upon his skull.

With a touching gesture of intimacy, for which she gave him a sympathetic apologetic little smile, she moistened the two small electrodes with her own spit, touching her finger to her tongue and then to the electrode. These went to his temples.

She adjusted the verniered dials on the helmet itself, lifted the rear wire, and applied it to her forehead.

Casher heard the click of a switch.

"That did it," he heard T'ruth's voice saying, very far away.

He was too busy looking into the gun-cabinet. He knew them all and loved some of them. He knew the feel of their stocks on his shoulder, the glimpse of their barrels in front of his eyes, the dance of the target on their various sights, the welcome heavy weight of the gun on his supporting arm, the rewarding thrust of the stock against his shoulder when he fired. He knew all this, and did not know how he knew it.

"The Hechizera, Agatha herself, was a very accomplished sportswoman," murmured T'ruth to him. "I thought her knowledge would take a second printing when I passed it along to you. Let's take these."

She gestured to little Harry Hadrian, who unlocked the cabinet and took out two enormous guns, which looked like the long muskets mankind had had on Earth even before the age of space began.

"If you're going to shoot children," said Casher with his new-found expertness, "these won't do. They'll tear the bodies completely to pieces."

T'ruth reached into the little bag which hung from her belt. She took out three shotgun shells. "I have three more," she said. "Six children is all we need."

Casher looked at the slug projecting slightly from the shotgun casing. It did not look like any shell he had ever seen before. The workmanship was unbelievably fine and precise.

"What are they? I never saw these before."

"Proximity stunners," she said. "Shoot ten centimeters above the head of any living thing and the stunner knocks it out."

"You want the children alive?"

"Alive, of course. And unconscious. They are a part of your final test."

Two hours later, after an exciting hike to the edge of the weather controls, they had the six children stretched out on the floor of the great hall. Four were little boys, two girls; they were fine-boned, soft-haired people, very thin, but they did not look too far from Earth-normal.

T'ruth called up a doctor-underman from among her servants. There must have been a crowd of fifty or sixty undermen and robots standing around. Far up the staircase, John Joy Tree stood hidden, half in shadow. Casher suspected that he was as inquisitive as the others but afraid of himself, Casher, "the man of blood."

T'ruth spoke quietly but firmly to the doctor. "Can you give them a strong euphoric before you waken them? We don't want to have to pluck them out of all the curtains in the house, if they go wild when they wake up."

"Nothing simpler," said the doctor-underman. He seemed to be of dog origin, but Casher could not tell.

He took a glass tube and touched it to the nape of each little neck. The necks were all streaked with dirt. These children had never been washed in their lives, except by the rain.

"Wake them," said T'ruth.

The doctor stepped back to a rolling table. It gleamed with equipment. He must have pre-set his devices, because all he did was to press a button and the children stirred into life.

The first reaction was wildness. They got ready to bolt. The biggest of the boys, who by Earth-standards would have been about ten, got three steps before he stopped and began laughing.

T'ruth spoke the Old Common Tongue to them, very slowly and with long spaces between the words:

"Wind-children—do—you—know—where—you—are?"

The biggest girl twittered back to her so fast that Casher could not understand it.

T'ruth turned to Casher and said, "The girl said that she is in the Dead Place, where the air never moves and where the Old Dead Ones move around on their own business. She means us." To the wind-children she spoke again.

"What—would—you—like—most?"

The biggest girl went from child to child. They nodded agreement vigorously. They formed a circle and began a little chant. By the second repetition around, Casher could make it out.

> *Shig—shag—shuggery,*
> *shuck shuck shuck!*
> *What all of us need is*
> *an all-around duck.*
> *Shig—shag—shuggery,*
> *shuck shuck shuck!*

At the fourth or fifth repetition they all stopped and looked at T'ruth, who was so plainly the mistress of the house.

She in turn spoke to Casher O'Neill: "They think that they want a tribal feast of raw duck. What they are going to get is inoculations against the worst diseases of this planet, several duck meals, and their freedom again. But they need something else beyond all measure. *You know what that is, Casher, if you can only find it.*"

The whole crowd turned its eyes on Casher, the human eyes of the people and underpeople, the milky lenses of the robots.

Casher stood aghast.

"Is this a test?" he asked, softly.

"You could call it that," said T'ruth, looking away from him.

Casher thought furiously and rapidly. It wouldn't do any good to make them into forgetties. The household had enough of them. T'ruth had announced a plan to let them loose again. Mister and owner Murray Madigan must have told her, sometime or other, to "do something" about the wind-people. She was trying to do it. The whole crowd watched him. What might T'ruth expect?

The answer came to him in a flash.

If she were asking *him,* it must be something to do with himself, something which he—uniquely among these people, underpeople, and robots—had brought to the storm-sieged mansion of Beauregard.

Suddenly he saw it.

"Use me, my Lady Ruth," said he, deliberately giving her the wrong title, "to print on them nothing from my intellectual knowledge, but everything from my emotional makeup. It wouldn't do them any good to know about Mizzer, where the Twelve Niles work their way down across the Intervening Sands. Nor about Pontoppidan, the Gem Planet. Nor about Olympia, where the blind brokers promenade under numbered clouds. Knowing things would not help these children. But *wanting*—"

He was unique. He had wanted to return to Mizzer. He had wanted to return beyond all dreams of blood and revenge. He had wanted things fiercely, wildly, so that even if he could not get them, he zig-zagged the galaxy in search of them.

T'ruth was speaking to him again, urgently and softly, but not in so low a voice that the others in the room could not hear.

"And what, Casher O'Neill, should I give them from you?"

"My emotional structure. My determination. My desire. Nothing else. Give them that and throw them back into the winds. Perhaps if they want something fiercely enough, they will grow up to find out what it is."

There was a soft murmur of approval around the room.

T'ruth hesitated a moment and then nodded. "You answered, Casher. You answered quickly and perceptively. Bring seven helmets, Eunice. Stay here, doctor."

Eunice, the forgetty, left, taking two robots with her.

"A chair," said T'ruth to no one in particular. "For him."

A large powerful underman pushed his way through the crowd and dragged a chair to the end of the room.

T'ruth gestured that Casher should sit in it.

She stood in front of him. *Strange,* thought Casher, *that she should be a great lady and still a little girl.* How would he ever find a girl like her? He was not even afraid of the mystery of the Fish, or the image of the man on two pieces of wood. He no longer dreaded space-three, where so many travelers had gone in and so few had come out. He felt safe, comforted by her wisdom and authority. He felt that he would never see the likes of this again—a child running a planet and doing it well; a half-dead man surviving through the endless devotion of his maidservant; a fierce woman hypnotist living on with all the anxieties and angers of humanity gone, but with the skill and obstinacy of turtle genes to sustain her in her re-imprinted form.

"I can guess what you are thinking," said T'ruth, "but we have already said the things that we had to say. I've peeped your mind a dozen times and I know that you want to go back to Mizzer so bad that space-three will spit you out right at the ruined fort where the big turn of the Seventh Nile begins. In my own way I love you, Casher, but I could not keep you here without turning you into a forgetty and making you a servant to my master. You know what always comes first with me, and always will."

"Madigan."

"Madigan," she answered, and with her voice the name itself was a prayer.

Eunice came back with the helmets.

"When we are through with these, Casher, I'll have them take you to the conditioning room. Good-bye, my might-have-been!"

In front of everyone, she kissed him full on the lips.

He sat in the chair, full of patience and contentment. Even as his vision blacked out, he could see the thin light sheath of a smock on the girlish figure, he could remember the tender laughter lurking in her smile.

In the last instant of his consciousness, he saw that another figure had joined the crowd—the tall old man with the worn bathrobe, the faded blue eyes, the thin yellow hair. Murray Madigan had risen from his private-life-in-death and had come to see the last of Casher O'Neill. He did not look weak, nor foolish. He looked like a great man, wise and strange in ways beyond Casher's understanding.

There was the touch of T'ruth's little hand on his arm and everything became a velvety cluttered dark quiet inside his own mind.

∾ XIV ∾

When he awoke, he lay naked and sunburned under the hot sky of Mizzer. Two soldiers with medical patches were rolling him onto a canvas litter.

"Mizzer!" he cried to himself. His throat was too dry to make a sound. "I'm home."

Suddenly the memories came to him and he scrabbled and snatched at them, seeing them dissolve within his mind before he could get paper to write them down.

Memory: there was the front hall, himself getting ready to sleep in the chair, with the old giant of Murray Madigan at the edge of the crowd and the tender light touch of T'ruth—his girl, his girl, now uncountable light-years away—putting her hand on his arm.

Memory: there was another room, with stained glass pictures and incense, and the weepworthy scenes of a great life shown in frescoes around the wall. There were the two pieces of wood and man in pain nailed to them. But Casher knew that scattered and coded through his mind, there was the ultimate and undefeatable wisdom of the Sign of the Fish. He knew he could never fear fear again.

Memory: there was a gaming table in a bright room, with the wealth of a thousand worlds being raked toward him. He was a woman, strong, big-busted, bejewelled, and proud. He was Agatha Madigan, winning at the games.

(*That must have come,* he thought, *when they printed me with T'ruth.*) And in that mind of the Hechizera, which was now his own mind, too, there was clear sure knowledge of how he could win men and women, officers and soldiers, even underpeople and robots, to his cause without a drop of blood or word of anger.

The man, lifting him on the litter, made red waves of heat and pain roll over him.

He heard one of them say, "Bad case of burn. Wonder how he lost his clothes."

The words were matter-of-fact; the comment was nothing special; but the cadence, that special cadence, was the true speech of Mizzer.

As they carried him away, he remembered the face of Rankin Meiklejohn, enormous eyes staring with inward despair over the brim of a big glass. That was the Administrator. On Henriada. That was the man who sent me past Ambiloxi to Beauregard at two seventy-five in the morning. The litter jolted a little.

He thought of the wet marshes of Henriada and knew that soon he would never remember them again. The worms of the tornadoes creeping up to the edge of the estate. The mad wise face of John Joy Tree.

Space-three? Space-three? Already, even now, he could not remember how they had put him into space-three.

And space-three itself—

All the nightmares which mankind has ever had pushed into Casher's mind. He twisted once in agony, just as the litter reached a medical military cart. He saw a girl's face—what *was* her name?—and then he slept.

∾ XV ∾

Fourteen Mizzer days later, the first test came.

A doctor colonel and an intelligence colonel, both in the workaday uniform of Colonel Wedder's Special Forces, stood by his bed.

"Your name is Casher O'Neill and we do not know how your body fell among the skirmishers," the doctor was saying, roughly and emphatically. Casher O'Neill turned his head on the pillow and looked at the man.

"Say something more!" he whispered to the doctor.

The doctor said, "You are a political intruder and we do not know how you got mixed up among our troops. We do not even know how you got back among the people of this planet. We found you on the Seventh Nile."

The intelligence colonel, standing beside him, nodded agreement.

"Do you think the same thing, Colonel?" whispered Casher O'Neill to the intelligence colonel.

"I ask questions. I don't answer them," said the man gruffly.

Casher felt himself reaching for their minds with a kind of fingertip which he did not know he had. It was hard to put into ordinary words, but it felt as though someone had said to him, Casher: "That one is vulnerable at the left forefront area of his consciousness, but the other one is well armored and must be reached through the mid-brain." Casher was not afraid of revealing anything by his expression. He was too badly burned and in too much pain to show nuances of meaning on his face. (Somewhere he had heard of the wild story of the Hechizera of Gonfalon! Somewhere endless storms boiled across ruined marshes under a cloudy yellow sky! But where, when, what was that . . . ? He could not take time off for memory. He had to fight for his life.)

"Peace be with you," he whispered to both of them.

"Peace be with you," they responded in unison, with some surprise.

"Lean over me, please," said Casher, "so that I do not have to shout."

They stood stock straight.

Somewhere in the resources of his own memory and intelligence, Casher found the right note of pleading which could ride his voice like a carrier wave and make them do as he wished.

"This is Mizzer," he whispered.

"Of course this is Mizzer," snapped the intelligence colonel, "and you are Casher O'Neill. What are you doing here?"

"Lean over, gentlemen," he said softly, lowering his voice so that they could barely hear him.

This time, they did lean over.

His burned hands reached for their hands. The officers noticed it, but since he was sick and unarmed, they let him touch them.

Suddenly he felt their minds glowing in his as brightly as if he had swallowed their gleaming, thinking brains at a single gulp.

He spoke no longer.

He *thought* at them—torrential, irresistible thought.

I am not Casher O'Neill. You will find his body in a room, four doors down. I am the civilian Bindaoud.

The two colonels stared, breathing heavily.

Neither said a word.

Casher went on: "Our fingerprints and records have gotten mixed. Give me the fingerprints and papers of the dead Casher O'Neill. Bury him then, quietly, but with honor. Once he loved your leader and there is no point in stirring up wild rumors about returns from out of space. I am Bindaoud. You will find my records in your front office. I am not a soldier. I am a civilian technician doing studies on the salt in blood chemistry under field conditions. You have heard me, gentlemen. You hear me now. You will hear me always. But you will not remember this, gentlemen, when you awaken. I am sick. You can give me water and a sedative."

They still stood, enraptured by the touch of his tight burned hands.

Casher O'Neill said, "Awaken."

Casher O'Neill let go their hands.

The medical colonel blinked and said amiably, "You'll be better, mister and doctor Bindaoud. I'll have the orderly bring you water and a sedative."

To the other officer he said, "I have an interesting corpse four doors down. I think you had better see it."

Casher O'Neill tried to think of the recent past, but the blue light of Mizzer was all around him, the sand-smell, the sound of horses galloping. For a moment, he thought of a big child's blue dress and he did not know why he almost wept.

On the Sand Planet

This is the story of the sand planet itself, Mizzer, which had lost all hope when the tyrant Wedder imposed the reign of terror and virtue. And its liberator, Casher O'Neill—of whom strange things were told, from the day of blood in which he fled from his native city of Kaheer, until he came back to end the shedding of blood for all the rest of his years.

Everywhere that Casher had gone, he had had only one thought in his mind—deliverance of his home country from the tyrants whom he himself had let slip into power when they had conspired against his uncle, the unspeakable Kuraf. He never forgot, whether waking or sleeping. He never forgot Kaheer itself along the First Nile, where the horses raced on the turf with the sand nearby. He never forgot the blue skies of his home and the great dunes of the desert between one Nile and the others. He remembered the freedom of a planet built and dedicated to freedom. He never forgot that the price of blood is blood, that the price of freedom is fighting, that the risk of fighting is death. But he was not a fool. He was willing, if he had to, to risk his own death, but he wanted odds on the battle which would not merely snare him home, like a rabbit to be caught in a steel trap, by the police of the dictator Wedder.

And then, he met the solution of his crusade without knowing it at first. He had come to the end of all things, all problems, all worries. He had also come to the end of all ordinary hope. He met T'ruth. Now her subtle powers belonged to Casher O'Neill, to do with as he pleased.

It pleased him to return to Mizzer, to enter Kaheer itself, and to confront Wedder.

Why should he not come? It was his home and he thirsted for revenge. More than revenge he hungered for justice. He had lived many years for this hour and this hour came.

He entered the north gate of Kaheer.

∾ | ∾

Casher walked into Mizzer wearing the uniform of a medical technician in Wedder's own military service. He had assumed the appearance and the name of a dead man named Bindaoud. Casher walked with nothing more than his hands as weapons, and his hands swung freely at the end of his arms. Only the steadfastness of his feet, the resolute grace with which he took each step, betrayed his purpose. The crowds in the street saw him pass but they did not see him. They looked at a man and they did not realize that they saw their own history going step by step through their various streets. Casher O'Neill had entered the city of Kaheer; he knew that he was being followed. He could feel it.

He glanced around.

He had learned in his many years of fighting and struggle, on strange planets, countless rules of unremembered hazards. To be alert, he knew what this was. It was a suchesache. The suchesache at the moment had taken the shape of a small witless boy, some eight years old, who had two trails of stained mucus pouring down from his nostrils, who had forever-open lips ready to call with the harsh bark of idiocy, who had eyes that did not focus right. Casher O'Neill knew that this was a boy and not a boy. It was a hunting and searching device often employed by police lords when they presumed to make themselves into kings or tyrants, a device which flitted from shape to shape, from child to butterfly or bird, which moved with the suchesache and watched the victim; watching, saying nothing, following. He hated the suchesache and was tempted to throw all the powers of his strange mind at it so that the boy might die and the machine hidden within it might perish. But he knew that this would lead to a cascade of fire and splashing of blood. He had already seen blood in Kaheer long ago; he had no wish to see it in the city again.

Instead he stopped the pacing which had been following his cadenced walk through the street. He turned calmly and kindly and looked at the boy, and he said to the boy and to the hideous machine within the boy, "Come along with me; I'm going straightway to the palace and you would like to see that."

The machine, confronted, had no further choice.

The idiot boy put his hand in Casher's hand and somehow or other Casher O'Neill managed to resume the rolling deliberate march which had marked so many of his years, while keeping a grip on the hand of the demented child who skipped beside him. Casher could still feel the machine watching him from within the eyes of the boy. He did not care; he was not afraid of guns; he could stop them. He was not afraid of poison; he could resist it. He was not afraid of hypnotism; he could take it in and spit it back. He was not afraid of fear; he had been on Henriada. He had come home through space-three. There was nothing left to fear.

Straightway went he to the palace. The midday gleamed in the bright yellow sun which rode the skies of Kaheer. The whitewashed walls in the arabesque design stayed as they had been for thousands of years. Only at the door was he challenged, but the sentry hesitated as Casher spoke: "I am Bindaoud, loyal servant to Colonel Wedder, and this is a child of the streets whom I propose to heal in order to show our good Colonel Wedder a fair demonstration of my powers."

The sentry said something into a little box which sat in the wall.

Casher passed freely. The suchesache trotted beside him. As he went through the corridors, laid with rich rugs, military and civilians moving back and forth, he felt happy. This was not the palace of Wedder, though Wedder lived in it. It was his own palace. He, Casher, had been born in it. He knew it. He knew every corridor.

The changes of the years were very few. Casher

turned left into an open courtyard. He smelled the smell of salt water and the sand and the horses nearby. He sighed a little at the familiarity of it, the good and kind welcome. He turned right again and ascended long, long stairs. Each step was carpeted in a different design.

His uncle Kuraf had stood at the head of these very stairs while men and women, boys and girls were brought to him to become toys of his evil pleasures. Kuraf had been too fat to walk down these stairs to greet them. He always let the captives come up to himself and to his den of pleasures. Casher reached the top of the stairs and turned left.

This was no den of pleasures now.

It was the office of Colonel Wedder. He, Casher, had reached it.

How strange it was to reach this office, this target of all his hopes, this one fevered pinpoint in all the universe for which his revenge had thirsted until he thought himself mad. He had thought of bombing this office from outer space, or of cutting it with the thin arc of a laser beam, or of poisoning it with chemicals, or of assaulting it with troops. He had thought of pouring fire on this building, or water. He had dreamed of making Mizzer free—even at the price of the lovely city of Kaheer itself—by finding a small asteroid somewhere and crashing it, in an interplanetary tragedy, directly into the city itself. And the city, under the roar of that impact, would have blazed into thermonuclear incandescence and would have become a poison lake at the end of the Twelve Niles. He had thought of a thousand ways of entering the city and of destroying the city, merely in order to destroy Wedder.

Now he was here. So too was Wedder.

Wedder did not know that he, Casher O'Neill, had come back.

Even less did Wedder know who Casher O'Neill had become, the master of space, the traveler who traveled without ships, the vehicle for devices stranger than any mind on Mizzer had ever conceived.

Very calm, very relaxed, very quiet, very assured, the doom which was Casher O'Neill walked into the antechamber of Wedder. Very modestly, he asked for Wedder.

The dictator happened to be free.

He had changed little since Casher last saw him, a little older, a little fatter, a little wiser—all these perhaps. Casher was not sure. Every cell and filament in his living body had risen to the alert. He was ready to do the work for which the light-years had ached, for which the worlds had turned, and he knew that within an instant it would be done. He confronted Wedder, gave Wedder a modest assured smile.

"Your servant, the technician Bindaoud, sir and colonel," said Casher O'Neill. Wedder looked at him strangely. He reached out his hand, and, even as their hands touched, Wedder said the last words he would ever say on his own.

Within that handclasp, Wedder spoke again and his voice was strange: "Who are you?"

Casher had dreamed that he would say, "I am Casher O'Neill come back from unimaginable distances to punish you," or that he would say, "I am Casher O'Neill and I have ridden starlanes for years upon years to find your destruction." Or he had even thought that he might say, "Surrender or die, Wedder, your time has come." Sometimes he had dreamed he would say, "Here, Wedder," and then show him the knife with which to take his blood.

Yet this was the climax and none of these things occurred.

The idiot boy with the machine within it stood at ease.

Casher O'Neill merely held Wedder's hand and said quite simply, "Your friend."

As he said that, he searched back and forth. He could feel inner eyes within his own head, eyes which did not move within the sockets of his face, eyes which he did not have and with which he could nevertheless see. These were the eyes of his perception. Quickly, he adjusted the anatomy of Wedder, working kinesthetically, squeezing an artery there, pinching off a gland here. Here, harden the tissue, through which the secretions of a given endocrine material had to come. In less time than it would take an ordinary doctor to describe the process, he had changed Wedder. Wedder had been tuned down like a radio with dials realigned, like a spaceship with its locksheets reset.

The work which Casher had done was less than any pilot does in the course of an ordinary landing; but the piloting he had done was within the biochemical system of Wedder himself. And the changes which he had effected were irreversible.

The new Wedder was the old Wedder. The same mind. The same will, the same personality. Yet its permutations were different. And its method of expression already slightly different. More benign. More tolerant. More calm, more human. Even a little corrupt, as he smiled and said, "I remember you, now, Bindaoud. Can you help that boy?"

The supposed Bindaoud ran his hands over the boy. The boy wept with pain and shock for a moment. He wiped his dirty nose and upper lip on his sleeves. His eyes came into focus. His lips compressed. His mind burned brightly as its old worn channels became human instead of idiot. The suchesache machine knew it was out of place and fled for another refuge. The boy, given his brains, but no words, no education yet, stood there and hiccupped with joy.

Wedder said very pleasantly, "That is remarkable. Is it all that you have to show me?"

"All," said Casher O'Neill. "You were not he."

He turned his back on Wedder and did so in perfect safety.

He knew Wedder would never kill another man.

Casher stopped at the door and looked back. He could tell from the posture of Wedder that that which had to be done, had been done: the changes within the man were larger than the man himself. The planet was free and Casher's own work was indeed done. The suddenly frightened child, which had lost the suchesache, followed him out of blind instinct.

The colonels and the staff officers did not know whether to salute or nod when they saw their chief stand at the doorway, and wave with unexpected friendliness at Casher O'Neill as Casher descended the broad carpeted steps, the child stumbling behind him. At the furthest steps, Casher looked one last time at the enemy who had become almost a part of himself. There stood Wedder, the man of blood. And now, he himself, Casher O'Neill, had expunged the blood, had redone the past, and reshaped the future. All Mizzer was heading back to the openness and freedom which it had enjoyed in the time of the old Republic of the Twelve Niles. He walked on, shifting from one corridor to the other and using short-cuts to the courtyards, until he came to the doorway of the palace. The sentry presented arms.

"At ease," said Casher. The man put down his gun.

Casher stood outside the palace, that palace which had been his uncle's, which had been his own, which had really been himself. He felt the clear air of Mizzer. He looked at the clear blue skies which he had always loved. He looked at the world to which he had promised he would return, with justice, with vengeance, with thunder, with power. Thanks to the strange and subtle capacities which he had learned from the turtle-girl, T'ruth, hidden in her own world amid the storm-churned atmosphere of Henriada, he had not needed to fight.

Casher turned to the boy and said, "I am a sword which has been put into its scabbard. I am a pistol with the cartridges dropped out. I am a wirepoint with no battery behind it. I am a man, but I am very empty."

The boy made strangled, confused sounds as though he were trying to think, to become himself, to make up for all the lost time he had spent in idiocy.

Casher acted on impulse. Curiously, he gave to the boy his own native speech of Kaheer. He felt his muscles go tight, shoulders, neck, fingertips, as he concentrated with the arts he had learned in the palace of Beauregard where the girl T'ruth governed almost-forever in the name of Mister and Owner Murray Madigan. He took the arts and memories he sought. He seized the boy roughly but tightly by the shoulders. He peered into frightened crying eyes and then, in a single blast of thought, he gave the boy speech, words, memory, ambition, skills. The boy stood there dazed.

At last the boy spoke and he asked, "Who am I?"

Casher could not answer that one. He patted the child on the shoulder. He said, "Go back to the city and find out. I have other needs. I have to find out who I myself may be. Good-bye and peace be with you."

∽ II ∽

Casher remembered that his mother still lived here. He had often forgotten her. It would have been easier to forget her. Her name was Trihaep, and she had been sister to Kuraf. Where Kuraf had been vicious, she had been virtuous. Where Kuraf had sometimes been grateful, she had been thrifty and shifty. Where Kuraf, with all his evils, had acquired a toleration for men and things and ideas, she remained set on the pattern of thought which her parents had long ago taught her.

Casher O'Neill did something he thought he would never do. He had never really even thought about doing it. It was too simple. He went home.

At the gate of the house, his mother's old servant knew him, despite the change in his face, and she said, with a terrible awe in her voice, "It seems to me that I am looking at Casher O'Neill."

"I use the name Bindaoud," said Casher, "but I am Casher O'Neill. Let me in and tell my mother that I am here."

He went into the private apartment of his mother. The old furniture was still there. The polished bricabrac of a hundred ages, the old paintings and the old mirrors, and the dead people whom he had never known, represented by their pictures and their mementos. He felt just as ill at ease as he felt when he was a small boy, when he had visited the same room, before his uncle came to take him to the palace.

His mother came in. She had not changed.

He half-thought that she would reach out her arms to him, and cry in a deliberately modern passion, "My baby! My precious! Come back to me!"

She did no such thing.

She looked at him coldly as though he were a complete stranger.

She said to him, "You don't look like my son, but I suppose that you are. You have made trouble enough in your time. Are you making trouble now?"

"I make no malicious trouble, Mother, and I never have," said Casher, "no matter what you may think of me. I did what I had to do. I did what was right."

"Betraying your uncle was right? Letting down our family was right? Disgracing us all was right? You must be a fool to talk like this. I heard that you were a wanderer, that you had great adventures, and had seen many worlds. You don't sound any different to me. You're an old man. You almost seem as old as I do. I had a baby once, but how could that be you? You are an enemy of the house of

Kuraf O'Neill. You're one of the people who brought it down in blood. But they came from outside with their principles and their thoughts and their dreams of power. And you stole from inside like a cur. You opened the door and you let in ruin. Who are you that I should forgive you?"

"I do not ask your forgiveness, Mother," said Casher. "I do not even ask your understanding. I have other places to go and other things yet to do. May peace be upon you."

She stared at him, said nothing.

He went on, "You will find Mizzer a more pleasant place to live in, since I talked to Wedder this morning."

"You talked to Wedder?" cried she. "And he did not kill you?"

"He did not know me."

"Wedder did not know you?"

"I assure you, Mother, he did not know me."

"You must be a very powerful man, my son. Perhaps you can repair the fortune of the house of Kuraf O'Neill after all the harm you have done, and all the heartbreak you brought to my brother. I suppose you know your wife's dead?"

"I had heard that," said Casher. "I hope she died instantly in an accident and without pain."

"Of course it was an accident. How else do people die these days? She and her husband tried out one of those new boats, and it overturned."

"I'm sorry, I wasn't there."

"I know that. I know that perfectly well, my son. You were outside there, so that I had to look up at the stars with fear. I could look up in the sky and stare for the man who was my son lurking up there with blood and ruin. With vengeance upon vengeance heaped upon all of us, just because he thought he knew what was right. I've been afraid of you for a long long time, and I thought if I ever met you again I would fear you with my whole heart. You don't quite seem to be what I expected, Casher. Perhaps I can like you. Perhaps I can even love you as a mother should. Not that it matters. You and I are too old now."

"I'm not working on that kind of mission any longer, Mother. I have been in this old room long enough and I wish you well. But I wish many other people well, too. I have done what I had to do. Perhaps I had better say good-bye, and much later perhaps, I will come back and see you again. When both of us know more about what we have to do."

"Don't you even want to see your daughter?"

"Daughter?" said Casher O'Neill. "Do I have a daughter?"

"Oh, poor fool, you. Didn't you even find that out after you left? She bore your child, all right. She even went through the old-fashioned business of a natural birth. The child even looks something like the way you used to look. Matter of fact, she's rather arrogant, like you. You can call on her if you want to. She lives in the house which is just outside the square in Golden Laut in the leather workers' area. Her husband's name is Ali Ali. Look her up if you want to."

She extended a hand. Casher took the hand as though she had been a queen. And he kissed the cool fingers. As he looked her in the face, here, too, he brought his skills from Henriada in place. He surveyed and felt her personally as though he were a surgeon of the soul, but in this case there was nothing for him to do. This was not a dynamic personality struggling and fighting and moving against the forces of life and hope and disappointment. This was something else, a person set in life, immobile, determined, rigid even for a man with healing arts who could destroy a fleet with his thoughts or who could bring an idiot to normality by mere command. He could see that this was a case beyond his powers.

He patted the old hand affectionately and she smiled warmly at him, not knowing what it meant. "If anyone asks," said Casher, "the name I have been using is that of the Doctor Bindaoud. Bindaoud the technician. Can you remember that, Mother?"

"Bindaoud the technician," she echoed, as she led him out the door to walk in the street.

Within twenty minutes he was knocking at his daughter's door.

∽ III ∽

The daughter herself answered the door. She flung it open. She looked at the strange man, surveyed him from head to heels. She noted the medical insignia on his uniform. She noted his mark of rank. She appraised him shrewdly, quickly, and she knew he had no business there in the quarters of the leather workers.

"Who are you?" she sang out, quickly and clearly.

"In these hours and at this time, I pass under the name of the expert Bindaoud, a technician and medical man back from the special forces of Colonel Wedder. I'm just on leave, you see, but sometime later, madam, you might find out who I really am, and I thought you better hear it from my lips. I'm your father."

She did not move. The significant thing is that she did not move at all. Casher studied her and could see the cast of his own bones in the shape of her face, could see the length of his own fingers repeated in her hands. He had sensed that the storms of duty which had blown him from sorrow to sorrow, the wind of conscience which had kept alive his dreams of vengeance, had turned into something very different in her. It, too, was a force, but not the kind of force he understood.

"I have children now and I would just as soon you not meet them. As a matter of fact, you have never done me a good deed except to beget me. You have never done me an ill deed except to threaten my life from beyond the stars. I am tired of you and I am tired of everything you were or might have been. Let's forget it. Can't you go your way and let me be? I may be your daughter, but I can't help that."

"As you wish, madam. I have had many adventures, and I do not propose to tell them to you. I can see quickly enough that you have what is seemingly a good life, and I hope that my deeds this morning in the palace will have made it better. You'll find out soon enough. Good-bye."

The door closed upon him and he walked back through the sun-drenched market of the leather workers. There were golden hides there. Hides of animals which had then been artfully engraved with very fine strips of beaten gold so that they gleamed in the sunlight. Casher looked upward and around.

Where do I go now? thought he. *Where do I go when I've done everything I had to do? When I've loved every-one I have wanted to love, when I have been everything I have had to be? What does a man with a mission do when the mission is fulfilled? Who can be more hollow than a victor? If I had lost, I could still want revenge. But I haven't. I've won. And I've won nothing. I've wanted nothing for my self from this dear city. I want nothing from this dear world. It's not in my power to give it or to take it. Where do I go when I have nowhere to go? What do I become when I am not ready for death and I have no reason whatsoever for life?*

There sprang into his mind the memory of the world of Henriada with the twisting snakes of the little tornadoes. He could see the slender, pale, hushed face of the girl T'ruth and he remembered at last that which it was which she had held in her hand. It was the magic. It was the secret sign of the Old Strong Religion. There was the man forever dying nailed to two pieces of wood. It was the mystery behind the civilization of all these stars. It was the thrill of the First Forbidden One, the Second Forbidden One, the Third Forbidden One. It was the mystery on which the robot, rat, and Copt agreed when they came back from space-three. He knew what he had to do.

He could not find himself because there was no himself to be found. He was a used tool. A discarded vessel. He was a shard tossed on the ruins of time, and yet he was a man with eyes and brains to think and with many unaccustomed powers.

He reached into the sky with his mind, calling for a public flying machine. "Come and get me," he said, and the great winged birdlike machine came soaring over the rooftops and dropped gently into the square.

"I thought I heard you call, sir."

Casher reached into his pocket and took out his imaginary pass signed by Wedder, authorizing him to use all the vehicles of the republic in the secret service of the regime of Colonel Wedder. The sergeant recognized the pass and almost popped out his eyes in respect.

"The Ninth Nile, can you reach it with this machine?"

"Easily," said the sergeant. "But you better get some shoes first. Iron shoes because the ground there is mostly volcanic glass."

"Wait here for me," said Casher. "Where can I get the shoes?"

"Two streets over and better get two water bottles, too."

∾ IV ∾

Within a matter of minutes he was back. The sergeant watched him fill the bottles in the fountain. He looked at his medical insignia without doubt and showed him how to sit on the cramped emergency seat inside the great machine bird. They snapped their seat belts and the sergeant said, "Ready?" and the ornithopter spread out its wings, and flew into the air.

The huge wings were like oars digging into a big sea. They rose rapidly and soon Kaheer was below them, the fragile minarets and the white sand with the racing turf along the river, and the green fields, and even the pyramids copied from something on Ancient Earth.

The operator did something and the machine flew harder. The wings, although far slower than any jet aircraft, were steady, and they moved with respectable speed across the broad dry desert. Casher still wore his decimal watch from Henriada, and it was two whole decimal hours before the sergeant turned around, pinched him gently awake from the drowse into which he had fallen, shouted something, and pointed down. A strip of silver matched by two strips of green wandering through a wilderness of black, gleaming glittering black, with the beige sands of the everlasting desert stretching everywhere in the distance.

"The Ninth Nile?" shouted Casher. The sergeant smiled the smile of a man who had heard nothing but wanted to be agreeable, and the ornithopter dived with a lurching suddenness toward the twist in the river. A few buildings became visible. They were modest and small. Verandas, perhaps, for the use of a visitor. Nothing more.

It was not the sergeant's business to query anyone on secret orders from Colonel Wedder. He showed the cramped Casher O'Neill how to get out of the ornithopter, and then, standing in his seat, saluted, and said, "Anything else, sir?"

Casher said, "No. I'll make my own way. If they ask you who I was, I am the Doctor Bindaoud and you have left me here under orders."

"Right, sir," said the sergeant, and the great machine reached out its gleaming wings, flapped, spiraled, climbed, became a dot, and vanished.

Casher stood there alone. Utterly alone. For many years he had been supported by a sense of purpose, by a drive to do something, and now the drives and the purpose were gone, and his life was gone, and the use of his future was gone, and he had nothing. All he had was the ultimate imagination, health, and great skills. These were not what he wanted. He wanted the liberation of all Mizzer. But he had gotten that, so what was it? He almost stumbled towards one of the nearby buildings.

A voice spoke up. A woman's voice. The friendly voice of an old woman.

Very unexpectedly, she said, "I've been waiting for you, Casher; come on in."

∼ V ∼

He stared at her. "I've seen you," he said. "I've seen you somewhere. I know you well. You've affected my fate. You did something to me and yet I don't know who you are. How could you be here to meet me when I didn't know I was coming?"

"Everything in its time," said the woman. "With a time for everything and what you need now is rest. I'm D'alma, the dog-woman from Pontoppidan. The one who washed the dishes."

"Her," cried he.

"Me," she said.

"But you—but you—how did you get here?"

"I got here," she said. "Isn't that obvious?"

"Who sent you?"

"You're part of the way to the truth," she said. "You might as well hear a little more of it. I was sent here by a lord whose name I will never mention. A lord of the underpeople. Acting from Earth. He sent out another dog-woman to take my place. And he had me shipped here as simple baggage. I worked in the hospital where you recovered and I read your mind as you got well. I knew what you would do to Wedder and I was pretty sure that you would come up here to the Ninth Nile, because that is the road that all searchers must take."

"Do you mean," he said, "that you know the road to—" He hesitated and then plunged into his question, "—the Holy of Unholies, the Thirteenth Nile?"

"I don't see that it means anything, Casher. Except that you'd better take off those iron shoes; you don't need them yet. You'd better come in here. Come on in."

He pushed the beaded curtains aside and entered the bungalow. It was a simple frontier official dwelling. There were cots hither and yon, a room to the rear which seemed to be hers; a dining room to the right and there were papers, a viewing machine, cards, and games on the table. The room itself was astonishingly cool.

She said, "Casher, you've got to relax. And that is the hardest of all things to do. To relax, when you had a mission for many many years."

"I know it," said he. "I know it. But knowing it and doing it aren't the same things."

"Now you can do it," said D'alma.

"Do what?" he snapped.

"Relax, as we were talking about. All you have to do here is to have some good meals. Just sleep a few times, swim in the river if you want to. I have sent everyone away except myself, and you and I shall have this house. And I am an old woman, not even a human being. You're a man, a true man, who's conquered a thousand worlds. And who has finally triumphed over Wedder. I think we'll get along. And when you're ready for the trip, I'll take you."

The days did pass as she said they would. With insistent but firm kindness, she made him play games with her: simple, childish games with dice and cards. Once or twice he tried to hypnotize her. To throw the dice his own way. He changed the cards in her hand. He found that she had very little telepathic offensive power, but that her defenses were superb. She smiled at him whenever she caught him playing tricks. And his tricks failed.

With this kind of atmosphere he really began to relax. She was the woman who had spelled happiness for him on Pontoppidan when he didn't know what happiness was. When he had abandoned the lovely Genevieve to go on with his quest for vengeance.

Once he said to her, "Is that old horse still alive?"

"Of course he is," she said. "That horse will probably outlive you and me. He thinks he's on Mizzer by galloping around a patrol capsule. Come on back; it's your turn to play."

He put down the cards, and slowly the peace, the simplicity, the reassuring, calm sweetness of it all stole over him and he began to perceive the nature of her therapy. It was to do nothing but slow him down. He was to meet himself again.

It may have been the tenth day, perhaps it was the fourteenth, that he said to her, "When do we go?"

She said, "I've been waiting for that question and we're ready now. We go."

"When?"

"Right now. Put on your shoes. You won't need them very much," she said, "but you might need them where we land. I am taking you part way there."

Within a few minutes, they went out into the yard. The river in which he had swum lay below. A shed, which he did not remember having noticed before, lay at the far end of the yard. She did something to the door, removing a lock, and the door flung open. And she pulled out a skeletonized ornithopter motor, wings, tails. The body was just a bracket of metal. The source of power was as usual an ultra-miniaturized, nuclear-powered battery. Instead of seats, there were two tiny saddles, like the saddles used in the bicycles of old, old Earth which he had seen in museums.

"You can fly that?" he asked.

"Of course I can fly it. It's better than going 200 miles over broken glass. We are leaving civilization now. We are leaving everything that was on any map. We are flying directly to the Thirteenth Nile, as you well knew it should be that."

"I knew that," he said. "I never expected to reach it so soon. Does this have anything to do with that Sign of the Fish you were talking about?"

"Everything, Casher. Everything. But everything in its place. Climb in behind me." He sat on top of the ornithopter, and this one ran down the yard on its tall, graceful mechanical legs before the flaps of its wings put it in the air. She was a better pilot than the sergeant had been; she soared more and beat the wings less. She flew over country that he, a native of Mizzer, had never dreamed about.

✧✧✧

They came to a city gaudy in color. He could see large fires burning alongside the river, and brightly painted people with their hands lifted in prayer. He saw temples and strange gods in them. He saw markets with goods, which he never thought to see marketed.

"Where are we?" he asked.

D'alma said, "This is the City of Hopeless Hope." She put the ornithopter down and, as they climbed out of the saddles, it lifted itself into the air and flew back, in the direction from whence they had come. "You are staying with me?" asked Casher.

"Of course I am. I was sent to be with you."

"What for?"

"You are important to all the worlds, Casher, not just Mizzer. By the authority of the friends I have, they have sent me here to help you."

"But what do you get out of it?"

"I get nothing, Casher. I find my own destruction, perhaps, but I will accept that. Even the loss of my own hope if it only moves you further on in your voyage. Come, let us enter the City of Hopeless Hope."

∽ VI ∽

They walked through the strange streets. Almost everyone in the streets seemed to be engaged in the practice of religion. The stench of the burning dead was all round them. Talismans, luck charms, and funeral supplies were in universal abundance.

Casher said, speaking rather quietly to D'alma, "I never knew there was anything like this on any civilized planet."

"Obviously," she replied, "there must be many people who believe in worry about death; there are many who do know about this place. Otherwise there would not be the throngs here. These are the people who have the wrong hope and who go to no place at all, who find under this earth and under the stars their final fulfillment. These are the ones who are so sure that they are right that they never will be right. We must pass through them quickly, Casher, lest we, too, start believing."

No one impeded their passage in the streets, although many people paused to see that a soldier, even a medical soldier, in uniform, had the audacity to come there.

They were even more surprised that an old hospital attendant who seemed to be an off-world dog walked along beside him.

"We cross the bridge now, Casher, and this bridge is the most terrible thing I've ever seen, whereas now we are going to come to the Jwindz, and the Jwindz oppose you and me and everything you stand for."

"Who are the Jwindz?" asked Casher.

"The Jwindz are the perfect ones. They are perfect in this earth. You will see soon enough."

∾ VII ∾

As they crossed the bridge, a tall, blithe police official, clad in a neat black uniform, stepped up to them and said, "Go back. People from your city are not welcome here."

"We are not from that city," said D'alma. "We are travelers."

"Where are you bound?" asked the police official.

"We are bound for the source of the Thirteenth Nile."

"Nobody goes there," said the guard.

"*We* are going there," said D'alma.

"By what authority?"

Casher reached into his pocket and took out a genuine card. He had remade one, from the memories he had retained in his mind. It was an all-world pass, authorized by the Instrumentality.

The police official looked at it and his eyes widened.

"Sir and master, I thought you were merely one of Wedder's men. You must be someone of great importance. I will notify the scholars in the Hall of Learning at the middle of the city. They will want to see you. Wait here. A vehicle will come."

D'alma and Casher O'Neill did not have long to wait. She said nothing at all in this time. Her air of good humor and competence ebbed perceptibly. She was distressed by the cleanliness and perfection around her, by the silence, by the dignity of the people.

When the vehicle came, it had a driver, as correct, as smooth, and as courteous as the guard at the bridge. He opened the door and waved them in. They climbed in and they sped noiselessly through the well-groomed streets: houses, each one in immaculate taste; trees, planted the way in which trees should be planted.

In the center square of the city, they stopped. The driver got out, walked around the vehicle, opened their door.

He pointed at the archway of the large building and he said, "They are expecting you."

Casher and D'alma walked up the steps reluctantly. She was reluctant because she had some sense of what this place was, a special dwelling for quiet doom and arrogant finality. He was reluctant because he could feel that in every bone of her body she resented this place. And he resented it, too.

They were led through the archway and across a patio to a large, elegant conference room.

Within the room a circular table had already been set in preparation of a meal.

Ten handsome men rose to greet them.

The first one said, "You are Casher O'Neill. You are the wanderer. You are the man dedicated to this planet and we appreciate what you have done for us, even though the power of Colonel Wedder never reached here."

"Thank you," said Casher. "I am surprised to hear that you know of me."

"That's nothing," said the man. "We know of everyone. And you, woman," said the same man to D'alma, "you know full well that we never entertain women here. And you are the only underperson in this city. A dog at that. But in honor of our guest we shall let you pass. Sit down if you wish. We want to talk to you."

A meal was served. Little squares of sweet unknown meat, fresh fruits, bits of melon, chased with harmonious drinks which cleared the mind and stimulated it, without intoxicating or drugging.

The language of their conversations was clear and

elevated. All questions were answered swiftly, smoothly, and with positive clarity.

Finally, Casher was moved to ask, "I do not seem to have heard of you, Jwindz; who are you?"

"We are the perfect ones," said the oldest Jwindz. "We have all the answers; there is nothing else left to find."

"How do you get here?" said Casher.

"We are selected from many worlds."

"Where are your families?"

"We don't bring them with us."

"How do you keep out intruders?"

"If they are good, they wish to stay. If they are not good, we destroy them."

Casher—still shocked by his experience of fulfilling all his life's work in the confrontation with Wedder—though his life might be at stake, asked casually, "Have you decided yet whether I am perfect enough to join you? Or am I not perfect and to be destroyed?"

The heaviest of all the Jwindz, a tall, portly man, with a great bushy shock of black hair, replied ponderously.

"Sir, you are forcing our decision, but I think that you may be something exceptional. We cannot accept you. There is too much force in you. You may be perfect, but you are more than perfect. We are men, sir, and I do not think that you are any longer a mere man. You are almost a machine. You are yourself dead people. You are the magic of ancient battles coming to strike among us. We are all of us a little afraid of you, and yet we do not know what to do with you. If you were to stay here a while, if you calmed down, we might give you hope. We know perfectly well what that dog-woman of yours calls our city.

She calls it the City of the Perfect Ones. We just call it Jwindz Jo, in memory of the ancient Rule of the Jwindz, which somewhere once obtained upon old Earth. And therefore, we think that we will neither kill you nor accept you. We think—do we not, gentlemen?—that we will speed you on your way, as we have sped no other traveler. And that we will send you, then, to a place which few people pass. But you have the strength and if you are going to the source of the Thirteenth Nile, you will need it."

"I will need strength?" Casher asked.

The first Jwindz who had met them at the door said, "Indeed you will need strength, if you go to Mortoval. We may be dangerous to the uninitiated. Mortoval is worse than dangerous. It is a trap many times worse than death. But go there if you must."

∞ VIII ∞

Casher O'Neill and D'alma reached Mortoval on a one-wheeled cart, which ran on a high wire past picturesque mountain gorges, soaring over two serrated series of peaks and finally dropping down to another bend in the same river, the illegal and forgotten Thirteenth Nile.

When the vehicle stopped, they got out. No one had accompanied them. The vehicle, held in place by gyroscopes and compasses, felt itself relieved of their weight and hurried home.

This time there was no city: just one great arch. D'alma clung close to him. She even took his arm and pulled it over her shoulder as though she needed protection. She whined a little as they walked up a low hill and finally reached the arch. They walked into the arch and a voice not made of sound cried out to them.

"I am youth and am everything that you have been or ever will be. Know this now before I show you more."

Casher was brave, and this time he was cheerfully hopeless, so he said, "I know who I am. Who are you?"

"I am the force of the Gunung Banga. I am the power of this planet which keeps everyone in this planet and which assures the order which persists among the stars, and promises that the dead shall not walk among the men. And I serve of the fate and the hope of the future. Pass if you think you can."

Casher searched with his own mind and he found what he wanted. He found the memory of a young child, T'ruth, who had been almost a thousand years on the planet of Henriada. A child, soft and gentle on the outside, but wise and formidable and terrible beyond belief, in the powers which she had carried, which had been imprinted upon her.

As he walked through the arch he cast the images of truth here and there. Therefore he was not one person but a multitude. And the machine and the living being which hid behind the machine, the Gunung Banga, obviously could see him and could see D'alma walking through, but the machine was not prepared to recognize whole multitudes of crying throngs.

"Who are you thousands that you should come here now? Who are you multitudes that you should be two people? I sense all of you. The fighters and the ships and the men of blood, the searchers and the forgetters, there's even an Old North Australian renunciant here. And the great Go-Captain Tree, and there are even a couple of men of Old Earth. You are all walking through me. How can I cope with you?"

"Make us, us," said Casher firmly.

"Make you, you," replied the machine. "Make you, you. How can I make you, you, when I do not know who you are, when you flit like ghosts and you confuse my computers? There are too many, I say. There are too many of you. It is ordained that you should pass."

"If it is so ordained, then let us pass." D'alma suddenly stood proud and erect.

They walked on through.

She said, "You got us through." They had indeed passed beyond the arch, and there, beyond the arch, lay a gentle riverside with skiffs pulled up along the beach.

"This seems to be next," said Casher O'Neill.

D'alma nodded. "I'm your dog, master. We go where you think."

They climbed into a skiff. Echoes of tumult followed from the arch.

"Good-bye to troubles," the echoes said. "Had they been people they would have been stopped. But she was a dog and a servant, who had lived many years in the happiness of the Sign of the Fish. And he was a combat-ready man who had incorporated within himself the memories of adversaries and friends, too tumultuous for any scanner to measure, too complex for any computer to assess." The echoes resounded across the river.

There was even a dock on the other side. Casher tied

the skiff to the dock and he helped the dog-woman go
toward the buildings that they saw beyond some trees.

∼ IX ∼

D'Alma said, "I have seen pictures of this place; this is
the Kermesse Dorgeil, and here we may lose our way,
because this is the place where all the happy things of this
world come together, but where the man and the two
pieces of wood never filter through. We shall see no one
unhappy, no one sick, no one unbalanced; everyone will
be enjoying the good things of life; perhaps I will enjoy it,
too. May the Sign of the Fish help me that I not become
perfect too soon."

"You won't be," Casher promised.

At the gate of this city, there was no guard at all. They
walked on past a few people who seemed to be promenad-
ing outside the town. Within the city they approached
what seemed to be a hotel and an inn or a hospital. At any
rate it was a place where many people were fed.

A man came out and said, "Well, this is a strange sight;
I never knew that the Colonel Wedder let his officers get
this far from home, and as for you, woman, you're not
even a human being. You're an odd couple and you're not
in love with each other. Can we do anything for you?"

Casher reached into his pocket and tossed several
credit pieces of five denominations in front of the man.

"Don't these mean anything?" asked Casher.

Catching them in his fingers, the man said, "Oh, we
can use money! We use it occasionally for important

things; we don't need yours. We live well here, and we have a nice life, not like those two places across the river, which stay away from life. All men who are perfect are nothing but talk—Jwindz they call themselves, the perfect ones—well, we're not that perfect. We've got families and good food and good clothes, and we get the latest news from all the worlds."

"News," said Casher. "I thought that was illegal."

"We get anything. You would be surprised at what we have here. It's a very civilized place. Come on in; this is the hotel of the Singing Swans and you can live here as long as you wish. When I say that, I mean it. Our treasure has unusual resources, and I can see that you are unusual people. You are not a medical technician, despite that uniform, and your follower is not a mere dog-underperson or you wouldn't have gotten this far."

They entered a promenade two stories high; little shops lined each side of the corridor with the treasures of all the worlds on exhibit. The prices were marked explaining them, but there was no one in the stalls.

The smell of good food came from a cool dining room in the inn.

"Come into my office and have a drink. My name is Howard."

"That's an old Earth name," said Casher.

"Why shouldn't it be?" asked Howard. "I came here from old Earth. I looked for the best of all places, and it took me a long time to find it. This is it—the Kermesse Dorg,eil. We have nothing here but simple and clean pleasures; we have only those vices which help and support. We accomplish the possible; we reject the impossible. We live life, not death. Our talk is about things and not about ideas. We have nothing but scorn for that city behind you, the City of the Perfect Ones. And we have nothing but pity for the holier than holies far back where they claim to have Hopeless Hope, and practice nothing but evil religion. I passed through those places too, although I had to go around the City of the Perfect Ones. I know what they are and I've come all the way from Earth, and if I have come all the way from old old Earth I should know what this is. You should take my word for it."

"I've been on Earth myself," said Casher, rather dryly. "It's not that unusual."

The man stopped with surprise.

"My name," said Casher, "is Casher O'Neill."

The man halted and then gave him a deep bow.

"If you are Casher O'Neill, you have changed this world; you have come back, my lord and master. Welcome. We are no longer your host. This is your city. What do you wish of us?"

"To look a while, to rest a while, to ask directions for the voyage."

"Directions? Why should anyone want directions away from here? People come here and ask directions from a thousand places to get to Kermesse Dorgeil."

"Let's not argue this now," said Casher. "Show us the rooms, let us clean ourselves up. Two separate rooms."

Howard walked upstairs. With an intricate twist of his hand he unlocked two rooms.

"At your service," he said. "Call me with your voice; I can hear you anywhere in the building."

Casher called once for sleeping gear, toothbrushes,

shaving equipment. He insisted that they send the shampooer, a woman of apparent Earth origin, in to attend to D'alma; and D'alma actually knocked at his door and begged that he not shower her with these attentions.

He said, "You with your deep kindness have helped me so far. I am helping you very little."

They ate a light repast together in the garden just below their two rooms, and then they went to their rooms and slept.

It was only on the morning of the second day that they went with Howard into the city to see what could be found.

Everywhere the city was strong with happiness. The population could not have been very large, twenty or thirty thousand persons at most.

At one point, Casher stopped; he could smell the scorch of ozone in the air. He knew the atmosphere itself had been burned and that meant only one thing, spaceships coming in or going out.

He asked, "Where is the spaceport for Earth?"

Howard looked at him quickly and keenly. "If you were not the lord Casher O'Neill, I'd never tell you. We have a small spaceport there. That is the way that we avoid our traffic with most of Mizzer. Do you need it, sir?"

"Not now," said Casher. "I just wondered where it was." They came to a woman who danced as she sang to the accompaniment of two men with wild archaic guitars. Her feet did not have the laughter of ordinary dance, but they had the positiveness, the compulsion of a meaning.

Howard looked at her appreciatively; he even ran the tip of his tongue across his upper lip.

"She is not yet spoken for," said Howard. "And yet she is a very unusual thing. A resigned ex-lady of the Instrumentality."

"I find that unusual, indeed. What is her name?"

"Celalta," said Howard. "Celalta, the other one. She has been in many worlds, perhaps as many worlds as you have, sir. She's faced dangers like the ones you've faced. And oh, my lord and master, forgive me for saying it, but when I look at her dancing, and I see you looking at her, I can see a little bit into the future; and I can see you both dead together, the winds slowly blowing the flesh off your bones. And your bones anonymous and white, lying two valleys over from this very place."

"That's an odd enough prophecy," said Casher. "Especially from someone who seems not to be poetic. What is that?"

"I seem to see you in the Deep Dry Lake of the Damned Irene. There's a road out of here that goes there and some people, not many, go there, and when they go there, they die. I don't know why," said Howard. "Don't ask me."

D'alma whispered, "That is the road to the Shrine of Shrines. That's the place to the Quel itself. Find out where it starts."

"Where does that road start?" asked Casher.

"Oh, you'll find out; there's nothing you won't find out. Sorry, my lord and master. The road starts just beyond that bright orange roof." He pointed to a roof and then turned back.

Without saying anything more, he clapped his hands at the dancer and she gave him a scornful look. Howard clapped his hands again; she stopped dancing and walked over.

"And what is it you want now, Howard?"

He gave her a deep bow. "My former lady, my mistress, here is the lord and master of this planet, Casher O'Neill."

"I am not really the lord and master," said Casher O'Neill. "I merely would have been if Wedder had not taken the rule away from my uncle."

"Should I care about that?" asked the woman.

Casher smiled back. "I don't see why you should."

"Do you have anything you want to say to me?"

"Yes," said Casher. He reached over and seized her wrist. Her wrist was almost as strong as his.

"You have danced your last dance, madam, at least for the time. You and I are going to a place that this man knows about, and he says that we are going to die there, and our bones will be blown with the wind."

"You give me commands," she cried.

"I give you commands," he said.

"What is your authority?" she asked scornfully.

"Me," he said.

She looked at him, he looked back at her, still holding her wrist.

She said, "I have powers. Don't make me use them."

He said, "I have powers, too; nobody can make me use mine."

"I'm not afraid of you; go ahead."

Fire shot at him as he felt the lunge of her mind

toward his, her attack, her flight for freedom, but he kept her wrist and she said nothing.

But with his mind responding to hers he unfolded the many worlds, the old Earth itself, the gem planet, Olympia of the blind brokers, the storm planet, Henriada, and a thousand other places that most people only knew in stories and dreams. And then, just for a little bit, he showed her who he was, a native of Mizzer who had become a citizen of the Universe. A fighter who had been transformed into a doer. He let her know that in his own mind he carried the powers of T'ruth the turtle-girl, and behind T'ruth herself, he carried the personalities of the Hechizera of Gonfalon. He let her see the ships in the sky turning and twisting as they fought nothing at all, because his mind, or another mind which had become his, had commanded them to.

And then with the shock of a sudden vision, he projected to her the two pieces of wood, the image of a man in pain. And gently, but with the simple rhetoric of profound faith, he pronounced: "This is the call of the First Forbidden One, and the Second Forbidden One, and the Third Forbidden One. This is the symbol of the Sign of the Fish. For this you are going to leave this town, and you are going with me, and it may be that you and I shall become lovers."

Behind him a voice spoke. "And I," said D'alma, "will stay here."

He turned around to her. "D'alma, you've come this far; you've got to come further."

"I can't, my lord. I read my duty as I see it. If the authorities who sent me want me enough, they will send me back to my dishwasher on Pontoppidan, otherwise they will leave me here. I am temporarily beautiful and I'm rich and I'm happy and I don't know what to do with myself, but I know I have seen you as far as I can. May the Sign of the Fish be with you."

Howard merely stood aside, making no attempt to hinder them or to help them.

Celalta walked beside Casher like a wild animal which had never been captured before.

Casher O'Neill never let go of her wrist.

"Do we need food for this trip?" he asked of Howard.

"No one knows what you need."

"Should we take food?"

"I don't see why," said Howard. "You have water. You can always walk back here if you have disappointments. It's really not very far."

"Will you rescue me?"

"If you insist on it," said Howard. "I suppose somewhere people will come out and bring you back, but I don't think you will insist—because that is the Deep Dry Lake of the Damned Irene, and the people who go in there do not want to come out, and do not want to eat, and they do not want to go forward. We have never seen anyone vanish to the other side, but you might make it."

"I am looking," said Casher, "for something which is more than power between the worlds. I am looking for a sphinx that is bigger than the sphinx on old Earth. For weapons which cut sharper than lasers, for forces that move faster than bullets. I am looking for something which will take the power away from me and put the simple humanity back into me. I am looking for something which will be nothing, but a nothing I can serve and can believe in."

"You sound like the right kind of man," said Howard, "for that kind of trip. Go in peace, both of you."

Celalta said, "I do not really know who you are, my lord, master, but I have danced my last dance. I see what you mean. This is the road that leads away from happiness. This is the path which leaves good clothes and warm shops behind. There are no restaurants where we are going, no hotels, no river anymore. There are neither believers nor unbelievers; but there is something that comes out of the soil which makes people die. But if you think, Casher O'Neill, that you can triumph over it, I will go with you. And if you do not think it, I will die with you."

"We are going, Celalta, I didn't know that it was just going to be the two of us, but we are going and we are going now."

∝ X ∝

It was actually less than two kilometers to get over the ridge away from the trees, away from the moisture-laden air along the river, and into a dry, calm valley which had a clean blessed quietness which Casher had never seen before. Celalta was almost gay.

"This, this is the Deep Dry Lake of the Damned Irene?"

"I suppose it is," said Casher, "but I propose to keep on walking. It isn't very big."

As they walked their bodies became burdensome; they carried not only their own weight but the weight of every month of their lives. The decision seemed good to them that they should lie down in the valley and rest amid the skeletons, rest as the others had rested. Celalta became disoriented. She stumbled, and her eyes became unfocused.

Not for nothing had Casher O'Neill learned all the arts of battle of a thousand worlds. Not for nothing had he come through space-three. This valley might have been tempting if already he had not ridden the cosmos on his eyes alone.

He had. He knew the way out. It was merely through. Celalta seemed to come more to life as they reached the top of the ridge. The whole world was suddenly transformed by not more than ten steps. Far behind them, several kilometers, perhaps, there were still visible the last rooftops of the Kermesse Dorg̣eil. Behind them lay the bleaching skeletons, in front—

In front of them was the final source and the mystery, the Quel of the Thirteenth Nile.

∽ XI ∽

There was no sign of a house, but there were fruits and melons and grain growing, and there were deep trees at the edges of caves, and there were here and there signs of people that had been there long ago. There were no signs of present occupancy.

"My lord," said the once-lady Celalta, "my lord," she repeated, "I think this is it."

"But this is nothing," said Casher.

"Exactly. Nothing is victory, nothing is arrival, nowhere is getting there. Don't you see now why she left us?"

"She?" asked Casher.

"Yes, your faithful companion, the dog-woman D'alma."

"No, I don't see it. Why did she leave this to us?"

Celalta laughed. "We're Adam and Eve in a way. It's not up to us to be given a god or to be given a faith. It's up to us to find the power and this is the quietest and last of the searching places. The others were just phantoms, hazards on our route. The best way to find freedom is not to look for it, just as you obtained your utter revenge on Wedder by doing him a little bit of good. Can't you see it, Casher? You have won at last the immense victory that makes all battles seem vain. There is food around us; we can even walk back to the Kermesse Dorg,eil, if we want clothing or company or if we want to hear the news. But, most of all, this is the place in which I feel the presence of the First Forbidden One, the Second Forbidden One, and the Third Forbidden One. We don't need a church for this, though I suppose there are still churches on some planets. What we need is a place to find ourselves and be ourselves and I'm not sure that this chance exists in many other places than this one spot."

"You mean," said Casher, "that everywhere is nowhere?"

"Not quite that," said Celalta. "We have some work to do getting this place in shape, feeding ourselves. Do you know how to cook? Well, I can cook better. We can catch a few things to eat; we can shut ourselves in that cave and then"—and then Celalta smiled, her face more beautiful than he ever expected he would find a face to be—"we have each other."

Casher stood battle-ready, facing the most beautiful

dancer he had ever met. He realized that she had once been a part of the Instrumentality, a governor of worlds, a genuine advisor in the destination of mankind. He did not know what strange motives had caused her to quit authority and to come up to this hard-to-find river, unmarked on maps. He didn't even know why the man Howard should have paired them so quickly: perhaps there was another force. A force behind that dog-woman which had sent him to his final destination.

He looked down at Celalta and then he looked up at the sky, and he said, "Day is ending; I will catch a few of those birds if you know how to cook them. We seem to be a sort of Adam and Eve, and I do not know whether this is paradise or hell. But I know that you are in it with me, and that I can think about you because you ask nothing of me."

"That is true, my lord, I ask nothing of you. I, too, am looking for both of us, not myself alone. I can make a sacrifice for you, but I look for those things which only we two, acting together, can find in this valley."

He nodded in serious agreement.

"Look," she said, "that is the Quel itself, there the Thirteenth Nile comes out of the rocks, and here are the woods below. I seem to have heard of it. Well, we'll have plenty of time. I'll start the fire, but you go catch two of those chickens. I don't even think they're wild birds. I think they are just left over people-chickens that have grown wild since their previous owners left. . . ."

"Or died," said Casher.

"Or died," repeated Celalta. "Isn't that a risk anybody has to take? Let us live, my lord, you and me, and let us find the magic, the deliverance which strange fates have thrown in front of you and me. You have liberated Mizzer, is that not enough? Simply by touching Wedder, you have done what otherwise could have been accomplished at the price of battle and great suffering."

"Thank you," said Casher.

"I was once Instrumentality, my lord, and I know that the Instrumentality likes to do things suddenly and victoriously. When I was there we never accepted defeat, but we never paid anything extra. The shortest route between two points might look like the long way around; it isn't. It's merely the cheapest human way of getting there. Has it ever occurred to you, that the Instrumentality might be rewarding you for what you have done for this planet?"

"I hadn't thought of it," said Casher.

"You hadn't thought of it?" She smiled.

"Well . . ." said Casher, embarrassed and at a loss for words.

"I am a very special kind of woman," said Celalta. "You will be finding that out in the next few weeks. Why else do you think that I would be given to you?"

He did not go to hunt the chickens, not just then. He reached his arms out to her and, with more trust and less fear than he had felt in many years, he held her in his arms, and kissed her on the lips. This time there was no secret reserve in his mind, no promise that after this he would get on with his journey to Mizzer. He had won, his victory was behind him, and in front of him there lay nothing, but this beautiful and powerful place and . . . Celalta.

Three to a Given Star

∽|∽

"Stick your left arm straight forward, Samm," said Folly.

He stretched his arm out.

"I can sense it!" cried Folly. "Now wiggle your fingers!"

Samm wiggled them.

Finsternis said nothing, but both of them caught from his mind, riding clear and wise beside them, a "sense of the situation." His "sense of the situation" could be summed up in the one-word comment, which he did not need to utter:

"Foolishness!"

"It is not foolishness, Finsternis," cried Folly. "Here are the three of us, riding empty space millions of kilometers from nowhere. We were people once, Earth people from Old Earth itself. It is foolish to remember what we used to be? I was a woman once. A beautiful woman. Now I'm this—this thing, bent on a mission of murder and destruction. I used to have hands myself, real hands. Is

659

it wrong for me to enjoy looking at Samm's hands now and then? To think of the past which all three of us have left behind."

Finsternis did not answer; his mind was blank to both of them. There was nothing but space around them, not even much space dust, and the bluish light of Linschoten XV straight ahead. From the third planet of that star they could occasionally hear the cackle and gabble of the man-eaters.

Once again Folly cried to Finsternis, "Is that so wrong, that I should enjoy looking at a hand? Samm has well-shaped hands. I was a person once, and so were you. Did I ever tell you that I was a beautiful woman once?"

She had been a beautiful woman once and now she was the control of a small spaceship which fled across emptiness with two grotesque companions.

She was now a ship only eleven meters long and shaped roughly like an ancient dirigible. Finsternis was a perfect cube, fifty meters to the side, packed with machinery which could blank out a sun and contain its planets until they froze to icy, perpetual death. Samm was a man, but he was a man of flexible steel, two hundred meters high. He was designed to walk on any kind of planet, with any kind of inhabitant, with any kind of chemistry or any kind of gravity. He was designed to bring antagonists, whomever they might be, the message of the power of man. The power of man . . . followed by terror, followed if necessary by death. If Samm failed, Finsternis had the further power of blocking out the sun, Linschoten XV. If either or both failed, Folly had the job of adjusting them so that they could win. If they had no chance of winning, she then had the task of destroying Finsternis and Samm, and then herself.

Their instructions were clear:

"You will not, you will not under any circumstances return. You will not under any conditions turn back toward Earth. You are too dangerous to come anywhere near Earth, ever again. You may live if you wish. If you can. But you must not—repeat *not*—come back. You have your duty. You asked for it. Now you have it. Do not come back. Your forms fit your duty. You will do your duty."

Folly had become a tiny ship, crammed with miniaturized equipment.

Finsternis had become a cube blacker than darkness itself.

Samm had become a man, but a man different from any which had ever been seen on Earth. He had a metal body, copied from the human form down to the last detail. That way the enemies, whoever they might be, would be given a terrible glimpse of the human shape, the human voice. Two hundred meters high he stood, strong and solid enough to fly through space with nothing but the jets on his belt.

The Instrumentality had designed all three of them. Designed them well.

Designed them to meet the crazy menace out beyond the stars, a menace which gave no clue to its technology or origin, but which responded to the signal "man" with the counter-signal, "gabble cackle! eat, eat! man, man! good to eat! cackle gabble! eat, eat!"

That was enough.

The Instrumentality took steps. And the three of

them—the ship, the cube, and the metal giant—sped between the stars to conquer, to terrorize, or to destroy the menace which lived on the third planet of Linschoten XV. Or, if needful, to put out that particular sun.

Folly, who had become a ship, was the most volatile of the three.

She had been a beautiful woman once.

∾ II ∾

"You were a beautiful woman once," Samm had said, some years before. "How did you end up becoming a ship?"

"I killed myself," said Folly. "That's why I took this name—Folly. I had a long life ahead of me, but I killed myself and they brought me back at the last minute. When I found out I was still alive, I volunteered for something adventurous, dangerous. They gave me this. Well, I *asked* for it, didn't I?"

"You asked for it," said Samm gravely. Out in the middle of nothing, surrounded by a tremendous lot of nowhere, courtesy was still the lubricant which governed human relationships. The two of them observed courtesy and kindness toward one another. Sometimes they threw in a bit of humor, too.

Finsternis did not take part in their talk or their companionship. He did not even verbalize his answers. He merely let them know his sense of the situation and this time, as in all other times, his response was—"Negative. No operation needed. Communication nonfunctional. Not needed here. Silence, please. I kill suns. That is all I do. My part is my business. All mine." This was communicated in a single terrible thought, so that Folly and Samm stopped trying to bring Finsternis into the conversations which they started up, every subjective century or so, and continued for years at a time.

Finsternis merely moved along with them, several kilometers away, but well within their range of awareness. But as far as company was concerned, Finsternis might as well not have been there at all.

Samm went on with the conversation, *the* conversation which they had had so many hundreds of times since the planoform ship had discharged them "near" Linschoten XV and left them to make the rest of their way alone. (If the menace were really a menace, and if it were intelligent, the Instrumentality had no intention of letting an actual planoform ship fall within the powers of a strange form of life which might well be hypnotic in its combat capacities. Hence the ship, the cube, and the giant were launched into normal space at high velocity, equipped with jets to correct their courses, and left to make their own way to the danger.)

Samm said, as he always did, "You were a beautiful woman, Folly, but you wanted to die. Why?"

"Why do people ever want to die, Samm? It's the power in us, the vitality which makes us want so much. Life always trembles on the edge of disappointment. If we hadn't been vital and greedy and lustful and yearning, if we hadn't had big thoughts and wanted bigger ones, we would have stayed animals, like all the little things back on Earth. It's strong life that brings us so close to death. We can't stand the beauty of it, the nearness of the things we want, the remoteness of the things that we can have. You and me and Finsternis, now, we're monsters riding out between the stars. And yet we're happier now than we were when we were back among people. I was a beautiful woman, but there were specific things which I wanted. I wanted them myself. I alone. For me. Only for me. When I couldn't have them, I wanted to die. If I had been stupider or happier I might have lived on. But I didn't. I was me— intensely me. So here I am. I don't even know whether I have a body or not, inside this ship. They've got me all hooked up to the sensors and the viewers and the computers. Sometimes I think that I may be a lovely woman still, with a real body hidden somewhere inside this ship, waiting to step out and to be a person again. And you, Samm, don't you want to tell me about yourself? Samm. SAMM. That's no name for an actual person—Superordinated Alien Measuring and Mastery device. What were you before they gave you that big body? At least you still look like a person. You're not a ship, like me."

"My name doesn't matter, Folly, and if I told it to you, you wouldn't know it. You never knew it."

"How wouldn't I know?" she cried. "I've never told you my name either, so perhaps we did know each other back on Old Earth when we were still people."

"I can tell something," said Samm, "from the shape of words, from the ring of thoughts, even when we're not out here in nothing. You were a lady, perhaps high-born. You were truly beautiful. You were really important. And I—I was a technician. A good one. I did my work and I loved my family, and my wife and I were happy with every child which the Lords gave us for adoption. But my wife died first. And after a while my children, my wonderful boy and my two beautiful, intelligent girls—my own children, they couldn't stand me anymore. They didn't like me. Perhaps I talked too much. Perhaps I gave them too much advice. Perhaps I reminded them of their mother, who was dead. I don't know. I won't ever know. They didn't want to see me. Out of manners, they sent me cards on my birthday. Out of sheer formal courtesy, they called on me sometimes. Now and then one of them wanted something. Then they came to me, but it was always just to get something. It took me a long time to figure out, but I hadn't done anything. It wasn't what I had done or hadn't done. They just plain didn't like me. You know the songs and the operas and the stories, Folly, you know them all."

"Not all of them," thought Folly gently, "not all of them. Just a few thousand."

"Did you ever see one," cried Samm, his thoughts ringing fiercely against her mind, "did you ever see a single one about a rejected father? They're all about men and women, love and sex, but I can tell you that rejection hurts even when you don't ask anything of your loved ones but their company and their happiness and their simple genuine smiles. When I knew that my children had no use for me, I had no use for me either. The Instrumentality came along with this warning, and I volunteered."

"But you're all right now, Samm," said Folly gently. "I'm a ship and you are a metal giant, but we're off doing work which is important for all mankind. We'll have adventures together. Even black and grumbly here," she added, meaning Finsternis, "can't keep us from the excitement of companionship or the hope of danger. We're doing something wonderful and important and exciting. Do you know what I would do if I had my life again, my ordinary life with skin and toenails and hair and things like that?"

"What?" asked Samm, knowing the answer perfectly well from the hundreds of times they had touched on this point.

"I'd take baths. Hundreds and hundreds of them, over again. Showers and dips in cold pools and soaks in hot bathtubs and rinses and more showers. And I would do my hair, over and over again, thousands of different ways. And I would put on lipstick, in the most outrageous colors, even if nobody saw me, except for my own self looking in the mirror. Now I can hardly remember what it used to be to be dry or wet. I'm in this ship and I see the ship and I do not really know if I am a person or not any more."

Samm stayed quiet, knowing what she would say next.

"Samm, what would you do?" Folly asked.

"Swim," he said.

"Then swim, Samm, swim! Swim for me in the space between the stars. You still have a body and I don't, but I can watch you and I can sense you swimming out here in the nothing-at-all."

Samm began to swim a huge Australian crawl, dipping his face to the edge of the water—as if there were water there. The gestures made no difference in his real motion, since they were all of them in the fast trajectory computed for them from the point where they left the Instrumentality's ship and started out in normal space for the star listed as Linschoten XV.

This time, something very sudden happened, and it happened strangely.

From the dark gloomy silence of the cube, Finsternis, there came an articulate cry, called forth in clear human speech:

Stop it! Stop moving right now. I attack.

Both Samm and Folly had instruments built into them, so they could read space around them. The instruments, quickly scanned, showed nothing. Yet Folly felt odd, as though something had gone very wrong in her ship-self, which had seemed so metal, so reliable, so inalterable.

She threw a thought of inquiry at Samm and instead got another command from Finsternis. *Don't think.*

∾ III ∾

Samm floated like a dead man in his gargantuan body. Folly drifted like a fruit beside his hand.

At last there came words from Finsternis:

"You can think now, if you want to. You can chatter at each other again. I'm through."

Samm thought at him, and the thought-pattern was troubled and confused. "What happened? I felt as though the immaculate grid of space had been pinched together in a tight fold. I felt you do something, and then there was silence around us again."

"Talking," said Finsternis, "is not operational and it is not required of me. But there are only three of us here, so I might as well tell you what happened. Can you hear me, Folly?"

"Yes," she said, weakly.

"Are we on course," asked Finsternis, "for the third planet of Linschoten XV?"

Folly paused while checking all her instruments, which were more complicated and refined than those carried by the other two, since she was the maintenance unit. "Yes," said she at last. "We are exactly on course. I don't know what happened, if anything did happen."

"Something happened, all right," said Finsternis, with the gratified savagery of a person whose quick-and-cruel nature is rewarded only by meeting and overcoming hostility in real life.

"Was it a space dragon, like they used to meet on the old, old ships?"

"No, nothing like that," said Finsternis, communicative for once, since this was something operational to talk about. "It doesn't even seem to be in this space at all. Something just rises up among us, like a volcano coming out of solid space. Something violent and wild and alive. Do you two still have eyes?"

"Seeing devices for the ordinary light band?" asked Samm.

"Of course we do!" said Finsternis. "I will try to fix it so that you will have a visible input."

There was a sharp pause from Finsternis.

The voice came again, with much strain.

"Do not do anything. Do not try to help me. Just watch. If it wins, destroy me quickly. It might try to capture us and get back to Earth."

Folly felt like telling Finsternis that this was unnecessary, since the first motion toward return would trigger destruction devices which had been built into each of the three of them, beyond reach, beyond detection, beyond awareness. When the Instrumentality said, "Do *not* come back," the Instrumentality meant it.

She said nothing.

She watched Finsternis instead.

Something began to happen.

It was very odd.

Space itself seemed to rip and leak.

In the visible band, the intruder looked like a fountain of water being thrown randomly to and fro.

But the intruder was not water.

In the visible light-band, it glowed like wild fire rising from a shimmering column of blue ice. Here in space there was nothing to burn, nothing to make light: she knew that Finsternis was translating unresolvable phenomena into light.

She sensed Samm moving one of his giant fists uncontrollably, in a helpless, childish gesture of protest.

She herself did nothing but watch, as alertly and passively as she could.

Nevertheless, she felt wrenched. This was no material phenomenon. It was wild unformed life, intruding out of some other proportion of space, seeking material on which to impose its vitality, its frenzy, its identity. She could see Finsternis as a solid black cube, darker than mere darkness, drifting right into the column. She watched the sides of Finsternis.

On the earlier part of the trip, since they had left the people and the planoform ship and had been discharged in a fast trajectory toward Linschoten XV, Finsternis' side had seemed like dull metal, slightly burnished, so that Folly had to brush him lightly with radar to get a clear image of him.

Now his sides had changed.

They had become as soft and thick as velvet.

The strange volcano-fountain did not seem to have much in the way of sensing devices. It paid no attention to Samm or to herself. The dark cube attracted it, as a shaft of sunlight might attract a baby or as the rustle of paper might draw the attention of a kitten.

With a slight twist of its vitality and direction, the whole column of burning, living brightness plunged upon Finsternis, plunged and burned out and went in and was seen no more.

Finsternis' voice, clear and cheerful, sounded out to both of them.

"It's gone now."

"What happened to it?" asked Samm.

"I ate it," said Finsternis.

"You what?" cried Folly.

"I ate it," said Finsternis. He was talking more than he ever had before. "At least, that's the only way I can describe it. This machine they gave me or made me into or whatever they did, it's really rather good. It's powerful. I can feel it absorbing things, taking them in, taking them apart, putting them away. It's something like eating used to be when I was a person. That wild thing attacked me, wrapped me up, devoured me. All I did was to take it in, and now it's gone. I feel sort of full. I suppose my machines are sorting out samples of it to send away to rendezvous points in little rockets. I know that I have sixteen small rockets inside me, and I can feel two of them getting ready to move. Neither one of you could have done what I do. I was built to absorb whole suns if necessary, break them down, freeze them down, change their molecular structure, and shoot their vitality off in one big useless blast on the radio spectrum. You couldn't do anything like that, Samm, even if you do have arms and legs and a head and a voice—if we ever get into an atmosphere for you to use it in. You couldn't do what I have just done, Folly."

"You're *good*," said Folly, with emphasis. But she added: "I can repair *you*."

Obviously offended, Finsternis withdrew into his silence.

Samm said to Folly, "How much further to destination?"

Said Folly promptly, "Seventy-nine earth years, four months and three days, six hours and two minutes, but you know how little that means out here. It could seem like a single afternoon or it could feel to us like a thousand lifetimes. Time doesn't work very well for us."

"How did Earth ever find this place, anyhow?" asked Samm.

"All I know is that it was two very strong telepaths, working together on the planet Mizzer. An ex-dictator named Casher O'Neill and an ex-Lady named Celalta. They were doing a bit of psionic astronomy and suddenly this signal came in strong and clear. You know that telepaths can catch directions very accurately. Even over immense distances. And they can get emotions, too. But they are not very good at actual images or things. Somebody else checked it out for them."

"M-m-m," said Samm. He had heard all this before. Out of sheer boredom, he went back to swimming vigorously. The body might not really be his, but it made him feel good to exercise it.

Besides, he knew that Folly watched him with pleasure—great pleasure, and a little bit of envy.

Casher O'Neill and the Lady Celalta had finished with making love.

They had lain with their bodies tired and their minds clear, relaxed. They had stretched out on a blanket just above the big gushing spring which was the source of the Ninth Nile. Both telepaths, they could hear a bird-couple quarreling inside a tree, the male bird commanding the female to get out and get to work and the female answering by dropping deeper and deeper into a fretful and irritable sleep.

The Lady Celalta had whispered a thought to her lover and master, Casher O'Neill.

"To the stars?"

"The stars?" thought he with a grumble. They were both strong telepaths. He had been imprinted, in some mysterious way, with the greatest telepath-hypnotist of all time, the Honorable Agatha Madigan. In the Lady Celalta he had a companion worthy of his final talents, a natural telepath who could herself reach not only all of Mizzer but some of the nearer stars. When they teamed up together, as she now proposed, they could plunge into dusty infinities of depth and bring back feelings or images which no Go-Captain had ever found with his ship.

He sat up with a grunt of assent.

She looked at him fondly, possessively, her dark eyes alight with alertness, happiness, and adventure.

"Can I lift?" she asked, almost timidly.

When two telepaths worked together, one cleared the vision for both of them as far as their combined minds could reach and then the other sprang, with enormous effort, as far and as fast as possible toward any target which presented itself. They had found strange things, sometimes beautiful or dramatic ones, by this method.

Casher was already drinking enormous gulps of air, filling his lungs, holding his breath, letting go with a gasp, and then inhaling deeply and slowly again. In this way he reoxygenated his brain very thoroughly for the huge effort of a telepathic dive into the remote depth of space. He did not even speak to her, nor did he telepath a word to her; he was conserving his strength for a good jump.

He merely nodded to her.

The Lady Celalta, too, began the deep breathing, but she seemed to need it less than did Casher.

They were both sitting up, side by side, breathing deeply.

The cool night sands of Mizzer were around them, the harmless gurgle of the Ninth Nile was beside them, the bright star-cluttered sky of Mizzer was above them.

Her hand reached out and took hold of his. She squeezed his hand. He looked at her and nodded to her again.

Within his mind, Mizzer and its entire solar system seemed to burst into flame with a new kind of light. The radiance of Celalta's mind trailed off unevenly in different directions, but there, almost 2° off the pole of Mizzer's ecliptic, he felt something wild and strange, a kind of being which he had never sensed before. Using Celalta's mind as a base, he let his mind dive for it.

The distance of the plunge left them both dizzy, sitting on the quiet night sands of Mizzer. It seemed to both of them that the mind of man had never reached so far before.

The reality of the phenomenon was undoubtable.

There were animals all around them, the usual categories: runners, hunters, jumpers, climbers, swimmers, hiders, and handlers. It was some of the handlers who were intensely telepathic themselves.

The image of man created an immediate, murderous response.

"Cackle gabble, gabble cackle, man, man, man, eat them, eat them!"

Casher and Celalta were both so surprised that they let the contact go, after making sure that they had touched a whole world full of beings, some of them telepathic and probably civilized.

How had the beings known "man"? Why had their response been immediate? Why anthropophagous and homicidal?

They took time, before coming completely out of the trance, to make a careful, exact note of the direction from which the danger-brains had shrieked their warning.

This they submitted to the Instrumentality, shortly after the incident.

And that was how, unknown to Folly, Samm, and Finsternis, the inhabitants on the third planet of Linschoten XV had come to the attention of mankind.

∾ IV ∾

As a matter of fact, the three wanderers later on felt a vague, remote telepathic contact which they sensed as being warmhearted and human, and therefore did not try to track down, with their minds or their weapons. It was O'Neill and Celalta, many years later by Mizzer time, reaching to see what the Instrumentality had done about Linschoten XV.

Folly, Samm, and Finsternis had no suspicion that the two most powerful telepaths in the human area of the galaxy had stroked them, searched them, felt them through, and seen things about them which the three of them did not know about themselves or about each other.

Casher O'Neill said to the Lady Celalta, "You got it, too?"

"A beautiful woman, encased in a little ship?"

Casher nodded. "A redhead with skin as soft and transparent as living ivory? A woman who was beautiful and will be beautiful again?"

"That's what I got," said the Lady Celalta. "And the tired old man, weary of his children and weary of his own life because his children were weary of him."

"Not so old," said Casher O'Neill. "And isn't that a spectacular piece of machinery they put him into? A metal giant. It felt like something about a quarter of a kilometer high. Acid-proof. Cold-proof. Won't he be surprised when he finds that the Instrumentality has rejuvenated his own body inside that monster?"

"He certainly will be," said the Lady Celalta happily, thinking of the pleasant surprise which lay ahead of a man whom she would never know or see with her own bodily eyes.

They both fell silent.

Then said the Lady Celalta, "But the third person . . ." There was a shiver in her voice as though she dared not ask the question. "The third person, the one in the cube." She stopped, as though she could neither ask nor say more.

"It was not a robot or a personality cube," said Casher O'Neill. "It was a human being all right. But it's crazy. Could you make out, Celalta, as to whether it was male or female?"

"No," said she, "I couldn't tell. The other two seemed to think that it was male."

"But did *you* feel sure?" asked Casher.

"With that being, I felt sure of nothing. It was human, all right, but it was stranger than any lost hominid we have ever felt around the forgotten stars. Could you tell, Casher, whether it was young or old?"

"No," said he. "I felt nothing—only a desperate human mind with all its guards up, living only because of the terrible powers of the black cube, the sun-killer in which it rode. I never sensed someone before who was a person without characteristics. It's frightening."

"The Instrumentality are cruel sometimes," said Celalta.

"Sometimes they have to be," Casher agreed.

"But I never thought that they would do that."

"Do what?" asked Casher.

Her dark eyes looked at him. It was a different night,

and a different Nile, but the eyes were only a very little bit older and they loved him just as much as ever. The Lady Celalta trembled as though she herself might think that the all-powerful Instrumentality could have hidden a microphone in the random sands. She whispered to her lover, "You said it yourself, Casher, just a moment ago."

"Said what?" He spoke tenderly but fearlessly, his voice ringing out over the cool night sands.

The Lady Celalta went on whispering, which was very unlike her usual self. "You said that the third person was 'crazy.' Do you realize that you may have spoken the actual literal truth?" Her whisper darted at him like a snake.

At last, he whispered back, "What did you sense? What could you guess?"

"They have sent a madman to the stars. Or a mad woman. A real psychotic."

"Lots of pilots," said Casher, speaking more normally, "are cushioned against loneliness with real but artificially activated psychoses. It gets them through the real or imagined horrors of the sufferings of space."

"I don't mean that," said Celalta, still whispering urgently and secretly. "I mean a real psychotic."

"But there aren't any. Not loose, that is," said Casher, stammering with surprise at last. "They either get cured or they are bottled up in thought-proof satellites somewhere."

Celalta raised her voice a little, just a little, so that she no longer whispered but spoke urgently.

"But don't you see, that's what they must have done. The Instrumentality made a star-killer too strong for any normal mind to guide. So the Lords got a psychotic somewhere, a real psychotic, and sent a madman out among the stars. Otherwise we could have felt its gender or its age."

Casher nodded in silent agreement. The air did not feel colder, but he got gooseflesh sitting beside his beloved Celalta on the familiar desert sands.

"You're right. You must be right. It almost makes me feel sorry for the enemies out near Linschoten XV. Do you see nothing of them this time? I couldn't perceive them at all."

"I did, a little," said the Lady Celalta. "Their telepaths have caught the strange minds coming at them with a high rate of speed. The telepathic ones are wild with excitement but the others are just going cackle-gabble, cackle-gabble with each other, filled with anger, hunger, and the thought of man."

"You got that much?" he said in wonder.

"My lord and my lover, I dived this time. Is it so strange that I sensed more than you did? Your strength lifted me."

"Did you hear what the weapons called each other?"

"Something silly." He could see her knitting her brows in the bright starshine which illuminated the desert almost the way that the Old Original Moon lit up the nights sometimes on Manhome itself. "It was Folly, and something like 'Superordinated Alien Measuring and Mastery machine' and something like 'darkness' in the Ancient Doyches Language."

"That's what I got, too," said Casher. "It sounds like a weird team."

"But a powerful one, a terribly powerful one," said the Lady Celalta. "You and I, my lover and master, have seen strange things and dangers between the stars, even before we met each other, but we never saw anything like this before, did we?"

"No," said he.

"Well, then," said she, "let us sleep and forget the matter as much as we can. The Instrumentality is certainly taking care of Linschoten XV, and we two need not bother about it."

And all that Samm, Folly, and Finsternis knew was that a light touch, unexplained but friendly, had gone over them from the far star region near home. Thought they, if they thought anything about it at all, "The Instrumentality, which made us and sent us, has checked up on us one more time."

∽ V ∼

A few years later, Samm and Folly were talking again while Finsternis—guarded, impenetrable, uncommunicating, detectable only by the fierce glow of human life which shone telepathically out of the immense cube— rode space beside them and said nothing.

Suddenly Folly cried out to Samm loudly, "I can *smell* them."

"Smell who?" asked Samm mildly. "There isn't any smell out here in the nothingness of space."

"Silly," thought Folly back, "I don't mean really smell. I mean that I can pick up their sense of odor telepathically."

"Whose?" said Samm, being dense.

"Our enemies', of course," cried Folly. "The man-rememberers who are not man. The cackle-gabble creatures. The beings who remember man and hate him. They smell thick and warm and alive to each other. Their whole world is full of smells. Their telepaths are getting frantic now. They have even figured out that there are three of us and they are trying to get our smells."

"And we have no smell. Not when we do not even know whether we have human bodies or not, inside these things. Imagine this metal body of mine smelling. If it did have a smell," said Samm, "it would probably be the very soft smell of working steel and a little bit of lubricants, plus whatever odors my jets might activate inside an atmosphere. If I know the Instrumentality, they have made my jets smell awful to almost any kind of being. Most forms of life think first through their noses and then figure out the rest of experience later. After all, I was built to intimidate, to frighten, to destroy. The Instrumentality did not make this giant to be friendly with anybody. You and I can be friends, Folly, because you are a little ship which I could hold like a cigar between my fingers, and because the ship holds the memory of a very lovely woman. I can sense what you once were. What you may still be, if your actual body is still inside that boat."

"Oh, Samm!" she cried. "Do you think I might still be alive, really alive, with a real me in a real me, and a chance to be myself somewhere again, out here between the stars?"

"I can't sense it plainly," said Samm. "I've reached as much as I can through your ship with my sensors, but I can't tell whether there's a whole woman there or not. It might be just a memory of you dissected and laminated between a lot of plastic sheets. I really can't tell, but sometimes I have the strangest hunch that you are still alive, in the old ordinary way, and that I am alive too."

"Wouldn't that be wonderful!" She almost shouted at him. "Samm, imagine being us again, if we fulfill our mission and conquer this planet and stay alive and settle there! I might even meet you and—"

They both fell silent at the implications of being ordinary-alive again. They knew that they loved each other. Out here, in the immense blackness of space, there was nothing they could do but streak along in their fast trajectories and talk to each other a little bit by telepathy.

"Samm," said Folly, and the tone of her thought showed that she was changing a difficult subject. "Do you think that we are the furthest out that people have ever gone? You used to be a technician. You might know. Do you?"

"Of course I know," thought Samm promptly. "We're not. After all, we're still deep inside our own galaxy."

"I didn't know," said Folly contritely.

"With all those instruments, don't you know where you are?"

"Of course I know where I am, Samm. In relation to the third planet of Linschoten XV. I even have a faint idea of the general direction in which Old Earth must lie, and how many thousands of ages it would take us to get home, traveling through ordinary space, if we did try to turn around." She thought to herself but didn't add in her thought to Samm, "Which we can't." She thought again to him, "But I've never studied astronomy or navigation, so I couldn't tell whether we were at the edge of the galaxy or not."

"Nowhere near the edge," said Samm. "We're not John Joy Tree and we're nowhere near the two-headed elephants which weep forever in intergalactic space."

"John Joy Tree?" sang Folly; there was joy and memory in her thoughts as she sounded the name. "He was my idol when I was a girl. My father was a Subchief of the Instrumentality and always promised to bring John Joy Tree to our house. We had a country house and it was unusual and very fine for this day and age. But Mister and Go-Captain Tree never got around to visiting us, so there I was, a big girl with picture-cubes of him all over my room. I liked him because he was so much older than me, and so resolute-looking and so tender too. I had all sorts of romantic day-dreams about him, but he never showed up and I married the wrong man several times, and my children got given to the wrong people, so here I am. But what's this stuff about two-headed elephants?"

"Really?" said Samm. "I don't see how you could hear about John Joy Tree and not know what he did."

"I knew he flew far, far out, but I didn't know exactly what he did. After all, I was just a child when I fell in love with his picture. What *did* he do? He's dead now, I suppose, so I don't suppose it matters."

Finsternis cut in, grimly and unexpectedly, "John Joy Tree is not dead. He's creeping around a monstrous place on an abandoned planet, and he is immortal and insane."

"How did you know that?" cried Samm, turning his enormous metal head to look at the dark burnished cube which had said nothing for so many years.

There was no further thought from Finsternis, not a ghost, not an echo of a word.

Folly prodded him.

"It's no use trying to make that thing talk if it doesn't want to. We've both tried, thousands of times. Tell me about the two-headed elephants. Those are the big animals with large floppy ears and the noses that pick things up, aren't they? And they make very wise, dependable under-people out of them?"

"I don't know about the underpeople part, but the animals are the kind you mention, very big indeed. When John Joy Tree got far outside our cosmos by flying through Space^3 he found an enormous procession of open ships flying in columns where there was nothing at all. The ships were made by nothing which man has ever even seen. We still don't know where they came from or what made them. Each open ship had a sort of animal, something like an elephant with four front legs and a head at each end, and as he passed the unimaginable ships, these animals howled at him. Howled grief and mourning. Our best guess was that the ships were the tombs of some great race of beings and the howling elephants, the immortal half-living mourners who guarded them."

"But how did John Joy Tree ever get back?"

"Ah, that was beautiful. If you go into Space^3, you take nothing more than your own body with you. That was the finest engineering the human race has ever done. They designed and built a whole planoform ship out of John Joy Tree's skin, fingernails, and hair. They had to change his body chemistry a bit to get enough metal in him to carry the coils and the electric circuits, but it worked. He came back. That was a man who could skip through space like a little boy hopping on familiar rocks. He's the only pilot who ever piloted himself back home from outside our galaxy. I don't know whether it will be worth the time and treasure to use space-three for intergalactic trips. After all, some very gifted people may have already fallen through by accident, Folly. You and Finsternis and I are people who have been built into machines. We are now ourselves the machines. But with Tree they did it the other way around. They made a machine out of *him*. And it worked. In that one deep flight he went billions of times further than we will ever go."

"You think you know," said Finsternis unexpectedly. "That's what you always do. You think you know."

Folly and Samm tried to get Finsternis to talk some more, but nothing happened. After a few more rests and talks they were ready for landing on the third planet of Linschoten XV.

They landed.

They fought.

Blood ran on the ground. Fire scorched the valleys and boiled the lakes. The telepathic world was full of the cackle-gabble of fright, hatred throwing itself into suicide, fury turning into surrender, into deep despair, into hope-lessness, and at last into a strange kind of quiet and love.

Let us not tell that story.

It can be written some other time, told by some other voice.

The beings died by thousands and tens of thousands while Finsternis sat on a mountain-top, doing nothing. Folly wove death and destruction, uncoded languages, drew maps, showed Samm the strong-points and the weapons which had to be destroyed. Part of the technology was very advanced, other parts were still tribal. The dominant race was that of the beings who had evolved into handlers and thinkers; it was they who were the telepaths.

All hatred ceased as the haters died. Only the submissive ones lived on.

Samm tore cities about with his bare metal hands, ripped heavy guns to pieces while they were firing at him, picking the gunners off the gun carriages as though they were lice, swimming oceans when he had to, with Folly darting and hovering around or ahead of him.

Final surrender was brought by their strongest telepath, a very wise old male who had been hidden inside a deep mountain.

"You have come, people. We surrender. Some of us have always known the truth. We are Earth-born, too. A cargo of chickens settled here unimaginable times ago. A time-twist tore us out of our convoy and threw us here. That's why, when we sensed you far across space, we caught the relationship of eat-and-eaten. Only, our brave ones had it wrong. You eat us: we don't eat you. You are the masters now. We will serve you forever. Do you seek our death?"

"No, no," said Folly. "We came only to avert a danger, and we have done that. Live on, and on, but plan no war and make no weapons. Leave that to the Instrumentality."

"Blessed is the Instrumentality, whoever that may be. We accept your terms. We belong to you."

When this was done, the war was over.

Strange things began to happen.

Wild voices sang from within Folly and Samm, voices not their own. *Mission gone. Work finished. Go to hill with cube. Go and rejoice!*

Samm and Folly hesitated. They had left Finsternis where they landed, halfway around the planet.

The singing voices became more urgent. *Go. Go. Go now. Go back to the cube. Tell the chicken-people to plant a lawn and a grove of trees. Go, go, go now to the good reward!*

They told the telepaths what had been said to them and voyaged wearily up out of the atmosphere and back down for a landing at the original point of contact, a long low hill which had been planted with huge patches of green turf and freshly transplanted trees even in the hours in which they flew off the world and back on it again. The bird-telepaths must have had strong and quick commands.

The singing became pure music as they landed, chorales of reward and rejoicing, with the hint of martial marches and victory fugues woven in.

Alan, stand up, said the voices to Samm.

Samm stood on the ridge of the hill. He stood like a colossus against the red-dawning sky. A friendly, quiet crowd of the chicken-people fell back.

Alan, put your hand to your right forehead, sang the voices.

Samm obeyed. He did not know why the voices called him "Alan."

Ellen, land, sang the rejoicing voices to Folly. Folly, herself a little ship, landed at Samm's feet. She was bewildered with happy confusion and a great deal of pain which did not seem to matter much.

Alan, come forth, sang the voices. Samm felt a sharp pain as his forehead—his huge metal forehead, two hundred meters above the ground—burst open and closed again. There was something pink and helpless in his hand.

The voices commanded, *Alan, put your hand gently on the ground.*

Samm obeyed and put his hand on the ground. The little pink toy fell on the fresh turf. It was a tiny miniature of a man.

Ellen, stand forth, sang the voices again. The ship named Folly opened a door and a naked young woman fell out.

Alma, wake up. The cube named Finsternis turned darker than charcoal. Out of the dark side, there stumbled a black-haired girl. She ran across the hill-slope to the figure named Ellen. The man-body named Alan was struggling to his feet.

The three of them stood up.

The voices spoke to them: *This is our last message. You have done your work. You are well. The boat named Folly contains tools, medicine, and the other equipment for a human colony. The giant named Samm will stand forever as a monument to human victory. The cube named Finsternis will now dissolve. Alan! Ellen! Treat Alma lovingly and well. She is now a forgetty.*

The three naked people stood bewildered in the dawn.

Good-bye and a great high thanks from the Instrumentality. This is a pre-coded message, effective only if you won. You have won. Be happy. Live on!

Ellen took Alma—who had been Finsternis—and held her tight. The great cube dissolved into a shapeless slag-heap. Alan, who had been Samm, looked up at his former body dominating the skyline.

For reasons which the travelers did not understand until many years had passed, the bird-people around them broke into ululant hymns of peace, welcome, and joy.

"My house," said Ellen, pointing at the little ship which had spat forth her body just minutes ago, "is now a home for all of us."

They climbed into the successful little ship which had been called Folly. They knew, somehow, that they would find clothes and food. And wisdom, too. They did.

∽ VI ∽

Ten years later, they had the proof of happiness playing in the yard before their house—a substantial building, made of stone and brick, which the local people had built under Alan's directions. (They had changed their whole technology in the process of learning from him, and—thanks to the efficiency and power of the telepathic priestly caste—things learned at any one spot on the planet were swiftly disseminated to the whole group of races on the planet.) The proof of happiness consisted of the thirty-five human children playing in the yard. Ellen had had nine, four sets of twins and a single. Alma had had twelve, two sets of quintuplets and a pair of twins. The other fourteen had been bottle-grown from ova and sperm which they found in the ship, the frozen donations of complete strangers who had done their bit for the offworld settling of the human race. Thanks to the careful genetic coding of both the womb-children and the bottle-children, there was a variety of types, suitable for natural breeding over many generations to come.

Alan came to the door. He measured the time by the place where the great shadow fell. It was hard to realize that the gigantic, indestructible statue which loomed above them all had once been his own self. A small glacier was beginning to form around the feet of Samm and the night was getting cold.

"I'm bringing the children in already," said Ch-tikkik, one of the local nurses they had hired to help with the huge brood of human babies. She, in return, got the privilege of hatching her eggs on the warm shelf behind the electric stove; she turned them every hour, eagerly awaiting the time that sharp little mouths would break the shell and humanlike little hands would tear an opening from which a humanlike baby would emerge, oddly-pretty-ugly like a gnome, and unusual only in that it could stand upright from the moment of birth.

One little boy was arguing with Ch-tikkik. He wore a warm robe of vegetable-fiber veins knitted to serve as a base for a feather cloak. He was pointing out that with such a robe he could survive a blizzard and claiming, quite justly, that he did not have to be in the house in order to stay warm. *Was that Rupert?* thought Alan.

He was about to call the child when his two wives came to the door, arm in arm, flushed with the heat of the kitchen where they had been cooking the two dinners together—one dinner for the humans, now numbering thirty-eight, and the other for the bird-people, who were tremendously appreciative of getting cooked food, but who had odd requirements in the recipes, such as "one quart of finely ground granite gravel to each gallon of oatmeal, sugared to taste and served with soybean milk."

Alan stood behind his wives and put a hand on the shoulder of each.

"It's hard to think," he said, "that a little over ten years ago, we didn't even know that we were still people. Now look at us, a family, and a good one."

Alma turned her face up to be kissed, and Ellen, who was less sentimental, lifted her face to be kissed, too, so that her co-wife would not be embarrassed at being babied separately. The two liked each other very much. Alma came out of the cube Finsternis as a forgetty, conditioned to remember nothing of her long sad psychotic life before the Instrumentality had sent her on a wild mission among the stars. When she had joined Alan and Ellen, she knew the words of the Old Common Tongue, but very little else.

Ellen had had some time to teach her, to love her, and to mother her before any of the babies were born, and the relationship between the two of them was warm and good.

The three parents stood aside as the bird-women, wearing their comfortable and pretty feather cloaks, herded the children into the house. The smallest children had already been brought in from their sunning and were being given their bottles by bird-girls who never got tired of watching the cuteness and helplessness of the human infant.

"It's hard to think of that time at all," said Ellen, who had been "Folly." "I wanted beauty and fame and a perfect marriage and nobody even told me that they didn't go together. I have had to come to the end of the stars to get what I wanted, to be what I might become."

"And me," said Alma, who had been "Finsternis," "I had a worse problem. I was crazy. I was afraid of life. I didn't even know how to be a woman, a sweetheart, a female, a mother. How could I ever guess that I needed a sister and wife, like the one you have been, to make my life whole? Without you to show me, Ellen, I could never have married our husband. I thought I was carrying murder among the stars, but I was carrying my own solution as well. Where else could I turn out to be me?"

"And I," said Alan, who had been "Samm," "became a metal giant between the stars because my first wife was dead and my own children forgot me and neglected me. Nobody can say I'm not a father now. Thirty-five, and more than half of them mine. I'll be more of a father than any other man of the human race has ever been."

There was a change in the shadow as the enormous right arm swung heavily toward the sky as a prelude to the sharp robotic call that nightfall, calculated with astronomical precision, had indeed come to the place where he stood.

The arm reached its height, pointing straight up.

"*I* used to do that," said Alan.

The cry came, something like a silent pistol-shot which all of them heard, but a shot without echoes, without reverberations.

Alan looked around. "All the children are in. Even Rupert. Come in, my darlings, and let us have dinner together." Alma and Ellen went ahead of him and he barred the heavy doors behind them.

This was peace and happiness; that at last was goodness. They had no obligation but to live and to be happy. The threat and the promise of victory were far, far behind.

Down to a Sunless Sea

High, oh, high, oh, they jingle in the sky oh! Bright how bright the light of those twin moons of Xanadu, Xanadu the lost, Xanadu the lovely, Xanadu the seat of pleasure. Pleasure of the senses, body, mind, soul. Soul? Who said anything about soul?

∞|∞

Where they were standing the wind whispered softly. From time to time Madu in an ageless feminine gesture tugged at her tiny silver skirt or adjusted her equally nominal open sleeveless jacket. Not that she was cold. Her abbreviated costume was appropriate to Xanadu's equable climate.

She thought: "I wonder what he will be like, this Lord of the Instrumentality? Will he be old or young, fair or dark, wise or foolish?" She did not think "handsome or ugly." Xanadu was noted for the physical perfection of its inhabitants, and Madu was too young to expect anything less.

Lari, waiting beside her, was not thinking of the Space Lord. His mind was seeing again the video tapes of the dancing, the intricate steps and beautiful frenzy of movement of the group from ancient days of Manhome, the group labeled "Bawl-shoy." "Someday," he thought, "oh, perhaps someday I too can dance like that . . ."

Kuat thought: "Who do they think they're fooling? In all the years I've been governor of Xanadu this is the first time a Lord has been here. War hero of the battle of Styron IV indeed! Why, that's been over substantive months ago. . . . He's had plenty of time to recover if it's really true he was wounded. No, there's something more . . . they know or suspect something . . . Well, we'll keep him busy. Shouldn't be hard to do here with all the pleasures Xanadu has to offer . . . and there's Madu. No, he can't complain or he'll blow his cover. . . ."

And all the while, as the ornithopter neared, their destiny was approaching. He did not know that he was to be their destiny; he did not intend to be their destiny, and their destiny had not been predetermined.

The passenger in the descending ornithopter reached out with his mind to try to perceive the place, to sense it. It was hard, terribly hard . . . there seemed to be a thick cloud-like cover—a mist—between his mind and the minds he tried to feel. Was it himself, his mind damage from the war? Or was it something more, the atmosphere of the planet—something to deter or prevent telepathy?

Lord bin Permaiswari shook his head. He was so full

of self-doubt, so confused. Ever since the battle . . . the mind-scarring probes of the fear machines . . . how much permanent damage had they done? Perhaps here on Xanadu he could rest and forget.

As he stepped from the ornithopter Lord bin Permaiswari felt an even greater sense of bewilderment. He had known that Xanadu had no sun, but he was unprepared for the soft shadowless light which greeted him. The twin moons hung, seemingly, side by side, while their light was reflected by millions of mirrors. In the near distance li after li of white sand beaches stretched, while farther on stood chalk cliffs with the jet-black sea foaming on their bases. Black, white, silver, the colors of Xanadu.

Kuat approached him without delay. Kuat's sense of apprehension had diminished appreciably at the first glimpse of the Space Lord. The visitor did indeed look ill and confused; correspondingly, Kuat's amiability increased without conscious effort on his part.

"Xanadu extends you welcome, oh Lord bin Permaiswari. Xanadu and all that Xanadu contains is yours." The traditional greeting sounded strange in his rough tones. The Space Lord saw before him a huge man, tall and correspondingly heavy, muscles gleaming, his longish reddish hair and beard showing magenta in the light of the moons and mirrors.

"It gives me pleasure, Governor Kuat, merely to be in Xanadu, and I return the planet and its contents to you," replied Lord Kemal bin Permaiswari.

Kuat turned and gestured toward his two companions.

"This is Madu, a distant relative, and so my ward. And this is Lari, my brother, son of my father's fourth wife—she who drowned herself in the Sunless Sea." The Space Lord winced at Kuat's laugh, but the young people appeared not to notice it.

Gentle Madu hid her disappointment and greeted the Lord with becoming modesty. She had expected (hoped for?) a shining figure, a blazing armor, or perhaps simply an aura which proclaimed "I am a hero." Instead she saw an intellectual-looking man, tired, looking somehow older than his substantive thirty years. She wondered what he had done, how this man could be the talk of the Instrumentality as the savior of human culture in the battle of Styron IV.

Lari, because he was a male, knew more of the facts of the battle than Madu, and he greeted Lord bin Permaiswari with grave respect. In his dream world, second only to dancers and runners of easy grace, Lari looked up to intelligence. This was the man who had dared to pit himself, his living mind, his intellect against the dread fear machines . . . and won! The price was evident in his face, but he had WON. Lari placed his hands together and held them to his forehead in a gesture of homage.

The Lord reached out in a gesture which won Lari's heart forever. He touched Lari's hand and said, "My friends call me Kemal." Then he turned to include Madu and, almost as an afterthought, Kuat.

Kuat did not notice the near omission. He had turned and was walking toward what appeared to be a huge lump of yellow and black striped fur. He made a peculiar hissing sound, and at once the lump separated into four enormous cats. Each cat was saddled, and each saddle was equipped with a holding ring, but there was no apparent means of guiding the cats.

Kuat answered Kemal's question. "No, of course there's no way to guide them. They're pure cat, you know, unmodified except for size. No underpeople here! I think we're the only planet in the Instrumentality that doesn't have underpeople—except for Norstrilia, of course. But the reasons for Norstrilia and Xanadu are at the opposite ends of the spectrum. We enjoy our *senses* . . . none of that nonsense about hard work building character like the Norstrilians believe. We don't believe in austerity and all that malarkey. We just get more sensual pleasure out of our unmodified animals. We have robots to do the dirty work."

Kemal nodded. After all, wasn't that what he was here for? To allow his senses to repair his damaged mind?

Nonetheless, the man who had faced the fear machines with scarcely a tremble did not know how to approach the cat which was designated as his.

Madu saw his hesitation. "Griselda is perfectly friendly," she said. "Just wait a minute till I scratch her ears; she'll lie down and you can mount."

Kemal glanced up and caught an expression of disgust in Kuat's eyes. It did not help in his search for self-mending.

Madu, oblivious to Kuat's displeasure, had coaxed the great cat to kneeling position and smiled up at Kemal.

Kemal felt something like pain stab him at her glance. She was so beautiful and so innocent; her vulnerability wrenched at his heart. He remembered the Lady Ru's quotation of an ancient sage: "Innocence within is armor without," but a web of fear settled on his mind. He brushed it aside and mounted the cat.

As he lay dying nearly three centuries later, he remembered that ride. It was as thrilling as his first space jump. The leap into nothingness and then the sudden realization that he was traveling, traveling, traveling without volition, with no personal control over the direction his body might take. Before fear had the opportunity to assert itself it was converted into a visceral, almost orgasmic excitement, a gush of pleasure almost too strong to bear.

Lank dark hair flying in his face, the Lord bin Permaiswari would have been unrecognizable to the Lords and Ladies who gathered at the Bell on Old Earth in time of crisis. They would not have recognized the boyish glee in a face which they were accustomed to seeing as grave and preoccupied. He laughed in the wind and tightened his knees against Griselda's flanks, holding the saddle ring with one hand as he turned back to wave at the others who were somewhat behind.

Griselda seemed to sense his pleasure at her long effortless bounds. Suddenly the ride took on a new proportion. Overhead the ornithopter which had brought the Space Lord to Xanadu passed by on its way back to the spaceport. At once Griselda left the pride and leapt futilely after the ascending ornithopter. As she attempted to bat at it, Kemal was forced to use both hands on the holding ring in order not to fall off ignominiously. She continued to leap and bat hopelessly in its direction until it disappeared from sight. Then she sat down to lick herself and, inadvertently, her passenger.

Lord Kemal found her sandpaper tongue not unpleasant,

but he winced as her fang brushed his leg. At some distance Kuat sat laughing. Madu's face, even in the distance, showed concern, however, which cleared as the Lord waved to her. Lari, confident in the powers of the hero of Styron IV, was gazing dreamily at the distant city.

Slowly now, Griselda joined the rest of the pride, her attitude apparently one of some embarrassment at having performed such a kittenish prank when she had been entrusted with the welfare of the distinguished visitor.

In the distance the domes and towers of the city gleamed nacreous in the soft shadowless light of the moons and mirrors. Lord Kemal had his sense of unreality reinforced. The city looked so beautiful and so unreal that he had the feeling it might vanish as they approached. He was to learn that the city and all it stood for were all too real.

As they neared the city walls, Kemal could see that the stark whiteness of the city from afar was an illusion. The shimmering white walls of the buildings were set with gemstones in intricate patterns, flowers, leaves, and geometric designs all heightening the beauty of the incredible architecture. In all the worlds he had visited Lord Kemal had seen nothing to equal this city; Philip's palace on the Gem Planet was a hovel compared to these buildings.

Formal gardens with fountains and artificial pools separated the buildings. Shrubbery in an artful plan which gave the appearance of being natural was planted here and there. Suddenly the Space Lord realized another strange aspect of the planet: he had seen no trees.

Dogs yipped at them from safe distances as they entered the city, but this time Griselda refused to be tempted. Now that she was in the city she had assumed a certain dignity; it was as if she wanted to forget her previous dereliction. She headed straight for the palace steps.

Lord Kemal could feel the muscles of Griselda's haunches tighten as she prepared to hurdle up the steps and through the open door. It would be a tight squeeze for the two of them. Fortunately Kuat reached the steps first and hissed his command to her. Kemal could feel her reluctance. She would much have preferred bounding up the steps, but she obeyed. She lay belly down, back feet crouched, front feet stretched forward; the Lord Kemal dismounted easily but with reluctance, a regret almost as great as Griselda's that the ride was over. He reached over to scratch the cat's ears.

Madu smiled approvingly. "That's right. When you make friends with your cat, she'll obey you much more readily."

Kuat grunted. "I have my own way for making them obey if they get too many ideas of their own." For the first time the Space Lord noticed a small barbed whip tucked into Kuat's belt, to which Kuat pointed now.

"Kuat, you wouldn't," Madu protested. "You never have . . ."

"You haven't seen me," he said. Then as her face clouded he added as if reassuringly: "Up to now I haven't needed to. But don't think I wouldn't."

Kemal noticed that Kuat's reassurance was not quite adequate. A gauze of doubt or wonder seemed to obscure the open brightness of Madu's face. Once more the Lord Kemal felt a stab of fear for her and once more dismissed it.

It was her innocence he feared for. He found that her eyes reminded him of D'irena from the ancient days of his true youth—before he had been made wise in the ways of mankind, before he had been made to know that underpersons and true men could not mix as equals. D'irena with the fawnlike grace, the soft gentle mouth, the innocent eyes of the doe she was derived from. What had happened to her after he left? Did her eyes still hold that candid ingenuousness which he saw mirrored in Madu's eyes? Or had she mated with some gross stag and had some of his grossness transferred itself to her?

He hoped, remembering her fondly, that she had mated with a fine buck who had given her does as gentle and as graceful as she was in his memory. He shook his head. The fear machines had stirred up all kinds of strange memories and feelings. Absently, he petted the cat.

Servants came forward to unsaddle the cats. With a renewed start the Space Lord realized that these were true men, not underpersons, doing work, and he remembered Kuat's statement about enjoying the sensuality of animals. There was something else, something he had almost thought of, but he could not quite think . . . it was as if he tried to catch the tail of an elusive animal as it disappeared around the corner.

Led by Kuat and trailed by Madu and Lari, the Lord Kemal threaded his way through a maze of rooms and corridors. Each seemed more amazing than the last. The only time the Space Lord had seen anything similar had been on videotapes—a reconstruction of old Manhome as it had been before Radiation III. The walls were hung with tapestries and paintings based on reproductions of those from Earth; couches, statues, rugs of color and warmth brought here by Xanadu's founder, the original Kahn. Yes, Xanadu was a return to pleasure of the senses, to luxury and beauty, to the unnecessary.

Kemal felt himself beginning to relax in this atmosphere of enchantment, but the spell was broken when, upon reaching the main salon, Kuat unceremoniously flung himself into the nearest couch. As he stretched full length, he vaguely waved a hand to the rest of the party.

"Sit down, sit down," he said. Candles flickered and glowed; low tables and couches stood about invitingly.

For the first time since the introduction on the Space Lord's arrival Lari spoke spontaneously. "We welcome you to our home," he said, "and hope that we can do all possible to make your visit enjoyable."

Kemal realized that he had paid little attention to the youth because he had been so absorbed in new impressions, and (he had to admit it to himself) the girl Madu had fascinated him. Lari, in his own way, was as physically perfect as Madu. Tall, slender, lightly muscled, a golden boy. And, like Madu, he had a curious air of openness, of vulnerability. It seemed strange to the Lord Kemal that these two should grow up so innocent under the guardianship of a man as coarse and boorish as Kuat seemed.

Kuat interrupted his reverie. "Come! The dju-di!"

Madu immediately moved toward a table on which rested a copper-colored tray with silvery highlights. On the tray sat a dual-spouted pitcher of the same material and eight small matching goblets. A lid covered the top of the pitcher. As Madu picked up the pitcher, Kuat gave one of the grunts which the Space Lord was finding increasingly distasteful.

"Just be sure you put your thumb over the right hole."

Her answering tone was indulgent but as nearly scornful as Kemal could imagine her being. "I've been doing this since childhood. Is it likely I'd forget now?"

In after years it seemed to Kemal bin Permaiswari that this night was one of the important turns that his life took in its convoluted passage through time. He seemed removed from events as they occurred; he seemed a spectator, watching the actions, not only of the others but of himself, as if he had no control over them, as if in a dream . . .

Madu knelt gracefully and placed a thumb over one of the two holes at the top of the pitcher. Candlelight played over the light silvery dusting of powder which covered the entire area of her bare skin. As she poured the reddish liquid into four of the little goblets, Kemal noticed that even the nails of her small hands were painted silver.

Kuat raised his goblet. The first toast by the rules of politeness should have been to the guest of honor, or at the very least to the Instrumentality, but Kuat went by his own rules.

"To pleasure," he said, and drank the contents with one gulp.

While the rest of the party slowly sipped their drinks, Kuat roused himself to pour another cupful. He had swallowed the second cupful before the others had finished their first.

The Lord Kemal savored the taste of the dju-di.

Unlike anything he had ever tasted before, neither sweet nor sour, it was more like the juice of pomegranate than any other flavor he had tasted, and yet it was unique.

As he sipped he felt a pleasant tingling sensation pervade his body. By the time he had finished the cup he had decided that dju-di was the most delicious thing he had ever tasted. Instead of muddling his wits like alcohol or conferring nothing but sensual pleasure like the electrode, dju-di seemed to heighten all his senses, his awareness. All colors were brighter, background music of which he had been only dimly aware was suddenly piercingly lovely, the texture of the brocaded couch was a thing of joy, perfumes of flowers he had never known overwhelmed him. His scarred mind rejected Styron IV and all its implications. He felt a glow of comradeship, momentarily even toward Kuat, and suddenly felt he had come against a Daimoni wall.

Then he knew. His inability to sense or to read the other minds on this planet did not lie within himself or any defect incurred through the fear machines but was directly connected to Kuat, to some nonauthorized barrier which Kuat had erected. The barrier was imperfect, however. Kuat had not been able merely to keep his own thoughts from being read; he had had to set up a universal barrier. This was obvious from the fact that Kuat showed no indication that he could sense the Space Lord.

"And what," thought Kemal, "do you have to hide? What is so much against the laws of the Instrumentality that you have had to set up a universal mind barrier?"

Kuat, relaxed, smiled pleasantly.

For the first time since Styron IV the Lord Kemal bin

Permaiswari felt that he might in truth recover completely. It was the first time he had felt really interested in anything.

Madu brought him back to his present situation.

"You like our dju-di?" It was hardly a question.

Kemal nodded, blissful and still absorbed in the puzzle he had encountered.

"You may have one more," she said, "but that is all that is good for you. After that, one begins to lose one's senses, and *that*, after all, is *not* pleasurable, is it?"

She poured the second cup for Kemal, for Lari and herself.

Kuat reached for the pitcher, and she slapped playfully at his hand. "One more and you might pour yourself pisang by accident."

He laughed. "I am bigger than most men and can drink more than they."

"At least let me pour it then," she said, and proceeded to do so.

She turned again to the Space Lord with a playful gaiety which did not ring quite true. "He is one whom we must all indulge; but, really, it is dangerous to have too much. You see how this pitcher is made?"

She took off the lid to demonstrate the division of the pitcher. "In one half is dju-di; in the other there is pisang, which is identical in taste to dju-di, but it is deadly. One cup kills anyone drinking it within eefunjung." Involuntarily Kemal shuddered. The unit of time she mentioned was so small as to be almost instantaneous.

"No antidote?"

"None."

Lari, who had been sitting quietly, now spoke. "It is the same thing, really. Dju-di is the distilled pisang. They come from a fruit which grows here, only on Xanadu. Galaxy knows how many people must have died eating the fruit or drinking the fermented but undistilled pisang before the secret of dju-di was discovered."

"Worth every one of them," Kuat laughed. Any remaining warmth engendered by the dju-di which the Space Lord might have felt toward the Governor of Xanadu was dissipated. His curiosity regarding the duality of the pitcher, however, was aroused.

"But if you know that pisang is poison, why do you keep it in the same container with dju-di? For that matter, why do you keep it in its undistilled state at all?"

Madu nodded agreement. "I have often asked the same question, and the answers I get make no sense."

"It's the excitement of danger," Lari said. "Don't you enjoy the dju-di more knowing there's the element of chance you'll get pisang?"

"That's what I said," Madu repeated. "The answers make no sense."

At this point Kuat broke in. His speech was slightly slurred, but he spoke intelligently enough. "In the first place, there is tradition. In the old days, under the first Kahn and before Xanadu came under the jurisdiction of the Lords of the Instrumentality, there was a great deal of lawlessness on Xanadu. There were power struggles for leadership. People came here from other planets to plunder our richness. There had to be some simple way of eliminating them before they knew they were being eliminated. The double pitcher is copied, so they say, from a Chinesian one brought by the first Kahn. I don't know about that, but it has become traditional here. You won't find a dju-di holder on Xanadu without its corresponding pisang holder." He nodded wisely, as if he had explained everything, but the Space Lord was not satisfied.

"All right," he said, "you make the pitchers in the traditional way, but why, by Venus's clouds, must you continue to put pisang in them?"

Kuat's answer, when it came, was in even more slurred tones than his previous speech; the effects of too much dju-di began to make him sound intoxicated, and the Space Lord made mental note to heed Madu's injunctions not to exceed two cupfuls of the drink. Kuat gave a rather leering smile and wagged a finger admonishingly at Lord Kemal.

"Strangers mustn't ask too many questions. Might still be enemies around and we're all prepared. Anyway, that's the way we execute criminals on Xanadu." His laugh was uninhibited. "They don't know what they're getting. It's like a lottery. Sometimes I tease them a little. Give them dju-di first, and they start to think they're going to be freed. Then I give them another cup, and they don't suspect a thing. Drink it happily because nothing happened with the first cup. Then when the paralysis hits them—ha! you should see their faces!"

For an instant the latent dislike which the Space Lord had conceived for Kuat sprang full grown. But the man's intoxicated, in effect, he thought. And then: But is this the real man speaking?

"No, no, Kuat, you don't mean that!"

Realization seemed to return to Kuat. He gave his

brother's knee a reassuring pat. "No, no, course don't. Think I'll go to bed. You'll take care of our guest, won't you?"

He staggered slightly as he stood up but managed to walk fairly steadily from the room.

Suddenly the barrier was down slightly. He could not read Kuat's mind, but the Space Lord could sense, somewhere on the planet, something evil, strange, unlawful. A coldness seemed to replace the warmth of the dju-di in his veins.

Across the white dunes the wind was beginning to rise. Far from the city, protected by the ancient crater lake of the sunless sea, the laboratory had a deceptive exterior placidity. Within, the illegal diehr-dead, not yet quite sentient, stirred in their amniotic fluid; outside, trees bearing their deadly fruit seemed to quiver as if in dread anticipation.

Madu sighed. "I knew he shouldn't have had that last one, but he would do it." She turned toward Lari, oblivious of the Space Lord, and said reassuringly:

"Of course he didn't mean what he said about teasing the prisoners. He's been so good to us all these years . . . nobody could be so kind to us and cruel in other ways, could he?"

Once more the Space Lord glanced in Lari's direction. The handsome young face, vital but young, so young, held a look of uneasiness. "No, I suppose not, and still I've heard tales. . . ." He broke off, remembering the presence of the Space Lord. "Of course it's all nonsense," he concluded, but Lord Kemal had the feeling that he was trying as much to reassure himself as to erase the bad impression his brother had made.

"We will eat now," Madu said brightly, and stood up to go into the dining salon. Again the Space Lord felt as if the subject were being changed.

∽ II ∽

In after years the Space Lord remembered. Thoughts raced through his mind. *Oh, Xanadu, there is nothing with which to liken you in all the galaxies. The shadowless days and nights, the treeless plains, the sudden rainless blasts of thunder and lightning which somehow add to your charm. Griselda. The only pure animal I ever knew. The great rumbling purr, the soft pink nose with the black spot on one side, the eyes which seemed to look beyond the features of my face into my very being. Oh, Griselda, I hope that somewhere you still bound and leap . . .*

But now: the first few days of the Lord Kemal bin Permaiswari on Xanadu passed quickly as he was introduced to the infinite pleasures of Xanadu.

On the day following Kemal's arrival a footrace had been scheduled in which Lari was to run. The element of competition which had been brought back to Xanadu was part of a deliberate return to the simpler joys which mankind in its mechanization had forgotten.

Crowds at the stadium were gay and bright. Most of the young girls wore their hair loose and flowing; the

women, old and young alike, wore the typical costume of
Xanadu: tiny short skirt and open sleeveless jacket. On
most worlds the older women would have looked
grotesque or at least ludicrous in this costume, and the
younger women would have seemed lewd. But on Xanadu
there was a basic innocence and acceptance of the body,
and almost without exception the women of Xanadu,
irrespective of age, seemed to have retained their lovely
lithe figures, and there was no false modesty to call
attention to their seminudity.

Most of the young people, male and female alike, wore
the shimmering body powder which the Space Lord had
first noted on Madu; some matched the powder to their
clothes, others to their hair or eyes. A few wore a colorless
luminescent dusting. Of them all, the Space Lord thought
Madu the loveliest.

She radiated excitement, a portion of which communicated itself to Lord Kemal. Kuat seemed unemotional.

"How can you sit there so calmly?" she asked.

"The boy'll win, you know. Anyway horse racing is
more exciting."

"For you, maybe. Not for me."

Lord Kemal was interested. "I have never seen this
racing," he said. "What is it? The horses all run together
to see which is the fastest?"

Madu nodded agreement. "They all start at a given
signal and run a predetermined path. The one who reaches
the goal first is the winner. He," she nodded her head
playfully in Kuat's direction, "likes to bet, that is to wager,
that his horse will win. That is why he likes horse races
better than human races."

"And you have no wager on the human races?"

"Oh, no. It would be degrading to human beings to wager on their abilities or accomplishments!"

There were three races that day, each one narrowing the field of contestants. It became evident that there was no real competition; Lari so far outdistanced the others that it was almost embarrassing. If he had not been so obviously a superb runner, it would have been easy to assume that the others had held back in order to allow the brother of the governor of Xanadu to win.

Kuat went off to the center of the stadium to participate in a copy of an ancient ritual from old Manhome in which a crown of golden leaves was set on Lari's hair.

In his absence, Lord Kemal heard various whisperings behind him in which he caught the words "dance with the aroi," "old governor will not be pleased," "too bad his mother . . ." Madu seemed not to be listening.

After the celebrations, when the Governor and his party had returned to the palace, Lord Kemal remembered the curious phrases; in particular he was puzzled by the present or future tense of "old governor *will be* (not *would have been*) pleased." It stuck in his mind and fretted there, like a splinter in a sore finger. His mind was only just recovering from the wounds of the fear machines, and he decided he could not risk a further infection.

While Kuat was having his second goblet of dju-di, Lord Kemal said, most casually, "How long have you been governor of Xanadu, Kuat?"

The latter glanced up, sensing something beneath the casualness of the immediate question.

Lari interrupted. "I was a small baby—"

Kuat's gesture silenced him. "For many years," he said. "Does it matter how many?"

"No, I was curious," said the Space Lord, deciding on modified candor. "I thought that the governorship of Xanadu was hereditary, but I heard something today which made me believe that the governor your father was still alive."

Again Lari, before Kuat could silence him, rushed to answer. "But he is. He's with the aroi . . . that's why my mother—"

Kuat's frown silenced him.

"These are not matters for the Instrumentality. These are matters of Xanadu's local customs, protected by Article #376984, sub-article a, paragraph 34c of the instrument under which Xanadu agreed to come under the protection of the Instrumentality. I can assure the Lord that only domestic matters of purely autochthonous origin are concerned."

Lord Kemal nodded in ostensible agreement. He felt that he had somehow uncovered another small portion of the mystery which intrigued him, interested him as nothing else had done since Styron IV.

∾ III ∾

On the fourth "day" of his stay on Xanadu, Lord Kemal went out with Madu and Lari for his first experience beyond the walls of the city since his arrival. By this time, the Space Lord had become quite fond of the cat Griselda. It pleased him inordinately when she gave a great purr of pleasure and lay down for him to mount without awaiting a command.

He saw animals in a new light. With poignancy he knew that underpersons, modified animals in the shape of human beings, were truly neither one thing nor the other. Oh, there were underpersons of great intelligence and power but . . . he let the thought trail off.

They raced across the plains with a singular joy. Windswept, treeless, the small planet had a wild beauty of its own. The black sea lashed at the foot of the chalk cliffs. Kemal, watching the li of sand, felt the strangeness of the place once more. In the distance he saw a great bird rise, falter, then fall.

Later, much later, the song the computer wrote when he fed it the facts of time and place became known throughout the galaxies:

> On a dark mountain
> Alone in the cloud
> The eagle paused
> And the wind shrieked aloud
> The thunder rolled
> And the mist of the cloud
> Formed the eagle's shroud
> As it fell to the ground
> Wings battered and torn.
>
> And the surf
> At the foot
> Of the cliff
> Was white

That night,
And bright
The wings
Of the falling
Bird.

I heard
The cry.

Perhaps it was testimony to the depth of his feeling
that the Lord Kemal fed these facts to the computer in
such a way that some of his agony was expressed.

Madu and Lari watched also as the bird fell, their
bright joy overcast by something they could not quite
comprehend.

"But why?" Madu whispered. "It flew along as freely
as we were riding, we bounded as it soared, all free and
happy. And now . . ."

"And now we must forget it," said the Space Lord, of
a wisdom born of endless endurance and a wariness he
wished he did not feel. But he himself could not forget it.
Hence the computer.

"On a dark mountain . . ."

More slowly now, chilled by the death of beauty, of
life, they proceeded, each involved in thought.

"What waste!" the Space Lord thought. What waste of
beauty. The bird had soared free as a dream. Why? A
strange current of air? Or something more deadly?

"What did my mother feel?" thought Lari. "What were
her feelings and thoughts when she walked into the warm
deep dark sea—and knew she would never return?"

Madu felt confused and lonely. It was the first time that she personally had ever confronted death in any form. Her parents were unreal to her; she had never known them. But this bird—she had seen it alive and free, flying, concerned with nothing more important than its graceful glides and soaring; and now, suddenly, it was dead. She could not reconcile the two thoughts in her mind.

It was Lord Kemal who, because of his age and experience, recovered first. "You haven't told me," he said, "where we are going."

Madu's smile was a feeble echo of her usual glow, but she made the effort. "We're going to ride around the edge of the crater up there by the peak. It's a beautiful view, and when you stand there you can almost get the idea that you can see the whole planet."

Lari nodded, determined to participate in the conversation despite the dark thoughts which had clouded his mind. "It's true," he said. "You can even see the grove of buah trees from there. It's from the fruit of the buah trees that we get pisang and dju-di."

"I was curious about that," the Space Lord said. "I haven't seen a tree since I landed on the planet."

"No," said Madu and Lari simultaneously. It created a small diversion, and they both laughed spontaneously, acting more naturally than they had since the death of the bird. Unconsciously they communicated their more cheerful attitude to the cats, which now began to bound forward once more at increased speed.

The Space Lord's happiness at the upswing in spirits of his young companions was tempered with chagrin that the conversation, which had started to be interesting, could not continue while their steeds were proceeding at this breakneck speed.

As they continued uphill, however, the cats gradually began to slow. The change was imperceptible at first, but as the long climb continued, Lord Kemal could feel Griselda's increasing effort. He had begun to think that nothing could tire her, but the climb to the edge of the crater was considerably longer than it looked from below.

That the other cats were also feeling the strain was evident from their decreased pace.

The Space Lord reopened the conversation. "You were going to tell me about the trees," he said.

It was Lari who answered first. "You are quite right about not having seen any trees," he said. "The only trees which grow on Xanadu except the buah trees are the Kelapa trees, and they grow down in the craters of the smaller volcanoes. You can see some of *them* too when we get to the crater rim. But the buah trees always grow in groves—there must be both male and female to bear fruit, and the fruit can only be approached at certain times. Otherwise, even to inhale the scent is deadly."

Madu gravely concurred. "We must always keep at a distance from the buah grove until Kuat has consulted with the aroi, and when he tells us the time is right, then everyone on Xanadu participates in the harvest. The aroi dance, and it is the best time of all. . . ."

Lari shook his head, disapprovingly. "Madu, there are things we don't talk about to outsiders."

Her face suffused, eyes suddenly welling, she stammered, "But a Lord of the Instrumentality . . ."

Both men realized her unhappiness, and each in his

own way hastened to remedy it. The Space Lord said, "I'm good at not remembering things I shouldn't."

Lari smiled at her and put his right hand hard on her shoulder. "It's all right. He understands, and you didn't mean any harm. We won't either of us say anything to Kuat."

As he lay in his room after dinner, the Space Lord tried to reconstruct the afternoon. They had reached the rim of the crater and it had been as Madu said: one could feel as if the horizon was infinite. The Space Lord had felt an overwhelming sense of the magnitude of infinity, something he had never quite experienced to this degree before in all of his trips through space or time. And yet there had been a small nagging feeling that something was not quite right.

Part of the feeling was associated with the grove of buah trees. He was sure that he had glimpsed a building as the uncertain, sometimes gusting, sometimes gentle wind blew the buah branches. He had not mentioned this observation to the young people. It was probably something else autochthonous and therefore forbidden to discussion, or surely one of them would have mentioned it.

He searched his memory (yes, he felt, his mind was definitely recovering) for a person among the servants at the palace who might be willing to talk to a Lord of the Instrumentality. Suddenly he remembered something of which he must have made subliminal note at the time without being consciously aware. One of the men in the cat stable. What was it now? He had drawn a fish in the cat sand and then, glancing at the face of the Space Lord, had casually brushed it over. Later he had caught the gleam of metal at the man's neck. Could it have been a cross of the God Nailed High? Was there a member of the Old Strong Religion here on Xanadu? If so, he had a subject for blackmail.

Or did he? The man had been trying to communicate to him. Now that he thought of it, he was sure. Well, at least he had a possible colleague. Now all he had to do was remember the man's name.

He gave his mind free association; the face came to him; the man's hand fumbling at the chain at his neck . . . yes, certainly the cross, he could see it now . . . why hadn't he noticed it before? . . . but there it was, recorded on his mind . . . and, yes, the man's name: Mr.-Stokely-from-Boston. The unlikely suspicion that there was, after all, an underperson on Xanadu crossed his mind. Mr.-Stokely-from-Boston did not look as if he were animal-derived, but the name indicated something odd in his background.

Lord Kemal bin Permaiswari felt he could not wait until "morning" to try to further his acquaintance with Mr.-Stokely-from-Boston. What excuse could he have to go down to the cat stables at this hour? The gates of Xanadu were closed for the next eight hours. Then he realized that he had been thinking as an ordinary human being. He was a Lord of the Instrumentality. Why should he have to have an excuse for anything he chose to do? Kuat might be Governor of Xanadu, but in the schema of the Instrumentality he was a very small speck.

Nevertheless, the Space Lord felt it best to be circumspect in his movements. Kuat had demonstrated his ruthlessness, and certain of these "autochthonous" practices seemed very peculiar. A Space Lord who "accidentally" drank pisang while of a disordered mind might be written off. And there was the well-being of Mr.-Stokely-from-Boston to be considered.

Griselda. That was the answer. He had noticed that she was sneezing this afternoon . . . he had even mentioned it to Madu and Lari . . . and they had passed it off as dust or pollen. But it would serve as an excuse. He had become so obviously fond of Griselda as to be the subject of teasing of a mild sort on her behalf. Certainly no one would find his concern for her out of the ordinary.

The corridors seemed strangely deserted as he strode through on his way to the cat stable. He realized that he had not ventured from his living area after the final meal of the day since his arrival on Xanadu. Apparently everyone retired after this meal, servants and masters alike. He wondered if the stables would also be deserted.

It was his incredible good fortune to find Mr.-Stokely-from-Boston alone. At least, at the time, he assumed that the meeting was fortuitous. Later he questioned the bird-man. Mr.-Stokely-from-Boston had proved to be, as the Space Lord had wildly surmised, an underperson.

Mr.-Stokely-from-Boston's smile was wise and kindly. "You see, Governor Kuat has no suspicion at all that I am an underperson. And, of course, the universal mind barrier has no operative effect on me. It was a little difficult, but I see I did manage to get through to you. I was somewhat worried when my mind probe showed all the leftover scar tissue from Styron IV, but I've been using the latest methods to try healing your mind, and I'm sure we're succeeding very nicely."

The Space Lord felt an odd momentary resentment

that this animal-derived person had such an intimate acquaintance with his mind, but the anger was short-lived because he quickly equated the empathy he had built up with Griselda to the mental communication he was having with the bird-man.

Mr.-Stokely-from-Boston smiled even more broadly. "I was quite right about you, Lord bin Permaiswari. You are the ally we have been needing here on Xanadu. You look surprised?"

Lord bin Permaiswari nodded. "The governor was so firm that there were no underpersons on Xanadu—"

"Getting through has not been without its difficulties," Mr.-Stokely-from-Boston acknowledged, "but I am not alone. And we have other human families, of course, but none so powerful as a Space Lord up to now."

Lord Kemal found that he did not resent the assumption that he was an ally. Again the bird-man read his thoughts and smiled at him. He had a curiously winning smile, assured but kindly. He looked trustworthy, and Lord Kemal felt himself ready to accept whatever the bird-man might say.

Their thoughts locked. "Let me introduce myself properly," spieked the bird-man. "My real name is E'duard, and my progenitor was the great E'telekeli, of whom you may have heard."

Lord Kemal found the false modesty of this statement rather touching. He bowed his head momentarily in respect; the legendary bird-man, the E'telekeli, was known throughout the Instrumentality as the acknowledged leader and spiritual advisor of the underpersons. This egg-derived underperson could be a most helpful ally in carrying out the work of the Instrumentality or an opposition of fearful proportions. The Lords and Ladies who ruled the Instrumentality were anxious for his cooperation.

Many underpersons were known to have extraordinary medical and psychic powers, and it comforted the Space Lord to know that the animal-derived person who had been manipulating his mind was a descendant of the E'telekeli. He found that he was spieking his thoughts because E'duard could obviously hier them. It would certainly make the process of solving Xanadu's mystery simpler for the Space Lord if they cooperated, but first he wanted to know if their peculiar alliance violated any of the laws of the Instrumentality.

"No." E'duard was emphatic. "In fact, it is a correction of matters which are in direct conflict with the laws of the Instrumentality, with which we have to deal."

"Something 'autochthonous'?" asked the Space Lord shrewdly.

"Native culture is involved," E'duard agreed, "but it's really being used as a screen for something far more evil—and I use the word 'evil' not only in this sense" (he held up the cross of the God Nailed High) "but in its sense of the basic violation of the rights of the living. I mean the right of an entity to exist, to exist on its own terms provided they do not violate the rights of others, to come to its own terms with life, and to make its own decisions."

For a second time Lord Kemal bin Permaiswari nodded in respect and agreement. "These are inalienable rights."

E'duard shook his head. "They *should* be," he spieked, "but on Xanadu, Kuat has found a way around that inalienability. You are, of course, familiar with the diehr-dead?"

"Of course. 'And ne'er a life of their own . . .'" he quoted from an ancient song. "But what does that have to do with the rights of the living? The diehr-dead are grown from the frozen bits of flesh of remarkable achievers long dead. It's true that in regenerating the physical person of the dead one we have sometimes had extraordinary results with the diehr-dead in their second lives; but sometimes not—their achievements seem to have been a combination of circumstances and genes, not of genes alone. . . ."

Again E'duard shook his head. "It's not of the legal, scientifically controlled diehr-dead I spiek, although I sometimes feel very sorry for them. But what would you think of diehr-dead grown from the living?"

The Space Lord looked his wonder and horror as E'duard continued. "Diehr-dead who are controlled like puppets by Kuat, diehr-dead who are substituted for the originals, so that in truth neither the diehr-dead nor the original has a life of its own. . . ."

With quick realization the Space Lord knew what was in the building he had glimpsed in the grove of buah trees. "That's the laboratory, isn't it?"

E'duard nodded. "It's a perfect location. Kuat has spread the rumor that the scent of the buah tree is deadly except when, after consultation with the aroi, he pronounces it safe to harvest the fruit. So nobody dares approach the laboratory. All nonsense. There is only a very short period, just before harvest, when the scent of the buah fruit is deadly . . . in other words, just enough truth to the rumor to give it currency. You saw our scout killed this morning—"

Lord Kemal looked uncomprehending.

"The unmodified eagle you saw fall from the skies this morning on your ride. He was scouting the laboratory for us. He was shot with a pisang dart. It's things like that which make people believe they must stay away from the grove."

"You could communicate?"

For the first time the Space Lord thought that the smile of the bird-man was a little smug. "Of course." Then his face fell and his eyes became old and sad. "He was a brother of mine; we were hatched in the same nest, but I was chosen for genetic coding as an underperson, and he was not. Our feelings are somewhat different from those of true persons, but we are capable of love and loyalty, and sadness as well. . . ."

Lord Kemal saw again in memory the handsome soaring bird of his morning's ride, and he felt E'duard's sadness. Yes, he could believe in the feelings of the underpersons. E'duard touched his hand with a tentative finger.

"I could tell that you grieved for him without knowing any of the circumstances. It is one of the reasons I willed you to come tonight." There was a quick change in his mood. "We must deal first with the aroi."

"I have heard the word, but I don't know its meaning," the Space Lord acknowledged.

"I'm not surprised. The aroi lead a life of pleasure: they sing, they dance, they entertain, and they serve as a kind of priesthood. Both men and women make up the aroi, and they are respected and honored. But there's a singularly ghastly requirement for joining the aroi."

The Space Lord looked his question.

"All living descendants of the current mate of the

person joining the aroi must be sacrificed. Or the mate must die, and if there is more than one offspring of that union, an equivalent number of other volunteers must also die."

Lord Kemal comprehended. "So that is the reason that Lari's mother drowned herself in the sunless sea—to save her infant son. But why did the old Governor join the aroi?"

"Don't you see? With Kuat as governor and the old Governor with the aroi, that pair of conspirators wields a power over this planet so absolute—"

"So it was a conspiracy from the beginning."

"Of course. Kuat was the son of the first wife, when the governor was in his first youth. In his old age he wanted to continue the power but with the help of a viceroy, as it were."

"And the diehr-dead in the laboratory?"

"That is the reason that the matter is urgent. They are full-grown and almost sentient. They must be destroyed before they are substituted for the originals and the originals killed."

"I suppose there is no other way, but it seems almost like murder."

E'duard disagreed. "The substitution is both physical and spiritual murder. These diehr-dead are like robots without soul—" He saw the Space Lord's faint smile. "— I know you do not believe in the Old Strong Religion, but I think you know what I mean."

"Yes. They are not, in the sense you mean, living beings. They have no will of their own."

"The aroi are two villages away, about one hundred li.

After they have performed their entertainment in those villages, they will proceed here. That will be the signal for the harvest of the buah fruit and the substitution of the diehr-dead for their living counterparts. Then there will be no opposition to Kuat on the planet, and he can give his cruelty full rein . . . and plan for the conquest of other worlds. His brother Lari is one of the planned victims because he fears the boy's popularity with the crowds."

The Space Lord was almost incredulous. "But the two persons he has seemed to be truly fond of are Lari and the girl Madu."

"Nevertheless one of the diehr-dead in the laboratory is a replica of the boy Lari."

"Won't the old Governor, the father, object?"

"Possibly, although the mere fact that he joined the aroi when he knew what the cost would be in human terms argues against his interference."

"And Madu?"

"He will keep her as she is, for the time being, and try to mold her to his will. He so little respects individuality that if he cannot, he will obtain some bit of her flesh and eventually she too will be replaced by a diehr-dead. He could be satisfied with a physical replica without caring that the *person* was missing."

The Space Lord felt his tired mind attempting to ingest more than was possible at one time. Immediately E'duard was sympathetic.

"I have kept you too long. You must rest. We will be in touch. And don't worry; Kuat's mind barrier applies to him too; only underpersons and animals are exempt, and we are all in league."

As he made his way back to his living quarters, Lord bin Permaiswari was again aware of the silence, the absence of any human activity anywhere in the palace. He wondered how long it had been since he had left his room to seek Mr.-Stokely-from-Boston in the cat stables. He wished he had remembered to ask E'duard how he had acquired that unlikely name. Immediately he was aware of E'duard's voice spieking in his mind: "It was bestowed upon me for some small service I rendered the Instrumentality on old Manhome." The Space Lord started with surprise. He had forgotten that there were no space barriers to spieking if he left his mind open. He spieked "Thank you," then closed his mind.

∽ IV ∽

When he awoke from a dream-tormented sleep, the Space Lord felt a weariness which he knew E'duard would have termed a tiredness of the soul. There was no way in which he could communicate with the Instrumentality. The next scheduled spaceship for the spaceport above Xanadu was too far in the future to be of any use in the matter of the illegal diehr-dead. E'duard was right. The substitution must be stopped before it began. But how? He felt it somehow belittling to his position for a Space Lord to have to rely on an underperson; the only consolation was that the underperson involved was a descendant of the great E'telekeli.

As they ate their first meal of the day, Madu seemed subdued; Lari was not present. Lord Kemal, making his voice as pleasant as he could, queried Kuat about the boy.

"He's gone down to Raraku to dance with the aroi," Kuat said. Then, apparently, he realized that the Space Lord would not know the word "aroi." "It's a group of dancers and entertainers we have here on Xanadu," he explained kindly. Kemal felt a coldness about his heart.

He could hardly wait to communicate with E'duard. "Lari is missing," he spieked, as soon as he was sure that Kuat would not notice his expression.

"All the diehr-dead are still in place, our scouts report," E'duard spieked back. "We will try to locate him and communicate with you."

But time passed; the only things the underpersons were able to assure Lord Kemal were that Lari was not with the aroi at Raraku and that the diehr-dead replica of him was still in place in the laboratory. He seemed to have vanished from the planet.

Madu had taken Kuat's statement at its face value; she was much quieter now, but she apparently believed that Lari was dancing with the aroi. The Space Lord tried a gentle probing:

"I had gathered from what I heard that the aroi was a closed group which one had to join in order to participate."

"Oh, yes, to participate fully," Madu said, "but near harvest time the best dancers are allowed to dance with the aroi whether they are members or not. It will not be so long now. The aroi have moved from Raraku to Poike. Then they will come here. I will be so glad to see Lari again; I always miss him when he goes off to run or to dance."

"He has gone away before to dance?" the Space Lord asked.

"Well, no. Not to dance. To run, but not to dance before. But he is very good. He really hasn't been quite old enough before."

"And do you have other entertainment at the harvest besides the dancing?" the Space Lord asked, still seeking a clue as to the whereabouts of the vanished Lari.

Her smile had some of its old radiance. "Oh, yes. That is when we have the horse racing I told you about. It is Kuat's favorite sport. Only," her face clouded, "this time I'm afraid his horse doesn't have much chance of winning. Gogle has really been raced too long and too hard; his back legs are wearing out. The vet was talking about doing a muscle transplant if they had a suitable donor, but I don't think they've found one."

At the prospect of seeing Lari soon again, however, she seemed happier with some of the joy the Space Lord associated with her. They went for a cat ride, and Lord Kemal felt again the overwhelming sense of wonder and pleasure as he and the cat Griselda became as one being. Their feelings were in such close communication that he did not have to tighten his knees or hiss at her to obey his slightest wish. For the first time in days Lord bin Permaiswari was able to forget about E'duard and the diehr-dead, about his concern for Lari and his worry as to whether the Instrumentality would approve his cooperation with the bird-man.

For the first time, also, the Space Lord began to wonder to what extent Madu and Lari were committed to each other. Now that he had Madu to himself, he felt more than ever the strong attraction she held for him. He had never, in all the worlds he had known, felt such an attraction for a woman before. And, such was his honor, he began to feel it all the more imperative to restore Lari safely before he could express his feelings to her. He tried spieking to E'duard.

"Nothing," said the bird-man. "We have found no trace of him. The last time he was seen by one of our people was on the outskirts of the palace, headed in the direction of the stables. That is all."

On the day of the festival before the harvest the Space Lord, using Griselda as a pretext, once more went to the cat stables.

E'duard as Mr.-Stokely-from-Boston was hard at work. He looked gravely at the Space Lord, but his mind remained closed. He did not spiek. Lord bin Permaiswari found himself annoyed. He opened his mind and spieked, "Animals!"

E'duard winced slightly but did not spiek.

The Space Lord, apologetic, spieked, "I'm sorry. I didn't mean that."

This time E'duard spieked back. "Yes, you did. And we are, but why so much contempt? We are each what we are."

"I was annoyed that your mind was closed to me, a Space Lord. You have the right to close your mind to anyone. I apologize."

E'duard accepted the statement graciously. He said, "There was a reason that my mind was closed to you. I was trying to decide how to tell you something. And I needed to know your full feelings about the girl Madu and the boy Lari before I can spiek freely."

Lord bin Permaiswari felt a sense of shame; he had behaved, not as a Space Lord, but as a child. He tried to spiek with complete frankness. "I am truly worried about the boy Lari. As to Madu, you must know that there is a strong attraction, but I must first find out about the boy and see what her feelings are."

E'duard nodded. "You spiek as I hoped you would. We have found Lari. He is crippled for life."

Lord Kemal's intake of air hurt his throat. "What do you mean?"

"Kuat had his vet take the boy's calf muscles and transplant them to his favorite horse, Gogle. The horse will be able to run one more race at top speed, thus fooling all those who bet against Kuat. It's improbable that any surgery will enable the boy to walk again, much less to run or dance."

The Space Lord found his mind a blank. He realized that E'duard was still spieking.

"We will have the boy in his wheelchair at the horse race tomorrow. You will need Madu's help. Then you can decide what to do."

Until the time of the race next day Lord Kemal found himself moving as if in a dream, dispassionately observing his movements. E'duard spieked to him only once. "We must kill off the diehr-dead at once," he said. "After the race tomorrow, when everybody is celebrating, will be the time. Keep Kuat busy and I will take care of the matter."

Fearful, unhappy, feeling weaker than he had since Styron IV, Lord Kemal bin Permaiswari accompanied Madu and Governor Kuat to the horse race. At their box sat Lari, white-faced, thin, much older, in a wheelchair. "Why?" spiek-shrieked the Space Lord.

E'duard's voice came through much more calmly. "Kuat actually thought he was being kind. With the boy crippled, he can't be the racer-hero he has been to the people of Xanadu. Kuat thought that way he wouldn't need to substitute the diehr-dead. He didn't realize he's taken the boy's chief reason for wanting to live; he might almost as well have substituted the diehr-dead."

Madu was sobbing. Kuat, in what he intended as rough kindness, stroked her hair. "We'll take care of him. And, Venus! Will we fool the bettors today! They think Gogle can't run anymore. Will they be fooled! Of course, it's only for this one race, but it'll be worth it!"

"Be worth it," the Space Lord thought. Be worth the rest of Lari's life, spent crippled, unable to do what he loved most.

"Be worth it," Madu thought. Never to dance again, never to run, to feel the wind in his hair as the crowds cheered.

"Be worth it," Lari thought. What does anything matter anymore?

Gogle won by half a track.

Kuat, his mood expansive, said to the others, "See you in the main salon of the palace. Have to collect my wagers."

Madu's face was carved of marble as she wheeled Lari toward a special two-cat cart brought up beside the stadium. Lord Kemal, without a word, mounted Griselda. He felt the need, for a little while, at least, for solitude.

They loped, in silent communication, away from the

walls of the city. Lord Kemal heard a cry from the city gate, but he paid no attention. His mind was on Lari. Again the cry. Another lope. Suddenly Griselda faltered, stumbled, fell. At once the Space Lord was down, beside her face. Her eyes were glazing. He saw, then, the dart piercing her neck. Pisang. She tried to lick his hand; he petted her, his eyes filled with tears. She gave one great wrenching sigh, looked into her being, shuddered, and died. Part of him died with her.

When he reached the gate he queried the guard. No one was supposed to leave the city between the end of the races and the harvesting of the buah fruit. Griselda was the victim of an error of administrative oversight. No one had remembered to tell the Space Lord.

Silently he walked back through the pathways of the city. How beautiful it had seemed to him a short while ago. How empty and how sad it seemed now.

He reached the main salon shortly after Madu and Lari in his wheelchair arrived.

It was strange how all the budding desire for Madu had withered like a flower in the frost.

Kuat entered, laughing.

Lord Kemal would be tortured for more than two centuries by a question. When did the end justify the means? When was the law absolute? He saw in his mind's eye Griselda bounding over dunes and plains—a Madu innocent as dawn—Lari dancing under a sunless moon.

"Dju-di!" demanded Kuat.

Madu moved gracefully toward the low table. She picked up the two-holed pitcher. Lord Kemal saw, through E'duard's spiech, that the pisang flow was being let into the amniotic fluid of the diehr-dead. Soon they would be truly dead.

Kuat laughed. "I won every bet I made today."

He looked away from Madu toward the Lord Kemal.

Almost imperceptibly Madu's thumb moved from one hole to the other.

Lord Kemal did nothing in the endless night.

Section II:
Miscellaneous
Works

War No. 81-Q
(Original Version)

It came to war.

Tibet and America, each claiming the Radiant Heat Monopoly, applied for a War Permit for 2127 A.D.

The Universal War Board granted it, stating, of course, the conditions. It was, after a few compromises and amendments had been effected, accepted by the belligerent nations.

The conditions were:

a. Five 22,000-ton aero-ships, combinations of aero and dirigible, were to be the only combatants.

b. They were to be armed with machine-guns firing nonexplosive bullets only.

c. The War Territory of Kerguelen was to be rented by the two nations, the United American Nations and the Mongolian Alliance, for the two hours of the war, which was to begin on January 5, 2127, at noon.

d. The nation vanquished was to pay all the expenses of the war, excepting the War Territory Rent.

e. No human beings should be on the battlefield. The Mongolian controllers must be in Lhasa; the American ones, in the City of Franklin.

The belligerent nations had no difficulty in renting the War Territory of Kerguelen. The rent charged by the Austral League was, as usual, forty million dollars an hour.

Spectators from all over the world rushed to the borders of the Territory, eager to obtain good places. Q-ray telescopes came into tremendous demand.

Mechanics carefully worked over the giant war-machines.

The radio-controls, delicate as watches, were brought to perfection, both at the control stations in Lhasa and in the City of Franklin, and on the war-flyers.

The planes arrived on the minute decided.

Controlled by their pilots thousands of miles away, the great planes swooped and curved, neither fleet daring to make the first move.

There were five American ships, the *Prospero, Ariel, Oberon, Caliban,* and *Titania,* and five Chinese ships, rented by the Mongolians, the *Han, Yuen, Tsing, Tsin,* and *Sung.*

The Mongolian fleet incurred the displeasure of the spectators by casting a smoke screen, which greatly interfered with the seeing. The *Prospero,* every gun throbbing, hurled itself into the smoke screen and came out on the other side, out of control, quivering with incoordinating machinery. As it neared the boundary, it was blown up by its pilot, safe and sound, thousands of miles away. But the sacrifice was not in vain. The *Han* and *Sung,* both severely crippled, swung slowly out of the mist. The *Han,* with a list that clearly showed it was doomed, was struck by a lucky shot from the *Caliban* and fell several hundred feet, its left wing ablaze. But for a second or two, the pilot regained control, and, with a single shot, disabled the *Caliban,* and then the *Han* fell to its doom on the rocky islands below.

The *Caliban* and *Sung* continued to drift, firing at each other. As soon as it was seen that neither would be of any further use in the battle, they were, by common consent, taken from the field.

There now remained three ships on each side, darting in and out of the smoke screen, occasionally ascending to cool the engines.

Among the spectators, excitement prevailed, for it was announced from the City of Franklin that a new and virtually unknown pilot, Jack Bearden, was going to take command of three ships at once! And never before had one pilot commanded, by radio, more than two ships! Besides, two of the most famous Mongolian aces, Baartek and Soong, were on the field, while an even more famous person, the Chinese mercenary T'ang, commanded the *Yuen.*

The Americans among the spectators protested that a pilot so young and inexperienced should not be allowed to endanger the ships.

The Government replied that it had a thorough confidence in Bearden's abilities.

But when the young pilot stepped before the television screen, on which was pictured the battle, and the maze of controls, he realized that his ability had been overestimated, by himself and by everyone else.

He climbed up on the high stool and reached for the speed control levers, which were directly behind him. He leaned back, and fell! His head struck against two buttons: and he saw the *Oberon* and *Titania* blow themselves up.

The three enemy ships cooperated in an attack on the *Ariel.* Bearden swung his ship around and rushed it into the smoke screen.

He saw the huge bulk of the *Tsing* bear down upon him. He fired instinctively—and hit the control center.

Dodging aside as the *Tsing* fell past him, he missed the *Tsin* by inches. The pilot of the *Tsin* shot at the reinforcements of the *Ariel's* right wing, loosening it.

For a few moments, he was alone, or, rather, the *Ariel* was alone. For he was at the control board in the War Building in the City of Franklin.

The *Yuen,* controlled by the master-pilot T'ang, rose up from beneath him, shot off the end of his left wing, and vanished into the mists of the smoke screen before the astonished Bearden was able to register a single hit.

He had better luck with the *Tsin.* When this swooped down on the *Ariel,* he disabled its firing control. Then, when this plane rose from beneath, intending to ram itself into the *Ariel,* Bearden dropped half his machineguns overboard. They struck the *Tsin,* which exploded immediately.

Now only the *Ariel* and the *Yuen* remained! Masterpilot faced master-pilot.

Bearden placed a lucky shot in the *Yuen's* rudder, but only partially disabled it.

Yuen threw more smoke-screen bombs overboard.

Bearden rose upward; no, he was still safe and sound in America, but the *Ariel* rose upward.

The spectators in their helicopters blew whistles, shot off pistols, went mad in applause.

T'ang lowered the *Yuen* to within several hundred feet of the water.

He was applauded, too.

Bearden inspected his ship with the autotelevisation. It would collapse at the slightest strain.

He wheeled his ship to the right, preparatory to descending.

His left wing broke under the strain: and the *Ariel* began hurtling downward. He turned his autotelevisation on the *Yuen,* not daring to see the ship, which carried his reputation, his future, crash.

The *Yuen* was struck by his left wing, which was falling like a stone. The *Yuen* exploded forty-six seconds later.

And, by international law, Bearden had won the war for America, with it the honors of war and the possession of the enormous Radiant Heat revenue.

All the world hailed this Lindbergh of the twenty-second century.

Western Science Is So Wonderful

The Martian was sitting at the top of a granite cliff. In order to enjoy the breeze better he had taken on the shape of a small fir tree. The wind always felt very pleasant through non-deciduous needles.

At the bottom of the cliff stood an American, the first the Martian had ever seen.

The American extracted from his pocket a fantastically ingenious device. It was a small metal box with a nozzle which lifted up and produced an immediate flame. From this miraculous device the American readily lit a tube of bliss-giving herbs. The Martian understood that these were called *cigarettes* by the Americans. As the American finished lighting his cigarette, the Martian changed his shape to that of a fifteen-foot, red-faced, black-whiskered Chinese demagogue, and shouted to the American in English, "Hello, friend!"

The American looked up and almost dropped his teeth.

The Martian stepped off the cliff and floated gently

down toward the American, approaching slowly so as not to affright him too much.

Nevertheless, the American did seem to be concerned, because he said, "You're not real, are you? You can't be. Or can you?"

Modestly the Martian looked into the mind of the American and realized that fifteen-foot Chinese demagogues were not reassuring visual images in an everyday American psychology. He peeked modestly into the mind of the American, seeking a reassuring image. The first image he saw was that of the American's mother, so the Martian promptly changed into the form of the American's mother and answered, "What is real, darling?"

With this the American turned slightly green and put his hand over his eyes. The Martian looked once again into the mind of the American and saw a slightly confused image.

When the American opened his eyes, the Martian had taken on the form of a Red Cross girl halfway through a strip-tease act. Although the maneuver was designed to be pleasant, the American was not reassured. His fear began to change into anger and he said, "What the hell are you?"

The Martian gave up trying to be obliging. He changed himself into a Chinese Nationalist major general with an Oxford education and said in a distinct British accent, "I'm by way of being one of the local characters, a bit on the Supernatural side, you know. I do hope you do not mind. Western science is so wonderful that I had to examine that fantastic machine you have in your hand. Would you like to chat a bit before you go on?"

The Martian caught a confused glimpse of images in

the American's mind. They seemed to be concerned with something called *prohibition,* something else called "on the wagon," and the reiterated question, "How the hell did *I* get here?"

Meanwhile the Martian examined the lighter.

He handed it back to the American, who looked stunned.

"Very fine magic," said the Martian. "We do not do anything of that sort in these hills. I am a fairly low-class Demon. I see that you are a captain in the illustrious army of the United States. Allow me to introduce myself. I am the 1,387,229th Eastern Subordinate Incarnation of a Lohan. Do you have time for a chat?"

The American looked at the Chinese Nationalist uniform. Then he looked behind him. His Chinese porters and interpreter lay like bundles of rags on the meadowy floor of the valley; they had all fainted dead away. The American held himself together long enough to say, "What is a Lohan?"

"A Lohan is an Arhat," said the Martian.

The American did not take in this information either and the Martian concluded that something must have been missing from the usual amenities of getting acquainted with American officers. Regretfully the Martian erased all memory of himself from the mind of the American and from the minds of the swooned Chinese. He planted himself back on the cliff top, resumed the shape of a fir tree, and woke the entire gathering. He saw the Chinese interpreter gesticulating at the American and he knew that the Chinese was saying, "There are Demons in these hills . . ."

The Martian rather liked the hearty laugh with which the American greeted this piece of superstitious Chinese nonsense.

He watched the party disappear as they went around the miraculously beautiful little Lake of the Eight-Mouthed River.

That was in 1945.

The Martian spent many thoughtful hours trying to materialize a lighter, but he never managed to create one which did not dissolve back into some unpleasant primordial effluvium within hours.

Then it was 1955. The Martian heard that a Soviet officer was coming, and he looked forward with genuine pleasure to making the acquaintance of another person from the miraculously up-to-date Western world.

Peter Farrer was a Volga German.

The Volga Germans are about as much Russian as the Pennsylvania Dutch are Americans.

They have lived in Russia for more than two hundred years, but the terrible bitterness of the Second World War led to the breakup of most of their communities.

Farrer himself had fared well in this. After holding the noncommissioned rank of *yefreitor* in the Red Army for some years he had become a sublieutenant. In a technikum he had studied geology and survey.

The chief of the Soviet military mission to the province of Yunnan in the People's Republic of China had said to him, "Farrer, you are getting a real holiday. There is no danger in this trip, but we do want to get an estimate on the feasibility of building a secondary mountain highway along the rock cliffs west of Lake Pakou. I think well of you, Farrer. You have lived down your German name and you're a good Soviet citizen and officer. I know that you will not cause any trouble with our Chinese allies or with the mountain people among whom you must travel. Go easy with them, Farrer. They are very superstitious. We need their full support, but we can take our time to get it. The liberation of India is still a long way off, but when we must move to help the Indians throw off American imperialism we do not want to have any soft areas in our rear. Do not push things too hard, Farrer. Be sure that you get a good technical job done, but that you make friends with everyone other than imperialist reactionary elements."

Farrer nodded very seriously. "You mean, comrade Colonel, that I must make friends with *everything*!"

"Everything," said the colonel firmly.

Farrer was young and he liked doing a bit of crusading on his own. "I'm a militant atheist, Colonel. Do I have to be pleasant to priests?"

"Priests, too," said the colonel, "especially priests."

The colonel looked sharply at Farrer. "You make friends with everything, everything except women. You hear me, comrade? Stay out of trouble."

Farrer saluted and went back to his desk to make preparations for the trip.

Three weeks later Farrer was climbing up past the small cascades which led to the River of the Golden Sands, the Chinshachiang, as the Long River or Yangtze was known locally.

Beside him there trotted Party Secretary Kungsun.

Kungsun was a Peking aristocrat who had joined the Communist Party in his youth. Sharp-faced, sharp-voiced, he made up for his aristocracy by being the most violent Communist in all of northwestern Yunnan. Though they had only a squad of troops and a lot of local bearers for their supplies, they did have an officer of the old People's Liberation Army to assure their military well-being and to keep an eye on Farrer's technical competence. Comrade Captain Li, roly-poly and jolly, sweated wearily behind them as they climbed the steep cliffs.

Li called after them, "If you want to be heroes of labor let's keep climbing, but if you are following sound military logistics let's all sit down and drink some tea. We can't possibly get to Pakouhu before nightfall anyhow."

Kungsun looked back contemptuously. The ribbon of soldiers and bearers reached back two hundred yards, making a snake of dust clutched to the rocky slope of the mountain. From this perspective he saw the caps of the soldiers and the barrels of their rifles pointing upward toward him as they climbed. He saw the towel-wrapped heads of the liberated porters and he knew without speaking to them that they were cursing him in language just as violent as the language with which they had cursed their capitalist oppressors in days gone past. Far below them all the thread of the Chinshachiang was woven like a single strand of gold into the gray-green of the twilight valley floor.

He spat at the army captain, "If you had your way about it, we'd still be sitting there in an inn drinking the hot tea while the men slept."

The captain did not take offense. He had seen many

party secretaries in his day. In the New China it was much safer to be a captain. A few of the party secretaries he had known had got to be very important men. One of them had even got to Peking and had been assigned a whole Buick to himself together with three Parker 51 pens. In the minds of the Communist bureaucracy this represented a state close to absolute bliss. Captain Li wanted none of that. Two square meals a day and an endless succession of patriotic farm girls, preferably chubby ones, represented his view of a wholly liberated China.

Farrer's Chinese was poor, but he got the intent of the argument. In thick but understandable Mandarin he called, half laughing at them, "Come along, comrades. We may not make it to the lake by nightfall, but we certainly can't bivouac on this cliff either." He whistled *Ich hatt' ein Kameraden* through his teeth as he pulled ahead of Kungsun and led the climb on up the mountain.

Thus it was Farrer who first came over the lip of the cliff and met the Martian face to face.

This time the Martian was ready. He remembered his disappointing experience with the American, and he did not want to affright his guest so as to spoil the social nature of the occasion. While Farrer had been climbing the cliff, the Martian had been climbing Farrer's mind, chasing in and out of Farrer's memories as happily as a squirrel chases around inside an immense oak tree. From Farrer's own mind he had extracted a great many pleasant memories. He had then hastened back to the top of the cliff and had incorporated these in very substantial-looking phantoms.

Farrer got halfway across the lip of the cliff before he realized what he was looking at. Two Soviet military trucks were parked in a tiny glade. Each of them had tables in front of it. One of the tables was set with a very elaborate Russian *zakouska* (the Soviet equivalent of a smorgasbord). The Martian hoped he would be able to keep these objects materialized while Farrer ate them, but he was afraid they might disappear each time Farrer swallowed them because the Martian was not very well acquainted with digestive processes of human beings and did not want to give his guest a violent stomach ache by allowing him to deposit through his esophagus and into his stomach objects of extremely improvised and uncertain chemical makeup.

The first truck had a big red flag on it with white Russian letters reading "WELCOME TO THE HEROES OF BRYANSK."

The second truck was even better. The Martian could see that Farrer was very fond of women, so he had materialized four very pretty Soviet girls, a blonde, a brunette, a redhead, and an albino just to make it interesting. The Martian did not trust himself to make them all speak the correctly feminine and appealing forms of the Russian language, so having materialized them he set them all in lounge chairs and put them to sleep. He had wondered what form he himself should take and decided that it would be very hospitable to assume the appearance of Mao Tze-tung.

Farrer did not come on over the cliff. He stayed where he was. He looked at the Martian and the Martian said, very oilily, "Come on up. We are waiting for you."

"Who the hell are you?" barked Farrer.

"I am a pro-Soviet Demon," said the apparent Mr. Mao Tze-tung, "and these are materialized Communist hospitality arrangements. I hope you like them."

At this point both Kungsun and Li appeared. Li climbed up the left side of Farrer, Kungsun on the right. All three stopped, gaping.

Kungsun recovered his wits first. He recognized Mao Tze-tung. He never passed up a chance to get acquainted with the higher command of the Communist Party. He said in a very weak, strained, incredulous voice, "Mr. Party Chairman Mao, I never thought that we would see you here in these hills, or are you you, and if you aren't you, who are you?"

"I am not your party chairman," said the Martian. "I am merely a local Demon who has strong pro-Communist sentiments and would like to meet companionable people like yourselves."

At this point Li fainted and would have rolled back down the cliff knocking over soldiers and porters if the Martian had not reached out his left arm, concurrently changing the left arm into the shape of a python, picking up the unconscious Li, and resting his body gently against the side of the picnic trucks. The Soviet sleeping beauties slept on. The python turned back into an arm.

Kungsun's face had turned completely white; since he was a pale and pleasant ivory color to start with, his white-ness had a very marked tinge.

"I think this *wang-pa* is a counter-revolutionary impostor," he said weakly, "but I don't know what to do about him. I am glad that the Chinese People's Republic has a representative from the Soviet Union to instruct us in difficult party procedure."

Farrer snapped, "If he is a goose, he is a Chinese goose. He is not a Russian goose. You'd better not call him that dirty name. He seems to have some powers that do work. Look at what he did to Li."

The Martian decided to show off his education and said very conciliatorily, "If I am a *wang-pa* you are a *wang-pen*." He added brightly, in the Russian language, "That's an ingrate, you know. Much worse than an illegitimate one. Do you like my shape, comrade Farrer? Do you have a cigarette lighter with you? Western science is so wonderful, I can never make very solid things, and you people make airplanes, atom bombs, and all sorts of refreshing entertainments of that kind."

Farrer reached into his pocket, groping for his lighter.

A scream sounded behind him. One of the Chinese enlisted men had left the stopped column behind and had stuck his head over the edge of the cliff to see what was happening. When he saw the trucks and the figure of Mao Tze-tung he began shrieking, "There are devils here! There are devils here!"

From centuries of experience, the Martian knew there was no use trying to get along with the local people unless they were very, very young or very, very old. He walked to the edge of the cliff so that all the men could see him. He expanded the shape of Mao Tze-tung until it was thirty-five feet high. Then he changed himself into the embodiment of an ancient Chinese god of war with whiskers, ribbons, and sword tassels blowing in the breeze. They all fainted dead away as he had intended. He packed them snugly against the rocks so that none of them would fall back down the slope. Then he took on the shape of a Soviet WAC—a rather pretty little blonde with sergeant's insignia—and rematerialized himself beside Farrer.

By this point Farrer had his lighter out.

The pretty little blonde said to Farrer, "Do you like this shape better?"

Farrer said, "I don't believe this at all. I am a militant atheist. I have fought against superstition all my life." Farrer was twenty-four.

The Martian said, "I don't think you like me being a girl. It bothers you, doesn't it?"

"Since you do not exist you cannot bother me. But if you don't mind could you please change your shape again?"

The Martian took on the appearance of a chubby little Buddha. He knew this was a little impious, but he felt Farrer give a sigh of relief. Even Li seemed cheered up, now that the Martian had taken on a proper religious form.

"Listen, you obscene demonic monstrosity," snarled Kungsun, "this is the Chinese People's Republic. You have absolutely no business taking on supernatural images or conducting unatheistic activities. Please abolish yourself and those illusions yonder. What do you want, anyhow?"

"I would like," said the Martian mildly, "to become a member of the Chinese Communist Party."

Farrer and Kungsun stared at each other. Then they both spoke at once, Farrer in Russian and Kungsun in Chinese. "But we can't let you in the Party."

Kungsun said, "If you're a demon you don't exist, and if you do exist you're illegal."

The Martian smiled. "Take some refreshments. You may change your minds. Would you like a girl?" he said, pointing at the assorted Russian beauties who still slept in their lounge chairs.

But Kungsun and Farrer shook their heads.

With a sigh the Martian dematerialized the girls and replaced them with three striped Siberian tigers. The tigers approached.

One tiger stopped cozily behind the Martian and sat down. The Martian sat on him. Said the Martian brightly, "I like tigers to sit on. They're so comfortable. Have a tiger."

Farrer and Kungsun were staring open-mouthed at their respective tigers. The tigers yawned at them and stretched out.

With a tremendous effort of will the two young men sat down on the ground in front of their tigers. Farrer sighed. "What *do* you want? I suppose you won this trick . . ."

Said the Martian, "Have a jug of wine."

He materialized a jug of wine and a porcelain cup in front of each, including himself. He poured himself a drink and looked at them through shrewd, narrowed eyes. "I would like to learn all about Western science. You see, I am a Martian student who was exiled here to become the 1,387,229th Eastern Subordinate Incarnation of a Lohan and I have been here more than two thousand years, and I can only perceive in a radius of ten leagues. Western science is very interesting. If I could, I would like to be an engineering student, but since I cannot leave this place I would like to join the Communist Party and have many visitors come to see me."

By this time Kungsun made up his mind. He was a

Communist, but he was also a Chinese—an aristocratic Chinese and a man well versed in the folklore of his own country. Kungsun used a politely archaic form of the Peking court dialect when he spoke again in much milder terms. "Honored, esteemed Demon, sir, it's just no use at all your trying to get into the Communist Party. I admit it is very patriotic of you as a Chinese Demon to want to join the progressive group which leads the Chinese people in their endless struggle against the vicious American imperialists. Even if you convinced me I don't think you can convince the party authorities, esteemed sir. The only thing for you to do in our new Communist world of the New China is to become a counter-revolutionary refugee and migrate to capitalist territory."

The Martian looked hurt and sullen. He frowned at them as he sipped his wine. Behind him Li began snoring where he slept against the wheel of a truck.

Very persuasively the Martian began to speak. "I see, young man, that you're beginning to believe in me. You don't have to recognize me. Just believe in me a little bit. I am happy to see that you, Party Secretary Kungsun, are prepared to be polite. I am not a Chinese Demon, since I was originally a Martian who was elected to the Lesser Assembly of Concord, but who made an inopportune remark and who must live on as the 1,387,229th Eastern Subordinate Incarnation of a Lohan for three hundred thousand springs and autumns before I can return. I expect to be around a very long time indeed. On the other hand, I would like to study engineering and I think it would be much better for me to become a member of the Communist Party than to go to a strange place."

Farrer had an inspiration. Said he to the Martian, "I have an idea. Before I explain it, though, would you please take those damned trucks away and remove that *zakouska?* It makes my mouth water and I'm very sorry, but I just can't accept your hospitality."

The Martian complied with a wave of his hand. The trucks and the tables disappeared. Li had been leaning against a truck. His head went thump against the grass. He muttered something in his sleep and then resumed his snoring. The Martian turned back to his guests.

Farrer picked up the thread of his own thoughts. "Leaving aside the question of whether you exist or not, I can assure you that I know the Russian Communist Party and my colleague, Comrade Kungsun here, knows the Chinese Communist Party. Communist parties are very wonderful things. They lead the masses in the fight against wicked Americans. Do you realize that if we didn't fight on with the revolutionary struggle all of us would have to drink Coca-Cola every day?"

"What is Coca-Cola?" asked the Demon.

"I don't know," replied Farrer.

"Then why be afraid to drink any?"

"Don't be irrelevant. I hear that the capitalists make everybody drink it. The Communist Party cannot take time to open up supernatural secretariats. It would spoil irreligious campaigns for us to have a demonic secretary. I can tell you the Russian Communist Party won't put up with it and our friend here will tell you there is no place in the Chinese Communist Party. We want you to be happy. You seem to be a very friendly demon. Why don't you just go away? The capitalists will welcome you. They are very reactionary and very religious. You might even find people there who would believe in you."

The Martian changed his shape from that of a roly-poly Buddha and assumed the appearance and dress of a young Chinese man, a student of engineering at the University of the Revolution in Peking. In the shape of the student he continued, "I don't want to be believed in. I want to study engineering, and I want to learn all about Western science."

Kungsun came to Farrer's support. He said, "It's just no use trying to be a Communist engineer. You look like a very absent-minded demon to me and I think that even if you tried to pass yourself off as a human being you would keep forgetting and changing shapes. That would ruin the morale of any class."

The Martian thought to himself that the young man had a point there. He hated keeping any one particular shape for more than half an hour. Staying in one bodily form made him itch. He also liked to change sexes every few times; it seemed sort of refreshing. He did not admit to the young man that Kungsun had scored a point with that remark about shape-changing, but he nodded amiably at them and asked, "But how could I get abroad?"

"Just go," said Kungsun, wearily. "Just go. You're a Demon. You can do anything."

"I can't do that," snapped the student-Martian. "I have to have something to go by."

He turned to Farrer. "It won't do any good, your giving me something. If you gave me something Russian and I would end up in Russia, from what you say they won't want to have a Communist Martian any more than these

Chinese people do. I won't like to leave my beautiful lake anyhow, but I suppose I will have to if I am to get acquainted with Western science."

Farrer said, "I have an idea." He took off his wrist-watch and handed it to the Martian.

The Martian inspected it. Many years before, the watch had been manufactured in the United States of America. It had been traded by a G.I. to a fräulein, by the fräulein's grandmother to a Red Army man for three sacks of potatoes, and by the Red Army man for five hundred rubles to Farrer when the two of them met in Kuibyshev. The numbers were painted with radium, as were the hands. The second hand was missing, so the Martian materialized a new one. He changed the shape of it several times before it fitted. On the watch there was written in English "MARVIN WATCH COMPANY." At the bottom of the face of the watch there was the name of a town: "WATERBURY, CONN."

The Martian read it. Said he to Farrer, "Where is this place Waterbury, *Kahn?*"

"The Conn, is the short form of the name of one of the American states. If you are going to be a reactionary capitalist that is a very good place to be a capitalist in."

Still white-faced, but in a sickly ingratiating way, Kungsun added his bit. "I think *you* would like Coca-Cola. It's very reactionary."

The student-Martian frowned. He still held the watch in his hand. Said he, "I don't care whether it's reactionary or not. I want to be in a very scientific place."

Farrer said, "You couldn't go any place more scientific than Waterbury, Conn., especially Conn.—that's the most scientific place they have in America and I'm sure they are very pro-Martian and you can join one of the capitalist parties. They won't mind. But the Communist parties would make a lot of trouble for you."

Farrer smiled and his eyes lit up. "Furthermore," he added, as a winning point, "you can keep my watch for yourself, for always."

The Martian frowned. Speaking to himself the student-Martian said, "I can see that Chinese Communism is going to collapse in eight years, eight hundred years, or eighty thousand years. Perhaps I'd better go to this Waterbury, Conn."

The two young Communists nodded their heads vigorously and grinned. They both smiled at the Martian.

"Honored, esteemed Martian, sir, please hurry along because I want to get my men over the edge of the cliff before darkness falls. Go with our blessing."

The Martian changed shape. He took on the image of an Arhat, a subordinate disciple of Buddha. Eight feet tall, he loomed above them. His face radiated unearthly calm. The watch, miraculously provided with a new strap, was firmly strapped to his left wrist.

"Bless you, my boys," said he. "I go to Waterbury." And he did.

Farrer stared at Kungsun. "What's happened to Li?"

Kungsun shook his head dazedly. "I don't know. I feel funny."

(In departing for that marvelous strange place, Waterbury, Conn., the Martian had taken with him all their memories of himself.)

Kungsun walked to the edge of the cliff. Looking over, he saw the men sleeping.

"Look at that," he muttered. He stepped to the edge of the cliff and began shouting. "Wake up, you fools, you turtles. Haven't you any more sense than to sleep on a cliff as nightfall approaches?"

The Martian concentrated all his powers on the location of Waterbury, Conn.

He was the 1,387,229th Eastern Subordinate Incarnation of a Lohan (or an Arhat), and his powers were limited, impressive though they might seem to outsiders.

With a shock, a thrill, a something of breaking, a sense of things done and undone, he found himself in flat country. Strange darkness surrounded him. Air, which he had never smelled before, flowed quietly around him. Farrer and Li, hanging on a cliff high above the Chinshachiang, lay far behind him in the world from which he had broken. He remembered that he had left his shape behind.

Absentmindedly he glanced down at himself to see what form he had taken for the trip.

He discovered that he had arrived in the form of a small, laughing Buddha seven inches high, carved in yellowed ivory.

"This will never do!" muttered the Martian to himself. "I must take on one of the local forms . . ."

He sensed around in his environment, groping telepathically for interesting objects near him.

"Aha, a milk truck."

Thought he, Western science is indeed very wonderful. Imagine a machine made purely for the purpose of transporting milk!

Swiftly he transferred himself into a milk truck.

In the darkness, his telepathic senses had not distinguished the metal of which the milk truck was made nor the color of the paint.

In order to remain inconspicuous, he turned himself into a milk truck made of solid gold. Then, without a driver, he started up his own engine and began driving himself down one of the main highways leading into Waterbury, Connecticut . . . So if you happen to be passing through Waterbury, Conn., and see a solid gold milk truck driving itself through the streets, you'll know it's the Martian, otherwise the 1,387,229th Eastern Subordinate Incarnation of a Lohan, and that he still thinks Western science is wonderful.

Nancy

Two men faced Gordon Greene as he came into the room. The young aide was a nonentity. The general was not. The commanding general sat where he should, at his own desk. It was placed squarely in the room, and yet the infinite courtesy of the general was shown by the fact that the blinds were so drawn that the light did not fall directly into the eyes of the person interviewed.

At that time the colonel general was Wenzel Wallenstein, the first man ever to venture into the very deep remoteness of space. He had not reached a star. Nobody had, at that time, but he had gone farther than any man had ever gone before.

Wallenstein was an old man and yet the count of his years was not high. He was less than ninety in a period in which many men lived to one hundred and fifty. The thing that made Wallenstein look old was the suffering which came from mental strain, not the kind which came from anxiety and competition, not the kind which came from ill health.

It was a subtler kind—a sensitivity which created its own painfulness.

Yet it was real.

Wallenstein was as stable as men came, and the young lieutenant was astonished to find that at his first meeting with the commander in chief his instinctive emotional reaction should be one of quick sympathy for the man who commanded the entire organization.

"Your name?"

The lieutenant answered, "Gordon Greene."

"Born that way?"

"No, sir."

"What was your name originally?"

"Giordano Verdi."

"Why did you change? Verdi is a great name too."

"People just found it hard to pronounce, sir. I followed along the best I could."

"I kept my name," said the old general. "I suppose it is a matter of taste."

The young lieutenant lifted his hand, left hand, palm outward, in the new salute which had been devised by the psychologists. He knew that this meant military courtesy could be passed by for the moment and that the subordinate officer was requesting permission to speak as man to man. He knew the salute and yet in these surroundings he did not altogether trust it.

The general's response was quick. He countersigned, left hand, palm outward.

The heavy, tired, wise, strained old face showed no change of expression. The general was alert. Mechanically friendly, his eyes followed the lieutenant. The lieutenant was sure that there was nothing behind those eyes, except world upon world of inward troubles.

The lieutenant spoke again, this time on confident ground.

"Is this a special interview, General? Do you have something in mind for me? If it is, sir, let me warn you, I have been declared to be psychologically unstable. Personnel doesn't often make a mistake but they may have sent me in here under error."

The general smiled. The smile itself was mechanical. It was a control of muscles, not a quick spring of human emotion.

"You will know well enough what I have in mind when we talk together, Lieutenant. I am going to have another man sit with me and it will give you some idea of what your life is leading you toward. You know perfectly well that you have asked for deep space and that so far as I'm concerned you've gotten it. The question is now, 'Do you really want it?' Do you want to take it? Is that all that you wanted to abridge courtesy for?"

"Yes, sir," said the lieutenant.

"You didn't have to call for the courtesy sign for that kind of a question. You could have asked me even within the limits of service. Let's not get too psychological. We don't need to, do we?"

Again the general gave the lieutenant a heavy smile.

Wallenstein gestured to the aide, who sprang to attention.

Wallenstein said, "Send him in."

The aide said, "Yes, sir."

The two men waited expectantly. With a springy,

lively, quick, happy step a strange lieutenant entered the room.

Gordon Greene had never seen anybody quite like this lieutenant. The lieutenant was old, almost as old as the general. His face was cheerful and unlined. The muscles of his cheeks and forehead bespoke happiness, relaxation, an assured view of life. The lieutenant wore the three highest decorations of his service. There weren't any others higher and yet there he was, an old man and still a lieutenant.

Lieutenant Greene couldn't understand it. He didn't know who this man was. It was easy enough for a young man to be a lieutenant but not for a man in his seventies or eighties. People that age were colonels, or retired, or out.

Or they had gone back to civilian life.

Space was a young man's game.

The general himself arose in courtesy to his contemporary. Lieutenant Greene's eyes widened. This too was odd. The general was not known to violate courtesy at all irregularly.

"Sit down, sir," said the strange old lieutenant.

The general sat.

"What do you want with me now? Do you want to talk about the Nancy routine one more time?"

"The Nancy routine?" asked the general blindly.

"Yes, sir. It's the same story I've told these youngsters before. You've heard it and I've heard it, there's no use of pretending."

The strange lieutenant said, "My name's Karl Vonderleyen. Have you ever heard of me?"

"No, sir," said the young lieutenant

The old lieutenant said, "You will."

"Don't get bitter about it, Karl," said the general. "A lot of other people have had troubles, besides you. I went and did the same things you did, and I'm a general. You might at least pay me the courtesy of envying me."

"I don't envy you, General. You've had your life, and I've had mine. You know what you've missed, or you think you do, and I know what I've had, and I'm sure I do."

The old lieutenant paid no more attention to the commander in chief. He turned to the young man and said,

"You're going to go out into space and we are putting on a little act, a vaudeville act. The general didn't get any Nancy. He didn't ask for Nancy. He didn't turn for help. He got out into the Up-and-Out, he pulled through it. Three years of it. Three years that are closer to three million years, I suppose. He went through hell and he came back. Look at his face. He's a success. He's an utter, blasted success, sitting there worn out, tired, and, it would seem, hurt. Look at me. Look at me carefully, Lieutenant. I'm a failure. I'm a lieutenant and the Space Service keeps me that way."

The commander in chief said nothing, so Vonderleyen talked on.

"Oh, they will retire me as a general, I suppose, when the time comes. I'm not ready to retire. I'd just as soon stay in the Space Service as anything else. There is not much to do in this world. I've had it."

"Had what, sir?" Lieutenant Greene dared to ask.

"I found Nancy. He didn't," he said. "That's as simple as it is."

The general cut back into the conversation. "It's not that bad and it's not that simple, Lieutenant Greene. There seems to be something a little wrong with Lieutenant Vonderleyen today. The story is one we have to tell you and it is something you have to make up your own mind on. There is no regulation way of handling it."

The general looked very sharply at Lieutenant Greene.

"Do you know what we have done to your brain?"

"No, sir." Greene felt uneasiness rising in him.

"Have you heard of the *sokta* virus?"

"The *what*, sir?"

"The *sokta* virus. *Sokta* is an ancient word, gets its name from Chosenmal, the language of Old Korea. That was a country west of where Japan used to be. It means 'maybe' and it is a 'maybe' that we put inside your head. It is a tiny crystal, more than microscopic. It's there. There is actually a machine on the ship, not a big one because we can't waste space; it has resonance to detonate the virus. If you detonate *sokta*, you will be like him. If you don't, you will be like me—assuming, in either case, that you live. You may not live and you may not get back, in which case what we are talking about is academic."

The young man nerved himself to ask, "What does this do to me? Why do you make this big fuss over it?"

"We can't tell you too much. One reason is it is not worth talking about."

"You mean you really can't, sir?"

The general shook his head sadly and wisely.

"No, I missed it, he got it, and yet it somehow gets out beyond the limits of talking."

At this point while he was telling the story, many years

later, I asked my cousin, "Well, Gordon, if they said you can't talk about it, how can you?"

"Drunk, man, drunk," said the cousin. "How long do you think it took me to wind myself up to this point? I'll never tell it again—never again. Anyhow, you're my cousin, you don't count. And I promised Nancy I wouldn't tell anybody."

"Who's Nancy?" I asked him.

"Nancy's what it's all about. That is what the story is. That's what those poor old goops were trying to tell me in the office. They didn't know. One of them, he had Nancy; the other one, he hadn't."

"Is Nancy a real person?"

With that he told me the rest of the story.

The interview was harsh. It was clean, stark, simple, direct. The alternatives were flat. It was perfectly plain that Wallenstein wanted Greene to come back alive. It was actual space command policy to bring the man back as a live failure instead of letting him become a dead hero. Pilots were not that common. Furthermore, morale would be worsened if men were told to go out on suicide operations.

The whole thing was psychological and before Greene got out of the room he was more confused than when he went in.

They kept telling him, both of them in their different ways—the general happily, the old lieutenant unhappily—that this was serious. The grim old general was very cheerful about telling him. The happy lieutenant kept being very sympathetic.

Greene himself wondered why he could be so sympathetic toward the commanding general and be so perfectly carefree about a failed old lieutenant. His sympathies should have been the other way around.

Fifteen hundred million miles later, four months later in ordinary time, four lifetimes later by the time which he'd gone through, Greene found out what they were talking about. It was an old psychological teaching. The men died if they were left utterly alone. The ships were designed to be protected against that. There were two men on each ship. Each ship had a lot of tapes, even a few quite unnecessary animals; in this case a pair of hamsters had been included on the ship. They had been sterilized, of course, to avoid the problem of feeding the young, but nevertheless they made a little family of their own in a miniature of life's happiness on Earth.

Earth was very far away.

At that point, his copilot died.

Everything that had threatened Greene then came true.

Greene suddenly realized what they were talking about.

The hamsters were his one hope. He thrust his face close to their cage and talked to them. He attributed moods to them. He tried to live their lives with them, all as if they were people.

As if he, himself, were a part of people still alive and not out there with the screaming silence beyond the thin wall of metal. There was nothing to do except to roam like a caged animal in machinery which he would never understand.

Time lost its perspectives. He knew he was crazy and

he knew that by training he could survive the partial craziness. He even realized that the instability in his own personality which had made him think that he wouldn't fit the Space Service probably contributed to the hope that went in with service to this point.

His mind kept coming back to Nancy and to the *sokta* virus.

What was it they had said?

They had told him that he could waken Nancy, whoever Nancy was. Nancy was no pet name of his. And yet somehow or other the virus always worked. He only needed to move his head toward a certain point, press the resonating stud on the wall, one pressure, his mission would fail, he would be happy, he would come home alive.

He couldn't understand it. Why such a choice?

It seemed three thousand years later that he dictated his last message back to Space Service. He didn't know what would happen. Obviously, that old lieutenant, Vonderleyen, or whatever his name was, was still alive. Equally obviously the general was alive. The general had pulled through. The lieutenant hadn't.

And now, Lieutenant Greene, fifteen hundred million miles out in space, had to make his choice. He made it. He decided to fail.

But he wanted, as a matter of discipline, to speak up for the man who was failing and he dictated, for the records of the ship when it got back to Earth, a very simple message concluding with an appeal for justice.

". . . and so, gentlemen, I have decided to activate the stud. I do not know what the reference to Nancy signifies. I have no concept of what the *sokta* virus will do except that it will make me fail. For this I am heartily ashamed. I regret the human weakness that has driven me to this. The weakness is human and you, gentlemen, have allowed for it. In this respect, it is not I who is failing, but the Space Service itself in giving me an authorization to fail. Gentlemen, forgive the bitterness with which I say *good-bye* to you in these seconds, but now I do say good-bye."

He stopped dictating, blinked his eyes, took one last look at the hamsters—what might they be by the time the *sokta* virus went to work?—pressed the stud and leaned forward.

Nothing happened. He pressed the stud again.

The ship suddenly filled with a strange odor. He couldn't identify the odor. He didn't know what it was.

It suddenly came to him that this was new-mown hay with a slight tinge of geraniums, possibly of roses, too, on the far side. It was a smell that was common on the farm a few years ago where he had gone for a summer. It was the smell of his mother being on the porch and calling him back to a meal, and of himself, enough of a man to be indulgent even toward the woman in his own mother, enough of a child to turn happily back to a familiar voice.

He said to himself, "If this is all there is to that virus, I can take it and work on with continued efficiency."

He added, "At fifteen hundred million miles out, and nothing but two hamsters for years of loneliness, a few hallucinations won't hurt me any."

The door opened.

It couldn't open.

The door opened nevertheless.

At this point, Greene knew a fear more terrible than anything else he had ever encountered. He said to himself, "I'm crazy, I'm crazy," and stared at the opening door.

A girl stepped in. She said, "Hello, you there. You know me, don't you?"

Greene said, "No, no, miss, who are you?"

The girl didn't answer. She just stood there and she gave him a smile.

She wore a blue serge skirt cut so that it had broad, vertical stripes, a neat little waist, a belt of the same material, a very simple blouse. She was not a strange girl and she was by no means a creature of outer space.

She was somebody he had known and known well. Perhaps loved. He just couldn't place her—not at that moment, not in that place.

She still stood staring at him. That was all.

It all came to him. Of course. She was Nancy. She was not just that Nancy they were talking about, she was *his* Nancy, his own Nancy he had always known and never met before.

He managed to pull himself together and say it to her, "How do I know you if I don't know you? You're Nancy and I've known you all my life and I have always wanted to marry you. You are the girl I have always been in love with and I never saw you before. That's funny, Nancy. It's terribly funny. I don't understand it, do you?"

Nancy came over and put her hand on his forehead. It was a real little hand and her presence was dear and precious and very welcome to him. She said, "It's going to take a bit of thinking. You see, I am not real, not to anybody except you. And yet I am more real to you than anything else will ever be. That is what the *sokta* virus is, darling. It's me. I'm you."

He stared at her. He could have been unhappy but he didn't feel unhappy, he was so glad to have her there.

He said, "What do you mean? The *sokta* virus has made you? Am I crazy? Is this just a hallucination?"

Nancy shook her head and her pretty curls spun.

"It's not that. I'm simply every girl that you ever wanted. I am the illusion that you always wanted but I am you because I am in the depths of you. I am everything that your mind might not have encountered in life. Everything that you might have been afraid to dig up. Here I am and I'm going to stay. And as long as we are here in this ship with the resonance we will get along well."

My cousin at this point began weeping. He picked up a wine flask and poured down a big glass of heavy Dago Red. For a while he cried. Putting his head on the table, he looked up at me and said, "It's been a long, long time. It's been a very long time and I still remember how she talked with me. And I see now why they say you can't talk about it. A man has got to be fearfully drunk to tell about a real life that he had and a good one, and a beautiful one and let it go, doesn't he?"

"That's right," I said, to be encouraging.

Nancy changed the ship right away. She moved the hamsters. She changed the decorations. She checked the records. The work went on more efficiently than ever before.

But the home they made for themselves, that was

something different. It had baking smells, and it had wind smells, and sometimes he would hear the rain although the nearest rain by now was one thousand six hundred million miles away, and there was nothing but the grating of cold silence on the cold, cold metal at the outside of the ship.

They lived together. It didn't take long for them to get thoroughly used to each other.

He had been born Giordano Verdi. He had limitations.

And the time came for them to get even more close than lover and lover. He said, "I just can't take you, darling. That is not the way we can do it, even in space and not the way, even if you are not real. You are real enough to me. Will you marry me out of the prayer book?"

Her eyes lit up and her incomparable lips gleamed in a smile that was all peculiarly her own. She said, "Of course."

She flung her arms around him. He ran his fingers over the bones of her shoulder. He felt her ribs. He felt the individual strands of her hair brushing his cheeks. This was real. This was more real than life itself, yet some fool had told him that it was a virus—that Nancy didn't exist. If this wasn't Nancy, what was it? he thought.

He put her down and, alive with love and happiness, he read the prayer book. He asked her to make the responses. He said, "I suppose I'm captain, and I suppose I have married you and me, haven't I, Nancy?"

The marriage went well. The ship followed an immense perimeter like that of a comet. It went far out. So far that the sun became a remote dot. The interference of the solar system had virtually no effect on the instruments.

Nancy came to him one day and said, "I suppose you know why you are a failure now."

"No," he said.

She looked at him gravely. She said, "I think with your mind. I live in your body. If you die while on this ship, I die too. Yet as long as you live, I am alive and separate. That's funny, isn't it?"

"Funny," he said, an old new pain growing in his heart.

"And yet I can tell you something which I know with that part of your mind I use. I know without you that I am. I suppose I recognize your technical training and feel it somehow even though I don't feel the lack of it. I had the education you thought I had and you wanted me to have. But do you see what's happening? We are working with our brain at almost half-power instead of one-tenth power. All your imagination is going into making me. All your extra thoughts are of me. I want them just as I want you to love me but there are none left over for emergencies and there is nothing left over for the Space Service. You are doing the minimum, that's all. Am I worth it?"

"Of course you are worth it, darling. You're worth anything that any man could ask of the sweetheart, and of love, and of a wife and a true companion."

"But don't you see? I am taking all the best of you. You are putting it into me and when the ship comes home there won't be any me."

In a strange way he realized that the drug was working. He could see what was happening to himself as he looked at his well-beloved Nancy with her shimmering hair and he realized the hair needed no prettying or hairdos. He looked at her clothes and he realized that she wore clothes for which there was no space on the ship. And yet she changed them, delightfully, winsomely, attractively, day in and day out. He ate the food that he knew couldn't be on the ship. None of this worried him. And now he couldn't even be worried at the thought of losing Nancy herself. Any other thought he could have rejected from his subconscious mind and could have surrendered to the idea that it was not a hallucination after all.

This was too much. He ran his fingers through her hair. He said, "I know I'm crazy, darling, and I know that you don't exist—"

"But I do exist. I am you. I am a part of Gordon Greene as surely as if I'd married you. I'll never die until you do because when you get home, darling, I'll drop back, back into your deeper mind but I'll live in your mind as long as you live. You can't lose me and I can't leave you and you can't forget me. And I can't escape to anyone except through your lips. That's why they talk about it. That's why it is such a strange thing."

"And that's where I know I'm wrong," stubbornly insisted Gordon. "I love you and I know you are a phantom and I know you are going away and I know we are coming to an end and it doesn't worry me. I'll be happy just being with you. I don't need a drink. I wouldn't touch a drug. Yet the happiness is here."

They went about their little domestic chores. They checked his graph paper, they stored the records, they put a few silly things into the permanent ship's record. They then toasted marshmallows before a large fire. The fire was in a handsome fireplace which did not exist. The flames couldn't have burned but they did. There weren't any marshmallows on the ship but they toasted them and enjoyed them anyhow.

That's the way their life went—full of magic, and yet the magic had no sting or provocation to it, no anger, no hopelessness, no despair.

They were a very happy couple.

Even the hamsters felt it. They stayed clean and plump. They ate their food willingly. They got over space nausea. They peered at him.

He let one of them, the one with the brown nose, out and let it run around the room. He said, "You're a real army character. You poor thing. Born for space and serving out here in it."

Only one other time did Nancy take up the question of their future. She said,

"We can't have children, you know. The *sokta* drug doesn't allow for that. And you may have children yourself but it is going to be funny having them if you marry somebody else with me always there just in the background. And I will be there."

They made it back to Earth. They returned.

As he stepped out of the gate, a harsh, weary medical colonel gave him one sharp glance. He said,

"Oh, we thought that had happened."

"What, sir?" said a plump and radiant Lieutenant Greene.

"You got Nancy," said the colonel.

"Yes, sir. I'll bring her right out."

"Go get her," said the colonel.

Greene went back into the rocket and he looked.

There was no sign of Nancy. He came to the door astonished. He was still not upset. He said,

"Colonel, I don't seem to see her there but I'm sure that she's somewhere around."

The colonel gave him a strange, sympathetic, fatigued smile. "She always will be somewhere around, Lieutenant. You've done the minimum job. I don't know whether we ought to discourage people like you. I suppose you realize that you are frozen in your present grade. You'll get a decoration, Mission Accomplished. Mission successful, farther than anybody has gone before. Incidentally, Vonderleyen says he knows you and will be waiting over yonder. We have to take you into the hospital to make sure that you don't go into shock."

"At the hospital," said my cousin, "there was no shock."

He didn't even miss Nancy. How could he miss her when she hadn't left? She was always just around the corner, just behind the door, just a few minutes away.

At breakfast time he knew he'd see her for lunch. At lunch, he knew she'd drop by in the afternoon. At the end of the afternoon, he knew he'd have dinner with her.

He knew he was crazy. Crazy as he could be.

He knew perfectly well that there was no Nancy and never had been. He supposed that he ought to hate the *sokta* drug for doing that to him, but it brought its own relief.

The effect of Nancy was an immolation in perpetual hope, the promise of something that could never be lost, and a promise of something that cannot be lost is often better than a reality which can be lost.

That's all there was to it. They asked him to testify against the use of the *sokta* drug and he said,

"Me? Give up Nancy? Don't be silly."

"You haven't got her," said somebody.

"That's what you think," said my cousin, Lieutenant Greene.

The Fife of Bodidharma

Music (said Confucius) *awakens the mind, propriety finishes it, melody completes it.*
　　　　　　　　—The *Lun Yu*, Book VIII, Chapter 8

∽ | ∽

It was perhaps in the second period of the proto-Indian Harappa culture, perhaps earlier in the very dawn of metal, that a goldsmith accidentally found a formula to make a magical fife. To him, the fife became death or bliss, an avenue to choosable salvations or dooms. Among later men, the fife might be recognized as a chancy prediscovery of psionic powers with sonic triggering.

Whatever it was, it worked! Long before the Buddha, long-haired Dravidian priests learned that it worked.

Cast mostly in gold despite the goldsmith's care with the speculum alloy, the fife emitted shrill whistlings but it also transmitted supersonic vibrations in a narrow range—narrow and intense enough a range to rearrange synapses in the brain and to modify the basic emotions of the hearer.

The goldsmith did not long survive his instrument. They found him dead.

The fife became the property of priests; after a short, terrible period of use and abuse, it was buried in the tomb of a great king.

∽ II ∽

Robbers found the fife, tried it and died. Some died amid bliss, some amid hate, others in a frenzy of fear and delusion. A strong survivor, trembling after the ordeal of inexpressibly awakened sensations and emotions, wrapped the fife in a page of holy writing and presented it to Bodidharma the Blessed One just before Bodidharma began his unbelievably arduous voyage from India across the ranges of the spines of the world over to far Cathay.

Bodidharma the Blessed One, the man who had seen Persia, the aged one bringing wisdom, came across the highest of all mountains in the year that the Northern Wei dynasty of China moved their capital out of divine Loyang. (Elsewhere in the world where men reckoned the years from the birth of their Lord Jesus Christ, the year was counted as Anno Domini 554, but in the high land between India and China the message of Christianity had not yet arrived and the word of the Lord Gautama Buddha was still the sweetest gospel to reach the ears of men.)

Bodidharma, clad by only a thin robe, climbed across the glaciers. For food he drank the air, spicing it with prayer. Cold winds cut his old skin, his tired bones; for a cloak he drew his sanctity about him and bore within his indomitable heart the knowledge that the pure, unspoiled message of the Lord Gautama Buddha had, by the will of time and chance themselves, to be carried from the Indian world to the Chinese.

Once beyond the peaks and passes he descended into the cold frigidity of high desert. Sand cut his feet but the skin did not bleed because he was shod in sacred spells and magical charms.

At last animals approached. They came in the ugliness of their sin, ignorance, and shame. Beasts they were, but more than beasts—they were the souls of the wicked condemned to endless rebirth, now incorporated in vile forms because of the wickedness with which they had once rejected the teachings of eternity and the wisdom which lay before them as plainly as the trees or the night-time heavens. The more vicious the man, the more ugly the beast: this was the rule. Here in the desert the beasts were very ugly.

Bodidharma the Blessed One shrank back.

He did not desire to use the weapon. "O Forever Blessed One, seated in the Lotus Flower, Buddha, help me!"

Within his heart he felt no response. The sinfulness and wickedness of these beasts was such that even the Buddha had turned his face gently aside and would offer no protection to his messenger, the missionary Bodidharma.

Reluctantly Bodidharma took out his fife.

The fife was a dainty weapon, twice the length of a man's finger. Golden in strange, almost ugly forms, it hinted at a civilization which no one living in India now remembered. The fife had come out of the early beginnings of mankind, had ridden across a mass of ages, a legion of years, and survived as a testimony to the power of early men.

At the end of the fife was a little whistle. Four touch holes gave the fife pitches and a wide variety of combinations of notes.

Blown once the fife called to holiness. This occurred if all stops were closed.

Blown twice with all stops opened the fife carried its own power. This power was strange indeed. It magnified every chance emotion of each living thing within range of its sound.

Bodidharma the Blessed One had carried the fife because it comforted him. Closed, its notes reminded him of the sacred message of the Three Treasures of the Buddha which he carried from India to China. Opened, its notes brought bliss to the innocent and their own punishment to the wicked. Innocence and wickedness were not determined by the fife but by the hearers themselves, whoever they might be. The trees which heard these notes in their own treelike way struck even more mightily into the earth and up to the sky reaching for nourishment with new but dim and treelike hope. Tigers became more tigerish, frogs more froggy, men more good or bad, as their characters might dispose them.

"Stop!" called Bodidharma the Blessed One to the beasts.

Tiger and wolf, fox and jackal, snake and spider, they advanced.

"Stop!" he called again.

Hoof and claw, sting and tooth, eyes alive, they advanced.

"Stop!" he called for the third time.

Still they advanced. He blew the fife wide open, twice, clear and loud.

Twice, clear and loud.

The animals stopped. At the second note, they began to thresh about, imprisoned even more deeply by the bestiality of their own natures. The tiger snarled at his own front paws, the wolf snapped at his own tail, the jackal ran fearfully from his own shadow, the spider hid beneath the darkness of rocks, and the other vile beasts who had threatened the Blessed One let him pass.

Bodidharma the Blessed One went on. In the streets of the new capital at Anyang the gentle gospel of Buddhism was received with curiosity, with calm, and with delight. Those voluptuous barbarians, the Toba Tartars, who had made themselves masters of North China, now filled their hearts and souls with the hope of death instead of the fear of destruction. Mothers wept with pleasure to know that their children, dying, had been received into blessedness. The Emperor himself laid aside his sword in order to listen to the gentle message that had come so bravely over illimitable mountains.

When Bodidharma the Blessed One died he was buried in the outskirts of Anyang, his fife in a sacred onyx case beside his right hand. There he and it both slept for thirteen hundred and forty years.

∽ III ∽

In the year 1894 a German explorer—so he fancied

himself to be—looted the tomb of the Blessed One in the name of science.

Villagers caught him in the act and drove him from the hillside.

He escaped with only one piece of loot, an onyx case with a strange copperlike fife. Copper it seemed to be, although the metal was not as corroded as actual copper should have been after so long a burial in intermittently moist country. The fife was filthy. He cleaned it enough to see that it was fragile and to reveal the un-Chinese character of the declarations along its side.

He did not clean it enough to try blowing it: *he* lived because of that.

The fife was presented to a small municipal museum named in honor of a German grand duchess. It occupied case No. 34 of the Dorotheum and lay there for another fifty-one years.

∽ IV ∽

The B-29s had gone. They had roared off in the direction of Rastatt.

Wolfgang Huene climbed out of the ditch. He hated himself, he hated the Allies, and he almost hated Hitler. A Hitler youth, he was handsome, blond, tall, craggy. He was also brave, sharp, cruel, and clever. He was a Nazi. Only in a Nazi world could he hope to exist. His parents, he knew, were soft rubbish. When his father had been killed in a bombing, Wolfgang did not mind. When his mother, half-starved, died of influenza, he did not worry about her. She was old and did not matter. Germany mattered.

Now the Germany which mattered to him was coming apart, ripped by explosions, punctured by shock waves, and fractured by the endless assault of Allied air power.

Wolfgang as a young Nazi did not know fear, but he did know bewilderment.

In an animal, instinctive way, he knew—without thinking about it—that if Hitlerism did not survive he himself would not survive either. He even knew that he was doing his best, what little best there was still left to do. He was looking for spies while reporting the weak-hearted ones who complained against the Führer or the war. He was helping to organize the Volkssturm and he had hopes of becoming a Nazi guerrilla even if the Allies did cross the Rhine. Like an animal, but like a very intelligent animal, he knew he had to fight, while at the same time, he realized that the fight might go against him.

He stood in the street watching the dust settle after the bombing.

The moonlight was clear on the broken pavement.

This was a quiet part of the city. He could hear the fires downtown making a crunching sound, like the familiar noise of his father eating lettuce. Near himself he could hear nothing; he seemed to be all alone, under the moon, in a tiny forgotten corner of the world.

He looked around.

His eyes widened in astonishment: the Dorotheum museum had been blasted open.

Idly, he walked over to the ruin. He stood in the dark doorway.

Looking back at the street and then up at the sky to make sure that it was safe to show a light, he then flashed on his pocket electric light and cast the beam around the display room. Cases were broken; in most of them glass had fallen in on the exhibits. Window glass looked like puddles of ice in the cold moonlight as it lay broken on the old stone floors.

Immediately in front of him a display case sagged crazily.

He cast his flashlight beam on it. The light picked up a short tube which looked something like the barrel of an antique pistol. Wolfgang reached for the tube. He had played in a band and he knew what it was. It was a fife.

He held it in his hand a moment and then stuck it in his jacket. He cast the beam of his light once more around the museum and then went out in the street. It was no use letting the police argue.

He could now hear the laboring engines of trucks as they coughed, sputtering with their poor fuel, climbing up the hill toward him.

He put his light in his pocket. Feeling the fife, he took it out.

Instinctively, the way that any human being would, he put his fingers over all four of the touch holes before he began to blow. The fife was stopped up.

He applied force.

He blew hard.

The fife sounded.

A sweet note, golden beyond imagination, softer and wilder than the most thrilling notes of the finest symphony in the world, sounded in his ears.

He felt different, relieved, happy.

His soul, which he did not know he had, achieved a condition of peace which he had never before experienced. In that moment a small religion was born. It was a small religion because it was confined to the mind of a single brutal adolescent, but it was a true religion, nevertheless, because it had the complete message of hope, comfort, and fulfillment of an order beyond the limits of this life. Love, and the tremendous meaning of love, poured through his mind. Love relaxed the muscles of his back and even let his aching eyelids drop over his eyes in the first honest fatigue he had admitted for many weeks.

The Nazi in him had been drained off. The call to holiness, trapped in the forgotten magic of Bodidharma's fife, had sounded even to him. Then he made his mistake, a mortal one.

The fife had no more malice than a gun before it is fired, no more hate than a river before it swallows a human body, no more anger than a height from which a man may slip; the fife had its own power, partly in sound itself, but mostly in the mechano-psionic linkage which the unusual alloy and shape had given the Harappa goldsmith forgotten centuries before.

Wolfgang Huene blew again, holding the fife between two fingers, with none of the stops closed. This time the note was wild. In a terrible and wholly convincing moment of vision he reincarnated in himself all the false resolutions, the venomous patriotism, the poisonous bravery of Hitler's Reich. He was once again a Hitler youth, consummately a Nordic man. His eyes gleamed with a message he felt pouring out of himself.

He blew again.

This third note was the perfecting note—the note which had protected Bodidharma the Blessed One fifteen hundred and fifty years before in the frozen desert north of Tibet.

Huene became even more Nazi. No longer the boy, no longer the human being. He was the magnification of himself. He became all fighter, but he had forgotten who he was or what it was that he was fighting for.

The blacked-out trucks came up the hill. His blind eyes looked at them. Fife in hand, he snarled at them.

A crazy thought went through his mind. "Allied tanks . . ."

He ran wildly toward the leading truck. The driver did not see more than a shadow and jammed on the brakes too late. The front bumper burst a soft obstruction.

The front wheel covered the body of the boy. When the truck stopped the boy was dead and the fife, half crushed, was pressed against the rock of a German road.

∽ V ∽

Hagen von Grün was one of the German rocket scientists who worked at Huntsville, Alabama. He had gone on down to Cape Canaveral to take part in the fifth series of American launchings. This included in the third shot of the series a radio transmitter designed to hit standard wave radios immediately beneath the satellite. The purpose was to allow ordinary listeners throughout the world to take part in the tracking of the satellite. This particular satellite was designed to have a relatively short life. With good luck it would last as long as five weeks, not longer.

The miniaturized transmitter was designed to pick up the sounds, minute though they might be, produced by the heating and cooling of the shell and to transmit a sound pattern reflecting the heat of cosmic rays and also to a certain degree to relay the visual images in terms of a sound pattern.

Hagen von Grün was present at the final assembly. A small part of the assembly consisted of inserting a tube which would serve the double function of a resonating chamber between the outer skin of the satellite and a tiny microphone half the size of a sweet pea which would then translate the sound made by the outer shell into radio signals which amateurs on the Earth surface fifteen hundred miles below could follow.

Von Grün no longer smoked. He had stopped smoking that fearful night in which Allied planes bombed the truck convoy carrying his colleagues and himself to safety. Though he had managed to scrounge cigarettes throughout the war he had even given up carrying his cigarette holder. He carried instead an odd old copper fife he had found in the highway and had put back into shape. Superstitious at his luck in living, and grateful that the fife reminded him not to smoke, he never bothered to clean it out and blow it. He had weighed it, found its specific gravity, measured it, like the good German that he was, down to the last millimeter and milligram but he kept it in his pocket though it was a little clumsy to carry.

Just as they put the last part of the nose cone together, the strut broke.

It could not break, but it did.

It would have taken five minutes and a ride down the elevator to find a new tube to serve as a strut.

Acting on an odd impulse, Hagen von Grün remembered that his lucky fife was within a millimeter of the length required, and was of precisely the right diameter. The holes did not matter. He picked up a file, filed the old fife, and inserted it.

They closed the skin of the satellite. They sealed the cone.

Seven hours later the message rocket took off, the first one capable of reaching every standard wave radio on earth. As Hagen von Grün watched the great rocket climb he wondered to himself, "Does it make any difference whether those stops were opened or closed?"

Angerhelm

Funny funny funny. It's sort of funny funny funny to think without a brain—it is really something like a trick but not a trick to think without a brain. Talking is even harder but it can be done.

I still remember the way that phrase came ringing through when we finally got hold of old Nelson Angerhelm and sat him down with the buzzing tape.

The story began a long time before that. I never knew the beginnings.

My job is an assistant to Mr. Spatz, and Spatz has been shooting holes in budgets now for eighteen years. He is the man who approves, on behalf of the Director of the Budget, all requests for special liaison between the Department of the Army and the intelligence community.

He is very good at his job. More people have shown up asking for money and have ended up with about one-tenth of what they asked than you could line up in any one corridor of the Pentagon. That is saying a lot.

The case began to break some months ago after the Russians started to get back those odd little recording capsules. The capsules came out of their Sputniks. We didn't know what was in the capsules as they returned from upper space. All we knew was that there was something in them.

The capsules descended in such a way that we could track them by radar. Unfortunately they all fell into Russian territory except for a single capsule which landed in the Atlantic. At the seven-million-dollar point we gave up trying to find it.

The Commander of the Atlantic fleet had been told by his intelligence officer that they might have a chance of finding it if they kept on looking. The Commander referred the matter to Washington, and the budget people saw the request. That stopped it, for a while.

The case began to break from about four separate directions at once. Khrushchev himself said something very funny to the Secretary of State. They had met in London after all.

Khrushchev said at the end of a meeting, "You play jokes sometimes, Mr. Secretary?"

The Secretary looked very surprised when he heard the translation.

"Jokes, Mr. Prime Minister?"

"Yes."

"What kind of jokes?"

"Jokes about apparatus."

"Jokes about machinery don't sit very well," said the American.

They went on talking back and forth as to whether it

was a good idea to play practical jokes when each one had a serious job of espionage to do.

The Russian leader insisted that he had no espionage, never heard of espionage, and that his espionage worked well enough so that he knew damn well that he didn't have any espionage.

To this display of heat, the Secretary replied that he didn't have any espionage either and that we knew nothing whatever that occurred in Russia. Furthermore not only did we not know anything about Russia but we knew we didn't know it and we made sure of that. After this exchange both leaders parted, each one wondering what the other had been talking about.

The whole matter was referred back to Washington. I was somewhere down on the list to see it.

At that time I had "Galactic" clearance. Galactic clearance came a little bit after universal clearance. It wasn't very strong but it amounted to something. I was supposed to see those special papers in connection with my job of assisting Mr. Spatz in liaison. Actually it didn't do any good except to fill in the time when I wasn't working out budgets for him.

The second lead came from some of the boys over in the Valley. We never called the place by any other name and we don't even like to see it in the federal budget. We know as much as we need to about it and then we stop thinking.

It is much safer to stop thinking. It is not our business to think about what other people are doing, particularly if they are spending several million dollars of Uncle Sam's money every day, trying to find out what they think and most of the time ending up with nothing conclusive.

Later we were to find out that the boys in the Valley had practically every security agent in the country rushing off to Minneapolis to look for a man named Angerhelm. Nelson Angerhelm.

The name didn't mean anything then but before we got through it ended up as the largest story of the twentieth century. If they ever turn it loose it is going to be the biggest story in two thousand years.

The third part of the story came along a little later.

Colonel Plugg was over in G-2. He called up Mr. Spatz and he couldn't get Mr. Spatz so he called me.

He said, "What's the matter with your boss? Isn't he ever in his room?"

"Not if I can help it. I don't run him, he runs me. What do you want, Colonel?" I said.

The colonel snarled.

"Look, I am supposed to get money out of you for liaison purposes. I don't know how far I am going to have to go to liaise or if it is any of my business. I asked my old man what I ought to do about it and he doesn't know. Perhaps we ought to get out and just let the Intelligence boys handle it. Or we ought to send it to State. You spend half your life telling me whether I can have liaison or not and then giving me the money for it. Why don't you come on over and take a little responsibility for a change?"

I rushed over to Plugg's office. It was an Army problem.

These are the facts.

The Soviet Assistant Military Attache, a certain Lieutenant Colonel Potariskov, asked for an interview. When he came over he brought nothing with him. This time he didn't even bring a translator. He spoke very funny English but it worked.

The essence of Potariskov's story was that he didn't think it was very sporting of the American military to interfere in solemn weather reporting by introducing practical jokes in Soviet radar. If the American army didn't have anything else better to do would they please play jokes on each other but not on the Soviet forces?

This didn't make much sense.

Colonel Plugg tried to find out what the man was talking about. The Russian sounded crazy and kept talking about jokes.

It finally turned out that Potariskov had a piece of paper in his pocket. He took it out and Plugg looked at it.

On it there was an address. Nelson Angerhelm, 2322 Ridge Drive, Hopkins, Minnesota.

It turned out that Hopkins, Minnesota, was a suburb of Minneapolis. That didn't take long to find out.

This meant nothing to Colonel Plugg and he asked if there was anything that Potariskov really wanted.

Potariskov asked if the Colonel would confess to the Angerhelm joke.

Potariskov said that in Intelligence they never tell you about the jokes they play with the Signal Corps. Plugg still insisted that he didn't know. He said he would try to find out and let Potariskov know later on. Potariskov went away.

Plugg called up the Signal Corps, and by the time he got through calling he had a lead back into the Valley. The Valley people heard about it and they immediately sent a man over.

It was about this time that I came in. He couldn't get hold of Mr. Spatz and there was real trouble.

The point is that all three of them led together. The Valley people had picked up the name (and it is not up to me to tell you how they got hold of it). The name Angerhelm had been running all over the Soviet communications system. Practically every Russian official in the world had been asked if he knew anything about Nelson Angerhelm and almost every official, at least as far as the boys in the Valley could tell, had replied that he didn't know what it was all about.

Some reference back to Mr. Khrushchev's conversation with the Secretary of State suggested that the Angerhelm inquiry might have tied in with this. We pursued it a little further. Angerhelm was apparently the right reference. The Valley people already had something about him. They had checked with the F.B.I.

The F.B.I. had said that Nelson Angerhelm was a 62-year-old retired poultry farmer. He had served in World War I.

His service had been rather brief. He had gotten as far as Plattsburg, New York, broken an ankle, stayed four months in a hospital, and the injury had developed complications. He had been drawing a Veterans Administration allowance ever since. He had never visited outside the United States, never joined a subversive organization, never married, and never spent a nickel. So far as the F.B.I. could discover, his life was not worth living.

This left the matter up in the air. There was nothing whatever to connect him with the Soviet Union.

It turned out that I wasn't needed after all. Spatz came into the office and said that a conference had been called for the whole Intelligence community, people from State were sitting in, and there was a special representative from OCBM from the White House to watch what they were doing.

The question arose, "Who was Nelson Angerhelm? And what were we to do about him?"

An additional report had been made out by an agent who specialized in pretending to be an Internal Revenue man.

The "Internal Revenue agent" was one of the best people in the F.B.I. for checking on subversive activities. He was a real expert on espionage and he knew all about bad connections. He could smell a conspirator two miles off on a clear day. And by sitting in a room for a little while he could tell whether anybody had an illegal meeting there for the previous three years. Maybe I am exaggerating a little bit but I am not exaggerating much.

This fellow, who was a real artist at smelling out Commies and anything that even faintly resembles a Commie, came back with a completely blank ticket on Angerhelm.

There was only one connection that Angerhelm had with the larger world. He had a younger brother, whose name was Tice. Funny name and I don't know why he got it. Somebody told us later on that the full name tied in with Theiss Ankerhjelm, which was the name of a Swedish admiral a couple hundred years ago. Perhaps the family was proud of it.

The younger brother was a West Pointer. He had had

a regular career; that came easily enough out of the Adjutant General's Office.

What did develop, though, was that the younger brother had died only two months previously. He too was a bachelor. One of the psychiatrists who got into the case said, "What a mother!"

Tice Angerhelm had traveled a great deal. He had something to do, as a matter of fact, with two or three of the projects that I was liaising on. There were all sorts of issues arising from this.

However, he was dead. He had never worked directly on Soviet matters. He had no Soviet friends, had never been in the Soviet Union, and had never met Soviet forces. He had never even gone to the Soviet Embassy to an official reception.

The man was no specialist, outside of Ordnance, a little tiny bit of French, and the missile program. He was something of a Saturday evening Don Juan. It was then time for the fourth stage.

Colonel Plugg was told to get hold of Lieutenant Colonel Potariskov and find out what Potariskov had to give him. This time Potariskov called back and said that he would rather have his boss, the Soviet Ambassador himself, call on the Secretary or the Undersecretary of State.

There was some shilly-shallying back and forth. The Secretary was out of town, the Undersecretary said he would be very glad to see the Soviet Ambassador if there were anything to ask about. He said that we had found Angerhelm, and if the Soviet authorities wanted to interview Mr. Angerhelm themselves they jolly well could go to Hopkins, Minnesota, and interview him.

This led to a real flash of embarrassment when it was discovered that the area of Hopkins, Minnesota, was in the "no travel" zone proscribed to Soviet diplomats in retaliation against their "no travel" zones imposed on American diplomats in the Soviet Union.

This was ironed out. The Soviet Ambassador was asked, would he like to go see a chicken farmer in Minnesota?

When the Soviet Ambassador stated that he was not particularly interested in chicken farmers, but that he would be willing to see Mr. Angerhelm at a later date if the American government didn't mind, the whole thing was let go.

Nothing happened at all. Presumably the Russians were relaying things back to Moscow by courier, letter, or whatever mysterious ways the Russians use when they are acting very deliberately and very solemnly.

I heard nothing and certainly the people around the Soviet Embassy saw no unusual contacts at that time.

Nelson Angerhelm hadn't come into the story yet. All he knew was that several odd characters had asked him about veterans that he scarcely knew, saying that they were looking for security clearances.

And an Internal Revenue man had a long and very exhausting talk with him about his brother's estate. That didn't seem to leave much.

Angerhelm went on feeding his chickens. He had television and Minneapolis has a pretty good range of stations. Now and then he showed up at the church; more frequently he showed up at the general store.

He almost always went away from town to avoid the

new shopping centers. He didn't like the way Hopkins had developed and preferred to go to the little country centers where they still have general stores. In its own funny way this seemed to be the only pleasure the old man had.

After nineteen days, and I can now count almost every hour of them, the answer must have gotten back from Moscow. It was probably carried in by the stocky brown-haired courier who made the trip about every fortnight. One of the fellows from the Valley told me about that. I wasn't supposed to know and it didn't matter then.

Apparently the Soviet Ambassador had been told to play the matter lightly. He called on the Undersecretary of State and ended up discussing world butter prices and the effect of American exports of ghee to Pakistan on the attempts of the Soviet Union to trade ghee for hemp.

Apparently this was an extraordinary and confidential thing for the Soviet Ambassador to discuss. The Undersecretary would have been more impressed if he had been able to find out why the Soviet Ambassador just out of the top of his head announced that the Soviet Union had given about a hundred and twenty million dollars' credit to Pakistan for some unnecessary highways and was able to reply, therefore, somewhat tartly to the general effect that if the Soviet Union ever decided to stabilize world markets with the cooperation of the United States we would be very happy to cooperate. But this was no time to discuss money or fair business deals when they were dumping every piece of export rubbish they could in our general direction.

It was characteristic of this Soviet Ambassador that he took the rebuff calmly. Apparently his mission was to have no mission. He left and that was all there was from him.

✧✧✧

Potariskov came back to the Pentagon, this time accompanied by a Russian civilian. The new man's English was a little more than perfect. The English was so good that it was desperately irritating.

Potariskov himself looked like a rather horsey, brown-faced schoolboy, with chestnut hair and brown eyes. I got to see him because they had me sitting in the back of Plugg's office pretending just to wait for somebody else.

The conversation was very simple. Potariskov brought out a recording tape. It was standard American tape.

Plugg looked at it and said, "Do you want to play it right now?"

Potariskov agreed.

The stenographer got a tape recorder in. By that time three or four other officers wandered in and none of them happened to leave. As a matter of fact one of them wasn't even an officer but he happened to have a uniform on that very day.

They played the tape and I listened to it. It was *buzz, buzz, buzz*. And there was some hissing, then it went *clickety, clickety, clickety*. Then it was *buzz, buzz, buzz* again. It was the kind of sound in which you turn on a radio and you don't even get static. You just get funny buzzing sounds which indicate that somebody has some sort of radio transmission somewhere but it is not consistent enough to be the loud *whee, wheeeee* kind of static which one often hears.

All of us stood there rather solemnly. Plugg, thoroughly a soldier, listened at rigid attention, moving his eyes back and forth from the tape recorder to Potariskov's face.

Potariskov looked at Plugg and then ran his eyes around the group.

The little Russian civilian, who was as poisonous as a snake, glanced at every single one of us. He was obviously taking our measure and he was anxious to find out if any of us could hear anything he couldn't hear. None of us heard anything.

At the end of the tape Plugg reached out to turn off the machine.

"Don't stop it," Potariskov said.

The other Russian interjected, "Didn't you hear it?"

All of us shook our heads. We had heard nothing.

With that, Potariskov said with singular politeness, "Please play it again."

We played it again. Nothing happened, except for the buzzing and clicking.

After the fifteen-minute point it was beginning to get pretty stale for some of us. One or two of the men actually wandered out. They happened to be the bona fide visitors. The non-bona fide visitors slouched down in the room.

Colonel Plugg offered Potariskov a cigarette, which Potariskov took. They both smoked and we played it a third time. Then the third time Potariskov said, "Turn it off."

"Didn't you hear it?" said Potariskov.

"Hear what?" said Plugg.

"Hear the name and the address."

At that the funniest feeling came over me. I knew that I had heard something and I turned to the Colonel and said, "Funny, I don't know where I heard it or how I heard it but I do know something that I didn't know."

"What is that?" said the little Russian civilian, his face lighting up.

"Nelson," said I, intending to say, "Nelson Angerhelm, 2322 Ridge Drive, Hopkins, Minnesota." Just as I had seen it in the "galactic" secret documents. Of course I didn't go any further. That was in the document and was very secret indeed. How should I know it?

The Russian civilian looked at me. There was a funny, wicked, friendly, crooked sort of smile on his face. He said, "Didn't you hear 'Nelson Angerhelm, 2322 Ridge Drive, Hopkins, Minnesota,' just now, and yet did you not know *where* you heard it?"

The question then arose, "What had happened?"

Potariskov spoke with singular candor. Even the Russian with him concurred.

"We believe that this is a case of marginal perception. We have played this. This is obviously a copy. We have many such copies. We have played it to all our people. Nobody can even specify at what point he has heard it. We have had our best experts on it. Some put it at minute three. Others put it at minute twelve. Some put it at minute thirteen and a half and at different places. But different people under different controls all come out with the idea that they have heard 'Nelson Angerhelm, 2322 Ridge Drive, Hopkins, Minnesota.' We have tried it on Chinese people."

At that the Russian civilian interrupted. "Yes, indeed, they tried it on Chinese persons and even they heard the same thing, Nelson Angerhelm. Even when they do not know the language they hear 'Nelson Angerhelm.' Even when they know nothing else they hear that and they hear the street numbers. The numbers are always in English. They cannot make a recording. The recording is only of this noise and yet it comes out. What do you make of that?"

What they said turned out to be true. We tried it also, after they went away.

We tried it on college students, foreigners, psychiatrists, White House staff members, and passers-by. We even thought of running it on a municipal radio somewhere as a quiz show and offering prizes for anyone that got it. That was a little too heavy, so we accepted a much safer suggestion that we try it out on the public address system of the SAC base. The SAC was guarded night and day.

No one happened to be getting much leave anyhow and it was easy enough to cut off the leave for an extra week. We played that damn thing six times over and almost everybody on that base wanted to write a letter to Nelson Angerhelm, 2322 Ridge Drive, Hopkins, Minnesota. They were even calling each other Angerhelm and wondering what the hell it meant.

Naturally there were a great many puns on the name and even some jokes of a rather smutty order. That didn't help.

The troublesome thing was that on all these different tests we too were unable to find out at what point the subliminal transmission of the name and address came.

It was subliminal, all right. There's not much trick to that. Any good psychologist can pass along either a noise message or a sight message without the recipient knowing exactly when he got it. It is simply a matter of getting down near the threshold, running a little tiny bit under the threshold, and then making the message sharp and clear enough, just under the level of conscious notice, so that it slips on through.

We therefore knew what we were dealing with. What we didn't know was what the Russians were doing with it, how they had gotten it, and why they were so upset about it.

Finally it all went to the White House for a conference. The conference, to which my boss Mr. Spatz went along as a sort of rapporteur and monitor to safeguard the interests of the Director of the Budget and of the American taxpayer, was a rather brief affair.

All roads led to Nelson Angerhelm. Nelson Angerhelm was already guarded by about half of the F.B.I. and a large part of the local military district forces. Every room in his house had been wired. The microphones were sensitive enough to hear his heart beat. The safety precautions we were taking on that man would have justified the program we have for taking care of Fort Knox.

Angerhelm knew that some awful funny things had been happening but he didn't know what and he didn't know who was concerned with it.

Months later he was able to tell somebody that he thought his brother had probably done some forgery or counterfeiting and that the neighborhood was being thoroughly combed. He didn't realize his safeguarding was the biggest American national treasure since the discovery of the atomic bomb.

The President himself gave the word. He reviewed the evidence. The Secretary of State said that he didn't think that Khrushchev would have brought up the question of a joke if Khrushchev himself had not missed out on the facts.

We had even tried Russians on it, of course—Russians on our side. And they didn't get any more off the record than the rest of the people. Everybody heard the same blessed thing, "Nelson Angerhelm, 2322 Ridge Drive, Hopkins, Minnesota."

But that didn't get anybody anywhere.

The only thing left was to try it on the man himself.

When it came to picking inconspicuous people to go along, the Intelligence committee were pretty thin-skinned about letting outsiders into their show. On the other hand they did not have domestic jurisdiction, particularly not when the President had turned it over to J. Edgar Hoover and said, "Ed, you handle this. I don't like the looks of it."

Somebody over in the Pentagon, presumably deviled on by Air Intelligence, got the bright idea that if the Army and the rest of the Intelligence committee couldn't fit into the show the best they could do would be to get their revenge on liaison by letting liaison itself go. This meant Mr. Spatz.

Mr. Spatz has been on the job for many, many years by always avoiding anything interesting or dramatic, always watching for everything that mattered—which was the budget and the authorization for next year—and by ditching controversial personalities long before anyone else had any idea that they were controversial.

Therefore, he didn't go. If this Angerhelm fiasco was going to turn out to be a mess he wanted to be out of it.

It was me who got the assignment.

I was made a sort of honorary member of the F.B.I.

and they even let me carry the tape in the end. They must have had about six other copies of the tape so the honor wasn't as marked as it looked. We were simply supposed to go along as people who knew something about the brother.

It was a dry, reddish Sunday afternoon, looking a little bit as though the sunset were coming.

We drove up to this very nice frame house. It had double windows all the way around and looked as tight as the proverbial rug for a bug to be snug in in cold winter. This wasn't winter and the old gentleman obviously couldn't pay for air conditioning. But the house still looked snug.

There was no waste, no show. It just looked like a thoroughly livable house.

The F.B.I. man was big-hearted and let me ring the doorbell. There was no answer so I rang the doorbell some more. Again, nobody answered the bell.

We decided to wait outside and wandered around the yard. We looked at the car in the yard; it seemed in running order.

We rang the doorbell again, then walked around the house and looked into the kitchen window. We checked his car to see if the radiator felt warm. We looked at our watches. We wondered if he were hiding and peeking out at us. Once more we rang the doorbell.

Just then, the old boy came down the front walk.

We introduced ourselves and the preliminaries were the usual sort of thing. I found my heart beating violently. If something had stumped both the Soviet Union and the rest of the world, something salvaged possibly out of space itself, something which thousands of men had heard and none could identify, something so mysterious that the name of Nelson Angerhelm rang over and over again like a pitiable cry beyond all limits of understanding, what could this be?

We didn't know.

The old man stood there. He was erect, sunburned, red-cheeked, red-nosed, red-eared. Healthy as he could be, Swedish to the bone.

All we had to do was to tell him that we were concerned with his brother, Tice Angerhelm, and he listened to us. We had no trouble, no trouble at all.

As he listened his eyes got wide and he said, "I know there has been a lot of snooping around here and you people had a lot of trouble and I thought somebody was going to come and talk to me about it but I didn't think it would be this soon."

The F.B.I. man muttered something polite and vague, so Angerhelm went on. "I suppose you gentlemen are from the F.B.I. I don't think my brother was cheating. He wasn't that dishonest."

Another pause, and he continued. "But there is always a kind of a funny sleek mind—he looked like the kind of man who would play a joke."

Angerhelm's eyes lit up. "If he played a joke, gentlemen, he might even have committed a crime, I don't know. All I do is raise chickens and try to have my life."

Perhaps it was the wrong kind of Intelligence procedure but I broke in ahead of the F.B.I. and said, "Are you a happy man, Mr. Angerhelm? Do you live a life that you think is really satisfying?"

The old boy gave me a keen look. It was obvious that

he thought there was something wrong and he didn't have very much confidence in my judgment.

And yet underneath the sharpness of his look he shot me a glance of sympathy and I am sure that he suspected I had been under a strain. His eyes widened a little. His shoulders went back, and he looked a little prouder.

He looked like the kind of man who might remember that he had Swedish admirals for ancestors, and that long before the Angerhelm name ran out and ran dry there in this flat country west of Minneapolis there had been something great in it and that perhaps sparks of the great name still flew somewhere in the universe.

I don't know. He got the importance of it, I suppose, because he looked me very sharply and very clearly in the eye.

"No, young man, my life hasn't been much of a life and I haven't liked it. And I hope nobody has to live a life like mine. But that is enough of that. I don't suppose you're guessing and I suppose you've got something pretty bad to show me."

The other fellow then took over.

"Yes, but it doesn't involve any embarrassment for you, Mr. Angerhelm. And even Colonel Angerhelm, your brother, wouldn't mind if he were living."

"Don't be so sure of that," said the old man. "My brother minded almost everything. As a matter of fact, my brother once said to me, 'Listen, Nels, I'd come back from Hell itself rather than let somebody put something over on me.' That's what he said. I think he meant it. There was a funny pride to him and if you've got anything here on my brother, you'd better just show it to me."

With that, we got over the small talk and we did what we were told to do. We got out the tape and put it on the portable machine, the hi-fi one which we brought along with us.

We played it for the old man.

I had heard it so often that I think I could almost have reproduced it with my vocal cords. The *clickety-click* and the *buzz, buzz.* There wasn't any *whee, whee,* but there was some more *clickety-click* and there was some *buzz, buzz,* and long periods of dull silence, the kind of contrived silence which a recording machine makes when it is playing but nothing is coming through on it.

The old gentleman listened to it and it seemed to have no effect on him, no effect at all.

No effect at all? That wasn't true.

There was an effect. When we got through the first time, he said very simply, very directly, almost coldly, "Play it again. Play it again for me. There may be something there."

We played it again.

After that second playing he started to talk.

"It is the funniest thing, I hear my own name and address there and I don't know where I hear it, but I swear to God, gentlemen, that's my brother's voice. It is my brother's voice I hear there somewhere in those clicks and noises. And yet all I can hear is Nelson Angerhelm, 2322 Ridge Drive, Hopkins, Minnesota. But I hear that, gentlemen, and it is not only plain, it is my brother's voice and I don't know where I heard it. I don't know how it came through."

We played it for him a third time.

When the tape was halfway through, he threw up his hands and said, "Turn it off. Turn it off. I can't stand it. Turn it off."

We turned it off.

He sat there in the chair breathing hard. After a while in a very funny cracked tone of voice he said, "I've got some whiskey. It's back there on the shelf by the sink. Get me a shot of it, will you, gentlemen?"

The F.B.I. man and I looked at each other. He didn't want to get mixed up in accidental poisoning so he sent me. I went back. It was good enough whisky, one of the regular brands. I poured the old boy a two-ounce slug and took the glass back. I sipped a tiny bit of it myself. It seemed like a silly thing to do on duty but I couldn't risk any poison getting to him. After all my years in Army counterintelligence I wanted to stay in the Civil Service and I didn't want to take any chances on losing my good job with Mr. Spatz.

He drank the whisky and he said, "Can you record on this thing at the same time that you play?"

We said we couldn't. We hadn't thought of that.

"I think I may be able to tell you what it is saying. But I don't know how many times I can tell you, gentlemen. I am a sick man. I'm not feeling good. I never have felt very good. My brother had the life. I didn't have the life. I never had much of a life and never did anything and never went anywhere. My brother had everything. My brother got the women, he got the girl—he got the only girl I ever wanted, and then he didn't marry her. He got the life and he went away and then he died. He played jokes and he never let anybody get ahead of him. And, gentlemen, my brother's dead. Can you understand that? My brother's dead."

We said we knew his brother was dead. We didn't tell him that he had been exhumed and that the coffin had been opened and the bones had been X-rayed. We didn't tell him that the bones had been weighed, fresh identification had been remade from what was left of the fingers, and they were in pretty good shape.

We didn't tell him that the serial number had been checked and that all the circumstances leading to the death had been checked and that everybody connected with it had been interviewed.

We didn't tell him that. We just told him we knew that his brother was dead. He knew that too.

"You know my brother is dead and then this funny thing has his voice in it. All it's got is his voice . . ."

We agreed. We said that we didn't know how his voice got in there and we didn't even know that there was a voice.

We didn't tell him that we had heard that voice our-selves a thousand times and yet never knew where we heard it.

We didn't tell him that we'd played it at the SAC base and that every man there had heard the name, Nelson Angerhelm, had heard something saying that and yet couldn't tell where.

We didn't tell him that the entire apparatus of Soviet Intelligence had been swearing over this for an unstated period of time and that our people had the unpleasant feeling that this came out of a Sputnik somewhere out in the sky.

We didn't tell him all that but we knew it. We knew that if he heard his brother's voice and if he wanted to record, it was something very serious.

"Can you get me something to dictate on?" the old man said.

"I can take notes," the F.B.I. man replied.

The old man shook his head. "That isn't enough," he said. "I think you probably want to get the whole thing if you ever get it and I begin to get pieces of it."

"Pieces of what?" said the F.B.I. man.

"Pieces of the stuff behind all that noise. It's my brother's voice talking. He's saying things—I don't like what he is saying. It frightens me and it just makes everything bad and dirty. I'm not sure I can take it and I am not going to take it twice. I think I'll go to church instead."

We looked at each other. "Can you wait ten minutes? I think I can get a recording machine by then."

The old man nodded his head. The F.B.I. man went out to the car and cranked up the radio. A great big aerial shot up out of the car, which otherwise was a very inconspicuous Chevrolet sedan. He got his office. A recording machine with a police escort was sent out from downtown Minneapolis toward Hopkins. I don't know what time it took ambulances to make it but the fellow at the other end said, "You better allow me twenty to twenty-two minutes."

We waited. The old man wouldn't talk to us and he didn't want us to play the tape. He sat there sipping the whisky.

"This might kill me and I want to have my friends around. My pastor's name is Jensen and if anything happens to me you get a hold of him there but I don't think anything will happen to me. Just get a hold of him. I may die, gentlemen, I can't take too much of this. It is the most shocking thing that ever happened to any man and I'm not going to see you or anybody else get in on it. You understand that it could kill me, gentlemen."

We pretended that we knew what he was talking about, although neither one of us had the faintest idea, beyond the suspicion that the old man might have a heart condition and might actually collapse.

The office had estimated twenty-two minutes. It took eighteen minutes for the F.B.I. assistant to come in. He brought in one of these new, tight, clean little jobs, the kind of thing that I'd love to take home. You can pack it almost anywhere. And it comes out with concert quality.

The old man brightened when he saw that we meant business.

"Give me a set of headphones and just let me talk and pick it up. I'll try to reproduce it. It won't be my brother's voice. It will be my voice you're hearing. Do you follow me?"

We turned on the tape.

He dictated, with the headset on his head.

That's when the message started. And that's the thing I started with in the very beginning.

Funny funny funny. It's sort of funny funny funny to think without a brain—it is really something like a trick but not a trick to think without a brain. Talking is even harder but it can be done.

Nels, this is Tice. I'm dead.

Nels, I don't know whether I'm in Heaven or Hell, but

I think it's Hell, Nels. And I am going to play the biggest joke that anybody's ever played. And it's funny, I am an American Army officer and I am a dead one, and it doesn't matter. Nels, don't you see what it is? It doesn't matter if you're dead whether you're American or Russian or an officer or not. And even laughter doesn't matter.

But there's enough left of me, Nels, enough of the old me so that perhaps for one last time I'll have a laugh with you and the others.

I haven't got a body to laugh with, Nels, and I haven't got a mouth to laugh with and I haven't got cheeks to smile with and there really isn't any me. Tice Angerhelm is something different now, Nels. I'm dead.

I knew I was dead when I felt so different. It was more comfortable being dead, more relaxed. There wasn't anything tight.

That's the trouble, Nels, there isn't anything tight. There isn't anything around you. You can't feel the world, you can't see the world, and yet you know all about it. You know all about everything.

It's awfully lonely, Nels. There are some corners that aren't lonely, some funny little corners in which you feel friendship and feel things creeping up.

Nels, it's like kittens or the faces of children or the smell of the wind on a nice day. It's any time that you turn away from yourself and you don't think about yourself.

It's the times when you don't want something and you do want something.

It's what you're not resenting, what you're not hating, what you're not fearing, and what you're not jeering. That's it, Nels, that's the good part inside of death. And I suppose some people could call it Heaven. And I guess you get Heaven if you just get into the habit of having Heaven every day in your ordinary life. That's what it is. Heaven is right there, Nels, in your ordinary life, every day, day by day, right around you.

But that's not what I got. Oh, Nels, I am Tice Angerhelm all right, I am your brother and I'm dead. You can call where I am Hell since it's everything I hated.

Nels, it smells of everything that I ever wanted. It smells the way the hay smelled when I had my old Willys roadster and I made the first girl I ever made that August evening. You can go ask her. She's a Mrs. Prai Jesselton now. She lives over on the east side of St. Paul. You never knew I made her and if you don't think this is so, you can listen for yourself.

And you see, I am somewhere and I don't know what kind of a where it is.

Nels, this is me, Tice Angerhelm, and I'm going to scream this out loud with what I've got instead of a mouth. I am going to scream it loud so that any human ear that hears it can put it on this silly, silly Soviet gadget and take it back. TAKE THIS MESSAGE TO NELSON ANGER-HELM, 2322 RIDGE DRIVE, HOPKINS, MINNESOTA. And I'm going to repeat that a couple more times so that you'll know that it's your brother talking and I'm some-where and it isn't Heaven and it isn't Hell and it isn't even really out in space. I am in something different from space, Nels. It is just a somewhere with me in it and there isn't anything but me. In with me there's everything.

In with me there is everything I ever thought and everything I ever did and everything I ever wanted.

All the opposites are the same. Everything I hated and everything I loved, it's all the same. Everything I feared and everything I yearned for—that's the same. I tell you it's all the same now and the punishment is just as bad if you want something and get it as if you want something and don't get it.

The only thing that matters is those calm, nice moments in life when you don't want anything, Nels. You aren't anything. When you aren't trying for anything and the world is just around you, and you get simple things like water on the skin, when you yourself feel innocent and you are not thinking about anything else.

That's all there is to life, Nels. And I'm Tice and I'm telling you. And you know I'm dead, so I wouldn't be telling you a lie.

And I especially wouldn't be telling you on this Soviet cylinder, this Soviet gismo which will go back to them and bother them.

Nels, I hope it won't bother you too much, if everybody knows about that girl. I hope the girl forgives me but the message has got to go back.

And yet that's the message—everything I ever feared—I feared something in the war and you know what the war smells like. It smells sort of like a cheap slaughterhouse in July. It smells bad all around. There's bits of things burning, the smell of rubber burning and the funny smell of gunpowder. I was never in a big war with atomic stuff. Just the old sort of explosions. I've told you about it before and I was scared of that. And right in with that I can smell the perfume that girl had in the hotel there in Melbourne, the girl that I thought I might have wanted

*until she said something and then I said something and
that was all there was between us. And I'm dead now.*

And listen, Nels—

*Listen, Nels, I am talking as though it were a trick. I
don't know how I know about the rest of us—the other
ones that are dead like me. I never met one and I may
never talk to one. I just have the feeling that they are here
too. They can't talk.*

It's not that they can't talk, really.

They don't even want to talk.

*They don't feel like talking. Talking is just a trick. It is
a trick that somebody can pick up and I guess it takes a
cheap, meaningless man, a man who lived his life in spite
of Hell and is now in that Hell. That's the kind of silly man
it takes to remember the trick of talking. Like a trick with
coins or a trick with cigarettes when nothing else matters.*

*So I am talking to you, Nels. And Nels, I suppose you'll
die the way I do. It doesn't matter, Nels. It's too late to
change—that's all.*

*Good-bye, Nels, you're in pretty good shape. You've
lived your life. You've had the wind in your hair. You've
seen the good sunlight and you haven't hated and feared
and loved too much.*

When the old man got through dictating it, the F.B.I.
man and I asked him to do it again.

He refused.

We all stood up. We brought in the assistant.

The old man still refused to make a second dictation
from the sounds out of which only he could hear a voice.

We could have taken him into custody and forced him

but there didn't seem to be much sense to it until we took the recording back to Washington and had this text appraised.

He said good-bye to us as we left his house.

"Perhaps I can do it once again maybe a year from now. But the trouble with me, gentlemen, is that I believe it. That was the voice of my brother, Tice Angerhelm, and he is dead. And you brought me something strange. I don't know where you got a medium or spirit reader to record this on a tape and especially in such a way that you can't hear it and I could. But I did hear it, gentlemen, and I think I told you pretty good what it was. And those words I used, they are not mine, they are my brother's. So you go along, gentlemen, and do what you can with it and if you don't want me to tell anybody that the U.S. government is working on mediums, I won't."

That was the farewell he gave us.

We closed the local office and hurried to the airport. We took the tape back with us but a duplicate was already being teletyped to Washington.

That's the end of the story and that is the end of the joke. Potariskov got a copy and the Soviet Ambassador got a copy.

And Khrushchev probably wondered what sort of insane joke the Americans were playing on him. To use a medium or something weird along with subliminal perception in order to attack the U.S.S.R. for not believing in God and not believing in death. Did he figure it that way?

Here's a case where I hope that Soviet espionage is very good. I hope that their spies are so fine that they know we're baffled. I hope that they realize that we have come to a dead end, and whatever Tice Angerhelm did or somebody did in his name way out there in space recording into a Soviet Sputnik, we Americans had no hand in it.

If the Russians didn't do it and we didn't do it, who did do it?

I hope their spies find out.

The Good Friends

Fever had given him a boyish look. The nurse, standing behind the doctor, watched him attentively. Her half-smile blended tenderness with an appreciation of his manly attraction.

"When can I go, doc?"

"In a few weeks, perhaps. You have to get well first."

"I don't mean home, doc. When can I go back into space? I'm a captain, doc. I'm a good one. You know that, don't you?"

The doctor nodded gravely.

"I want to go back, doc. I want to go back right away. I want to be well, doc. I want to be well *now*. I want to get back in my ship and take off again. I don't even know why I'm here. What are you doing with me, doc?"

"We're trying to make you well," said the doctor, friendly, serious, authoritative.

"I'm not sick, doc. You've got the wrong man. We brought the ship in, didn't we? Everything was all right, wasn't it? Then we started to get out and everything went black. Now I'm here in a hospital. Something's pretty fishy, doc. Did I get hurt in the port?"

"No," said the doctor, "you weren't hurt at the port."

"Then why'd I faint? Why am I sick in a bed? Something must have happened to me, doc. It stands to reason. Otherwise I wouldn't be here. Some stupid awful thing must have happened, doc. After such a nice trip. Where did it happen?" A wild light came into the patient's eyes. "Did somebody do something to me, doc? I'm not hurt, am I? I'm not ruined, am I? I'll be able to go back into space, won't I?"

"Perhaps," said the doctor.

The nurse drew in her breath as though she were going to say something. The doctor looked around at her and gave her an authoritative frown, meaning *keep quiet*.

The patient saw it.

Desperation came into his voice, almost a whine. "What's the matter, doc? Why won't you talk to me? What's wrong? Something has happened to me. Where's Ralph? Where's Pete? Where's Jock? The last time I saw him he was having a beer. Where's Larry? Where's Went? Where's Betty? Where's my gang, doc? They're not killed, are they? I'm not the only one, am I? Talk to me, doc. Tell me the truth. I'm a space captain, doc. I've faced queer hells in my time, doc. You can tell me anything, doc. I'm not *that* sick. I can take it. Where's my gang, doc—my pals from the ship? What a cruise that was! Won't you talk, doc?"

"I'll talk," said the doctor, gravely.

"Okay," said the patient. "Tell me."

"What in particular?"

"Don't be a fool, doc! Tell me the straight stuff. Tell

me about my friends first, and then tell me what has happened to me."

"Concerning your friends," said the doctor, measuring his words carefully, "I am in a position to tell you there has been no adverse change in the status of any of the persons you mentioned."

"All right, then, doc, if it wasn't them, it's me. Tell me. What's *happened* to me, doc? Something stinking awful must have happened or you wouldn't be standing there with a face like a constipated horse!"

The doctor smiled wryly, bleakly, briefly at the weird compliment. "I won't try to explain my own face, young fellow. I was born with it. But you are in a serious condition and we are trying to get you well. I will tell you the whole truth."

"Then do it, doc! Right away. Did somebody jump me at the port? Was I hurt badly? Was it an accident? Start talking, man!"

The nurse stirred behind the doctor. He looked around at her. She looked in the direction of the hypodermic on the tray. The doctor gave her a brief negative shake of his head. The patient saw the whole interplay and understood it correctly.

"That's right, doc. Don't let her dope me. I don't need sleep. I need the truth. If my gang's all right, why aren't they here? Is Milly out in the corridor? Milly, that was her name, the little curlyhead. Where's Jock? Why isn't Ralph here?"

"I'm going to tell you everything, young man. It may be tough but I'm counting on you to take it like a man. But it would help if you told me first."

"Told you what? Don't you know who I am? Didn't you read about my gang and me? Didn't you hear about Larry? What a navigator! We wouldn't be here except for Larry."

The late-morning light poured in through the open window; a soft spring breeze touched the young ravaged face of the patient. There was mercy and more in the doctor's voice.

"I'm just a medical doctor. I don't keep up with the news. I know your name, age, and medical history. But I don't know the details of your cruise. Tell me about it."

"Doc, you're kidding. It'd take a book. We're famous. I bet Went's out there right now, making a fortune out of the pictures he took."

"Don't tell me the whole thing, young man. Suppose you just tell me about the last couple of days before you landed, and how you got into port."

The young man smiled guiltily; there was pleasure and fond memory in his face. "I guess I can tell you, because you're a doctor and keep things confidential."

The doctor nodded, very earnest and still kind. "Do you want," said he softly, "the nurse to leave?"

"Oh, no," cried the patient. "She's a good scout. It's not as though you were going to turn it loose on the tapes."

The doctor nodded. The nurse nodded and smiled, too. She was afraid that there were tears forming at the corners of her eyes, but she dared not wipe them away. This was an extraordinarily observant patient. He might notice it. It would ruin his story.

The patient almost babbled in his eagerness to tell the

story. "You know the ship, doc. It's a big one: twelve cabins, a common room, simulated gravity, lockers, plenty of room."

The doctor's eyes flickered at this but he did nothing, except to watch the patient in an attentive sympathetic way.

"When we knew we just had two days to Earth, doc, and we knew everything was all right, we had a ball. Jock found the beer in one of the lockers. Ralph helped him get it out. Betty was an old pal of mine, but I started trying to make time with Milly. Boy, did I make it! Yum." He looked at the nurse and blushed all the way down to his neck. "I'll skip the details. We had a party, doc. We were high. Drunk. Happy. Boy, did we have fun! I don't think anybody ever had more fun than we did, me and that old gang of mine. We docked all right. That Larry, he's a navigator. He was drunk as an owl and he had Betty on his lap but he put that ship in like the old lady putting a coin in the collection plate. Everything came out exactly right. I guess I should have been ashamed of landing a ship with the whole crew drunk and happy, but it was the best trip and the best gang and the best fun that anybody ever had. And we had succeeded in our mission, doc. We wouldn't have cut loose at the end of the mission if we hadn't known everything was hunky-dory. So we came in and landed, doc. And then everything went black, and here I am. Now you tell me your side of it, but be sure to tell me when Larry and Jock and Went are going to come in and see me. They're characters, doc. That little nurse of yours, she's going to have to watch them. They might bring me a bottle that I shouldn't have. Okay, doc. Shoot."

"Do you trust me?" said the doctor.

"Sure. I guess so. Why not?"

"Do you think I would tell you the truth?"

"It's something mean, doc. Real mean. Okay, shoot anyhow."

"I want you to have the shot first," said the doctor, straining to keep kindness and authority in his voice.

The patient looked bewildered. He glanced at the nurse, the tray, the hypodermic. Then he smiled at the doctor, but it was a smile in which fright lurked.

"All right, doctor. You're the boss."

The nurse helped him roll back his sleeves. She started to reach for the needle.

The doctor stopped her. He looked her straight in the face, his eyes focused right on hers. "No, intravenous. I'll do it. Do you understand?"

She was a quick girl.

From the tray she took a short length of rubber tubing, twisted it quickly around the upper arm, just below the elbow.

The doctor watched, very quiet.

He took the arm, ran his thumb up and down the skin as he felt the vein.

"Now," said he.

She handed him the needle.

Patient, nurse, and doctor all watched as the hypodermic emptied itself directly into the little ridge of the vein on the inside of the elbow.

The doctor took out the needle. He himself seemed relieved. Said he: "Feel anything?"

"Not yet, doc. Can you tell me now, doc? I can't

make trouble with this stuff in me. Where's Larry? Where's Jock?"

"You weren't on a ship, young man. You were alone on a one-man craft. You didn't have a party for two days. You had it for twenty years. Larry didn't bring your ship in. The Earth authorities brought it in with telemetry. You were starved, dehydrated, and nine-tenths dead. The boat had a freeze unit and you were fed by the emergency kit. You had the narrowest escape in the whole history of space travel. The boat had one of the new hypo kits. You must have had a second or two to slap it to your face before the boat took over. You didn't have any friends with you. They came out of your own mind."

"That's all right, doc. I'll be all right. Don't worry about me."

"There wasn't any Jock or Larry or Ralph or Milly. That was just the hypo kit."

"I get you, doc. It's all right. This dope you gave me, it's good stuff. I feel happy and dreamy. You can go away now and let me sleep. You can explain it all to me in the morning. But be sure to let Ralph and Jock in, when visiting hours open up." He turned on his side away from them.

The nurse pulled the cover up over his shoulders.

Then she and the doctor started to leave the room. At the last moment, she ran past the doctor and out of the room ahead of him. She did not want him to see her cry.

TIMELINE OF THE INSTRUMENTALITY OF MANKIND

A.D.	STORIES
1900-2500	No, No, Not Rogov Mark Elf (prelude only) War No. 81-Q

2500-6500	How the Dream
	  Lords Died
	  (projected story)

6500-8500	Mark Elf The Queen of the Afternoon

8500-9500	Scanners Live in Vain
	When the People Fell
	The Lady Who Sailed
	  the Soul
	Think Blue, Count Two
	The Colonel Came
	  Back from the
	  Nothing-at-All

9500-12,000	The Game of Rat and
	  Dragon
	The Burning of the Brain
	From Gustibles's Planet
	The Lady Who Sailed
	  the Soul
	  (prologue and epilogue)

SURROUNDING EVENTS

More than Ancient times. Forgotten first age of space,
War games to settle disputes. Chinese conquer
Australia, turning it into vast city state of Aojou Nan Bien.
Australians manage to flee to Paradise VII,
a hellish planet where they barely remain human.

The Ancient Wars, destruction of civilization and
erasure of all ancient nations save Chinesia in the Long
Nothing. Survivors include Others in the Earth—
saints morons and the Unforgiven. Beasts and
menschenjagers also inhabit the Wild, still plagued
by The Kaskaskia Effect.

Saints die off. The Dwellers restore cities,
but leave the Wild to remaining
Unforgiven, morons and Beasts. Fighting
trees and weeds planted to decontaminate
land and sea environments. Rule of the
Jwindz, ended after return to Earth of the
Vomacht (Vomact) sisters.

Return of vitality to history. Founding of
the Instrumentality. New age of space
begins. The Great Pain of Space and the
Scanners. Chinesians conquer Venus.
Two hundred worlds settled by sailship,
including Nostrilia (from Paradise VII).
Standard human lifespan is 160 years.
Discovery of planoforming towards the end.

Rapid interstellar flight and commerce by
planoforming. Thousands of worlds settled.
Adaptation of men to strange worlds like
Viola Sideria. Appearances of the Daimoni
at Earth and Nostrilia. Development of Norstrilian
immortality drug stroon. Instrumentality arbitrarily
sets maximum life span for ordinary people at 400 years.

TIMELINE OF THE INSTRUMENTALITY OF MANKIND

A.D.	STORIES
12,000-14,000	**No, No, Not Rogov** (prologue and epilogue)
	Golden the Ship Was, Oh! Oh! Oh!
	Himself in Anachron (?)
	The Crime and Glory of Commander Suzdal
14,000-16,000	**The Dead Lady of Clown Town**
	Under Old Earth
	Drunkboat
	Mother Hitton's Littul Kittons
	The Robot, the Rat and the Copt (projected story)
	Alpha Ralpha Boulevard
	The Ballad of Lost C'Mell
	Norstrillia
	A Planet Named Shayol
Post-Rediscovery of Man:	**On the Gem Planet**
	On the Storm Planet
	On the Sand Planet
	Three to a Given Star

SURROUNDING EVENTS

Creation of underpeople and robots for ordinary labor.
Succession of dynasties on Earth under the
Instrumentality, including the Bright, sponsors of
dance festivals and other artistic extravaganzas.
Bright later create Bright Empire in far reaches of space.
Instrumentality suppresses challenges from that empire
and any other potential rivals. Creation of Shayol as
place of punishment and source of organ transplants.

The pleasure revolution and stagnation of
utopia, Martyrdom of D'Joan and the
development of an underpeoples'
underground. Rediscovery of Man and
liberation of the Underpeople under Lord
Jestocost. Discovery of Space 3. Rebirth of
the Old Strong Religion, based in part on
revelations from Space 3 by the Robot,
the Rat and the Copt.

Note: With most of Smith's own notebooks lost, chronology
is largely a matter of guesswork, based on internal evidence.
But the order of stories and surrounding events can be fairly
well established. "Projected story" indicates stories planned
but not written.

PRAISE FOR
LOIS McMASTER BUJOLD

What the critics say:

The Warrior's Apprentice: "Now here's a fun romp through the spaceways—not so much a space opera as space ballet… It has all the 'right stuff.' A lot of thought and thoughtfulness stand behind the all-too-human characters. Enjoy this one, and look forward to the next."   —Dean Lambe, *SF Reviews*

"The pace is breathless, the characterization thoughtful and emotionally powerful, and the author's narrative technique and command of language compelling. Highly recommended."   —*Booklist*

Brothers in Arms: "…she gives it a genuine depth of character, while reveling in the wild turnings of her tale… Bujold is as audacious as her favorite hero, and as brilliantly (if sneakily) successful."   —*Locus*

"Miles Vorkosigan is such a great character that I'll read anything Lois wants to write about him… a book to re-read on cold rainy days."   —Robert Coulson, *Comics Buyers Guide*

Borders of Infinity: "Bujold's series hero Miles Vokosigan may be a lord by birth and an admiral by rank, but a bone disease that has left him hobbled and in frequent pain has sensitized him to the suffering of outcasts in her very hierarchical era…. Playing off of Miles's reserve and cleverness, Bujold draws outrageous and outlandish foils to color her high-minded adventures."   —*Publishers Weekly*

Falling Free: "In *Falling Free* Lois McMaster Bujold has written her fourth straight superb novel…. How to break down a talent like Bujold's into analyzable components? Best not to try. Best to say: 'Read, or you will be missing something extraordinary.'"
                                  —Roland Green, *Chicago Sun-Times*

The Vor Game: "The chronicles of Miles Vokosigan are far too witty to be literary junk food, but they rouse the kind of craving that makes popcorn magically vanish during a double feature."   —Faren Miller, *Locus*

MORE PRAISE FOR
LOIS McMASTER BUJOLD

What the readers say:

"My copy of *Shards of Honor* is falling apart I've reread it so often.... I'll read whatever you write. You've certainly proved yourself a grand storyteller.
                                            —Lisa Kolbe, Colorado Springs, CO

"I experience the stories of Miles Vorkosigan as almost viscerally uplifting... But certainly, even the weightiest theme would have less impact than a cinder on snow were it not for a rousing good story, and good story-telling with it. This is the second thing I want to thank you for... I suppose if you boiled down all I've said to its simplest expression, it would be that I immensely enjoy and admire your work. I submit that, as literature, your work raises the overall level of the science fiction genre, and spiritually, you work cannot avoid positively influencing all who read it."
                                            —Glen Stonebreaker, Gaithersburg, MD

"'The Mountains of Mourning' [in *Borders of Infinity*] was one of the best-crafted, and simply best, works I'd ever read. When I finished it, I immediately turned back to the beginning and read it again, and I can't remember the last time I did that."
                                            —Betsy Bizot, Lisle, IL

"I can only hope that you will continue to write, so that I can continue to read (and of course buy) your books, for they make me laugh and cry and think ... rare indeed."
                                            —Steven Knott, Major, USAF

What do you say?

Cordelia's Honor
pb • 0-671-57828-6 • $7.99
Contains *Shards of Honor* and Hugo-award winner *Barrayar* in one volume.

Young Miles
trade pb • 0-671-87782-8 • $17.00
pb • 0-7434-3616-4 • $7.99
Contains *The Warrior's Apprentice*, Hugo-award winner *The Vor Game*, and Hugo-award winner "The Mountains of Mourning" in one volume.

Cetaganda
0-671-87744-5 • $7.99

Miles, Mystery and Mayhem
pb • 0-7434-3618-0 • $7.99
Contains *Cetaganda, Ethan of Athos* and "Labyrinth" in one volume.

Brothers in Arms
pb • 1-4165-5544-7 • $7.99

Miles Errant
trade pb • 0-7434-3558-3 • $15.00
Contains "The Borders of Infinity," *Brothers in Arms* and *Mirror Dance* in one volume.

Mirror Dance
pb • 0-671-87646-5 • $7.99

Memory
pb • 0-671-87845-X • $7.99